"We have a job for you," I said to the magician, "and I suspect you might accomplish it."

"Is this a dangerous job?" he asked.

"It is one involving great risk and small prospect of success," I said. "It is also one in which, if you fail, you will be apprehended and subjected to ingenious, lengthy and excruciating tortures, to be terminated only months later with the mercy of a terrible death. Are you afraid?"

"Of course not," he said. "Beyond what you describe there is little to fear."

"What is this task?" asked the magician. "You wish the Central Cylinder moved? You wish the walls of Ar rebuilt overnight? You wish a thousand tarns tamed in one afternoon?"

"What do you think would happen," I asked, "if the Home Stone of Ar's Station, now on public display, disappeared from beneath the very noses of the authorities?"

"You wish me to obtain the Home Stone of Ar's Station for you?"

"For Ar," I said, "for Ar's Station, for the citizenry of Ar's Station, for the overthrow of Cos!"

John Norman titles published by DAW Books:

The Gor Novels

HUNTERS OF GOR
MARAUDERS OF GOR
TRIBESMEN OF GOR
SLAVE GIRL OF GOR
BEASTS OF GOR
EXPLORERS OF GOR
FIGHTING SLAVE OF GOR
ROGUE OF GOR
GUARDSMAN OF GOR
SAVAGES OF GOR
BLOOD BROTHERS OF GOR
KAJIRA OF GOR
PLAYERS OF GOR
MERCENARIES OF GOR
DANCER OF GOR
RENEGADES OF GOR
VAGABONDS OF GOR
MAGICIANS OF GOR

Other Norman Titles

TIME SLAVE
IMAGINATIVE SEX
GHOST DANCE

DAW BOOKS, INC.
DONALD A. WOLLHEIM, PUBLISHER
1633 Broadway, New York, NY 10019

Copyright © 1988 by John Norman.

All Rights Reserved.

Cover art by Ken Kelly.

DAW Book Collectors No. 746.

First Printing, June 1988

1 2 3 4 5 6 7 8 9

PRINTED IN THE U. S. A.

Contents

The Street

"Surely you understand the law, my dear," he said.

She struggled in the net, dropped from the ceiling, then held about her by guardsmen sprung from concealment at the sides of the room.

"No!" she cried. "No!"

She was then turned about, twice in the net, on the couch so that she was thoroughly entangled, doubly, in its toils.

"No!" she wept.

The guardsmen, four of them, held the net.

Her eyes were wild. Her fingers were in the knotted mesh. She was like a frightened animal.

"Please," she wept. "What do you want?"

The fellow did not then answer her, but regarded her. She was naked in the toils of the net, and now lay on her side, her legs drawn up in it, now seemingly small and very vulnerable, so bared and caught, on the deep furs of the huge couch.

"Milo!" she cried to a tall, handsome fellow to one side. "Help me!"

"But I am a slave," pointed out Milo, donning his purple tunic.

She looked at him, wildly.

"I am sure you are familiar with the law," said the first fellow, flanked by two magistrates.

"No!" she cried.

The magistrates were *ex officio* witnesses, who could certify the circumstances of the capture. The net was a stout one, and weighted.

"Any free woman who couches with another's slave, or readies herself to couch with another's slave, becomes herself a slave, and the slave of the slave's master. It is a clear law."

"No! No!" she wept.

"Think of it in this fashion, if you wish," he said. "You have given yourself to Milo, but Milo is mine, and can own nothing, and thus you have given yourself to me. An analogy is the coin given by a free person to a street girl, which coin, of course, does not then belong to the girl but to her master. What is given to the slave is given to the master."

She regarded him with horror.

"I loathe you!" she cried. "Bring me my clothing!" she wept to the guardsmen.

"When the certifications are approved, and filed, and in this case there will be no ambiguity or difficulty about the matter, you will be mine."

"No!" she wept.

"Put her on her knees, on the couch, in the net," he said.

This was done.

She looked wildly at Milo. There were tears in her eyes. "Will I then, as a slave, be your woman?" she asked.

"I do not think so," said Milo, smiling.

"The handsome, charming, suave, witty Milo," said the fellow, "is a seduction slave."

"A seduction slave?" she wept.

"Yes," he said. "He has much increased my stock of slaves."

She tore at the net, in tears, but was helpless.

"Had you, and your predecessors, not been so secretive, so much concerned to conceal your affairs with a slave, Milo's utility as a seduction slave would have doubtless been much diminished by now. On the other hand, the concern for your reputation and such, so natural in you free women, almost guarantees the repeatability, and the continued success, of these small pleasant projects."

"Release me!" she begged.

"Some of Milo's conquests are used in my fields, and others in my house," he said. "But most, and I am sure you will be one of these, are exported, sold out of the city to begin your new life."

"My new life?" she whispered.

"That of a female slave," he smiled.

She struggled, futilely.

"Raise the net to her waist, and lower it to her neck," he said, "and tie it about her. Then put her in a gag and hood."

"No!" she wept.

"By tonight," he said, "you will be branded and collared."

"No, please!" she wept.

The net was then adjusted on the female, in accordance with the fellow's instructions, in such a way that her legs and head were free, but her arms were confined. It was then bound tightly in place.

The fellow then glanced at the handsome slave. "You will leave by another exit," he said.

"Yes, Master," said the slave.

The free woman watched the slave withdraw. "Milo!" she whispered.

"You are now kneeling on a couch," said the fellow, "which, for a female slave, is a great honor. You may be months into your bondage before you are again permitted such an honor."

"Milo!" she wept, after the slave.

The leather bit of the gag, a fixture of the hood, was then forced back between her teeth, and tied in place.

She made a tiny noise, of protest.

The hood itself was then drawn over her head, covering it completely. It was then fixed on her, buckled shut, beneath her chin.

"What have you seen?" asked Marcus.

I stepped back from the crack in the shutters, through which I had observed the preceding scene.

"Nothing," I said.

We were in a street of Ar, a narrow, crowded street, in which we were much jostled. It was in the Metellan district, south and east of the district of the Central Cylinder. It is a shabby, but not squalid district. There are various tenements, or *insulae*, there. It is the sort of place, far enough from the broad avenues of central Ar, where assignations, or triflings, might take place.

"Is Ar this crowded always?" asked Marcus, irritably.

"This street, at this time of day," I said.

My companion was Marcus Marcellus, of the Marcelliani, formerly of Ar's Station, on the Vosk. We had come to Ar from the vicinity of Brundisium. He, like myself, was of the caste of warriors. With him, clinging closely, about him, as though she might fear losing him in the crowd, and attempting also, it seemed, not unoften, to make herself small and conceal herself behind him, was his slave, Phoebe, this name having been put on her, a slender exquisite, very lightly complexioned, very dark-haired girl. She had come into his keeping in the vicinity of Brundisium, some months ago.

"As we do have the yellow ostraka and our permits do not permit us to remain in the city after dark," said Marcus, "I think we should venture now to the sun gate."

Marcus was the sort of fellow who was concerned about such things, being arrested, impaled, and such.

"There is plenty of time," I assured him. Most cities have a sun gate, sometimes several. They are called such because they are commonly opened at dawn and closed at dusk, thus the hours of their ingress and egress being determined by the diurnial cycle. Ar is the largest city of known Gor, larger even, I am sure, than Turia, in the far south. She has some forty public gates, and, I suppose, some number of restricted smaller gates, secret gates, posterns, and such. Long ago, I had once entered the city through such a passage, its exterior access point reached by means of a putative Dar-Kosis pit, which passage, I had recently determined, descending into the pit on ropes, was now closed. I supposed that this might be the case with various such entrances, if they existed, given Ar's alarm at the announced approach of Cos. In a sense I regretted this loss, for it had constituted a secret way in and out of the city. Perhaps other such passages existed. I did not know.

"Let us go," suggested Marcus.

I saw a slave girl pass, in a brief, brown tunic, her back straight, her beauty protestingly full within her tiny, tight garment, balancing a jar on her head with one hand. The bottom of the jar rested in a sort of improvised shallow stand or mount, formed of a dampened, wrapped towel. In Schendi the white slave girls of black masters are sometimes taught to carry such vessels on their heads without the use of their hands or such devices as the towel. And woe to the girl who drops it. Such exercises are good for a girl's posture. To be sure, the lower caste black women of Schendi and the interior do such things commonly. I looked at the girl. Yes, I thought, she could be similarly trained, without doubt. If I owned her, I thought, I might so train her. If she proved clumsy or slow to learn she could be whipped. I did not think she would prove slow to learn. Our eyes met, briefly, and she lowered her eyes swiftly, still keeping her burden steady. She trembled for a moment. I think she had seen, in that glance, that I could be her master, but then, so, too, of course, could be many men. A slave girl is often very careful about meeting the eyes of a free man directly, particularly a stranger. They can be cuffed or beaten for such insolence. The collar looked well on her, gleaming, close-fitting, locked. She was barefoot. Her brief garment was all she wore. It would have no nether closure. Thusly on Gor are female slaves commonly garbed. She hurried on.

"Let us be on our way," said Marcus. Phoebe clung close to him, her tiny fingers on his sleeve.

"In a moment," I said.

"I do not like such crowds," said Marcus.

We were buffeted about a bit.

"There is a date on the permits," Marcus reminded me, "and they will be checking at the gate to see who has left the city and who has not."

"I think they will be coming out in a moment or two," I said, "there, at that door."

"Who?" he asked.

"There," I said.

I saw the fellow who had been in the room emerge through the door. He was followed by the two magistrates, who had probably now made the entries in their records. They were followed by four guardsmen, in single file. "Make way, make way!" said the fellow from the room, and the crowds parted a little, to let them pass. The third of the three guardsmen carried a burden on his right shoulder. It was a naked woman whose upper body was thoroughly and tightly wrapped in several turns on a heavy net, tied closely about her. Her head was covered with a buckled hood. She squirmed a little, helplessly. She was being carried with her head to the rear, as a slave is carried.

"So that is what you were watching," said Marcus, "a caught slave."

"In a sense," I said.

About at the same time, coming toward us, down the street, following the other party by several yards, was a large, graceful fellow, blond and curly-haired, who was astoundingly handsome, almost unbelievably so. Oh his left wrist, locked, there was a silver slave bracelet. His tunic was of a silken purple. He had golden sandals.

"Who is that?" I asked a fellow in white and gold, the colors of the merchants, when the handsome fellow had passed. Such a one, I assumed, might be generally known. He was no ordinary fellow.

"That is the actor, Milo," said the man.

"He is a slave," I said.

"Owned by Appanius, the agriculturalist, impresario and slaver," said the fellow, "who rents him to the managements of various theaters."

"A handsome fellow," I said.

"The handsomest man in all Ar," said the merchant. "Free women swoon at his feet."

"And what of slaves?" asked Marcus, irritably, scowling at Phoebe.

"I swoon at your feet, Master," she smiled, putting down her head.

"You may kneel and clean them with your tongue," said Marcus, angrily.

"Yes, Master," she said, and fell to her knees, putting down her head.

"The appearance of Milo in a drama assures its success," said the merchant.

"He is popular," I said.

"Particularly with the women," he said.

"I can understand that," I said.

"Some men do not even care for him," said the merchant, and I gathered he might be one of them.

"I can understand that," I said. I was not certain that I was enthusiastic about Milo either. Perhaps it was merely that I suspected that Milo might be even more handsome than I.

"I wish you well," said the merchant.

"Perhaps Milo serves, too, in capacities other than that of an actor," I said.

"What did you have in mind?" asked the merchant.

"Nothing," I said.

"It is Milo," whispered one free woman to another. They were together, veiled.

"Let us hurry after him, to catch a glimpse of him," said one of them.

"Do not be shameless!" chided the first.

"We are veiled," the second reminded her.

"Let us hurry," urged the first then, and the two pressed forward, through the crowd, after the purple-clad figure.

"Fellows as handsome as he," complained the merchant, "should be forced to go veiled in public."

"Perhaps," I granted him. Free women in most of the high cities on Gor, particularly those of higher caste, go veiled in public. Also they commonly wear the robes of concealment which cover them, in effect, from head to toe. Even gloves are often worn. There are many reasons for this, having to do with modesty, security, and such. Slave girls, on the other hand, are commonly scandalously clad, if clad at all. Typically their garments, if they are permitted them, are designed to leave little of their beauty to the imagination. Rather they are designed to call attention to it, and so reveal and display it, sometimes even brazenly, in all its marvelousness. Goreans are not ashamed of the luscious richness, the excitingness, the sensuousness, the femininity, the beauty of their slaves. Rather they prize it, treasure it and celebrate it. To be sure, it must be admitted that the slave girl is only an animal, and is under total male domination. To understand this more clearly, two further items might be noted. First, she must go about in public, denied face veiling. Men, as they please, may look freely upon her face, witnessing its delicacy, its beauty, its emotions, and such. She is not permitted to hide it from them. She must bare it, in all its revelatory intimacy, and with all the consequences of this, to their gaze. Second, her degradation is completed by the fact that she is given no choice but to be what she is, profoundly and in depth, a human female, and must thus, willing or not, sexually and emotionally, physically and psychologically, accept her fulfillment in the order of nature.

"I wish you well," I said to the merchant.

He turned away.

"Make way," I heard. "Make way!"

A house marshal was approaching, carrying a baton, with which he touched folks and made a passage among them. He was preceding the palanquin of a free woman, apparently a rich one, borne by some eight male slaves. I stepped to one side to let the marshal, the palanquin and its bearers move past. The sides of the palanquin were veiled.

"Odd that a palanquin of such a nature should be in the Metellan district," I said.

"Perhaps we should consider saving our lives now," said Marcus.

"Phoebe is not finished with your feet," I said.

Phoebe looked up, happily.

"Up," said Marcus irritably, snapping his fingers. Immediately she sprang to her feet. She stood beside him, her head down, docile. She, I noted, attracted her share of attention. I was not too pleased with this, as I did not wish to be conspicuous in Ar. On the other hand, it is seldom wise to interfere in the relationship between a master and a slave.

I looked back down the street. I could no longer see any sign of the fellow who had been in the room, the magistrates, or the guardsmen, with their shapely prisoner. She had been on a guardsman's shoulder, being carried, her head to the rear, as a slave. Later I did not think she would be often accorded the luxury of such transportation. Soon, perhaps in a day or two, she would be learning how to heel a man and to walk gracefully on his leash.

"Oh!" said Phoebe.

Someone in the crowd, in passing, had undoubtedly touched her. Marcus looked about, angrily. I did not know, really, what he expected.

I looked back down the street. I could see the head of Milo, with its blond curls, over the heads of the crowd, about fifty yards away. He was standing near a wall. The free woman's palanquin had stopped briefly by him, and then, after a time, continued on its way.

"Oh!" said Phoebe again.

Marcus turned about again, swiftly, angrily. There was only the crowd.

"If you do not care for such things," I said, "perhaps you should give her a garment."

"Let her go naked," he said. "She is only a slave."

"Perhaps some article of clothing would not be amiss," I said.

"She has her collar," he said.

"You may never have noticed," I said, "but she is an exquisitely beautiful female."

"She is the lowest and most despicable of female slaves," he said.

"Of course," I said.

"Too," said he, "do not forget that I hate her."

"It would be difficult to do that," I said, "as you have told me so many times."

Phoebe lowered her head, smiling.

"Too," said he, "she is my enemy."

"If ever she was your enemy," I said, "she is not your enemy now. She is now a slave. Look at her. She is simply an animal you own. Do you think she does not know that? She now exists for you, to please and serve you."

"She is Cosian," he said.

"Turn your flank to him, slave," I said. "Touch your collar."

Phoebe complied.

"You can see the brand," I said. "You can see the collar. Furthermore, it is yours."

He regarded the slave, docile, obedient, turned, her fingers, too, lightly on her collar, so closely locked on her lovely neck.

"And it is a pretty flank," I said, "and a lovely throat."

He moaned softly.

"I see that you think so," I said.

The feelings of the young warrior toward his slave were profoundly ambivalent. She was not only the sort of female that he found irresistibly, excruciatingly attractive, as I had known before I had shown her to him the first time, but, to my surprise and delight, there seemed to be a special mystery or magic, or chemistry, between them. Each was a dream come true for the other. She had been, it seemed, in some profound genetic sense, born for his chains. They fitted together, like a lock and its key. She loved him profoundly, helplessly, and from the first time she had seen him. He, too, had been smitten. Then he had discovered that she was from Cos, that ubarate which was his hated foe, at the hands of whose mercenary and regular forces he had seen his city destroyed. It was no wonder that in rage he had vowed to make the lovely slave stand proxy for Cos, that he might then vent upon her his fury, and his hatred, for Cos, and all things Cosian. And so it was that he had determined to reduce and humiliate her, and make her suffer, but with each cuffing, with each command, with each kick, with each blow of the whip, she became only the more his, and the more loving. I had known for a long time, even as long ago as the inn of the Crooked Tarn, on the Vosk Road, before the fall of Ar's Station, that she had profound slave needs, but I had never suspected their depth until I had seen her in a camp outside Brundisium, kneeling before Marcus, looking up at him, unbelievingly. She had known then that she was his, and in perfection. I had no doubt they fitted together, in the order of nature, in the most intimate, beautiful and fulfilling relationship possible between a man and a woman, that of love master and love slave. To be sure, she was Cosian.

Phoebe put down her head, shyly smiling.

"Cosian slut!" snarled Marcus.

He seized her by the arms and lifted her from her feet, thrusting her back against the wall of the building.

He held her there, off her feet, her back pressed back, hard, against the rough wall.

"Yes," she cried. "Yes!"

"Be thusly used, and as befits you," said he, "slave, and slut of Cos!"

"Yes, my Master!" she wept. She clung about him, her eyes closed, her head back, gasping.

Then he cried out, and lowered her to the stones of the street.

She knelt there, gratefully, sobbing. Her back was bloody. Marcus had not been gentle with the slave. She was holding to his leg.

"Disgusting," said a free woman, drawing her veil more closely about her face.

Did she not know that she, too, if she were a slave, would be similarly subject to a master's pleasure?

"This is a very public place," I said to Marcus.

A small crowd, like an eddy in the flowing stream of folks in the street, had gathered about.

"She is a slut of Cos," said Marcus to a fellow nearby.

"Beat her for me," said the man.

"She is only a slave," I said.

"A Cosian slut," said one man to another.

"She is only a slave," I said again.

The crowd closed in a bit more, menacingly. Phoebe looked up, frightened.

In the press there was not even room to draw the sword, let alone wield it.

"Let us kill her," said a fellow.

"Move back," said Marcus, angrily.

"A slut of Cos," said another man.

"Let us kill her!" said another fellow.

Phoebe was very small and helpless, kneeling on the stones, near the wall.

"Continue on your way," I said to the men gathered about. "Be about your business."

"Cos is our business," said a man.

The ugliness of the crowd, its hostility, and such, was, I think, a function of recent events, which had precipitated confusion, uncertainty and terror in Ar, in particular the military catastrophe in the delta, in which action, absurdly, the major land forces of Ar had been invested, and the news that the Cosian forces at Torcadino, one of the largest assemblages of armed men ever seen of Gor, under their polemarkos, Myron, cousin to Lurius of Jad, Ubar of Cos, had now set their standards toward Ar. Torcadino had been a supply depot for the forces of Cos on the continent. It had been seized by the mercenary, Dietrich of Tarnburg, to forestall the march on Ar. Ar, however, had failed to act. She had not relieved the siege at Torcadino nor that in the north, at Ar's Station. Dietrich, finally understanding the treason in Ar, in high places, had managed to effect a withdrawal from Torcadino. His location was now unknown and Cos had put a price on his head. Now there lay little or nothing between the major forces of Cos on the continent, now on the march, and the gates of Ar. Further, though there was much talk in the city of resistance, of the traditions or Ar, of her Home Stone, and such, I did not think that the people of Ar, stunned and confused by the apparently inexplicable succession of recent disasters, had the will to resist the Cosians. Perhaps if there had been a Marlenus of Ar in the city, a Ubar, one to raise the people and lead them, there might have been hope. But the city was now under the governance of the regent, Gnieus Lelius, who, I had little doubt, might have efficiently managed a well-ordered polity under normal conditions, but was an unlikely leader in a time of darkness, crisis and terror. He was, I thought, a good man and an estimable civil servant, but he was not a Marlenus of Ar. Marlenus of Ar had vanished months ago on a punitive raid in the Voltai, directed against the tarnsmen of Treve. He was presumed dead.

"Kill her," said a man.

"Kill her!" said another.

"No!" said Marcus.

"No," I said.

"There are only two of them," said a fellow.

"Listen!" I said, lifting my hand.

In that instant the crowd was silent. More than one man lifted his head. We turned down the street. Phoebe, very small and vulnerable, naked, in her collar, crawled more behind the legs of Marcus.

We could hear the bells, the chanting. In a moment we could see the lifted golden circle, on its staff, approaching. The people in the street hurried to press against the walls.

"Initiates," I said to Marcus.

I could now see the procession clearly.

"Kneel," said a fellow near me.

"Kneel," I said to Marcus.

We knelt, on one knee. It surprised me that the people were kneeling, for, commonly, free Goreans do not kneel, even in the temples of the Initiates. Goreans commonly pray standing. The hands are sometimes lifted, and this is often the case with praying Initiates.

"I do not kneel to such," said Marcus.

"Stay down," I said. He had caused enough trouble already.

We could now smell the incense. In the lead of the procession were two lads in white robes, with shaved heads, who rang the bells. Following them were two more, who shook censers, these emitting clouds of incense. These lads, I assumed, were novices, who had perhaps taken their first vows.

"Praise the Priest-Kings!" said a man, fervently.

"Praise the Priest-Kings," said another.

I thought that Misk, the Priest-King, my friend, might have been fascinated, if puzzled, by this behavior.

An adult Initiate, in his flowing white robe, carried the staff surmounted with the golden circle, a figure with neither beginning nor end, the symbol of Priest-Kings. He was followed by some ten or so Initiates, in double file. It was these who were chanting.

A free woman drew back her robes, hastily, frightened, lest they touch an Initiate. It is forbidden for Initiates to touch women, and, of course, for women to touch them. Initiates also avoid meat and beans. A good deal of their time, I gather, is devoted to sacrifices, services, chants, prayers, and the perusal of mystic lore. By means of the study of mathematics they attempt to purify themselves.

"Save Ar!" wept a man, as they passed.

"Save us, oh intercessors with Priest-Kings!" cried a woman.

"Pray to the Priest-Kings for us," cried a man.

"I will bring ten pieces of gold to the temple!" promised another.

"I will bring ten verr, full-grown verr, with gilded horns!" promised another.

But the Initiates took no note of these not inconsiderable pledges. Of what concern could be such things to them?

"Keep your head down," I muttered to Marcus.

"Very well," he growled. Phoebe was behind us, on her stomach, shuddering, covering her head with her hands. I did not envy her, a naked slave, caught inadvertently in such a place.

In a few moments the procession had passed and we rose to our feet. The crowd had dissipated about us.

"You are safe now," I said to Phoebe, "or at least as safe as is ever a female slave."

She knelt timidly at the feet of Marcus, holding to his leg.

"We cannot resist Cos," said a man, a few feet from us.

"We must place our trust in the Priest-Kings," said another.

"Our lads will protect us," said a man.

"A few pitiful regiments and levies of peasants?" asked another.

"We must place our trust in the Priest-Kings," said a man.

Across from us, about seven feet away, on the other side of the narrow street, was the free woman who had secured her robes, that they might not touch an Initiate. She rose to her feet, looking after the procession. We could still hear the bells. The smell of incense hung in the air. Near the free woman was a female slave, in a short gray tunic. She, too, had been caught, like Phoebe, in the path of the procession. She had knelt with her head down to the street, the palms of her hands on the stones, making herself small, in a common position of obeisance. The free woman looked down at her. As the girl saw she was under the scrutiny of a free person she remained on her knees. "You sluts have nothing to fear," said the free woman to her, bitterly. "It is such as I who must fear." The girl did not answer. There was something in what the free woman had said, though in the frenzy of a sacking, the blood of the victors racing, flames about, and such, few occupants of a fallen city, I supposed, either free or slave, were altogether safe. "It will only be a different collar for you," said the free woman. The girl looked up at her. She was a lovely slave I thought, a red-haired one. She kept her knees tightly together before the free woman. Had she knelt before a man she would probably have had to keep them open, even if they were brutally kicked apart, a lesson to her, to be more sensitive as to before whom she knelt. "Only a different collar for you!" cried the free woman, angrily. The girl winced, but dared not respond. To be sure, I suspected, all things considered, that the free woman was right. Slave girls, as they are domestic animals, are, like other domestic animals, of obvious value to victors. It is unlikely that they would be killed, any more than tharlarion or kaiila. They would be simply chained together, for later distribution or sale. Then the free woman, in fury, with her small, gloved hand, lashed the face of the slave girl, back and forth, some three or four times. She, the free woman, a free person, might be trampled by tharlarion, or be run through, or have her throat cut, by victors. Such things were certainly possible. On the other hand, the free women of a conquered city, or at least the fairest among them, are often reckoned by besiegers as counting within the yield of prospective loot. Many is the free female in such a city who has torn away her robes before enemies, confessed her natural slavery, disavowed her previous masquerade as a free woman, and begged for the rightfulness of the brand and collar. This is a scene which many free woman have enacted in their imagination. Such things figure, too, in the dreams of women, those doors to the secret truths of their being. The free woman stood there, the breeze in the street, as evening approached, ruffling the hems of her robes. The free woman put her fingers to her throat, over the robes and veil. She looked at the slave, who did not dare to meet her eyes.

"What is it like to be a slave?" she asked.

"Mistress?" asked the girl, frightened.

"What is it like, to be a slave?" asked the free woman, again.

"Much depends on the master, beautiful Mistress," said the girl. The slave could not see the face of the free woman, of course, but such locutions, "beautiful Mistress," and such, on the part of slave girls addressing free women, are common. They are rather analogous to such things as "noble Master," and so on. They have little meaning beyond being familiar epithets of respect.

"The *master*?" said the free woman, shuddering.

"Yes, Mistress," said the girl.

"You must do what he says, and obey him in all things?" asked the free woman.

"Of course, Mistress," said the girl. "He is the Master."

"You may go," said the free woman.

"Thank you, Mistress!" said the girl, and leaped to her feet, scurrying away.

The free woman looked after the slave. Then she looked across at us, and at Phoebe, who lowered her eyes, quickly. Then, shuddering, she turned about and went down the street, to our left, in the direction from whence the Initiates had come.

"The people of Ar are frightened," said Marcus.

"Yes," I said.

We saw a fellow walk by, mumbling prayers. He was keeping track of these prayers by means of a prayer ring. This ring, which had several tiny knobs on it, was worn on the first finger of his right hand. He moved the ring on the finger by means of his right thumb. When one, turning the ring by means of the knobs, keeping track of the prayers that way, comes to the circular knob, rather like the golden circle at the termination of the Initiate's staff, one knows one has completed one cycle of prayers. One may then stop, or begin again.

"Where do you suppose the Initiates were bound?" I asked Marcus.

"To their temple, I suppose," he said.

"What for?" I asked.

"For their evening services, I presume," he said, somewhat irritably.

"I, too, would conjecture that," I said.

"The sun gate!" he cried. "We must be there before dark!"

"Yes," I agreed.

"Is there time?" he asked.

"I think so," I said.

"Come!" he said. "Come quickly!"

He then, leading the way, hurried up the street. I followed him, and Phoebe raced behind us.

2 The Tent

"You may turn about," said Marcus, standing up.

Phoebe, kneeling, gasping, unclasped her hands from behind her neck, and lifted her head from the dirt, in our small tent, outside the walls of Ar, one of hundreds of such tents, mainly for vagabonds, itinerants and refugees.

"Thank you, Master," said Phoebe. "I am yours. I love you. I love you."

"Stand, and face me," he said. "Keep your arms at your sides."

Marcus took a long cord, some five feet or so in length, from his pouch, and tossed it over his shoulder.

"Am I to be bound now?" she asked.

"The air seems cleaner and fresher outside the walls," I said.

We could hear the sounds of the camp about us.

"It is only that we do not have the stink of incense here," smiled Marcus.

"Do you know what this is?" he asked Phoebe. He held in his hand, drawn forth from his pouch, a bit of cloth.

"I am not certain," she said, timidly, hopefully, "Master." Her eyes lit up.

I smiled.

"It is a tunic!" she cried, delightedly.

"A *slave* tunic," he said, sternly.

"Of course, Master," she said, delightedly, "for I am a slave!"

It was a sleeveless, pullover tunic of brown rep cloth. It was generously notched on both sides at the hem, which touch guarantees an additional baring of its occupant's flanks.

I saw that Phoebe wanted to reach out and seize the small garment but that she, under discipline, kept her hands, as she had been directed, at her sides.

The cord over Marcus' shoulder, of course, was the slave girdle, which is used to adjust the garment on the slave. Such girdles may be tied in various ways, usually in such ways as to enhance the occupant's figure. Such girdles, too, like the binding fiber with which a camisk is usually secured on a girl, may be used to bind her.

"It is to be mine, is it not?" asked Phoebe, eagerly, expectantly, hopefully. She would not be fully certain of this, of course. Once before, in the neighborhood of Brundisium, far to the north and west, when she had thought she was to recieve a similar garment, one which had previously been worn by another slave, Marcus had refused to permit it to her. He had burned it. She was from Cos.

"I own it," said Marcus, "as I own you, but it is true that it was with you in mind that I purchased it, that you might wear it when permitted, or directed."

"May I touch it, Master?" she asked, delightedly.

"Yes," he said.

I watched her take the tiny garment in her hands, gratefully, joyfully.

It is interesting, I thought, how much such a small thing can mean to a girl. It was a mere slave tunic, a cheap, tiny thing, little more than a ta-teera or camisk, and yet it delighted her, boundlessly. It was the sort of garment which free women profess to despise, to find unspeakably shocking, unutterably scandalous, the sort of garment which they profess to regard with horror, the sort of garment which they seem almost ready to faint at the sight of, and yet to Phoebe, and to others like her, in bondage, it was precious, meaning more to her doubtless than the richest garments in the wardrobes of the free women. To be sure, I suspect that free women are not always completely candid in what they tell us about their feelings toward such garments. The same free woman, captured, who is cast such a garment, and regarding it cries out with rage and frustration, and dismay, and hastens to don it only when she sees the hand of her captor tighten on his whip, is likely, in a matter of moments, to be wearing it quite well, and with talent, moving gracefully, excitingly and provocatively within it. Such garments, and their meaning, tend to excite women, inordinately. Too, they are often not such strangers to such garments as they might have you believe. Such garments, and such things, are often found among the belongings of women in captured cities. It is presumed that many women wear them privately, and pose in them, before mirrors, and such. Sometimes it is in the course of such activities that they first feel the slaver's noose upon them, they surprised, and taken, in the privacy of their own compartments. On Gor it is said that free women are slaves who have not yet been collared. In Phoebe's case, of course, the garment represented not only such things, confirmation of her bondage, her subjection to a master, and such, but, more importantly, at the moment, the considerable difference between being clothed and unclothed. She, a slave, and not entitled to clothing, any more than other animals, was, by the generosity of her master, to be permitted a garment.

"Thank you, Master! Thank you, Master!" wept Phoebe, clutching the garment.

Marcus had, of his own thinking in the matter, purchased the garment. It was, in my opinion, high time he had done so. Not only would Phoebe be incredibly fetching in a slave garment, garments permitting a female in many ways to call attention to, accentuate, display and enhance her beauty, but it would make her, and us, less conspicuous on the streets of Ar. Also, of course, she would then be no more susceptible than other, similarly clad slaves of the pinches, and other attentions, of passers-by in the streets.

"May I put it on?" she asked, holding the garment out.

"Yes," said Marcus. He was beaming. I think he had forgotten that he hated the wench, and such.

"Why have you come to Ar?" I asked Marcus.

"Surely you know," he said.

"But that is madness," I said.

During the siege of Ar's Station its Home Stone had been smuggled out of the city and secretly transported to Ar for safekeeping. This was done in a wagon owned by a fellow named Septimus Entrates. We had learned, however, after the fall of Ar's Station, that the official rumor circulated in the south was to the effect that Ar's Station had opened its gates to the Cosian expeditionary force, this in consideration of substantial gifts of gold. Accordingly, those of Ar's Station were now accounted renegades in the south. This supposed treachery of Ar's Station was then used, naturally, to explain the failure of Ar's might in the north to raise the siege. it was supposed that Ar's dilemma in the north was then either to attack their former colony or deal with the retreating expeditionary force. On the supposition that the latter action took priority the might of Ar in the north entered the delta in pursuit of the Cosians, in which shifting, trackless morass column after column was lost or decimated. The devastation of Ar's might in the delta was perhaps the greatest military disaster in the planet's history. Of over fifty thousand men who had entered the delta it was doubted that there were more than four or five thousand survivors. Some of these, of course, had managed to find their way back to Ar. As far as these men knew, of course, at least on the whole, the circulating rumors were correct, namely, that Ar's Station had betrayed Ar, that it was still intact and that it was now a Cosian outpost. Such things they had been told in their winter camp, near Holmesk, south of the Vosk.

Phoebe slipped the garment over her head.

Marcus observed, intently.

Understandably enough, given these official accounts of doings in the north, Ar's Station and those of Ar's Station were much despised and hated in Ar. Happily Marcus' accent, like most of Ar's Station, was close enough to that of Ar herself that he seldom attracted much attention. Too, of course, these days, in the vicinity of Ar, given the movements of Cos on the continent, and the consequent displacements and flights of people, there were medleys of accents in and about Ar. Not even my own accent, which was unusual on Gor, attached much attention.

Phoebe drew down the tunic about her thighs, and turned before Marcus, happily.

"Aii!" said Marcus.

"Does the slave please you?" inquired Phoebe, delighted. The question was clearly rhetorical.

"It is too brief," said Marcus.

"Nonsense," I said.

"It is altogether too brief," said Marcus.

"The better that my master may look upon my flanks," said

Phoebe. They were well exposed, particularly with the notching on the sides.

"And so, too, may other men," he said, angrily.

"Of course, Master," she said, "for I am a slave!"

"She is extraordinarily beautiful," I said. "Let her be so displayed and exposed. Let others seethe with envy upon consideration of your property."

"She is only a slut of Cos!" said Marcus, angrily.

"Now only your slave," I reminded him.

"You are a pretty slave, slut of Cos," said Marcus to the girl, grudgingly.

"A girl is pleased, if she is found pleasing by her master," said Phoebe.

"Surely, by now," I said to Marcus, "you have thought the better of your mad project."

"No," said Marcus, absently, rather lost in the rapturous consideration of his lovely slave.

The Home Stone of Ar's Station, as I have suggested, was in Ar. It was primarily in connection with this fact that Marcus had come to Ar.

"She is marvelously beautiful," said Marcus.

"Yes," I said.

"For a Cosian," he said.

"Of course," I said.

Given the anger in Ar at Ar's Station, and the fact that the Home Stone of Ar's Station had been sent to Ar, supposedly, according to the rumors, not for safekeeping, given the imminent danger in the city, but in a gesture of defiance and repudiation, attendant upon the supposed acceptance of a new Home Stone, one bestowed upon them by Cosians, the stone was, during certain hours, publicly displayed. This was done in the vicinity of the Central Cylinder, on the Avenue of the Central Cylinder. The purpose of this display was to permit the people of Ar, and elsewhere, if they wished, to vent their displeasure upon the stone, insulting it, spitting upon it, and such.

"The stone," I said, "is well guarded."

We had ascertained that this morning. We had then gone to the Alley of the Slave Brothels of Ludmilla, on which street lies the *insula* of Achiates. I did not enter the *insula* itself, but made an inquiry or two in its vicinity. Those whom I had sought there were apparently no longer in residence. I did not make my inquiries of obvious loungers in its vicinity. I went back, with Marcus and Phoebe, later in the afternoon. The loungers were still in evidence. I had assumed then they had been posted. There was a street peddler nearby, too, sitting behind a blanket on which trinkets were spread. I did not know if he had been posted there or not. It did not much matter. Normally in such arrangements there are at least two individuals. In this way one can report to superiors while the other keeps his vigil. As far as I knew, no one knew that I was in the vicinity of Ar. I did know I could be recognized by certain individuals. The last time I had come to Ar, before this time, I had come with dispatches to Gnieus Lelius, the regent, from Dietrich of Tarnburg, from Torcadino. I had later carried a spurious message which had nearly cost me my life to Ar's Station, to be delivered to its commanding officer at the time, Aemilianus, of the same city. I had little doubt that I had inadvertently become identified as a danger to, and an enemy of, the party of treason in Ar. I did not know if the regent, Gnieus Lelius, were of this party or not. I rather suspected not. I was certain, however, from information I had obtained at Holmesk, at the winter camp of Ar, that the high general in the city, Seremides, of Tyros, was involved. Also, secret documents earlier obtained in Brundisium, and deciphered, gave at least one other name, that of a female, one called Talena, formerly the daughter, until disowned, of Marlenus of Ar. Her fortunes were said to be on the rise in the city.

"I am well aware," said Marcus, "that the stone is well guarded."

"Then abandon your mad project," I said to him.

"No," said he.

"You can never obtain the stone," I said.

"Have you come to Ar for a reason less likely of fruition?" he asked.

I was silent.

The girl did not understand our conversation as we had not spoken before her of these things. She was a mere slave and thus appropriately kept in ignorance. Let them please and serve. That is enough for them.

"Well?" smiled Marcus.

I did not respond to him. I thought of a woman, one now high in Ar, one for whom I had once mistakenly cared, a vain, proud woman who had once, thinking me helpless and crippled, mocked and scorned me. I thought of her, and chains. It would be impossible to obtain her, of course. Yet, if somehow, in spite of all, I should obtain her it was not even my intention to keep her but rather, as a gesture, merely dispose of her, giving her away or selling her off as the least of slaves.

"I see," said Marcus.

"Master?" asked Phoebe, turning before Marcus.

"Yes," he said, "you are very pretty."

"Thank you, Master," she said, "for giving me a garment."

"For permitting you to wear one," Marcus corrected her.

"Yes, Master," she said.

"For at least a moment or two," he said.

"Yes, Master!" she laughed.

"You have an exquisitely beautiful slave, Marcus," I said.

Phoebe looked at me, gratefully, flushed.

Marcus made an angry noise, and clenched his fists. I saw that he feared he might come to care for her.

He whipped the cord, some five feet in length, from his shoulder.

Phoebe approached him and held her wrists, crossed, before her. "Am I to be bound, Master?" she asked. In extending their limbs so readily, so delicately, for binding, slaves express, and demonstrate, their submission.

"Do you like the garment?" he asked.

"Whose use I may have, if only for a moment," she smiled. "Yes, Master. Oh, yes, my Master!"

"Are you grateful?" he asked.

"Yes, Master," she said. "A slave is grateful, so very grateful."

"It is not much," he said.

"It is a treasure," she said. I smiled. To her, I supposed, a slave, such a tiny thing, little more than a brief rag, would indeed be a treasure.

"You understand, of course," he said, "that its use may be as easily taken from you as given to you."

"Yes, Master," she said.

"Do you wish to retain its use?" he asked.

"Of course, Master," she said.

"You now have an additional motivation for striving to please," he said.

"Yes, Master," she smiled. The control of a girl's clothing, and many other things, such as her diet, chaining, name, whether or not her head is to be shaved, and so on, are all within the purview of the master. His power over the slave is unqualified and absolute. Phoebe, of course, was muchly in love with Marcus, and he, in spite of himself, with her. On the other hand, even if she had been, as he sometimes seemed to want her, the hating slave of a hating master, she would still have had to strive with all her power to please him, and in all things, and with perfection. It is such to be a Gorean slave girl.

"Do you think me weak?" he asked.

"No, Master!" she said.

He regarded her, torn with his love for her, and his hatred of the island of Cos.

She lifted her crossed wrists to him, for binding.

But he did not move to pinion them. The cord, of course,

was not for such a purpose, though that was a purpose which it could surely serve.

She separated her wrists timidly, and looked at him, puzzled, with love in her eyes.

"I am eager to be pleasing to you," she whispered.

"That is fitting," he said.

"Yes, Master," she whispered.

"For you are a slave," he said.

"And yours," she said, suddenly, breathlessly, "yours, your slave!"

He looked at her, angrily.

"I exist for you," she said, "and it is what I want, to please and serve you." She was much in love. She wanted to give all of herself to Marcus, irreservedly, to hold nothing back, to live for him, if need be, to die for him. It is the way of the female in love, for whom no service is too small, no sacrifice too great, offering herself selflessly as an oblation to the master.

He regarded her, in fury.

She extended her arms a little, toward him, timidly, hoping to be permitted to embrace him. "Accept the devotion of your slave," she begged.

I saw his fists clench.

"I love you. I love you, my Master!" she said.

"Sly, lying slut!" he said.

"No!" she wept.

"Mendacious slut of Cos!" he cried.

"I love you! I love you, my Master!" she cried.

He then struck her with the back of his hand, striking her to one side, and she fell, turning, to her knees. She looked up at him from all fours, blood at her lips.

"Were you given permission to speak?" he asked.

"Forgive me, Master," she whispered. She then crawled to his feet and, putting her head down, kissed them. "A slave begs the forgiveness of her Master," she said.

Marcus looked down at her, angrily. Then he turned to me. "Her use, of course," he said, "is yours, whenever you might please."

"Thank you," I said, "but I think that I can find a rent wench outside in the camp, or, if I wish, buy a slut, for they are cheap in the vicinity of Ar these days."

"As you wish," said Marcus.

Although Marcus was harsh with his slave, pretending even to a casual and brutal disdain for her, he was also, it might be mentioned, extremely possessive where she was concerned. Indeed, he was almost insanely jealous of her. She was not the sort of girl, for example, whom he, as a host, even at the cost of a certain rudeness and inhospitality, would be likely to hand over for the nightly comfort of a guest. It would be at his slave ring alone that she would be likely to find herself chained.

"Stand up," said Marcus to the girl.

"I hear some music outside," I said.

"Yes," said Marcus.

"At least someone in the neighborhood seems cheerful," I said.

"Probably peasants," said Marcus.

I thought this might be true. There were many about, having fled before the march of Cos. Driven from their lands, their stock muchly lost, or driven before them, they had come to the shelter of Ar's walls. Still they were ready to sing, to drink and dance. I admired peasants. They were hardy, sturdy, irrepressible.

Phoebe now stood humbly before Marcus, as she had been commanded.

"Wipe your face," said Marcus.

She wiped the blood away, or smeared it, with her right forearm.

"This cord," said Marcus, "may function as a slave girdle. Such may be tied in several ways. You, as a slave, doubtless know the tying of slave girdles."

I smiled. Marcus would know, of course, that Phoebe would not be likely to know much, if anything, of such matters. Only recently she had been a free woman, though, to be sure, one who had been long kept, languishing, it seemed, and, of course, incompletely fulfilled, in the status of a mere captive. Only a few weeks ago had she been branded and collared, and thusly liberated into total bondage.

"No, Master," said Phoebe. "I am not trained, save in so far as you, and before you, Master Tarl, have deigned to impart some understandings to me."

"I see," said Marcus. I think he was just as pleased that Phoebe had not been muchly trained. From one point of view this suggested that she had presumably been less handled before coming into his keeping than might have been otherwise the case. Also, of course, if she was to strive to please, and squirm, under strict training disciplines, he would prefer that she do so under his personal tutelage, and in the lights of his personal taste, she thus being kept more to himself, and also being trained to be a perfect personal slave, one honed to the whims, preferences and needs of a particular master. To be sure, this sort of thing can be done with any woman. It is part of her "learning the new master."

"Master is undoubtedly familiar with many slaves, and things having to do with slaves," said Phoebe. "Perhaps then Master can teach his slave such things."

Though Marcus was a young man and, as far as I knew, had never owned a personal slave before Phoebe, he, as a Gorean, would be familiar with slaves. Not only were they in his culture but he probably, as he was of the Marcelliani, which had been a prominent, wealthy family in Ar's Station, would have had them in his house, in growing up, the use of some perhaps being accorded to him after puberty. Similarly he would be familiar with them from his military training, which would include matters such as the hunting and capture of women, who count as splendid trophies of the chase, so to speak, and his military life, as officers and men commonly have at their disposal barracks slaves, camp slaves, and such. Too, of course, he would be familiar with the lovely properties encountered in paga taverns, and such places. Indeed, together we had frequented such establishments, for example, in Port Cos, after our landing there, as refugees from Ar's Station. The Gorean slave girl seldom needs to fear that her master will not be fully familiar with, and skilled in, the handling, treatment and discipline of slaves.

"I am not a professional slave trainer," said Marcus, "or costumer or cosmetician, but I will show you two of the most common ties. Others you might inquire of, when the opportunity permits, of your sister slaves."

"Yes, Master," she said.

Phoebe, because of the nature of her acquisition and holding, and our movements, and such, had had very little chance to associate with, or meet, other slaves. On the other hand this deprivation might be soon remedied, I supposed, if Marcus should take up a settled domicile. Indeed, even if we remained in the camp for a few days, it was likely that Phoebe would soon find herself in one group or another of female slaves, conversing, working together, perhaps laundering, or such. From her sisters in bondage a girl, particularly a new girl, can learn much. In such groups there are normally numerous subtle relationships, hierarchies of dominance, and such, but when a male appears they are all instantly reduced, before him, to the commonality of their beauty and bondage.

"Also," said Marcus, sizing up the slim beauty before him, "we can always, if we wish, extend our repertoire of ties by experiment."

"Yes, Master," said Phoebe, eagerly. It seemed she had forgotten her cuffing. Yet I had little doubt that its admonitory sting lingered within her, not only as a useful memorandum of her bondage but recalling her to the prudence of caution.

Marcus looped the cord and put it over her, so that the loop hung behind her back and two loose ends before her.

Already, it seemed, Phoebe had returned to her normal mode of relating to him, as a mere, docile slave, not daring to confess her love openly. Yet I think there was now something subtly different in their relationship. Phoebe now, given his recent intensity, his denunciation of her mendacity, his fury, his excessive response to her protestations of love, the violence of his reaction to them, had more than ample evidence of the depth of his feelings toward her. She was more than satisfied with what had occurred. Such things, to the softness and intelligence of her woman's heart, spoke clearly to her. She was not in the position of the helplessly loving female slave at the feet of a beloved master who regarded her with indifference as merely another of his women, or was even cold to her, perhaps disdaining her as a trivial, meaningless possession.

Marcus now, roughly, took the forward ends of the cord, where they dangled before her, and put them back, beneath her arms, through the back loop, and drew them forward where he tied them, snugly, beneath her breasts.

"Oh!" she said.

"You are pretty, slut of Cos," he said, standing back, admiring his handiwork.

"I wish that I had a mirror," she said.

"You may see yourself, in a sense," I said, "in the mirror of his desire."

"Yes," she whispered, shyly.

"And this," said Marcus, loosening the cord, "is perhaps the most common way of wearing the slave girdle." He then took the forward ends of the cord, again free, and this time crossed them, over the bosom, before placing them again through the loop at the back, drawing them forward and, once more, fastening them, perhaps more snugly than was necessary, before her.

"Ohh," he said. "Yes."

"Aii," I whispered. I then needed a woman. I must leave the tent and search for one, perhaps a girl in one of the open-air brothels, forbidden without permission to leave her mat or even to rise to her knees.

"Is it pretty?" asked Phoebe.

"It is a perhaps not unpleasing effect," said Marcus.

"Yes," I agreed.

"There are, of course, numerous other ways in which to tie slave girls," said Marcus.

"True," I said. To be sure they tended to have certain things in common, such as the accentuation and enhancement of the slave's figure.

Phoebe moved about in the tent, delighted. She could perhaps suspect what she might look like.

"You see," I said, "there is some point in permitting a female clothing."

"Yes," said he, "providing it may be swiftly, and at one's will, removed."

"Of course," I said.

Phoebe then, beside herself with passion, knelt swiftly before Marcus. "Please, Master!" she said.

I saw that Marcus was in agony to have her. He could scarcely control himself.

"Please!" wept the slave.

I expected him to leap upon her and fling her to her back to the dirt, ravishing her with the power of the master.

"Please, please, Master!" wept the slave, squirming in piteous need before him.

"What do you want?" asked Marcus then, drawing himself up, coldly, looking down at her. It amazed me that he was capable of this.

"Master?" she asked.

He regarded her, coldly.

"I beg use," she whispered.

"Do you protest your love?" he inquired. His hand was open, where she could see it. It was poised. She saw it. He was ready, if necessary, again to cuff her.

"No, Master," she said, hastily.

"Not even the love of a slave girl?" he asked.

"No, Master," she said.

"And in any event," he said, "the love a slave girl is worthless, is it not?"

"Yes, Master," she whispered, tears in her eyes. This was absurd, of course, as the love of a slave girl is the deepest and most profound love that any woman can give a man. Love makes a woman a man's slave, and the wholeness of that love requires that she be, in truth, his slave. With nothing less can she be fully, and institutionally, content.

"You do not then protest your love," he said, "not even the love of a slave girl?"

"No, Master," she whispered.

"What then?" asked he, casually.

"I beg simple use," she said.

"I see," he said.

"I am a slave in desperate need," she said. "I am at your mercy. You are my master. In piteous need I beg use!"

"So," said he, scornfully, "the slut of Cos, on her knees, begs use of her Master, one of Ar's Station."

"Yes, Master!" she said.

"You will wait," he said.

"Yes, Master," she moaned.

"I hear music outside, the instruments of peasants, I believe," said Marcus, turning to me. "Perhaps they are holding fair or festival, such as they may, in such times."

"Perhaps," I said.

"Let us investigate," suggested Marcus.

"Very well," I said.

"Oh, yes," said he, looking down, "what of this slave?" She squirmed. It seemed she had slipped his mind.

"Bring her along," I suggested.

"You are an ignorant and unworthy slave, are you not?" asked Marcus.

"Yes, Master," she said. She was flushed and helplessly needful, even trembling.

'Better surely," said Marcus, "that she be stripped and left here, behind, alone, bound hand and foot."

"Perhaps if you have a slave ring to chain her to," I said.

"You think there is danger of theft?" he asked.

"Yes," I said.

"You think she might be of interest to others?" he asked.

"Undoubtedly," I said.

"On your feet," he said to the girl.

Groaning, scarcely able to stand straight, so wrought with need she was, she stood.

"There will be darkness and crowds," mused Marcus. "Do you think you will try to escape?" he asked the girl.

"No, Master," she said.

"Straighten up," he said, "put your shoulders back, pull in your belly, thrust forth your breasts."

"She is a delicacy," I said, "worth at least two silver tarsks, in any market."

"I will not try to escape, Master," said the girl.

"I wonder," mused Marcus.

"I am collared," she said. "I am branded."

"True," said Marcus.

In this way she had suggested that even if she might desire to escape such a hope would be forlorn for her. She was reminding him of the categoricality of her condition, of its absoluteness, of the hopelessness of escape for such as she, a female held in Gorean bondage. For example, there are not only such obvious things as the brand and collar, and the distinctive garbing of the slave, or the lack of garbing, but, far more significantly, the extreme closeness of the society, with its scrutiny of strangers, and the general nature of an uncompromising culture, with its social, legal and institutional recognition of, and inflexible enforcement of, her condition. There is, accordingly, for all practical purposes, no escape for the Gorean slave girl. At best she might, at great risk to her own life, succeed in obtaining a new chaining, a new master, and one who, in view of her flight, will undoubtedly see to it that she is incarcerated in a harsher bondage than that from which she fled, to which now, under her new strictures, she is likely to look back upon longingly. Similarly the penalties for attempted escape, particularly for a second attempt, are severe, usually involving hamstringing. Only the most stupid of women dares to even think of escape, and then seldom more than once.

"Will it be necessary to bind you?" asked Marcus.

"No, Master," she said.

"Turn about, and put your hands, wrists crossed, behind you," he said.

He then, whipping a short length of binding fiber from his pouch, with two simple loops, and a double knot, a warrior's capture knot, tied her hands together.

"Will it be necessary to leash you?" he asked.

"No, Master," she said.

He then turned her about and put a leather leash collar, with its attached lead, now dangling before her, on her neck.

Although I did not think that Phoebe, who was a highly intelligent girl, would be likely to attempt an escape, even if she were not bound to Marcus by chains a thousand times stronger than those of iron, the chains of love, she might be stolen. Slave girls are lovely properties, and slave theft, the stealing of beautiful female slaves, is not unknown on Gor.

She tried to press against him, but he pressed her back, with one hand.

"Yes, Master," she sobbed. She was not now, without his permission, to so much as touch him.

"Let us be on our way," said Marcus.

The girl moaned with need.

"Very well," I said.

"Outside," said Marcus to the girl, "stand and walk well."

"Yes, Master," she said.

She was flushed, and needful, but I did not know if this would be readily apparent outside, among the moving bodies, in the darkness, in the wayward shadows, in the uncertain light of campfires.

"You are sure you do not wish to remain in the tent for a bit?" I asked.

"Please, Master!" begged Phoebe.

"No," said Marcus.

Phoebe was quite beautiful in the tunic. It was adjusted on her by a slave girdle, in one of its common ties.

The girl looked at her master, piteously.

"Let us be on our way," said Marcus.

We left the tent, the girl following, bound, on the leash. She whimpered once, softly, piteously, beggingly, to which sound, however, her master, if he heard it, paid no heed.

3 The Camp

"Stones! Guess stones!" called a fellow. "Who will play stones?"

This is a guessing game, in which a certain number of a given number of "stones," usually from two to five, is held in the hand and the opponent is to guess the number. There are many variations of "Stones," but usually one receives one point for a correct guess. If one guesses successfully, one may guess again. If one does not guess successfully, one holds the "stones" and the opponent takes his turn. The game is usually set at a given number of points, usually fifty. Whereas the "stones" are often tiny pebbles, they may be any small object. Sometimes beads are used, sometimes even gems. Intricately carved and painted game boxes containing carefully wrought "stones" are available for the affluent enthusiast. The game, as it is played on Gor, is not an idle pastime. Psychological subleties, and strategies, are involved. Estates have sometimes changed hands as a result of "stones." Similarly, certain individuals are recognized as champions of the game. In certain cities, tournaments are held.

I wiped my mouth with my forearm and rose to my feet. I was now much refreshed.

"Do not leave me, I beg you" said the girl at my feet, on the mat. Her hands were about my ankle. "I would kneel to you!" she said.

"You do not have permission even to rise to your knees," I reminded her. She groaned.

"Paga! Paga!" called a fellow, with a large bota of paga slung over his shoulder.

"I belly to you!"said the girl, her head down, over my foot.

She held still to my ankle, her small hands about it. Her hair was about my foot. I felt her hot lips press again and again to my foot. She looked up. "Buy me," she begged. "Buy me!" The marks of the rush mat were on her back. She was a blonde, and short, voluptuously curvaceous. She drew her legs up then, and lay curled on her side, looking up at me, her hands still on my ankle. "Buy me," she begged.

"Lie on your back," I told her, "your arms at your sides, the palms of your hands up, your left knee raised."

She did so.

"Buy me!" she begged.

I could now walk away from her.

"Please," she begged.

Her words puzzled me. Why would she want me to buy her? Certainly I had not accorded her dignity or respect, or such things. Indeed, it had not even occurred to me to do so, nor would it have been appropriate, as she was a mere slave. Similarly I had not handled her gently. Indeed, at least in my second usage of her, purchased with a second tarsk bit placed in the shallow copper bowl beside her, she had been put through fierce, severe, uncompromising slave paces. Once, when she had seemed for an instant hesitant, I had even cuffed her.

"I want to be your slave," she said. "Please buy me!"

I considered her. She was certainly a hot slave.

"Please, Master," she begged.

"Are you finished?" asked a fellow behind me.

I looked again at the female, luscious, collared, on the mat.

"Please buy me!" she begged.

I considered my purposes in coming to Ar, the dangers that would be involved.

"I do not think it would be practical," I said.

She sobbed.

"Are you finished?" asked the fellow, again.

"Yes," I said.

"Master!" she wept.

As I left, slinging about me my accouterments, I heard a new coin entered into the copper bowl.

Some peasants were to one side. Every now and then, presumably at some joke, or recounted anecdote, perhaps one about some tax collector thrown into a well, they would laugh uproariously.

A fellow brushed past me, drawing behind him two slaves, their wrists extended before them, closely together, pulled forward, the lead chains attached to their wrist shackles.

I was looking about for Marcus and Phoebe.

I glanced over to the walls of Ar, some hundred or so yards away, rearing up in the darkness. Here and there fires were lit on the walls, beacons serving to guide tarnsmen. The last time I had been to Ar, that time I had received the spurious message, to be delivered to Aemilianius, in Ar's Station, there had been no need of yellow ostraka, or permits, to enter the city. Such devices, or precautions, had in the interim apparently been deemed necessary, doubtless for purposes of security or to control the number of refugees pouring into the city which, even earlier, had been considerable. Many had slept in the streets. I had rented, at that time, a room in the *insula* of Achiates. One permitted residence in Ar received the identificatory ostrakon, for example, citizens, ambassadors, resident aliens, trade agents, and such. Such ostraka, of course, were only for free persons. The permitted residency of slaves, in their kennels, and such, was a function of their owner's possession of such ostraka. Others might enter the city on permits, usually for a day, commencing at dawn and concluding at sundown. Records were kept of visitors. A visitor whose permit had expired was the object of the search of guardsmen. Too, guardsmen might, at their option, request the presentation of either ostraka or permits. Ostraka were sometimes purchased illegally. Sometimes men killed for them. The nature of the ostraka, in virture of such possibilities, was changed periodically, for example, taking different shapes, having different colors, being recoded, and so on.

I saw some fellows gathered about a filled, greased wineskin. There was much laughter. I went over to watch. He who manages to balance on it for a given time, usually an Ehn, wins both the skin and its contents. One pays a tarsk bit for the chance to compete. It is extremely difficult, incidentally, to balance on such an object, not only because of the slickness of the skin, heavily coated with grease, but even more so because of its rotundity and unpredictable movements, the wine surging within it. "Aii!" cried a fellow flailing about and then spilling from its surface. There was much laughter. "Who is next?" called the owner of the skin. This sort of thing is a sport common at peasant festivals, incidentally, though there, of course, usually far from a city, within the circle of the palisade, the competition is free, the skin and wine being donated by one fellow or another, usually as his gift to the festival to which all in one way or another contribute, for example, by the donation of produce, meat or firewood. At such festivals there are often various games, and contests and prizes. Archery is popular with the peasants and combats with the great staff. Sometimes there is a choice of donated prizes for the victors. For example, a bolt of red cloth, a tethered verr or a slave. More than one urban girl, formerly a perfumed slave, sold into the countryside, who held herself above peasants, despising them for their supposed filth and stink, has found herself, kneeling and muchly roped, among such a set of prizes. And, to her chagrin, she is likely to find that she is not the first chosen.

I was brushed by a fellow in the darkness. While I could still see him I checked my wallet. It was there, intact. The two usual modalities in which such folks work are to cut the strings of the wallet from the belt, carrying it away, or to slit the bottom of the wallet, allowing the contents to slip into their hand. Both actions require skill.

I saw a line of five slave girls, kneeling, abreast, their hands tied behind their backs. Bits of meat were thrown to them, one after the other, A catch scored two points for the master. A missed piece might be sought by any of the girls, scrambling about, on their bellies. She who managed to obtain it received one point for her master. The girls were encouraged from the sidelines, not only by their masters but by the crowd as well, some of whom placed bets on the outcome.

"Would you like to purchase a yellow ostrakon?" asked a fellow. I had hardly heard him. I looked about, regarding him. His hood was muchly pulled about his face. Were his offer genuine, I would indeed be eager to purchase such an object.

"Such are valuable," I said.

"Only a silver tarsk," he said.

"Are you resident in Ar?" I asked.

"I am leaving the city," he said. "I fear Cos."

"But Cos is to be met and defeated on the march to Ar," I said.

"I am leaving the city," he said. "I have no longer a need for the ostrakon."

"Let me see it," I said.

Surreptitiously, scarcely opening his hand, he showed it to me.

"Bring it here, by the light," I said.

Unwillingly he did so. I took it from his hand.

"Do not show it about so freely," he whispered.

I struck him heavily in the gut and he bent over, and sank to his knees. He put down his head. He gasped. He threw up into the dirt near the fire.

"If you cannot hold your paga, go elsewhere," growled a peasant.

The fellow, in pain, in confusion, in agony, looked up at me.

"It is indeed a yellow ostrakon," I said, "and oval in shape, as are the current ostraka."

"Pay me," he gasped.

"Only this morning I was at the sun gate," I told him, "where the current lists are posted, the intent of which is to preclude such fraud as you would perpetrate."

"No," he said.

"The series of this ostrakon," I said, "was discontinued, probably months ago."

"No," he said.

"You could have retrieved from a carnarium," I said. This was one of the great refuse pits outside the walls.

I broke the ostrakon in two and cast the pieces into the fire.

"Begone," I said to the fellow.

He staggered to his feet and, bent over, hobbled quickly away. I had not killed him.

"They may have to give up ostraka," said the peasant sitting cross-legged by the fire.

"Why?" I asked.

"It is dangerous to carry them," he said. "Too many folks are killed for them."

"What then will Ar do?" I asked.

"I think she will shut her gates," he said.

"But her forces are interposed between her gates and Cos," I said.

"True," said the peasant.

I then continued my search for Marcus and Phoebe. He was, of course, quite proud of her. I did not doubt but what he was circulating about, seemingly merely wandering about, but showing her off. She would surely be one the most fetching slaves in the area.

How lofty, I thought, are the walls of Ar. Yet they were only of stone and mortar. They could be breached. Her bridges could be, as the Goreans have it, washed in blood. But there were forces of Ar between her walls and the banners of Cos. It was well.

I stopped for a moment to watch an amusing race. Several slave girls are aligned, on all fours, poised, their heads down. Then, carefully, a line of beans, one to a girl, is placed before them. She must then, on all fours, push the bean before her, touching it only with her nose. The finish line was a few yards away. "Go!" I heard. The crowd cheered on its favorites. On this sport, as well as on several others, small bets were placed. Sometimes a new slave, one who has recently been a haughty, arrogant free woman, is used in such a race. Such things, aside from their amusing, and fitting, aspects, are thought to be useful in accommodating her to her new reality, that of the female slave. In them she learns something more of the range of activities that may be required of her.

I passed two fellows wrestling in a circle, others watching.

Another group, gathered about a fire, were singing and passing about a bota, I presume, of paga.

I passed a pair of fellows intent over a Kaissa board. It seemed they were in their own world.

A female slave passed me, looking shyly down. She moved, excellently. I saw another regarding me. She was on her master's leash. I recalled that Phoebe, too, had been on a leash. Perhaps by now, I thought, Marcus would have returned with his slave, suffering in her need, to the tent, if only to satisfy himself with her, for he, too, I was certain, was in an agony to have her. Yet, in spite of his need, his intense desire for her, which it seemed he would choose to conceal from her, and her obvious, even explicitly expressed piteous need, which he chose to ignore, thereby supposedly, I suppose, indicating to her its meaninglessness to him, he had, as though nothing were afoot, simply taken her from the tent, as though merely to take in the sights, to see what might be seen in the camp. If Marcus had returned to the tent by now, of course, I did not think it would do for me to drop back, at least just yet. I wondered if, even now, Phoebe might be writhing at his mercy in an intricate slave binding, one which might make her so much the more helpless under his touch. Yet, given what I knew of Marcus, and his will, and determination, he was probably still about in the camp. But how long, I wondered, could he hold out. Certainly Phoebe had been superb in her tunic, adjusted on her by the slave girdle. The mere sight of her had led me to hurry to the mats. I supposed, however, that they were somewhere about. Knowing Marcus I would suppose so. He was excellent at gritting his teeth. I wondered if Phoebe had dared yet, in her need, to come close to him, on her leash, or even, perhaps, to brush against him, perhaps as though inadvertently. If Marcus thought such a thing deliberate on her part it might have earned her another cuffing. To be sure, it doubtless amused Marcus, or seemed fitting to him, to lead her about on her leash, suffering in a need which might be detectable even in the darkness and the shifting shadows. He might regard that as quite appropriate for a "slut of Cos."

There was, from one side, a sudden sound of grunting and the cracking of great staffs, and urging cries from men. Two fellows, brawny lads, in half tunics, were doing staff contest.

Both were good. Sometimes I could scarcely follow the movement of these weapons. "Watch him!" called a fellow to one of the contestants. "Cheers for Rarir!" called another. "Aii!" cried one of the lads, blood at the side of his head and ear, stumbling to the side. "Good blow!" cried an onlooker. But the lad came back with redoubled energy. I stayed for a moment. The lad from Rarir, as I understood it, then managed to pierce the guard of his opponent and thrust the staff into the fellow's chest. He followed this with a smiting to the side of the fellow's head which staggered him. He then, at the last moment, held back. The opponent, dazed, sat back in the dirt, laughing. "Victory for Rarir!" cried a man. "Pay us!" called another. Extending his hand to the foe the victor pulled him to his feet. They embraced. "Paga! Paga for both!" called a fellow.

I circled about a bit.

I saw no sight of Marcus or his lovely slave. Perhaps they had returned to the tent.

In one place, hearing a jangling of bells, I went over to a large open circle of fellows to watch a game of "girl catch." There are many ways in which this game, or sort of game, is played. In this one, which was not untypical, a female slave, within an enclosure, her hands bound behind her back, and hooded, is belled, usually with common slave bells at the collar, wrists and ankles and a larger bell, a guide bell, with its particular note, at her left hip. Some fellows then, also hooded, or blindfolded, enter the enclosure, to catch her. Neither the quarry nor the hunters can see the other. The girl is forbidden to remain still for more than a certain interval, usually a few Ihn. She is under the control of a referee. His switch can encourage her to move, and, simultaneously, of course, mark her position. She is hooded in order that she may not determine into whose power she comes. When she is caught that game, or one of its rounds, is concluded. The victor's prize, of course, is the use of the slave.

I continued to walk about.

Two fellows were haggling over the price of a verr.

I saw a yoked slave girl, two buckets attached to the ends of the yoke. She was probably bearing water for draft tharlarion. There were some in the camp. I had smelled them.

A fellow stumbled by, drunk.

I looked after the girl. She was small, and comely. She would probably have to make several trips to water the tharlarion.

I wondered if the drunken fellow knew where his camp was. Fortunately there were no carnaria in this vicinity. It would not do to stumble into one.

Around one of the campfires there was much singing.

I heard the sound of a lash, and sobs. A girl was being disciplined. She was tied on her knees, her wrists over her head, tied to a horizontal bar between two poles. I gathered that she had been displeasing.

In a tent I heard a heated political discussion.

"Marlenus of Ar will return," said a fellow. "He will save us."

"Marlenus is dead," said another.

"Let his daughter then, Talena, take the throne," said another.

"She is no longer his daughter," said a fellow. "She has been disavowed by Marlenus. She was disowned."

"How is it then her candidacy for the throne is taken seriously in the city?" asked a man.

"I do not know," admitted the other.

"Some speak of her as a possible Ubara," said a man.

"Absurd," said another.

"Many do not think so," said the man.

"She is an arrogant and unworthy slut," said another. "She should be in a collar."

"Beware, lest you speak treason," said one of the men.

"Can it be treason to speak the truth?" inquired a fellow.

"Yes," said the other fellow.

"Indeed," said a man, heatedly, "she may even know the whereabouts of Marlenus. Indeed, she, and others, may be responsible for his disappearance, or continued absence."

"I have not heard what you said," said a man.

"And I have not said it," was the rejoinder.

"I think it will be Talena," said a man, "who will sit upon the throne of Ar."

"How marvelous for Cos!" said a fellow. "That is surely what they would wish, that a female should sit upon the throne of Ar."

"Perhaps they will see to it that she does," said a man.

"Ar is in great peril," said a man.

"She has might between Cos and her gates," said a fellow. "There is nothing to fear."

"Yes!" said another man, fervently.

"We must trust in the Priest-Kings," said another.

"Yes," said another.

"I can remember," said a fellow, "when we trusted in our steel."

I then left the vicinity of this tent.

I wondered if I could balance on the greased wineskin. I knew a fellow who, I had little doubt, could have done so, Lecchio, of the troupe of Boots Tarsk-Bit.

I recalled the free female whose capture I had noted in Ar, that which had taken place in a street-level room in the Metellan district. Surely she must have known the law. The consorting of a free female with another man's slave renders her susceptible to the collar of the slave's master. The net had been cunningly arranged, that it might, when released, activated perhaps by springs or the pulling of a lever, fall and drape itself over the couch. It was clearly a device designed for such a purpose. The net and the room doubtless constituted a capture cubicle, simpler perhaps, but not unlike those in certain inns, in which a woman, lulled by the bolting on the doors, and feeling herself secure, may complete her toilet at leisure, bathing, combing her hair, perfuming herself and such, before the trap doors, dropped from beneath her, plunge her into the waiting arms of slavers. Guardsmen and magistrates, I had noted, had been in immediate attendance. She had had light brown hair and had been excellently curved. Yet I did not doubt but what her figure, even then of great interest, would be soon improved by diet and exercise, certainly before she would be put upon the block. To one side, in the half darkness, I heard the grunting of a man, and a female's gasping, and sobbing. There, to one side, in the shadows, difficult to make out, a slave girl, I could see the glint of her collar, writhed in a fellow's arms. I wondered if he owned her, or had simply caught her in the darkness. She was gasping, and squirming, and clutching at him. Her head twisted back and forth in the dirt. Her small, sweet, bared legs thrashed. Such responsiveness, of course, is not unusual in a female slave. It is a common function of the liberation of bondage. It comes with the collar, so to speak. Indeed, if a new slave does not soon exhibit profound and authentic sexual responsiveness, which matter may be checked by the examination of her body, within, say, an Ahn or so, the master's whip will soon inquire why. One blow of the whip is worth six months of coaxing. I thought again of the captured free woman, she taken in the net. Doubtless she, too, soon, given no choice, would become similarly responsive. Indeed, she, like other female slaves, would soon learn to be, and discover that she had become, perhaps to her initial dismay and horror, helplessly responsive to the touch of men, any man.

The pair thrashed in the darkness. She was pinioned, she sobbed with joy.

To be sure, if one prefers an inert, or frigid, or anesthetic, so to speak, woman, one may always make do with a free female, inhibited by her status, and such. They are plentiful, dismally so. Goreans, incidentally, doubt that any female is, *qua* female, irremediably or ultimately frigid. It is a common observation, even on Earth, that one man's petulant and frigid wife is another man's, to be sure, a different sort of man's, passionate, begging, obedient slave.

"I yield me, Master!" wept the slave, softly.

"It is known to me," he said.

"Yes, Master," she said.

I heard the sound of a tabor several yards away, and the swirl of a flute, and the clapping of hands.

I went in that direction.

"Marcus," I said, pleased, finding him in the crowd there.

"Women are dancing," he said.

"Superb," I said.

Behind Marcus was Phoebe, standing very straight, and very close to him, but not touching him. She was holding her lower lip between her teeth, presumably to help her keep control of herself. Also there was a little blood at the left side of her mouth. I gathered she must have dared in her need to brush hopefully or timidly against her master, or whimpered a bit more than he cared to hear. Indeed, perhaps she had even dared to importune him. Her wrists were still bound behind her. The lead on her leash looped up to Marcus' grasp.

"The camp is in a holiday mood," I said.

"Yes," he said.

I saw more than one fellow looking at Phoebe. She had marvelous legs and ankles, and a trim figure. She stood very straight. It was not difficult to tell now, even by glancing at her, that she was in need. One of the fellows looking her over laughed. Phoebe trembled, and bit her lip a little more.

A fellow tore off the tunic of a slave girl and thrust her out, into the circle.

"Aii!" cried men.

The female danced.

"I entered Phoebe in "meat catch," " said Marcus, "but she failed to catch even a single morsel."

"I am not surprised," I said. "She can hardly stand."

"That one is pretty," said Marcus. He referred to a redhead, thrust into the circle.

"I had thought you might have taken Phoebe to the tent by now," I said.

"No," said Marcus.

There were now some four or five girls in the circle. One wore a sign that said, "I am for sale."

Phoebe made a tiny noise.

"I think Phoebe is ready for the tent now," I said.

"She did not even want to leave it," said Marcus.

"True," I said.

Two more girls entered the circle.

"Perhaps you should take Phoebe back to the tent," I said. "She is hot."

"Oh?" asked Marcus.

"Yes," I said.

"Perhaps I should put her into the circle," he said.

"She can scarcely move," I said.

"Oh," he said. But I think he was pleased.

"She is in desperate need of a man's touch," I said.

"It does not matter," he said. "She is only a slave."

"Look," said Marcus. He referred to a new girl, joining the others in the circle. She wore ropes and performed on her knees, her sides, her back and stomach.

"She is very good," said Marcus.

"Yes," I said.

The dance in the circle, as one might have gathered, was not the stately dance of free maidens. even in which, of course, the maidens, though scarcely admitting this even to themselves, experience something of the stimulatory voluptuousness of movement, but slave dance, that form of dance, in its thousands of variations, in which a female may excitingly and beautifully, marvelously and fulfillingly, express the depths and profoundities of her nature. In such dance the woman moves as a female, and shows herself as a female, in all her excitingness and beauty. It is no wonder that women love such dance, in which dance they are so desirable and beautiful, in which dance they feel so free, so sexual, so much a slave.

Another woman entered the circle. She, too, was excellent.

"How do you like them?" Marcus asked Phoebe. It was no accident, surely, that he had brought her here to watch the slave dance.

"Please take me to the tent, Master," she begged.

As Marcus had undoubtedly anticipated the sight of the slave dance would have its effect on his little Cosian. She saw how beautiful could be slaves, of which she was one. On the other hand, I suspected he had not counted on the effect on himself.

Another girl, a slim blonde, was thrust into the circle. Her master, arms folded, regarded her. She lifted her chained wrists above her head, palms facing outward, this, because of the linkage of the manacles, tightening it, bringing the backs of her hands closely together. She faced her master. Desperate was she to please him. There was a placatory aspect to her dance. It seemed she wished to divert his wrath.

"Ah," said Marcus, softly.

The girl who wore the sign, "I am for sale," danced before us, as she had before others, displaying her master's proffered merchandise. I saw that she wanted to be purchased. That was obvious in the pleading nature of her dance. Her master was perhaps a dealer, and one, as are many, who is harsh with his stock. Her dance, thusly, was rather like the "Buy me, Master" behavior of a girl on a chain, the "slaver's necklace," or in a market, the sort of behavior in which she begs purchase. A girl on such a chain, or in a market, who is too much passed over has reason for alarm. Not only is she likely to be lowered on the chain, perhaps even to "last girl," which is demeaning to her, and a great blow to her vanity, but she is likely to be encouraged to greater efforts by a variety of admonitory devices, in particular, the switch and whip. Earth-girl slaves brought to Gor, for example, are often, particularly at first, understandably enough, I suppose, afraid to be sold, and accordingly, naturally enough, I suppose, sometimes attempt, usually in subtle ways, to discourage buyers, thereby hoping to be permitted to cling to the relative security of the slaver's chain. Needless to say, this behavior is soon corrected and, in a short time, only too eager now to be off the slaver's chain, they are displaying themselves, and proposing themselves, luscious, eager, ready, begging merchandise, to prospective buyers.

The girl for sale was a short-legged brunet, extremely attractive. I considered buying her, but decided against it. This was not a time for buying slaves. I gestured for her to dance on. She whirled away. A tear moved diagonally down her cheek.

She might, of course, not belong to a dealer.

There are many reasons why a master might put his girl, or girls, up for sale, of course. He might wish, for example, if he is a breeder, to improve the quality of his pens or kennels, trying out new blood lines, freshening his stock, and such. He might wish, casually, merely to try out new slaves, perhaps ridding himself of one to acquire another, who may have caught his eye. Perhaps he wants to keep a flow of slaves in his house, lest he grow too attached to one, always a danger. Too, of course, economic considerations sometimes become paramount, these sometimes dictating the selling off of chattels, whose value, of course, unlike that of a free woman, constitutes a source of possible income. Indeed, there are many reasons for the buying and selling of slaves, as there are for other forms of properties.

I continued to watch the female, the sign about her neck, dance. No, I said to myself, it would not do to bring her into peril. Then I chastised myself for weakness. One would not wish to purchase her, of course, because she might constitute an encumbrance. Still, she was attractive. Even as I considered the matter she received a sign from a fellow, her master, I suppose, and she tore open her silk, and danced even more plaintively before one fellow and then another. She seemed frightened. I suspected she had been warned as to what might befall her if she should prove unsuccessful in securing a buyer. I saw her glance at her master. His gaze was stern, unpitying. She danced in terror.

"Ahh," said Marcus. "Look!"

He was indicating the slim blonde, she with the chained wrists, whose dance before her master seemed clearly placatory in nature. She had perhaps begged to be permitted to appear before him in the dancing circle, that she might attempt to please him. He had perhaps acquiesced. I recalled he had thrust her into the circle, perhaps in this generously according her, though perhaps with some impatience, and misgivings, this chance to make amends for some perhaps unintentional, miniscule transgression. Perhaps his paga had not been heated to the right temperature. Women look well in collars.

'See?" asked Marcus.

I wondered how long he could hold out.

"I can do that, Master," sobbed Phoebe, trying to stand very still.

The blonde was now on her knees, extending her hands to her master, piteously, all this with the music in her arms, her shoulders, her head and hair, her belly.

"Aii!" said Marcus.

Her master seized her from the circle then and hurried her from the light, her head down, held by the hair, at his left hip. This is a common leading position for female slaves being conducted short distances. As the master holds her hair in the left hand, it leaves his right hand, commonly the sword hand, free.

Another woman was thrust into the circle.

I thought the blonde had very successfully managed to divert the master's wrath, assuming that was what she was up to. The only whip she need fear now, muchly, at any rate, would seem to be the "whip of the furs." To be sure, she might be given a stroke or two, if only to remind her that she was a slave.

"Look," said Marcus, interested.

I saw that the girl with the sign about her neck had taken a leaf from the book of the blonde, and cunningly, too. She, too, was now on her knees, advertising her charms, attesting mutely to the joys and delicacies that would be attendant upon her ownership. I saw her owner look at her, startled. She, of course, did not now see him. I gathered he had never seen her in just this fashion or way before, her silk parted, writhing on her knees, kissing, lifting her hands, her head moving, her hair flung about. "I will buy her!" called a fellow. "How much do you want?" inquired another, eagerly. Her master rushed into the circle. "Close your silk, lascivious slut!" he ordered her. Swiftly she clutched the silk about her, startled, confused, kneeling small before him. He looked about, angrily. He jerked her by one arm to her feet. She struggled to keep her silk closed with the other hand. "She is not for sale!" he said. He then drew her rapidly from the light, into the darkness outside the circle. We heard a tearing of silk. There was much laughter.

"He did not know what he owned!" laughed a man.

"No!" agreed another.

I guessed that the possession of such a wench might not, after all, even in my situation, have been too burdensome. After all, one could always have gotten a great deal of good out of her, and a great deal of work. On the other hand, she was no longer for sale.

"I can do that," said Phoebe.

"Nonsense," said Marcus.

"I can!" she said.

Marcus and I watched the women in the circle. I think perhaps about two Ihn passed. Perhaps one might have wiped one's nose, quickly, in the interval.

"Well," said Marcus, wearily, "it is getting late,"

"It is still early, Master," said Phoebe.

"I think that I shall return to the tent," said Marcus.

"A good idea," I said. "But I think I shall dally a bit outside."

"Oh?" said Marcus, concerned, but, I think, not excessively disappointed.

"Yes," I said.

"Perhaps we will return to the tent now," said Marcus to Phoebe.

"As Master wishes," she said, lightly. I thought she had carried that off rather well.

"I thought you wished to return to the tent," said Marcus.

"I am a slave," she said. "I must obey my master."

"Do you not want my touch?" asked Marcus.

"I am a slave," she said. "I must submit to the will of my master."

"I see," said Marcus.

Phoebe moved her lovely little head in the leash and collar, and looked off into the distance. "I am at your disposal," she said.

"I am well aware of that," said Marcus.

"Yes, Master," she said.

Phoebe's mistake, of course, was to look away. In this fashion she did not anticipate Marcus' touch. Too, it was firm, uncompromising, and not soon released. "Ohh!" she cried.

Marcus regarded her.

She, eyes wide, looked at him, startled, reproachfully, unbelievingly. She was half bent over. The leash dangled down from her collar.

She then began to tremble. Her small wrists pulled at the binding fiber, pinioning her hands behind her. Then, not even daring to move, she stood, partly bent from the waist, before him.

"Please," she whispered. "Please, my Master!"

"Perhaps you can move interestingly on your knees?" he said.

"Yes!" she said. "Anything! Anything!"

"And on your back and stomach?" he asked.

"Yes!" she said.

"And your sides?" he asked.

"Yes!" she said.

"Perhaps you desire to do these things," he said.

"Yes," she said. "Yes!"

"Perhaps you will be bound," he said.

"Yes, Master!" she said. "Bind me!"

It is common to bind slave girls.

"Do you have any petitions, any supplications?" inquired Marcus.

"Take me to the tent!" she begged. "Take me to the tent!"

He regarded her.

"I beg your touch, my Master!" she gasped.

"Oh?" he said.

"I beg it! I beg it! I beg it, my Master," she wept.

"Slut of Cos!" snarled Marcus suddenly.

"Your slave, only your slave, Master!" she wept.

He then, angrily, picked her up and threw her over his shoulder, her head to the rear. It is in this fashion that slaves are commonly carried. I saw her eyes for a moment, wild, but frightened, and grateful. Then he had sped with her from the place.

"A hot little vulo," said a man.

"Quite so," said a man.

"She could light a fire," said another.

"I wonder what he wants for her," said another.

"I do not think she is for sale," I said.

We then returned our attention to the dancing circle. New women entered it upon occasion, as others were withdrawn. There were now some ten to fifteen slaves in in the circle. How beautiful are women!

"How disgusting," said a free woman, nearby. I had not noticed her standing there until now.

"Begone, slut!" said a peasant.

The free woman gasped, and hurried away. Peasants are not always tolerant of gentlewomen. To be sure, they do not always object to them when they come into their possession, as, say, they might after the fall of a city, or if one, say, has been captured and deliberately sold to them, perhaps by some male acquaintance, for one reason or another. Indeed, I suspect the hardy fellows upon occasion rather enjoy owning such elegant women, women who are likely in their loftiness to have hitherto disparaged or despised their caste. It is pleasant to have them in ropes, naked at their feet. Sometimes they are asked if they rejoice to now be owned by peasants. If they respond negatively they are beaten. If they respond affirmatively they are also beaten, for lying. Quickly then will the women be taught the varied labors and services of the farm. Interestingly these women, under the domination of their powerful masters, often become excellent farm slaves. Sometimes they are even permitted to sleep in the hut, at their masters' feet.

"That is an excellent dancer there," said a fellow.

"Yes," I said.

"I think she has auburn hair," said another fellow. It was difficult to tell in the light.

"Yes," said another.

Auburn hair is highly prized in the slave markets. I recalled the slave, Temione, now, as I understood it, a property of Borton, a courier for Artemidorus of Cos. Her hair was a marvelous auburn. Too, by now, it would have muchly grown out, after having been shaved off some months ago, for catapult cordage.

I noted that the free female had gone a bit about the outside of the circle, and now stood there, back a bit from the circle, where there was a space between some men. From that position of vantage she continued to watch the dancers. This puzzled me. If she found such beauty, such sensuous liberation, such fulfilling joy, such reality, such honesty, the marvelousness of owned women before their masters, offensive or deplorable, why did she watch? What did she see there in the circle, I wondered.

What so drew her there, what so fascinated her there? Like most free women she was perhaps inhibited, frustrated and unhappy. She continued to gaze into the circle. Perhaps she saw herself there, clad in a rag and collar, if that, moving, turning with the others, like them so beautiful, so much alive, so vulnerable, so helpless, so owned. Does her master lift his whip? She must then redouble her efforts to please, lest she be lashed. I supposed that she, even there, standing so seemingly still, pretending to be a mere observer, could feel the dance in her body, in its myriad incipient movements, tiny movements in her legs, in her belly, in her body, in herself, in the wholeness of her womanhood. Perhaps she wished for her robes to be torn off and to be collared, and to be thrust, in her turn, into the circle. I did not doubt but what she would be zealous to please. Indeed, she had best be! But how strange that she, a free woman, would even linger in this place. Perhaps free women are incomprehensible. A Gorean saying came to mind, that the free woman is a riddle, the answer to which is the collar.

"Away!" called a fellow, who had turned about and seen the free woman. He waved his arm, angrily. "Away!" he said. The free woman then turned about and left the vicinity of the circle, hurriedly. I felt rather sorry for her, but then, I thought, surely the fellow was right, that the circle, or its vicinity, was no place for a free female. It was a place, rather, for the joy of masters and their slaves. Similarly, the vicinity of such places, though I did not think it would be so in this camp, at this particular time, can be dangerous for free women. For example, sometimes free women attempt, sometimes even disguising themselves, to spy on the doings of masters and slaves. For example, they might attempt, perhaps disguised as lads, to gain entrance to paga taverns. And often such entrance is granted them but later, to their horror, they may find themselves thrown naked to the dancing sand and forced to perform under whips. Similarly if they attempt to enter such establishments as pretended slaves they may find themselves leaving them by the back entrance, soon to become true slaves. In many cities, such actions, attempting to spy on masters and slaves, disguising oneself as a slave, garbing oneself as a slave, even in the supposed secrecy of one's own compartments, lingering about slave shelves and markets, even exhibiting an interest in, or fascination with, bondage, can result in a reduction to bondage. The theory is apparently that such actions and interests are those of a slave, and that the female who exhibits them should, accordingly, be imbonded.

I noted a fellow approaching the circle, who had behind him, heeling him, an unusually lovely slave.

"Teibar!" called more than one man. "Teibar!"

I have, more than once, I believe, alluded to the hatred of free women for their imbonded sisters, and to how they profess to despise them and hold them in contempt. Indeed, they commonly treat such slaves with what seems to be irrational and unwonted cruelty. This is particularly the case if the slave is beautiful, and of great interest to men. I have also suggested that this attitude of the free female toward the slave seems to be motivated, paradoxically enough, by envy and jealousy. In any event, slave girls fear free women greatly, as they, being mere slaves, are much at their mercy. Once in Ar, several years ago, several free women, in their anger at slaves, and perhaps jealous of the pleasures of masters and slaves, entered a paga tavern with clubs and axes, seeking to destroy it. This is, I believe, and example, though a rather extreme one, of a not unprecedented sort of psychological reaction, the attempt, by disparagement or action, motivated by envy, jealousy, resentment, or such, to keep from others pleasures which one oneself is unable, or unwilling, to enjoy. In any event, as a historical note, the men in the tavern, being Gorean, and thus not being inhibited or confused by negativistic, antibiological traditions, quickly disarmed the women. They then stripped them, bound their hands behind their back, put them of a neck rope, and, by means of switches, conducted them swiftly outside the tavern. The women were then, outside the tavern, on the bridge of twenty lanterns, forced to witness the burning of their garments. They were then permitted to leave, though still bound and in coffle. Gorean men do not surrender their birthright as males, their rightful dominance, their appropriate mastery. They do not choose to be dictated to by females. The most interesting portion of this story is its epilogue. In two or three days the women returned, mostly now barefoot, and many clad now humbly in low-caste garments. Some had even wrapped necklaces or beads about their left ankle. They begged permission to serve in the tavern in servile capacities, such as sweeping and cleaning. This was granted to them. At first the slaves were terrified of them but then, when it became clear that the women were not only truly serving humbly, as serving females, but that they now looked timidly up to the slaves, and desired to learn from them how to be women, and scarcely dared to aspire to their status, the fears of the slaves subsided, at least to a degree. Indeed, it was almost as though each of them, though perhaps a low girl in the tavern rosters, and much subject to the whip, had become "first girl" to some free woman or other, a rare turnabout in the lives of such collared wenches. Needless to say, in time, the free women, learning the suitable roles and lessons of womanhood, for which they had genetic predispositions, and aided by their lovely tutors, were permitted to petition for the collar. It was granted to them. It seems that this was what they had wanted all the time, though on a level not fully comprehensible to them at the beginning. One does not know what has become of them for, in time, as one might expect, they being of Ar, they were shipped out of the city, to be disposed of in various remote markets.

"Greetings, Teibar!" called a fellow.

"Hail, Teibar!" called another.

From the latter manner of greeting, I gathered this Teibar might be excellent with the staff, or sword. Such greetings are usually reserved for recognized experts, or champions, at one thing or another. For example, a skilled Kaissa player is sometimes greeted in such a manner. I studied Teibar. I would have suspected his expertise to be with the sword.

"His Tuka is with him," said a fellow.

"Tuka, Tuka!" called another, rhythmically.

'Tuka' is common slave name on Gor. I have known several slaves with that name.

The girl who had come with Teibar, Tuka, I supposed, now knelt at his side, her back straight, her head down. Her collar, like most female slave collars, particularly in the northern hemisphere, was close fitting. There would be no slipping it. I had no doubt that this Teibar was the sort of fellow who would hold his slave, or slaves, in perfect discipline.

"Tuka, Tuka!" called another fellow.

"She is extremely pretty," I said.

"She knows something of slave dance," said a fellow, licking his lips.

"Oh?" I said.

"Yes," he said.

"Tuka, Tuka, Tuka!" called more men.

The fellow, Teibar, looked down at his slave, who looked up at him, and quickly, timidly, kissed at his thigh. How much she was his, I thought.

"Tuka, to the circle!" called a fellow.

"She is a dancer," said a man.

"She is extraordinary," said another.

"Put Tuka in the circle!" called a fellow.

"Tuka, Tuka!" called another.

Teibar snapped his fingers once, sharply, and the slave leaped to her feet, standing erect, her head down, turned to the right, her hands at her sides, the palms facing backward. She might have been in a paga tavern, preparing to enter upon the sand or floor. I considered Teibar's Tuka. She had an excellent figure for slave dance.

"Clear the circle!" called a fellow.

The other dancers hurried to the side, to sit and kneel, and watch.

I considered the slave. She was beautiful, and well curved.

Teibar gestured to the circle.

"Ahh!" said men.

"She moves like a dancer," I said.

"She is a dancer," said a fellow.

I considered the girl. She now stood in the circle, relaxed, yet supple and vital, her wrists, back to back, over her head, her knees flexed.

"She is a bred passion slave," I said, "with papers and a lineage going back a thousand years."

"No," said a man.

"Where did he pick her up," I asked, "at the Curulean?"

"I do not know," said a fellow.

I supposed she was perhaps a capture. I did not know if a fellow such as this Teibar, who did not seem of the merchants, or rich, could have afforded a slave of such obvious value. A fellow, for example, who cannot afford a certain kaiila might be able to capture it, and then, once he has his rope on its neck, and manages to make away with it, it is his mount.

"Aii!" cried a fellow.

"Aii!" said I, too.

Dancing was the slave!

"She is surely a bred passion slave," I said. "Surely the blood lines of such an animal go back a thousand years!"

"No! No!" said a man, rapt, not taking his eyes from the slave.

I regarded her, in awe.

"She is trained, of course," said a man.

Only too obviously was this a trained dancer, and yet, too, there was far more than training involved. Too, I speak not of such relatively insignificant matters as the mere excellence of her figure for slave dance, as suitable and fitting as it might be for such an art form, for women with many figures can be superb in slave dance, or that she must possess a great natural talent for such a mode of expression, but something much deeper. In the nature of her dance I saw more than training, her figure, and her talent. Within this woman, revealing itself in the dance, in its rhythm, its joy, its spontaneity, its wonders, were untold depths of femaleness, a deep and radical femininity, unabashed and unapologetic, a rejoicing in her sex, a respect of it, a love of it, an acceptance of it and a celebration of it, a wanting of it, and of what she was, a woman, a slave, in all of its marvelousness.

"Tuka, Tuka!" called men.

Men clapped their hands.

The slave danced.

Much it seemed to me, though there might be two hundred men about the circle, she danced for her master.

Once he even indicated that she should move more about which, instantly, commanded, she did.

"Tuka, Tuka!" even called some of the other slaves about the edges of the circle, sitting and kneeling there, unable to take their eyes from her, clapping, too. Teibar's Tuka, it seemed, was popular even with the other slaves, of which she was such a superb specimen.

I watched her moving about the circle.

"Aii!" cried men, as she would pause a moment to dance before them. I had little doubt she might once have been a tavern dancer. Such dancers must present themselves in such a fashion before customers. This gives the customer an opportunity to assess them, and to keep them in mind, if he wishes, for later use in an alcove.

"Aii," cried another fellow.

I speculated that she would not have languished for attention in the alcoves.

"She is superb," said the fellow next to me.

"Yes," I said.

She was working her way about the circle.

It was interesting to me that a master would dare to display such a slave publicly. I gathered that he was quite confident of his capacity to keep her. He must then, I suspected, be excellent with the sword.

"Ah," said the fellow next to me.

The dancer approached.

How marvelous are the Gorean women, I thought. And I thought then, too, sadly, of the women of Earth, so many of them so confused, so miserable, so unhappy, women not knowing what they were, or what they might be, women trapped in a maze of ultimately barren artifices, women subjected to inconsistent directives and standards, women subjected to social coercions, women subjected to antibiological constraints, women forced to deny themselves and their depth natures in the name of freedom, women trying to be men, not knowing how to be women, women torturing themselves and others with their confusions, their inhibitions, their pain, their frustrations. But I did not blame them for they were the victims of pathological conditioning programs. Any beautiful, natural creature can be clipped and cut, and formed into monstrous shapes, torn from nature, and then instructed to rejoice in its mutilations and mishapenness. It was little wonder that so many of the women of Earth were so inhibited, so frigid, so inert, so anesthetic. That so many of them could even feel their pain was, I supposed, a hopeful sign. If their culture was correct, or judicious, why did it contain so much unhappiness and pain? In a body, pain is an indication that something is wrong. So, too, it is in a culture.

Then the dancer was before me, and I was awed with beauty.

I kept her there before me for a moment, not letting her move away, my gaze holding her.

I wept then for the men of Earth, that they could not know such beauties. How utterly marvelous are the Gorean females! How utterly different they are from the women of Earth! How impossible it would be for a female of Earth to match them!

I watched the dancer then move to the next fellow, and turn about.

Suddenly I was stunned. High on her left arm there was a small, circular scar. It was not, surely, in that place, and given its nature, the result of a marking iron. Indeed, it is by means of such tiny indications, fillings in the teeth, and such, that a certain sort of girl, for which there is a market on Gor, is often recognized.

"She is not from Gor!" I said.

"She is from far away," said the fellow next to me.

"From a distant land," said another.

"Called "Earth," " said another.

"Yes," I said.

"They make excellent slaves," said another. I wondered if this might not be true. The Earth female, starved for sexual fulfillment, suddenly plunged into the gorgeous world of Gor, subject to masculine pleasure, taught obedience, and such, might well, I supposed, after a period of adjustment and accommodation, rejoice in self-discovery, in her true liberation, in her finding herself at last in her place in nature, the beautiful and desirable slave of strong and uncompromising masters.

"I think we should send an army there and bring them all back in chains," said another.

"That is where they belong," said another.

"Yes," said another.

The mark on the girl's arm had not been the result of the imprint of a master's iron. It had been a vaccination mark. I had noted, too, interestingly, just before she had whirled away, that she was shy. I assessed her as being quite intelligent, extremely sensitive, and an excellent slave.

She had now, as the music swirled to its finish, returned to move before her master. Then, the dance ended, men striking their left shoulders in Gorean applause, shouting their vociferous approval, some armed warriors striking their shields with spear blades, she sank to the ground, on her back, breathless, breasts heaving, covered with a sheen of sweat, before her master, her left knee raised, her head turned toward him, the palms of her hands, at her sides, vulnerably exposed.

She had been superb. My shoulder was sore where I had much struck it.

Then with a sensuous, fluid movement she rose to her knees before her master. She spread her knees, widely. She regarded him, beggingly. The dance had much aroused her, and she was totally his, completely at his will, his pleasure and mercy.

"Our gratitude, Teibar!" called a fellow.

"Hail, Teibar!" called another.

He called Teibar then waved to the men about, and turning about, took his way from the area of the circle. The slave rose to her feet and hurried after him, to heel him. More than one man touched her, and as a slave may be touched, as she moved through them, hurrying to catch up with her master. To even these touches I could see her respond, even in her flight. I saw that she was a hot slave, and one who would be, whether she wished it or not, uncontrollable, helplessly responsive, in a man's arms. Then she was with her master, seeming to heel him, but yet so close to him that she touched him, brushing against him. I had little doubt that she would soon be lengthily used, ravished with all the attention, detail and patience with which Gorean masters are wont to exploit their helpless chattels.

After the dance of Tuka, men and slaves departed from the circle, many doubtless to hurry to their blankets and tents. I, too, though I had taken comfort earlier with the blond mat girl, was uncomfortable.

"Use me, Master?" said a coin girl.

I looked down at her, a small brunet, half naked in a ta-teera, a slave rag. About her neck, over her collar, close about it, was a chain collar, padlocked shut, with its coin box, and slot.

"Master?" she smiled.

I was angry. She had doubtless come to a circle, knowing that fellows in need, ones without slaves, such as I, might be found there. Her attitude seemed to me insufficiently respectful. She was not even kneeling.

"Oh!" she cried, spinning to the side, cuffed.

I snapped my fingers. "There," I said, pointing, indicating a place before me, "kneel there, facing away from me." Swiftly she crawled to the place, obeying. "On your belly," I snapped. Swiftly did she fling herself, a slave who might have been displeasing, in terror, to her belly. I seized her ankles and parted them, widely, pulling her toward me. "Perhaps you deserve a full lashing," I said. "No, please, Master!" she wept. "How much are you?" I asked. "Only a tarsk bit, Master!" she wept. I considered the matter. I could afford that. I dragged her back to me. She gasped, mine. "Oh!" she cried. "Oh! Oh!" Then I thrust her from me, and stood. She was then on her side, looking back at me. She was grasping. I kicked her, angrily, with the side of my foot. She winced. "Forgive me, Master," she wept. "I beg forgiveness!" "Perhaps you will learn manners," I said. "Yes, Master," she said. "Perhaps you will know enough next time to be respectful, and to kneel before men," I said. "Yes, Master," she said. "Forgive me, Master!" I looked down upon her, angrily. I think she feared she might be again cuffed, or kicked. Then he crawled to my feet, and kissed them. Then she looked up at me. "Buy me," she begged, suddenly, "It is to a man such as you that I wish to belong!" I dragged her to her knees by the hair and, she sobbing, trying to hold me, thrust a coin, a tarsk bit, into the coin box. I then thrust her back to the dirt, on her side, and, turning about, angrily, left her. "Master!" she called after me. "Please, Master!" In a time I turned back to regard her. She was where I had left her, except that she was now kneeling. Her shoulders shook with sobs. She had the coin box, on its chain, lifted in her hands. Her head was down, and her hair fell about the coin box. She pressed her lips to it, again and again, sobbing. I did not think that she was a poor slave. I think rather that she merely needed a strong master.

"Well done," said a fellow, passing me.

I looked back at the girl again. She did have pretty thighs, well revealed in the ta-teera. But then I steeled myself against softness, and reminded myself that this was no time to acquire a bond maid, even one with a lovely little figure and pretty thighs, one who was now clearly ready to obey instantly, and with perfection.

I looked to the lofty walls of Ar. Within them lay what danger, what treachery, what intrigue I dared not guess.

"Oh!" said a slave, slapped below the small of the back by a peasant.

"She is in the iron belt," said the fellow, looking at me, grinning.

The girl hurried on.

"Perhaps it is just as well," I said.

He laughed.

She looked well in the tunic.

I passed a couple, the master enjoying his slave.

I looked up at the moons of Gor. They have, it seems, an unusual effect on women. Sometimes female slaves, or captured free women, are chained beneath them. I do not know the nature of this effect. Perhaps it is merely aesthetic, for surely the moons are very beautiful. On the other hand the effects may also be psychological or biological. On the psychological approach the moons may have a profound subconscious effect on the female, an effect achieved through symbolism, a symbolism, in its waxings and wanings, clearly suggestive of feminine sexual cycles. But even more interestingly the effect on the female is possibly biological. There are many biological vestiges in the human being. One which is typical and interesting is the tendency of the skin to erupt in tiny protuberances, "goose bumps," when it is cold. This response presumably harkens back to a time when the human animal, or its forebear, had a great deal more hair than is now typical. This eruption of the skin would then lift hair from the flesh, thusly forming an insulating layer against the cold. So, too, the sight of the moons, and their rhythms, and such, so interestingly approximating the periods of feminine sexual cycles, may at one time have played a role in mating cycles. Perhaps the female came out into the moonlight, in her need, where she might be located and appraised, though not in the harsh light of day. Perhaps in the moonlight, away from darkness, with its dangers of predators and such, she cried out, or moaned, her needs, attempting to attract attention to herself, calling for the attentions of the male. Perhaps those which would seek to mate in the fullness of light distracted the group from feeding, or were too much fought over. Perhaps those who sought the darkness were not as easily found or succumbed to predators. Perhaps, in time, as a matter of natural selections, operative upon a relatively, at that time, helpless species, those tended to survive whose mating impulses became synchronized with the moons. This might explain why, even today, and doubtless numerous genetic codings later, codings obviously favoring frequent and aperiodic sexuality, some women are, so to speak, in addition, still "called by the moon." It would be a vestige, like the rising of hair on "goose bumps." Aside from this, it might be noted, of course, that the sexual cycles of various species do tend to be correlated with the cycles of the moon, presumably through one natural selection or another. The Kurii, for example, seem to have retained some vestiges along these lines, for in that species, as I understand it, it is not unusual for females to go to the mating cliffs in the moonlight, where, helpless in their sexuality, they cry out, or howl, their needs.

I passed a few fellows playing dice. There are many forms of dice games on Gor, usually played with anywhere from a single die to five dice. The major difference, I think, between the dice of Earth and those of Gor is that the Gorean dice usually have their numbers, or letters, or whatever pictures or devices are used, painted on their surfaces. It is difficult to manufacture a pair of fair dice, of course, in which the "numbers," two, three and so on, are represented by scooped out indentations. For example, the "one" side of a die is likely to have less scooped-out material missing than the "six" side of a die. Thus the "one" side is slightly heavier and, in normal play, should tend to land face down more often than, say, the "six" side, this bringing up the opposite side, the "six" side in Earth dice, somewhat more frequently. To be sure, the differences in weight are slight and, given the forces on the dice, the differential is not dramatic. And, of course, this differential can be compensated for in a sophisticated die by trying to deduct equal amounts of material from all surfaces, for example, an amount from the "one" side which will equal the amount of the "six" side, and, indeed, on the various sides. At any rate, in the Gorean dice, as mentioned, the numbers or letters, or pictures or whatever devices are used, are usually painted on the dice. Some gamesmen, even so, attempt to expend the same amount of paint on all surfaces. To be sure, some Gorean dice I have seen to use the "scooped-out" approach to marking the dice. And these, almost invariably, like the more sophisticated Earth dice, try to even out the material removed from each of the surfaces. Some Gorean dice are sold in sealed boxes, bearing the city's imprint. These, supposedly, have been each cast six hundred times, with results approximating the ideal mathematical probabilities. Also, it might be mentioned that dice are sometimes tampered with, or specially prepared, to favor certain numbers. These, I suppose, using the Earth term, might be spoken of as "loaded." My friend, the actor, magician, impresario and whatnot, Boots Tarsk-Bit, once narrowly escaped an impalement in Besnit on the charge of using false dice. He was, however, it seems, framed. At any rate the charges were dismissed when a pair of identical false dice turned up in the pouch of the arresting magistrate, the original pair having, interestingly, at about the same time, vanished.

I stayed to watch the fellows playing dice for a few Ehn. I do not think they noticed me, so intent they were on their game. The stakes were small, only tarsk bits, but one would not have gathered that from the earnestness of the players. A slave girl was kneeling nearby, in a sort of improvised slave brace, a short, stout pole, drilled through in three places. Her ankles were fastened to the pole, by means of a thong threaded through one of the apertures, near its bottom, her wrists by another thong passing through a hole a few inches higher than the bottom hole, and her neck by a thong passed through the aperture in the top part of the pole, behind her neck. There are many arrangements for the keeping of slaves, bars, harnesses, and such. I will mention two simple ones, first, the short, hollow tube, usually used with a sitting slave, whose wrists are tied, the thong then passing through the tube to emerge at the far end, where it is used to secure her ankles, and, second, the longer pole, drilled four times, used with a prone or supine slave, in which it is impossible for her to rise to her feet. Her ankles are fastened some six inches or so from one end, and she is then, of course, secured, in one fashion or another, back or belly to the pole, as the master might please, at suitable intervals, by the wrists, belly and neck, the pole usually extending some six inches or so beyond her head. The girl near the gamblers was apparently not a stake in the game. On the other hand, it is not unusual for female slaves, like kaiila and other properties, to serve as stakes in such games, as in races, contests and such. Indeed, in many contests, female slaves are offered as prizes. I had once won one myself, in Torvaldsland, in archery. I had subsequently sold her to a warrior. I trust that she is happy, but it does not matter, as she is only a slave.

"Larls, larls!" called a fellow. "I win!"

"Alas," moaned the other. "I have only verr."

"Larls" would be maximum highs, say, double highs, if two dice were being used, triple highs if three dice were in play, and so on. The chances of obtaining a "larl" with one throw of one die is one in six, of obtaining "larls"with two dice, one in thirty-six, of obtaining "larls" with three dice, one in two hundred and sixteen, and so on. Triple "larls is a rare throw, obviously. The fellow had double "larls." Other types of throws are "urts," "sleen," "verr," and such. The lowest value on a single die is the "urt." The chances of obtaining, say, three "urts" is very slim, like that of obtaining three "larls" one in two hundred and sixteen. "Verr" is not a bad throw but it was not good enough to beat "larls." If two dice are in play a "verr" and a "larl" would be equivalent on a numerical scale to ten points, or, similarly, if the dice are numbered, as these were, one would simply count points, though, of course, if, say, two sixes were thrown, that would count as "larls."

A lad danced past, pounding on a tabor.

I stood there, in the camp, looking about, at the various fires and the folks about them. Mostly, as I have suggested, these folks were of the peasants, but, among them were representatives of many other castes, as well, mostly refugees from Torcadino and its environs, in the west, and from the vicinity of Ar's Station, in the north, folks who had fled before the marches of Cos.

"Ai!" cried a fellow a few yards away, tumbling off the filled, greased wineskin. He would not win the skin and its contents. There was much laughter.

"Next!" called the owner of the skin. "Next!" As it cost a tarsk bit to try the game I think he had already made more than the cost of the wineskin and its contents.

I wondered if I could balance on the skin. It is not easy, of course, given the surgent fluid and the slippery surface.

Another fellow addressed himself to the task, but was on his back in the dirt in an instant. There was more laughter about the skin.

"An excellent effort," called the owner of the skin, "would you care to try again?"

"No," said the fellow.

"We will hold you while you mount," volunteered the owner.

But the fellow waved good-naturedly and left.

"A tarsk bit," called the owner. "Only a tarsk bit! Win wine, the finest ka-la-na, a whole skinful, enough to treat your entire village."

"I will try," said a fellow, determinedly.

I walked over to the circle to watch.

The fellow was helped to the surface of the wineskin. But only an Ihn or so later he tumbled off into the dirt. Fellows about slapped their thighs and roared with laughter.

"Where is more wine?" called one of his friends.

There was laughter.

How odd it was, I thought, that these folks, who had so little, and might, were it not for the forces of Ar, such as they were, between Cos and the city, be in mortal jeopardy, should disport themselves so delightedly.

I watched another fellow being helped to the surface of the skin.

I supposed it might be safe, now, to return to the tent. Presumably, by now, it would not be a violation of decorem to return to the tent. Indeed, by now, Marcus and Phoebe might be asleep. Marcus usually slept her at his feet, in which case her ankles would be crossed and closely chained, or at his thigh, in which case, she would be on a short neck chain, fastened to his belt. A major advantage of sleeping the girl at your thigh is that you can easily reach her and, by the hair, or the chain, if one is used, pull her to you in the night. These measures, however, if they were intended to be precautions against her escape, were in my opinion unnecessary. Phoebe, as I have suggested, was held to her master by bonds compared to which stout ropes, woven of the strongest, coarsest fibers, and chains or iron, obdurate, weighty and unbreakable, were mere gossamer strands. She was madly, helplessly, hopelessly in love with her master. And he, no less, rebellious, moody, angry, chastising himself for his weakness, was infatuated with his lovely slave.

The fellow struggled to stay on the bulging, shifting wineskin, and then slipped off. He had actually done quite well. Nearly had he won the wine.

There was applause about the small circle.

I heard a fellow advertising the booth of a thought reader. This reader probably read coins. One, presumably without the knowledge of the reader or a confederate, selects one coin from several on a tray or platter, usually tarsk bits, and then, holding it tightly in his hand, concentrates on the coin. Then, after the coin has been replaced on the tray or platter, the thought reader turns about and, more often than not, far more than the probabilities would suggest, locates the coin. One then loses one's tarsk bit. If the reader selects the wrong coin, one receives all the tarsk bits on the tray or platter, usually several. I assumed there must be some sort of trick to this, though I did not know what it was. Goreans, on the other hand, often accept, rather uncritically, in my mind, that the reader can actually read thoughts, or usually read them. They reason that if one fellow can see farther than another, and such, why can't someone, similarly, be able to "see" thoughts. Similarly, less familiar with tricks, prestidigitation, illusions, and such, than an Earth audience, some Goreans believe in magic. I have met Goreans who really believed, for example, that a magician can make a girl vanish into thin air and then retrieve her from the same. They accept the evidence of their senses, so to speak. The taking of auspices, incidentally, is common on Gor before initiating campaigns, enterprises, and such. Many Goreans will worry about such things as the tracks of spiders and the flights of birds. Similarly, on Gor, as on Earth, there is a clientele, particularly in uncertain, troubled times, for those who claim to be able to read the future, to tell fortunes, and such.

"Noble Sir!" called the owner of the wineskin. "What of you?"

I regarded him, startled.

"A tarsk bit a chance!" he invited me. "Think of the whole skin of wine for you and your friends!"

A skin of wine might bring as much as four or five copper tarsks.

"Very well," I said.

There was some commendation from others about. "Good fellow," said more than one fellow.

"Surely you do not intend to wear your sandals," said the owner of the wineskin.

"Of course not," I said, slipping them off. I then rubbed my feet well in the dirt near the skin.

"Let me help you up," said the fellow.

"That will not be necessary," I said.

"Here, let me help you," he said.

"Very well," I said. I had not been able to get on the skin.

"Are you ready?" asked the owner, steadying me.

"—Yes," I said. I wished Lecchio, of the troupe of Boots Tarsk-Bit, were about. He might have managed this.

"Ready?" asked the owner.

"Yes," I said.

"Time!" he cried, letting go of me.

"How well you are doing!" he cried, at which point I slipped from the skin. I sat in the dirt, laughing. "How marvelously he did!" said a fellow. "Has he gotten on the skin yet?" asked another, a wag, it seems. "He has already fallen off," he was informed. "He did wonderfully," said another. "Yes," said another, "he must have been on the skin for at least two Ihn." I myself thought I might have managed a bit more than that. To be sure, on the skin, an Ihn seems like an Ehn. Before one becomes too critical in these matters, however, I recommend that one attempt the same feat. To be sure, some fellows do manage to stay on the skin and win the wine.

"Next?" inquired the owner of the wineskin.

I looked about, and picked up my sandals. I had scarcely retrieved them when I noticed a stillness about, and the men looking in a given direction. I followed their gaze. There, at the edge of the circle, emerged from the darkness, there was a large man, bearded, in a tunic and cloak. I took him as likely to be of the peasants. He looked about himself, but almost as though he saw nothing.

"Would care to try your luck?" asked the owner of the wineskin. I was pleased that he had addressed the fellow.

The newcomer came forward slowly, deliberately, as though he might have come from a great distance.

"One tries to stand upon the skin," said the owner. "It is a tarsk bit."

The bearded man then stood before the owner of the wineskin, who seemed small before him. The bearded fellow said nothing. He looked at the owner of the wineskin. The owner of the wineskin trembled a little. Then the bearded man placed a tarsk bit in his hand.

"One tries to stand on the skin," said the owner again, uncertainly.

The large man looked at him.

"Perhaps you will win," said the owner.

"What are you doing?" cried the owner.

No one moved to stop him, but the large man, opening his cloak, drew a knife from his belt sheath and slowly, deliberately, slit the skin open. Wine burst forth from the skin, onto the ankles of the large fellow, and, flowing about, seeking its paths, sank into the dirt. The dust was reddened. It was not unlikc blood.

The large fellow then sheathed his knife, and stood on the rent, emptied skin.

"I have won," he said.

"The skin is destroyed," said the owner. "The wine is lost."

"But I have won," said the bearded man.

The owner of the rent skin was silent.

"Twenty men were with me," said the large, bearded man. "I alone survived."

"He is of the peasant levies!" said a fellow.

"Speak, speak!" cried men, anxiously.

"The skin is rent," said the man. "The wine is gone."

"Speak!" cried others.

The fellow pulled his cloak away and put it over his arm.

"He is wounded!" said a man. The left side of the fellow's tunic was matted with blood. The cloak had clung to it a bit, when he removed it.

"Speak!" cried men.

"I have won," said the man.

"He is delirious," said a fellow.

"No," I said.

"I have won," said the man, dully.

"Yes," I said. "You have stood upon the skin. You have won."

"But the skin is gone, the wine is gone," said a fellow.

"But he has won," I said.

"What occurred in the west?" demanded a man.

"Ar has lost," he said.

Men looked at one another, stunned.

"The banners of Cos incline toward the gates of Ar," said the man.

"No!" cried a man.

"Ar is defenseless," moaned a fellow.

"Let the alarm bars sound," wept a man. "Let her seal her gates!"

I had some concept of the forces of Cos. Too, I had some concept of the forces of Ar in the city, now mostly guardsmen. She could never withstand a concerted siege.

"I have won," said the bearded man.

"How have you won?" asked a man, angrily.

"I have survived," he said.

I looked at the rent skin and the reddened dust. Yes, I thought, he was the sort of man who would survive.

Men now fled away from the circle. In Ihn, it seemed, the camp was in consternation.

A slave girl fled by.

Tents were being struck.

Now, from within Ar, I could hear the sounding of alarm bars. There was lamentation in the camp from some. But most, peasants, seemed to be gathering together their goods.

The large, bearded fellow was now sitting on the ground, the wet wineskin clutched to his breast, weeping.

I stood there, for a time, holding my sandals.

Men moved past me, pulling their carts and wagons. Some had slave girls chained to them. Some of these women, in their manacles, attached to the rear of the vehicles, thrusting and pushing, helped to hurry them ahead. I heard the bellowing of tharlarion being harnessed.

"How far is Cos?" I asked the man.

"Two, three days," he said.

I gathered this would depend on Myron's decision as to the rate and number of marches. I did not think he would press his men. He was an excellent commander and, from what I had gathered, there need be no haste in the matter. He might even rest his men for a day or two. In any event, an excellent commander, he would presumably bring them fresh to the gates of Ar.

I donned my sandals.

Many of the fires in the camp had now been extinguished. It might be difficult finding my way back to the tent.

"Are you all right?" I asked the bearded fellow.

"Yes," he said.

I looked to the walls of Ar. Here and there, on the walls, like shadows flickering against the tarn beacons, I could see the return of tarnsmen.

I looked to the west. Out there, somewhere, were the forces of Cos, their appetites whetted by victory. Within a week, surely, they would be within sight of Ar, eager for war, zestful for loot. I listened to the alarm bars in the distance, from within the city. I wondered how well, tonight, would sleep her free women. Would they squirm and toss in fear in their silken sheets? I wondered if they better understood, this night, perhaps better than other nights, their dependence on men. Surely they knew in the bottoms of their lovely bellies that they, too, as much as the slaves in their kennels, were spoils.

"Pray to the Priest-Kings! Pray to the Priest-Kings!" wept a man.

I thrust him aside, moving through the press, the throngs, the carts and wagons, the tharlarion. In a few Ehn I had come to our tent.

4 Within Ar

"Revile the Home Stone of Ar's Station while you may," said the guard to a tradesman. "We do not know what the future may hold."

"No," said the tradesman, looking about. He knew not who might be in that crowd, nor what their sympathies might be. He did not enter between the velvet ropes, forming their corridor to the roped enclosure within which rested the stone.

"I do not fear to do so, even now," said a brawny fellow of the caste of metal workers.

"Steady," I said to Marcus, beside me.

"Nor do I fear," said the brawny fellow, "the legions of Cos, nor her adherents or spies! I am of Ar!" He then strode between the ropes to the stone, which rested upon a plank, itself resting on two huge terra-cotta vats, of the sort into which slop pots in *insulae* are dumped. Such vats are usually removed once or twice a week, emptied in one carnarium or another, outside the walls, rinsed out and returned to the *insula*. Companies have been organized for this purpose. "Curses upon Ar's Station," he cried, "city faithless and without honor, suborned ally, taker of bribes, refuge of scoundrels, home of cowards, betrayer of the mother city! Down with Ar's Station. Curses upon her!" He then spat vigorously upon the stone.

"Steady," I whispered to Marcus. "Steady."

The fellow then, not looking about, exited between the velvet ropes on the other side.

Only yesterday there had been lines, though smaller than when we had first come to Ar, to revile the stone. Today almost no one approached it. The enclosure was within sight of the Central Cylinder, on the Avenue of the Central Cylinder.

I put my hand on Marcus' wrist, not permitting him to draw his sword. "Remember," I said. "They think that Ar's Station opened her gates to Cos."

"Cursed lie!" said he.

"Yes, indeed," I said, rather loudly, for I saw some fellows look about at Marcus, "it is a cursed lie for any to suggest that the men of Ar might lack courage. Surely they are among the bravest on all Gor!"

"True, true," said more than one fellow, returning his attention to his own business.

"Come away from here," I said to Marcus.

Phoebe was not with us. We had stopped at one of the depots for fee carts on Wagon Street, in southeast Ar. There we had backed her into a slave locker, reached by a catwalk, on all fours, inserted the coin, a tarsk bit, turned and removed the key. It is a simple device, not unlike the slave boxes used in certain storage areas. Unlike the slave boxes they do not require the immediate services of an attendant. The lockers open outward, as opposed to the slave boxes, which open upward. The lockers, thus, like slave cages, may be tiered. The gate of the locker, like the lid of the slave box, is perforated for the passage of air, usually, like the slave box, with a design in the form of a cursive 'Kef', the first letter of 'Kajira', the most common Gorean expression, among several, for a female slave. The usual, and almost universal, temporary holding arrangement is a simple slave ring, mounted in the wall. These are conveniently available in most public places. The slave is usually chained to them. Marcus had decided to keep Phoebe today in a box or locker, rather than at an open ring. "Down on all fours, crawl within, backward!" Marcus had ordered the slim beauty. She had obeyed, instantly. Gorean slave girls swiftly learn not to demur at the orders of masters. I recalled her face, looking up at Marcus. "Let this help you to keep in mind that you are a slave," said Marcus. "Yes, Master," she had said. He had then closed the door, turning the key, removing it, placing it in his pouch. I did not object to this incarceration of his beauteous slave as such things are excellent for their discipline. Also, it seemed to me, aside from the value of its effect of Phoebe, an excellent idea. If he were successful in his mad attempt to obtain the Home Stone of his city he would doubtless be a recognized wanted man. Some might recall that Phoebe was his slave, and thus attempt to trace him through her. In the locker she would not be as easily recognized, surely not as easily as if she were kneeling at a wall, braceleted to a ring. The keeping her in a box or locker seemed to me superior, too, incidentally, to renting a tenement room, even though these were now cheaper and more available than when I had been last in Ar, because of the new egress of refugees, now from Ar herself. We might be remembered by the proprietor or other tenants in such a place. Had we used such a room we could have left her there, chained to a slave ring. In such a room, assuming slaves are allowed in the building, there are usually two of these, one at the wall and one at the foot of a straw-filled pallet. The depot, incidentally, had been muchly crowded, though not with fee carts. Most of the wagons, coaches, fee carts, and such were gone. No longer were the schedules, within and outside of the city, being kept. Tharlarion, and such transportation, were now said to be worth their weight in gold. I had heard that certain rich men had exchanged as many as fifteen high slaves, choice "flowers" from their pleasure gardens, trained even to Curulean quality, for a single tharlarion and wagon. But I did not know, even then, how far they might get, what with the need of such conveyances, brigands on the road, advance scouts of Cos, and such. Some, I had had heard, had been turned back even by guardsmen of Ar, outside the city. That seemed hard to understand. In any event, most of those in the city, surely the largest part, by far, of its population, had no practical way to leave the city, lest it be on foot. Even then they would have surely, most of them, nowhere to go, or stay. Who knew what dangers might lie outside the walls? Too, they could always be overtaken by tharlarion cavalry or Cosian tarnsmen. The citizenry of Ar, for the most part, was trapped in the city. Indeed, there were even rumors circulating that the gates of the city would soon be closed, and even sealed, reinforced against siege weapons. There was much talk, too, of course, about defending the city. Indeed, it was with this in mind, that I had come this morning to the city, to lend my sword, a modicum of mercenary iron, to her defense. On the other hand, this cause, I suspected, was doomed. It was not that I doubted that those of Ar, suitably rallied and led, might effect a stout and fierce resistance, but that I had some concept, as many did not, Marcus, for example, of the arithmetic of war. In any normalcy of combat, assuming the equivalence of the units, the comparability of weaponry, the competence of the commanders, and such, Ar would be doomed. The army of Cos was the largest ever brought to the field on Gor, and it was now, after the fall of Ar's Station, abetted by numerous reinforcements from the north. Furthermore, it had had the winter to restore its siege train, the original train burned in Torcadino, fired by Dietrich of Tarnburg, and, because of its recent success in the field, west of Ar, it could draw on thousands of square pasangs for its logistical support. Further, its lines of communication, from the palace at Telnus, in Cos, to the tent of Myron, the polemarkos, were swift and reliable. I doubted that Ar, even if rallied by a Marlenus of Ar, could hold out for more than a few weeks. And, once one added to the reckoning of these dismal tables the skewing factor of treachery in Ar, and that her high general, Seremides, of Tyros, was traitorous to his oaths, as I had learned at Holmesk, in the north, Ar. I was sure, was doomed.

"Look!" said a man, pointing upward. "Tarnsmen!"

"They are clad in blue," cried a man.

"Cosian tarnsmen over the city!" cried another.

"The tarn wire will protect us!" said another.

"Where are our lads?" asked a man.

"They cannot be everywhere," said another, angrily.

Yet the appearance of Cosian tarnsmen over Ar indicated to me that Cos must now control the skies, as she had in the north.

"The tarn wire will protect us," repeated the fellow.

"Wire can be cut," said a man.

"No one must be permitted to again revile the Home Stone of Ar's Station!" said Marcus.

"Come away from here," I said. I pulled him from the knot of men, to the side.

I looked back to the enclosure within which was the Home Stone of Ar's Station, it resting on the plank, supported by the two terra-cotta vats. There were at least ten guards in the vicinity, as well as perhaps fifty to a hundred men.

"I do not think you are likely, at this time," I said, "to seize the Home Stone by force. Even if you could cut your way to it, you would not be likely to get more than a few feet with it, before you were brought down, by spear or quarrel, if not by blade."

"I can die in the attempt of its rescue," he said, grimly.

"Yes, I suppose you could," I said, "and probably without much difficulty, but if your intent is its rescue, and not your death in its attempted rescue, this is not the time to strike."

He looked at me, angrily.

"You have many of the virtues of the warrior," I said, "but there is yet one you must learn—patience."

"It is not your Home Stone," he said.

"And that," I said, "is perhaps why it is easier for me to consider these matters with more objectivity than you."

"The Stone may be moved, or hidden," he said.

"That is a possibility," I said.

"We must strike now," he said.

"We must wait," I said.

"I do not want to wait," he said.

"I have an idea," I said. This had occurred to me as I had considered the Stone, its placement, the arrangement of guards and such.

"What is your idea?" he asked.

"You would not approve of it," I said, "as it involves something other than a bloody frontal assault."

"What is it?" he asked.

"It is really only a possibility," I said. "I shall discuss it with you later."

I then turned back toward Wagon Street, and Marcus, reluctantly, joined me.

"Our permits to be within the city expire at sundown," he said. "And the camp outside is largely struck. Indeed, there may well be scouts and skirmishers of Cos under the walls tonight. The gates will be closed, we will be outside. We may not even be able to regain entrance to the city."

"It is my intention," I said, "to remain within the city, putting my sword at its service."

"You owe Ar nothing," he said.

"True," I said.

"She is doomed," he said.

"Perhaps," I said.

"Why would you wish to remain here then?" he asked.

"I have a reason," I said.

"Shall we discuss it," he asked, "its rationality, and such, with objectivity?"

"Certainly not," I said.

"I thought not," he said.

We clasped hands, and then continued on our way, to fetch Phoebe.

5 Outside The Gate

"And so, tonight," said Marcus, huddling beside me, in a blanket, Phoebe covered in another, completely, so that she could not see, beside him, in the darkness and cold outside the sun gate, with perhaps two or three hundred others, "I thought you were to be warm and snug in Ar."

"There were no recruiting tables," I admitted.

"The services of your sword were not accepted," he said.

"No," I said.

"Interesting," he said.

"They did ask for my permit and told me I should be out of the city by sundown."

"Cos may be hiring," said a fellow.

"They do not need any more," said another.

I supposed that was true.

"It is strange," said Marcus. "I would have thought they might even free and arm male slaves."

I shrugged.

"But then," he said, "I suppose there are not too many male slaves in the city who might serve in that capacity."

"Perhaps not," I said. It was not like the city contained large numbers of dangerous, powerful, virile male slaves, such as might be found on the galleys, in the quarries, on the great farms, and so on. Such, in numbers, would be dangerous in the city. Most male slaves in the city were pampered silk slaves, owned by Gorean women who had not yet learned their sex. Such slaves, when captured, if not slain in disgust by the victors, were usually herded together like slave girls, and chained for disposition in markets catering to their form of merchandise, markets patronized largely by free women. To be sure, there were virile male slaves in Ar. For example, many of the fellows who attended to the great refuse vats usually kept at the foot of the stairs in *insulae* were male slaves. Usually they worked under the direct or indirect supervision of free men. Occasionally they would be treated to a dram of paga or thrown a kettle girl for the evening.

"I would have thought," said Marcus, "that Ar might have rejoiced these days to obtain even the services of a lad with a beanshooter."

"Apparently not," I said.

"You understand what this means?" asked Marcus.

"Yes," I said. "I think I understand what it means."

"Do you think they will open the gate in the morning?" asked a man.

"Yes," said another.

"How far is Cos?" Marcus asked a fellow stirring around in his blankets.

"Two days," said the fellow.

"They may be closer," said a man.

"Ar will be defended to the death," said a man.

"Perhaps," said another.

"You are not sure of it?" asked the first.

"No," said the second.

"Have you heard the latest news?" asked a fellow.

"What?" inquired another.

"It was suddenly in Ar," said the fellow. "I heard it just before I was expelled from the city, the gate then closed."

"What?" asked a man.

"Talena, the daughter of Marlenus, has offered to sacrifice herself for the safety of the city."

"I do not understand," said a fellow.

"Tell me of this!" I said.

"Talena has agreed to deliver herself naked, and in the chains of a slave, to the Cosians, if they will but spare Ar!"

"She must never be permitted to do so!" cried a man.

"No!" said another.

"Noble woman!" cried a man.

"Noble Talena!" cried another.

"It is absurd," said another fellow. "She is not the daughter of Marlenus. She was disowned by him."

"And thus," I said, "her offer is of no more import than would be the similar offer of any other free woman of Ar."

"Treason!" said a fellow.

"It is said," said a fellow, "that she has been a slave."

"I have heard that," said a man.

"Marlenus did disown her," said a man.

"She does not even have her original name restored," said a man, "but the merely same name, permitted her, after she was freed."

"Long was she sequestered in the Central Cylinder," said another.

"As is Claudia Tentia Hinrabia, of the Hinrabians," said a man. "Remember her?"

"Yes," said a fellow. Claudia Tentia Hinrabia had been the

daughter of a former Ubar of Ar, Minus Tentius Hinrabius. When Marlenus had regained the throne he had freed her from a bondage to which Cernus, his foe, who had replaced Minus Tentius Hinrabius on the throne, had seen that she was reduced. I recalled her. She had been a slender, dark-haired beauty, with high cheekbones, She still lived, as I understood it, in the Central Cylinder.

"I, too, have heard it said," I said, "that Talena was once a slave, and I have heard it said, as well, that even now she wears on her thigh the mark of Treve, a souvenir of her former bondage to a tarnsman of that city."

"She is the daughter of Marlenus," said a man, sullenly.

"She should be Ubara," said another.

"Her offer to deliver herself to the Cosians, that the city may be spared," said a fellow, "is preposterous. "When they take the city they can have her, and any other number of free women. The whole thing is absurd."

"But incredibly noble!" said a fellow.

"Yes," said another.

"It is an act worthy of one who should be Ubara," said a man.

I considered these matters, rather interested in them. In making an offer of this sort, of course, Talena was implicitly claiming for herself the status of being a Ubar's daughter, else the offer would have been, as one of the fellows had suggested, absurd. This was, in its way, presenting a title to the throne. It was not as though she were merely one, say, of a thousand free women who were making the same offer.

"Is she asking, say, a thousand other free women to join her in this proposal?" I asked.

"No," said the fellow.

The extremely interesting thing to my mind would be the Cosian response to this offer. I had little doubt, personally, from what I had learned of the intrigues in Ar that this offer had some role to play in the complicated political games afoot in that metropolis.

At this point a fellow hurried among us. He had come from the darkness, away from the gate. "Cosians!" he said. Men cried out. Some slaves among us screamed. Some men ran to the wall. Some went to pound and cry at the gate.

"Where?" I asked, standing, my sword drawn. Marcus thrust Phoebe's head farther down, she covered totally by the blanket. He was then beside me, his weapon, too, unsheathed. These were two of the few weapons in the group. These fellows, I realized, could be pinned against the wall and gate, and slaughtered. I made as though to kick the tiny fire out. "No," said the man. "No!"

"Scatter in the darkness!" I said.

"No," he said.

"They will be on us with blades in an instant!" said a man.

"Let us in!" cried a fellow, upward to the wall, where there were guards.

"They are scouts, skirmishers?" asked Marcus.

"I think so," said the man.

"Surely they will attack," said a man.

"Perhaps we can be defended from the walls," said a man. I did not think that quarrel fire from the walls would be much to our advantage. We would be as likely to be hit, I supposed, as Cosians. Too, it was very dark. Few archers will waste quarrels in such light.

"I think we are in no danger, at least now," said the man.

"Why do you say that?" I asked.

"Look," he said. He held his hand near the fire and opened it.

"A sliver tarsk!" said a man.

"It was given to me by a Cosian, in the shadows," said the man, wonderingly.

"I do not understand," said a man.

"He pressed it into my hand," said the man, "when I thought to be spitted on his blade."

"What did he say?" asked a man.

"That Cos was our friend," said the man.

"How many were there?" I asked.

"Only a few, I think," said the man.

"Scouts, or skirmishers," I said to Marcus.

"It would seem so," he said.

"What shall we do now?" asked a man.

"We will wait here," said a man, "until the gate opens."

"It is only an Ahn until dawn," said a man.

I looked out into the darkness. Out there, somewhere, were Cosians. I then looked at the fellow who had recently joined us. He was sitting by the tiny fire now, trembling. He was perhaps cold. His fist was clenched. In it, I gathered, was a silver tarsk.

"I do not think Ar will choose to defend itself," I said.

"I do not think so either," said Marcus, softly.

"Doubtless that is why there were no recruiting tables," I said.

"Undoubtedly," he said.

6 The Public Boards

Marcus and I turned to the street for a moment, to watch a company of guardsmen, at quick march, hasten by, their bootlike sandals, coming high on the calf, resounding on the stones.

"Ar will defend herself to the death," said a man.

"Yes," said another.

I looked after the retreating guardsmen. I doubted if there were more than fifteen hundred such in the city.

"There is no danger," said a man.

"No," said another.

"The tarn wire will protect us," said a man.

"Our gates are impregnable," said another. "Our walls cannot be breached.

"No," said another.

How little these fellows knew of the ways of war, I thought.

"Here it is," said Marcus, calling back to me, "on the public boards." The public boards are posting areas, found at many points in Ar, usually in plazas and squares. These boards were along the Avenue of the Central Cylinder, and were state boards, on which official communiqués, news releases, announcements and such, could be posted. Some boards are maintained by private persons, who sell space on them for advertising, notifications, and personal messages. To be sure, many folks, presumably poorer folks, or at least folks less ready to part with a tarsk bit, simply inscribe their messages, in effect as graffiti, on pillars, walls of buildings, and such. Too, posters, and such, usually hand-inked, are common in public places, usually put up by the owners or managers of *palestrae*, or gymnasiums, public baths, taverns, race courses, theaters, and such. Sales of tharlarion and slaves, too, are commonly thusly advertised. Heralds and criers, too, and carriers of signs, are not unknown. Some proprietors rent space in their shops or places of business for small postings. So, too, similarly, some homeowners who live on busy streets charge a fee for the use of their exterior walls. There are many other forms of communication and advertising as well, such as the parades of acrobats, jugglers, clowns, animal trainers, mimes and such, and the passage of flatbedded display wagons through the streets, on which snatches of performances, intended to whet the viewer's interests, are presented, or, say, slaves are displayed, usually decorously clad, in connection with imminent sales at various markets and barns. The viewer, or the male viewer, at any rate, understands that the decorous attire of the imbonded beauties of the moving platform is not likely to be worn in the exposition cages or on the block. There is a Gorean saying that only a fool buys a woman clothed. On these platforms the women are usually chained only by an ankle, that there will be but little interference with their movements and their appeals to the crowds. On the other hand, some owners, who prefer more obvious restraints for their women, who are, after all, slaves, use flatbedded wagons with mounted slave bars of various sorts, sometimes with intricate chainings or couplings. Similarly, stout, multiply locked cage wagons may be used for a similar purpose.

"I see," I said, reading the boards.

"I have heard," said a man, near me, speaking to another, "that many other free women, like Talena herself, have offered themselves as slaves, that the city be spared.

"There is nothing to that effect here on the public boards," said the other fellow.

"True," said the first.

"Read to me," begged a fellow looking up at the boards. "I cannot read. What does it say?"

" 'Greetings from Lurius of Jad, Ubar of Cos, to the people of Glorious Ar,' " read a man, rather slowly, pointing to letters with his fingers, which led me to believe that his literacy was not likely to be much advanced over that of the other. To be sure, I myself did not read Gorean fluently, as the alternate lines change direction. The first line is commonly written left to right, the second from right to left, and so on. Cursive script is, of course, at least for me, even more difficult. In particular I find it difficult to write. In defense I might point out that I can print Gorean fairly well, and can sign my name with a deftness which actually suggests to those who do not know better that I am fully literate in the language. In further defense I might point out that many warriors, for no reason that is clear to me, seem to take pride in a putative lack of literacy. Indeed, several fellows I have known, of the scarlet caste, take pains to conceal their literacy, seemingly ashamed of an expertise in such matters, regarding such as befitting scribes rather than warriors. Thus, somewhat to my embarrassment, I found I fitted in well with such fellows. I have known, incidentally, on the other hand, several warriors who were quite unapologetic about literary interests and capacities, men who were, for example, gifted historians, essayists and poets.

" 'Know, people of Glorious Ar,' " the man continued to read, " 'that Cos is your friend.' "

"Does it say that?" asked a man.

"Yes," said the fellow, determinedly. He then continued to read. " 'Cos has no quarrel with the people of Ar, whom it reveres and respects. The quarrel of Cos is rather with the wicked and corrupt regime, and the dishonest and ruthless policies, of Gnieus Lelius, subverter of peace, enemy of amity between our states. It was only with the greatest reluctance and most profound regret that Cos found herself, after all avenues of conciliation and negotiation were exhausted, forced to take up arms, in the name of free peoples everywhere, to resist, and call to account, the actions and policies of the tyrant, Gnieus Lelius, enemy to both our states.' "

"I did not know Gnieus Lelius was a tyrant," said a fellow.

"That is absurd," said another.

"But it is on the public boards!" said another.

"It must be true," said another.

"Who made these postings?" asked a man.

"The members of the palace guard, the Taurentians themselves," said another.

"They must then be true," said another.

"No," said a fellow. "All that is being done here is to inform us of the message of Lurius of Jad."

"True," said another, relievedly.

"Read on," said a man.

" 'Now, with sadness, given no choice, with the support and encouragement of all the world, now allied with me, I, Lurius of Jad, who would be your friend and brother, have been forced to come before your gates. The Priest-Kings are with me. My arms are invincible. I have conquered in the delta. I have conquered in Torcadino. I have conquered but three day's march from your very gates. Resistance to me is useless. Yet, although Ar, under the tyranny of Gnieus Lelius, has been guilty of many crimes and my patience has been sorely tried, I am prepared to be merciful. I offer you the alternatives of annihilation or friendship, of devastation or prosperity. Make your decision not rashly, but with care. Do not force me to give Ar to the flames. Rather let us live in peace and brotherhood.' "

"Is there more?" asked a man.

"A little," said the fellow who was reading.

"What?" he was asked by several about.

" 'If Ar desires peace, and would survive, if she desires peace, and would be freed of the onerous yoke of a tyrant, let her deliver to my plenipotentiary, Myron, polemarkos of the continental forces of the Cosian ubarate, some sign of her desire for peace, some evidence of her hope for reconciliation, some token of her good will.' "

"What does he want?" asked a man.

"Is Gnieus Lelius a tyrant?" asked a fellow.

"There is the matter of the ostraka," said a man.

"And the permits!" said another.

"Tyrannical actions!" said another.

"Gnieus Lelius is a tyrant," said another.

"Absurd," said a fellow.

"He is soft, weak, vacillating," said a man.

"He is not a Ubar," said another, "but, too, he is surely not a tyrant."

"He is a weak fool," said another.

"But not a tyrant," said a man.

"No," said another.

"There is the matter of the ostraka, the permits, the restrictions," said another.

"That is true," said another.

"Perhaps he is a tyrant,"said a man.

"Perhaps," said another.

"Yes," said another. "He us a tyrant!"

From the public postings, I had now gathered that Gnieus Lelius was not likely to have been of the party of treachery in Ar, which I was pleased to learn. To be sure, he might have been of that party, and might have been, in the developments within that party, outmaneuvered, to find himself suddenly cast in the role of a scapegoat, something to be thrown to the crowd, to satisfy it and protect others. On the other hand, from what I knew of Gnieus Lelius, whom I had met, I guessed he was an honest man. Indeed, in another time and place, it was my speculation that he might have served as an efficient, beloved administrator. I suspected that he was at worst a dupe, a trusting man, perhaps even one of considerable talent, who had found himself, through no real fault of his own, a pawn in games of state, games in which there seemed to be no rules other than survival and victory.

"Read further," demanded a man.

"That is the message," said the fellow who had been reading it. "There is no more."

"No more?" asked a man.

"Only 'I wish you well. Lurius of Jad, Ubar of Cos,' " said the fellow.

"But what does Cos want?" asked a man.

"Apparently she wants some sign of our desire for peace," said a fellow, looking up at the posting.

"Tell them to go back to Cos," said a fellow, angrily, "and we shall consider the matter."

"The posting refers to some evidence of our hope for reconciliation," said the first fellow, "some token of our good will."

"Give them our steel in their neck!" said a fellow.

"And with good will!" said another, a fellow of the potters.

"That is a token they will understand," added another.

"But what do they want?" asked another.

"They may want our Talena," said a man.

"That brave and noble woman, we will never surrender her!" said another.

"I myself would block the gate," said a fellow, "before I would see her leave the city at the stirrup of a Cosian envoy."

"She has offered so to sacrifice herself," said a man.

"It is here on the public postings," said another, "over here."

"They cannot have our Talena," said a man.

"I do not think it is Talena they want," said a man.

"But what, then?" asked another.

"What could be a suitable token of Ar's desire for peace?" asked another.

"Who wants peace?" said a man.

"I do not understand what is going on," said a fellow.

"Those who are high in the city," said a fellow, "will inquire into these matters. They are wiser than we and will do what is best."

At this point there was much shouting in side streets, coming from the west. In moments, too, men were shouting about us.

"Cos!" they cried. "Cos can be seen from the walls!"

I did not think, in these times, that they would let civilians ascend the walls. Otherwise I might have hastened to the ramparts. From them, I gathered, might be viewed the legions of Cos. Such armies appear first like small lines at the horizons. It is often difficult, at first, to mark out the units. Sometimes, on sunny days, there is a flashing along the horizon, from lifted standards. At night one can usually see the fires of the camps, three of four pasangs away. To be sure, what might be visible from the walls now might be only smoke from fired fields or, more likely, dust from tharlarion cavalries.

"Are the Cosians numerous?" asked a man.

"They are like the leaves of trees, like the sands of the sea," said a man.

"Look, overhead!" cried a man.

We saw a Cosian tarnsman over the city.

"Ar is doomed," said a man.

"We will fight to the death," said another.

"Perhaps we can treat with the Cosians," said another.

"Never!" said another.

"Way, make way!" we heard. Now, moving south on the Avenue of the Central Cylinder, toward the great gate of Ar, were several riders of tharlarion.

"That is the personal banner of Seremides!" said a man.

The riders were muchly cloaked. From the precision of their lines, however, and the ease and discipline of their seat on the tharlarion, I took them to be soldiers. Too, if the fellow was right, that one of the banners in the group was that of Seremides, then presumably he, or his empowered agent, was one of the riders.

"Save us, Seremides!" cried a man.

Then the riders had passed.

"Where is Gnieus Lelius, the regent?" asked a man.

"He has not been seen in public in days," said another.

"Perhaps he has fled the city!" suggested another.

"Tonight," said another, "let our gates be sealed."

"I have heard," said a fellow, "that Cos is our friend, and that it is Gnieus Lelius who is the enemy."

"That is absurd," said a man.

"Last night, Cosian scouts, outside the walls," said a man, "distributed silver tarsks to the homeless, assuring them of the good intentions and friendships of the maritime ubarate!"

"That is preposterous," said a man.

"I know a fellow who received one," said the first fellow.

"Unfortunately," said a fellow, "I was home in bed."

"You should have been outside the walls," said another.

"I could use a silver tarsk," said a man.

"Do you think that Cos is truly our friend?" asked a man.

"No," said a fellow.

Men looked at him.

"Why do you say that?" asked a man.

"I was in the delta," he said, and turned away.

"Ar's Station," said a man, "has been well treated by Cos."

"Do not respond to that," I said to Marcus, and drew him back a bit from the public boards, to the edge of the crowd. The young warrior's face was flushed.

"Perhaps Seremides can save us," said a man.

"Or the intercessions of our beloved Talena," said another.

"We must fight to the death," said a man.

"Cos will show us no mercy," said another.

"Perhaps the city will be spared if we confess our wrongs, and make clear our desire for peace."

"What wrongs?" asked a man.

"Surely we must have wrongs," said a man.

"I suppose so," said another.

I myself could think of at least three, the failure to meet Cos at Torcadino, the failure to relieve the siege at Ar's Station, and the unprepared entry into the delta, in putative pursuit of the Cosian expeditionary force in the north.

"We can do nothing," said a man.

"We are helpless under the tyranny of Gnieus Lelius," said another.

"Who can free us from the grip of this tyrant?" asked a man.

"Perhaps our friends in Cos," said a fellow.

"Where is he?" asked a man.

"Hiding in the Central Cylinder," said another.

"He has fled the city," said another.

"Ar cannot be indefinitely defended, said a man.

"We must declare ourselves an open city," said another.

"I do not know what is to be done," said a man.

"Others wiser than we will know," said another.

"How can we make Cos know we wish to be their friend?" asked another.

"I do not wish to be their friend," said a man, angrily.

"Our military situation is hopeless," said a man. "We must prove our desire for peace to the Cosians."

"How can we do that?" asked a man.

"I do not know," he said.

"They will wish some clear, explicit token," said a man.

"Yes," said another.

"But what?" asked a man.

"I do not know," said the first fellow.

"Come along," I said to Marcus.

In a few moments we had come to a slave ring where we had left Phoebe.

The ring to which she was attached was set quite close to the ground level, a ring to which it was presumed a slave might be fastened by the ankle. Marcus, however, using a pair of slave bracelets, had fastened her to it by the neck, one bracelet about the ring, the other about her collar, pressing into her neck. She lay on her stomach on the stones, her neck held close to the ring, her eyes closed against glare. Marcus kicked her, not gently, with the side of his foot. "Master," she said, and rose to her knees, bent over, her head held down to the stones.

"She is Cosian," he said to me.

"No," I said. "She is only a slave."

"Are you hungry?" Marcus asked Phoebe.

"Yes, Master," she said.

"Perhaps then," he said, "you will not be fed today."

"I am not permitted to lie to my master," she said.

"A slave, like any other animal," I said, "may grow hungry."

"True," said Marcus.

He then crouched down and removed the bracelets from the ring and collar.

"I, too, am hungry," I said.

"Very well," he said.

"There are food shops on Emerald Street," I said.

"Is it far?" he asked.

"No," I said.

Then, in a moment we left, retracing our steps, moving north on the Avenue of the Central Cylinder, past shops, fountains, columns and such, until we would make our left turn, toward Emerald Street, Phoebe heeling him, her hands now fastened behind her in the bracelets.

"Look," I said, while still on the Avenue of the Central Cylinder, pointing upward.

"Another Cosian tarnsman," he said.

"Yes," I said.

"Coppers, coppers for the temple," called an Initiate, rattling some tarsk bits in a tray.

"What do you think Cos wants?" asked Marcus.

"I think," I said, "the destruction of the gates of Ar."

"That is absurd," said Marcus.

"True," I said.

"They will never be given that," he said.

"No," I said.

7 Ar Is Liberated

We were muchly jostled.

"Hear the bars?" asked Marcus.

"They are sounding out peals of rejoicing," I said.

It was now two days after we had read the first postings of the conciliatory message of Lurius of Jad on the public boards.

"Hail Ar! Hail Cos!" cried folks about.

It was difficult to keep our feet.

"Are they coming?" asked a man.

"Yes," said another, moving out further onto the avenue.

"Back," said a guardsman. "Back."

We had come to this coign of vantage, such as it was, very early this morning, even at the second Ahn. Yet, even at that time, many had been about, some with blankets to sleep on the stones. It was in the open area near the Central Cylinder, which loomed in the center of a circular park, the territory open enough for defense, midway in the avenue.

"Hail Ar! Hail Cos!" cried a man.

Many folks held small Cosian banners which they might wave. Banners, too, of Ar were much in evidence.

The night before last, the night of that day on which we had taken note of the postings, the gates of Ar had been dismantled and burned. Some citizens had attempted to interfere with this, but were discouraged with clubs and blades. There had even been sporadic mutinies of small contingents of guardsmen, determined to hold their posts, but these for the most part dissipated when it became clear that the orders were from the Central Cylinder itself. Two of these armed reluctances, yielding neither to reason nor orders, were quelled bloodily by Taurentians. Gnieus Lelius, it seems, had been deposed, and Seremides, in a military coup he himself characterized as regrettable, had seized temporary power, a power to be wielded until the High Council, now the highest civilian authority in Ar, could elect a new leader, be it Administrator, Regent, Ubar or Ubara.

"I had not thought to see the gates of Ar burned, not by her own," said Marcus.

"No," I said.

The metal plating had been pried from them, to be melted down. The great timbers then, shattered and separated, had been formed into gigantic pyres and burned. I think the light of these would have been visible for fifty pasangs. Marcus and I, and Phoebe, had watched the burning of the great gate for a time. Many folks from the city, too, some in numbness, some in sorrow, some in disbelief, had come out to watch. We could see their faces in the reflected light. Many had wept. Some uttered lamentations, tearing their hair and clothes. It had been uncomfortably hot even within a hundred paces of the flames, so great was the heat generated. I had come through that gate many times.

We could hear cheering in the distance.

"Cos is within the city," said Marcus.

"At last we are free!" cried a man.

"We have been liberated!" cheered another, waving a Cosian banner on a small stick.

The city was festooned with ribbons and garlands. It was

hard to hear Marcus beside me, what with the sound of the bars ringing and the shouts of the crowd.

"Has there ever been such a day for rejoicing in Ar?" asked a man.

"I do not know," I admitted. After all, I was not of Ar.

I could hear trumpets and drums in the distance.

"Do you think Cos will now sack and burn the city?" asked Marcus.

"No," I said.

"They are within the walls," he said.

"Selected, controllable contingents, probably mostly regulars," I said.

"You do not expect them to burn Ar?" he asked.

"No," I said. "Ar is a prize, surely more valuable as she is, rather than in ashes."

"Is the population not to be slaughtered?" he asked.

"I would doubt it," I said. "There is a great pool of skills and talent in Ar. Such things, too, are prizes."

"But surely they will sack the city," he said.

"Perhaps little by little," I said.

"I do not understand," he said.

"Study the campaigns of Dietrich of Tarnburg," I said.

Marcus looked at me.

"I do not doubt but what Myron, polemarkos of Cos, or his advisors, have done so."

"You speak in riddles," said Marcus.

"I can see them!" cried a man.

"Look, too, the Central Cylinder!" cried a man!

At the edge of the circular park, within which rears the lofty Central Cylinder, a platform had been erected, presumably that thousands more, gathered on the streets, could witness what was to occur. We were within a few yards of this platform. This platform could be ascended by two ramps, one in the back, on the side of the Central Cylinder, and one in front, opposite to the Central Cylinder, on the side of the Avenue of the Central Cylinder. Phoebe was close behind Marcus, clinging to him, that she not be swept from us in the throngs.

"Look there, at the foot of the platform!" said a man.

"The sleen, the scoundrel, the tyrant!" cried men.

There were cries of rage and hatred from the crowd. Being dragged along the side of the platform, conducted by a dozen chains, each attached to, and radiating out from, a heavy metal collar, each chain held by a child, was a pathetic figure, stumbling and struggling, its ankles shackled and its upper body almost swathed in chains, Gnieus Lelius. Other children too, some five of them, with switches, hung about him like sting flies. At intervals, for which they watched eagerly, receiving the permission of a supervising Taurentian, they would rush forward, striking the helpless figure. Muchly did the crowd laugh at this. Gnieus Lelius was barefoot. Too, he had been placed in motley rags, not unlike the sort that might be worn by a comedic mime upon the stage. I supposed this was just as well. Gnieus Lelius, thus, might have some hope of evading impalement on the walls of Ar. He would perhaps rather be sent to the palace of Lurius of Jad, in Telnus, to be kept there for the amusement of Lurius and his court, as a caged buffoon.

"Sleen! Tyrant!" cried men.

Some fellows rushed out to cast ostraka at him. "Take your ostraka, tyrant!" they cried. Gnieus flinched, several of these small missiles striking him. These were the same ostraka, I supposed, which, a few days ago, would have been worth their weight in gold, permits, passes, in effect, to remain in the city. After the burning of the gates, of course, one need no longer concern oneself with ostraka and permits.

"We are free now!" cried one of the men, flinging his ostrakon at Gnieus Lelius.

Other men rushed out to fall upon the former regent with blows but Taurentians swiftly, with proddings and blows of their spears, drove them back.

Gnieus Lelius was then, by the front ramp, conducted to the surface of the platform. Many in the crowd, now first seeing him, shrieked out their hatred. There he was put on his knees, to one side, the children locking their chains to prepared rings, set in a circle, then withdrawing. The five lads with switches were given a last opportunity, to the amusement of the crowd, to strike the former regent, then they, too, were dismissed.

The sounds of the drums and trumpets to our right were now closer.

"Look!" said a fellow. He pointed in the direction of the Central Cylinder from which, but moments before, Gnieus Lelius, and his escort, had emerged.

"It is Seremides, and members of the High Council!" said a fellow.

Seremides, whom I had not seen this clearly since long ago in Ar, in the days of Minus Tentius Hinrabius, and Cernus, of Ar, with others, members of the High Council, I gathered, now, from the side of the Central Cylinder, ascended the platform.

"He is not in the robes of a penitent or suppliant!" shouted a fellow, joyfully.

"No!" cried others.

"He is in uniform!" cried a man.

"Yes!" said others.

"Look," cried a man. "He has his sword!"

"Seremides retains his sword!" cried a man, calling back to those less near the platform.

There was much cheering greeting this announcement.

Then the High Council stood to one side, and Seremides himself returned to the point on the platform where the rear ramp, that near the Central Cylinder, ascended to its surface.

The ringing of the bars then ceased, first those of the Central Cylinder and then those near it, and then those farther away, about the city. This happened so quickly, however, that it was doubtless accomplished not by the fellows at the bells apprehending that those most inward in the city had ceased to ring but rather in virture of some signal, presumably conveyed from the Central Cylinder, a signal doubtless relayed immediately, successively, by flags or such, to other points.

The crowd looked at one another.

No longer now, the bars now quiet, did I even hear the drums and trumpets of the approaching Cosians. Those instruments, too, were silent. I did not doubt, however, that the approach north on the Avenue of the Central Cylinder was still in progress.

Seremides now, at the rear of the platform, where the rear ramp ascended to its surface, extended his hand downward, to escort a figure clad and veiled in dazzling white to the surface of the platform. It was a graceful figure who, head down, the fingers of her left hand in the light grasp of Seremides, now came forward upon the platform.

"No! No!" cried many in the crowd. "No!"

"It is Talena!" wept a man.

The figure, to be sure, was robed in white, and veiled, but I had little doubt that it was indeed Talena, once the daughter of Marlenus of Ar, Ubar of Ubars.

"She is not gloved!" cried a man.

"She is barefoot!" cried another.

Marcus looked down, sharply, at Phoebe, who clung to his arm. Instantly Phoebe looked down. In that crush she could scarcely have knelt. She might have been forced from her knees and trampled. Phoebe, of course, was much exposed in the brief slave tunic, her arms and legs. I looked at her calves, ankles and feet. She, too, was barefoot. This was appropriate for her, of course, as she was a slave. Slaves are often kept barefoot. I then looked up, continuing to regard her, she clinging to Marcus. Yes, she was quite lovely. She looked up a moment, saw my eyes upon her, and then looked down again, quickly. The slave girdle too, tied high on her, crossed, emphasized the loveliness of her small breasts. I was pleased for Marcus. He had a lovely slave. I was lonely. I wished that I, too, had a slave.

"She is in the robes of a penitent or suppliant!" cried another in dismay.

"No, Talena!" cried a man.

"No, Talena," cried another, "do not!"

"We will not permit it!" cried a man.

"Not our Talena!" wept a woman.

"The crowd grows ugly," observed Marcus.

"Ar is not worth such a price!" cried a man.

"Better give the city to flames!" cried another.

"Let us fight! Let us fight!" cried men.

Several men broke out, into the street, where Taurentians, with spears held across their bodies, struggled to restrain them.

"Good," said Marcus. "There is going to be a riot."

"If so," I said, "let us withdraw."

"It will give me a chance to slip a knife into a few of these fellows," said Marcus.

"Phoebe might be hurt," I said.

"She is only a slave," said Marcus, but I saw him shelter her in his arms, preparing to move back through the crowd.

"Wait," I said.

Talena herself, on the height of the platform, had her hands out, palms up, shaking them negatively, even desperately.

I smiled.

This behavior on her part seemed scarcely in keeping with the dignity of the putative daughter of a Ubar, not to mention her mien as a penitent or suppliant.

"She urges us to calm!" said a man.

"She pleads with us to stand back," said a man. "Come back."

"Noble Talena!" wept a fellow.

The crowd wavered. Several of the men in the street backed away, returning to the crowd.

Talena then, now that the crowd, divided and confused, seemed more tractable, put her head down and to one side, and, lifting her arms, the palms up, made a gesture as of resignation and nobility, pressing back the crowd.

"She does not wish succor," said a fellow.

"She fears that we may suffer in her behalf," moaned a man.

It had been a narrow thing, I thought. Had Talena herself not suddenly interposed her own will, clearly, vigorously, even desperately, signaling negatively to the crowd, the platform and avenue might have swarmed with irate citizens, intent upon her rescue. The handful of Taurentians about would have been swept back like leaves before a hurricane.

"Do not let this be done, Seremides!" cried a fellow.

"Protect Talena!" cried several men.

But now Seremides held forth his hands, calmly, palms down, and raised and lowered them, gently, several times.

The crowd murmured, uneasily, threateningly.

"Talena intends to sacrifice herself for us, for the city, for the Home Stone!" wept a man.

"She must not be permitted to do so," said a fellow.

"We will not permit it!" said another, suddenly.

"Let us act!" cried a man.

Again the crowd wavered. There was a sudden pressing forth toward the platform, a tiny, incipient surgency. Taurentians braced themselves and pressed back against the crowd with the shafts of their spears.

Seremides' calming hands continued to beg for patience.

Then, again, the crowd was quiet, tense. I did not think that it would take much to precipitate violence. Yet, for the moment, at least, it was still, if seething. There is often a delicate balance in such things, and sometimes in such situations even a small action, even a seemingly insignificant stimulus, can trigger a sudden, massive response.

Seremides then, again, held out his hand to Talena. He then led her forward, as before, toward the front ramp. As they neared the figure of Gnieus Lelius, kneeling in his chains near the front ramp, Talena seemed to hesitate, to shrink back with distaste. One small hand, even, extended, palm out, toward the former regent, as though she would fend away the very sight of him, as though she could not bear the thought of his nearness. She even turned to Seremides, doubtlessly imploring him with all the piteous vulnerability of the penitent or suppliant, that she not be stationed close to that odious object, which had brought such lamentable catastrophe and misery upon her city.

Seremides seemed to hesitate for a moment and then, as though he had made a determined decision, however unwise it might be, graciously, and with great courtesy, conducted Talena to a place further from the kneeling Gnieus Lelius.

The crowd murmured its approval.

"Good, Seremides!" cried a man.

As Talena was conducted to her place, a few feet from Gnieus Lelius, she drew up the white robes a little with her right hand, so that they were above her ankles. In this way those who might not have noticed this fact before could now note that she was barefoot. I supposed this tiny act of exposure, so apparently natural, if not inadvertent, as though merely to aid her footing, this act so delicately politic, must have cost the modesty of the putative daughter of Marlenus of Ar much.

A man near me put his head in his hands and wept. Marcus glanced at him, contemptuously.

In a moment then, startling me, and doubtless many others in the crowd, there was a blast of trumpets and a roll of drums to our right. Regulars of Cos, regiments of them, in ordered lines, in cleaned, pressed blue, with polished helmets and shields, preceded by numerous standard bearers, representing far more units than were doubtless in the city at the moment, and musicians, advanced. Tharlarion cavalrymen, of both bipedal and quadrupedal tharlarion, flanked the lines. The street shook under the tread of these beasts. Turned on the crowd they might, in their passage, have trampled hundreds.

The crowd, now that it had segments of the forces of Cos before it, seemed strangely docile. These were not a handful of Taurentians that might have been swept from their path like figures off a kaissa board. These were warriors in serried ranks, many of whom had doubtless seen battle. To move against such would have been much like throwing themselves onto the knife walls of Tyros. Similarly, should the troops wheel to the sides, charging, blades drawn, they might have slaughtered thousands, harvesting the crowds, trapped by their own numbers, like sa-tarna.

With a roll of drums and a blast of trumpets, and the distinct, uniform sound of hundreds of men coming simultaneously to a halt, the Cosian array arrested its march not yards from the forward ramp.

I thought I saw the figure of Talena, standing on the platform, with others, tremble. Perhaps now she realized, I thought, what it might mean to have Cosians in the city. Did she now, suddenly, I wondered, realize how vulnerable she really was, and Ar, and how such fellows could now do much what they pleased. She was in the white robes of a penitent or suppliant. The penitent or suppliant, incidentally, is supposed to be naked beneath such robes. I doubted, however, that Talena was naked beneath them. On the other hand, she would surely wish the good citizens of Ar to believe that she was.

It seemed terribly quiet for a moment. If I had spoken, even softly, I am sure I would have been heard for yards, so still were the pressed throngs.

"Myron," I heard whispered. "Myron, polemarkos of Cos!"

I saw nothing for a time but the crowd, the platform, the people on the platform, and Cosians, for several yards to the right, standard bearers, some even bearing the standards of mercenary companies, probably not in the march, such as that of Raymond Rive-de-Bois, musicians, and soldiers, both foot and cavalry.

"He is coming!" I heard.

The polemarkos, if it were indeed he, I thought, must be very confident, to so enter Ar. I did not think that Lurius of Jad, Ubar of Cos, would have done so. To be sure, Lurius seldom left the precincts of the palace in Telnus. More than one triumph in a Gorean city has been spoiled by the bolt of an assassin.

"I see him!" I said to Marcus.

"Yes," he said. Phoebe stood on her tiptoes, clinging to Marcus' arm, her slim, lovely body very straight. She craned her neck. She could still see, I thought, very little. The close-fitting steel collar was lovely on her throat. The collar, with its lock, muchly enhances a woman's beauty.

In a moment a large bipedalian saddle tharlarion, in golden panoply, its nails polished, its scales brushed bright, wheeled to a halt before the standard bearers. Behind it came several other tharlarion, resplendent, too, but lesser in size and panoply, with riders. Myron, or he who was acting on his behalf, then, by means of a dismounting stirrup, not the foot stirrup, the rider's weight lowering it, descended to the ground. It was curious to see him, as I had heard much of him. He was a tall man, in a golden helmet, plumed, too, in gold, and a golden cloak. He was personally armed with the common gladius, the short sword, the most common infantry weapon on Ar, and a dagger. In a saddle sheath, remaining there, was a longer weapon, a two-handed scimitar, the two-handed *scimitarus*, useful for reaching other riders on tharlarion. There was no lance in the saddle boot. He removed his helmet and handed it to one of his fellows. He seemed a handsome fellow, with long hair. I recalled he had once been under the influence of the beautiful slave, Lucilina, even to the point of consulting her in matters of state. She had been privy to many secrets. Indeed, her influence over the polemarkos had been feared, and her favor had been courted even by free men. Her word or glance might mean the difference between advancement and neglect, between honor and disgrace. Then Dietrich of Tarnburg had arranged for her to be kidnapped and brought to him, stripped. He had soon arranged for her to be emptied of all sensitive information. He had then renamed her 'Luchita', an excellent name for a slave and quite different from the prestigious name 'Lucilina', which might have graced a free woman. he had then given her to one of his lowest soldiers, as a work and pleasure slave. The last time I had seen her had been in Brundisium, among the slaves belonging to various mercenaries, men of the company of a fellow who was then identifying himself as Edgar, of Tarnwald. I did not know where this Edgar, of Tarnwald, now was, nor his men. I suspected that by now Myron had come to understand, and to his chagrin, how he had been the pliant dupe of a female, and even one who was a slave. I did not think it likely that this would happen again. He now doubtless had a much better idea of the utilities and purposes of females.

Myron now, as I suppose it was Myron, with two fellows behind him, each bearing a package, ascended the platform.

Seremides approached him and, drawing his sword from its sheath, extended it to him, hilt first.

"Myron does not accept his sword!" said a man.

Myron, indeed, with a magnanimous gesture, had demurred to accept the weapon of Seremides, the high general of Ar. Seremides now sheathed the sword.

"Hail Cos! Hail Ar!" whispered a fellow.

The crowd then hushed as Seremides extended his hand to Talena and conducted her before Myron, her head down.

"Poor Telena," whispered a man.

The daughters of conquered ubars often grace the triumphs of victorious generals. This may be done in many ways. Sometimes they are marched naked at their stirrups, in chains; sometimes they are marched similarly but among slaves holding other loot, golden vessels, and such; sometimes they are displayed on wagons, or rolling platforms, caged with she-verr or she-tarsks, and so on. Almost always they will be publicly and ceremoniously enslaved, either before or after the triumph, either in their own city or in the city of the conqueror.

Myron, however, bowed low before Talena, in this perhaps saluting the loftiness and honorableness of her status, that of the free female.

"I do not understand," said Marcus.

"Wait," I said.

"Will he not now strip her and have her put in chains?" asked Marcus.

"Watch," I said.

"She will be in his tent, as one of his women, before nightfall," he said.

"Watch," I said.

"To be sure," he said, "perhaps she will be kept for the

pleasure gardens of Lurius of Jad, or the kennels of his house slaves, if she is not beautiful enough for his pleasure gardens."

"Watch a moment," I said.

Talena, as I knew, was an exquisitely beautiful female, with that olive skin, and dark eyes and hair. I did not doubt but what she was worthy of a ubar's pleasure gardens, and even if, all things considered, she was not quite of that quality, she would still, undoubtedly, find herself there. Allowances are often made for special women, former enemies, and such, and I had little doubt that an allowance of one sort or another would be made for a ubar's daughter, or one taken to be such. It must be remembered, too, that the contents of a pleasure garden are not necessarily always viewed in only one light. For example, such a garden may contain women who are, in a sense, primarily trophies. Surely Talena might count, say, from the standpoint of a Lurius of Jad, as such a trophy. Indeed, some men, collectors, use their gardens mainly for housing their collections, say, of different types of women, selected perhaps primarily with an eye to illustrating, and exhibiting, various forms of female beauty, or, indeed, even for their unique or rare brands.

Myron then turned about to one of the two fellows who had ascended the ramp with him, each of which held a package.

"What is in the package?" asked a man.

"A slave collar, slave bracelets, shackles, such things," said a man.

"No, look!" said a man.

"Ai!" said Marcus.

Myron, from the package held by one of the two fellows who had ascended the ramp with him, drew forth a shimmering veil. He shook this out and displayed it to the crowd.

"It is the veil of a free woman!" said a man.

Myron handed this to Talena, who accepted it.

"I do not understand," said Marcus.

"It will be all she will be given," said a man, angrily.

"A Cosian joke," said another, "then to be removed from her when they wish."

"Cosian sleen," said a man.

"We must fight," said another.

"We cannot fight," said another. "It is hopeless."

Another fellow moaned.

Myron then, however, from the same package, drew forth a set of the ornate robes of concealment, displaying these to the crowd, as he had done with the veil. These, too, he then delivered to Talena.

"Why are they giving her such garments?" asked a man.

"They are Cosian garments," said a man.

"Perhaps it is that Lurius of Jad is to be the first to look upon her fully, in his pleasure chambers," said a man.

"Woe is Talena," whispered a man.

"Woe is us, woe is Ar!" said another.

"We must fight," said the man, again.

"No, it is hopeless!" said the other.

"No, see!" said another. "He again bows before her. Myron, the polemarkos, bows before our Talena!"

Talena then bowed her head, too, as though shyly, gratefully, before the polemarkos.

"She accepts his respects!" said a man.

"It seems she now wishes to withdraw," said a man.

"Poor modest little Talena!" said another.

To be sure, it seemed that Talena now, overcome with modesty, clutching the garments to her gratefully with one hand and with the other seeming to try to pull down the white robes, to more cover her bared feet, wished to leave the platform.

The hand of Seremides however gently stayed her.

"Modest Talena!" exclaimed a man.

"She is not a slave," said another, glaring angrily at Phoebe who, frightened, in her slave tunic, pressed herself more closely against Marcus.

"Myron will speak," said a man.

The polemarkos, or him I took to be he, then advanced to the front of the platform. Gnieus Lelius, chained, was kneeling to his right.

At the front of the platform, after a pause, Myron began to speak. He spoke in a clear, strong, resounding voice. His accent was Cosian, of course, but it was a high-caste Cosian accent, intelligible to all. Too, he spoke deliberately, and slowly. "I bring greetings," said he, "from my ubar, your friend, Lurius of Jad." He then turned to Talena, who stood somewhat behind him, the hand of Seremides on her arm, as though to supply her with perhaps much-needed kindly support in these trying moments. "First," said Myron, "I bring greetings from Lurius of Jad to Talena of Ar, daughter of Marlenus of Ar, Ubar of Ubars!" Talena inclined her head, accepting these greetings.

"Hail Cos!" cried a fellow in the crowd.

Myron now turned to the crowd.

The impressiveness of greeting Talena first, I had no doubt, had its significance. Also, I noted that she was being accepted as the daughter of Marlenus of Ar by Cos, in spite of the fact that Marlenus had disowned her. In accepting her as the daughter of Marlenus, of course, Cos had made it reasonably clear that they would not be likely to challenge any claims she, or others on her behalf, might make with respect to the succession in Ar. Also, though I did not think Lurius of Jad himself would have approved of Marlenus being spoken of as the ubar of ubars, as he perhaps thought that he himself might better deserve that title, the reference seemed a judicious one on the part of Myron. It was a clear appeal to patriotic sentiment in Ar. And, naturally, this sort of reference to Marlenus would scarcely be expected to tarnish the image of Talena, who was thus implicitly being characterized as the daughter of the ubar of ubars.

"And greetings, too," called Myron, "to our friends and brothers, the noble people of Ar!"

The crowd looked at one another.

"Today," said Myron, "you are free!"

"Hail Cos! Hail Ar!" cried a fellow in the crowd.

"The tyrant, our common enemy," cried Myron, gesturing to Gnieus Lelius, "has been defeated!"

"Kill him!" cried men in the crowd!

"To the walls with him!" cried a fellow.

"Fetch an impaling spear!" cried another.

"Peace, friendship, joy and love," called Myron, "to our brothers in Ar!"

One of the members of the High Council, presumably its executive officer, who would have had been directly subordinate to Gnieus Lelius, the regent, in a civilian capacity, as Seremides would have been in a military capacity, stepped forth to respond to Myron, but he was warned back by Seremides. "I speak on behalf of Talena of Ar, daughter of Marlenus of Ar, Ubar of Ubars," called Seremides. "She, in her own name, and in the name of the people and Home Stone of Ar, gives thanks to our friends and brothers of Cos, for the delivery of her city from the tyranny of Gnieus Lelius and for the liberation of her people!"

At this point, doubtless by a prearranged signal, the great bars of the Central Cylinder began to ring, and, in moments, so, too, did the other bars about the city, near and far. But it seemed, too, then, for a time, one could scarcely hear the bars, so loud, so unrestrained, so wild, so grateful, so elated and tumultuous, were the cheers of the crowd.

"Hail Cos! Hail Ar!" we heard.

The cries seemed deafening.

On the platform Myron then, and the fellows with him, now reached into the second package, seizing out handfuls of coins, even silver tarsks, and showered them into the crowd. Men seized them as they could. Taurentians stepped back from the crowd's perimeter. No longer was there danger of seething, ignitable surgency. I noted that while Myron and his fellows scattered these coins about, Seremides, waving to the crowd, and Talena, lifting her hand, too, and the High Council, withdrew from the surface of the platform. Also, almost unnoticed a squad of fellows from Cos ascended to the platform. The head of Gnieus Lelius was pushed down to the platform. A chain, about two feet Gorean in length, was put on his neck and attached to the short chain linking his shackles. Too, he was leashed. He was then pulled to his feet. Because of the length of the new chain on his neck he could not stand upright, but must, rather, remain bent over, deeply, from the waist. A Taurentian then freed his neck of the heavy collar with the radiating chains, by means of which the children had conducted him to the height of the platform. Gnieus Lelius, then, former regent of Ar, in the motley rags suitable to a comedic mime, his ankles shackled, his upper body wrapped in chains, bent far over, held in this fashion by the short chain between his neck and ankles, trying to keep his balance, taking short steps, was dragged by Cosians from the platform on the leash. He fell twice in my view, after which incidents he was struck by spear butts and pulled rudely again to his feet, to be again hastened, with more blows, on his way south on the Avenue of the Central Cylinder. Some in the crowd, seeing him as he passed, so clad, so hobbled, so helpless, so conducted, pointed and roared with mirth; others cried out hatred and insults, shrieked imprecations upon him, spat upon him, and tried to strike him. "Fool!" cried some. "Buffoon!" cried some. "Tyrant! Tyrant!" cried others. Dressing Gnieus Lelius in the garments of a comedic mime, in effect, a fool, a buffoon, seemed to me a politic decision on the part of the party of treachery in Ar. This would almost certainly preclude not only his return to power, if he should manage to regain his freedom, but even the formation of a party that might favor this. Indeed, even his closest supporters were inclined to grant his dupery. Too, the party of treachery must have realized that many in Ar would know, or surely eventually come to understand, that Gnieus Lelius, whatever might have been his faults as a leader in a time of crisis, was a far cry from a tyrant. If anything, his faults had been on the lines of tolerance, compromise and permissiveness, policies which had allowed Cos and her partisans to operate almost unopposed in the city, policies which had allowed Ar to be taken from him, and from herself. No, they would be likely to say to themselves, he was not a tyrant, but, indeed, he was perhaps a fool.

"Tyrant! Tyrant!" cried men.

Lurius of Jad, of course, would know that Gnieus Lelius was not a tyrant.

"Tyrant!" cried men. "Tyrant!"

I looked after Gnieus Lelius.

I assumed he would be taken to Cos.

Perhaps he would eventually adorn the court of Lurius of Jad, as a chained fool. Perhaps he might eventually entertain at banquets, pretending on his leash to be a dancing sleen.

The coins cast forth, Myron lifted his arms to the crowd.

Muchly was he cheered.

Then he, with his fellows, descended the ramp and were in a moment again, utilizing the mounting rings, in the saddle. They then wheeled their mounts and began to move south. His helmet bearer, on his own beast, followed him. Showing his face to the crowd was judicious, I thought. It suggested openness, candor, trust, rejoicing. Too, the common Gorean helmet, with its "Y"-shaped aperture, of which his helmet was a variant, tends to have somewhat formidable appearance. He smiled. He waved. Peals of rejoicing rang from the signal bars about the city. The crowds, on both sides of the avenue, cheered. Then the musicians struck up a martial air, and the standards turned about. The forces of Cos, too, about-faced. Then they withdrew, south on the avenue, between cheering crowds. Girls rushed out to give flowers to the soldiers. Some of the men tied them on their spears. "Hail Cos! Hail Ar! cried hundreds of men. "We are free!" cried others. "Hail our liberators!" called others. "Gratitude to Cos!" cried others. "Hail Lurius of Jad!" cried others. Children were lifted on shoulders to see the soldiers. Thousands of small Cosian pennons, together with pennons of Ar, appeared, waving. Both sides of the street were riots of color and sound. "Hail Lurius of Jad!" cried men. "Hail Seremides!" cried others. "Hail Talena!" cried others. "Hail Talena!"

I looked at Marcus.

Phoebe had her head down, her eyes shut, covering her ears with her hands, so great was the din.

But, in a few Ehn, with the passage of the Cosians south on the avenue, the crowd melted away from us.

Phoebe opened her eyes and removed her hands from her ears, but she kept her head down.

We could trace the withdrawal of the Cosians by the sounds of the crowd, ever farther away.

I looked at the platform, deserted now. On that platform, barefoot, Talena had stood. She had worn the robe of a penitent or suppliant. She should have been by custom naked beneath that robe, but I doubted that she had been. I wondered what might have occurred had things turned out differently, and not as planned, say, had Myron removed that robe and found her clothed. I smiled to myself. She might have been killed. At the least she would have soon learned the lash of a man's displeasure, in detail and liberally. But I did not think that she, or Seremides, had feared that eventuality. Surely she was of more use to the party of treachery, in which she doubtless stood high, and to the Cosians, on the throne of Ar than as merely another woman, naked and in chains, gracing a conqueror's triumph. Seremides, too, and Myron, as well, I thought, had played their parts well.

As I pondered these things some workmen came forth to dismantle the platform. It had served its purpose. Too, at this time the great bars in the Central Cylinder ceased their ringing. We could still hear the ringing of other bars elsewhere in the city, farther away. Too, far off now, like the sounds of Thassa breaking on a distant shore, we could hear the crowds.

I again considered the platform. On it Talena, of Ar, had stood barefoot. I trusted that she had not injured her feet.

Phoebe now knelt beside Marcus, her head down.

"It is strange," I said to Marcus. "The war betwixt Cos and Ar has ended."

"Yes," he said.

"It is done," I said. "It is over."

"With victory for Cos," said Marcus.

"Complete victory," I said.

Marcus looked down at Phoebe. "You have won," he said.

"Not I," she said.

"Cos has won," he said.

"Cos," she said, "not I."

"You are Cosian," he said.

"No longer," she said. "I am a slave."

"But doubtless you rejoice in her victory," he said.

"Perhaps Master rejoices," she said, "that Ar, who refused to succor Ar's Station, the city of the slave's master, has now fallen?"

Marcus looked down upon her.

"Am I to be now slain?" she asked, trembling.

"No," he said.

She looked up at him.

"You are only a slave," he said.

Swiftly, weeping, she put down her head to his feet. She laughed and cried, and kissed his feet. Then she looked up at him, through her tears. "But am I no longer to be your little "Cosian"?" she asked, laughing.

"You will always be my little Cosian," he said.

"Yes, Master," she said.

"Spread your knees, Cosian," he said.

"Yes, Master!" she laughed.

"More widely," said he.

"Yes, Master!" she said.

"Slave," said he.

"Your slave, my Master!" she said.

I heard the sound of hammers as the workmen struck boards from the platform.

"We should seek lodging," said Marcus.

"Yes," I said.

Phoebe rose to her feet beside her master, clinging to him, pressing herself to him, soft, her head down. He nestled her in his arms. How much she was his!

"Tomorrow," said Marcus, "I would conjecture that Myron will have a triumph."

"More likely the Ubar of Cos, by proxy," I said.

"Doubtless its jubilation and pomp will dwarf the celebrations of this morning."

"Ar will do her best, I am sure, to officially welcome, and express her gratitude to, her liberator, the great Lurius of Jad," I said.

"Represented by his captain, and cousin, Myron, polemarkos of Temos," he said. This was Myron's exact title, incidentally. Temos is one of the major cities on the island of Cos. The crowd, of course, or many in it, regarded him simply as the polemarkos, or, say, understandably enough, and, I suppose, correctly enough, as the polemarkos of Cos.

"Of course," I said.

"Seremides will doubtless participate in the triumph," he said.

"He should," I said. "It is his, as well. He has doubtless worked hard and long to realize such a day."

"And Talena," he said.

"Yes," I said.

"You sound bitter," he said.

"Perhaps," I said.

"Myron did not accept the sword of Seremides," he said.

"That is understandable," I said.

"I suppose so," he said.

"Certainly," I said.

The acceptance of the sword would have constituted a public token of the surrender of Ar's forces, foot and cavalry, both tarn and tharlarion. That Myron had refused to accept it publicly on the platform was fully in keeping with the pretense of liberation.

"It is my speculation," I said, "that the sword was surrendered yesterday, in the tent of Myron, or, more likely, before his troops, outside the city, and then, later, privately returned."

"Yes!" said Marcus. "I wager you are right!"

"The troops of the polemarkos would expect such a thing," I said.

"Of course," he said.

"So, too, would Lurius of Jad," I said.

"Yes," he said.

"In any event," I said, "with or without such tokens, the surrender of Ar is complete. It has been clearly and indisputably effected. Resistance to Cos has been ordered to cease. The forces of Ar, such as remain of them, have laid down their arms. They will presumably be soon reduced in numbers, perhaps to handfuls of guardsmen subject to Cosian officers, if not completely disbanded and scattered. Weapons will presumably, in time, be outlawed in the city. Her gates have been burned. I would expect, eventually, that her walls, stone by stone, will be taken down. She will then be utterly vulnerable, dependent completely on the mercies of Cos or her puppets."

"It will be the end of a civilization," said Marcus.

"A civilization of sorts will remain," I said, "and arts of a sort, a literature of a sort, and such things."

"Perhaps Gor will be the better for it," said Marcus, bitterly.

I was silent.

"How will the men retain their manhood?" he asked.

"Perhaps they will manage," I said. I had great respect for the men of Ar.

"And what will become of the women?" he asked.

"I do not know," I said. "If the men do not retain their manhood, it will be difficult, or impossible, for the women, at least those who are in relationship to such men, to be women."

"Yes," he said.

"Cos," I said, "is master on Gor." I recalled that Dietrich of Tarnburg had feared such an eventuality, the coming to sovereignty of a major power. Such might mean the end of the free companies.

"Only in a sense," said Marcus.

I regarded him.

"In many cities and lands, indeed, in most parts of the world," he said, "things will be surely much as they were before."

I considered such things as the difficulties of communication, the difficulties of maintaining supply lines, the lengths of marches, the paucity of roads, the isolation of cities, the diversities of cultures and such.

"I think you are right," I said.

It would be merely that Cos would now be the dominant force on the continent. Also, geopolitically, it did not seem likely that Cos could indefinitely maintain her power. Her seat of power was overseas and her forces were largely composed of mercenaries who were difficult to control and expensive to maintain. The recent campaigns of Lurius of Jad must have severely drained the treasury of Cos, and perhaps of Tyros, too, her ally. To be sure, her outlays might now be recouped here and there, for example, from conquered Ar. Cos had succeeded in defeating Ar. It was not so clear, I now realized, that she had managed to guarantee and secure her own hegemony indefinitely. Indeed, with Ar vulnerable and helpless, nullified militarily, if the power of Cos should collapse, a new barbarism might ensue, at least within the traditional boundaries of Ar, a lawless barbarism broken here and there by the existence of minor tyrannies, places where armed men imposed their will.

"I do not hear the bars any longer," said Marcus. "Nor the crowds."

"Nor do I," I said.

It now seemed quiet at the park of the Central Cylinder, save for the sounds of the workmen, striking apart the boards of the platform. Few people, too, were about. Some papers blew across the park, some of them tiny banners of colored paper, banners of both Cos and Ar.

Again I considered the platform. On it Talena had stood, barefoot.

"Look," I said to Marcus, indicating some of the boards removed from the platform and piled to one side.

"What?" he asked.

"The boards," I said, "on their upper surfaces, they are smoothed."

"And from the reflection of light, sealed," he said.

"Yes," I said.

"Doubtless prepared for the feet of the noble Talena,' he said.

"Yes," I said.

"Unusual solicitation for a penitent or suppliant," said Marcus.

"Yes," I granted him.

"But we would not wish to risk her little feet, would we?" Marcus asked Phoebe.

"No, Master," said Phoebe.

Although Marcus had spoken in irony, Phoebe's response was quite serious, and appropriately so. She did not even begin to put herself in the category of a free woman. An unbridgeable and, to the slave, terrifying chasm separates any free woman on Gor from a slave, such as Phoebe.

"It is regrettable, is it not," Marcus asked Phoebe, "that she was forced to appear degradingly unshod?"

"Yes, Master," said Phoebe, "for she is a free woman."

Indeed, I suppose that it had cost Talena much to be seen in public, barefoot.

Phoebe, of course, was barefoot. That is common with slaves.

I watched another board being thrown on the pile.

For the most part the platform was held together by wooden pegs, pounded through prepared holes. In this way I supposed it might be easily reassembled. Perhaps there was some intention that it might be used again, perhaps, say, for the coronation of a ubara.

Then the portion of the platform nearest us was down.

I wondered how Talena might look on another sort of platform, say, on an auction platform, stripped and in chains, being bid upon by men. Such a surface would be likely to be quite smooth to her feet, too, presumably having been worn smooth by the bared feet of numerous women before her.

"Let us seek lodging," said Marcus.

"Very well," I said.

8 The Wall

"I have had the good fortune to be chosen for wall duty," said a youth to his fellow.

"I myself volunteered for it," answered the other.

"Such things are the least we can do," said the first.

"By means of them Ar will become great," said the other.

"Not all values are material," said the first.

"By means of such things we shall visibly demonstrate our love of peace," said the second.

"Without such things," said the first, "our protests of love and brotherhood would be empty."

"Of course," said the other.

"I am weary," said Marcus.

"It is the wagons," I said.

In Gorean cities it is often the case that many streets, particularly side streets, little more than alleys, are too narrow for wagons. Local deliveries in such areas are usually made by porters or carts. Similarly, because of considerations such as congestion and noise, and perhaps aesthetics, which Goreans take seriously, wagons are not permitted on certain streets, and on many streets only during certain hours, usually at night or in the early morning. Indeed, most deliveries, as of produce from the country, not borne on the backs of animals of peasants, are made at night or in the early morning. This is also often the case with goods leaving the city, such as shipments of pottery and linens.

We were walking in the Metellan district, and then turned east toward the Avenue of Turia. Phoebe was heeling Marcus.

This morning, some Ahn before dawn, a convoy of wagons had rattled past our lodgings in the Metellan district, in the *insula* of Torbon on Demetrios Street. Our room, like many in an *insula*, had no window, but I had gone to the hall and thrust back the shutters of a window there, overlooking the street. Below, guided here and there by lads, with lanterns, were the wagons. There had been a great many of them. Demetrios Street, like most Gorean streets, like no sidewalks or curbs but sloped gently from both sides to a central gutter. The lads with the lanterns, their light casting dim yellow pools here and there on the walls and paving stones, performed an important function. Without some such illumination it is only too easy to miss a turn or gouge a wall with an axle. Marcus had joined me after a time. The wagons were covered with canvas, roped down. It was not the first such convoy which we had seen in the past weeks.

"Well," Marcus had asked, "what is being borne?"

"Who knows?" I had said.

He laughed.

To be sure, we knew, generically, what was being borne. It was not difficult to tell. Normal goods, exports of bar iron, and such, do not move in the city in such numbers. It is true, of course, that sometimes wagons would congregate at meeting places near gates, the wagons, say, of various manufacturers and merchants, and then travel on the roads in convoys, as a protection against brigandage, but in such a case the wagons, having different points of origin, would not form their convoy until in the vicinity of the gates, and, indeed, sometimes outside them, in order to avoid blocking streets. But the formation of such convoys, too, are usually advertised on the public boards, this information being of interest to various folks, say, merchants who might wish to ship goods, teamsters, guards, and such, who might wish employment, and folks wishing to book passage. Sometimes, incidentally, rich merchants can manage a convoy by themselves, but even so they will usually accommodate the wagons of others in their convoys. There is commonly safety in numbers and the greater the numbers usually the greater the safety. A fee is usually charged for entering wagons in a convoy, this primarily being applied to defray the costs of guards. Too, in some cases, it may be applied to tolls, drinking water, provender for animals, and such. Some entrepreneurs make their living by the organization, management and supply of convoys. But these convoys, those of the sort now passing, were not such convoys. For example, they were not advertised. Indeed, many in Ar might not even be aware of them. Another clue as to the sort of convoys they were was that the wagons were not uniform but constituted rather a diverse lot. Some were even street wagons, and not road wagons, the latter generally of heavier construction, built for use outside the city where roads may be little more than irregular paths, uneven, steep, rugged and treacherous. Some Gorean cities, for example, perhaps as a military measure, in effect isolate themselves by the refusal to allocate funds for good roads. Indeed, they often go further by neglecting the upkeep of even those tracks that exist. It can be next to impossible to reach such cities in the spring, because of the rains. Besnit is an example. Beyond this, although many of the wagons were unmarked, many others, in the advertising on their sides, bore clear evidence of their origins, the establishments of chandlers, carders, fullers, coopers, weavers, millers, bakers, and so on, wagons presumably commandeered for their present tasks. As a last point this convoy, and those which had preceded it on other days, seemed overstaffed, particularly for the city. Instead of having one driver, or a driver and a fellow, a relief driver or one to help with the unloading, and perhaps a lad to help through the city in the darkness, each wagon had at least four or five full-grown men with it, armed, usually two or three on the wagon box, and another two or three on the cargo itself, on the canvas, or, in some cases, holding to the wagon, riding on sideboards or the step below the wagon gate. Others, too, here and there, were afoot, at the sides.

"Ar bleeds," said Marcus.

"Yes," I had said.

"Where are we going?" asked Marcus, following me.

"I want to see what is going on at the walls," I said.

"The same thing," said he, "as was going on last time."

"I wish to see what progress is being made," I said.

"You merely wish to observe the flute girls," he said.

"That, too," I admitted.

In a few Ehn we were on the Avenue of Turia, one of the major avenues in Ar. It is lined with Tur trees.

"What a beautiful street!" exclaimed Phoebe. The vista, when one comes unexpectedly on it, particularly after the minor side streets, is impressive.

Marcus turned about, sharply, and regarded her. She stopped.

"Are you in a collar?" he asked.

"Yes, Master!" she said.

"Are you a slave?" he asked.

"Yes, Master!" she said.

"Do you think," he asked, "that just because I did not slay you on the day of the victory of Cos, that I am weak?"

"No, Master!" she said.

"Or that you may do as you please?"

"No, Master!"

"I decided then to think of you as merely what you are, a slave girl."

"Of course, Master," she said.

"Do you think that any of the fellows of Cos about would free you because you were once of Cos?" he asked.

"No, Master," she said, "for I am now no longer of Cos. I am now no more than an animal, no more than a slave."

"Perhaps then," he said, "you will consider such matters before you next speak without permission."

"Yes, Master," she said.

We then continued on our way.

Marcus, enamored even as he was with every glance and movement, every word and wisp of hair, of his slave, was determined, I was pleased to note, to keep her under perfect discipline. To be sure, he had not beaten her. On the other hand, she had had her warning, and might, the next time, be taught the penalties for such an infringement, in a sense, a daring to exceed her station. Sometimes a girl will court the whip, and even provoke a lashing, just to reassure herself that her master is truly her master. After her whipping, reassured of the strength of her master, and that she will be kept in her place, where she belongs, and wishes to be, she curls gratefully, lovingly, at his feet, eager to serve in all ways, his to command. To be sure, I think that Phoebe's outburst was genuinely inadvertent. I was not sure what I would have done in Marcus' place. Perhaps the same thing. Perhaps, on the other hand, I would have cuffed her. I do not know. There are, of course, inadvertences and inadvertences. Usually a girl can tell when she has an implicit permission to speak, that is, for example, when the master would not be likely to object to it, or would even welcome it, and when it would be wise to ask for such permission explicitly. When she is in doubt it would be wise to ask. I myself, incidentally, am occasionally inclined to encourage a certain inventiveness and spontaneity on the part of slaves. On the other hand the girl must always be clearly aware that she is subject to discipline, and that it may be imposed upon her instantly, at any time. She is, after all, a slave.

"Did you notice the haircut of that young fellow we just passed?" I asked.

"Yes," he said. "It is done in the style of Myron, the polemarkos."

"Yes," I said.

"Here are public boards," said Marcus.

Such are found at various points in Ar, such as the vicinity of squares and plazas, near markets, and on major streets and avenues.

"Is there anything new?" I inquired. I would prefer for Marcus to make out the lettering. He read Gorean fluently.

"Not really," said Marcus. "The usual things, quotations from various officials, testimonials of fidelity to both Cos and Ar, declarations of chagrin and shame by various men of note concerning the crimes of Ar under Gnieus Lelius."

"I see," I said. It was now some two months since the entry of Myron into the city and the subsequent triumph of Lurius of Jad, celebrated a day later in his name by Myron, the polemarkos, in which triumph he, Myron, acting as proxy for Lurius of Jad, was joined by Seremides and Talena, and several weeks after the ascension of Talena to the throne of Ar, as Ubara. Her coronation may have been somewhat less spectacular than Myron's entry into the city and Lurius' subsequent triumph, which may have grated upon her somewhat, but I think it had been impressive enough. The crown of Tur leaves was placed upon her head by Myron, but on behalf of the people and councils of Ar. Seremides and most members of the High Council were in attendance. Certain other members of the High Council were asserted to be indisposed. Some rumors had it that they were under house arrest. A medallion of Ar was also placed about Talena's neck but the traditional medallion, which had been worn by Marlenus, and which he had seldom permitted out of his keeping, and which he may have had with him upon his departure from the city long ago, had not been found. Too, the ring of the Ubar, which in any event would have been too large for the finger of Talena, was not found. But that ring, it was said, had not been in Ar for years. Indeed, it had been rumored in Ar, even before the disappearance of Marlenus, that it had once been lost in the northern forests, upon a hunting expedition. After the medallion, Talena had been given the Home Stone of Ar, that she might hold it in her left hand, and a scepter, a rod of office, signifying power, that she might hold in her right. Her coronation was followed by a declaration of five holidays. The triumph of Lurius of Jad, as I recall, had been followed by ten such days. The chief advisors of the new ubara were Myron, of Cos, and Seremides, once of Tyros.

"Here is something," said Marcus, "though I do not gather its import."

"What?" I asked.

"There is a charge to the citizens and councils of Ar to consider how they might make amends for their complicity in the crimes of their city."

"Reparations?" I asked.

"I do not know," said Marcus.

"I would have thought that Ar had already made considerable amends," I said.

I recalled the convoys of wagons which had passed by the *insula* of Torbon on the street of Demetrios.

"Be careful what you say," said a man near me.

"We are guilty," said a man.

"Yes," said another.

"It is only right," said another, "that we should attempt to make amends to our good friends of Cos and others whom we may have injured."

"True," said another man.

Marcus and I then, followed by Phoebe, continued on our way.

"The Home Stone of Ar's Station is no longer exhibited publicly," said Marcus, gloomily.

"I think it will be again," I said.

"Why do you say that?" he asked, interested.

"I have my reasons," I said. "Do not concern yourself with it now."

"The wall seems very bare there," said Marcus, as we passed a public edifice, a court building.

There were also numerous small holes in the wall, chipped at the edges.

"Surely you have noted similar walls," I said.

"Yes," he said.

"Decorative reliefs, in marble, have been removed from them," I said. "As I recall the ones here, they celebrated the feats of Hesius, a perhaps legendary hero of Ar."

"He for whom the month of Hesius is named," said Marcus.

"I presume so," I said. The month of Hesius is the second month of the year in Ar. It follows the first passage hand. In Ar, as in most cities in the northern hemisphere, the new year begins with the vernal equinox.

"Were the marbles here well done?" asked Marcus.

"Though I am scarcely a qualified judge of such things," I said, "I would have thought so. They were very old, and reputed to be the work of the master, Aurobion, though some have suggested they were merely of his school."

"I have heard of him," said Marcus.

"Some think the major figures profited from his hand and that portions of the minor detail, and some of the supportive figures, were the work of students."

"Why would the marbles be removed?" asked Marcus.

"They have antiquarian value, as well as aesthetic value," I said. "I would suppose that they are now on their way to a museum in Cos."

"The decorative marbles on the Avenue of the Central Cylinder, and those about the Central Cylinder itself, and on the Cylinder of Justice are still there," he said.

"At least for the time," I said. The building we had just passed was an extremely old building. Many in Ar were not sure of its age. It may have dated to the first ubarate of Titus Honorious. Many of the functions originally discharged within its precincts had long ago been assumed by the newer Cylinder of Justice, located in the vicinity of the Central Cylinder. Incidentally, many buildings, particularly public buildings, in this part of the city, which was an older part of the city, were quite old. Many smaller buildings, dwellings, shops, *insulae*, and such, on the other hand, were relatively new. I might also mention, in passing, if only to make the controversy concerning the "Aurobion marbles" more understandable, that many Gorean artists do not sign or otherwise identify their works. The rationale for this seems to be a conviction that what is important is the art, its power, its beauty, and so on, and not who formed it. Indeed many Gorean artists seem to regard themselves as little more than vessels or instruments, the channels or means, the tools, say, the chisels or brushes, so to speak, by means of which the world, with its values and meanings, in its infinite diversities, in its beauties and powers, its flowers and storms, its laughters and rages, its delicacy and awesomeness, its subtlety and grandeur, expresses itself, and rejoices. Accordingly the Gorean artist tends not so much to be proud of his work as, oddly enough perhaps, to be grateful to it, that it consented to speak through him. As the hunters of the north, the singers of the ice pack and of the long night have it, "No one knows from whence songs come." It is enough, and more than enough, that they come. They dispel the cold, they illuminate the darkness. They are welcomed, in the darkness and cold, like fire, and friendship and love. The focus of the Gorean artist then, at least on the whole, tends to be on the work of art itself, not on himself as artist. Accordingly his attitude toward his art is less likely to be one of pride than one of gratitude. This makes sense as, in his view, it is not so much he who speaks as the world, in its many wonders, great and small, which speaks through him. He is thus commonly more concerned to express the world, and truth, than himself.

"Let us turn right, here," I said.

We then left the Avenue of Turia and were once again on a side street. Many Gorean streets, incidentally, do not have specific names, particularly from one end to the other, some being known by one designation here and another there. Indeed, sometimes a long, winding street will have several names, depending on its turns and so on. Others may have no names really, in themselves, but are referred to, for example, as the street on which Sabor has his smithy, and so on. This becomes more intelligible if one thinks of "alleys." For example, alleys seldom have names. So, too, many Gorean streets, particularly those that are smaller and much like alleys, may not have names. One may usually hire a lad from the district to direct one to particular points. Similarly, of course, one may make inquiries of fellows in the area. In such inquiries, the male will normally speak to a male, and the female to a female. This has to do not only with matters of propriety, enshrined in Gorean custom, but also with common-sense security measures. For example, a woman would not wish to seem forward, nor, in effect, to be calling herself to the attention of a strange male, which can be dangerous on Gor, and a woman, a free woman, might be well advised not to respond to the accostings of a strange male. He might even be a slaver or a slaver's man, interested in seeing if she has a pleasing voice, one suitable for a slave. Similarly if she responds to a strange male this may be taken as evidence that she is eager to please a man and obey, two attributes which suggest her readiness, even immediately, for his collar. One may, of course, make such inquiries of slave girls. In such a case they are expected to kneel immediately, being in the presence of a free man, or person, and be as helpful as possible. It is desirable, incidentally, for the girls of a district to know the district rather well, in case they are asked for directions and such. If they do not know the information desired, it is sensible on their part to keep their head very low, even to the stones, or even to belly to the interlocutor. This may save them a cuffing or kick. This street, however, had a name. It was Harness Street, apparently so called from long ago when it was once a locale of several harness makers. The harness makers are members of the caste of leather workers. The "harness makers" on Gor, provide not just harnesses but an entire line of associated products, such as saddles, bridles, reins, hobblings and tethers. Presumably the harness makers on this street would not have dealt in slave harnesses. That product would have been more likely to have been, as it still was, available on the "Street of Brands," a district in which are found many of the houses of slavers, sales barns, sales arenas, holding areas, boarding accommodations, training facilities, and shops dealing with product lines pertinent to slaves, such as collars, cosmetics, jewelry, perfumes, slave garb, chains, binding fiber and disciplinary devices. In such a district one may have a girl's septum or ears pierced. There are many varieties of slave harness, incidentally, with various purposes, such as discipline, display and security. Many of them are extremely lovely on a woman, and many, by such adjustments as cinching, tightening, and buckling, may be fitted closely and exquisitely to the individual slave.

"Look," I said, "there is a woman in garments of Cosian cut."

"I wonder how she would look on her knees, in a slave rag," said Marcus.

"I do not know," I said.

"Undoubtedly quite well," he said.

"I would suppose so," I said. After all, most women do.

"Talena of Ar, as you know," said Marcus, "now affects the garments of Cos."

"I have heard that," I said.

We now crossed the Alley of the Slave Brothels of Ludmilla, actually a reasonably large street.

"You need not look at the establishments on this street," Marcus informed Phoebe.

"Yes, Master," she said, putting her head down, smiling.

As a slave, of course, anything could done with her. She could be, for example, sold to a brothel.

I recalled my first visit to one of the slave brothels on the street, the Tunnels. I recalled one of its slaves, a former Earth girl. She had been slight but well curved for her size and weight. She had had red hair. Her name, perhaps originally her

Earth name, but now on her as a slave name, had been 'Louise'. In my arms, as I recalled, she had learned to be pleasing. I also recalled a blond free woman acquired later in the same place, the Lady Lydia, of the High Merchants, whose wealth had been in gems and land, a tenant even of the Tabidian Towers. I had sold her to a slaver. A few nights ago I had returned to the Tunnels but had learned that Louise had been purchased long ago by some sturdy young fellow who had been quite taken with her, finding her extraordinarily pliant, eager and exciting. The brothel mistress could not recall his name. On the other hand, she had speculated that he would prove to be an exacting, stern and strong master to the former Earth girl, such as she required. She did inform me that the girl had accompanied her new master joyfully. I hoped that my instruction to the girl had been of some use in bringing about this development, instruction primarily profitable to her with respect to her nature and its correct relationship to that of the male. The blonde, who had been highly placed in the society of Ar, would presumably have been sold out of the city long ago. In another city, of course, she would be only another slave.

We then continued east on Harness Street.

"Did you enjoy the performance at the great theater last night?" I asked.

"Of course," said Marcus. "It was just the way to spend a long evening, prior to having one's sleep interrupted before dawn by a wagon convoy."

"I thought you might like it," I said.

The performance, a pageant, had been called "The Glory of Cos" and the famed Milo, the city's most famous actor, though a slave, had played the part of Lurius of Jad. The roofed stage of the great theater, usually called that, though technically, it was the theater of Pentilicus Tallux, a poet of Ar, of over a century ago, best known for his poems in the delicate trilesiac form and two sensitive, intimate dramas, was over a hundred yards in width, and some twenty yards in depth. This incredible stage, although only the center portions of it were used on many occasions, lent itself to large-scale productions, such as circuses and spectacles. It could easily accommodate a thousand actors. Too, given its strength, ponderous tharlarion, together with numerous other beasts, wagons and such, could appear on it, as they had last night, for example, in staged battles, in which Lurius of Jad, by personal intervention and at great personal risk, again and again turned the tide, and triumphal processions, as at the climax of the pageant.

"Did you enjoy the pageant?" I asked Phoebe.

"Yes, Master!" she said.

"I thought I heard you gasp when Milo first appeared on the stage," said Marcus.

"He is very handsome in his costume, Master," she said.

"Undoubtedly," said Marcus.

"Surely master is not jealous?" inquired Phoebe, delightedly.

"No," he snarled.

"You may beat me tonight, if you wish," she said.

"I may beat you any night, if I wish," he said.

"Yes, Master," she said.

"By count," I said, "I think that some eleven free women were carried fainted, or helpless, from the theater."

"Surely no more than one or two," said Marcus.

"No, eleven," I said.

"Master is a thousand times more handsome than Milo," said Phoebe.

"Apparently you do wish the lash," he said.

"No, Master!" she said.

"Am I really so handsome?" asked Marcus.

"To me, Master," she said.

"Hmmm,' said Marcus, considering this, I speculate. He was, I think, a good-looking young chap. To be sure, he may not have been quite as handsome as I.

"Of course I am only one woman," she said.

"And only a female slave," he said.

"Yes, Master," she said.

"Still," he said, "you are a woman."

"But only a female slave," she said.

"True," he said.

Phoebe, I think, in her way, was having her vengeance. For example, when we had passed by various open-air markets, shelf markets, and such, many of the girls, nude in their chains, usually fastened by the neck or ankle to heavy iron rings, had clearly, to the fury of Phoebe, in posings, and by means of subtle glances, and such, attempted to call themselves to the attention of the young warrior. Only too obviously would they have welcomed being his slaves.

"Probably some women would regard me as being less handsome than Milo," he mused.

"Perhaps, Master," she said.

"Probably at least eleven," I said.

"I did not note women swooning over the sight of you," said Marcus.

"It was dark," I reminded him.

To be sure, as is well known, and doubtless fortunately for

we who are not Milos, the attractiveness of a man to woman is seldom based on physiognomical regularities. For example, men who are not in any normal sense handsome, sometimes even grotesquely irregular men, often exercise an enormous fascination over beautiful women. Women tend to respond to a great variety of properties in a male, few of which are directly correlated with facial symmetries. Among such properties are initiative, will, command, intelligence, strength, and power, in short, with characteristics appropriate to a master. Too, of course, women, who are enormously sensitive, complex, marvelous creatures, can hope for, welcome, and respond to, such things as tenderness, gentleness, and softness. Here one must be careful, however, to distinguish between the tenderness of the strong man, who is truly strong, and the softness of the weakling, who is merely weak. Tenderness, gentleness, and such, become meaningful only in the context of, and against a background of, a temporarily suspended, perhaps even momentarily suspended, strength and command. Only she who is truly at the mercy of a male, and his slave, and under his discipline, can truly appreciate the value of such things.

"We are coming to the Wall Road," said Marcus. This is the longest road, or street, in Ar. It follows the interior circumference of the wall. It is not only a convenience to citizens but it enables troops to be moved rapidly from point to point in the defenses.

I could hear the flutes.

In attending the great theater last night we had conceded to public opinion, or, more particularly, to the sensibilities of free women, clothing Phoebe modestly, or at least somewhat modestly. Indeed, had we not, we would probably not have been permitted within with her. First we draped a sheet about her. Then, with a piece of cloth, we rigged a veil. After this we drew the sheet up in the back and put it about her head, that it might also serve as a hood. Phoebe herself, of course, held the sheet about her. When we were finished we thought it a job rather well done, an approximation to the robes of concealment, hood and veil. Little more than Phoebe's soft, dark eyes and the bridge of her nose could be seen, except, of course, at the bottom, where one might detect her bared ankles and feet. We did not think that Phoebe would relax her vigilence in clutching the sheet about her. She was naked beneath it. Marcus did not want her to forget that she was a slave. Slaves, incidentally, may attend various such functions, particularly those intended for a general audience. Indeed, sometimes masters, with their individual slave or slaves, and even owners of feast slaves, managers of slave houses, taverns and brothels, and such, will bring a chain of slaves to various events, such as races, contests, games or performances. Private masters, for example, often relish the company of their slaves at such events, and public masters, so to speak, recognize the value of such outings for slaves, as stimulation and recreation. Also they give the master more power over the girl. What girl wishes to be left behind, in her kennel, while her chain sisters enjoy an evening at the theater or games? Marcus had had a brief altercation with the taker of ostraka at the entrance, not wishing to pay an entrance fee, or at least the entire entrance fee, for a slave. The taker of ostraka, however, had been adamant, pleading policy and arguing cogently that even a sleen or verr would have to pay, as they would occupy space in the house. Too, what if a fellow were to bring in ten thousand free slaves? Then there would be little room even for free folk. Too, think of all the money the house would lose. Slaves are not permitted at all public events, of course. For example, their presence is sometimes prohibited at certain song dramas and concerts. Similarly, they may not enter temples. In such cases, facilities are usually provided for their custody, usually a walled enclosure, sometimes adjoining the structure, or sets of posts or rings, for their chaining.

"Hold!" said a voice.

Marcus and I stopped, and Phoebe knelt beside Marcus, back a bit, in close heeling position.

"You are armed," said the voice. He was in the uniform of a guardsman of Ar, but his accent was Cosian. There were still guardsmen of Ar, native guardsmen of Ar, in the city, but their numbers had been considerably reduced and they were generally assigned duties of low responsibility. Even then they were under the command of Cosian officers. Putting Cosians in the uniforms of guardsmen of Ar, of course, did suggest that they were, at least in one sense or another, guardsmen of Ar. Surely, at least, they were guardsmen *in* Ar. Perhaps the folks of Ar found this sort of thing reassuring, or, at least, less objectionable than if the fellows seemed a foreign garrison force, clad openly in Cosian uniform. This is not to deny that there were Cosian regulars, in Cosian uniform, in the city, in numbers. Too, many Cosian mercenaries were in the city, with their identifying armbands, scarves, and such. Myron, probably intelligently, however, had limited the numbers of such mercenaries who might enter the city at any one time. Some incidents had occurred nonetheless, such as the destruction of property in various taverns and the vandalization of certain buildings, for example, baths and libraries. Certain shops had apparently also been looted, though no mention of this had appeared on the public boards. The armed forces of Ar had been disbanded, of course, both foot and cavalry, both tharlarion and tarn. Not even border patrols had been retained. Beasts and equipment were acquired by Cos. Most of these men had left the vicinity of the city. I did not know what might become of them. Doubtless they would seek various employments. Perhaps some would become brigands. Some, of course, remained in the city, perhaps hoping to hire into the guardsmen.

"Yes," I said.

"Are you of Ar?" asked the guardsman.

"No," I said.

"What is your employment?" asked the guardsman.

"I seek employment," I said.

"You are not of Ar?"

"No," I said.

"Can you use that blade?" he asked.

"Passably," I said.

"There may be employment for such as you," he said. "Men are needed."

"May we pass?" I asked.

"What do you wish here," he asked, "if you are not of Ar?"

"To see the progress of the works," I said.'

He laughed. "And the flute girls?" he said.

"Surely," I said.

"Pass," he said.

We then continued on our way. The carrying of weapons, and even their possession, was now illegal for citizens of Ar, exceptions being made for guardsmen and such. The populace of Ar, then, was disarmed. This was reputedly for its own protection. Compliance with the disarmament laws was also taken as a fitting token of good will on the part of those of Ar, and an indication both of their good intentions and of their zealous desire for peace. Too, it was called to their attention that arms were now unnecessary, given the blessings of peace, attendant upon the liberation.

"It will be only a matter of time," said Marcus, "before weapons will be altogether illegal in the city."

"Except for those authorized to carry them," I said.

"Cosians," he said.

"And such," I said.

"You noticed how he inquired into our employments?" said Marcus.

"Of course," I said.

"Soon," he said, "there will be regulations about such things, and papers, and permits, and ostraka, and such."

"I would suppose so," I said. To be sure, I had an idea that an employment, and in the fee of Cos, might fit in with my plans, and perhaps those of Marcus, as well.

"It will be worse than under Gnieus Lelius," he said.

"Yes," I said. I supposed that Gnieus Lelius was now on his way to Cos. Perhaps he was already there.

"Perhaps Milo can save Ar," he said.

"Do not be bitter," I said.

I myself had rather enjoyed the pageant glorifying Cos, or, as it actually turned out, Lurius of Jad. The production had been well designed, well staged, brilliantly costumed, and impressively acted. Indeed, it is hard to get a thousand actors on a stage without being impressive in one way or another. Too, I had to admit, in spite of misgivings on the subject, that Milo was a handsome fellow, and certainly played a part well. It was somewhat ironic to see Lurius of Jad, whom I had once seen, a corpulent slug of a man, portrayed by such a godlike fellow as Milo, but then that was probably in the best interests of the drama's intent, and artistic license, as I understand it, permits such occasional thespic peccadilloes.

"I think the drama must have lasted five Ahn," said Marcus.

"Probably no more than three," I said. "Did you enjoy the fellow who played the wicked, conniving Gnieus Lelius?"

"Of course," said Marcus. "I had not realized thitherto that even a demented sleen could be so wicked."

"You just did not have your mind on the drama," I said.

"That is perhaps true," said Marcus, perking up.

"You just did not realize that Phoebe could be so fetching, completely concealed," I said.

"But underneath the sheet naked," Marcus reminded me.

"You could not wait to get her home," I said.

"Perhaps," he said.

No sooner had he had Phoebe inside the door to our room in the *insula* than he had torn the sheet and veil from her and flung her on her belly to the straw-filled mat, then leaping upon her with a cry of joy.

"Do you think others knew she was naked?" he asked.

"From their glances, and expressions, I think a free woman or two suspected it," I said. One had sneered "Slave!" to Phoebe, to which Phoebe had put down her head, saying "Yes, Mistress." There had been little difficulty, of course, in folks knowing that Phoebe was a slave, given, for example, that her primary covering was a sheet and that her feet were bared.

Too, during intermissions Marcus knelt her at his feet, with her head down.

"Let them crawl naked before a man, fearing his whip," said Marcus.

"Free women?" I said.

"Well," said Marcus, irritably, "collar them first."

"I would hope so," I said.

To be sure, it is pleasant to have free women in such a predicament. It helps them to understand that fate which is to be shortly theirs.

"I do not like Milo," said Marcus.

"You are just angry because he is such a handsome fellow," I said.

"The drama was a poor one," said Marcus.

"Not at all," I said.

"It was a waste of money," said Marcus.

"Phoebe liked it," I said.

"What does she know?" asked Marcus.

"She is a highly intelligent, well-educated woman," I said.

"A slave," he said.

"Now," I said. Many Goreans enjoy owning highly intelligent, well-educated women. It is pleasant to have them at your feet, yours, begging, eager to please you, knowing, too, that if they do not, they will be punished. To be sure, thousands of sorts of women make excellent slaves, each in their different ways.

It had cost three full copper tarsks for our admission to the pageant, and one of those was for Phoebe. The first performance of the pageant, several days ago, had been attended by Talena, the Ubara. I had not been able to obtain admission ostraka for that performance, as it was apparently restricted. I had lingered by her path to the theater, with others in a crowd, but I had been able to see only her palanquin, its curtains drawn, borne not by slaves but by stout fellows apparently of the staff of the Central Cylinder. The palanquin, too, was surrounded by guardsmen, either of Ar or Cos. It interested me that the Ubara, so popular in the city, presumably, should require so much security. Behind the palanquin, on tharlarion, side by side, had ridden Seremides, formerly high general of Ar, now, in peacetime, first minister to her majesty, the Ubara, and Myron, the polemarkos of Temos. Seremides, to be sure, now as captain, high captain, retained command of the palace guard, the Taurentians. There were probably some twenty-five hundred of these fellows in the city. I had not seen Talena when she had left the palanquin, for she had done so within the theater's outer concourse, hidden from the street. That she now wore the garments of Cos I had heard, but I had not seen her in them.

We could now hear the flute music quite clearly.

"There!" I said, startled.

I had not realized that so much had been done since my last visit to this area.

I hurried forward, to the Wall Road.

A gigantic breach, over four hundred yards in width, had been made in the wall. The bottom of the breach was still some forty or fifty feet high. The edges of it tapered up to the height of the wall on each side, in this area, some hundred to a hundred and twenty feet Gorean above the pavement. The breach swarmed with human beings. Stone after stone was being tumbled down from the walls, to the outside of the city. These, I had heard, on the other side, were being lifted to wagons and carted away. On the walls were not only men of Ar, and male youth, but women and girls, as well.

I stood on the Wall Road, back near Harness Street. Here I was about a hundred feet back from the wall. In moment or two Marcus was again beside me, and Phoebe behind him, on his left. The girl normally heels a right-handed master on the left, that she not encumber the movements of the weapon hand.

"Much progress has been made since last we came here," I said.

"About the walls, here and there, thousands apply themselves," he said.

This was not the only breach in the walls, of course, but it was that which was nearest to our lodgings. Here some hundreds, at least, were laboring. Others, of course, on the other side of the wall, would be gathering up tumbled stone, loading it and removing it from the area. The walls of Ar, in effect, had become a quarry. This would, I suppose, depress the market for stone in various cities, perhaps even as far away as Venna. There were many uses for such stone, but most had to do with materials for building, paving and fill. Much of the stone would be pounded into gravel by prisoners and slaves far from the city. This gravel was used mainly for bedding primary roads and paving secondary roads. There were, at present, nineteen such breaches about the city. These breaches, multiplying the avenues of possible assault on the city, were not randomly located. They were set at tactically optimum sites for such assaults and distributed in such a manner as to require the maximum dispersal of defensive forces. The pursued objective, of course, was to multiply and join breaches, until the razing of the walls of Ar was complete.

"Although I hate Ar," said Marcus, "this sight fills me with sorrow."

"You hate not Ar," I said, "but those who betrayed her, and Ar's Station."

"I despise Ar, and those of Ar," he said.

"Very well," I said.

We continued to regard the work on the walls.

Here and there upon the walls, among those working, were silked flute girls, sometimes sitting cross-legged on flat stones, rather even with or even below the heads of workers, sometimes perched cross-legged on large stones, above the heads of workers, sometimes moving about among the workers, sometimes strolling, playing, at other times turning and dancing. Some were also on the lower level, even on the Wall Road.

"Many of the flute girls seem pretty," said Marcus.

"Yes," I said. To be sure, we were rather far from them.

"It is a joke of Lurius of Jad, I gather," said Marcus, "that the walls of Ar should be torn down to the music of flute girls."

"I would think so," I said.

"What an extreme insult," he said.

"Yes," I said.

"You will note," he said, "that many of the girls sit cross-legged."

"Yes," I said.

"They should be beaten," he said.

"Yes," I said.

On Gor men sit cross-legged, not women. The Gorean female, whether free or slave, whether of low caste or high caste, kneels. This posture on the part of a woman, aping that of men, is a provocation. I had seen panther girls in the north, in their desire to repudiate their own nature, and in their envy of men, adopt such a posture. To be sure, such women, reduced to slavery, quickly learn to kneel and usually, considering their new status, with their knees widely apart. The cross-legged posture of several of the flute girls was undoubtedly an insolence, intended as a further insult to the citizens of Ar.

"Why is it that the men do not punish them?" asked Marcus.

"I do not know," I said.

"Perhaps they are afraid to," he said.

"I think rather it has to do with the new day in Ar, and the new understandings."

"What do you mean?" he said.

"Officially," I said, "the music of the flute girls is supposed to make the work more pleasant."

"Who believes that?" asked Marcus.

"Many may pretend to, or even manage to convince themselves of it," I said.

"What of the provocative posture?" asked Marcus. "Surely the insult of that is clear enough to anyone."

"It is supposedly a time of freedom," I said. "Thus why should a good fellow of Ar object if a flute girl sits in a given fashion? Is not everyone to be permitted anything?"

"No," said Marcus, "freedom is for the free. Others are to be kept in line, and exactly so. Society depends on divisions and order, each element stabilized perfectly in its harmonious relationship with all others."

"You do not believe, then," I asked, "that everyone is the same, or must be supposed to be such, despite all evidence to the contrary, and that society thrives best as a disordered struggle?"

Marcus looked at me, startled.

"No," I said. "I see that you do not."

"Do you believe such?" he asked.

"No," I said. "Not any more."

We returned our attention to the wall.

"They work cheerfully, and with a will," said Marcus, in disgust.

"It is said that even numbers of the High Council, as a token, have come to the wall, loosened a stone, and tumbled it down."

"Thus do they demonstrate their loyalty to the state," he said.

"Yes," I said.

"The state of Cos," he said, angrily.

"Many high-caste youth, on the other hand, work side by side with low-caste fellows, dismantling the wall."

"They are levied?" asked Marcus.

"Not the higher castes," I said.

"They volunteer?" he asked.

"Like many of these others," I said.

"Incredible," said he.

"Youth is idealistic," I said.

"Idealistic?" he asked.

"Yes," I said. "They are told that this is a right and noble work, that it is a way of making amends, of atoning for the faults of their city, that it is in the interests of brotherhood, peace, and such."

"Exposing themselves to the blades of strangers?" he asked.

"Perhaps Cos will protect them," I said.

"And who will protect them from Cos?" he asked.

"Who needs protection from friends?" I asked.

"They were not at Ar's Station," he said. "They were not in the delta."

"Idealism comes easiest to those who have seen least of the world," I said.

"They are fools," said Marcus.

"Not all youth are fools," I said.

He regarded me.

"You are rather young yourself," I said.

"Anyone who cannot detect the insanity of dismantling their own defenses is a fool," said Marcus, "whether they are a young fool or an old one."

"Some are prepared to do such things as a proof of their good will, of their sincerity," I said.

"Incredible," he said.

"But many youth," I said, "as others, recognize the absurdity of such things."

"Perhaps Gnieus Lelius was such a youth," said Marcus.

"Perhaps," I said.

"Perhaps he may reconsider his position, in his cage," said Marcus.

"He has undoubtedly already done so," I said.

"Much good it will do him now," said Marcus.

"Look," I said, "the children."

We saw some children to one side, on the city side of the Wall Road. They had put up a small wall of stones, and they were now pushing it down.

On the wall, in the trough of the breach, we saw four men rolling a heavy stone toward the field side of the wall. A flute girl was parodying, or accompanying, their efforts on the flute, the instrument seeming to strain with them, and then, when they rolled the stone down, she played a skirl of descending notes on the flute, and, spinning about, danced away. The men laughed.

"I have seen enough," said Marcus.

There was suddenly near us, startling us, another skirl of notes on a flute, the common double flute. A flute girl, come apparently from the wall side of the Wall Road, danced tauntingly near us, to our right, and, with the flute, while playing, gestured toward the wall, as though encouraging us to join the others in their labor. I, and Marcus, I am sure, were angry. Not only had we been startled by the sudden, intrusive noise, which the girl must have understood would have been the case, but we resented the insinuation that we might be such as would of our own will join the work on the wall. Did she think we were of Ar, that we were of the conquered, the pacified, the confused and fooled, the verbally manipulated, the innocuous, the predictable, the tamed? She was an exciting brunet, in a short tunic of diaphanous silk. She was slender, and was probably kept on a carefully supervised diet by her master or trainer. Her dark eyes shone with amusement. She pranced before us, playing. She waved the flute again toward the wall.

We regarded her.

She again gestured, playing, toward the wall.

I had little doubt that she assumed from our appearance in this area that we were of Ar.

We did not move.

A gesture of annoyance crossed her lovely features. She played more determinedly, as though we might not understand her intent.

Still we did not move.

Then, angrily, she spun about, dancing, to return to her former post near the wall side of the Wall Road. She was attractive, even insolently so, at the moment, in the diaphanous silk.

"You have not been given permission to withdraw," I said, evenly.

She turned about, angrily, holding the flute.

"You are armed," she suddenly said, perhaps then for the first time really noting this homely fact.

"We are not of Ar," I said.

"Oh," she said, standing her ground, trembling a little.

"Are you accustomed to standing in the presence of free men?" I asked.

"I will kneel if it will please you," she said.

"If you not kneel," I said, "it is possible that I may be displeased."

She regarded me.

"Kneel," I said.

Swiftly she knelt.

I walked over to her and, taking her by the hair, twisting it, she crying out, turned her about and threw her to her belly on the Wall Road.

She sobbed in anger.

Marcus and I crouched near her.

"Oh!" she said.

"She is not in the iron belt," said Marcus.

"That is a further insult to those of Ar," I said, "that they would put unbelted flute girls among them."

"Yes," growled Marcus.

The tone of his voice, I am sure, did nothing to set our fair prisoner at ease. Flute girls, incidentally, when hired from their master, to entertain and serve at parties, are commonly unbelted, that for the convenience of the guests.

"She is not unattractive," I said.

"Oh!" she said, as I pulled her silk muchly away, tucking it then in and about the slender girdle of silken cord at her waist.

"No," said Marcus. "She is not unattractive."

"What are you going to do with me?" she asked.

"You have been an insolent slave," I said.

"No," she said. "No!"

"You have not been pleasing," I said.

"You do not own me!" she said. "You are not my master!"

"The discipline of a slave," I said, "may be attended to by any free person, otherwise she might do much what she wished, provided only her master did not learn of it." The legal principle was clear, and had been upheld in several courts, in several cities, including Ar.

I then stood.

"Lash her," I said to Marcus.

"Please no, Master!" she suddenly cried.

I was pleased to note that she, as she was a slave, had now recollected to address free men by the title of 'Master'.

Marcus used his belt for the business, slipping the knife in its sheath, and his pouch, from it, and handing them to me. He also gave me his over-the-shoulder sword belt as well, that he might not be encumbered.

Then the disciplined slave lay trembling on her belly, her eyes wide, her cheeks tear-stained, her hands beside her head, the tips of her fingers on the stones.

"I gather," I said, "that the discipline to which you have been recently subject has been lax. Perhaps therefore you should be further beaten."

"No, Master!" she cried. "Please no, master! Forgive me, Master! Forgive me, Master!"

"Are you are sorry for the error of your ways?" I asked.

"Yes, Master!" she said. "Please forgive me, Master!"

Her contrition seemed to me authentic.

"What is your name?" I asked.

"Whatever Master pleases!" she sobbed.

"Come now," I said.

"Tafa, if it pleases Master," she said. That is a common slave name on Gor.

"Do you repent of the error of your ways?" I asked.

"Yes, Master," she said.

"Who repents of the error of her ways?" I asked.

"Tafa repents of the error of her ways," she said.

"Who is sorry, who begs forgiveness?" I asked.

"Tafa is sorry! Tafa begs forgiveness!" she said.

"I wonder if you should be further beaten," I said.

The belt, doubled, hung loose in Marcus' hand.

"Please, no, Master," begged the girl.

I turned to Phoebe. "Are you distressed?" I asked.

"No, Master," said Phoebe, "certainly not. She was an errant slave. She should have been punished."

Tafa groaned.

"Indeed," said Phoebe, "it seems to me that she got off quite lightly. I myself believe she should have been whipped even more."

"Please no, Mistress," begged Tafa.

"I am not "mistress," " said Phoebe. "I, too, am only a slave."

It was natural enough, in the circumstances, for Tafa to have addressed Phoebe as "Mistress." As Tafa was currently subject to us, and Phoebe was with us, this put Phoebe in a position of *de facto* priority to her. For example, in a group of female slaves, for example, in a pleasure gardens, a fortress or a tavern, there will usually be a girl appointed First Girl. Indeed, if there is a large number of slaves, there are sometimes hierarchies of "first girls," lower-level first girls reporting to higher-level first girls, and so on. The lower-level slaves will commonly address their first girl as "Mistress." Thus, in some situations, the same girl may be first girl to certain girls and be subordinated herself to another, on a higher level, whom she will address as "Mistress." Sometimes a hierarchy is formed in which girls are ranked in such a manner that each must address the girls above her as "Mistress." More commonly, it is only the lowest slave, usually the newest slave, who must do this with all the others, whereas the others will address only their first girl as "Mistress," and, of course, any free woman whom they might, to their risk, or peril, encounter. Technically the lowest of free women, of the lowest caste, is immeasurably above even the highest of slaves, even the preferred slave of a ubar. Sometimes a ubar will even have his preferred slave serve in a low-caste hovel one day a year, under the command, and switch, of a low-caste free woman, performing her labors, and such, that she may be reminded that she is truly, when all is said and done, only a slave, as much as the lowest of the kettle-and-mat girls in the most wretched of hovels, crowded about the walls of a small city.

"The decision as to the discipline of slave will be made by the masters," I reminded Phoebe.

"Yes, Master," said Phoebe. "Forgive me, Master."

Phoebe's zeal to see an errant slave punished, and suitably, was a quite natural one, of course. The girl was a slave, and had not been pleasing. Thus it was appropriate, even imperative, that she be punished. More broadly, order and structure in human life, stability in society, even, in a sense, civilization itself, depends upon sanctions. A civilization must be willing to impose sanctions, and to impose them reliably and efficiently. A lapse in such resolve and practice is a symptom of decline, even of impending disintegration. Ultimately civilization depends upon power, moral and physical, upon, so to speak, the will of masters and the reality of the whip and sword. It might be added, incidentally, that Phoebe, herself a slave, in moral consistency, fully accepted this same principle, at least intellectually, in her own case. She accepted, in short, as morally indisputable, the rightfulness of herself being punished if she should fail to be pleasing. Also, accepting this principle, and knowing the strength and resolve of her master, and the uncompromising reality of the discipline under which she herself was held, she was naturally disinclined to see others escape sanctions and penalties to which she herself was subject. Why should others be permitted lapses, faults and errors, particularly ones in which they took arrogant pride, for which she herself would promptly and predictably suffer? Accordingly, slave girls are often zealous to see masters immediately and mercilessly correct even small lapses in the behavior of their chain sisters. It pleases them. Phoebe herself, it might be mentioned, had very seldom been lashed, particularly since the day of Myron's entrance into the city when Marcus had finally accepted her as a mere slave, as opposed to a Cosian woman in his collar, to be sure, enslaved, on whom he could vent his hatred for Cos and all things Cosian. The general immunity to the lash which was experienced by Phoebe, of course, was a function of her excellence as a slave. Excellent slaves are seldom beaten, for there is little, if any, reason to do so. To be sure, such a girl, particularly a love slave, occasionally desires to feel the stroke of the lash, wanting to feel pain at the hands of a beloved master, wanting to be whipped by him because she loves him, in this way symbolizing to herself her relationship to him, that of slave to master, her acceptance of that relationship, and her rejoicing in it. To be sure, she is soon likely to be merely, again, a whipped slave, begging her master for mercy.

"Look!" laughed Phoebe, looking toward the prone slave.

The slave, sobbing, had lifted her body.

"Scandalous slave!" laughed Phoebe.

The slave groaned.

"Apparently you do not wish to be further beaten," I said.

"No, Master," said the slave.

"You wish to placate masters?" I asked.

"Yes, Master," she said.

"Slave, slave!" laughed Phoebe.

"Yes, Mistress," whispered the salve.

"She is such a slave," said Phoebe.

"She is a female," I said.

"Yes, Master," said Phoebe.

I was amused by Phoebe's attitude. Indeed, I found it delightfully ironic. Many was the time I had seen her so lift herself to Marcus, hoping to avert his wrath.

I looked down at the slave.

She was tense, and hardly moved.

I handed Marcus his things, piece by piece, the sheath, with its knife, and the pouch, both for his belt, and the sword belt, with its scabbard and blade, to be slung over the left shoulder. I then crouched down beside the slave.

"Master?" she asked.

I pushed her down to the stones, so that her belly was flat on them.

"Master?" she asked.

"Do you beg use?" I asked.

"Yes, Master!" she whispered, tensely.

"Perhaps some other time," I said.

"Do not kill me," she said.

I took my knife and, from the back of her head, gathered together a large handful of her long dark hair, and then cut it off, close to the scalp. I then, using his hair, bound her hands together behind her back.

"You have not earned a use," I said.

I then cut another gout of her hair from the back of her head and used it to tie the flute about her neck. I did not crop the hair about her head with the knife, rather in the manner of shaving it off, as is sometimes done as a punishment for female slaves. I did no more than take the two gouts. To be sure, these two gouts, thick as they were, cleared an irregular space of several square inches of the back of her head. This cleared area, though not evident from the front, was only too obvious from the back. It would doubtless occasion much merriment upon its discovery by her chain sisters, as she was a beauty, and might be envied by them. Too, given her personality, I suspected that they would be likely to find her plight even more amusing. Perhaps she could wear a scarf for a time, or have her hair shortened or tied in such a way as to conceal or minimize the rather liberal extent of this local cropping. One advantage of shaving a girl's head, incidentally, is the duration of the punishment. It is recalled to her, for example, every time she touches her head or sees her reflection. By the time it has grown out, and even by the time that it begins to grow out a little, she has usually determined to do all in her power to be such that her master will permit her to keep her hair. If he wishes, or thinks it judicious, of course, he may keep her with a shaved head. It might also be noted that certain slaves, rather as an occupational mark or precaution, for example, girls working in foundries and mills, often have their heads shaved. Too, it is common to shave a girl completely if she is to be transported in a slave ship. This is to protect her against vermin of various sorts, in particular, lice.

I dragged the slave up to her knees and knelt her before us. She trembled, daring not to meet our eyes.

"Go to the other flute girls," I said, "to all those about, whether on the street or on the wall. Inform them that their work for the day is finished."

"Master?" she said.

"Tell them to hurry home to their chains."

"Master!" she said.

"Do you understand?" I asked.

"Yes, Master," she said.

"Do you dally in the carrying out of a command?" I asked.

"No, Master!" she said, and leaped to her feet, running across the Wall Road, her hands tied behind her, wisps of silk fluttering about her waist, the flute dangling from her neck.

"She is very pretty," said Marcus.

"More so than I?" asked Phoebe.

"Is the slave jealous?" inquired Marcus, teasingly.

"Please, Master," begged Phoebe.

"Are you jealous?" he said.

"Yes, Master!" said Phoebe, defiantly.

"You do not sound humble," he said.

"Forgive me, Master," she said, quickly, frightened.

"Who is jealous?" he inquired.

"Phoebe is jealous," she whispered.

"You are a thousand times more beautiful than she," said Marcus.

"Master sports with his helpless slave," pouted Phoebe.

"To me," said Marcus, teasingly.

"How shall I ever hold you, Master?" she wept. "I am yours, and only a slave. You may put me aside, or keep me with others, as you might please. There are thousands of intelligent, pretty women who would be eager to serve you. You may have your pick. You may buy and sell as you please. How shall I ever keep you?"

"It is mine to keep you—if I wish," said Marcus.

"Yes, Master!" she wept.

I considered the unilaterality of the master/slave relationship. All power is with the master. This, of course, has its effect upon the slave. Let her strive to be such that her master will keep her.

"Look," I said, pointing to the foot of the wall, where the flute girl was together with others of her station. She seemed distraught, bound, turning about, to look at me. They all, excited, confused, looked in this direction. To be sure, several of them, and many on the wall, too, both flute girls and laborers, had paused in their various activities, to follow the sequence of events on the Wall Road. But Marcus and Phoebe paid me no attention. They were in one another's arms.

"I love you, Master," was saying Phoebe, looking up at him, "totally and helplessly."

"And I," he was saying, brushing back hair from her forehead, "fear that I might find myself growing fond of you."

"Use me, Master, use me!" she begged.

"Not here," said Marcus. "Perhaps in a darkened doorway, on the way back to our lodging."

Quickly she pulled from him, and hurried a few steps back, toward Harness Street, turning them to look back, pleadingly at him.

I was pleased to see that she was much in his power.

"I see," said Marcus. The flute girls at the foot of the wall, looking this way, knelt, putting their heads down to the stones, doing obeisance in our direction. They then, one by one, leapt to their feet and hurried away. The command of a free man had been conveyed to them. I then saw the lovely brunet picking her way with difficulty up a path to the higher part of the breach. She was communicating my message, I gather, to the girls she encountered, on the different levels. I looked up toward the height of the breach. There, girl after girl, especially as she saw my eyes upon her, knelt, putting her head down.

Those that were sitting cross-legged swiftly abandoned that position, also performing obeisance. Then, one by one, as the brunet hurried among them, they picked their way down the paths from the breach to the Wall Road and hurried away. In a few moments the breach was cleared of flute girls. Doubtless all of them, at one time or another, had been under an excellent discipline and now, fearful of an impending restoration of such rigors, would lose no time in recalling, and manifesting, suitable attitudes and behaviors. No woman who has ever felt the whip forgets it.

"Was this wise?" asked Marcus.

"No," I said.

"Tomorrow they will be back, and things will be the same," he said.

"Undoubtedly," I said.

"Nothing will be changed," he said.

"True," I said.

"Then why did you do it?" he asked.

"I felt like it," I said.

"I was afraid you might not have had a good reason," he said.

"Master," said Phoebe, pleadingly.

"It could be dangerous here," said Marcus.

"For whom?" I asked.

"I see," said Marcus.

"Master," begged Phoebe.

"The men of Ar, and the women, and youth," he said, looking over to the wall, "remain on the breach."

"Yes," I said.

"Interesting," he said.

"Master!" said Phoebe, suddenly, again. But this time, from the note in her voice, we turned about, instantly.

"You there, hold!" cried an angry voice, that of a guardsman in the uniform of Ar, hurrying toward us. His hand was on the hilt of his sword.

We turned to face him, separating ourselves. This permits outflanking, the engagement by one, the death stroke by the other.

Instantly the guardsman stopped. He was then some four or five yards from us.

"You are armed," he said.

"It is lawful," I said. "We are not of Ar."

He drew his blade.

We, too, drew ours.

"You have drawn before a guardsman!" he said.

"Did you think we would not?" I asked.

"It is against the law," he said.

"Not our law," I said.

"What have you done here?" he asked.

"The flute girls have worked enough today," I said. "We have sent them home."

"By whose authority?" he asked.

"By mine," I said.

"You are an officer?" he said.

"No," I said.

"I do not understand," he said.

"You are Cosian," said Marcus.

"I am a guardsman of Ar," said the fellow.

"You are Cosian," said Marcus.

"You have drawn a weapon against me," I said.

"You are of the warriors?" said the fellow. He wavered. He, too, knew the codes.

"Yes," I said.

"And he?" asked the fellow.

"He, too," I said.

"You are not in scarlet," he said.

"True," I said. Did he think that the color of a fellow's garments was what made him a warrior? Surely he must realize that one not of the warriors might affect the scarlet, and that one who wore the grimed gray of a peasant, one barefoot, and armed only with the great staff, might be of the scarlet caste. It is not the uniform which makes the warrior, the soldier.

"There are two of you," he said, stepping back a pace.

"Yes," I said.

"Be off," said he, "before I place you under arrest."

"Perhaps you fellows should go about in squads of ten," I said.

"It is not necessary," he said.

"No," I said. "I suppose it is not necessary."

"Are you going to kill him?" Marcus asked me.

"I have not decided," I said.

"There are two of you," he said.

"You are a brave fellow," I said, "not to turn about, and flee." The odds, you see, were much against him, even were we mediocre swordsmen. One need only engage and defend, and the other strike.

"You dare not attack," he said. "It is day. Those of Ar watch."

"Is it true?" I asked Marcus, not taking my eyes off the fellow.

Marcus stepped back, shielding himself behind me. "Yes," he said.

"Interesting," I said.

"You see," he said. "There are many witnesses."

"They are not rushing for aid are they?" I asked Marcus.

"No," he said.

"I suspect they will have seen nothing," I said.

The fellow turned pale.

"You are cowards!" he said.

"Which of us will kill him?" asked Marcus.

"It does not matter," I said.

The fellow stepped back another pace.

"Why do you not run?" I asked.

"Those of Ar watch," he said.

"And not to show fear before them you would stand your ground against two?"

"I am Cosian," he said.

"Now," I said to Marcus, "perhaps the victory of Cos is clearer to you."

"Yes," said Marcus.

"Under the circumstances," I said to the guardsman, "I would nonetheless recommend a discretionary withdrawal."

"No," said the man.

"We are prepared to permit it," I said.

"No," he said.

"No dishonor is involved in such a thing," I said.

"No," he said.

"You need not even make haste," I said.

"Those of Ar watch," he said.

"I have decided not to kill you," I said.

"I do not fear you singly," he said.

"On guard," I said.

He immediately entered readiness.

"Stay back," I said to Marcus.

I had scarcely uttered my injunction to Marcus when, Phoebe screaming, the fellow lunged. Our blades met perhaps three times and I was under his guard. He drew back, shaken, white faced. Again we engaged and, again, in a moment, I was behind his guard. Again he drew back, this time staggering, off balance. "Aii" he wept and lunged again, and then, tripped, scrambling about, pressed back with my foot, was on his back, my sword at his throat. He looked up, wildly. "Strike!" he said.

"Get up," I said. "Sheath your sword."

He staggered to his feet, watching me, and sheathed his sword. I then sheathed mine.

"Why did you not kill me?" he asked.

"I told you earlier," I said, "I had decided not to kill you."

"I am an expert swordsman," he said, looking at me.

"I agree," I said.

"I have never seen such speed, such subtlety," he said. "It is like defending oneself against wind, or lightning."

I did not respond to him. In a way I felt sad, and helpless. In many ways I am a very average man, if that. Too, I have many lacks, and many faults. How ironic then it was, I thought, that among the few gifts which I might possess, those few things which might distinguish me among other men, were such as are commonly associated with destructiveness. Of what value is it, I asked myself, to have certain talents. Of what dreadful value are such skills? Of what value, really, is it to be able to bring down a running man with the great bow at two hundred yards, to throw the quiva into a two-hort circle at twenty paces, to wield a sword with an agility others might bring to the handling of a knife? Of what use are such dreadful skills? Then I reminded myself that such skills are often of great use and that culture, with its glories of art, and music and literature, can flourish only within the perimeters of their employments. Perhaps there is then a role for the lonely fellows on the wall, for the border guards, for the garrisons of far-flung outposts, for the guardsmen in the city treading their lonely rounds. All these, too, in their humble, unnoticed way, serve. Without them the glory is not possible. Without them even their critics could not exist.

"Are you all right?" I asked.

"Yes," he said.

I recalled, too, the games of war. They, too, in their awesomeness, must not be forgotten. Why is it that some men seek wars, traveling to the ends of the earth to find them? It is because they have a taste for such things. It is because there, where others fear to tread, they find themselves most alive. He who has been on the field of battle knows the misery, the terror, the tenseness, the racing of the blood, the pounding of the heart, the exhileration, the meaningfulness. In what other arena, and for what lesser stakes, can so much of man be summoned forth, man with his brutality, his cruelty, his mercilessness, his ruthlessness, his terribleness, these ancient virtues, and man with his devotion, his comraderie, his fellowship, his courage, his discipline, his glory? In what other endeavor is man, in his frailty and strength, in his terribleness and nobility, so fully manifested? What is the meaning of war to the warrior? Surely it is not merely to be found in the beholding of flaming cities and the treading of bloody fields. Surely it is not merely to be found in silver plate and golden vessels, nor even in women lying naked in their chains, huddled together, trembling, in the mud, knowing that they are now properties and must please. It is rather, I think, primarily, the contest, and that for which all is risked, victory. To be sure, this is a war of warriors, not of technicians and engineers, a war of men, not of machines, not of explosives, not of microscopic allies, not of poisoned atmospheres, wars in which the tiny, numerous meek, in their swarms, crawling on six legs, will inherit the earth.

"You are not of Ar, said the guardsman.

"No," I said.

"I did not think so," he said.

I shrugged.

"Cos," he said, "can use blades such as yours."

"I seek employment," I said.

"Go the barracks of guardsman," said he.

"Perhaps," I said.

"I would now leave this area," he said. "Too, I would not attempt to interfere with the work on the walls."

"I understand," I said.

"That is a pretty slave," he said.

"She belongs to my friend," I said. Phoebe shrank back a bit, closer to Marcus. Female slaves on Gor must grow used to being looked upon frankly by men, and assessed as the properties they are. They know they can be acquired, and disposed of, and bought and sold, and traded, and such, with ease, even at a moment's notice.

"Is she of Ar?" he asked.

"No," said Marcus.

"Are you sure?" asked the guardsman.

"Yes," said Marcus.

"Many women of Ar look well in slave tunics, barefoot and collared," he said.

"Undoubtedly," I said.

"They should all be slaves," he said.

"So should all women," I said.

"True," he said.

To be sure, it did amuse me to think of the proud women of Ar, of "Glorious Ar," as slaves. Such a fate seemed to me fully appropriate for them, and in particular for some of them.

"Let us return to our lodgings," I said to Marcus.

"I wish you well," said the guardsman.

"I, too, wish you well," I said.

"I must now put these tame cattle of Ar back to work," he said.

"One man alone?" I asked.

"No more are needed," he said.

Indeed, there were no guardsmen on the walls themselves. We had encountered one on the way to the wall, on Harness Street, who had detained us briefly, apparently primarily to determine whether or not we were of Ar.

"We shall leave now," said Marcus.

"Yes, Master," said Phoebe.

We then turned about, and left the vicinity of the Wall Road. Near the entrances to Harness Street, off the Wall Road, I turned about.

"Continue your work for peace!" called the guardsmen to those on the wall.

The men on the wall then, and the youth, and women, returned to their labors.

"Incredible," marveled Marcus.

"Master," moaned Phoebe.

Things were then much as they had been before. Nothing had changed. To be sure, the work was not now being performed to the music of flute girls. Tomorrow, however, I did not doubt but what the flute girls would be back, and numerous guards in attendance, at least on the street.

"Is your sword for hire?" I asked Marcus.

"It could be," he said.

"Good," I said.

"You have some plan?" he asked.

"Of course," I said.

"Master," whimpered Phoebe.

Marcus stopped and looked at her.

She, too, stopped, and looked up at him.

"Strip," he said.

She looked at him, suddenly, wildly, and then about herself. "This is a public street," she said.

He did not speak.

She squirmed. "Is there no doorway? No sheltered place?" she asked.

He did not respond to her.

"I was a woman of Cos," she said, tears springing to her eyes. "This is a public street in *Ar*!"

His expression remained impassive. He maintained his silence.

"Cos has defeated Ar!" she wept.

He did not speak.

"Am I to suffer because you are angry with the men of Ar?" she asked.

"Does the slave dally in her obedience?" he inquired.

"No, Master!" she said, frightened.

"Must a command be repeated?" he inquired.

"No, Master!" she cried. Her tiny fingers began to fumble with the knot of the slave girdle, on her left. Then she had the knot loose and pulled away the girdle. She then, hastily, struggling a little with it, pulled the tunic, a light pullover tunic, off, over her head. "The slave obeys her master!" she gasped, frightened, kneeling before him. He then tied her hands behind her back with the slave girdle and thrust the tiny tunic, folded, crosswise, in her mouth, so that she would bite on it. He then pushed her head down to the stones.

"Are you now less angry with the men of Ar?" I asked him, in an Ehn or two.

Marcus stood up, adjusting his tunic.

"Yes," he said.

Phoebe turned about, from her knees, the tunic between her teeth, and looked back at us.

"This has little to do with you," I told her. "Too, it is immaterial that you were once of Cos. A slave, you must understand, must sometimes serve such purposes." Her eyes were wide. But one of the utilities of a slave, of course, is to occasionally serve as the helpless object upon which the master may vent his dissatisfaction, his frustration or anger. Too, of course, they may serve many other related purposes, such as the relief of tensions, to relax oneself and even to calm oneself for clear thought.

"Do you understand?" I asked.

She nodded.

I regarded her.

She whimpered, once.

"Good," I said.

One whimper signifies "Yes," and two signifies "No." This arrangement, at any rate, was the one which Marcus had taught to Phoebe long ago,, quite early in her slavery to him, at a time when she had been much more often kept bound and gagged than now.

Marcus then snapped his fingers that she should rise.

She leaped to her feet.

We turned our steps once more toward our lodging. Phoebe hurried behind. Once she tried, whimpering, to press herself against her master. She looked up at him, tears in her eyes, her hands tied behind her, the tunic between her teeth. She feared that she might have now, because of her earlier behavior, lapsed in his favor. Too, compounding her misery, was doubtless the fact that Marcus, in his casual usage of her, had done little more than intensify her needs, the helpless prisoner of which, as a slave girl, she was. He thrust her back. We then continued on our way, Phoebe heeling her master. I heard her gasp once or twice, and sob. She was now, I was sure, much more aware, in her own mind, of what it was to be a slave. I do not think, then, she thought of herself any longer, really, as a woman of Cos, or even one who had once been of Cos, but rather now as merely a slave, only that, and one who had perhaps, frighteningly, to her trepidation and misery, failed to be fully pleasing. I did not doubt that later, when we had reached the room, and she was unbound and freed of the gag, that she would crawl to Marcus on all fours, the whip between her teeth, begging. Too, though he loved her muchly, I did not doubt but what he would use it on her. She was, after all, his slave, and he, after all, was her master.

9 The Plaza of Tarns

"She," said Talena, Ubara of Ar, "she is chosen."

The woman uttered a cry of anguish.

There were cheers, and applause, the striking of the left shoulder, from the crowd standing about the edges of the huge, temporary platform, the same which had earlier served near the Central Cylinder for the welcoming of Myron, in his entrance into the city.

The woman, held now by the upper left arm, by a guardsman, was conducted to a point on the platform, erected now in the Plaza of Tarns, a few feet from a rather narrow, added side ramp, where she was knelt, to be manacled. This smaller, added ramp would be on the left side of the platform, as one would face it. My own position was near to, and rather at the foot of this ramp, such that I would be on the right of a person descending the ramp. Talena, with certain aides and counselors, and guardsmen and scribes, was on a dais, it mounted on the surface of the platform, a few feet away, rather to its left, as one would face it. There was a similar added ramp on the other side, by means of which the women, barefoot, and clad at that point in the robe of the penitent, would ascend to its surface.

The manacles were closed about the wrists of the kneeling woman. One could clearly hear the decisive closure of the devices, first the one, then the other. She lifted them, regarding them, unbelievingly.

"Have you never worn chains?" asked a man.

First with one hand and then the other, suddenly, frenziedly, first from one wrist, and then from the other, sobbing, she tried to force the obdurate iron from her wrist.

Then, again, she lifted the manacles, regarding them, disbelievingly.

"Yes, they are on you," laughed a fellow.

"You cannot slip them," said a man.

"They were not made to be slipped by such as you," said another.

There was much laughter.

The woman sobbed.

"Do not blubber, female," said a man. "Rejoice, rather, that you have been found suitable, that you have been honored by having been chosen!"

The woman then, conducted by another fellow, with an armband, signifying the auxiliary guardsmen, the first fellow, a uniformed guardsman, returning to the group on the platform, was conducted down the ramp. She was knelt before me. "Wrists," I said. She lifted her chained wrists. I then, by means of the chain, pulled her wrists toward me. I inserted the bolt of a small, sturdy, padlocklike joining ring through a link in the coffle chain. This would hold it in a specific place on the chain, preventing slippage. I then snapped the ring shut about her wrist chain. She looked up at me, coffled.

"On your feet, move," said another auxiliary guardsman.

She rose to her feet and moved ahead, to the first line scratched in the tiles of the plaza. There were some one hundred such lines, each about four or five feet apart, marking places for women to stand. As she moved ahead, so, too, did others. Beyond these hundred spaces the chain moved to the side, and was doubled, and folded back upon itself, again and again, in this fashion keeping its prisoners massed, different lines facing different directions, and all in the vicinity of the platform.

"It angers me," said a fellow nearby, "that these women should complain. It is a simple enough duty to perform, and a worthy enough act, as female citizens, given the guilt of Ar, her complicity in the wicked schemes of Gnieus Lelius, to offer themselves for reparation consideration."

"Few enough are chosen anyway," said a fellow.

"Yes," said another, angrily.

"Are all burdens to be borne only by men?" asked a man.

"What of the work levies and such?" said another.

"Yes," said another.

"And the taxes and special assessments," said another.

"True," said a fellow.

"They are citizens of Ar," said another. "It is only right that they, too, pay the price for our misdeeds."

"And theirs," said another.

"Yes," said a fellow.

"They supported members of councils, and members to elect members of councils," said a man.

"Yes!" said another.

"Look at noble Talena," said a man. "How bravely she performs this duty."

"How onerous it must be for her," said a man.

"Poor Talena," said a fellow.

"She, too, it might be recalled," said a man, "appeared in public barefoot, in the garb of a penitent, prepared to offer herself to save Ar."

"Of course," said a man.

"Noble woman," breathed a man.

Auxiliary guardsmen do not wear helmets. I had, accordingly, covered my head and, loosely, the lower portion of my face with a scarf, rather in the manner of the fellows in the Tahari. This fitted in well with the motley garbs of auxiliary guardsmen who, on the whole, had little in common except that they were not of Ar. Regular guardsmen of Ar were, as I have suggested, fellows of Ar under Cosian command, or, often, Cosians, in the uniform of Ar. Too, as mentioned, there were regulars of Cos in the city, and, at any given time, various mercenaries, usually on passes. Some mercenaries, it might be mentioned, had been transferred into the auxiliary guardsmen. Some others, discharged, had enlisted in these units. A good deal of the sensitive work in Ar, work which might possibly produce resentment, or even enflame resistance, was accorded to auxiliary guardsmen. Their actions, if necessary, could always be deplored or disavowed. If necessary, some units might even be disbanded, as a token of conciliation. Such units are, after all, difficult to control. In this I saw further evidence of attention on the part of Myron, or his advisors, to the principles and practices of Dietrich of Tarnburg. A similar device, incidentally, though not one employed by Dietrich of Tarnburg, at least to my knowledge, is to recruit such forces from the dregs of a city itself, utilizing their resentment of, and their hatred for, their more successful fellow citizens to constitute a vain, suspicious and merciless force. This force then may later be disbanded, or even destroyed, to the delight of the other citizens, who then will see their conqueror as their protector, not even understanding his use of, and sacrifice of, such instrumentalities as the duped dregs of their own community, first making use of them, then disposing of them.

"No," said Talena, "not her."

A guardsman, on the surface of the platform, before the dais, draped the robe of the penitent about the shoulders of the woman before Talena. He did this deferentially. She was shuddering. Another guardsman quickly ushered her to the rear and down the large ramp at the rear of the platform. She would now return home.

"No, Talena!" called a fellow from the crowd, a few feet away.

Talena regally turned her head in his direction.

"Be silent," said a man to he who had called out.

"Hail Talena!" called a man from the vicinity of the fellow who had called out before.

"Glory to Talena!" called another.

"Glory to Talena!" cried others.

She then returned her attention to her duties on the platform

"How merciful is Talena," said a fellow.

"Yes," said another.

At a gesture from one of the guardsmen on the platform another woman in a white robe came forward, leaving the long line behind her, one extending across the platform to the small ramp on the other side, down the ramp, across the far side of the Plaza of Tarns, and thence down down Gate Street, where I could not see its end.

"Lady Tuta Thassolonia," read a scribe.

Lady Tuta then, unaided, removed her robe and stood before her Ubara. Then she knelt before her.

Men gasped.

She knelt back on her heels, her knees spread, her back straight, her head up, the palms of her hands on her thighs.

"It seems you are a slave," said Talena.

"I have always been a slave, Mistress," said Lady Tuta.

Talena turned to one of her counselors, and they conferred.

"Are you a legal slave, my child?" asked one of the counselors, a scribe of the law.

"No, Master," said the woman.

"You are then a legally free female?" asked the scribe.

"Yes, Master," she said.

"It is then sufficient," said the scribe to Talena.

"You are chosen," said Talena, graciously.

"Thank you, Mistress!" said the woman.

Cheers commended the decision of the Ubara.

Another of Talena's aides, or counselors, one in the garb of Cos, then spoke to Talena, shielding his mouth with his hand.

Talena nodded, and he then addressed himself to the kneeling woman.

"Rise up," said he, in a kindly fashion, "and do not address us as Master and Mistress."

She rose up.

"Do you wish, as a free female, before you join your sisters to our right, to say anything?"

"Hail Talena!" she cried. "Glory to Talena!"

This cry was taken up by hundreds about. Then she was conducted to the side, to be manacled.

"It will be a lucky fellow who will get her," said a man.

"She is already a slave," said another.

"She will train speedily and well," said another.

"I would like to get my hands on her," said a fellow.

"She will go to some Cosian," said another.

The woman was then drawn to her feet by an auxiliary guardsman and conducted down the ramp.

The auxiliary guardsman on the other side of the ramp, then, who was working with me, said to her, "Kneel, slut."

She knelt.

"You were rich, were you not?" he asked her.

"Yes," she said.

"Yes—what?" he said, angrily.

"Yes, I was rich!" she said, frightened.

"Do not strike her," I said to the fellow. "She is not yet a slave."

"She is a slut of Ar," he said.

"Yes," I said.

He lowered his hand.

"Wrists," I said to her.

She lifted her chained wrists, and I attached her to the coffle with a joining ring.

"Why is he angry with me?" she asked.

"It might be wise to accustom yourself, even though you are legally free now," I said, "to addressing free men as "Master" and free women as "Mistress."

"He is only an auxiliary guardsman," she said.

"He is a man," I said, "and you are female."

"Yes!" she said.

"You see the fittingness of it?" I asked.

"Yes," she said.

"You used such expressions on the platform," I said.

"But to my Ubara," she said, "and to men of high station."

"Accord such titles of respect to all free persons, even the lowliest of free persons," I said, "for you will be more beneath them than the dirt beneath their sandals."

"Forgive me, Master," she said to the other fellow. "Forgive me, Master!"

He regarded her, his arms folded, somewhat mollified.

"It seems the slut of Ar learns rapidly," I said.

"Get up," he said to her. "Move!"

"Yes, Master," she said. Then she looked back. "Thank you, Master," she said.

The line moved to its next position.

I then put the next woman on the chain, and she, too, was ordered to her feet, and moved to the next position.

"Not her," said Talena to another woman, revealed before her.

This other woman was then conducted to the rear of the platform, and permitted to leave.

"Nor she," said Talena of another, who had been announced. "Nor she," said she of another.

As I have mentioned, there were scribes on, or near, the dais with Talena. Lists were being kept, and referred to. One list, for example, had the names of the women upon it, in the order in which they ascended the platform. It was from this list that one of the scribes announced the names. Another list, presumably a duplicate list, was kept as a record of the results of Talena's decisions. The most interesting lists, however, seemed to be lists referred to as the various names were called. There were at least five such lists. Three of them, I think, are worth mentioning. One of these was held by a member of the High Council. Another was held by a Cosian counselor. Another was held by one of Talena's aides, at her side.

There was suddenly a scuffle near the far ramp and a guardsman seized a woman who had suddenly turned about and attempted to run.

"Bring her forward," said Talena.

The guardsman, who now had her well in hand, holding her from behind, by the upper arms, literally lifting her off the surface of the platform, carried her forward, before Talena. The woman's small bared feet were five inches off the wood. She was held as helplessly as a doll. The guardsman then put her down.

"Strip her," said Talena.

This was done, and the woman was flung on her knees before the Ubara of Ar.

"Mercy, my Ubara!" cried the woman, lifting her hands, clasped, to Talena.

"What is your name, child?" asked Talena.

"Fulvia!" she wept. "Fulvia, Lady of Ar!"

"We are all ladies of Ar," said Talena.

"Mercy, Ubara!" she wept, lifting her clasped hands. "Spare us! Spare your sisters of Ar!"

"Alas, my child," cried Talena, "we are all guilty. All of us are implicated in the iniquities of the infamous Gnieus Lelius. Why had we not adequately opposed him? Why did we follow his heinous policies?"

"You opposed him, beloved Ubara!" cried a man. "You tried to warn us! You did what you could! We would not listen to you! It is we, the others, who are guilty, not you!"

This sort of cry was taken up elsewhere in the crowd, as well. There were numerous protests concerning Talena's apparent willingness to accept, and share, the guilt of Ar.

"No," cried Talena. "I should have acted. Rather than witness the shame of Ar I should have plunged a dagger into my own breast!"

"No! No!" cried men.

"It would have been a tiny, if futile, symbolic gesture," she cried, "but I did not do it. Thus I, too, am guilty!"

Roars of protest greeted this remark on the part of the Ubara. I saw several men weeping.

"You chose to live, to work for the salvation of Ar!" cried a man.

"We owe everything to you, beloved Ubara!" cried another.

"And now," said Talena, "in spite of all, and the most outrageous provocation, our brother, Lurius of Jad, Ubar of Cos, has spared our city. The Home Stone is safe! The Central Cylinder stands! How shall we make amends to our Cosian brother? What gift would be great enough to thank him for our Home Stone, our lives and honor? What sacrifice would be too much to express our gratitude?"

"No gift would be too great!" cried men.

"No sacrifice would be too great!" cried others.

"And now, my child," said Talena to Lady Fulvia, "do you begin to understand why you have been requested to come here this day?"

Lady Fulvia, it seemed, could not speak. She looked up, frightened, at her Ubara.

"Surely you regret the crimes of Ar," said Talena. "Else why would you have come here, as a penitent?"

Lady Fulvia put down her head.

The women, of course, had been ordered to report. Indeed, they had been ordered to report yesterday afternoon to the great theater, from whence, to their surprise, they had been transported in cage wagons, actually locked, to the Stadium of Blades more than a pasang away. Beneath the stands of the Stadium of Blades were numerous holding areas, suitable for wild beasts, dangerous men, criminals, and such. In such areas, the women, having been checked, arranged and counted, were incarcerated for the night. They had also, at that time, been given the robes of penitents, that they might spend the night in them. They had then, this morning, been transported to a location on Gate Street, in the vicinity of the Plaza of Tarns. Some women who had failed to report to the great theater were brought later that evening to the Stadium of Tarns by guardsmen, both regulars and auxiliaries. I myself, with some other auxiliaries, had brought in two of these women. One we had had to tie and leash, almost like a rebellious slave girl, save that slave girls are seldom rebellious more than once.

"Surely you wish to do your best to expiate the crimes of Ar?" said Talena to the kneeling woman.

Her interlocutor was silent.

"Are you not eager to atone for the crimes of Ar, to make amends for her iniquities?" asked the Ubara, kindly.

Lady Fulvia was silent.

"Do you not wish to do what you can to set these things right?" asked the Ubara.

Silence.

"Speak, you slut!" cried a man from the side, angrily.

"Please!" cried Talena, holding forth her hand. "Desist, noble citizen! You speak of a free woman of Ar!"

"Yes, my Ubara," said Lady Fulvia.

"You do not wish to be selfish, do you?" asked the Ubara.

"No, Ubara," she wept.

"And is this sacrifice we ask of you, in the name of the city, and its Home Stone, any more than that which I myself was prepared to make?"

"No, my Ubara," wept the Lady Fulvia.

Talena, with a small, reluctant, almost tragic gesture, indicated that Lady Fulvia might be taken to the side.

"Next," called a scribe.

The small wrists of Fulvia, now kneeling near me, her knees about at my chest level, on the platform, were locked in manacles. In another moment she was pulled down the ramp and knelt before me. She seemed numb, in shock.

"Wake up," said a fellow.

"The cut of the whip is excellent for waking them up," said a man.

I added her to the chain with a joining ring.

She looked at the ring, and the chain to which she was now attached.

"And when they awaken they find themselves in their place," said another.

"Yes," said another.

"Stand, move," said the auxiliary opposite me.

"I would like to have her," said a fellow.

"She will go to a Cosian," said a fellow, bitterly.

"I wonder if the women of Cos are so desirable," said another.

In my opinion, though I did not speak, not having been addressed, they were. I had, from time to time, used, rented or owned various women of Cos, or former women of Cos. I had found them superb. Phoebe, of course, had been Cosian. What the women of Ar and those of Cos have in common, of course, despite their numerous political, cultural and dialectical differences, is that they are all females. Stripped in a slave market it is hard to tell the difference, one from the other. But this is true of all women. Any woman, properly mastered, makes an excellent slave.

"No," said Talena, again. She had now, in the three or four Ehn which had passed since the selection of the Lady Fulvia, rejected four women. I gather that this may have been to compensate, before the crowd, for the selection of the Lady Fulvia, to indicate that in spite of the Lady Fulvia's concerns and protests, how very few women, actually, all in all, were being selected.

Talena seemed then prepared to dismiss another woman, for she had her hand half lifted, as though, with the customary small gesture, to do so, when one of her counselors, a Cosian, near her, in the uniform of a high captain, bent quickly toward her, his eyes glinting on the female in question, she standing before the Ubara, the robes of the penitent about her ankles. I saw the female stiffen, suddenly, almost in disbelief. At the same time a guardsman seized her from behind by the upper arms. She moved a little bit but found herself helpless in his grasp. Then, as she gasped, her arms were pulled back a little, rather behind her, this accentuating her figure.

"You are chosen," said Talena.

The woman uttered a small noise, as of disbelief or protest, but was quickly conducted to the place of manacling.

In what the Cosian had said to the Ubara I had made out the expression 'slave curves'.

Manacles were put on the woman.

I saw the Cosian's eyes still on her as she was manacled. I suspected she would not long remain on the chain, after I had added her to it. When she was before me, having descended the ramp and being knelt in place, I considered her. Yes, she had excellent slave curves. She would doubtless soon learn that those curves were such as would be muchly exploited by masters. Then I had added her to the chain, and she had been ordered to her feet, and moved to the next position.

"No," said Talena, again and again.

I began to suspect then that the quotas, whatever they might be, had perhaps been reached for the day. But then another woman was selected, and subsequently manacled and, in due course, added to the coffle.

Several other women were then passed over.

Then a slim woman took her place gracefully before the Ubara.

"Claudia Tentia Hinrabia, Lady of Ar," read the scribe.

A stir, a thrill of recognition, coursed through the crowd. Men pressed more closely about the platform. "Claudia!" said men. "The Hinrabian," said others.

I myself moved closer to the platform, pressing even against it. Claudia Tentia Hinrabia was the daughter of a former Administrator of Ar, Minus Tentius Hinrabius. She had figured as a pawn in the dark games of Cernus of Ar, to bring down the house of Portus, his major economic rival in the city. Later, the machinations of Cernus had brought him even to the throne of the Ubar, which he held until his deposition by Marlenus of Ar. Claudia, at the time of the deposition of Cernus, had been a slave in his house. Marlenus, upon his return to the throne, had freed her, even arranging for her support at state expense. For several years, she had been a resident of the Central Cylinder. She was the last of the Hinrabians.

Claudia, with a toss of her head, freed her hair of the hood. She had long black hair, swirling and beautiful. It cascaded behind her. I remembered it that way from the house of Cernus, the first time I had seen her. When I had seen her later in the house of Cernus, it had been much shorter, as, in the intervening time, he had had it shaved off, and then, later, it had regrown somewhat. In her freeing herself of the hood she had, too, bared her face. She, as the others, had not been separately veiled. I well remembered the dark eyes of the Hinrabian, and the high cheekbones.

She then, gracefully, slipped the robe of the penitent back from her shoulders, letting it drop behind her.

"Ahhh," said several men.

She was slimly beautiful. She stood very straight before her Ubara, it seemed defiantly, it seemed insolently.

"See her," said a man to others.

Claudia smiled. She knew that she was unusually beautiful, even on a world where beauty is not rare.

Talena seemed displeased.

To be sure, if she were stripped and put beside the Hinrabian, I did not think she would need to fear, or much fear, the comparison.

Claudia looked up at Talena, on the dais.

"You will choose me," she said.

"Perhaps, if you are suitable," said Talena, in fury.

"You have waited long for this day," said Claudia, "to have me, the daughter of Minus Tentius Hinrabius, in your power, your rival."

"I," said Talena, "am the daughter of Marlenus of Ar!"

"You are not!" cried Claudia. "You are disowned. You have no more right to the throne of Ar than a sleek, pretty little she-urt!"

"Treason!" cried men. "Treason!"

"Your father sent men to the Voltai, to seek out and destroy Marlenus of Ar!" cried Talena.

"I do not deny that my father was enemy to Marlenus of Ar," said Claudia. "That is well known, and so, too, at the time, were many in Ar!"

"Cernus!" cried Talena.

"Yes," said Claudia.

"To whom you were a slave!" said Talena, scornfully.

"She-urt!" cried Claudia.

"Turn about, slowly," said Talena.

Men gasped.

Angrily, Claudia complied. Then she again faced Talena. "I stood higher in the Central Cylinder than you," she said. "I was the daughter of a former Administrator of Ar! You were nothing, a disowned disgrace, rescued from the north. They brought you back in a sheet, with not even a tarsk bit to your name, and dishonored. No longer had you even citizenship! Because of what you once had been, the daughter of Marlenus of Ar, you were permitted to live in the Central Cylinder. But you were kept hidden there, sequestered, that you not bring further embarrassment upon Marlenus of Ar and the city! Do not compare yourself with me. You are nothing! I am the daughter of Minus Tentius Hinrabius!"

"Do not listen to her, beloved Talena!" called a man.

"You are an upstart," said Claudia. "You are a Cosian puppet!"

"I am your Ubara!" cried Talena.

"You are a Cosian puppet!" said Claudia.

"Treason!" cried men.

"You even wear Cosian garments!" cried Claudia.

"In this fashion we may demonstrate our respect for Cos, our gratitude to her, our friendship with her," said Talena.

"Dance on their strings, puppet!" screamed Claudia.

"Perhaps it is you will dance," cried Talena, "and as a slave, before my officers!"

"And I would do so more excitingly than you!" said Claudia.

I rather doubted that. To be sure, Talena was not trained. I supposed that both might look quite well, in a jewel or two, writhing as salves before strong men.

"Slave! Slave!" cried Talena.

"Marlenus of Ar freed me of bondage!" said Claudia.

"I am not Marlenus of Ar!" cried Talena.

"He treated me with honor," she said, "and gave me support and residence!"

"I am not he," said Talena.

"Nor are you, disowned and disgraced, any longer his daughter!" cried Claudia.

"Treason!" cried men.

Talena turned to the crowd. "Should this woman's caste, and her lofty birth, and that she was the daughter of an administrator, a mere administrator, permit her to shirk her duties to the state?"

"No!" cried men. "No!"

"To the state of Cos?" inquired Claudia.

"Treason!" cried men.

"Do you think you should be shown special privileges?" asked Talena.

This took Claudia aback.

"Hah!" cried a fellow. "Look, she is silent!"

Claudia, of course, was of high caste, and a member of the aristocracy. Gorean society tends to value tradition and is carefully structured. Accordingly, it would never have occurred to her that she was not, in fact, in virtue of her position, entitled to customary privileges. Such privileges, of course, in theory at least, are balanced by duties and demands far beyond those devolving on others. The Cosians, as many conquerors, made a point of enlisting class jealousies in their cause, utilizing them to secure their ends, for example, the replacement of a given aristocracy, or elite, with one of their own, preferably in as covert a fashion as is possible. This has to do with structure in human society, without which such society is not possible.

"Do you think you are better than other women of Ar?" asked Talena.

"I am better than at least one," said Claudia, "Talena, who would be tyranness of Ar, save only that her Cosian masters will not permit her such power!"

"Treason!" cried men. "Kill the Hinrabian! Death to her! Let her be impaled! Weight her ankles!"

"And at night, do you serve your masters in the furs?" inquired Claudia.

It seemed that Talena might swoon at the very thought of this. She was supported by two of her aides.

"Death to the Hinrabian!" cried men.

A guardsman behind Claudia had his sworn half drawn from its sheath.

"No! No!" cried Talena to the crowd. "Do not cry out so, against a woman of Ar!"

"Merciful Talena!" wept a man.

The guardsman sheathed his sword.

The crowd was then silent.

"I regret that I cannot," said Talena, "despite my love for you, exempt you from your duties to the state."

"Hail Talena!" cried a man.

"Nor in this matter treat you differently from other women of Ar."

"Glory to Talena!" cried a man.

"For I, too, have my duties to perform, for I am Ubara."

Here the Plaza of Tarns rang with the cheering of men.

"Be done with your farce!" cried Claudia. "Here I am before you, naked and in your power! Have you not waited for this moment? Is my name not first on your list? Relish your triumph! Do with me as you will!"

"My decision will be made," said Talena, "as it would be in the case of any other woman of Ar. You will be treated with absolute fairness."

Talena then seemed to ponder the matter of Claudia, assessing her fittingness to be included among items to be accorded to Cos, in atonement for, and in reparation for, the crimes of Ar.

"Turn about, again, my dear, slowly," said Talena, musingly.

Men laughed.

Once again the Hinrabian turned slowly before her Ubara, as might have an assessed slave.

Talena then seemed to hesitate. She turned to her advisors, as though troubled, as though seeking their council. Would the

Hinrabian be suitable, did they think, as a conciliatory offering, or a partial reparation payment, to the offended Cosians? Would she be acceptable? Would she be adequate? Or would such an offering insult them, or offend them, in its lack of worth, in its paltriness? I smiled. I did not doubt what their opinion, that of men, would be, in the case of the lovely Hinrabian.

Claudia stood in fury before the dais, her fists clenched.

With no other woman, of all of them, had such consultation been deemed necessary.

Brilliant insult thusly did Talena to the Hinrabian.

Talena then turned again to face her.

"The decision has been made," said Talena.

Claudia drew herself up, proudly.

"The matter was an intricate one," said Talena, "and required the weighing of several subtle factors. Against you, as you might imagine, were the defects of your face and figure."

The Hinrabian gasped.

"In virtue of them alone I would have disqualified you. Yet there was also the matter of your treachery to Ar, which only now, with reluctance, do I make public."

The Hinrabian looked at her, startled.

"What treachery?" cried men.

"Conspiracy, seditious assertions, betrayal of the Home Stone, support of the wicked regime of Gnieus Lelius, former tyrant of Ar."

"I am innocent!" cried Claudia.

"Did you not support the regime of Gnieus Lelius?" asked Talena.

"I did not oppose him," said Claudia. "Nor did others! He was regent."

"In not opposing such wicked policies, you betrayed the Home Stone of Ar," said Talena.

"No!' wept Claudia.

"You wished to use him to further your own political ambitions," said Talena.

"No!" said Claudia.

"But your political ambitions are soon to be at an end," said Talena.

"Citizens, I implore you not to listen to her," cried Claudia to the crowd.

"You even slept at his slave ring!" cried Talena.

"No!" cried Claudia.

"In the future," said Talena, "perhaps you will grow accustomed to sleeping at such rings."

Claudia seemed about to faint. She was supported by the

guardsman behind her, and not gently. Then she was stood again, wavering, on her small feet.

"And, citizens," called Talena to the crowd, "have you not heard her, even here, on this very platform, in my very presence, utter shamelessly seditious discourse!"

"Yes!" cried men.

"Kill her," cried others. "Kill her!"

"But," said Talena to the horrified Hinrabian, "I am prepared, on my own responsibility, and in spite of your crimes, in recollection of our former affection for one another, which I still entertain for you, and in respect of your exalted lineage, and the contributions of your family to Ar, before the accession of your father, the infamous Minus Tentius Hinrabius, to the chair of the Administrator, to permit you, instead, to make amends to us all, by permitting you the honor of serving your city."

"I am innocent!" wept Claudia.

"Kill her!" cried men.

"Prepare to hear yourself sentenced," said Talena.

"No!" cried Claudia.

"It is with a heavy heart and tearful eyes that I utter these words," said Talena.

"Marlenus of Ar freed me from bondage!" cried Claudia.

"We have observed you before us," said Talena, "carefully and closely, how you move and such."

"He freed me!" cried Claudia.

"That was a mistake," said Talena.

"Perhaps!" said Claudia.

Men regarded one another.

"Speak," said Talena, amused.

"Twice I have been a slave," said Claudia. "I have had my head shaved. I have felt the whip. I have worn the collar. I have served men."

"Doubtless such experiences will put you in good stead," said Talena. "Perhaps they will even save your life."

"In the Central Cylinder," said Claudia, "I have been lonely, more lonely than I ever knew a woman could be. My life was empty. I was unhappy. I was miserable. I was unfulfilled. In those long years I remembered my time in bondage, and that it had been, in spite of its terrors and labors, the most real, and the happiest, of my life. I had learned something in the collar that I was afraid even to tell myself, that I, Claudia Tentia Hinrabia, of the Hinrabians, belonged at the feet of men."

"You will not object then when I return you to your proper place," laughed Talena.

But there was little laughter from about her, for the men attended to the Hinrabian.

"I confess," wept Claudia, "now, publicly, and before men, that I am in my heart and belly a slave!"

"Then rejoice as I order you imbonded!" said Talena.

"No!" wept Claudia. "It is one thing to be captured by a man and taken to his tent, and put to his feet and made to serve, or to be sentenced by a magistrate in due course of law to slavery for crimes which I have actually committed, and another to stand here publicly shamed, before my enemy, a woman, in her triumph, to be consigned by her to helpless bondage."

"What difference does it make?" asked a man.

"True," wept Claudia. "What difference does it make!"

"Put the slave on her knees!" cried Talena.

"I am a free woman!" wept Claudia. "I am not yet legally imbonded!"

"Thus," cried Talena, "will you learn to kneel before free persons!"

Claudia struggled, but, in a moment, her small strength, that of a mere female, availing her nothing, by two guardsman, was thrown to her knees.

"You look well there, Hinrabian!" said Talena.

"False Ubara!" screamed Claudia, held on her knees.

Talena made an angry sign and a guardsman withdrew his blade from its sheath. In a moment Claudia's head was held down and forward by another guardsman.

"She is to be beheaded!" said a man.

I tensed.

Talena made another sign, and the fellow who held Claudia's hair pulled her head up, that she might see Talena.

Talena's eyes flashed with fury, and Claudia's eyes, then, were filled with terror.

"Who is your Ubara?" asked Talena.

"You are my Ubara!" cried Claudia.

"Who?" asked Talena.

"Talena," she cried. "Talena of Ar is my Ubara!"

This response on the part of Claudia seemed to me judicious, and, indeed, suitable. Talena of Ar was her Ubara.

"Do you confess your faults?" inquired Talena.

"Yes, my Ubara!" said Claudia.

"And do you beg forgiveness of your Ubara?" asked Talena.

"Yes, yes, my Ubara," sobbed Claudia.

"Who begs forgiveness?" asked Talena.

"I, Claudia Tentia Hinrabia, of the Hinrabians, beg forgiveness of Talena of Ar, my lawful Ubara!" she wept.

"I am prepared to be merciful," said Talena.

The guardsman with the drawn blade resheathed it. The guardsman holding Claudia's hair released it, angrily, pushing her head down. The other two guardsmen, one holding each arm, retained their merciless grip on the Hinrabian.

"Talena, Ubara of Ar," announced a scribe, "will now pronounce judgment on the traitress, Claudia Tentia Hinrabia.

"Enemy of Ar, enemy of the people of Ar, enemy of the Home Stone of Ar, Claudia Tentia Hinrabia," said Talena, "you are to be imbonded, and before nightfall."

Claudia's body shook with sobs.

"Send her to the chain," said Talena.

Claudia was pulled to the side and rudely manacled. She, on her knees, looked back at Talena.

"You look well in the chains of men," said Talena.

"You, too, Talena of Ar, my Ubara," wept the Hinrabian, "would doubtless look well in the chains of men!"

Men gasped, in fury.

"Take her away," said Talena.

"Beware the chains of men!" cried the Hinrabian. Then she was pulled down the ramp and, men jeering her and striking at her, buffeting and bruising her, was thrown on her knees before me, to be added to the chain.

"As she is poor stuff," said Talena, loudly, "let a silver tarsk be added to the reparations, to compensate, if it can, for her inadequacies of face and figure."

There was much laughter.

The Hinrabian put down her head, and I took her wrist chain and, in a moment, with the joining ring, had attached her to the coffle chain.

She looked up at me, tears in her eyes. She gasped. My eyes warned her to silence. Doubtless she remembered me from years before. She turned back then, and looked toward the platform. She looked at me then, again, wonderingly.

"Stand, slut of Ar," said the auxiliary guardsman opposite me. "Move to the first position."

"Yes, Master," she said, obeying.

"No, my dear," Talena was saying to another woman on the platform. "You are too young."

That woman was conducted to the rear of the platform. Earlier in the morning, it might be noted, Talena had consigned women as young, or younger than that one, to the chain.

"No, not she," said Talena, as the next woman was presented. "We must keep some beauty in Ar," she explained.

The woman looked at her, gratefully, and quickly pulled the proffered robe again about herself, and hurried from the platform.

Men expressed approval of the decision of their Ubara.

"Master," whispered Claudia to me, standing about a yard behind me, and to my right.

I went to stand beside her. "Yes?" I said.

She looked up at me, her cheeks stained with tears. "Am I beautiful?" she asked, frightened.

"Yes," I said.

"Thank you, Master," she said.

"Years ago," I said, "even in your time of power and cruelty, you were beautiful."

"Such things are behind me now," she said.

"Yes," I said.

She smiled.

"And you are still beautiful," I said.

"Thank you, Master," she said.

"Never doubt your beauty," I said.

"Yes, Master," she said.

"You are still free," I said. "You need not address me as 'Master.' "

"Surely," she said, "it would be well for me to accustom myself, once again, to the utterance of such appropriate deferences."

"True," I said.

"Not she, either," said Talena.

"How merciful is Talena," marveled a man.

"Cornelia, Lady of Ar," said the scribe.

"Do not bare me to men, I beg you," said the woman to Talena, clutching the robe about her.

Talena consulted a list held by a scribe near her. It was not one of the copies of the master list, so to speak, which contained the full list of names.

"Please," begged the woman.

Talena looked up from the list. "Strip her," she said.

The woman cried out with anguish as the single garment was removed from her. She put down her head. She blushed, totally, from the roots of her hair to her toes.

I did not think the woman would be chosen. Like many free women, she had not taken care of her figure. Perhaps that was why she had not wished to be bared before men. To be sure, if she were imbonded it was likely that masters would remedy her oversights in this area, enforcing upon her exact, even merciless, regimens of diet and exercise. They would see that she was soon brought into prime condition, both with respect to physical health and sexual responsiveness.

"It seems," said Talena to the woman, "that two years ago, in the great theater, you were overheard making a remark concerning your future Ubara, one in which you expressed disapproval of her restoration to citizenship."

The woman regarded her, aghast.

"You are chosen," said Talena.

The woman was dragged to the side, to be knelt and manacled. In a moment or so I had added her to the chain.

"No," said Talena, "not that one, dismissing the next woman.

I looked after the woman who had just been added to the chain, who had now been ordered to her feet, and moved to the first scratch mark on the tiles. In three or four months, if not sooner, I suspected she would have become a hot, obedient, excitingly curved slave.

"No," said Talena, "not this one either."

Talena was then ready to dismiss another woman, but something was called to her attention from the list held by the representative of the High Council, and that woman, too, was consigned to the chain. I gathered that she, or perhaps some relative of hers, had offended some member of the current council. Another woman, similarly, later, whom Talena seemed prepared to dismiss, she reconsidered and selected, apparently at the request or suggestion of one of the Cosians on the dais. As he was not likely to be a party to the internal intrigues in Ar, and such, I supposed it was merely that the woman had appealed to him. Perhaps he regarded her as the sort whom Cosians would enjoy having serve their banquets, moving among the tables, bearing platters of viands, or pouring wine, or such, or perhaps merely lying on their bellies or backs beside their small tables at such banquets, ready, too, to serve.

"No," said Talena, apropos of the next female, "not she."

The free, native population of Ar, though there are no certain figures on the matter even in the best of times, and, given the flight of many from the city, conjectures have become even more hazardous, is commonly estimated at between two and three million people. Itinerants, resident aliens and such would add, say, another quarter million to these figures. It is, at any rate, clearly the most populous city of known Gor, exceeding even Turia, in the southern hemisphere. Slaves, incidentally, are not counted in population statistics, any more than sleen, verr, tarsks and such. There were perhaps a quarter million slaves in Ar, the great majority of which were female.

"Nor she, either," said Talena.

What was going on on the platform was of great interest to me. As is probably well known, females on Gor, like gold and silver, and domestic animals, and such, commonly count as legitimate loot. Certainly there is no doubt about this in the case of the female slave, who is a property, a domestic animal, to begin with. On the other hand, it should also be understood that the free women of a conquered city, or territory, if spared, are also commonly understood as, and ranked as, in their own minds and in that of the conquerors, as loot. It is one thing, of course, for a fellow in a flaming city to throw a woman against a wall and tear off her clothes and then, if he likes her, keep her, and quite another for the women of a conquered city, levied, and in the name of reparations, atonement, and such, to line up for their assessment.

"Yes," said Talena, "she is chosen." Another woman then, a blonde, was manacled, brought down the ramp and, by me, added to the chain.

The rumor was that Cos had set the first levy on free females from Ar at only ten thousand. If one supposes, as a conservative estimate, that there were now some two million native citizens in Ar, and that half of them, say, are female, then the levy on free females in Ar was thus only about one in every one hundred. To be sure, this was merely the first levy. It was difficult to estimate the numbers of female slaves seized by Cos, just as the number of verr and such. There were apparently levies for such slaves but, as certain forms of looting or taxation, they were not much publicized. Such slaves, like jewelry, Torian rugs, silver plate, verr, and such, tended to be seized largely as a result of house-to-house searches. More than once I had seen a begging, tearful slave torn from the arms of a beloved master, to be bound and led away on a Cosian leash. Similarly there were numerous confiscations of slaves.

"Ludmilla, Lady of Ar," called the scribe. "Ludmilla, Lady of Ar!"

Guardsmen looked at one another.

"No," said Talena. "Ludmilla, Lady of Ar, has been excused, because of her contributions to Ar, because of her service to the state."

The two scribes, holding the copies of the master list, made appropriate notations. The guardsmen relaxed.

I wondered if the Ludmilla in question was the woman who owned several slave brothels on the street known as The Alley of the Slave Brothels of Ludmilla, the street receiving its name, of course, from the fact that several of its slave brothels were hers. They are, or were, I believe, the Chains of Gold, supposedly the best, or at least the most expensive, and then, all cheap tarsk-bit brothels, the Silken Cords, the Scarlet Whip, the

Slave Racks and the Tunnels. I had once patronized the Tunnels. That was where, as I have mentioned, I had met, and improved, the Earth-girl slave, Louise. I had also once resided in the *insula* of Achiates, which is located on the same street.

At that point the bar for the fifteenth Ahn sounded from the Central Cylinder, across the city.

"I am weary," said Talena.

"Such work is trying," said the representative of the High Council, solicitously.

The scribes put their marking sticks away. They closed their wood-bound tablets, tying them shut. The women yet to be assessed looked at one another. "Turn about," said a guardsman. "Am I to be selected or not?" asked the second woman in the line, anxiously. "Doubtless, given your position in line," said the guardsman, "you will learn tomorrow." "I must wait?" she asked. "Yes," he said. "Now turn about, do not look back." The assessments, of course, would continue for several days. "Oh!" said she who had been the next to be assessed, then the first in the line, now, turned about, at the rear of the long line, stretching still across the platform, down the ramp, and across the Plaza of Tarns. "Oh!" said the woman who had spoken to the guardsman, who had been second in line, and now, turned about, was second to last in the long line. The light cord, little more than twine, but strong enough not to be broken by a woman's strength, had been knotted about her neck and then carried forward to the woman before her, where it was tied similarly, and thence forward again, being unwound from a long spool. It is common to coffle women from the back of the line forward, to minimize the temptation to bolt. I did not know if the women were to be marched back to the Stadium of Blades or only to a rendezvous with cage wagons, to be thence transported to the stadium's holding areas. I did not think, at any rate, that the Cosians would send cage wagons for them in full daylight to the Plaza of Tarns, in the view of a crowd. After all, these were free women of Ar, not female slaves. An additional security in which the women were held, aside from the coffling and guardsmen, auxiliary and regular, was the fact that they were barefoot and clad only in the robes of penitents. In this way was their status well marked out. More women, tonight, incidentally, and doubtless for the next few nights, at least, would be reporting to the great theater. Thence I supposed they would be transported to the Stadium of Tarns, as had been the first batch of women, in their turn to be incarcerated, given the robes of penitents and assigned their place in line.

"Captain," said Talena, "in the room of the Ubar, in the Central Cylinder, we are planning a small supper this evening. I do hope you will honor us with your presence."

The Cosian regarded her.

"There will be delicacies from as far away as Bazi and Anango," she said, "and we shall open vessels of Falarian from the private stores of the Ubar."

"A sumptious supper, indeed," he commented.

"Nothing pretentious," she said, "but nice."

"There is hunger in the city," he said.

"Unfortunately," said the Ubara, "there is not enough for everyone."

"I see," said he.

"Let them suffer for their crimes against Cos," she said.

"Of course," said he.

"Shall we expect you?" she asked.

"Is there to be entertainment?" he asked.

"Czehar music," she said, "and, later, the recitation of poetry by Milo, the famed actor, to the music of the double flute." The instrument which is played by the flute girls is a double flute, too, but I had little doubt that the player involved would not be a flute girl but someone associated with one or another of the theaters of Ar. Similarly the instrument would undoubtedly be far superior, in both range and tone, to those likely to be at the disposal of flute girls.

"I was referring," said he, "to *entertainment*."

"Whatever, Captain, could you have in mind?" she asked.

"I have duties," he said.

"Surely you do not mean "entertainment" in which females might figure," she said.

"Is there another sort?" he asked.

"You have free women in mind," she asked, "perhaps lute players."

"No," said he. "*Females*, female slaves."

"I see," she said.

"Dancers," he said.

"I see," she said.

"Or perhaps such as might figure as contestants in games, or as prizes, and such."

"Of course," she said.

"Perhaps Earth-girl slaves," he suggested.

"That would not do at all," said Talena. "They are the lowest of the low."

"Some are rather nice," he said.

"Perhaps we could find some girls from Turia," she said.

"Or Ar," he said.

"Captain!" she exclaimed.

"Ubara?" he asked.

"The women of Ar," she said, "are not suitable for such things."

"What of the women you consigned to the chain?" he asked.

"Well," she conceded, "such as those—"

"I assure you," he said, "that the women of Ar, imbonded, grovel, and lick and kiss, as well as other women."

"Undoubtedly," she said.

"It is necessary only to put them in their place," he said, "the place of females. The woman of Ar, in her place, the place of a female, is as hot and helpless, as eager and obedient, as devoted and dutiful, as any other slave."

"Undoubtedly," she said, angrily.

"Forgive me, Ubara," said he, "if I have offended you. I am not a courtier, not a diplomat. I am a soldier, a plain man, and I speak bluntly."

"I take no offense, of course," said Talena, Ubara of Ar.

"I meant only to suggest," said he, "that there are women in Ar who are marvelously beautiful and exciting."

"I understand," she said.

"Ubara?" he said.

"I was thinking," she said. "What you say is undoubtedly true, that there must be some women of Ar at least, in all Ar, who are not only suitable for the collar, but belong in it."

"Of course," he said.

"I can think of some entertainment in which you might be interested," she said.

"Ubara?" he asked.

"By nightfall," she said, "Claudia Tentia Hinrabia, of the Hinrabians, will be a collared slave."

"Yes," he said.

"Would you not be curious to see her dance?" she asked.

"She is not a dancer," he said.

"Surely she could be put through slave paces, and made to perform, under a whip," she said.

"Of course," he said.

"And do you men not say that any woman can dance?" she laughed.

"To one extent or another," he said.

"And to the extent that her performance is unsatisfactory, she may be whipped," she said.

"Of course," he said.

"And perhaps I myself shall reserve the judgment on that matter," she said.

"As is your prerogative, Ubara," he said.

"I think that will be amusing," she said, "to have the Hinrabian brought as an entertainer to my supper party, and have her perform as a slave, before men, in my viewing."

"Quite amusing," he said.

"When you return to your headquarters," she said, "please request your polemarkos, Myron, to also honor us with his presence."

"Your wish," he said, bowing, "is my command."

"I wish to have her perform as a slave before him, as well," she said.

"Your vengeance on the Hinrabian is profound indeed, Ubara," he said.

She laughed.

"The performance of the Hinrabian will be reserved for late in the evening, I gather?" he said.

"Yes," she said. "To accompany dessert."

"That seems fitting," he said.

"Superbly fitting," she laughed. "But come early. You would not wish to miss the czehar music nor the performance of Milo."

"You are retaining the czehar player and the actor then," he asked.

"Yes," she said. "I promised him."

"I shall come early," he promised, "and I do not doubt but what I shall be accompanied by Myron, my polemarkos."

"I shall look forward to seeing you both," she said.

"By the way," said he, "how will the supper be served?"

"By slave girls, of course," she said.

"Good," he said.

"Decorously clad," she said. "In long, white gowns."

"I see," he said.

"But their arms will be bared," she said.

"Oh, excellent," he smiled.

"Do not fret, Captain," she laughed. "The decorum of their attire will contrast nicely with that of the Hinrabian."

"Which will consist of a collar and a brand?" he asked.

"Precisely," she said.

"Excellent," he said.

"Let her see the contrast between herself and higher slaves," said Telena.

"Superb," he said.

"After I withdrew for the evening, you may, of course," she said, "do what you wish with the serving slaves, and the Hinrabian."

"Our thanks, Ubara," said he, "those of myself and my polemarkos, and, too, of course, those of our staff members, guards and accompanying officers."

"It is nothing," said Talena.

The captain bowed once again, and then withdrew.

In a few moments the dais, and then the platform, was cleared. The crowd had long ago drifted away.

The long chain of women had been permitted to kneel after the last additions had been made to it. An auxiliary guardsman had come back up the line making certain that the women knelt with their knees widely apart. The heavy chain came to the belly of each, and then lay over the right leg of each, as she knelt, passing back then to the woman behind her. Their wrists, held closely together, were before their bodies. When they were to move out they would pass through a certain station where a Cosian slaver's man, with a marking tape, would measure them for their collar size. This number then would be written by another fellow, with a grease pencil, on their left breast, for the convenience of the fitter. The left breast is the usual place for the temporary recording of such information, presumably because most men are right-handed. In the Street-of-Brands district over a hundred braziers would be waiting, from each of which would project several irons. They were all to be marked with the cursive Kef, as common girls. That is the most common brand for female salves on Gor. Claudia Tentia Hinrabia had already been branded, of course, long ago, so she needed only to be recollared. Her brand, if it is of interest, was also the cursive Kef. It had amused Cernus to have that put on her, such a common brand, she a Hinrabian. But I did not think she objected to it. It is not merely a familiar brand, but, more importantly, a particularly lovely one.

I heard, from several yards away, perhaps fifty yards away, the sound startling me even so, the crack of a whip. Several women in the chain cried out, and some wept. Yet I did not think the leather had touched any of them. To be sure, the fearsome sound of it undoubtedly informed them of what might befall them later, hinting clearly of the rigors of discipline, and the attendant sanctions, to which they were to be soon subject. The women then, with the sounds of chain, began to get to their feet. It was interesting to see the varying alacrities of their response to this signal. Judging by those nearest to me, those who seemed to be the most female were the quickest to respond. It was almost as though they, somehow, in some hitherto untapped portion of their brain, or in some hitherto concealed, or suspected but perhaps not explicitly recognized, portion of their brain, were prepared for, and understood, certain relationships, relationships which might be exemplified by, or symbolized by, such things as the chains on their wrists, or the sound of the whip. By contrast certain others of the women, who seemed to me simpler, or more sluggish in body, or perhaps merely, at this time, less in touch with themselves, were reactively slower. Slavery, of course, is the surest path by means of which a woman can discover her femininity. The paradox of the collar is the freedom which a woman experiences in at last finding herself, and becoming herself. She is a woman, really, you see, not a man, and not something else, either, also different from a woman, and she will never be fully content until she finds her personal truth, until she becomes, so to speak, what she is.

"What is to become of us?" asked the blonde of me, she who had been the last to be added to the chain.

I stayed my hand. She shrank back.

"You may beg forgiveness," I said.

She looked at me wildly.

I had not struck her, at least yet. She was, after all, a free woman.

The whip then, again, further ahead, down the line, cracked.

"I beg forgiveness!" she said.

"You beg forgiveness—what?" I asked.

"I beg forgiveness, Master!" she said.

I lowered my hand.

I thought it well for her to accustom herself to such utterances.

She still had her hands lifted. She had lifted her wrists, as she could, in the manacles, to fend the blow which I had not struck.

"Put your hands down," I said.

"Yes, Master," she said.

"Stand straight," I said. "Shoulders back."

"Yes, Master," she said.

I regarded her.

She had tiny, fine hair on the back of her wrists. One could see it, in its golden fineness, extending toward the dark, clasping iron, beneath which it vanished. She was nicely curved. I thought she would bring a good price. I continued to regard her and she became acutely aware of my scrutiny. She stood even straighter, and more beautifully. Yes, I thought to myself, she is starting to understand. Doubtless in time she will do quite well at a man's slave ring.

The whip cracked again, this time quite close, as the fellow with the device had been approaching, stopping here and there. Another fellow with him was checking the manacles and joining rings.

"The beads are on the string," said the second fellow, he who was checking the security of the chain. This was an oblique allusion to the "slaver's necklace," as a coffle of female slaves is sometimes called. The reference there, in effect, is usually to "jewels" on a chain. To be sure, the women on this chain, as they were merely free woman, had only been referred to, in rude humor, as "beads" and not "jewels." I did not doubt, however, but what in a few months' time these same women, properly disciplined, trained and brought into touch with their most profound and fundamental realities would also, in the same fashion as other female salves, become "jewels."

"Bring the extra chain back through the coffle," said the fellow with the ship.

There was coil of unused chain near my feet, left from the coffling. We could probably have added forty or fifty more women to the coffle had we wished.

My fellow guardsman lifted the far end of the chain and threaded it through the arms of the blonde. I then drew it forward and put it through the arms of the next woman. Then, in time, with the help of three or four other fellows, locating themselves along the coffle line, most of the weight being shortly borne by the wrist chains of the lovely "beads" themselves, we had doubled the chain, bringing it forward. In this way we distributed the weight of the unused length of chain over the wrist chains of the last forty women or so, this constituting no unusual burden to any one of them. We did not wish to cut the chain. Moreover it would be needed the next day. Coffle chains are usually adjusted, of course, to the number of women to be placed on it. To be sure, women can be spaced more or less closely on such a chain. A slaver's joke, one which free women are likely to hear with apprehension, has it that there is always room for another female on the chain.

In a few Ehn I had returned to my place at the end of the line.

The chain, ahead, to the crack of a whip, began to move. The blonde, however, at the end of the chain, given the length of the chain, did not move until at least two Ehn later.

Some of the women at the front of the chain had probably had to be informed that the first step taken in coffle is with the left foot. Later, of course, such things would become second nature to them.

As we moved from the Plaza of Tarns the streets seemed muchly deserted. Among the people we did pass, or who were passing by, few seemed to take much interest in the coffle. Many even looked away. It now had little, or nothing, to do with them. Its contents, in effect, were no longer of Ar. Some fellows in Turian garb did stand by a wall, their arms folded, considering the coffle, much as might have assessing slavers. Twice some children addressed themselves to the coffle, jeering its captives, spitting upon them, stinging them with hurled pebbles, rushing forward, even, to lash at them with switches. Already, it seemed, to these children, the women were no more than mere slaves.

When I had threaded the chain back through the arms of Claudia Tentia Hinrabia, incidentally, I did not mention to her that she had been selected to entertain at a late supper to be given by Talena of Ar, her Ubara, in the room of the Ubar, in the Central Cylinder. She would find out, soon enough.

10 The Sword Is Thirsty

"I can remember when the men of Ar, those I saw of them in the north, walked proudly," said Marcus.

The city was subdued, save for some idealistic youth, who seemed to take pride in its downfall.

"Yes," I said.

It was now some months after the entry of Myron, polemarkos of Temos, into Ar. The systematic looting of Ar had proceeded apace. More levies of women, free and slave, had been conducted. Work on the destruction of the walls had continued.

Marcus and I were on the Avenue of the Central Cylinder, the major thoroughfare in Ar.

"The major blow," said he, "was doubtless the movement of the Home Stone to Telnus."

This had been admitted on the public boards at last. Originally it had been rumored, which rumors had been denied, that only a surrogate for the stone had appeared in the Planting Feast. Later, however, when the ceremony of citizenship, in which the Home Stone figures, was postponed, speculation had become rampant. There had been demands by minor Initiates, of smaller temples, outside the pomerium of the city, first, for the ceremonies to be conducted, and, later, these ceremonies not taking place, for the Home Stone to be produced. In the furor of speculation over this matter the secular and ecclesiastical authorities in the city had remained silent. At last, in view of the distinct unrest in the city, and the possible danger of riots and demonstrations, a communication was received from the Central Cylinder, jointly presented by Talena, Ubara of Ar; Seremides, captain of the guard; Antonius, executive officer of the High Council; Tulbinius, Chief Initiate; and Myron, polemarkos of Temos, to the effect that Ar might now rejoice, as in these unsettled times Lurius of Jad, in his generosity and wisdom, at the request of the governance of Ar, and in the best interests of the people and councils of Ar, had permitted the Home Stone to be brought to Telnus for safekeeping. A surrogate stone was subsequently used for the ceremony of citizenship. Certain youth refused then to participate in the ceremony and certain others, refusing to touch the surrogate stone, uttered the responses and pledges while facing northwest, toward Cos, toward their Home Stone.

Marcus and I, with the armbands of auxiliary guardsmen, saluted a Cosian officer whom we passed.

"Tarsk," grumbled Marcus.

"He is probably a nice enough fellow," I said.

"Sometimes I regret that you are a dear friend," he said.

"Why is that?" I asked.

"It makes it improper to challenge you to mortal combat," he said.

"Folks have occasionally slain their dearest friends," I said.

"That is true," he said, brightening up.

"Just because someone is your mortal enemy," I said, "does not mean that you have to dislike him."

"I suppose not," said Marcus.

"Of course not," I said.

We walked on.

"You are just in a bad mood," I said. Such moods were not uncommon with Marcus.

"Perhaps," he said.

"Does Phoebe have her period?" I asked.

"No," he said.

"You were out late last night," I said.

"Yes," he said.

"Frequenting the taverns?" I asked.

"No," he said. "I was wandering about."

"It is now dangerous to walk the streets of Ar at night," I said.

"For whom?" he said.

"For anyone, I suppose," I said.

"Perhaps," he said.

"Where did you walk?" I asked.

"In the Anbar district," he said.

"That is a dangerous district," I said, "even formerly." It and the district of Trevelyan were two of the most dangerous districts in Ar, even before the fall of the city.

"Oh?" he said.

"Yes," I assured him. "It is frequented by brigands."

"It is now frequented by two less than yesterday," he said.

"Why do you do these things?" I asked.

"My sword," he said, "was thirsty."

"I am angry," I said.

"I made a profit on the transaction," he said.

"You robbed the brigands?" I asked.

"Their bodies," he said.

"We do not need the money," I said. Indeed, we had most of a hundred gold pieces left, a considerable fortune, which we had obtained last summer in the vicinity of Brundisium.

"Well, I did not really do it for the money," said Marcus.

"I see," I said.

"Not all values are material," Marcus reminded me.

"You should not risk your life in such a way," I said, angrily.

"What else is there to do?" he asked.

"I am sure you could think of something," I said, "if you seriously put your mind to it."

"Now it is you who seem in an ill humor," he remarked.

"If you find yourself spitted in the Anbar district that will not much profit the Home Stone of Ar's Station," I said.

"You told me that the Home Stone of Ar's Station would be exhibited again," he said.

"I am sure it will be," I said.

"That was months ago," he said.

"Be patient," I said.

"I do not even know where it is," he said. "It may be in Telnus by now."

"I do not think so," I said.

"At least those of Ar know where their Home Stone is," he said.

"Do not be surly," I said.

"You do not think it is in Telnus?" he asked.

"No," I said. "I think it is still in Ar.

"Why?" he asked.

"I have an excellent reason," I said.

"Would you be so kind as to share this reason with me?" asked Marcus.

"No," I said.

"Why not?" he asked.

"You are too noble to take it seriously," I said.

"Thank you," said he, "perhaps."

We paused to drink, from the upper basin of a fountain.

"Listen," I said.

"Yes," he said.

We turned about.

Some twenty men, stripped, in heavy metal collars, these linked by heavy chains, their hands behind their backs, presumably manacled, prodded now and then by the butts of guards' spears, were approaching. Behind the line came a flute girl, sometimes turning about, playing the instrument. It was this sound we had heard. Some folks stopped to watch.

"Political prisoners," said Marcus.

That could be told by the fact that the ears and noses of the prisoners had been painted yellow, to make them appear ridiculous.

"Interesting," said Marcus, "that they would parade them so publicly down the Avenue of the Central Cylinder."

"It is to be expected," I said. "If they were conducted out of the city in secret there would be much inquiry, much resentment, much clamor, much objection. It would be as though the Central Cylinder wished to conceal the fate imposed upon them, as though they were afraid of its becoming public, as though it might not be legitimately defensible. In this way, on the other hand, it performs its action openly, without special attention but, too, without stealth. It says, thusly, the action is in order, that it is acceptable, even trivial. Too, of course, it hopes to enlist public approbation by the painting of the ears and noses, thus suggesting that any who might disagree with its policies must be mad or dunces, at best objects of caricature and ridicule."

"Those in the Central Cylinder are clever," said Marcus.

"They may miscalculate," I said.

"Whence are these fellows bound?" asked Marcus.

"Probably the quarries of Tyros," I said.

"There must be many in Ar who will have scores to settle with the Ubara," he said.

"I suspect," I said, "that these arrests are more the work of Seremides, and Antonius, of the High Council."

"You would defend Talena of Ar?" he asked.

"I would not blame her for more than that for which she is responsible," I said.

"Surely her complicity is clear," he said.

I was silent.

"She is an arch conspirator in the downfall of Ar," he said.

"Perhaps," I said.

"What does she mean to you?" he asked.

"Nothing," I said.

The men were now filing past, with their guards. Their hands, indeed, were manacled behind their backs.

"Some of those men may have been high in the city," said Marcus.

"Undoubtedly," I said.

"Some even have signs about their necks," said Marcus.

"I am not familiar with the politics of Ar," I said, "so I do not recognize the names."

"I know the name of the last fellow," said Marcus, "Mirus Torus."

The sign about his neck had that name on it, and also the word, "Traitor."

"Who is he?" I asked.

"I assume," said Marcus, "that he is the Mirus Torus who was the executive officer of the High Council before Gnieus Lelius, and later held the same office under the regency of Gnieus Lelius."

"I think I have heard of him," I said.

"For some months he was under house arrest," said Marcus.

"The Central Cylinder," I said, "seems now to be very sure of its power."

"Doubtless it was encouraged by its success in the matter of the Home Stone," said Marcus.

"Undoubtedly," I said.

"You seem troubled," he said.

"It is nothing," I said.

We watched the coffle of prisoners move away, south on the Avenue of the Central Cylinder. For a long time we could hear the music of the flute girl who brought up the rear.

"What is it?" asked Marcus.

"There seems nothing to rouse Ar," I said.

"Forget Ar," said Marcus. "The men of Ar have become spineless urts."

"These men," I said, were once among the strongest and finest in the world."

"Ar died in the delta," said Marcus.

"Perhaps," I said. There seemed much to the sobering suggestion of the young warrior.

"What is Ar to you?" he asked.

"Nothing," I said.

"Cos loots with impunity," said Marcus, "tearing even the marbles from the walls. She disguises her depredations under absurd, meretricious rhetorics. It is as though the sleen pretended to be the friend of the verr. And what do the men of Ar do? They smile, they hasten to give up their riches, they beat their breasts, they lament their unworthiness, they cannot sufficiently praise those who despoil them, they rush to sacrifice at the great temples. They burn their gates, they dismantle their walls, they hide in their houses at night. They cheer while women who might be theirs are instead marched to Cosian ports. Do not concern yourself with them, my friend. They are unworthy of your concern."

I looked at Marcus.

He smiled. "You are angry," he said.

"Ho! One side, buffoons of Ar!" said a voice, that of a mercenary, one of two, with blue armbands.

We stepped to one side as they swaggered past.

"I am not of Ar," I said to Marcus.

"Nor am I," he said.

"Thus they could not have been speaking to us," I said.

"We could kill them," said Marcus.

"In broad daylight?" I asked.

"Perhaps they are nice fellows," said Marcus.

"Perhaps," I said.

"But then one cannot always permit oneself to be deterred by such considerations," he said.

"True," I said.

"They think they own the street," he said.

"Doubtless an impression they have gathered from those of Ar," I said.

"Surely," he said.

"There is nothing to rouse Ar," I said.

"No," he said.

"If Marlenus were alive, and might return," I said, "that might bring Ar to her feet, angry and mighty, like an awakened larl."

"If Marlenus were alive," said Marcus, "he would have returned to Ar long ago."

"Then there is no hope," I said.

"No," said Marcus. "There is no hope."

I regarded him.

"Ar died last summer," he said, "in the delta."

I did not respond to him. I feared he was right.

We walked on then, not speaking, south on the Avenue of the Central Cylinder.

In an Ehn I cried out, inadvertently, with rage, a helpless warrior's fury irrepressibly welling up within me.

A passer-by regarded me, startled, and hurried quickly past.

"You are angry," said Marcus.

"Are you not angry?" I asked.

"Perhaps," he said:

We heard then, behind us, running feet, laughter, a tearing of cloth, and a woman's cry. A group of young fellows was running past. We, too, were buffeted but I seized one of the lads by the wrist and, drawing him quickly across and about my body, and over my extended right leg, flung him to the stones, where I held him, my grip shifted now to the palm of his hand, on his knees, his head down, his arm high, twisted behind him, his wrist bent, far back. He screamed with pain. Another fraction of a hort, the least additional pressure, and his wrist would be broken. Almost at the same instant I heard Marcus' sword leave its sheath, warning back the other lads, some six of them. Marcus, I noted, was suddenly, relievedly, in an eager, elated mood. He hoped for their advance. He was quite ready, even eager, for the release of shedding blood. I felt my own nostrils flare as I suddenly, excitedly, drank in the air of Ar, exhilerated, fiercely alive. The six lads backed away. I had little doubt he would have cut them down had they come with the compass of his blade. One of the lads, their leader it seemed, clutched the woman's pouch, torn from her belt, and another held her veil. I looked back to the woman, who had been struck to her knees. She had drawn her hood about her face, that her features not be exposed publicly. Her eyes were wild in the opening within the hood.

"Do not hurt me!" screamed the lad on his knees.

I paid him little attention. He was going nowhere. At least two of the other lads had knives.

"You are "Cosians"?" I said to them.

They looked at one another.

Certain gangs of youths, young ruffians, roamed the streets, affecting Cosian garmets and haircuts. These were called "Cosians." Such things are common where an enemy is feared. They ape the feared enemy, and hope thereby, as though by some alchemy, to obtain his strength and success. Such charades serve, too, as a form of cowardly camouflage. Knowing they have nothing to fear from their own people, they pretend they are like the enemy, perhaps in the hope that then they will have nothing to fear from him, as well. Too, such postures, costumes and mannerisms provide an easy way to attract attention to oneself, a welcome feature to one who may otherwise be unworthy of attention. Similarly, such charades provide, in more serious cases, a way of expressing one's alienation from one's own society, one's repudiation of it, and one's contempt of it. From this point of view then, such things may constitute a comprehensible, if somewhat silly, or ineffectual, form of protest. Too, of course, such costumes can intimidate weaklings, which some would undoubtedly rate as an additional advantage.

"Do not hurt him!" said the leader.

"You are "Cosians"?" I asked.

"No," said their leader, "we are of Ar."

"I can probably reach at least two of them," said Marcus.

The six stepped back further, preparing to take to their heels.

"We are only lads!" said the leader, keeping his distance.

I gestured with my head back toward the woman behind us. She had risen to her feet. She still clutched the folds of her hood about her face, to conceal her features.

"Do you think she is some slave girl," I asked, "that you may strip her on the street, for your sport?"

"No," said one of the lads.

"She is a free woman, of your own city," I said.

"There is no Home Stone in Ar," he said.

"That is true," said Marcus.

"Do you make war on boys?" asked the leader.

"Now you are "boys," " I said.

They were silent.

"Sheath your knives," I said.

They did so. I was now pleased that they did this. I was not certain, really, of the responses of Marcus. He was not a fellow of Earth, but a Gorean. Too, he was of the Warriors, and his codes, in a situation of this sort, their weapons drawn, entitled him, even encouraged him, to attack, and kill. Moreover I thought he could really reach at least three of them, the first with a thrust, and the second two, each with a slash to the neck, first to the right, the blade withdrawn, and then to the left, before they could adequately break and scatter. Marcus was very fast, and trained. In this way I was encouraging them to protect themselves. They were, after all, as their leader had pointed out, a bit plaintively, and somewhat belatedly, only lads. To be sure this would not mean much to Marcus, who was probably not more than three or four years older than they were.

"And bring forward the pouch and veil."

"Release Decius," said the leader.

"I am not bargaining," I said.

The leader brought forward the pouch, and put it down on the stones. He then signaled to the lad with the veil. That fellow then brought the veil forward, too, and put it on the stones. Both of them then backed away. I then released the hand of the other lad, Decius, it seemed, and he scrambled away, holding his wrist.

"Give me my veil!" demanded the woman, coming forward.

I handed it to her.

She turned about, adjusting it.

"Pick up my pouch," she said, her back to us. "Give it to me."

I picked up the pouch. The lads had now withdrawn some forty yards or so away. They were gathered about the fellow whom I had had down on his knees, his arm behind him, the wrist bent. He was still undoubtedly in pain.

"Give me my pouch!" she demanded.

I looked at the group of youths.

The fellow's wrist had not been broken. I had not chosen to do that.

One or another of the lads, from time to time, looked back at us. I did not think they would return, however. To be sure, Marcus might have welcomed that. His sword was still unsheathed. Too, I did not think they would be interested in causing the lady further inconvenience.

I felt the woman's hand snatch at the pouch and my own hand, almost reflexively, closed on the pouch.

Her eyes flashed angrily over the veil, an opaque street veil, now readjusted.

"Give it to me!" she said.

"It was our mistake to interfere," said Marcus, dryly. He resheathed his blade.

"Give it to me!" said the woman.

"You are rude," I said.

She tugged at the pouch.

"Are you not grateful?" I asked.

"It demeans a free woman to express gratitude," she said.

"I do not think so," I said.

"Are you not paid for your work?" she asked.

"Are you not grateful?" I asked.

"I am not a slave!" she asked.

"Are you not grateful?" I asked, again.

""Yes," she said. "I am grateful! Now, give it to me!"

"Ah," I said, "Perhaps you are a slave."

"No!" she said.

"What do you think of this free woman?" I asked Marcus.

"It is difficult to tell, clothed as she is," he said.

She reacted angrily, but did not release the pouch.

"Do you think she might be more civil," I asked, "if she were stripped?"

"Yes," he said, "particularly if she were also branded and collared."

"She would then learn softness, as opposed to hardness," I said.

"It would be in her best interest to do so," said Marcus.

"Yes," I said.

She released the pouch and stepped back a little.

Her eyes were now wide, over the veil.

"Perhaps she is the sort of woman who is best kept in a kennel," I said, "to be brought forth when one wishes, for various labors."

"Such women are all haughty wenches," he said. "But they quickly lose their haughtiness in bondage."

"Please," she said. "Give me the coins."

I did not release them.

"Give them to me!" she said, angrily.

"Would you not like to learn softness, as opposed to hardness?" I asked.

She looked at me, angrily.

"Women learn it quickly in bondage," I said.

"It is in their best interest to do so," said Marcus.

"Yes," I said.

"Surely you have wondered what it would be, to be a slave?" inquired Marcus.

She gasped. Only too obviously had she considered such matters.

"But then," I said, "you may not be attractive enough to be a slave."

She did not speak.

I put the pouch inside my tunic.

"Oh!" she said, for I had then reached up and taken her hood in my hands.

"We shall see," I said.

"Oh!" she said, startled.

Marcus held her from behind, by the arms.

I pushed back her hood and thrust it down. I then jerked away the veil, and surveyed her features.

"I think you, like most women, would make an adequate slave," I said.

She squirmed.

"Hold her wrists together," I said. I then tied them together, behind her back, with her veil.

She moaned.

She could not now readjust the veil.

"Please," she begged. "Let me veil myself. Slavers might see me!"

"You were not pleasing," I said.

I then took the pouch of coins in my hand and lofted it to the group of lads some forty yards away. Their leader caught it. They then turned about, and ran.

The woman looked at me, astonished, aghast.

"Your lips are pretty," I said. "They could probably be trained to kiss well.'"

Tears sprang to her eyes.

"And lest you return home too quickly," I said, "we shall do this." I then crouched down and tore off a bit of the hem of her robes, but not enough to offend her modesty, for example, revealing her ankles, and, using the cloth as a bond, fastened her ankles together, leaving her some four or five inches of slack, rather like a slave girl's hobble chains.

"Return home now," I said.

We watched her withdraw, sobbing. She had not been pleasing.

'She is not unattractive," said Marcus.

"No," I said. "To be sure, her face now is a bit cold, and tight, and strained, as seems her body, as well, common in free women, but I do not doubt but what, in time, relaxed, brought into touch with herself, and her fundamental realities, no longer permitted to deny them, obliged then rather to express and fulfill them, she will blossom in softness and beauty."

"She might even bring a good price in a market," said Marcus.

"I am sure of it," I said.

"Sleen!" said a free woman, bundled in the robes of concealment, heavily veiled, hurrying by. Doubtless she had witnessed, from a distance, the fate of her compatriot.

"The woman of Ar should be slaves," said Marcus.

"Yes," I said. I could think of one in particular.

"It would much improve them," he said.

"Yes," I said. Slavery, of course, much improves any woman. This is because of the psychological dimorphism of the human species, that the female's fulfillment lies in her subjection to, and subjugation by, a strong male.

"But do not confuse the men of Ar with the women of Ar," I said.

"I do not feel sorry for them," he said.

"I do," I said. "They have been confused, misled, and robbed."

"And not only of their goods," said Marcus.

"No," I said, "but of their pride, as well."

"And their manhood," said Marcus, bitterly.

"I do not know," I said. "I do not know."

"Their women belong at the feet of men," said Marcus.

"So, too, do all women," I said.

"True," said Marcus.

Women taken in a given city, incidentally, are usually sold out of the city, to wear their collars elsewhere. In this fashion the transition from their former to their subsequent condition is made particularly clear to them. They must begin anew, as a new form of being, that of a lovely animal, the female slave. Also, given the xenophobia common on Gor, often obtaining among cities, the distrust of the stranger, the contempt for the outsider, and such, there is a special ease in a master's relating to a foreign slave, one with whom he has never shared a Home Stone. Similarly, of course, there is a special urgency and terror on the part of the slave, in finding that she now belongs helplessly to one of a different polity. She understands that it may be difficult to please such a master, one likely to be harsh and demanding, who may despise her, who may think nothing of subjecting her to cruel punishments, and that she must accordingly, if she would even live, strive desperately to be pleasing to him. They can thus, the girl's antecedents, like her name and clothing, stripped away, and his unknown to her, begin as pure master and slave. What, if anything, will then, from this basic fiat of their relationship, develop between them? Will she, in and of herself, alone, aside from the trivia of her now-irrelevant history, become his special, unique slave? Will he, on his part, in and of himself, alone, aside from his antecedents, his station, caste, and such, become to her a very special, very individual master, perhaps even her master of masters?

We then continued on.

"You are still troubled," said Marcus.

"It is like seeing a larl tricked into destroying himself," I said, "as though he were told that the only good larl is a sick, apologetic, self-suspecting, guilt-ridden larl. It is like vulos legislating for tarns, the end of which legislation is the death of the tarn, or its transformation into something new, something reduced, pathological and sick, celebrated then as the true tarn."

"I do not even understand what you are saying," said Marcus.

"That is because you are Gorean," I said.

"Perhaps," he shrugged.

"But you see such things occurring in Ar," I said.

"Yes," he said.

"The larl makes a poor verr," I said. "The tarn makes a pathetic vulo. Cannot you imagine it hunching down, and pretending to be little and weak? Is the image not revolting? Why is it not soaring among the cliffs, uttering its challenge scream to the skies?"

Marcus looked at me, puzzled.

"The beast who was born to live on flesh is not to be nourished on the nibblings of urts," I said.

"It is hard to understand you," he said.

"It is long since I have heard the roar of the larl, the cry of the tarn," I said.

"In Ar," he said, "there are no larls, there are no tarns."

"I do not know if that is true or not," I said.

"There are only women here," he said, "and men pretending to be like women."

"Each should be true to himself," I said.

"Perhaps neither should be true to himself, or to the other," said Marcus.

"Perhaps each should try to be true to those who can be true to neither."

"Perhaps," said Marcus.

I drove my fist into the palm of my hand.

"What is wrong?" he asked.

"Ar must be roused!" I said.

"It cannot be done," he said.

"Ar lacks leadership, will, a resistance!" I said.

"Lead Ar," suggested Marcus.

"I cannot do that," I said. "I am not even of Ar."

Marcus shrugged.

"There must be another!" I said.

"Marlenus is dead," he said.

"There must be another!" I wept.

"There is no other," said Marcus.

"There must be a way," I said.

"There is no way," said Marcus.

"There must be!" I said.

"Do not concern yourself," said Marcus. "Ar is dead. She died in the delta."

"In the delta?" I said.

"In the delta," said Marcus. "Indeed, we were there."

"That is possibly it," I whispered. "The delta."

Marcus looked at me, a little wildly. Perhaps he suspected that I had gone mad. Indeed, perhaps I had.

"That may be the key," I said. "The delta!"

"I do not understand," he said.

"Are you with me?" I asked.

"Has this anything to do with the recovery of the Home Stone of Ar's Station?" he asked.

"Oh, yes," I said. "Yes, indeed!"

"Then I am surely with you," he said.

"Is your sword still thirsty?" I asked.

"Parched," he said, smiling.

"Good," I said.

11 The Delka

"Stop babbling, man!" ordered the guardsman, an officer in the scarlet of Ar, though his accent proclaimed him Cosian.

"It was so quick!" wept the merchant. "My shop, my wares, ruined!"

"Aii," said another of the guardsmen with the officer. There were four such men with him. They were, I think, of Ar. They were looking about the shop, one of ceramics. There were many shards about. Shelves had been pulled down. Among the shards and wreckage, by count, there were seven bodies, all Cosian mercenaries.

"Who are you?" asked the officer, looking up.

"Auxiliaries, Captain," said I, "in the vicinity."

"See what carnage has been wrought here," said the officer, angrily.

"Looters?" I asked.

"Explain now," said the captain to the merchant, "what occurred. Control yourself. Be calm."

"I am sick!" wept the merchant.

"I am not of the physicians," said the officer. "I must have an account of this. There must be a report made."

"It was at the ninth Ahn," said the merchant, sitting on a stool.

"Yes?" said the officer.

"These fellows entered the shop," he said. "They claimed to be tax collectors."

"They presented their credentials?" asked the captain.

"They are not tax collectors," said one of the guardsmen. "They are fellows come in from the camp, on passes. They are well known on the avenue. They pose as tax collectors, and then, in that guise, take what they wish."

"What did they want?" asked the captain of the merchant.

"Money," he said.

"You gave it to them?" asked the officer.

"I gave them what I had," he said, "but it was little enough. The collectors had come only five days earlier. They leave us destitute!"

"You murdered these men?" inquired the captain, skeptically.

"I did nothing," said the merchant. "They grew angry at not receiving more money. To be sure, had I any, I would have given it to them readily. Glory to Cos!"

"Glory to Cos," growled the officer. "Continue."

"Angry at the pittance they obtained they began to wreck the shop."

"Yes?" inquired the officer.

"My shop! My beautiful wares!" he moaned.

"Continue!" said the officer.

"It was then that two fellows entered the shop, in silence, like darkness and wind, behind them," he said.

"And?" inquired the officer.

"And this was done!" said the merchant, gesturing to the floor.

"There were only two who entered behind them?" asked the officer.

"Yes," said the merchant.

"I do not believe you," said the officer. "These fallen fellows are swordsmen, known in the camp."

"I swear it!" said the merchant.

"There appears to be only one mark on the body of each of these fellows," said one of the guardsmen, who had been examining the bodies.

"Warriors," said another of the guardsmen.

"I do not even know if they realized what was among them," said the merchant.

"It seems to have been professionally done," said the captain.

"Yes, Captain," said one of the men.

"Whose work could it be?" asked the captain.

"Surely there is little doubt about the matter," said another of the guardsmen.

The captain regarded the guardsman.

"See, Captain?" asked the guardsman. He rolled one of the bodies to its back. On the chest was a bloody triangle, the "delka." That is the fourth letter in the Gorean alphabet, and formed identically to the fourth letter of the Greek alphabet, the 'delta', to which letter it doubtless owes its origin. In Gorean, the delta of a river is referred to as its "delka." The reasoning here is the same as in Greek, and, derivatively, in English, namely the resemblance of a delta region to a cartographical triangle.

"It was the same five days ago," said one of the men, "with the five brigands found slain in the Trevelyan district, and the two mercenaries cut down on Wagon Street, at the second Ahn, only the bloody delka left behind, scrawled on the wall."

"In the blood of the brigands, and of the mercenaries," said one of the men."

"Ar takes vengeance," said one of the guardsmen.

"Sooner could a verr snarl!" snapped the officer.

"We are not all urts," said one of the men.

"Your swords are pledged to Ar," said the officer, "Ar under the hegemony of Cos!"

"Is that other than to Cos herself?" asked a man.

"We obey our Ubara," said another.

"And whom does she obey?" asked the fellow.

"Silence," said the officer.

"Glory to Cos," I said.

"Let an auxiliary teach you your manners, your duties to the alliance," said the officer.

The guardsman shrugged.

"Good fellow," said the officer.

"Thank you, Captain," I said.

The officer turned to the tradesman. "Those assailants who slew these poor lads and wrecked your shop, surely several of them, not two, could you recognize them?"

"There were but two, as I said," said the tradesman, "and it was not they but those who now lie about, drenched in their own blood, who disturbed my wares."

"I see," said the officer, angrily.

"I would follow Marlenus," said a guardsman.

"Follow his daughter," said the officer.

"One whom he himself repudiated?" asked the man.

"False," said the officer.

"She was disowned, said the man.

"False!" said the officer.

"As you say, Captain," said one of the guardsmen.

"In following his daughter, you follow him," said the officer.

"Never would his footsteps have led to Cos unless there were an army at his back," said another.

"Hail Talena, Ubara of Ar," I said.

"Well said," said the Captain.

"Glory to Ar," said one of the men.

This sentiment was echoed by those present with the exception, I think, of the captain, myself and, if I am not mistaken, Marcus.

"Search the shop," said the officer.

Three guardsmen then went into the back of the shop, and one climbed the ladder to the second floor.

"Two many things of this sort have occurred," said the captain to me, looking about himself.

"Captain?" I asked.

"Yes," he said. "More than the men know of."

There was at that moment a girl's scream, coming from the back room.

The shopkeeper cried out in misery.

"Captain!" called a man.

The captain then strode to the rear room. The shopkeeper, Marcus and myself followed him.

In the back there were many ceramic articles about, vessels of numerous sorts, on tiers, and stacks of shallow bowls. The ruffians who had assaulted the shop had not reached the rear room. Further it seemed likely the merchant was not as poorly off as might have been supposed.

"See, Captain?" said one of the men, lifting up the lid of a narrow, oblong chest. Within it, huddled there, looking up, over her right shoulder, terrified, there crouched a girl. Her veil had become somewhat disarranged, and in such a way that one could see her lips and mouth.

"Cover yourself, immodest girl!" scolded the shopkeeper. She pulled the veil more closely about her features. "She is my daughter," said the shopkeeper. She was probably not more than sixteen or seventeen years old.

"Do you always keep her in a chest?" asked the captain, angrily. Keeping female slaves in small confines, of course, in properly ventilated chests, in slave boxes, and such, is not that unusual, but this girl, as far as we knew, was free. Apparently the chest had not been locked, and, too, of course, she was clothed, rather than naked, as slaves are usually kept in such places. To be sure, they are sometimes granted a sheet or blanket for comfort or warmth.

"Of course not," said the shopkeeper, frightened. "But when the ruffians came to the shop she was in the back and I told her to hide in the chest.

" 'Ruffians'?" asked the officer.

"Yes, Captain," said the man.

"And yet you did not have her emerge from the chest when the danger was past," observed the officer.

"It slipped my mind," said the shopkeeper.

"Of course," said the captain, ironically.

The shopkeeper was silent.

"You feared us, your defenders, your neighbors and allies," said the captain.

"Forgive me, Captain," said the shopkeeper, "but there are the levies, and such."

"And have you concealed your daughter from the authorities, in such matters?" asked the captain.

"Of course not, Captain," he said. "I am a law-abiding man. She is on the registries."

"There is nothing upstairs," said the man who had come down the ladder from the second floor.

The girl made no attempt to leave the chest. I did not know if this was because she was mature enough, and female enough, to understand that she had not yet been given permission to do so, or if there were a deeper reason.

"Turus, Banius," said the captain, addressing two of the men, "clear the front of the shop, remove the bodies, put them on the street."

"May I submit, Captain," I said, "that it might be preferable to leave the bodies in the shop until they can be properly disposed of. If they are displayed on the street, the power of those of the delta might be too manifestly displayed."

"Excellent," said the officer. "Desist," he said to the men.

"I am considering my report," said the officer to the merchant. "It seems that some good fellows of Cos, esteemed mercenaries, in the service of her Ubar, with all good will and innocence, entered this shop, to purchase wares for loved ones, and were treacherously set upon by assailants, some twenty in number."

"They came pretending to be collectors," said the merchant, "to rob me under this pretense, and dissatisfied with my inability to fill their purses, set out to destroy the shop and goods, and then two fellows whom I did not know, their features concealed in wind scarves, entered and did what you see in the front of the shop."

"I like my version better," said the captain.

"As you will," said the merchant.

"I do not care for what occurred here," said the captain, "and I find you uncooperative."

"I will cooperate in any way I can," said the merchant.

The captain then went to the sides of the back room and suddenly, angrily, kicked and struck goods about, shattering countless articles.

"Stop!" cried the merchant.

The captain swept kraters from a shelf.

In futility did the merchant wring his hands.

"I suspect," said the captain, overturning a stack of bowls, treading upon several of them, "you are in league with the brigands, that your shop served as a trap!"

"No!" cried the shopkeeper, anguished. "Would I have myself ruined? Stop! I beg you, stop!"

"Impalement would be too good for you, traitor to Ar!" said the officer.

"No!" wailed the merchant.

"If your story is true," said the officer, thrusting over a rack of ceramics, and a cabinet, "why were these goods not destroyed, as well?" He hurled a kylix to the wall. In his anger, his destructive fury, doubtless the belated eruption of precedent frustrations, he kicked articles about, and trod even on bowls. Even his ankles and legs were bloodied.

"They did not come so far," said the merchant. "But you, it seems, are determined to complete their work."

"Do you have rope, or hammers and nails?" asked the officer.

"Of course, Captain," said the man.

"Strip her," said the captain to one of the men.

"No!" cried the merchant. He was restrained by two guardsmen.

The girl, crying out, shrieking, pulled half from the chest, had her veil and clothing torn from her.

She was then trust down again, now naked, trembling, in the chest.

"No!" wept the shopkeeper, throwing himself to his knees before the officer.

"This will teach you to put her on the registries," said the officer.

"She is on the registries!" wept the merchant.

"I have found hammers, and nails," said the other of the guardsmen.

"Please, no!" cried the merchant.

"Is this where free men of Ar belong," asked the captain, "at the feet of Cos?"

"Get off your knees!" said one of the guardsmen.

The merchant could not move, but sobbed helplessly.

"Nail shut the chest," said the officer.

"I will say anything you want," said the shopkeeper, looking up piteously at the officer, "anything! I will render whatever testimony you desire. I will sign anything, anything!"

The room rang with the blows of the hammers.

"It will not be necessary," said the officer. The merchant collapsed.

The lid was now hammered shut on the chest.

The officer left the fellow on the floor of the rear room, and signaled for two of his men to pick up the chst and follow him.

He then, followed by the rest of us, including the two fellows with the chest, threaded his way through the front of the shop and to the street outside.

"Captain!" said one of the men outside, pointing to the exterior wall of the building.

There, on the wall, scratched on the stone, was a delka.

The captain cried out with rage.

"I am sure that was not there when we entered, Captain," said one of the guardsmen.

"No, it was not," said the captain.

That was true. As it might be recalled, Marcus and I had entered the shop after the captain and his men, having been on our rounds in the neighborhood.

Some men were about, but seeing the captain and his men, and Marcus and myself, hurried away, perhaps fearing that the delka might be blamed on them.

I did not doubt but what some of these folks had peeped within the shop and seen the bodies about. That would have been easy enough to do when we were in the back of the shop.

The two fellows carrying the chest put it down.

"I fear they are everywhere," said the captain.

"Who?" I asked.

"The Delta Brigade," he said.

I myself, in a paga tavern or two, some days ago, had dropped this expression, mentioning it as though it were one I had heard somewhere, and was curious to understand. I was pleased to note that it was now common currency in Ar. Such are the wings of rumors.

"You think this afternoon's attack was the work of this Delta Brigade?" I asked.

"Surely," he said.

"Who are they?" I asked.

"Dissidents, or renegades, doubtless," said the captain, "traitors to both Cos and Ar."

"I see," I said.

"I suspect veterans of the delta compaign," he said, "or scions of disaffected cities, such as Ar's Station."

"I am from Ar's Station," said Marcus.

"But you are an auxiliary," said the captain.

"True," said Marcus.

"Perhaps Marlenus of Ar has returned," I said. I thought that an excellent rumor to start.

"No," said the captain. "I do not think so. Marlenus was not, as far as we know, in the delta. I think it is more likely to be veterans of the delta, of which there are many in the city, or fellows from the north, from Ar's Station or somewhere."

"Perhaps you are right," I said. The captain was a shrewd fellow, and thusly an unlikely candidate to enlist in my efforts to initiate rumors, or at least this particular one. To be sure, even a fellow of genuine probity, one who is unlikely to nourish, reproduce, transmit, or credit a rumor in its infancy, may find himself uncritically accepting it later on, when it becomes "common knowledge," so to speak. Are we not all the victims of hearsay, even with respect to many of our most profound "truths"? Of our thousands, and hundreds of thousands, of such "truths," how many have we personally earned? How many of us can determine the distance of a planet or the structure of a molecule?

"I will have a wagon sent for the bodies," said the captain.

"Yes, Captain," I said.

The captain regarded the delka, scrawled on the wall, with anger.

"It is only a scratching, a mark," I said.

"No," he said. "It is more. It is a defiance of Cos, and of Ar!"

"Of Ar?" I asked.

"As she is today," he said.

"But perhaps not of the old Ar," I said.

"Perhaps not," he said.

"You have met men of Ar in battle?" I asked.

"Yes," he said. "And it is a mark of the old Ar, the Ar I knew in war, the Ar of spears and standards, of rides and marches, of dust and trumpets, of tarns and tharlarion, the Ar of imperialism, of glory, of valor, and pride. That is why it is so dangerous. It is a recollection of the old Ar."

"The true Ar?"

"If you wish," he said. Then he exclaimed, angrily. "They have been defeated! She is dead! She is gone! How dare they remember her?"

He looked up and down the street. It now seemed deserted. I did not doubt but what word of what had occurred had spread.

"How dare they resist?" he asked.

"There seem few here now," I said.

"They are there, somewhere," he said.

"Perhaps," I said.

"Guard yourselves," he said.

"Thank you, Captain," I said.

"They may be anywhere," he said.

"Surely there are only a few," I said, "perhaps a few madmen who cannot understand the barest essentials of the most obvious realities, political and prudential."

"They are verr," he said. "But not all of them. Some pretend to be verr. Some are sleen, disguised in the skins of verr."

"Or larls," I said, "patient, unreconciled, dangerous, capable of action."

"Cos, too, has her larls," said the captain.

"I do not doubt it," I said.

"Had I my way," he said, "we would have finished Ar. She would have been done with then, forever. There would be nothing here now but ashes and salt. Even her name would be excised from the monuments, from the documents, from the histories. It would be as though she had not been."

"It is hard for a man to be great who does not have great enemies," I said.

"And so Cos and Ar require one another, that each may be greater than they could otherwise be?" he asked.

"Perhaps," I said.

"There was no glory here," he said. "We did not win this victory in storm and fire, surmounting walls, breaching gates, winning Ar street by street, house by house. It was not we who defeated Ar. It was her putative own who betrayed her, in jealousy and intrigue, in ambition and greed. Ideas and lies defeated Ar. It was done through the sowing of confusion, the propagation of self-doubt and guilt, all suitably bedizened in the meretricious rhetorics of morality. We taught them that evil was good, and good evil, that strength was weakness, and weakness strength, that health was sickness, and sickness health. We made them distrust themselves, and taught them to believe that their most basic instincts and elemental insights, the most essential and primitive promptings of their blood, were to be repudiated in favor of self-denial and frustration, in favor of vacuous principles, used by us as weapons against them, in favor of stultifying verbalisms, to cripple and bleed them, and entrap them in our toils. And thus, betrayed by those who sought advancement in the destruction and dissolution of their own community, abetted by the well-intentioned, the simple-minded, the idealists, the fools, they put themselves at our mercy, at that of another community, one not so foolish, or not so sickened, as theirs. I saw strong men gladly setting aside their weapons. I saw citizens of Ar singing as their gates burned, as they tore down their walls with their own hands. That is no honest victory for Cos, won at the walls, at the gates, in the streets, That is not a victory of which we can be proud. That is a victory not of steel, but by poison."

"You are a warrior," I said.

"Once," he said.

He turned and looked at the shop. "When the bodies are removed," he said, "I think I shall have this shop burned."

"There are adjoining buildings," I said.

"Ah, yes," he said. "We must avoid incidents. We must keep the verr pacified, lest they learn how they are milked and shorn."

"Surely you do not believe the merchant is involved with the Delta Brigade," I said.

"No," he said. "I do not really believe that."

"And the slain men?" I asked.

"Well-known brigands," he said, "insults to the armbands they wear."

"And what report will you make of this?" I asked.

"Heroes, of course," said he, "slain by overwhelming odds."

"I see," I said.

"There is a game here," he said, "which I shall play. I have no wish to lose my post. You see, the sickness of Ar infects even her conquerors. We must pretend to believe the same lies."

"I understand," I said.

"And even if I did not make such a report I do not doubt but what it would be something to that effect which would eventually reach the tent of Myron, my polemarkos."

"He is a good officer," I said.

"Yes," said the captain. I had always heard this of Myron. To be sure, I had gathered that he had once been too much under the influence of a woman, a mere slave, who had been named Lucilina. She had been captured and was now owned by a common soldier in the retinue of Dietrich of Tarnburg. No longer was she a high slave, pampered and indulged. She was now a low slave, and among the lowest of the low, and was worked hard. She must often kneel and fear whipping. It was said, too, that in the arms of her master, well handled and mastered, she had discovered her womanhood. I doubted that Myron, for his part, would again make the mistake he had made with her. I did not doubt but what his women would now be well kept in their place, at his feet. They would kneel there, I did not doubt, in all trembling and subservience, and be in no doubt as to their collaring.

Again the captain looked angrily at the furrowed wall, the tracing of that triangle, the delka.

"Captain?" I said.

"How many do you think are in the Delta Brigade?" he asked.

"I do not know," I said. "Surely no more than a few."

"A few today may become a regiment tomorrow, and after that, who knows?"

"The merchant spoke of only two men," I reminded him.

"There had to be more than that," said the captain, "though how many it is difficult to say, perhaps ten, perhaps twelve."

"Why do you say that?" I asked.

"The victims were not civilians, not tradesmen, not potters or bakers. They were skilled swordsmen," he said.

"Perhaps then there are ten in the Delta Brigade," I said.

"I am sure there are many more," he said.

"Oh?" I said, interested.

"This sign turns up frequently in the city, and more often from day to day," he said. "It is a symbol of resistance, smeared on a wall, scratched on a flagstone, carved into a post, found inscribed on an unfolded napkin."

I had not known these things. I myself had not seen much evidence of this sort of thing. To be sure, Marcus and I usually prowled in the darkness, protected from suspicion by our armbands, as though we might be on duty. And during the day we had normal duties, guarding portals and such, or, when assigned them, rounds, usually in public areas, as today, where the inscribing of the delka would be more likely to be noticed. I suspected these delkas were mostly to be found in the alleys and the back streets of Ar.

"The scratching of the delka," I said, "might even be permitted, as an outlet for meaningless defiance, as a futile token of protest from those too helpless or weak to do more."

"I am sure you are right, for the most part," said the captain.

"Then I would not concern myself with them," I said.

"Four soldiers were found murdered this morning," said the officer, "off the Avenue of Turia. The delka was found there, too."

"I see," I said. I had certainly known nothing of this. Marcus and I, it seemed, had allies.

The officer's men, the guardsmen, looked at one another. I gathered that this was information to them, too.

"Do you wish for us to remain on duty here, my fellow and myself," I asked, "until the arrival of the wagon?"

"No," he said.

"Is there any way we may be of service?" I asked.

"We have our rounds," said the officer. He glanced at the chest on the street, outside the door of the shop.

"Yes, Captain?" I said.

"What do you think of the contents of this chest?" he asked.

"A pretty lass," I said, "though young."

"Do you think she would look well in slave silk and a collar?"

I thought about it. "Yes," I said. "But perhaps more so in a year or so."

"Did you not see how, when the lid of the chest was held open, her veil had been disarranged, that her lips and mouth might be visible?"

"It was impossible not to notice it," I said. I recalled her father had chided her about this. Such a lapse I was sure, had not been inadvertent, not on Gor, with a free woman. If it had not been overtly intentional, consciously arranged, so to speak, it had surely been covertly so, unconsciously so, a pathetic sign manifested outwardly of a dawning sexuality and an innate need whose first powerful promptings were doubtless felt even now.

"Do you think she would make a slave?" he asked.

"I assume you do not mean as a child might be a slave," I said, "carried into bondage to be trained as a mere serving girl or page, to be in effect held for true bondage later, say, to be auctioned as a pleasure object, if a female, or say, to be sent to the fields or quarries, if a male."

"No," he said.

"Yes," I said, "I suppose she is ready for the block now."

"Do you think she is on the registries?" he asked,.

"Probably," I said.

"But it does not really matter one way or another," he said, "as she is a girl of Ar."

"True," I said. Ar, and its contents, belonged to Cos.

"Do you know where the loot area is," he asked, "that in the district of Anbar?"

"Yes," I said.

"I would be obliged if you would see to the chest, and the slave," he said.

I suppose the young woman within the chest could hear our conversation. I would have supposed that she would then have pounded and wept, and scratched at the inside of the chest, begging mercy, but she did not. Slaves, those fit by nature for this elegant disposition, and whose minds and bodies crave it profoundly, and will not be happy without it, pretending that they are actually free women, commonly do such things. They are often among the most express in their protestive behaviors, the most demonstrative in their lamentations, and such, believing such things are expected of them, fearing only that they will be taken seriously. But this girl was actually very quiet, lying like a caressable, silken little urt in the chest. Indeed, for a moment, I feared there might be insufficient air in the chest and that she might have fainted, or otherwise lost consciousness. But then I noted that the chest was well ventilated, as made sense, considering it had probably been prepared to conceal her days ago, if not months ago. She had doubtless not, however, expected to have its lid nailed shut, and to find herself helplessly, nakedly, at the mercy of strong men, imprisoned within it. It interested me that she lay as quietly within her small, stout wooden prison as she did. I suspected she was trembling within it, and perhaps timidly, fearfully, trying to understand her feelings.

"My fellow and I," I said, "if you wish, will see to the chest, and the girl."

"The slave," he said.

"Yes," I said, "the slave."

"I wish you well," said the captain.

"I wish you well," I said.

He then, and his men, took their leave.

"Why did you not wish the bodies placed outside the shop?" Marcus asked of me, when the officer with his small squad had departed.

I motioned him to one side, that the girl in the chest might not overhear our conversation.

"Surely it would have been better if the bodies had been put outside," said Marcus, "that the strength of the Delta Brigade, as it is spoken of, and the effectiveness of its work, might seem displayed."

I spoke softly. "No, dear friend," I said. "Better that the carnage wrought within the shop should seem such that those of Cos feared it to be known, that they were concerned to conceal it from the public."

"Ah!" said Marcus.

"But, too," I said, "do not fear that it is not known. The shop is muchly open. The door was ajar. I am confident men have spied within and seen what lies strewn upon its tiles. And even if they have not, the bodies will presumably be removed and be seen then. And, too, if not this either, surely we may depend upon the tradesman to speak of such things."

"That the bodies were not put outside," said Marcus, "makes it seem as though Cos feared the Delta Brigade, and did not wish that the effectivenss of its work be known, and that is much more to the advantage of the Brigade."

"Yes," I said. "I think so."

"Accordingly," said Marcus, "its work is known, or likely to be known, but it is also made to seem that Cos fears the making broadcast of such intelligence."

"Precisely," I said.

"Thusly increasing the reputation of the Delta Brigade," he said.

"Yes," I said.

"Is is a form of Kaissa, is it not?" he asked.

"Of course," I said.

"Well played," he said.

"Perhaps," I said. "But it is difficult to foresee the continuations."

"I do not like such games," he said.

"You prefer a fellow at sword point, in an open field, at noon?" I asked.

"Of course," he said.

I was sympathetic with his view. The board had a thousand sides, and surfaces and dimensions, the pieces were of unknown number, and nature and value, the rules were uncertain, often you did not know whom you played, or where they were, often the moves must be made in darkness, in ignorance of your opponent's position, his pieces, his strengths, his skills, his moves.

"Perhaps I, too," I mused. Yet I had known men who enjoyed such Kaissa, the games of politics and men. My friend, Samos, of Port Kar, was one such.

"You enjoy such things," said Marcus.

"Perhaps," I said. "I am not sure." It is often easier to know others than ourselves. Perhaps that is because there is less need to tell lies about them. Few of us recognize the stranger in the shadows, who is ourself.

"I am a simple warrior," said Marcus. "Set me a formation, or a field, or a city. I think I know how to solve them, or set about the matter. Let things be clear and plain. Let me see my foe, let me meet him face to face."

"Subtlety and deception are not new weapons in the arsenal of war," I said. "They are undoubtedly as ancient as the club, the stone, the sharpened stick."

Marcus regarded me, angrily.

"Study the campaigns of Dietrich of Tarnburg," I said.

Marcus shrugged, angrily.

"He has sowed silver and harvested cities," I said.

" 'More gates are opened with gold than iron,' " he said.

"You pretend to simplicity," I said. "Yet you quote from the Diaries." These were the field diaries attributed by many to Carl Commenius, of Argentum. The reference would be clear to Marcus, a trained warrior.

"That I do not care for such games," said Marcus, "does not mean I cannot play them."

"How many are in the Delta Brigade?" I asked him.

"Two," he smiled. "We are the Delta Brigade."

"No," I said, "there are more."

He looked at me, puzzled.

"This morning," I said, "four soldiers, doubtless Cosians, were found slain in the vicinity of the Avenue of Turia. The delka was found there."

Marcus was silent.

"We have allies," I said. "Too, I have learned that the delka appears elsewhere in Ar, presumably mostly in poorer districts."

"I do not welcome unknown allies," he said.

"At least we cannot betray them under torture, nor they us."

"Am I to derive comfort from that thought?" he asked.

"Why not?" I asked.

"We cannot control them," he said.

"Nor they us," I said.

"We began this," said Marcus. "But I do not know where it will end."

"Cos will be forced to unsheath her claws."

"And then?" he asked.

"And then we do not know where it will end," I said.

"What of the Home Stone of Ar's Station?" he asked.

"Is that your only concern?" I asked.

"For all I care, traitorous Ar may be burned to the ground," he said.

"It will be again publicly displayed," I said.

"That is part of your Kaissa?" he asked.

"Yes," I said.

"You see far ahead," he said.

"No," I said. "It is a forced continuation."

"I do not understand," he said.

"Ar will have no choice," I said.

"And if the Home Stone of Ar's Station is again displayed, what then?" he asked. "It was displayed before."

"I know a fellow who can obtain it for you," I said.

"A magician?" he asked.

I smiled.

"The Delta Brigade," he asked, "all two of us?"

"I think there are more," I said.

"Enough to take the Central Cylinder?" he asked.

"Certainly not now," I said.

He looked at the delka, scratched on the exterior wall of the shop.

"You are curious as to its meaning, and its power?" I asked.

"Yes," he said.

"So, too, am I," I said.

"I am afraid," he said.

"So, too, am I," I said.

"And what of this?" asked Marcus, indicating the chest on the street, near us.

"Bring it along," I said.

"What are we going to do with it?" he asked.

"You will see," I said.

"You saw her mouth was uncoverd," he said. "She belongs with other lewd women in the loot pits of the Anbar district, awaiting their brands and collars."

"With other needful women," I said.

"She is a slave slut," he said.

"And will perhaps one day find her rightful master," I said.

"What are we going to do with her?" he asked.

"You will see," I said.

We then went to the chest. "Help me lift it," I said.

In a moment we had it in hand. It was a bit bulky to be easily carried by one man, but it was not heavy.

We felt its contents move within it.

12 The Countries Of Courage

"Put it down here," I said.

We were in a deserted alleyway, about two pasangs from the shop, rather between it and the Anbar district. It might well appear that we had been on our way to that district.

"Over here, more," I said. Marcus and I put the chest against one wall, that it might not move further in that direction. I then stepped back a bit and forcibly, with the flat of my foot, with four or five blows, kicked back the side of the chest, forcing it some inches inward, breaking it muchly from the ends, tearing it free of the nails and the lid. I delivered similar blows to the two ends of the chest, splintering it loose of nails and the back. The girl within cried out in misery. I then, with my hands, seizing it, now muchly freed, flung up the lid, revealing her within, and she cried out again, and hid her head, putting her hands over it. She lay there, terrified, among the splinters and nails, the sides and ends muchly loosened, collapsed about her. I then turned the shambles of the chest to its side, spilling her to the stones of the alley. Shuddering she was on her belly to us and crawled to my feet, pressing her lips to them.

"She desires to please, as a slave," observed Marcus.

"Do you object?" I asked.

She now pressed her lips similarly upon the feet of Marcus.

"No," he said. "She is obviously a slave, and is both comely and desirable. Too, she is of Ar, and all of the women of Ar should be slaves."

She then knelt before us, the palms of her hands on the stones, her head down to them, as well.

"Doubless she has seen slaves kneel in such a way," said Marcus.

"Probably," I said. It was a common position of slave obeisance.

"She is a slave," he said.

"She is frightened," I said.

"She is a slave," he said.

"That, too," I granted him.

"Look up, girl," said Marcus.

She looked up, frightened.

"Are you a slave?" asked Marcus.

Her lip trembled.

"She is legally free," I pointed out.

"Are you a slave?" pressed Marcus.

"Yes," she whispered.

" 'Yes', *what*?" he asked.

"Yes, *Master*," she whispered. I suspected she had used that word to men before only in her imagination, or speaking it softly to her pillow in the night.

"Legally free," he said, "but still a slave, and rightfully so?" he asked.

"Yes, Master," she said.

"Lacking only the legalities of the brand and collar?" he asked.

"Yes, Master!" she said.

"Yet she is young to be a slave," I said.

"Do you think we cannot be slaves?" she asked.

"Some men enjoy them," said Marcus, "squirming in the furs, panting, begging for more."

The girl closed her eyes, and sobbed. I wondered if she understood these things.

"She is young," I said.

"Do you scorn me for my youth?" she asked. "Do you think we do not have feelings? Do you think we are not yet capable of love, that we are not yet women? You are wrong! How little you understand us! We are young and desirable, and ready to serve!"

"You are young," I said. "Your surrender cannot be the full surrender of the mature woman, the woman experienced in life, the woman who has come to understand the barrenness of the conventions by which she is expected to abide, who has discerned the vacuity of the principles to which she is expected to mindlessly subscribe, who has learned the emptiness of the roles imposed upon her by society, roles alien to, and inimical to, the needs of her deepest self. You are not such a woman, a full, mature, knowledgeable, cognizant woman, a woman profoundly in touch with her passions and deepest self, one who has come to understand that her only hope for true happiness and fulfillment lies in obedience, love and service, one craving the collar, one yearning for a master."

"No, no, no!" she wept. "I am young, but I am a woman, and alive! Do you think that intelligence and maturity are prerogatives only of such as you! No! I am quick at my studies! I am alert! I think much! I am dutiful! I want to make a man happy, truly happy, in the fullest dimensions of his being, not a part of him, leaving the rest to hide, or shrivel and die! I cannot know my bondage if he does not learn his mastery! Why should his birthright be denied to him, and mine to me? As the master needs the slave so, too, the slave needs the master!"

I was taken aback by her words. I recalled how quietly she had lain in the box, that her veil had been disarranged when first the guardsmen, and Marcus and myself, had looked upon her. She was undoubtedly of high intelligence. Such is valued considerably, of course, in a slave. It makes them much better slaves. How much more tactful, sensitive and inventive are intelligent slaves! Indeed, the intelligence of some slaves blossoms in bondage, seemingly at last finding the apt environment for its flowering. To be sure, when a girl knows she may feel the lash for a mistake, she tends to become considerably more alert.

"What have we here," asked Marcus, "a little scribe?"

"I am no stranger to scrolls," she said.

"You are still young," I said.

"That does not mean I cannot feel," she said. "That does not mean I am stupid."

I had no doubt that in time she would make an excellent slave. Indeed, I could well imagine her, even now, serving in a house, deferentially, with belled ankles.

"I heard one speaking earlier," she said, "of the loot area in the district of Anbar."

"Can you not wait to be shackled and thrown into the loot pits with other women, to await the collar and brand?" inquired Marcus.

"Take me there!" she demanded.

Instantly, appropriately, he lashed her head to the side with the back of his right hand.

She was struck to the ground with the force of the blow and at a snapping of his fingers, and his gesture, she struggled again to her knees before us, her mouth bloody. Her eyes were wide. It was perhaps the first time she had been cuffed.

Marcus glared down at her. He did not have much patience with slaves. Phoebe had often learned that to her dismay. To be sure, she was scarcely ever struck or beaten now. She had become a superb slave in the past few months, under Marcus' tutelage.

"Forgive me, Master," she said. "I was not respectful. It was appropriate that I be cuffed."

In her eyes there were awe and admiration for Marcus. She saw that he would not hesitate to impose discipline upon her.

"It is common," I said, "for a slave to request permission to speak."

"Forgive me, Master," she said, putting down her head.

"You said you were no stranger to scrolls," I said.

"To some, Master," she said. "I did not mean to be arrogant. If I have not been pleasing, lash me."

"Have you read," I asked, "the *Manuals of the Pens of Mira, Leonora's Compendium*, the *Songs of Dina*, or Hargon's *The Nature and Arts of the Female Slave*?"

"No, Master," she said, eagerly. Such texts, and numerous others, like them, are sometimes utilized in a girl's training, particularly by professional slavers. Sometimes they are read aloud in training sessions by a scribe, a whip master in attendance. Most girls are eager to acquire such knowledge. Indeed, they often ply one another for secrets of love, makeup, costuming, perfuming, dance, and such, as each wishes to be as perfect for her master as it lies within her power to be. Also, of course, such diligence is prudential on her part. She will be lashed if she is not pleasing. Also, her very life, literally, is in his hands. Perhaps a word is in order pertaining to the *Songs of Dina*. Some free women claim that this book, which is supposedly written by Dina, "a slave," which continues to appear in various editions and revisions, because of its intelligence and sensitivity, is actually, and must be, written by a free woman. I suspect, on the other hand, that it is truly by a slave, as is claimed on the title page. There are two reasons for this. First, 'Dina' is a common slave name, often given to girls with the "Dina" brand, which is a small roselike brand. Second, the nature of the songs themselves. No free woman could have sung of chains and love, and the lash, and the glory of masters as she. Those are songs which, in my opinion, could be written only by a woman who knew what it was to be at a man's slave ring. As to the matter of the poetess' intelligence and sensitivity, I surely grant them to the free women, but maintain that such are entirely possible in a slave, and even more to expected in her than in them. I suspect their position may even be inconsistent. When a woman is enslaved, for example, surely they do not suppose that her intelligence and sensitivity disappear. Surely they would not expect theirs to do so, if they had them. No, she still has them. Also, it has been my personal experience, for what it is worth, that slaves are almost always more intelligent and sensitive than free women, who often, at least until taken in hand, tend to be ignorant, smug, vain and stupid. Also, it might be noted that many women are enslaved not simply because it is convenient to do so, the ropes are handy, so to speak, or because they are beautiful of face and figure, but actually *because* of their intelligence and sensitivity, qualities which appeal to many Gorean men. Indeed, such qualities commonly raise a girl's price. Also, as I have suggested, the intelligence and sensitivity of many women actually tends to blossom in bondage, finding within it the apt environment for its expression, for its flowering. This may have to do with such matters as the release of inhibitions, happiness, fulfillment, and such. I do not know.

"What of the *Prition* of Clearchus of Cos?" I asked.

"A Cosian?" said Marcus.

"Yes," I said.

"That will not be found in Ar," he said.

"It used to be," I said, "at least before the war."

"Yes, Master," she beamed. "I have read it!"

"You, a free girl, have read it?" I asked. To be sure, the book is a classic.

"Yes, Master!" she smiled.

"Does your father know you have read it?" I asked.

"No, Master," she said.

"What do you suppose he would do to you, if he found out?" I asked.

"I think he would sell me, Master," she said.

"And appropriately," I said.

"Yes, Master," she smiled.

"Stand," I said. "Turn about. Cross your wrists behind you."

"Yes, Master!" she said, eagerly, complying.

"Oh!" she said, bound.

"Turn about," I said.

Swiftly she did so, and looked shyly up at me. She tested the fiber on her wrists, subtly, attempting to do so inconspicuously, trying its snugness and strength, its effectiveness. She put down her head and suddenly, inadvertently, shuddered with pleasure. I had used capture knots. She knew herself helpless. I supposed it was the first time she had ever been bound.

"May I speak?" she asked.

"Yes," I said.

"I am tied as a slave is tied, am I not?" she asked.

"As slaves are sometimes tied," I said.

This comprehension was sudenly reflected, or exhibited, in her entire body, in fear, and desire and pleasure, she flexing her knees, twisting, her shoulders moving, and then, again, she stood before me, looking up at me, but now trembling.

"It is appropriate is it not?" I asked.

"Yes, Master," she said.

I regarded her.

She looked away.

She was trying to deal with her helplessness, to understand it, and its import. I wondered what her feelings would have been had she been a legal slave, and known herself totally at our mercy.

"Will it be necessary to leash you?" I asked.

"No," she said.

I then leashed her. "Now you will not run away," I said.

"I will not run away!" she said.

"I know," I said. I looped the long end of the leash three times. She looked at the swinging loops, apprehensively. Most slave leashes are long enough to serve not only as a leash but also as a lash. The length, too, permits them to facilitate a binding, both of hand and foot. A common technique is to run the leash through a slave ring and then complete the tie as one pleases, simply or complexly. Many leashes, such as the one I had just put on the girl, are cored with wire. This prevents them from being chewed through.

"Tarry here a moment," I said to Marcus. To the girl I said, "Precede me."

She went ahead of me some paces down the alley before I stopped her. "Do not turn about," I said.

I then turned back to face Marcus. I pointed to the remains of the chest and touched the knife at my side.

He nodded and drew his knife. On the lid of the chest he carved a delka, and then set the lid against the remains of the chest, that the sign might be prominently displayed. As we were not in the officer's chain of command, he in charge of the guardsmen of Ar whom we had earlier encountered, I did not think he would be likely to follow up the matter of the girl's disposition. He would presumably take it for granted, that she might even now be in the loot pits of the district of Anbar, awaiting the technicalities of her enslavement. Had he been interested in the matter he would doubtless have seen to it himself, or had his men see to it. Perhaps, on the other hand, he did not trust them, as they were of Ar. I did not know. If an investigation were initiated, which seemed to me unlikely, as many women were delivered on one pretext or another to the loot pits, and there would not be likely to be much interest in any particular one of them, Marcus and I could always claim that she had come into the power of the Delta Brigade, and we had thought it best not to gainsay their will in the matter, and indeed, I suppose, in a sense, that was true, as Marcus and I were, or were of, as it seemed better to put it now, given the most recent information at our disposal, the Delta Brigade. Too, even if the matter were not persued further, there would now be at least one one more delka in Ar.

In a few moments we were out on the streets. Even though such sights were not rare in Ar, in the past months, a free woman, leashed, in the custody of guardsmen or auxiliaries, presumably having been appropriated for levies, or perhaps merely having been subjected to irrevocable, unappealable seizure at an officer's whim, yet men turned to regard her as we passed. In spite of her youth she was well formed. In four or five years I had no doubt she would constitute an extraordinarily luscious love bundle helplessly responding in a master's arms. A fellow made a quick noise with his mouth as he passed her. She lifted her head, startled, in the leash collar. The meaning of the sound would be unmistakable, even to a girl, signifying as it did the eagerness and relish which the mere sight of her inspired in him. Her face was soft and lovely, gently rounded. Her hair was long and dark.

"She moves well," commented Marcus.

"Yes," I said.

"I think she has just begun to sense how men might view her," mused Marcus.

"I think so," I said.

"It is interesting," he said, "when a woman first begins to sense her desirability."

"True," I said.

"And hers is such that a price can be put on it," he said.

"Yes," I said. Her desirability was so exciting that it could only be that of a slave.

"Look at her," he said.

"Yes," I said.

"She is ready for the block now."

"Perhaps," I said.

"I am sure she would perform well," said Marcus. "And if she were reluctant to do so, or hesitated for a moment, I am sure any lingering scruples would be promptly dissipated by the auctioneer's whip."

"Undoubtedly," I said. I had seen such transformations take place many times at the sales. It is not so much, I think, that the lash, in such a situation, as a punishment, changes the woman's behavior, that she obeys because she does not wish to be whipped, but rather that the whip convinces her that she is now free to be the sensuous, sexual, marvelous creature which she is in herself and has always desired to be. In this sense the whip does not oppress the woman but rather liberates her to be herself, wild, uninhibited, free in a sense, even though she may be bound in chains, and sexual. To be sure, the whip is also used to punish women, and they do fear it, and mightily, for such a reason. Sometimes it is used, too, of course, merely to remind them of what they are, slaves.

"How graceful she is," he commented.

"Yes," I said.

I suspected that a perceptive master might have a woman such as she trained in slave dance, that she might please him also in this way. I could imagine her, even now, in the floor movements of slave dance. I wiped sweat from my brow.

How beautifully walked the girl, how conscious now, how proud, how pleased, she seemed, in the abundance of her beauty, her desirability and power. How different she was from many of the free women we had seen earlier being led through the streets, piteous, overfed, stumbling creatures following behind on their leashes, their heads down, loudly bemoaning their fate. But even those, I suspected, given diet, exercise and training, could, in time, be transformed into dreams of pleasure.

"Slave!" hissed a free woman to the girl. Then she was behind us. Her voice had been fraught with hatred.

"She thinks you are a slave," I said.

"Yes," laughed the girl, delightedly.

For some reason free women hate female slaves. They are often quite cruel even to those whom they themselves own. I am not certain of the explanation of this seemingly unreasoning, inexplicable hatred. Perhaps they hate the slave for her beauty, for her joy, her truth, her perfections, her desirability, her happiness. At the root of their hatred, perhaps, lies their own unhappiness and lack of fulfillment, their envy of the slave, joyful in her rightful place in nature. In any event, this attack on the part of the free woman, which happily had been only verbal, as they often are not, and the abused slave in any event dare not protest or object, as they are at the mercy of free persons, was in its way a profound compliment. So beautiful and exciting was the girl that the woman had naturally assumed she was that most marvelous, helplsss, lovely and degraded of objects, the female slave.

"Turn left here," I said to the girl.

"Masters?" she asked, stopping.

"Left," I said. As she was free I did not demur to repeat a command. Also, punishment for having to repeat a command is always at the option of the master. For example, a command might not be clearly heard, or might not be clear in itself, or might appear inconsistent with the master's presumed intentions. Whether punishment is in order or not is then a matter for judgment on the master's part. In this case, of course, as we were on Tarngate, at Lorna, she had every reason to question my direction.

"Masters," said the girl, "may I speak?"

"Yes," I said.

"This is not the way to the district of Anbar," she said. Perhaps she thought we were strangers, brought in as auxiliaries, and did not know the city. To be sure, there were many areas in Ar which I did not know.

"That is known to me," I said.

"Where are we going!" she asked.

"We are taking you home," I said.

"No!" she cried, aghast.

I regarded her.

"You are to take me to the loot area in the district of Anbar!" she said. "When I was within the chest I heard it so said!"

"You are going home," I said.

"We could sell her," said Marcus.

"Yes!" cried the girl. "Sell me!"

"No," I said. "You are going home."

She tried to back away but in an instant was stopped, the inside of the leash collar tight against the back of her neck. "Perhaps you have forgotten that you are leashed, female," I said.

She approached me and fell to her knees before me, the leash looping up to my hand. She put her head to the stones, at my feet. I think she then, better than before, understood her helplessness, and the meaning of the leash, and why I had put it on her.

"I thought you said you would not run away," I said.

She lifted her head. "I cannot run away," she said. "I am leashed!"

"Yes," I said.

"I am in your power," she said. "You can do with me as you wish. I beg to be taken to the loot pits. I beg to be taken there, or sold!"

"No," I said.

"Keep me then for yourselves!" she said, looking from me to Marcus, and back again.

"No," I said.

"Surely you do not doubt that I am a slave, and need to be a slave!" she wept.

"I do not doubt that," I said. "But I think it is a bit early to harvest you."

"Surely that is a matter of opinion," said Marcus.

"True," I granted him.

"Surely you have seen such slips of girls chained in the loot lines of conquered cities," he said.

"Yes," I admitted.

"They do not discriminate against them there, do they?" he said.

"No," I said.

"And surely you have been pleasured in various taverns by such," he said.

"Yes," I said.

"And they are excellent in their way, are they not?" he asked.

"Yes," I said. "Even though they do not yet have the full perfections of their femaleness upon them."

"What scruple then," asked he, "gives you pause?"

"She is rather young," I said. "Also we owe something to her father."

"What is that?" he asked.

"He is a brave man," I said.

" 'Brave'?" asked Marcus. "Did you not observe his wringing of hands, his wailing unmanliness, his terror, his obsequiousness, not see to to what extent he would go to accomodate himself to Cosian will?"

"It is true, Masters," said the girl, "if I may speak, as I gather I may, as you seem to insist upon treating me as a free woman. My father is a negligible coward."

"No," I said. "He is a brave man."

"I believe I know him better than you," she said.

"Surely Marcus," I said, "you would not begrudge the fellow

a certain dismay over the destruction of his shop and the grievous impairment of his means of livelihood."

"His reaction was excessive," said Marcus.

"Exaggerated, you think?"

"If you wish," he said.

"For the benefit of whom, do you suppose?" I asked.

"I do not understand," said Marcus.

"What would you have done?" I asked.

"I would have scorned the Cosian openly," said Marcus, "or set upon him, and the others, with my sword."

"Are you a tradesman?" I asked.

"No," said he. "I am of the Scarlet Caste."

"And what if you were a tradesman?"

"I?" he asked, angrily.

"Do you think that in castes other than your own there are no men?"

"I would have scorned them even if I were a confectioner," said Marcus.

"And hurled sweets at them?"

"Be serious," said he, irritably.

"And presumably, by now," I said, "You would have been beaten, or maimed or slain, and your property confiscated. At the least you would have been entered on one of the lists of suspicion, your movements subject to surveillance, your actions the objects of reports."

"This is more of your Kaissa," said he, distastefully.

"As a warrior," said I, "surely you are aware of the virtues of concealment, of subterfuge."

"No," said the girl. "My father is a coward. I know him."

"You have mistaken concern for cowardice," I said.

"My father does not understand me," she said.

"No fathers understand their daughters," I said. "They only love them."

"You saw to what an extent he would go to accomodate himself to Cosian will," said Marcus.

"To protect his daughter," I said. "Surely you, in his place, in his helplessness, lacking your sword, your skills, would have done as much, or more."

"I do not want his protection," said the girl. "He keeps me from myself!"

"He sees you in terms of one ideal," I said, "while it is actually another, one more profound, which you manifest."

"I do not want to go back to him," she said.

"He loves you," I said.

"I despise him!" she said.

"It is true that sometimes strangers understand a woman better than those closest to her, and see what she is, and needs. They see her more directly, more as herself, and less through their own distorting lenses, lenses they themselves have ground, lenses which would show her not as she is but as they require her to be."

"I hate him!" she said.

"And love him," I said. "You will always love him."

"He is a coward!" she cried.

"No," I said.

"I know him!" she said.

"You do not," I said.

"Surely you do not claim he is a brave man?" said Marcus.

"He did not identify us," I said.

"He did not recognize us," said Marcus.

"But he did," I said.

Marcus looked at me, angrily.

"Yes," I said.

"Our features were concealed," said Marcus.

"Do you think he would not recognize our builds," I asked, "our clothing, our sandals? Do you think this would be so hard to do, within moments of having seen us before?"

"If you feared this," he asked, "why did you reenter the shop?"

"Because of the patrol," I said. "I feared they might kill him, in vengeance for the carnage wrought in the shop. Too, we were in the vicinity, and it might seem unusual, surely, if we did not add our presence to the investigation. That might have attracted comment and inquiry, had it been noticed. Too, who knows, perhaps there could be more swordplay within."

"But you did not attack the patrol," he said.

"They were, as it turned out," I said, "mostly lads of Ar, and thusly it would have been not only impolitic but, in my opinion, actually objectionable to have done so. After all, we are, in our way, acting in support of Ar, the old Ar, the true Ar, and the officer, though obviously a Cosian sleen, was not a bad fellow. We cannot blame him for being angry that the carnage was wrought within his precinct, almost under his nose, and he could, at least, recognize, as her father could not, the true nature of this little slave slut before us."

The girl put down her head.

"You think the tradesman recognized us?" asked Marcus.

"Yes," I said.

"How do you know?" he asked.

"I saw it, in a flash, at first, in his eyes," I said.

"But he did not betray us."

"No," I said.

"He might have won much favor with Cos had he done so," said Marcus.

"Undoubtedly," I said.

"He is a brave man," said Marcus.

"And only a tradesman," I reminded him.

"There are brave men in all castes," smiled Marcus.

"Look," I said, pointing to a wall on Lorna, near where we stood. I had not seen it before. "The delka," I said.

"We did not put it there," said Marcus.

"And Lorna is a muchly frequented street," I said.

"Interesting," said he.

"Yes," I said.

I looked down at the kneeling, leashed girl.

"I want to be forced to fear, and serve, and yield totally to my master," she said.

"And undoubtedly in time it will be so," I told her.

"I am not yet ready, you think?" she said.

"No," I said.

"Perhaps in a day or or two," grumbled Marcus.

"Why will you return me to my father?" she asked.

"Because you are young," I said.

"And?" she asked, skeptically.

"Because we owe your father something," I said.

"And you owe me nothing?" she said.

"No," I said. "We owe you nothing." Then I added, "Nothing is owed a slave."

"Yes, Master," she said.

"On your feet," I said.

"I will get my collar!" she said. "If necessary I will slacken my veil. I will lift my robes in ascending a curb, that my ankles may be glimpsed. I will dare to walk the remote districts, and to tread high bridges!"

"Must a command be repeated?" I asked.

"No, Master," she said, quickly, rising.

"I will get my collar!" she repeated.

"I wonder if you will be as eager to wear it," I said, "when it is locked on your throat and you cannot remove it, when you find that you are truly a helpless slave."

She turned white.

"I will try to serve my master well," she whispered.

"Let us hope he is a kind one," I said.

She looked at me, frightened.

"You could be bought by anyone," I said.

"Yes, Master," she whispered.

"Precede us," I said.

She went left, as I had directed, on Lorna.

"Walk well," I cautioned her.

"Yes, Master," she said.

"Surely it is an error to let such a lovely slut go free," said Marcus.

"One as attractive as she will probably not be permitted to go free for long," I said.

We would keep to the main streets for a time. It would attract more attention, I feared, to march our captive between buildings, through backways and alleys, as though we wished to hide her. As it was, she was, in her way, well disguised, as her clothing could not be recognized nor, as she would customarily, at her age, be veiled, her face. When we reached the vicinity of the shop I would take her around the back, to conceal her delivery. In the meantime I thought it would do the exciting little chit good to be marched naked through the streets. Too, it was not unpleasant to walk behind her.

In time we had come to the vicinity of the shop and I directed her to the alley behind it.

We paused before the rear door of the shop.

I took up some of the slack in the leash and she turned and faced me, defiantly.

"So I am rejected as a female," she said, "and you return me here?"

I handed the leash to Marcus.

I turned her about and freed her hands. The leash was still on her neck.

"Do you think I am not beautiful enough, or intelligent enough," she said, angrily, not facing me, "to be a slave?"

"Oh!" she gasped, suddenly turned about, rudely, forcibly, by me, and held helplessly before me, by the upper arms. She was frightened. "You're hurting me," she whispered. "Oh!" she said, wincing, as I tightened my grip. She knew herself helpless. "Yes, Master," she suddeny breathed, her eyes closed. I saw that she understood masculine power, and would respond well to it.

I then, reluctantly, with some force of will, removed my hands from her.

"You are both beautiful enough and intelligent enough to be a slave," I said.

She looked at me. The prints of my grip lingered on her arms.

"Yes," I assured her.

"Then do not bring me back here," she whispered. "Take me to the loot pits, or keep me, or sell me, but do not bring me back here. No longer is this my home. My home I now know is in my master's house, or, if he will have it so, in his kennels."

I reguarded her.

"Shall I knock?" asked Marcus.

I looked at the girl. She looked well, leashed.

"Yes," I said.

"If it were not for what you owed my father," she asked, "would you have brought me here?"

I considered the matter, and regarded her. "No," I said.

She smiled, through her tears, almost defiantly.

I suddenly seized her by the hair, and twisted her head back, and regarded her, her lovely throat and face. "No," I said.

"Then I am beautiful enough and intelligent enough to be a slave," she said.

"Yes," I said.

She sobbed.

"Beauty and intelligence are all well and good," I said, "but the best slave is she who loves most deeply."

"My master will be all to me," she said. I regarded her. She would never be truly happy until she was in her place, at a man's feet.

"Someone is coming," said Marcus.

I released her.

"So it is all the will of men?" she said, through her tears. "All the debts, all the owing, all the payments? And nothing is owed to me?"

"No," I said. "Nothing is owed to you. You are a slave."

"Yes, Master!" she said.

We heard a fumbling with the bolts and chains on the door, and a lifting of the two bars. Gorean doors are often firmly secured.

"Remove the leash," I said to Marcus. In a moment he had freed her neck of it.

"Kneel here," I said to the girl, "head down, and cover yourself."

"Yes, Master," she whispered.

The door opened.

"Hurry inside," said the tradesman to the girl. She rose up and sped within, covering herself as she could. She turned once, inside the threshold, cast a wild glance at Marcus and myself, and hurried further within.

"I have been waiting for you," said the tradesman.

"How did you know we would return?" asked Marcus.

"You are men of honor," he said.

"I think it would be well," I said, "if you changed your name, and set up your business elsewhere."

"I have already considered the arrangements" he said.

We heard the girl cry out, startled inside.

"They have not yet come for the bodies," said the tradesman.

"They are sending a wagon," I said. "Doubtless it will not arrive until after dark." The girl, of course, would have only a very imperfect idea of what had occurred, as her father had doubtless hurried her to the chest upon the entry of the brigands. The details of the afternoon, however, would presumably be made clear to her by her father. He too, would presumably be interested in her afternoon. I suspected that her account to him would not be accurate or, at least, complete, in all respects.

Marcus and I turned to go.

"Warriors," said he.

We again faced him.

"My thanks," said he.

"It is nothing," I said.

"Warriors!" said he.

"Yes?" I said.

"Glory to the Delta Brigade," he whispered.

"Glory to Ar," I said.

"Yes, to Ar!" he said, though naught but a simple tradesman.

"Glory, too, to Ar's Station," said Marcus, angrily.

"As you say," said the tradesman, puzzled. "Glory, too, then, to Ar's Station!"

We then took our leave. It was time to report back to our headquarters, after which we would return to our quarters in the Metellan district.

"He does not even know that his daughter is a slave," said Marcus.

"She is legally free," I reminded him.

"A mere technicality," he said.

"It is not a mere technicality to those who find themselves in legal bondage," I said.

"I suppose not," he granted me.

"Of course not," I said.

"But she is a slave anyway," he said.

"Yes," I said.

"Do you think he knows?" he asked.

"I do not know," I said.

"But she knows," he said

"Obviously," I said.

13 A Difference Seems Afoot In Ar

"There is another delka," I said to Marcus.

"Bold that it should be in such a place," said Marcus.

Marcus and I, some days after the incident of the shop, were strolling on the Avenue of the Central Cylinder, which is, I suppose, in a sense, the major thoroughfare in Ar. It is at any rate her most famous, if not busiest, avenue, and it gives access to the park of the Central Cylinder, which edifice is itself, of course, located within the park of that name. It is a long, shaded, wide, elegant avenue, with expensive shops and fountains.

"A barracks was burned last night," said Marcus. "I heard that."

"If it is true," I said, "I do not think it will be found on the public boards."

"Does there not seem a new spirit in Ar?" he asked.

"It seems quiet here," I said.

"Nonetheless," he said. "Things are different."

"Perhaps," I said.

"There, listen!" said Marcus.

We turned to look at the street. Approaching, singing, was a group of youths, in rows, a sports team, marching together. Their colors were of both Ar and Cos. Such teams, drawn from various parts of the city, competed in various games, in hurling the stone, in hurling the thonged javelin, both for distance and accuracy, in races of various sorts, in jumping, in wrestling, and such. There were meets, and local championships, with awards, such as fillets of the wool of the bounding hurt, dyed different colors, and for champions, crowns woven of the leaves of the mighty Tur tree. Eventually various teams, in their respective age brackets, would become city champions. Such sports as these were familiar to Goreans, and had for years been privately practiced at numerous *palestrae* throughout the city. Indeed, such *palestrae*, upon occasion, would compete with one another.

"That is different," said Marcus.

"There used to be such teams," I said.

"They have been revived," said Marcus.

"You see in this something of significance?" I asked.

"Of course," he said. "Why would Cos revive such things?"

"To help them rule?" I asked. "To appear noble, well disposed, benevolent? To give the public baubles and toys, items of interest with which to beguile themselves? To create diversions, to distract Ar's attention from her defeat and sorry state?"

"They did not do this before," he said. "Why just now?"

We watched the youths as they passed us and continued on, down the street.

"Why?" I asked.

"To counteract the Delta Brigade," he said. "To lessen its influence!"

"Cos does not even know we exist," I said.

"The Ubara knows," he said, "and Seremides, and the Polemarkos."

"I think you are mad," I said.

"This time," he said, "I think my Kaissa is more subtle than yours."

"I should like to think so," I said.

"What of the new art center?" he said.

"What of it?" I asked.

"That is the same thing," he said.

I laughed.

"No," he said. "I am serious! That is the same thing, but for the intellectuals, the scribes, the high castes!"

"And will they bring back the marbles from Cos for the art center?" I asked.

"I am serious, Tarl," he said.

"Perhaps you are right," I said. "I hope so."

"I tell you things are changing in Ar now," he said. "They are becoming different."

"Perhaps," I said.

"The Initiates do not seem as welcome in the streets now," he said. "Men avoid them. Even some women avoid them. Some even demand they remain in their temples where they belong, away from honest, healthy folk."

"Interesting," I said.

"Now they often ring their bells and swing their censers to deserted streets," said Marcus. "In vain they chant their litanies to indifferent walls."

"I am sure it is not so bad as all that," I said.

"Are you so fond of the unproductive, parasitic caste?" he asked.

"I do not think much about them," I said.

"Surely you regret the minds they have stunted and spoiled," he said.

"If there are any such, of course," I said.

"They prey on credulity, they exploit fear, they purvey superstition," he said.

"It is their way of making a living," I said.

Marcus grunted angrily.

"And doubtless many of them, or at least the simpler ones, do not even understand what they are doing. Thus it is hard to blame them, unless, say, for stupidity, or a failure to undertake inquiries or, if undertaking them, a failure to pursue them in an objective manner."

Agan Marcus made an angry noise. He was one of those fellows who had not yet wearied of denouncing hypocrisy and fraud. He did not yet see the roll which such things served in the complex tapestry of life. What if some folks required lies, as the price of mental security? Should they be nonetheless denied their comforts, robbed of their illusions? Is their happiness worth less than that of others? Is it not better to tell them, if they are capable of no more, that the illusions are reality, that the lies are truth? If many desired such things, and cried out for them, is it any wonder that fellows would be found, perhaps even from noble motives, to sell them such wares, keeping the truth to themselves, as their burden and secret? I pondered the matter. I knew, as Marcus did not, of many civilizations which were unnatural, which had taken wrong paths, which were founded on myths and lies. Perhaps that is why Marcus dispproved so sternly of the Initiates. To him, they seemed anomalous in the world he knew, pointless, dangerous and pathological. In the end few things are real, perhaps the weight and glitter of gold, the movement and nature of weapons, a slave at one's feet, and, too, perhaps in spite of all, if we will have it so, defiant, honor, responsibility, courage, discipline, such things, such baubles, such treasures.

"Do you believe in Priest-Kings?" asked Marcus.

"Certainly," I said.

"I do not," he said.

"As you will," I said.

"But how are we to explain the Weapons Laws, the Flame Death?" he asked.

"That would seem to be your problem, not mine," I said, "as I accept their existence."

"Something exists," he said, "but they are not Priest-Kings."

"That is an interesting thought," I said.

"It is only that they possess the power of Priest-Kings!" he said.

"That is a second interesting thought," I said. "But if they posess the power of Priest-Kings, why not call them Priest-Kings?"

"Do you think they would mind, if I did not?" he asked, somewhat apprehensively.

"Probably not," I said. Indeed, provided men kept their laws the Priest-Kings were content to let them do much what they wished. The major concern of Priest-Kings with men, it seemed, was to have as little to do with them as possible. That had always seemed to me understandable.

"But what is the relation of the Initiates to the Priest-Kings, if there are such?" he asked.

"One which is rather remote, I suspect," I said, "if it exists at all."

"You do not think the Priest-Kings are on intimate terms with the Initiates, do you?"

"Would you wish to be on intimate terms with an Initiate?" I asked.

"Certainly not," he said.

"There you are," I said.

"Look at that fellow," said Marcus, indicating a baker striding by. The fellow fixed a fearless gaze upon us.

"He is only one man," I said.

"There is something different in Ar these days," he said.

"He is only one man," I said.

"Who walks proudly," said Marcus.

"He will not walk so proudly if he is beaten by a Cosian patrol," I said.

"In any event," said Marcus, "the power of the Initiates is certainly less now than before in the city."

"At least for the time," I said.

" 'For the time'?" he asked.

"If men should become again confused, and fearful, and lose confidence in themselves, if they should again begin to whine, and to beg for authority and reassurance," I said, "the white robes will again appear in the streets."

"Initiates are not needed for such a purpose," he said.

"True," I said. It could be a caste, the state, a leader, many things.

"The Initiates might have provided a core of resistance to Cos," he said.

"Cos saw to it, with offerings, and hetacombs, and such, that they would not do so."

"So they preached their passivity, their resignation?"

"Of course," I said. "But reduce their offerings, threaten their coffers, imperil their power, and it will not be long before they locate their patriotism."

"Cos is very clever," said Marcus.

"Clearly," I said.

"I hate Initiates," he said.

"I had gathered that," I admitted.

"I despise them" he said.

"Perhaps it is merely that you find yourself reluctant to rejoice in dishonesty, and to celebrate blatant fraud and hypocrisy," I said.

"Do you think it could be so easily explained?" he asked.

"Possibly," I said.

"I do have my limitations," he said.

"We all do," I said.

"And yet," he said, "the world is very mysterious."

"True," I said.

"What is its nature?" he asked.

"I am sure I do not know," I said.

He suddenly struck his fist into the palm of his hand. It must have stung. A fellow turned about, looking at him, and then continued on his way. "But it is here I am," he exclaimed, looking about himself, at the street, the avenue, the buildings, the trees, the fountains, the sky. "And it is here I will live!"

"That seems to me wise," I said.

"I have enjoyed this conversation, Tarl," he said. "It has meant a great deal to me."

"I haven't understood it in the least," I said.

"Some folks are so shallow," he said.

"But perhaps you are right," I said. "Perhaps things are different in Ar."

"Certainly!" he said, observing her.

"Hold, female!" said I.

The slave stopped, apprehensively.

"And surely she is not the first such you have seen of late," he said.

"No," I said. "Do not kneel," I told her. I wished the better to consider her legs.

Marcus and I walked about her.

"Consider the brevity of her tunic," he said, "its cleavage, its sleevelessness, the slashes at the hem of the skirt.

"Yes," I said.

The girl blushed crimson.

"This is a sign," he said, 'that the virility of the men of Ar is reviving."

"Yes," I said.

"And surely you have not failed to notice that in the last few days many slaves, many, indeed, are scantier garmented than before," he said.

"Yes," I said.

"I think it is clear that the men of Ar are beginning to recollect their manhood," he said. "They becoming more dangerous."

"Yes," I said.

Several weeks ago in Ar there had been some hints of an attempt on the part of the Ubarate, as a social-control procedure, to facilitate its governance, a venture doubtless emanating from Cos, which had reason to fear an alert, healthy foe, to reduce the vitality and virility of the men of Ar, to further crush and depress them. This was to be done under the initial guise of sumptuary laws, ostensibly to limit the adornment and display of slaves, as though there could be much of that sort of thing in the defeated city. This was to be followed by legislation encouraging, and then apparently to later require, more modest garmenture for slaves. There were even suggestions of attempting to regulate the relationships obtaining between masters and slaves. There was some talk of greater "respect" for slaves, that they might be permitted to drink from the higher bowls at the public fountains, even the insanity that one might not be able to make use of them without their permission, thus turning the master into a slave's slave. Naturally the motivation of this, putting aside the standard camouflage of moralistic prose which may be conveniently invoked for any purpose whatsoever, even those most antithetical to nature, health, reason, truth and life, was no concern for slaves but rather a desire to diminish the men of Ar, to make them easier to manage and exploit. Naturally they were expected to accept their own castration, so to speak, as a cause for rejoicing, as a long-overdue improvement of their condition. How glorious things were to be, once men had succeeded in achieving their own destruction. On the other hand the first straws testing the winds of Ar, cast in the streets, in the baths, in the taverns and markets, had been blown back with such fierceness that these castrative proposals had been almost immediately withdrawn. Indeed, a small announcement had even appeared on the boards, in the name of Ubara herself, that slave girls should obey their masters and try to be pleasing to them. Revolution, I do not doubt, would have occurred in the city. The men of Ar would have died rather than give up at least the retained semblance of their manhood. They had experienced the dominance, the mastery. This, once tasted, is never relinquished. The mistake of the Central Cylinder in this case, of course, was in attempting to impose such reductionism on adult males, even defeataed ones, who actually understood what was involved. The best prospects for the success of such policies are to implement them among men who have never tasted the mastery or, ideally, on innocent children who, if the programs are successful, will never taste them. Putatively this might be accomplished in virture of extensive conditioning programs aimed at demasculinization, programs which, if successful, will lead the child to suspect and fear himself, to experience shame and guilt at the very promptings of his own body and nature. It is a question, of course, as to the feasibility of these distortions, and the long-range consequences of them, if they prove feasible. Irreparable damage would result to the gene pool and the human race might actually, interestingly, eventually, for lack of will and joy, cease to thrive, and perhaps later become extinct. But then perhaps that is just as well, for if the human being cannot be a human being, why should it be anything else? Indeed, there is more than one way for a race to become extinct. The prehistoric wolf hunts now only in the corridors of the past. The poodle survives. Does the poodle remember? Does the wolf live in the poodle yet? I do not know. Would it not be interesting if the wolf were not dead but sleeping, and returned. Does this fear disturb the sleep of sheep?

"Kneel," I said to the female, "now."

Swiftly she knelt.

"You are pretty," I said.

"Thank you, Master," she said, frightened.

"Head to the pavement," I said, "palms on it."

She complied, losing no time. She looked well, in this position of obeisance.

"You seem fulfilled," I said.

"My master handles me well," she said.

"What would occur if you were not pleasing?" I asked.

"I would be beaten," she said.

"Stand," I said.

"Yes, Master," she said.

"Put your head back, your hands clasped behind it," I said.

"Oh!" she said.

"She is in the iron belt," I said to Marcus.

"Excellent," he said. This, too, in its way, was a sign that manhood, or the suspicion of it, might be reasserting itself in the streets of Ar, that masters, or some of them at least, would no longer take for granted the safety of their girls in the streets. Naturally self-pride and health stimulates sexual vitality. Contrariwise, of course, as sexual vitality is stunted and crippled, so, too, will be masculine pride and health. One cannot poison a part of an animal without poisoning the whole animal.

"Speed off!" I said.

The girl sped away.

"I envy the fellow his slave," said Marcus.

"And he would probably envy you yours," I said.

"I would not trade Phoebe for her," he said.

"And he might not trade her for Phoebe," I smiled.

"Perhaps not," he said.

I wondered if a man could be a man without a slave. I supposed that he might be a strong fellow, and a good fighter, and such, without a slave. Similarly, one might have lived, I supposed, without having eaten meat, without having heard music. I wondered if a woman knew what it was to be a woman without ever having had a master. It did not seem to me likely.

"Surely Cos will take note of these changes in Ar," I said.

"I have heard that there are fights among youth in Ar," he said, "that the gangs of youths called "Cosians" are now set upon by others, who speak of themselves by eccentric names, such as "The Ubars," "The Larls," and such."

"I have head that," I said.

"And, too, interestingly," he said, "it seems that some of those lads who were "Cosians" now wander about under quite different colors, now affecting beards and hair styles reminiscent of those once associated with veterans, hirsute and shabby, returned from the delta."

"I have heard that, too," I said.

I could recall when I had first come to Ar months ago that these veterans had not been welcome in the city. In spite of the hardships they had endured and the risks they had taken on behalf of Ar, both for the Home Stone and city, they had been held in contempt. They had been insulted, spat upon, ridiculed, and despised. Emotions which might better have been spent on the enemy were ventilated on one's own brothers. Some had scorned them as embarrassments and failures, as defeated men and fools, tricked, humiliated and decimated in the north, men who had dared to return to Glorious Ar without the crown of victory. Better, said some, that they should have died in the marshes or remained in the north than return home in defeat and disgrace. But those who said that had perhaps not themselves been in the delta, or even held weapons. Others, adopting the political ruses of Cos, had scorned them as little better than criminals, and as purveyors of imperialism, as though the ambitions of Cos were not the equal of those of Ar. Many of these men were confused and bitter. Was it for this that they had done their duty, was it for this that they had faced the delta, the tracklessness, the tharlarion, the insects, the hunger, the arrows of rencers, the blades of Cos?

"Some of these lads, former "Cosians" and others," I said, "are apparently little better, still, than vandals, "but, others, interestingly, it is rumored, track troop movements, shadow Cosian patrols and record the rounds of watchmen, reporting to the Delta Brigade."

"If so," said he, "that is a dangerous game for boys. I do not think Cos, in spite of their youth, will hesitate to impale them or have them at the ends of ropes."

"Others set themselves to different tasks," I said, "such as the supervision and protection of their own neighborhoods."

"A hopeful sign," said he, "if Ar, if only in her youth, should once again begin to look after herself."

"There is the Delta Brigade," I said.

"We are not of Ar," he said.

"But others, whosoever they may be, must be," I said.

"Cos cannot be ignorant of these many changes in Ar," he said.

"It seems she pretends to official ignorance," I said.

"That cannot long continue."

"No," I said.

"And it she who holds the sword," he said.

"Gross Lurius of Jad, Ubar of Cos, and many of his ministers," I said, "are doubtless in favor of wielding it. Until now they have doubtless been restrained only by the general effectiveness of their political warfare, the policies of spreading guilt, confusion and self-doubt in the enemy, pretending to be not the foe but the concerned friend and ally."

"Let those beware," smiled Marcus, "who are invited to dine with the sleen."

"There is a crowd ahead," I said, "at the public boards."

"They seem angry," he said.

"Let us see what is afoot," I said, and together we hurried forward, toward the boards.

14 In The Vicinity Of The Public Boards

Before the boards, rather in a circle before them, there was a crowd. Whereas there may have been unwelcome information on the boards, the immediate attention of the crowd was not at this moment upon them.

"Here is the insolent slut!" cried a fellow.

We pushed in, toward the center of the circle.

"Make way," I said. "Guardsmen! Guardsmen!"

Men cried out with anger, but drew back.

Marcus and I had our armbands, those of auxiliary guardsman, a band of red beneath one of blue, Ar under the supervison of Cos.

"Cosian sleen," I heard. But the fellow did not make himself prominent.

"One side!" I said.

I glimpsed the face of a girl, white and frightened, in the center of the crowd. She was standing, being held by two fellows, one wrist in the care of each.

To one side, quite close, there knelt four other girls, three in tunics of the wool of the bounding hurt, one in silk.

"Guardsmen!" I repeated, angrily, and forced myself forward.

The face of the standing, captive girl manifested sudden relief.

"Would you not know?" said one of the men, disgustedly.

One of the kneeling girls, too, cried out with joy.

"We are saved!" said another.

"What is going on here?" I demanded, not pleasantly.

"First the curfew," grumbled a fellow to another.

"Then the forbidding of the delka," said another.

"Now this!" exclaimed another.

I resolved I must learn more of what was on the boards. Marcus could read them much more rapidly than I.

"Release me," said the standing girl, angrily. The two fellows who had seized her wrists let them go, and she rubbed her wrists, as though to push away even the memory of their grip.

"Greetings, and welcome, noble guardsmen of Cos!" said she, delightedly. "I think you have arrived just in time!"

The other four girls made as though to rise, righteously, but a glance from Marcus put them back instantly on their knees.

This, I think, was not noticed by the girl who was standing, who was, I take it, a sort of leader amongst them.

"What is the difficulty?" I asked.

"We caught her drinking from the top bowl of the fountain," said one, pointing to a nearby fountain.

"You are not kneeling," I said to the girl in the center.

"I am a woman," she said, "why should I kneel?"

This seemed to me a strange response. I would have supposed it in excellent reason to kneel, being in the presence of men, if one were a woman. If she were a free woman, of course, fitting or not, there would be no legal proprieties involved. A free woman, as long as she remains free, can stand to the fullness of her short, graceful height before men.

"What is your status?" I asked.

"Slave," she said, tossing her lovely head, her hair swirling.

To be sure, my question was somewhat rhetorical, as her neck was appropriately banded.

I considered her.

She met my eyes for a moment, and then, angrily, looked away.

She was rather modestly garbed, I thought, her tunic coming to her knees. Too, it was not belted. This was presumably to conceal her figure. On the other hand, I conjectured that beneath that garment, woven of the wool of the bounding hurt, her figure might not be without interest. She wore no makeup. She had been given sandals. I considered her mien. I did not doubt but what she had a weak master.

"As you are slave," I asked, "how is it that you are not kneeling?"

"A strange question," she said, "coming from a guardsman of Cos."

"Yes," said a man, angrily.

"Tell me of your master," I said.

"He is liberated," she said, "and of the times! He knows my worth!"

"You would not be insolent in Cos, or Anango, or Venna!" said a man.

"I am in Ar!" she laughed. "Cos' Ar!"

"Hold!" I said angrily to the men, holding them back.

"Let her be punished!" said a fellow.

"No!" she laughed. "You do not dare touch me now! There are guardsmen of Cos present ! I am safe!"

Inwardly I smiled, wondering what her attitude might be, had she found herself anywhere but where she was, and in the presence of the power of Cos, in the form of Marcus and myself. What if she had found herself, for example, tied with wire in an alcove in Brundisium, almost concealed in ropes on a submission mat in the Tahari, wearing a body cage in Tyros, bound to a wheel in the land of the Wagon Peoples, shackled on a sales platform in Victoria, fearing the auctioneer's whip, or prone and chained on one of the swift ships of the black slavers of Schendi?

"Is it true that you have drunk from the higher bowl of the fountain?" I asked.

"Yes!" she said.

"How is it that you have done such a thing?" I asked. Slaves, of course, like other animals, are expected to drink from the lower level of a fountain, and, generally, on all fours.

"My master permits such things!" she said. "He is noble and kind!"

"A weakling and a fool," said a man. "I know him."

"He conforms to the proprieties of the new Ar!" she cried. "And he celebrates them! He grabs me modestly. He accords me sandals! He respects me!"

There was laughter.

"He accords me an allowance, and my own hours, and my own room!" she said.

"And does he require your permission before he puts you to use?" I asked.

"Of coruse," she said.

There was a reaction of amazement from the men present.

"And does he receive this permission when he wishes it?" I asked.

"Sometimes," she laughed.

"I can well imagine his anxiety," I said, "as to whether or not it will be granted."

She laughed. "Glory to Cos!" she said.

But neither Marcus nor myself, nor any other there, echoed this sentiment.

"You are not always in the mood?" I said.

"Of course not," she said.

"Sometimes you are weary," I conjectured, "or are afflicted with a headache?"

"Yes," she laughed. "But I do not need an excuse!"

"I see," I said.

"Sometimes," she said, "I deny him, to win my way, to punish him, to teach him a lesson." She laughed, and threw a meaningful look at the other girls kneeling near her. One or two of them looked up at her, smiling.

"I understand," I said. "Does your master trouble you often in this regard."

"Not so much now," she said, angrily.

"You are aware that he can sell you," I said.

"He would not dare to do so," she said.

"But you know he has this legal power?"

"In a sense," she said.

"In the fullest of senses," I said.

"Yes," she said, drawing back a little.

"And you know that he can do with you as he pleases?" I asked.

"Yes," she said.

"And that you are dependent upon him, even with respect to your very life?"

"In a sense," she said.

"Actually," I said, "and in the fullest of senses."

"Yes!" she said.

"Interesting," I said.

"Do you forget the proposed laws of respect!" she said.

"They were never enacted," I said.

"They should have been!" she said.

There was an angry mutter in the crowd.

"My master," she said, "is a kind, liberated, noble, enlightened master! He accepts such laws, or laws much like them, as much as if they had been proclaimed by the councils and promulgated by the Ubara herself!"

"The actual words of the Ubara," I said, "or at least as reported on the boards, where to the effect that slave girls should be obedient and try to please their masters."

"It is well," said a man, "or Ar would have gone up in flames."

"I do not know of such things," she said.

"Are you pleased with your master?" I asked.

"He is noble and kind, and liberated and enlightened," she said.

"You seem deprived, and unfulfilled."

"I?"

"Yes," I said. "Are you content and happy?"

"Of course!" she said, angrily.

"How long have you been a slave?" I asked.

"Two months," she said.

"How came it aout?" I asked.

"I was taken in the suburbs," she said, "by mercenaries, collected with others. The levy was unannounced."

I nodded. There had been many such, the soldiers appearing

with their ropes, often late at night, bursting into houses, bringing their catches forth, in various states of undress and nightwear, to the waiting wagons.

"You have had only one master?" I asked.

"Yes," she said. "He was one who had sought my hand in the free companionship but whose renewed suits I had consistently scorned."

"And now you are his slave?" I said.

"Yes," she said.

"Or he is yours," laughed a fellow.

"If you say so," she said.

Again anger coursed about the circle.

"What is your name?" I asked.

"Lady Filomela," she said, "of Ar."

"You are a slave," I said.

"Filomela, then," she said, "of Ar."

"Of Ar?" I asked.

"Simply Filomela then," she said, angrily.

"And you may be given any name your master pleases," I said.

"Yes!" she said, angrily.

"Why are you not happy?" I asked.

"I am happy!" she cried.

"I see," I said.

"I am going now," she said.

"Really?" I said.

She turned about, to leave, but the men did not move to let her pass. Then she turned about, again, to face me.

"May I go now?" she asked.

"Come here," I said.

She regarded me.

"Now," I said.

She did not move.

I snapped my fingers.

She hurried angrily to stand before me. She was now close to me, and I had good feelings, feelings of energy, possessiveness and manhood, good feelings, powerful feelings, at her closeness, and she, on her part, looked up at me, and then, looking quickly away, trembled a little. Then she blushed. There was some laughter.

"You sense in yourself slave feelings?" I asked.

"No!" she said.

"Turn about, and keep your hands at your sides," I said.

With two hands I brushed her hair forward, putting it before her shoulders. I then checked her collar. It was a standard collar, of a sort familiar in the north, flat, narrow, light, sturdy, close-fitting. I did not bother reading the engraving on the collar, as it would be of no interest, her master being a weakling. The collar was closed at the back of her neck with a small, heavy lock. This is common. It was attractive on her, as such things are on any woman.

"You are collared like a slave," I said.

"I am a slave," she said.

"Clasp your hands on the top of your head," I said.

She trembled.

"Common kajira brand," said a fellow.

"Yes," I said.

"Please," she said.

"You are branded like a slave," I said.

"I am a slave!" she said, angrily.

I permitted the hem of her rather-too-long tunic to fall again into place. She was left-thigh-branded, high on the thigh, a bit below the hip, like most girls.

I glanced to the four other girls kneeling to the side. They were apprehensive, frightened.

"Are you the leader of these others?" I asked her.

"We are friends," she said, evasively.

This was surely not impossible. Slave girls have much in common, such as their brands and collars, their typical garmentures, their entire condition and status, the sorts of labors they must perform, and the problems of pleasing masters. It is natural then, given such commonalities, and abused and despised by free women, that they should often seek out one another's company. It is not unusual to see them together, for example, laundering at the stream side or long basins, or sitting about in a circle, mending and sewing, or polishing silver. Sometimes they arrange their errands so that they may accompany one another. Sometimes, too, in the abundance of free time enjoyed by most urban slaves, they simply wander about, seeing the city, chatting, exchanging gossip, and such. To be sure, it would be remiss not to remark also that, as one would expect, some of the pettiest of jealousies, the most absurd of resentments, the vilest of acrimonies and the most inveterate of hatreds can obtain among these beautiful, vain, vital creatures, who are, after all, only females. This is particularly the case within the same house where contests often rage, sometimes subtly and sometimes not, for the favor of the master, on which contests, needless to say, considerable shiftings in rank and hierarchy may hinge. And there can be intrense competitions, it might be mentioned, not only for such treasures as the master's attentions and affections but for articles as ordinary as combs and brushes and prizes which, whatever may be their symbolic value, are often as small in themselves as a sweet or pastry. In this case, however, I suspected this was no typical grouping of slaves, of the normal sort, but a tiny covey of girls either with weak masters or masters whom they suspected might be weak, a natural enough suspicion in an Ar where the men of the city, betrayed and defeated, helpless and confused, were for most practical purposes, at least until recently, prostrate before the might of Cos. If one is in effect a slave oneself it is hard to be a strong master to one's female. It is much easier to rationalize one's weaknesses and struggle to view them as virtues.

"Is she your leader?" I asked one of the girls kneeling to the side, one of those in a tunic of the wool of the bounding hurt.

"Yes," she said.

"No!" swiftly said another, one also in a tunic of the wool of the bounding hurt. "Our mastes are our leaders!"

" 'Leaders'?" I asked.

"Owners!" she swiftly said.

"What are you?" I asked the first kneeling girl, sternly.

"Properties!" she said. And she added, quickly, seeing my eyes still upon her, "And animals!"

"Yes!" said the girl beside her, she who had spoken second earlier.

"And what are you?" I asked the slave, Filomela.

"A slave," she said, not turning around, standing facing away from me, her hands clasped on her head.

"Turn about," I said.

She obeyed.

"And?" I asked.

She was standing quite close to me, in the posture I had dictated.

"A property, and animal!" she said.

I looked upon her, savoring her. She looked away. I also observed, carefully, her tension, the tonicity of her body.

"Straighten your body," I said.

She did so.

The line of her beasts was lovely under her simple garment.

"You seem uneasy," I said.

She did not respond.

One of the kneeling girls gasped.

It was not difficult to detect her discomfort, her uneasiness, attendant on the proximity of a male. I loomed over her, letting this closeness work upon her. Others, too, now had moved in more closely about her.

"You are a slave?" I asked.

"Yes!" she said, tensely.

"Perhaps now you sense in yourself slave feelings?" I said.

She cast a frightened, pathetic, shamed glance at the other girls, those kneeling to the side.

"No!" she said. "No!"

"Spread your legs," I said.

"Please!" she said.

"Keep your hands as they are," I said.

"Ah," I said, "you are a lying slave girl."

She cried out with misery.

I stepped back from her.

"You may stand straight again," I informed her.

Quickly she stood straight. She kept her hands on her head.

"And what of you others?" I asked, looking to the other four. "Perhaps you sense in yourself slave feelings?"

They did not meet my eyes but clenched their knees closely together, as though by this means to suppress and control their sensations. They hunched down, they made themselves small. I did not think that there was one there who, in proper hands, would not squirm well, yielding herself up in grateful joy to a master.

"You may put your hands down," I informed Filomela, their leader.

"May I go now?" she said.

"You are charged," I said, "with drinking from one of the higher levels of a fountain."

"That fountain there," said a fellow, pointing back.

"Is it true?" I asked her.

She was silent.

"It is true," said a fellow.

"Yes," said another.

Assent to this was added, also, by others.

"Do you deny this?" I asked her.

She was silent.

"She is a slave," said a man.

"Let her testimony be taken under torture," said another.

The testimony of slaves is commonly taken under torture in Gorean law courts.

"Let us find a rack," said another.

The girl turned white. Perhaps when she was a free woman she had seen girls on the rack, though, of course, they would have been mere slaves.

"I drank from the high bowl," she said.

"Although you are a slave?" I said.

"Yes," she said.

"Why?" I asked.

"I was thirsty," she said.

"Speak truthfully," I said.

"I was thirsty!" she said.

"Thirst may be quenched at the lower bowl as well," I said.

She looked at me, angrily.

"Perhaps you forgot?" I said. "You were, after all, recently a free woman."

She did not answer.

I did not seriously consider the possibility, of course, that she might have forgotten the matter. Too, slaves are not permitted to forget such things. It is up to them to remember them. Too, obviously one could claim to have forgotten the most elementary duties, tokens of respect, and such. Accordingly, forgetfulness does not excuse the commission of such acts. A slave seldom forgets them more than once. The whip is an excellent mnemonic device. I did, of course, wish to accord her the recourse of pretending to forgetfulness, if she cared to take advantage of it. It might serve to mitigate the wrath of the men about, at least somewhat. After all, she did not seem to realize that her life was in danger.

She threw a look at the other girls.

"You did not forget then," I said. "And you must have known that free men were about. Your act then was intended as some sort of provocation, or insult, or insolency or challenge?"

"She knew herself observed," said a fellow, "and then with intent, and deliberation, drank from the third level."

"My master would permit it!" she cried.

"That is probably true," laughed a fellow, contemptuously.

"Kneel, errant slave," I said.

She knelt, in terror.

I looked down at her and pointed the first two fingers of my right hand to the ground, and then opened them. "You do not know the meaning of that sign?" I asked.

"No," she said, trembling.

"Her master is indeed weak," said a fellow.

I supposed her master must be a low-drive male.

"Spread your knees, widely," said another.

Frightened, the girl complied.

"Take her in hand," I said.

A fellow on either side of her then held her, each by a lifted wrist.

I looked at the other girls.

They, too, at my glance, knelt with their knees spread, widely.

"See!" said the one in silk. "My master has silked me! He has put me in silk, as the slave I am! Do not hurt me! I am only a silked slave! That is all I have been given to wear. He is a man, a man!" The first girl in line, one of the three clad in the wool of the bounding hurt, did not dare to meet my eyes but drew the hem of her tunic up and back, higher on her legs, that more of her beauty might be bared. She, too, did not wish to face the wrath of masters. The other two in the wool of the bounding hurt quickly followed her example. They then all adjusted their tunics further in one way or another, one pulling down a bit on the "V" at her neck, the others pushing up the sleeves of their tunics to reveal more of their gracefuly curved upper arms.

"Slaves!" chided the girl before me. She saw herself losing her grip upon them.

"And what are you?" I inquired.

"A slave!" she said.

I regarded her.

"—Master," she added.

"It is a serious thing you are charged with," I said.

She looked at me, angrily.

"You have drunk," I said, "from the wrong level of a fountain."

"What difference does it make," she asked, "what bowl of a fountain I drank from? It is a small thing!"

Anger coursed through the men present.

"It is not a small thing," I said. "Such things are symbols of rank and hierarchy, of difference and distance. They lie at the foundation of a natural society, one in accord with the aristocracy of nature, a society in which there are places for both heroes and slaves. They speak of ordered arrangements. All are not the same. All are not leveled, nor must they pretend to be. Such a flat, crushed world, without difference and meaning, lies to the ruled and makes liars of the rulers. It imposes fraud upon one and hypocrisy upon the other. In the unnatural world, as all cannot be the best, there is no alternative, if all are to be the same, then to reduce the best to the level of the worst, at least in pretense. Do you not think the intelligent, the strong, the aggressive, even the evil, will rule, under whatever forms are convenient? The larl, as a larl, must survey verr, or sleen will tend them, pretending to be themselves verr."

She looked up at me.

"You did not truly think it a small thing," I said, "otherwise you would not have done it."

She struggled a little, but could not, of course, free herself from the grip of the men. Then, under my stern gaze, she again spread her knees, so that they were again in the position, precisely, in which I had instructed her to have them.

"You challenged the men of Ar," I said. "But you did not expect the challenge to be accepted. You expected them to yield to their defeat, perhaps pretending not to notice it."

She struggled again a bit, and was then again as she was before.

"But it has been noticed," I said.

"I saw girls drinking from the high bowls last month!" she said.

"That was last month," I said.

"You cannot punish me!" she cried. "You are not my masters!"

"Any free person can punish an errant slave girl," I said. "Surely you do not think that her behavior fails to be subject to supervison and correction as soon as she is out of her master's sight?"

"Take me to my master!" she begged. "Let him punish me, if he wishes to do so!"

"We will attend to the matter," I said.

"No!" she wept.

"But you are an errant slave," I reminded her.

"No!" she cried.

I looked at the others. "And you, too," I suggested, "are errant slaves."

"No, Master!" they wept. "No, Master!"

"You cannot seriously intend to punish me!" said Filomela. "I was a free woman!"

"That is where most slaves come from," I said. I turned to the other slaves. "Were you not all once free women?" I asked.

"Yes, Master!" they said.

"But I was of high caste!" said Filomela.

"What was your caste?" I asked.

"The Builders!" she said.

"But you are not now of the Builders, or of any other caste, are you?" I asked.

"No," she said.

"What are you?"

"A slave," she said.

"Accordingly," I said, "you may be punished as what you are, a slave."

Suddenly she laughed, in hysterical relief.

"What is wrong?" I asked.

"It is a joke!" she said. "It is a game you are playing, to turn about and trick these fools, to humiliate these defeated, bedraggled beasts!"

"I do not understand," I said.

"You, and your fellow, are of Cos!" she said. "I see it on your armbands! It is your business to pacify the men of Ar, to keep them down, to suppress them, to keep them helpless, futile, confused, domesticated, tamed, subdued! Surely you have your orders to that effect. You can succeed in this. Ar is defeated. She is helpless. She is crushed. The entire might of Cos backs your authority! Grind down the men of Ar, as you should. Continue to keep them, as they have been kept, intimidated herds of prisoners incarcerated in their own city, encouraged to view the wretchedness of their lot as the evidence of some new triumph. And it is your intention to use me to help you in this, by permitting me to insult them, by permitting me to mock their manhood, to reduce their virility. Of course! I now understand! So now disband this rabble and release me!"

She made as though to rise.

"Remain on your knees, slave girl," I said.

"You must let me go, you must order my release, you must take me from these brutes, you must scold them, speak to them of laws and such, or something, anything!" she cried. "Defend me, us! I demand it! Release me! You must! I beg it! The men of Ar have been defeated! No longer are they men! No longer are they mighty and masters! They are now nothing, they are all weaklings! You are of Cos! You must keep them that way! It is important to you to keep them that way! Arrest them if they dare think again of pride and manhood, tangle them in rulings, trip them with laws, lie to them, confuse them, put them in prison, do not let them understand themselves, or become themselves, if necessary, put them to the sword! Burn Ar! Destroy it! Salt its ashes! Do you not understand how dangerous might prove to be manhood in Ar? You must not permit it! And you can use women like us to help you in your schemes, protecting us, and using us to diminish men! Let us be your allies in the conquest and subjugation of Ar! Surely you understand me? You are of Cos! You are of Cos!"

"But I am not of Cos," I said.

"Aiii!" cried several of the men about.

"You have drunk from a high bowl," I said, "and more than once you have spoken untruthfully, for example, in denying that you sensed slave feelings in yourself."

"Forgive me, Masters!" she cried.

"Too," I said, "you have demeaned the men of Ar."

"Forgive me, Masters!" she wept. "You are men! You are men! A slave begs forgiveness!" Her concern was certainly not out of place. The demeaning of men, whereas it is permitted to, and not unknown among, free women, is not permitted to female slaves. Such, on their part, can be a capital offense.

"More importantly," I said, "you have not been pleasing."

She looked at me, wildly.

"Remove her tunic," I said.

She was then amongst us, on her knees, a stripped slave. She was comely.

I then turned away from her. "What is new on the public boards?" I asked a fellow.

"Master! Master!" cried the girl, behind me.

"What of the slave?" asked a man.

"You are men," I said. "Doubtless you will know what to do with her."

One of the fellows looked at me.

"For example," I said, "she was thirsty. Perhaps you can see, then, that her thirst is quenched."

"That we will," said a fellow, taking charge of the matter.

"What of these others?" asked another man.

"Read their collars," I said. "And then instruct them to return to their masters and give them such a night of slave pleasure as they would not have conceived possible. Then be certain to follow up the matter the next day, to make certain they have complied fully."

"We shall," said a fellow.

"What of the next day, and the next?" asked a man.

"I would expect," I said, "that the masters, seeing what their slaves are truly capable of, and what may be obtained of them, will not be shortchanged in the future. On the other hand, if they are not strong enough to obtain the best and finest from their properties I am sure the girls themselves, they then needing true masters, will in one way or another soon obtain a new disposition. Perhaps the weak masters, unable to satisfy them, will weary of seeing the bondage knot in their hair, will weary of their importunities, their moans and whinings in the night, their beggings for use, and either give them, or sell them, to another. Or perhaps the weak masters, whether unable to satisfy them, or merely unwillilng to do so, will simply yield to their entreaties to be given away or sold, that they may receive an opportunity for their love, service and beauty to be put at the mercy of someone who can appreciate it and knows what to do with it."

"You heard?" inquired a fellow of the kneeling slaves.

"Yes, Master!" said one of them. "We will give our masters such a night of slave pleasure as they never knew could exist."

"Read the collars," said another fellow.

Names were read, and domiciles. Men were assigned to follow up on each slave the next morning and report back to a certain metal-worker's shop.

"Speed off!" said a fellow.

Quickly, released, the four girls leaped up and hurried away.

Tonight, I thought, there would be at least four astonished fellows in Ar, and four slaves who, by morning, if only by teaching themselves, by their own actions, would have a much better conception of the profoundities, and sensations involved, and significances, of their condition.

"What is new on the boards?" I asked Marcus. I did not really wish to make it clear to the men about that I did not read Gorean as well as I might.

Men crowded happily about me.

"There is to be a curfew," said Marcus. "It begins tonight. The streets are to be kept clear between the eighteenth and the fourth Ahn."

"What is the reason for that?" I asked a fellow.

"To limit the movements of the Delta Brigade," he whispered.

"Is there such a thing?" I asked.

"Seremides thinks so," said a man.

"I heard a barracks was burned last night," said a fellow.

"I heard that, too," said Marcus.

"Is it on the boards?" I asked.

"No," said a man.

"No," said Marcus. "I do not think so."

"Then it must not have happened," said a fellow, grimly.

"Of course," said another.

I heard the slave, some yards off, at the fountain, crying out. She had been taken to the lower bowl of the fountain. There she was sputtering and gasping, and crying out for mercy. Again and again was her head, held by the hair, forced down, held under the water and then jerked up again. "Please, Masters! Mercy, Masters!" she wept.

"The delka has been forbidden!" said Marcus. "It says so, here!"

"Interesting," I said.

"That is the first public recognition of the Delta Brigade," said a fellow.

I now heard the sound of a lash. The girl had her head down, her wet hair forward. She was held on her knees by the fountain, a wrist in the hands of each of two fellows. She shook under each blow. Then, when they had finished, she was on her hands and knees, her head down. Her entire body was trembling. She slipped to the pavement. Her hair was about. She lay there. It seemed she could hardly believe what had been done to her. I supposed this was the first time she had been lashed. It is something no slave girl forgets. A fellow then drew her up again, by the hair, to all fours and, looming over her, pointed to the fountain. She now, slowly, painfully, crawled to the fountain, between the men, and then, putting her head down, and as was fitting for her, and as she should have done earlier in the afternoon, drank from the lower bowl. She was then pulled back and put prone on the pavement. Her hands were pulled behind her back and fastened there, with a short thong.

"Is there more on the boards?" I asked Marcus.

"I think those are the main items of interest," he said.

I saw the girl placed on her belly over the stone lip of the lower bowl of the fountain. She cried out. Her small hands twisted in the thongs, behind her back. Men crowded about her.

"Glory to the Delta Brigade," said a man.

"Who are of the Delta Brigade?" asked a man.

"Who knows?" said another.

"They must be veterans of the delta campaign," said a man.

"Perhaps others, too," said a fellow.

"A fellow was asking me where he could join the Delta Brigade," said a man.

"Probably a spy," conjectured a fellow.

That seemed to me likely.

"I heard that they tried to take in a veteran for questioning," said a man.

"What happened?" I asked a fellow.

"He drew a sword from beneath his cloak," said a man.

"Swords are forbidden," said a fellow.

"Doubtless there are some about," said a man.

"What happened?" I asked.

" "He slew two Cosians, and disappeared," said the man.

"It may be dangerous to try to take in the veterans of the delta," said a man.

"They will send squads after them," said a man, "a squad to a man."

"Probably they should leave the city," I said.

"Why?" asked a man.

"They will be suspect," I said.

"There are warriors and guardsmen in the city," said a man, "who are not veterans of the delta."

"That is true," I said. Also, of course, it was not only in the delta that blood had been shed.

"Ah," said Marcus, glancing over toward the fountain, "here comes the insolent little slut now."

"She does not look so insolent now," said a fellow.

The girl, her hands still bound behind her, her head down, her hair about her face, shuddering, scarcely able to walk, her upper left arm in the grip of a fellow, by means of which grip she was being muchly supported, was being conducted into our presence.

Freed of his grip she immediately knelt, and in proper position.

"You may untie her," I said.

He jerked loose the thong from her wrists. Whereas it had confined her with perfection, she had not been able, of course, to reach either of the ends by means of which the knot could be expeditiously undone.

"To all fours," said her keeper.

Immediately she went to all fours.

"Describe a circle, of some five paces in diameter, on all fours, as you are now," said her keeper, "and return to this place."

I watched her.

In this way was she well displayed, and in the attitude of the she-quadruped.

She was then again before us, on all fours, head down.

"On all fours," remarked a fellow.

"In such a posture she does not seem as insolent," said another.

"She is not," said another.

"No, said another.

"A fitting posture for the little she-sleen," said a man.

"Yes," said a man.

"Look up," I said to the girl.

She looked up, through her hair.

"Have you learned to drink from the lower bowl?" I asked.

"Yes, Master," she said.

"You may lower your head," I said.

She put her head down, gratefully.

"You are not a little she-sleen, are you?" I said.

"No, Master," she said.

"You are more of a little vulo, aren't you?" I said.

"Yes, Master, now, Master," she said.

"What do you want to do, more than anything?" I asked.

"To please men," she said.

"What man?" I asked.

"Any man, Master," she said.

"I think she may be permitted to live," I said.

"I think so," said a fellow.

"Yes," said another.

She began to tremble. I did not think her arms and legs would support her.

"You may break position," I informed her.

Immediately she went to her belly before me, and reached to my ankle, and put her lips over my left sandal, pressing her lips to it.

"Do you think you will see your friends again?" I asked.

"I hope so, Master," she said.

"And how do you think they will find you?" I asked.

"They will find me a slave," she said.

"And how do you think you will find them?" I asked.

"I do not know, Master," she said.

"I think you will also find them slaves," I said.

"Yes, Master," she said.

"Do you still think that it might be well for the men of Ar to be put to the sword?" I asked.

"No, Master," she said. "It is rather that women such as I should be put to the sword of their manhood."

"Even if it should make them proud and powerful, and great?" I asked.

"It is hard for this humble slave to believe that her use, and the use of such as she, the use of meaningless chattels, should have so great a consequence, but, if it be so, then surely that would be an additional joy to me, and to my sisters in bondage."

"Even should it inevitably plunge you deeper and more irrevocably into your servitude, ensuring that it will become even more uncompromising and absolute?"

"Yes, Master," she said. "I now wish to live for the chain, the whip, and love."

I looked down at her.

"I beg you to buy me!" she suddenly wept.

"You beg to be purchased," I said.

"Yes, Master," he said, "I beg it!"

"Interesting," I said.

"Surely it is permissible for me to so beg. Indeed, it is fitting for me, as I am a slave."

"And it is just today, I gather," I said, "that you have learned this, that you are a slave."

"No, Master," she said. "I have known it for years, in my most secret heart. It is only that it is today, on this day, that I first admitted it to myself. It is only today that I ceased to lie to myself, that I ceased to be at war with myself. It is only today, today, that I ceased to pretend to be something which I knew I was not. It is only today that I have admitted to myself, honestly and openly, what I am."

"Bring her tunic," I said to a fellow.

He picked up what was left of it.

She looked up from my feet, frightened. "Surely you will keep me, or buy me!" she said.

"No," I said.

"But it is to you, or to one such as you that I must belong!" she wept.

I did not speak.

"Nature has designed my body, my mind, my dispositions, my needs, my beauty, if it be beauty, with one such as you in mind!"

I did not speak.

"It is for such as you that women such as I exist!" she wept.

I did not speak.

"Without one such as you," she wept "I canot obtain my happiness, my completion, my fulfillment!"

I remained silent.

"I am at your feet," she wept, "branded, collared, legally enslaved! I am helpless! Take pity on me! Surely you will not deny me the fulfillments of my condition!"

"Kneel," I said. "You will return to your master."

She screamed in misery. "Woe!" she wept. "This is my punishment, more grievous than the leather!"

"But he is kind, noble, liberated and enlightened," I reminded her.

"Woe!" she wept. "Woe!"

"Be the most abject and loving of slaves," I said. "Crawl at his feet. Weep for his mercy. Beg to serve him in the most intimate modalities of the slave girl."

"But he would lift me from my knees and chide me for my needs," she said. "He wants me to act like a man! I think he may want to relate a man, truly, but is afraid to do so. So he wants me to pretend to be one, or be like one. I do not know. I think he is afraid of a true woman, and what she is like. Perhaps he fears he is not man enough to satisfy her in the full spectrum of her needs, in her subtlety, depth and complexity. I do not know! Perhaps he is only weak, perhaps he is one of only infrequently active and diminutive drives. Perhaps he is emotionally shallow, unready to sound the depths of oceans, to measure the heights of a hundred skies. Perhaps it is all very simple. Perhaps he only lacks health, or virility, through no fault of his own. I do not know! Whatever it is, please do not send me back to him!"

"You will relate to him differently than you ever have before," I said. "Utterly differently. You will now be to him a true and perfect slave girl. You will be docile, dutiful and hard-working. You will serve, and be eager to serve, in all things. You will present yourself before him as a female slave, and truly and completely as such, and wholly at his mercy. You will crawl to him, the whip in your teeth. Surely he will understand this. You will petition to serve his pleasure, you will beg to squirm for him, and as the insignificant and meaningless slut, a mere slave, you now are."

She looked at me, clutching the remains of her tunic before her.

"I shall do as you say, Master," she said.

"And you may discover he is not the weakling you think," I said. "And you may find he will take the whip from your teeth and perhaps stand over you and howl with pleasure, sensing the joy of the mastery. You may even be struck with it, as he takes control of you, for the first time. Yes, you may even be put under the lash, that he punish you for what you have denied him before, and that he confirm upon you, and you be instructed in, and fully, the new relationship in which you stand to him."

"But what if he is weak?" she begged.

"Continue to serve him, in the fullness of your slavery, begging him for the least of his kisses, the most casual of his caresses."

"Yes, Master," she said, tears in her eyes.

"Even such small attentions, as you will discover, now that you have become sensitized to your slavery, will be precious to you."

"Yes, Master," she said.

I did not doubt but what she would soon be feeling the fullness of her needs, now that they were in the process of being liberated. In the pens it is not unusual for girls to bleed at the fingernails, from scratching at the walls of their kennels, or to bruise their lovely bodies against the bars of their cages, trying to reach out to a guard, if only to touch his sleeve. Sometimes a girl is deprived of attention for two or three days before her sale, that she will show well on the block, her body, and person, and aspect a helpless, piteous plea of need.

"If he continues to be inert," I said, "if he cannot be awakened or aroused, or fears to be, or does not wish to be, perhaps because of hostility toward you, or toward women, generally, he will presumably grow uneasy with you in the house and give you away, or sell you. Perhaps he will even trade you for a less needful woman, or one more in accord with his needs, whatever they might be."

"But what if he is stupid?" she asked.

"Beg him then to sell you, or give you away," I said, "that you may, if only in being sold off the block, come into the collar of another, one capable of satisfying what you are, a slave."

"But what if he will not sell me, or give me away?" she said. "What if he insists on keeping me, as he is, and as I now am? What if he will keep me only according to his own rules, and lights, and keep me from myself, denying me to myself, frustrating my deepest and most profound needs, as I am?"

"Then," said I, angrily, "that is how it will be, for it is you who wear the collar. He is the master. You are the slave."

"Yes, Master," she sobbed.

"But do not fear," I said. "I am certain, sooner or later, you will come into the possession of one who will not only accept your slavery, in its beauty, in its tenderness and needfulness, in its honesty and truth, but will celebrate it and relish it, and for whom you will be a treasure, an incredible and marvelous treasure, to be sure, one to be kept under the closest of disciplines."

"Yes, Master," she said, smiling through her tears.

"Rise up now, slave girl," I said, "and hurry to your master!"

"Yes, Master!" she said.

Clutching her tunic about her as best she could, she then rose up and hurried from the place of the public boards.

"I think she will make an excellent slave," said a fellow.

"Yes," said another.

I myself, too, thought that that was true. It is a beautiful moment when a woman comes to learn, and love, what she is, when she comes to understand herself, and has the courage to accept this understanding, when in joy the ice breaks in the rivers, when the glaciers melt, when spring comes, when she loves and kneels.

"It is a good thing you did here," said a man.

"For the girl?" I asked.

'She is only a slave," he said. "I mean for the men here."

"Oh," I said.

"You had an opportunity here to strike a blow for Cos, to humiliate the men of Ar, to further reduce and degrade them, to force them to submit even to the insolence and arrogance of slaves, to further subdue and crush them, to remind them of their sorry lot, their political and military weakness, of the loss of their goods, their city and pride, to injure them, to strike yet another blow at their staggering manhood, yet you did not do so. Rather you encouraged it, you permitted it to grow, if only a little. Word of this will be in all the taverns by nightfall!"

"Cos will not be pleased," warned a man.

"It is dangerous in these times to remind men of their past glories."

"What if we should be tempted to reclaim them?" asked another.

"Surely you understand how dangerous is the thing you do?" said another.

"How is it that you are in the fee of Cos?" asked another, indicating the armbands of Marcus and myself.

"Men may be in the fee of Cos," I said.

"True," said a fellow.

"Surely you are of Ar," said a man.

"No," I said. "I am of Port Kar."

"It is a lair of pirates," said a fellow, "a den of cutthroats."

"There is now a Home Stone in Port Kar," I said.

"That is more than there is in Ar," said a man.

"If you are of Port Kar," said a man, "I say 'Glory to Port Kar!' "

"Glory to Port Kar!" whispered another.

"Your fellow is surely of Ar," said another.

"No, his fellow is not," said Marcus, angrily. "I am of Ar's Station! Glory to Ar's Station!"

"The city of traitors?" asked a man.

Marcus' hand flew to the hilt of his sword, but I placed my hand quickly over his.

"Ar's Station is no city of traitors!" said he. "Rather by those of Ar was she betrayed!"

"Enough of this," I said.

"If you are of Ar's Station," said the fellow who had spoken before, "I say 'Glory, too, to Ar's Station!' "

Marcus relaxed. I removed my hand from his.

"Glory to Port Kar, and Ar's Station," said a man.

"Yes!" said another.

"Glory, too, to Ar," I said.

"Yes!" whispered men, looking about themselves. "Glory to Ar!"

I heard the ripping down of a sheet from the public boards and saw a young fellow casting it aside. Then, with a knife, he scratched a delka, deeply, into the wood. He turned to face us and brandished the knife. "Glory to Ar!" he cried.

"Gently, lad," I said.

Who knew who might hear?

Spies could be anywhere.

"I would cry out!" he said.

"The knife is no less a knife," I said, "because it makes no sound."

"Glory to Ar!" grumbled the lad, and sheathed the knife, and stalked away.

We regarded the delka.

"Glory to Ar!" whispered men. "Glory to Ar!"

I was pleased to see that not all the youth of Ar were in the keeping of Cos, that in the hearts of some at least there yet burned the fire called patriotism. Too, I recalled some would take the oath of citizenship only facing their Home Stone, now in far-off Cos. Others, in the streets and alleys, I speculated, could teach their elders courage.

"You spoke," I said to a man, "of a veteran who was to have been taken in for questioning, who drew forth a concealed weapon, who slew two Cosians, and disappeared."

"Yes," said the man.

"Know you his name?" I asked.

"Plenius," said a man.

I found that of interest, as I had known a Plenius in the delta. To be sure, there are many fellows with that name.

I looked again to the defiant delka cut into the boards.

"I do not think I would care to be found in the presence of this delka," I said, "so prominient on the public boards, so freshly cut."

"True," said more than one man.

The crowd dissipated.

Marcus regarded the delka.

"I fear reprisals," he said.

"Not yet," I said. "That is contrary to the fundamental policy of the government. The whole pretense here is that Cos is a friend and ally, that she and Ar, in spite of the earlier errors of Ar's ways, so generously forgiven now, are as sisters. This posture is incompatible with reprisals. It is one thing to tax, expropriate and confiscate in the name of various rights and moral principles, all interestingly tending to the best interests of particular parties, and quite another to enact serious reprisals against a supposedly allied citizenry."

"But sooner or later, surely, as you put it, Cos must unsheath her claws."

"I fear so," I said. "But by that time hopefully you will be free of the city with the Home Stone of Ar's Station."

"And when will you begin to work on this portion of your plan?" he asked.

"We have already been doing so," I said.

"Ho!" I cried out, hailing a squad of Cosian regulars. "Here! Here!"

They hurried across the avenue to the boards.

"Behold!" I said.

"Another cursed delka!" snapped the officer.

"And on the boards," I said.

"Have you been here long?" asked the officer.

"No," I said.

"Did you see who did this?" he asked.

"No," I said.

"The cowards are fled," he said, looking about.

"They are all urts," said a subaltern.

"It is only a delka," I said.

"There are too many about," said the officer.

"It is all they can do," laughed the subaltern.

The officer studied the delka.

"It was cut deeply, swiftly," he said, "with strength, probably in hatred."

"These signs are doubtless the works of only a few," said the subaltern.

"But they may be seen by many," said the officer.

"There is nothing to fear," said the subaltern.

"I will have this board replaced," said the officer.

"Shall we continue our rounds?" I asked the officer.

"Yes," said the officer.

Marcus and I turned about then, and continued as we had been originally, south on the Avenue of the Central Cylinder.

"What will be the move of Cos?" asked Marcus.

"The city championships in the *palestrae* games will take place soon," I said.

"So?" asked Marcus.

"That is her overt move, that things should proceed as though nothing had happened, as though nothing were afoot."

"I see," he said.

"And in the meantime, I expect," I said, "she will turn her attentions to matters of internal security."

"The officer was not pleased to see the delka," said Marcus.

"Do you think he was afraid?" I asked.

"No," he said. "I do not think so."

"Perhaps he would have been more afraid if it had been cut with more care, with more methodicality."

"Perhaps," said Marcus.

"It is one thing to deal with sporadic protest," I said. "It is another to deal with a determined, secret, organized enemy.

"Like the Cosian propagandists, infiltrators and spies during the war?" he asked.

"Yes," I said.

"But there is no such determined, secret, organized enemy to challenge Cos," he said.

"I do not know," I said.

"Certainly we are not such," he said.

"No," I said. "We are not such."

"I do not understand," he said.

"The matter may be no longer in our hands," I said.

"Interesting," he said.

15 Fire

"It will be dangerous," I said to Marcus.

"I am of Ar's Station," said he.

"What we do now will have little effect, I fear," I said, "on the fortunes of Ar's Station."

"Here is the rope," he said.

I took it. It was fastened to a one-pronged grappling iron, no more than a simple hook.

It was about the second Ahn, a dark, cloudy night. We had approached the house of records.

This afternoon, on the Avenue of Turia, a cart, putatively carrying the records of the veterans of the delta, supposedly on its way from the house of records to the war office in the Central Cylinder, had been surrounded by a group of youths, crying out against the veterans of the delta, almost as if it had been months ago, a time in which there had been several abusive demonstrations against the delta veterans, whose crime seemed to be that they had been loyal to the Home Stone and that they had been so foolish as to have served Ar, and suffered for her, in the north. These demonstrations, of course, had been instigated at the behest of Cos, and carefully planned and organized by Cosian agents. Such demonstrations, in spite of the apparent beliefs of many of their participants, do not somehow materialize by magic, in response to some requirement of appropriateness. They are structured events, serving certain purposes. In brief, however, these lads, some dozens of them, had surrounded the cart and its guards, screaming out reproaches against the delta veterans, spitting on the records, and such. The guards, I think, Cosians, were not certain how to respond to the demonstration. They tried to push back the youths but their lines were crowded through, while they themselves were being greeted as friends and brothers, saluted as allies and hailed as heroes. Soon one or two youths, seemingly overcome with hatred, had leaped upon the records and were tearing them apart and hurling them to the gathered crowd. In another moment a torch had been brought. Marcus and I, knowing the movement was to take place, and, indeed, it had been on the public boards, had come to watch. Men drew swords but the officer restrained them. The papers had then been burned and the youths had withdrawn in triumph, singing songs to the glory of Cos. I had recognized the first youth to spring upon the cart. It had been he who, some days before, had cut the defiant delka deeply into one of the public boards on the Avenue of the Central Cylinder.

"Those are brave lads," I had said to Marcus later.

"But surely," he said, "the destroyed papers were not the records of the delta veterans."

"No," I said. "They would have been moved secretly."

"What was the purpose of all this?" asked Marcus.

"Many associate the veterans of the delta with the Delta Brigade," I said. "This was undoubtedly a trap set by Seremides. In pretending to move the records, records from which the indentities of the delta veterans might be obtained, to a place of safer keeping, he hoped to lure an attack by the Delta Brigade. Certainly there were many guards near the cart, far more than one might expect, and there were a great many others, if I am not mistaken, in the crowd, in plain garments, with concealing cloaks. They moved, at any rate, with the cart."

"How will Cos understand this demonstration?" he asked.

"It was not an armed attack," I said. "The demonstrators were young, they seemed sincere. Cos may even take this action as one favorable to themselves. They have lost nothing and have apparently received a confirmation of the effectiveness of the their propaganda."

"Do you think Seremides will be fooled?" he asked.

"No," I said. "I do not think so."

"The Ubara?" he asked.

"I do not know," I said.

"She was at the *palestrae* games last week," he said.

"No," I said. "Some woman in her robes was."

"How do you know?" he asked.

"She was in sandals," I said, "and was a hort taller than the Ubara."

"You know the Ubara?" he asked.

"Once," I said.

"You are sure?" he asked.

"I know where she comes upon me."

"You were brave to approach her so closely," he said.

"I permitted her to approach me, as I stood to one side and she passed, with her guards."

"What if she had been the true Ubara, and recognized you?" he said.

"I was muchly hooded," I said, "but I did not think there was much danger. It would not be the true Ubara."

"Why not?" he asked.

"No longer would Cos choose to risk her in public," I said.

"Because of the Delta Brigade?"

"Of course," I said.

"They fear she would be struck down?"

"Of course," I said. "There is growing hatred in the city for our darling Ubara."

"Where is she, then?"

"In the Central Cylinder, I would conjecture," I said.

"As a virtual prisoner?" he asked.

"Probably as much so," I said, "as when she was kept there, sequestered in her shame by Marlenus."

"But she is still Ubara," he said.

"Of course," I said, "under Cos."

"Where do you think the records are?" he asked.

"I do not know," I said.

"Why then are we going to the house of records, with a rope and iron?" he asked.

"They may be there," I said.

"You would take such risks, ones which are not only unnecessary, but perhaps meaningless, just to keep the records out of the hands of Cos?"

"You do not need to accompany me," I said.

"Be serious," he said.

"The fact that Seremides, if I read him aright, set such a trap for the Delta Brigade, supposedly with the delta records, indicates if nothing else that he is quite serious in his suspicions of the delta veterans, and that he may act against them."

"They are not all bad fellows," admitted Marcus, "even though they be of Ar."

"There are good fellows in all cities," I said. "Even in Ar's Station."

"Perhaps," grumbled Marcus.

"Certainly," I assured him.

"What is your plan?" he asked.

"To approach the house of records over adjoining roofs, eschewing the use of patrolled streets," I said, "then to hurl the iron and rope from the roof of a nearby building to the roof of the house of records, and thence, later, by means of its displuviate atrium, to obtain entrance." The atrium in the house of records, I had learned, was open to the sky, which opening, as in many public and private Gorean buildings in the south, serves to admit light. The displuviate atrium is open in such a way as to shed rainwater outwards, keeping most of it from the flooring of the atrium below. This would also facilitate the use of the rope and iron. The alternative atrium, if unroofed, of course, is impluviate, so constructed as to guide rainwater into an awaiting pool below. This sort of atrium is less amenable to the rope and iron because of the pitch of the roof.

"You are confident you can recognize the records?"

"Not at all," I said.

"Surely you do not expect to carry them off?"

"Not at all," I said. "That would be impractical."

"You are going to burn them?"

"Yes," I said.

"How will you know what to burn?" he asked.

"I do not think that will present a problem," I said.

"Why not?" he asked.

"I plan on burning the entire building," I said.

"I see," he said. "What if the fire spreads throughout the entire district, and then burns down Ar?"

"I had not considered that," I admitted.

"Well," he said. "It is hard to think of everything."

"Yes," I granted him. He was right, of course.

"What if the records are in the Central Cylinder," he asked, "already at the war office?"

"That is where I expect they are," I said.

He groaned.

"But they may be here."

"You are not planning on burning down the Central Cylinder, are you?" he asked.

"Of course not," I said. "If they are there, with their facilities, they have probably already been copied, and perhaps more than once, and who knows where those copies might be stored, either there or about the city. Besides there are slave girls there."

"Such as the Ubara?" he asked.

"Yes," I said.

I suddenly stopped,.

"What is it?" he asked, instantly alert.

"Listen," I said.

"Yes," he said.

We could hear footsteps approaching, rapidly. We moved back, against a wall.

A brawny figure, in the darkness, passed.

I was not sure, but it seemed I had seen it somewhere, some place.

"Not everyone is observant of the curfew," remarked Marcus.

"You are out," I said.

"We have our armbands," he said.

"I think there is another coming," I said.

We kept back, in the shadows.

Another fellow was in the street, approaching, but suddenly detected us, shadows among shadows. He whipped free a sword and mine, and that of Marcus, too, left its sheath. He seemed startled, for a moment. I, too, was startled. Then, not sheathing the blade, he hurried on.

"Are there others?" whispered Marcus.

"Probably," I said, "but on other streets, each taking a separate way."

Marcus put back his sword. I, too, sheathed mine.

"Did you recognize the first fellow?" I asked.

"No," he said.

"I think he was of the peasant levies," I said. "I first saw him outside the walls. He had come from the west, and had survived the final defeat of Ar." I thought I rememberd him. He was a shaggy giant of a man. He had won the game of standing on the verr skin. He had cut the skin. I remembered the wine, soaking into the ground, like blood. He had stood upon the skin and regarded us. "I have won," he had said. He had been of the peasants. I would have expected him to have left the vicinity of city. To be sure, his village may have been one of several nearby villages put to the torch, its supplies gathered in by foragers, or burned. Such villages, after all, had furnished their quotas for the defensive levies. Indeed, a good portion of the civilian militia had been composed of such fellows, and youth, many not old enough to know how to handle a weapon.

"You recognized the second fellow?" said Marcus.

"I think so," I said.

"I think he may have recognized us as well," he said.

"Perhaps," I said.

"Plenius," said he, "from the delta."

"Yes," I said.

"I hear cries in the street," said Marcus.

"There is an alarm bar, as well," I said.

"Look there!" said Marcus.

"I see it," I said.

The sky was red in the east. It was a kind of radiance, flickering and pulsing.

"That is not the dawn," said Marcus grimly.

"I think we should return to our quarters," I said.

Some men ran past us now, toward the east, toward the light. We could hear more than one alarm bar now.

"Surely the curfew is still in effect," said Marcus.

"It will be hard to enforce now," I said.

"What is going on?" I called to a fellow hurrying past us, carrying a lantern,.

"Have you not heard?" he asked. "It is the house of records. It is afire!"

"Perhaps we should have gone to a tavern," said Marcus.

"They close at the eighteenth Ahn now," I said.

"True," he said, irritatedly.

I supposed that the taverners must be much put out by the curfew law, and would have lost much business. But perhaps they could open earlier.

I then, the rope and hook beneath my cloak, accompanied Marcus back toward the Metellan district. I could share his chagrin. Indeed, we might as well have spent the evening in a paga tavern, enjoying the swaying, pleading bodies of former free women of Ar, and considering on the ankles of which, on the cord there, wrapped several times about the ankle, and tied, we would consent to thread a pierced metal token, five of which might be purchased for a tarsk bit. At the time of the closing of the tavern these women were whipped if they did not have at least ten such tokens on their ankle cord. They jingled when they moved.

16 In The Vicinity Of The Teiban Market

"Ho!" cried the mercenary. "Behold! We have captured one of the Delta Brigade!"

"One side! One side!" cried his fellow, pushing men back.

"Will no one rescue me?" cried the bearded, bound fellow, struggling in the grasp of the mercenary who had first cried out. "Are you not men?"

We were at Teiban and Venaticus, at the southwest corner of the Teiban Sul Market. It was morning, the eighth Ahn, on the second day of the week. Naturally there were many folks about in such a place, at such a time.

"Careless," said Marcus, "that these fellows, not even guardsmen, should so boldly, so publicly, conduct their prisoner in this area, where hostility toward Cos might be rampant."

"Certainly an apparent lack of judgment," I granted him.

"Release me!" cried the bearded fellow to the two mercenaries. "I demand to be freed!"

"Silence, despicable sleen!" shouted one of the guardsmen, cuffing the prisoner, who reacted as though he might have been struck with great force.

"Sleen of a traitor to Cos!" said the other mercenary, adding a blow, to which the bearded prisoner once again reacted.

"I think I could have struck him harder than that," speculated Marcus.

"Release him!" cried a vendor of tur-pah, pushing through baskets of the vinelike vegetable.

"Do not interfere!" warned one of the mercenaries.

"Back, you disgusting patriots of Ar!" exclaimed the other.

"Strange," remarked Marcus, "that the prisoner has on his sleeve an armband with the delka upon it."

"Doubtless that is how the mercenaries recognized him as a member of the Delta Brigade," I said.

"The work of Seremides would be much simpler, to be sure," said Marcus, "if all the fellows in the Delta Brigade would be so obliging."

"Perhaps they could all wear a uniform," I suggested, "to make it easier to pick them out."

"There are only two of them!" cried the bearded prisoner. "Take me from them! Hide me! Glory to the Delta Brigade!"

None in the crowd, it seemed, dared echo this sentiment, but there was no mistaking its mood, one of sympathy for the fellow, and of anger toward the mercenaries, and there was a very definite possibility, one thing leading to another, that it might take action.

"Help! Help, if there be true men of Ar here!" cried the prisoner.

One of the fellows from the market pushed at a mercenary, who thrust him back, angrily.

"Make way! Make way!" cried the mercenary.

"We are taking this fellow to headquarters!" said the other.

"Let him go!" cried a man. Men surged about the two mercenaries.

"It is my only crime that I love Ar and am loyal to her!" cried the prisoner.

"Release him!" cried men. More than one fellow in the crowd had a staff, that simple weapon which can be so nimble, so lively, so punishing, in the hands of one of skill. This was only to be expected as many of the vendors in the market were peasants, come in with produce from outside the walls. Indeed, in many places they could simply enter through breaches in the wall, or climb over mounds of rubble, and enter the city. With respect to the staff, it serves of course not only as a weapon but, more usually, and more civilly, as an aid in traversing terrain of uncertain footing. Too, it is often used, yokelike, fore and aft of its bearer, to carry suspended, balanced baskets. Weaponwise, incidentally, there are men who can handle it so well that they are a match for many swordsmen. My friend Thurnock, in Port Kar, was one. Indeed, many sudden and unexpected blows had I received in lusty sport from that device in his hands. Eventually, under his tutelage, I had become proficient with the weapon, enabled at any rate to defend myself with some efficiency. But still I would not have cared to meet him, or such a fellow, in earnest, each of us armed only in such terms. I prefer the blade. Also, of course, all things being equal, the blade is a far more dangerous weapon. The truly dangerous peasant weapon is the peasant bow, or great bow. It is in virtue of that weapon that thousands of villags on Gor have their own Home Stones.

"Release him!" cried a man.

"What is to be done with him?" inquired another.

"Doubtless he will be impaled," said one of the mercenaries.

"No! No!" cried men.

"I wonder if those mercenaries realize they are in danger," said Marcus.

"I trust that they are being well paid," I said. "Otherwise they are certainly being exploited."

"Save me!" cried the bearded fellow. "Do not let them take me! Save me, if there be true men of Ar here!"

"Back, sleen of Ar!" cried the mercenary with the prisoner in hand.

"Back!" cried the other.

"Certainly they are not being very politic," said Marcus.

"Nor even courteous," I said.

"Help!" cried the prisoner, struggling. His hands were bound behind him and there were some ropes, as well, about his upper body, binding his arms to his sides.

"There is one hopeful sign here," said Marcus. "There is obviously sympathy for the Delta Brigade."

"Yes," I said.

"Help!" cried the prisoner.

"Does it seem to you that there are secret guardsmen about?" I asked Marcus. I had been trying to determine this.

He, too, surveyed the crowd, and area. "I do not think so," he said.

"Perhaps then," I said, "it is time to remove our armbands and reverse our cloaks, and adjust our wind scarves."

"Yes," said Marcus, grimly, "as the poor fellow is surely in desperate need of rescue."

In a moment then, our armbands removed, and certain adjustments effected in our garmenture, we thrust through the crowd.

"Unhand him!" I cried. It was not for nothing that I had once been granted a tryout with the troupe of Boots Tarsk-Bit. To be sure, the tryout had come to naught.

"Who are you?" cried one of the mercenaries. I did not think he was bad either. Surely he knew whom to expect, at any rate, in this situation. The prisoner's face suddenly beamed. With our wind scarves in place, and our blades drawn, there would be little doubt who we would be, at least in general.

"The Brigade!" whispered men, elated, about us.

"Unhand them!" cried one of the men about.

A fellow flourished a staff. I trusted the crowd would not now close with the mercenaries, for if it did I genuinely feared there would be little but pulp left of them. But, still, it seemed, they did not recognize that they were in actual danger. So little respect they had, it seemed, for the men of Ar. On the other hand perhaps they read the crowd better than I. But I really doubt it. I think I was much more aware, and had been earlier, from my position and perspective, and my awareness of the mood of Ar, of its tenseness, its readiness, its ugliness, like a dark sky that might suddenly, without warning, blaze and shatter with destruction and thunder. Indeed, it was the mercenaries whom Marcus and I, I believe, as it was turning out, were rescuing.

"We yield to superior force," said the first mercenary.

"We have no choice," said the second, apparently similarly resigned, the one who had the prisoner in hand.

A murmur of victory, of elation, coursed through the crowd.

"There are only two of us," I said to the mercenary who I took it was first of the two. "Let us have it out with blades."

"No, no, that is all right," he said.

"Here it seems you have many allies," said the second.

"I am sure they will be good fellows and not interfere," I said.

"No, we will not interfere!" said a fellow enthusiastically.
"Clear some space," said another.
The crowd began to move back.
"I tell you, we surrender the prisoner," said the first, somewhat unpleasantly. "We are surrendering him. Do you understand?"
"Yes," I said.
"We are yielding to superior force," he said.
"There is no choice for us," said the second.
"Very well," I said.
They then turned about, and expeditiously withdrew.
"You must now escape!" said a man. "They will inform guardsmen, they will return with reinforcements."
"I do not think so," I said.
Men looked at me, puzzled.
"My thanks, brothers!" said the prisoner. "But our brethren of Ar are right! We must flee! Take me with you, hide me!"
I sheathed my blade, and so, too, did Marcus his.
"Hurry! Untie me! Let us make away!" said the prisoner.
"You do not seem to be well tied," I said, inspecting his bonds.
"What are you doing?" he cried. "Ugh!"
"Now," I said, "you are well tied."
He struggled briefly, startled, frustratedly. Then he understood his helplessness.
"What is the meaning of this?" he said.
"What are you doing?" asked a fellow, puzzled.
I bent down and pushed the prisoner's ankles together, and then looped a thong about them, that they might not be able to move more than a hort or two apart. He could not now run. To be sure, he could stand.
"Untie me!" he said. "We must escape!"
"You are of the Delta Brigade!" I inquired.
"Yes," he said, "as must be you!"
"Why do you say that?" I inquired.
"You have rescued me," he said.
"You regard yourself as rescued?" I said.
"Surely you, like myself, are of the Delta Brigade!" he said.
"I do not think I know you," I said.
"I am not of your component," he said.
"But perhaps we are not of the Delta Brigade," I said.
"But who then?" he said.
"Perhaps we are loyal fellows of Ar," I said, "who, as is presumably appropriate for those of the new Ar, hate the Delta Brigade, and are opposed to it, who see in it a threat to Ar's

ignominous surrender, that is, to harmony and peace, who see in it a challenge to the imperious governance of Cos, that is, to the glorious friendship and alliance of the two great ubarates?"

"He speaks like the public boards," said a fellow.

"Like part of them, at any rate," said another.

"I thought only the pusillanimous, and naive adolescents, took such twaddle seriously," said another.

"I do not understand," said the prisoner uncertainly.

"Are you for the old Ar or the new Ar?" I asked.

"I am of the Delta Brigade!" he said. "And there is only one Ar, the old Ar, the true Ar!"

"Yes!" said a man.

"Brave fellow!" said a man.

"Release him and hide him!" urged another.

"No," said the prisoner. "They are right. They must make certain of me! In their place I would do the same."

"Make certain quickly then," said a man. "There may be little time!"

"Do not fear," I said.

The prisoner now stood straighter, more proudly, more assuredly. He now suspected he was being tested. Indeed, he was, but not in the sense he thought.

"You then acknowledge," I asked him, "that the only Ar, and the true Ar, is the Ar of old, the Ar which was betrayed and which stands in defiance of Cos?"

For a moment the prisoner turned white. Then he said, boldly, "Yes, that is the true Ar."

"And you further acknowledge that Seremides and the Ubara are traitors to Ar, and puppets of Cos?"

"Of course," he said, after a moment.

Here and there there were gasps in the crowd. Whereas presumably there were few in the crowd who were not prepared to resent, and as possible, oppose, Cos, not all were convinced of the depth and extent of the treason which had contributed so significantly to her victory. I thought it well to have the crowd hear these sentiments from the lips of the prisoner. To be sure, such understandings were surely not new to the Cosians in Ar, nor to many of the more reflective in Ar herself.

"Treason on the part of Seremides?" asked a man.

"Talena a traitor?" said another.

"Yes!" said the prisoner.

"Clearly he is of the Delta Brigade," said a man. "Release him!"

"You would have us hide you?" I asked.

"Yes," said the prisoner.

"Take you into our confidence, bring you to our secret places, tell you our plans, introduce you to our leaders, our pervasive, secret networks of communication?"

"Only if later you deem me worthy of such trust," he said.

I hoped by this last question to lead the crowd to believe that the Delta Brigade was a determined, disciplined, extensive, well-organized force in Ar, one which might realistically inspire hope in the populace and fear in the forces of occupation. Actually, of course, I had no idea of the nature or extent, or power, or resources, of the Delta Brigade. I was not even sure there was such an organization. At one time Marcus and I thought we were the Delta Brigade. Certainly at that time there had been no organization. Then, later, it seemed, there had been acts performed in the name of the Delta Brigade, sabotage, and such, in which we had had no part. These might have been the acts of individuals, or groups of individuals, for all we knew, perhaps patriots, or criminals, or fools, but not of an organization. There had apparently been concerted action in the burning of the house of records, but that did not necessitate the existence of a "Brigade." It could have been done by a small group of men, presumably mostly veterans of the delta, interested in making it difficult for Cos to trace their identities.

"Were you in the delta?" I asked.

"Certainly," said he.

"Who was commander of the vanguard?" I asked.

"Labienus," said he, "of this city."

"And his first subaltern?" I asked.

"I do know," he said. "I was not of the vanguard."

"Who commanded the 17th?" I asked.

"I do not remember," he said.

"Vinicius?" I said.

"Yes," he said. "Vinicius."

"And the 11th?"

"I do not know," he said.

"Toron, of Venna," I said.

"Yes," he said. "Toron, of Venna."

"In which command were you?"

"In the 14th," he said.

"Who commanded the 14th?"

"Honorius."

"And his first subaltern?"

"Falvius."

"His second?"

"Camillus."

"You were with the 14th then when it was defeated in the northern tracts of the delta?"

"Yes," he said.

"With the 7th, the 11th and the 9th?"

"Yes," he said.

I then removed the armband with the delka on it and tucked it in my belt. I then tore loose a part of his tunic and thrust it in his mouth. I then tied it in place with the armband. His eyes regarded me, questioningly, over it, frightened. I then crossed his ankles, causing him to fall, and tied them together, crossed. He tried, ineffectually, to speak. He tried to sit up but I thrust him back, my sandal to his chest, supine on the pavement, and looked down at him. He looked up at me. He was as helpless as a slave girl.

"Vicinius," I said, "did not command the 17th, nor Toron the 11th. Vicinius commanded the 4th, and Toron the 3rd. Your answers with respect to the chain of command in the 14th were correct, but the 14th was not defeated in the northern tracts, but in the southern tracts, with the 7th, 9th and 11th. It was the 3rd, the 4th and the 17th which were defeated in the north."

He struggled, futilely.

"He is a Cosian spy," I said.

Men cried out in fury.

The prisoner, now truly a prisoner, looked up at us, terrified. He tried to rise up a little, to lift his shoulders from the pavement, but angry staffs thrust him back down, and in a moment he was kept in place, on his back on the pavement, pinioned by staffs, some caging him at the sides, others pressing down upon him.

"Bring a sack," I said. "Put him in it."

"We shall bring one," said a fellow.

"Let it be a sack such as we use for tarsk meat," said another.

"Yes," said another.

"We will hang it with the meat," said a fellow. "In that way it will attract little notice."

"And we shall beat it well with our staffs," said a fellow, grimly, "as we tenderize the sacked meat of tarsks."

"That is fitting," laughed a fellow.

"That, too, will attract little attention," said another.

"We will break every bone in his body," said another.

"In the morning see that it is found on the steps of the Central Cylinder."

"It will be so," said a fellow.

"And on the sack," I said, "let there be inscribed a delka."

"It will be so!" laughed a man.

In moments a sack was brought and the fellow, his eyes wild, was thrust, bound and gagged, into it. I then saw it tied shut over his head, and saw it being dragged behind two peasants toward the far side of the market, to the area where the butchers and meat dressers have their stalls.

"What if he survives?" asked Marcus.

"I hope he does," I said. "I think his broken bones, his bruises, his blood, his groans, his gibbering, his accounts of what occurred, his terror, such things, would better serve the Delta Brigade than this death."

"It is for that reason that you have spared him?" he asked.

"Not only that," I said. "He seemed a nice fellow, and he did know the chain of command in the 14th."

"With you," said Marcus, "it is a game, but it is not so with certain others."

"You are referring to the two fellows who were found hung in an alley, near a tavern in the Anbar district?" I asked.

"Yes, with bloody delkas cut into their chests," he said.

"I heard of it, too," I said.

"It is speculated they were attempting to infiltrate the Delta Brigade."

"Interesting," I said.

"I fear there may actually be a Delta Brigade," he said.

"I do not know," I said. "'But I, too, think that it is possible."

"Did you discern the support of the crowd for the Delta Brigade?" he asked.

"Yes," I said. "And so, too, did the mercenaries."

"And the spy."

"Of course," I said. "Let us hope that he lives to make a report on the matter."

"And, further, their support for the delta veterans?"

"Yes," I said. "They were much in support of the spy when he claimed to be such."

"That is very different from a few months ago," said Marcus.

"Only lately has Ar become aware of what those men did for her, what they suffered, and how much she owes them."

"Better led they could have turned back Cos at the Vosk and stopped her at Torcadino," he said.

"You see what the Cosians here must now do, do you not?" I asked.

"What?" he asked.

"At this stage of the game?"

"What?"

"They must attempt to discredit the Delta Brigade."

"Of course," said Marcus.

"But no longer by identifying it with the veterans of the delta," I said.

"Why not?" he asked.

"Because of the popular support now rising in favor of the veterans," I said. "Seremides no doubt links the Delta Brigade with the veterans of the delta, and perhaps on the whole correctly, but he is clever enough to recognize that the popularity of the actions of the Delta Brigade has increased support for the veterans. He must now attempt to drive a wedge between the veterans and the Delta Brigade."

"In what fashion?" asked Marcus.

"Is it not obvious?" I asked.

"Speak," said Marcus.

"Seremides needs something, or someone, to dissociate the Delta Brigade from the veterans."

"Continue," said Marcus.

"He desires to turn the population away from the Delta Brigade."

"Yes?"

"Therefore the Delta Brigade must be presented as inimical to Ar, as the tool of her enemies."

"What enemies?" asked Marcus. "Surely not her true enemies, Cos and Tyros."

"Who betrayed Ar in the north?" I asked. "What city opened her gates to the expeditionary force of Cos?"

"No city," said Marcus, angrily.

"Ar's Station!" I smiled.

"I see," he said.

"This had to happen," I said. "Cos requires an enemy for Ar which is not herself. She must divert attention from her tyranny. If we dismiss the delta veterans the only practical choice is Ar's Station. As you know, many in Ar blame Ar's Station, and her supposed surrender in the north, not only for her current misfortunes but for the disaster in the delta."

"Absurd," said Marcus.

"Not if you do not know the truth," I said, "but have at your disposal only the propaganda of Cos and the lies of a traitorous government in the Central Cylinder."

"This is your Kaissa?" he said.

"Yes," I said. "In our way, and in what we began, for better or for worse, we have forced Seremides to renew the vilification of Ar's Station."

"And in this campaign of vilification will be brought forth once more the Home Stone of Ar's Station?"

"Exactly," I said.

"You have planned this?" he said.

"For both of our sakes," I said.

"For yours as well?"

"I, too, have a interest in these matters," I said.

"But I do not think it has to do with the Home Stone of Ar's Station."

"No," I said. "It has to do with something else."

"The crowd has dissipated," said Marcus. "I think it would be well for us, too, to withdraw."

"Yes," I said, and, in a few moments, in a sheltered place, between buildings, we had resumed our customary guise, that of auxiliary guardsmen, police in the pay of Cos.

"How do you plan on attacking the place of the Home Stone's display, if Seremides chooses to expose it once more to the abuse of Ar?"

"He will," I said.

"And how do you plan on attacking the place of its display?" asked Marcus.

"I do not plan on attacking anything," I said.

"How will you obtain it?" he asked.

"I intend to have it picked up," I said.

" 'Picked up'?"

"Yes," I said.

"Do you not think it might be missed?" he asked.

"No," I said.

"Why not?" he asked.

"Because it will still be there," I said.

"You are mad," he said.

17 Magic

"Where has she gone!" cried a man.

"My senses reel!" exclaimed Marcus. "But a moment ago she was within the palanquin!"

"Shhh," I said.

"I cannot understand what I have seen on this street!" he said.

Marcus and I stood in the pit, shoulder to shoulder with

others, before the low stage. There were tiers behind us for those who wished to pay two tarsk bits, rather than one, for the entertainments.

The four fellows, in turbans, with plumes, in stately fashion, as though nothing unusual had occurred, carried the palanquin, its curtains now open again, offstage.

"She has vanished," said a fellow, wonderingly.

"But to where?" asked another.

"She cannot disappear into thin air," said a fellow.

"But she has done so!" said another, in awe.

We were in a small, shabby theater. It had an open proscenium. The house was only some twenty yards in depth. This was the fourth such establishment we had entered this evening. To be sure, there were many other entertainments on the street outside, in stalls, and set in the open, behind tables, and such, in which were displayed mostly tricks with small objects, ostraka, rings, scarves, coins and such. I am fond of such things, and a great admirer of the subtlety, the adroitness, dexterity and skills which are often involved in making them possible.

"Alas," cried the ponderous fellow waddling about the stage, yet, if one noticed it, with a certain lightness and grace, considering his weight, "have I lost my slave?"

"Find her!" cried a fellow.

"Recover her!" cried another.

These fellows, I think, were serious. It might be mentioned, at any rate, that many Goreans, particularly those of lower caste, and who are likely to have had access only to the "first knowledge," take things of this sort very seriously, believing they are witnesses not to tricks and illusions but to marvelous phenomena consequent upon the gifts and powers of unusual individuals, sorcerers or magicians. This ingenuousness is doubtless dependent upon several factors, such as the primitiveness of the world, the isolation and uniqueness of cities, the disparateness of cultures and the tenuousness of communication. Also the Gorean tends neither to view the world as a mechanical clockwork of interdependent parts, as a great, regular, predictable machine, docile to equations, obedient to abstractions, nor as a game of chance, inexplicable, meaningless and random at the core. His fundamental metaphor in terms of which he would defend himself from the glory and mystery of the world is neither the machine nor the die. It is rather, if one may so speak, the stalk of grass, the rooted tree, the flower. He feels the world as alive and real. He paints eyes upon his ships, that they may see their way. And if he feels so even about this vessels, then so much more the awed and reverent must he feel when he contemplates the immensity and grandeur, the beauty, the power and the mightiness within which he finds himself. Why is there anything? Why is there anything at all? Why not just nothing? Wouldn't "nothing" be more likely, more rational, more scientific? When did time begin? Where does space end? On a line, at the surface of a sphere? Do our definitions constrain reality? What if reality does not know our language, the boundaries of our perceptions, the limitations of our minds? How is it that one wills to raise one's hand and the hand rises? How is it that an aggregation of molecules can cry out with joy in the darkness? The Gorean sees the world less as a puzzle than an opportunity, less as a datum to be explained than a bounty in which to rejoice, less as a problem to be solved than a gift to be gratefully received. It might be also be noted, interestingly, that the Gorean, in spite of his awe of Priest-Kings, and the reverence he accords them, the gods of his world, does not think of them as having formed the world, nor of the world being in some sense consequent upon their will. Rather the Priest-Kings are seen as being its children, too, like sleen, and rain and man. A last observation having to do with the tendency of some Goreans to accept illusions and such as reality is that the Gorean tends to take such things as honor and truth very seriously. Given his culture and background, his values, he is often easier to impose upon than would be many others. For example, he is likely, at least upon upon occasion, to be an easier mark for the fraud and charlatan than a more suspicious, cynical fellow. On the other hand, I do not encourage lying to Goreans. They do not like it.

"I could have reached out and touched her," said Marcus.

I really doubted that he could have done that. To be sure, we were quite close to the stage.

In this part of the performance a light, roofed, white-curtained palanquin had been carried on the stage by the four turbaned, plumed fellows. It had been set down on the stage and the curtains drawn back, on both sides, so that one could see through to the back of the stage, which was darkly draped. Within the palanquin, reclining there, as though indolently, on one elbow there had been a slim girl, veiled and clad in shimmering white silk.

"Surely this is some high-born damsel," had called out the ponderous fellow.

There had been laughter at this. Free women almost never appear on the Gorean stage. Indeed, in certain higher forms of drama, such as the great tragedies, rather than let women on the stage, either free or slave, female roles are played by men.

The masks worn, the costuming, the dialogue, and such, make it clear, of course, which roles are to be understood as the female roles. Women, of course, almost always slaves, may appear in mimings, farces and such.

The girl had then, aided by a hand from the ponderous fellow, risen from the palanquin and looked about herself, rather as though bored. She then regarded the audience, and at some length, disdainfully. There had been some hooting at this.

"Surely this cannot be my slave, Litsia?" wailed the fellow.

She tossed her head, in the hood and veil.

"If you be free, dear lady," said the fellow, "report me to guardsmen for my affrontery, that I may be flogged for daring to address you, but if you be my Litsia, remove your hood and veil."

As though with an almost imperial resignation she put back her hood and lowered her veil.

"She is pretty!" had exclaimed Marcus.

Others, too, expressed their inadvertent admiration of the woman.

"It is my Litsia!" cried the ponderous fellow, as though relieved.

The woman drew down her robes a bit, that her shoulders were bared. She held the robes together before her.

"She is not collared!" cried a fellow!

"Lash her!" cried another.

For an instant the girl blanched and trembled, clutching the robes together before her in her small fists, but then, in a moment, had recovered herself, and was back in character. It was easy to tell that she had, at some time or another, felt the lash, and knew what it was like.

"But surely we are to respect slaves in the new Ar?" inquired the ponderous fellow, anxiously, of the audience.

This question, of course, was greeted with guffaws and a slapping of the left shoulders.

"But my Litsia must have some token of her bondage upon her," said the fellow. "Please, Litsia, show us."

Quickly the girl thrust the lower portion of her left leg, lovely and curved, from the robe. On her left ankle was a narrow, locked slave anklet. Then, quickly, she concealed her leg and ankle again within the robe. The slave collar, of one form or another, band or bar, or chain and lock, is almost universal on Gor for slaves. On the other hand, some masters use a bracelet or anklet. Too, the slaves of others may wear as little to denote their condition as a ring, the significance of which may be known to few. The bracelet, the anklet and ring are often worn by women whose slavery is secret, largely hidden from the world, though not, of course, from themselves and their masters. And even such women, when in private with their masters, will usually be collared, as is suitable for slaves. Indeed, they will often strip themselves and kneel, or drop to all fours, to be collared, as soon as they enter their master's domicile. There are many points in favor of the collar, besides those of history and tradition. The throat is not only an ideal aesthetic showplace for the symbol of bondage, displaying it beautifully and prominently, but one which, because of the location, at the throat, and the widths involved, is excellently secure. It also makes it easier to leash the female. Also, of course, by means of it and a rope or chain one may attach her to various rings and holding devices. Some fellows even bracelet or tie her hands to it. The collar, too, of course, helps to make clear to the slave, and others, her status as a domestic animal.

"Show us a little more, Litsia," begged the ponderous fellow.

Litsia then, rather quickly, but holding the pose for a moment, opened the silken robes, and, her knees slightly flexed, and her head turned demurely to the left, held them out to the sides.

"She is lovely!" said Marcus.

"Yes," I agreed.

"Surely she is a bred slave, with lines like that," he said.

"No," I said. "She was a free woman, from Aspericke."

Marcus looked at me, puzzled.

"Yes," I said.

"Are you sure?" he asked.

"Yes," I said.

"Interesting," he said.

"In a sense, of course," I said, "she is a bred slave."

"True," he said.

It is a common Gorean belief that all females are bred slaves. It is only that some have their collars and some, as yet, do not.

The girl wore a modest slave tunic, which muchly covered her.

She now drew closed again the sides of the shimmering robe and, once more, tossed her head, and glanced disdainfully at the audience. Again there was hooting.

"Some folks," said the ponderous fellow, "think that I have spoiled her."

The girl then put out her small hand and was assisted by the ponderous fellow to the palanquin again. When she took her place in it it was lifted.

It was clearly off the floor. One could see the drapery at the back of the stage.

"I do trust you will be nice to me this evening!" said the ponderous fellow to the slim beauty on the palanquin.

She tossed her head and did not deign to respond to him.

He then drew shut the curtains of the palanquin. It was still off the floor.

"Do you think I am too easy with her?" the ponderous fellow inquired of the audience.

"Yes! Yes!" shouted several of the men.

"Oh, oh!" cried the ponderous fellow looking upward miserably and shaking his fists, helplessly, angrily, in the air. "If only I were not a devoted adherent of the new and wonderful Ar!"

There was much laughter.

"But alas I am such a devoted adherent!" he wept.

There was more laughter.

I gathered that much of the resentment toward the current governance of Ar tended to be expressed in such places, in shows, in farces, in bawdy travesties and such. Certain theaters had been closed down because of the articulateness and precision, and abusiveness, of such satire or criticism. Two had been burned. To be sure this fellow seemed technically within the bounds of acceptability, if only just so. Too, it was doubtless a great deal safer now than it had been a few weeks ago to indulge in such humor. Wisely I thought had the government withdrawn from its projected policies of devirilization, which, indeed, had never been advanced beyond the stage of proposals. It had discovered, simply, clearly, and immediately that most males of the city would not give up their manhood, even if they were praised for doing so. Indeed, even the Ubara herself, it seemed, had reaffirmed that slave girls should be obedient and try to please their masters. So narrowly, I suspected, had riots and revolution been averted. Still, I supposed, there might be spies in the audience. I doubted if the ponderous fellow would be popular with the authorities.

"If only some magician would aid me in my dilemma!" wept the ponderous fellow.

"Beware!" cried a fellow in the audience, alarmed.

"Yes, beware!" laughed another fellow.

"If only some magician would waft away my Litsia, if only for a moment, and teach her just a little of what is it to be a slave girl!" he said.

Several men laughed. I had to hand it to the ponderous fellow. He carried off the thing well.

"But of course there are no magicians!" he said.

"Beware," cried one fellow, he who had been so alarmed, so drawn into the drama, before. "Beware, lest one might be listening!"

"I think that I shall speak with her, and plead with her to be a better slave girl," said the fellow.

The palanquin was still of course where it had been last, near the center of the stage, lifted off the floor, by its four bearers. To be sure, as the ponderous fellow had drawn them, the curtains were now closed.

The audience was very still now.

The ponderous fellow then pulled back the curtains.

"Ai!" cried a fellow.

Several of the fellows, including Marcus, gasped.

"She is gone!" cried a fellow.

Once again, one could see through the open palanquin, to the draperies at the back of the stage.

The four fellows in turbans, with plumes, then, in stately fashion, as though nothing unusual had occurred, carried the palanquin offstage.

Men spoke excitedly about us.

I struck my left shoulder, commending the performer for the illusion.

Others, too, then applauded.

The ponderous fellow bowed to the crowd, and then resumed his character.

"I think there is but one chance to recover my slave," he confided to the audience, "but I fear to risk it."

"Why?" asked a fellow.

"Because," said the ponderous fellow, addressing his concerned interlocutor confidentially, with a stage whisper, "it might require magic."

"No matter!" said a fellow.

"There is a wicker trunk," said the ponderous fellow. "It was left with me by a fellow from Anango."

Some of the fellows in the audience gasped. The magicians of Anango are famed on Gor. If you wish to have someone turned into a turtle or something, those are the fellows to see. To be sure, their work does not come cheap. The only folks who are not familiar with them, as far as I know, are the chaps from far-off Anango, who have never heard of them.

"Of course, he may not be a magician," mused the ponderous fellow.

"But he might be!" pointed out an excited fellow in the audience.

"True," mused the ponderous fellow.

"It is worth a try," said a fellow.

"Anything to get your rope back on her," said another.

"Do you think he would mind?" asked the ponderous fellow.

"No!" said a fellow.

I wondered how he knew.

"He may be the very fellow who wafted her away!" said another.

"Yes," suggested another fellow.

"Perhaps he wants you to use the trunk to recover her!" said another.

"Yes!" said a man, convinced.

"He did say he was my friend," said the ponderous fellow.

"Fetch the trunk!" said a man.

"Fetch the trunk!" cried the ponderous fellow, decisively, to his fellows offstage.

Two of the fellows who had borne out the palanquin, their turbans and plumes now removed, appeared on stage, entering from stage right, the house left, each of them carrying a trestle. These were placed rather toward the back of the stage, at the center, about five feet apart. In a moment the other two fellows who had helped to bear the palanquin, they, too, now without the turbans and plumes, as there was now no point in such accouterments, their no longer being in attendance on the insolent slave, also emerged from stage right, bearing a long wicker trunk, some six feet in length, some two feet in height and two feet in depth. This was placed on the two trestles. One could, accordingly, see under the trunk, and about it. It was, thus, in full view, and spatially isolated from the floor, the sides of the stage and the drapery in the back, several feet behind it, supported on its two trestles.

"The trunk is not empty!" cried a fellow.

"The slave is within it!" called out another.

"That is no trick!" said another.

"I surely hope the slave is within it," called the ponderous fellow to the audience, "as I do wish to recover her!"

"She is there!" hooted a fellow.

"I hope so," said the ponderous fellow. "Let us look!"

He hurried to the trunk and lifted away the wicker lid, which covered it. He set the lid to one side, on the floor. He then unhinged the back of the trunk from the trunk sides. It then hung down in the back, being attached to the trunk bottom. One could see it, through the trestle legs. He then opened the left side of the trunk, letting it, too, hang free, except that it hung to the side. It, too, of course, was attached to the trunk's bottom. He treated the right side of the trunk in the same manner. It, too, naturally, was attached to the trunk bottom, in the same manner as was the left side. The trunk, in effect, was being disassembled before the audience. It was now completely open, the back hanging down in back, and the sides to the sides, except for the front panel, which the ponderous fellow held in place with one hand.

"Open the front panel!" cried a fellow.

"Show us the slave!" cried another.

"That is no trick!" said a fellow.

"Aii!" cried more than one fellow, as the ponderous fellow let the front panel drop forward, to the front. The trunk was now completely open.

"The slave is not there!" cried a man.

"She is not there," said another, startled.

"It would be a poor trick if she was there," said another.

"Why do you show us an empty trunk?" asked a man.

We could see through to the drapery behind.

"Alas, woe!" cried the ponderous fellow, running his hands about the empty space now exposed to view. "It is true! She is not here!" He got down on all fours and looked under the trunk, and then he lifted up the front panel, running his hand about under the trunk bottom, which was, say, about an inch in thickness. He then, seemingly distraught, let the front panel fall forward again. But even then he went again to his knees and thrust his hand about, to the floor, then between the trunk bottom and the floor. The front panel, even dropped forward, was still about eighteen inches from the floor. The floor could be seen clearly at all times beneath it. "She is not here!" wailed the ponderous fellow.

"Where is the slave?" asked a man.

"Perhaps she has been kept by the magician," proposed a fellow, seriously enough.

"But he is my friend!" protested the ponderous fellow.

"Are you sure of it?" asked one of the more earnest fellows in the audience.

"Perhaps the trunk is not really magic?" said the ponderous fellow.

"That would seem the most plausible explanation to me," whispered one fellow to another.

"I would think so," said Marcus, more to himself than to anyone else.

I looked at him sharply. I think he was serious.

"Do you not think so?" he asked. He was serious.

"Let us watch," I said. I smiled to myself. Marcus, I knew, was a highly intelligent fellow. On the other hand he did come from a culture which on the whole maintained a quite open mind on questions of this sort, and these illusions were, I take it, the first he had ever seen. To him they must have seemed awesome. Too, as a highly intelligent young man, from his particular background, he was prepared to accept what appeared to be the evidence of his senses. Would it not have seemed to him an even more grievous affront to rationality not to do so? I supposed that I, in his place, if I had had his background, and had known as little as he did about such things, might have been similarly impressed, if not convinced. Certainly many Goreans whom I regarded as much more intelligent than I took such things with great seriousness.

"What have I done wrong? What have I done wrong?" moaned the ponderous fellow. He then put up the front panel and latched it to the side panel on the left. "What have I done wrong?" he moaned. He then hooked up the right side of the trunk. It attached to the front panel. "I do not understand it," he moaned. He went to the back and lifted up the back panel and latched it to the side panels. He then reached down and put the wicker lid back on the trunk. He then faced the audience with comic misery. "What have I done wrong?" he queried.

"You did not call upon the magician!" cried a fellow.

"What?" cried the ponderous fellow, startled.

"No!" said the fellow in the audience. "Remember! You called out before, expressing a wish that you might be succored in your dilemma, that some magician might waft her away, if only for a moment, to teach her a little of what it was to be a slave girl!"

"Yes!" said the ponderous fellow. "Yes! That is true!"

"Perhaps the fellow from Anango, your friend," said the man, "who is perhaps a magician, heard you and did as you asked, as a favor."

"Is it possible?" inquired the ponderous fellow.

"It is possible!" averred the man.

"What must I then do?" inquired the ponderous fellow.

"Ask for her back!" said the man.

"Certainly," said another fellow in the audience.

"Do you think he would return her?" asked the ponderous fellow.

"Certainly," said the fellow who had been attempting to be of help in this matter.

"He is your friend," another reminded him.

"I think he is my friend," said the ponderous fellow.

"It is surely worth a try," said the first fellow.

The ponderous fellow then looked upward and called out,

"Oh, Saba Boroko Swaziloo, old chap, if you can hear me, and if it be you who has wafted away my little Litsia, perhaps for her instruction and improvement, please return her to me now!" Such names, of course, are nonsense, and are not really Anangan names but they do have several of the vowel sounds of such names, and, accordingly, upon occasions such as these, by fellows who are somewhat careless in such matters, are often prevailed upon to serve as such. It was highly unlikely, of course, that there would be any Anangans in the audience. I hoped not, at any rate, for the sake of the ponderous fellow.

There was silence.

"Nothing!" said the ponderous fellow, in disappointment. "Nothing!"

There was suddenly a rocking and bumping from the wicker trunk. It shook on the trestles.

"What is this?" cried the ponderous fellow, turning about.

The trunk rocked back and forth.

"Master!" came from within the trunk. "Master, oh, beloved Master, help me. I beg of you to help me, Master! Please, Master, if you can hear me, help me! Help me!"

"Open it!" cried a man.

"Open it!" called another.

The ponderous fellow threw off the wicker, basketlike lid of the trunk and gazed within, then staggering back as though in astonishment.

"Show us! Show us!" cried men.

Swiftly, losing not a nonce, he undid the side latches and dropped the front panel of the trunk. There, in the trunk, framed by the sides and back, as men cried out in wonder and delight, was descried the slave, Litsia, now not only in the least of slave rags but in sirik.

She was excitingly curvaceous, a dream of pleasure, such a sight as might induce a strong man to howl with joy, to dance with triumph.

Those on the tiers rose to their feet, applauding.

Yes, the woman was well turned. No longer now could there be the least doubt as to the promises of her lineaments. Almost might she have been on the block so little did her brief, twisted, scanty rags leave to the imagination of lustful brutes. And well did she move upon that wicker surface, in helpless desirability, in the grasp of the sirik, the metal on her neck, and on her wrists and ankles, the whole impeccably joined by its linkage of gleaming chain.

"The magician has returned her!" said a man.

"And she is in better condition than when he received her," laughed a man.

The ponderous fellow then, with a tug, tore away the bit of cloth which had provided its mockery of a shielding for her beauty and cast it aside.

Men cheered.

"It seems I have a new master," said the girl, squirming a little, naked, to the audience.

There was laughter.

She was then pulled from the trunk and flung to her knees on the stage.

She, kneeling, in sirik, turned to the audience. "I now know I have a new master!" she said.

There was more laughter.

"Where have you been?" demanded the ponderous fellow.

"I was in my palanquin," she said. "Then, in the blinking of an eye, I was in the castle somewhere, stripped and in chains!"

"In Anango, I wager," said the ponderous fellow.

"And at the feet of a magician!" she cried.

"That would be my old friend, Swaziloo," said the ponderous fellow.

"Yes," she said. "I think that is what he said his name was."

I was pleased that they had managed to get the name right the second time. I had known the ponderous fellow to slip up in such matters. The girl was not likely to make a mistake, of course. If she did so, she would probably be whipped.

"And for what purpose were you transported to his castle?" asked the ponderous fellow.

"To be taught, Master!" she said.

"And were you taught?" he asked.

"Yes, Master!" she said.

"And what were you taught?" he asked.

"To be a slave girl, Master!" she said.

Then, to the delight of the audience, she reached forth and, holding the fellow's leg, and pressing herself against it, kissed him humbly, timidly, lovingly, about the thigh.

"And I," said the ponderous fellow, "may have learned something, too, about how to be a master."

There was then applause and cheering, and bows were taken by the troupe, the assistants and the ponderous fellow, and the girl, for her part, performing obeisance to the audience, and then, to the delight of the audience, being conducted off, in her chains, with tiny, short steps, no more permitted her by the linkage on her ankle rings, in a common slave girl leading position, bent over at the waist, drawn along at the master's side by the hair.

Marcus had been shaken by the performance.

Afterward we were walking outside. We would not attend any more performances that evening, as the shows, and the street, would be soon closed, due to the curfew. Also, I had discovered what I had been searching for, the fellow I wished to contact.

"I am puzzled by what I have seen," he said.

"In what way?" I asked.

"Is he truly a magician, or in league with magicians?" asked Marcus.

"Much depends on what you mean by 'magician'," I said.

"You know what I mean," said Marcus.

"I do not think so,' I said.

"One who can do magic," said Marcus, irritably.

"Oh," I said.

"I do not know if it is wise to use magic in such a way," said Marcus, "for pay, as a show, for an audience."

"I do not understand," I said.

"Magic seems too strange and wonderful," he said.

"Why don't they just make gold pieces appear instead?" I asked.

"Yes, why not?" he asked.

"Indeed, why not?" I said.

"I do not understand the audience," he said. "Some men laughed much, and did not seem to understand the momentousness of what was occurring. Some seemed to take it almost for granted. Others were more sensitive to the wonders they beheld."

"Dear Marcus," I said, "such things are tricks. They are done to give pleasure, and amusement."

"The magician, or the magician, or magicians, the showman was in league with," said Marcus, "obviously possess extraordinary powers."

"In a sense, yes," I said, "and I would be the last to underestimate or belittle them. They have unusual powers. But you, too, have unusual powers. For example, you have unusual powers with tempered blades, with the steels of war."

"Such things," said he, quickly, "are mere matters of blood, of instinct, of aptitude, of strength, of reflexes, of training, of practice. They are skills, skills."

"The magician, too," I said, "has his skills. Let them be remarked and celebrated. Life is the richer for us that he has them. Let us rejoice in his achievements."

"I do not think I understand you," said Marcus.

"Would you like to know how the tricks were done?" I asked.

" 'Tricks'?" he said.

"Yes," I said. "If I tell you, will you then value them less?"

" 'Done'?" he said.

"Surely you do not believe that a slave disappeared into thin air and then reappeared out of thin air in a wicker trunk, do you?"

"Certainly it is difficult to believe," said Marcus, "but surely I must believe it, as it happened."

"Nonsense," I said.

"Did you not see what I saw?" he asked.

"I suppose that in one sense I saw what you saw," I said, "but in another sense I think it would be fair to say that I didn't. At the very least, we surely interpreted what we saw very differently."

"I know what I saw," said Marcus.

"You know what you think you saw," I said.

"There could be no tricks," said Marcus, angrily. "Not this time. Do not think I am naive! I have heard of such things as trapdoors and secret panels! I have even heard of illusions done with mirrors! But those are not done by true magic. They are only tricks. I might even be able to do them. But this was different. Here, obviously, there could have been only true magic."

"Why do you say that?" I asked.

"I do know that there is false magic, or only apparent magic, and false magicians, or only apparent magicians, but this was different."

"Why?" I asked.

"If there are so many false magicians," said Marcus, "then there must be at least one true magician."

"Have you reflected upon the logic of that?" I asked.

"Not carefully," he said.

"It might be well to do so," I said.

"Perhaps," he said, irritatedly.

"From the fact that most larls eat meat it does not follow that some larls do not," I said. "Rather, if one were to hazard an inference in such a matter, it would seem rational to suppose that they all eat meat."

"And from the fact that most magicians may not do real magic one should not infer that therefore some do?"

"That is it," I said.

"But some might!" he said, triumphantly.

"Perhaps," I said.

"I grant you the logic of matter," he said, "but in this case I must be granted the fact of the matter."

"What fact?" I asked.

"That there is real magic!"

"Why do you say that " I asked.

"Because tonight," he said, "we witnessed not tricks, but genuine magic."

"What makes you think so?" I asked.

"You saw the slave in the palanquin," he said. "It was moved about, it was lifted up in the air! Do you think the girl could have slipped through a trapdoor or something? There is no way that could have happened. Similarly the palanquin was moved about. Accordingly there could have been no mirrors."

"There could have been some," I said.

"Do you think it was done with mirrors?" he asked.

"No," I said. "It was not done with mirrors."

"It was done by magic," he said.

"Not by what you seem to mean by 'real magic'," I said, "whatever that might be."

"How then do you think it was done?" he asked, angrily.

"There were two illusions," I said, "the first in which the girl disappeared from the palanquin and the second in which she reappeared in the trunk."

"Or two wonders,' said Marcus, "the one of the palanquin and the other of the trunk."

"Very well," I said. "You noted, of course, that the palanquin was roofed, or canopied, and that the roof or canopy was supported by four poles."

"Of course," he said, warily.

"Those poles are hollow," I said, "and within them there are cords and weights."

"Continue," said he.

"The cords," I said, "are attached at one end to the weights within the poles and, at the other end, to the corners of a flat pallet at the bottom of palanquin, on which the girl reclines. When the curtains of the palanquin are drawn, as they were, you remember, the weights are disengaged by the bearers. These weights, the four of them, collectively, are much heavier than the pallet and the girl, whom, you will remember was slim and light. As the weights descend within the poles the cords move and draw the pallet up under the canopy."

"The girl was then being held at the top, concealed by the canopy?"

"Precisely," I said.

"I did not think of her as going up," said Marcus.

"Nor would most folks," I said. "After all, people do not normally fly upwards. Presumably most folks would think, if at all about these matters, in terms of a false bottom, or back, or something, but, as you saw, such considerations would have been immediately dismissed as the construction of the palanquin made them impractical, for example, its openness, and its bottom being too shallow to effect any efficacious concealment for the girl."

"It was not magic?" he said.

"Once the girl is offstage," I said, "there is no difficulty in changing her clothes and getting her in sirik."

"The trunk was real magic," he said, "as we saw it carried on, kept off the floor, and opened, and shown empty!"

"In the case of the trunk," I said, "you will recall that it was carried on, and opened in a certain way, in a certain order, and then that it was closed in a certain order, as well."

"Remind me," he said.

"Most significantly," I said, "after it was on the trestles, the back was lowered first, and then the sides and front."

"Yes," he said, "that is correct.'"

"When it was closed, however," I said, "it was the front which was first lifted and put in place, and then the sides, and then the back."

"Yes," he said.

"In short," I said, "in the opening of the trunk, the back was lowered first, and in its closing, it was lifted last."

"True," said Marcus.'

"You remember?" I asked.

"Yes," he said.

"The interior of the back was thus not seen by the audience in the beginning," I said, "because it was either concealed by the front panel as the trunk was carried onto the stage or was facing the back of the stage when it was hanging down in back. Similarly, later, the interior of the back was not seen by the audience because it was either facing away from them, when it hung down in back, or was concealed by the front panel and sides, which were first lifted, to keep it concealed."

"The slave was then carried onto the stage in the closed trunk, her body fastened somehow to the inside of the back panel."

"In a sling of straps," I said.

"She was then hanging down, fastened to the side of the back panel away from the audience, when the trunk was opened?"

"Yes," I said.

"And was returned to the interior of the trunk with the shielded lifting of the back panel?"

"Yes," I said. "And once within the trunk, it then closed again, she could, of course, her hands being free enough in the sirik to accomplish this, undo the straps, and conceal them in the flooring of the trunk, in a slot prepared for the purpose."

"Then it was not magic?" he said.

"That depends on what you mean by 'magic'," I said.

"You know what I mean," he said, somewhat disagreeably.

"No," I said. "It was not magic."

"But it could have been magic," he said.

"What do you mean?" I asked.

"Even those these wonders could have been accomplished so easily by mere trickery, that does not prove they were!"

"No," I said. "I suppose not."

"The same effect might have quite different causes," he said, "for example, in these cases, having been achieved either by mere charlatanry or by genuine magic."

"I have seen the equipment," I said. I had, in one of the wagons of the ponderous fellow several months ago. I had even diddled about with it, for my own amusement.

"But that does not prove it was used!" said Marcus.

"I suppose not," I said. "I suppose that these effects, so easily wrought by a skillful fellow, who knows how to bring them about, might actually, in these cases, have been produced not by familiar trickery but by the application of uncanny and marvelous powers."

"Certainly," said Marcus.

"Would you believe the fellow if he showed you how he did it?" I asked.

"He might show me how it could be done, but not how he actually did it," said Marcus. "He might lie to me, to conceal from me his possession of mysterious powers."

"Well," I said, "I never thought about that." I never had. "I guess you're right," I said.

Marcus walked on beside me for a way. Then suddenly he burst out, angrily, "The charlatan, the fraud!"

"Are you angry?" I asked.

"They are only tricks!" he said.

"Good tricks," I said.

"But only tricks!"

"I don't think he ever claimed they weren't," I said.'

"He should be boiled in oil!" cried Marcus.

"To me that seems somewhat severe," I said.

"Tricks!" said Marcus.

"I suppose you now respect them the less," I said.

"Charlatanry!" he murmured. "Trickery! Fraud!"

"I think that I myself," I said, "apparently responding to this sort of thing rather differently from yourself, admire them the more as I understand how ingenious and wonderful they are, as tricks. I think I should be awed by them, but would not find so much to admire in them, if I thought they were merely the manifestations of unusual powers, as, for example, the capacity to turn folks into turtles or something."

"Perhaps," he said.

"Certainly," I said.

"I would not wish to be a turtle," he said.

"So let us trust," I said, "that folks do not abound who can wreak such wonders."

"True," he said.

"Similarly," I said, "if there were such a thing as "real magic" in your sense, whatever that might be, the world would presumably be much different than it is."

"There might be a great many more turtles," he said.

"Quite possibly," I said.

I did not doubt, of course, from what I knew of them, that the science of Priest-Kings was such that many unusual effects could be achieved. And, indeed, I did not doubt but what many such were well within the scope of the several sciences of the Kurii, as well, But these effects, of course, were rationally explicable, at least to those with the pertinent techniques and knowledge at their disposal, effects which were the fruits of unusual sciences and technologies. I did not think that Marcus needed to know about such things. How inexplicable and marvelous to a savage might appear a match, a handful of beads, a mirror, a stick of candy, a tennis ball.

"The slave was not in Anango!" he cried.

"No," I said. "I would not think so."

"But she said so, or let it be thought!" he said. "She is thus a lying slave, and should be punished. Let her be whipped to the bone!"

"Oh, come now," I said. "She is playing her part in the show, in the entertainment. She is enjoying herself, along with everyone else. And she is a slave. What do you expect her to say? To tell the truth, and spoil the show, or perhaps have her master flogged? Do you not think such ill-thought-out intrepidity would swiftly bring her luscious hide into contact with the supple switch?"

"Yes," he said. "It is the master who is to blame."

"I do hope you get on with him," I said.

"What?" he cried.

"Yes," I said, "and, indeed, I would even recommend that you be nice to him."

"Why?" asked Marcus.

"Because," I said, "it is he who is going to obtain for you the Home Stone of Ar's Station."

18 Our Wallets Are in Order

"Here we are," I said.

"What place is this?" asked Marcus.

We had been walking about for some time after the show, even past the time of curfew the constraints of which, because of our affixed armbands, as auxiliary guardsmen, we had not the least difficulty in circumventing. Challenged, we challenged back. Questioned, we questioned. And if our challenges and questions were satisfactorily met, we would proceed further, first volunteering, of course, in deference to alternative authority, our own names and missions in turn. If notes were to be later compared at some headquarters, as I did not expect they would be, some officers might have been astonished to learn how many sets of auxiliary guardsmen and diverse missions had been afoot that night.

"This is the *insula*," I said, "at which resides the great Renato and his troupe."

"The magician?" said Marcus.

"Yes," I said. I had made inquiries into this matter prior to leaving the theater, Marcus waiting outside for me, pondering the wonders he was convinced he had beheld within.

"I would not keep the stripped, lashed Ubara of a captured city chained in a kennel such as this," he said.

"Surely you would do so," I said.

"Well, perhaps," he admitted.

Some believe such women should be prepared quickly for the collar and others that the matter may be drawn out, teasingly, until even she, trying to deny it to herself all the while, realizes what her eventual lot is to be.

"Not all folk in the theater and such live as well as they might," I said.

"It seems they cannot make gold pieces appear from thin air," said Marcus.

"Not without a gold piece to start with," I said.

"Getting one to start with is undoubtedly the real trick," he said.

"Precisely," I said. "Let us go in."

I shoved back the heavy door. It hung on its top hinge. It had not been barred. I gathered that not every one who lived within, interestingly, was necessarily expected back before curfew. On the other hand, perhaps the proprietor, or his manager, was merely lax in matters of security. The interior, the hall and foot of the stairs, was lit by the light of a tiny tharlarion-oil lamp.

"Whew!" said Marcus.

At the foot of the stairs, as is common in *insulae*, there was a great wastes pot, into which the smaller wastes pots of the many tiny apartments in the building are emptied. These large pots are then carried off in wagons to the carnaria, where their contents are emptied. This work is usually done by male slaves under the supervision of a free man. When the wastes pot is picked up, a clean one is left in its place. The emptied pot is later cleaned and used again, returned to one *insula* or another. There is sewerage in Ar, and sewers, but on the whole these service the more affluent areas of the city. The *insulae* are, on the whole, tenements.

"This is a sty," said Marcus.

"Do not insult the caste of peasants," I said. "It is the ox on which the Home Stone rests." Thurnock, one of my best friends, was of that caste.

Not everyone is as careful as they might be in hitting the great pot. Lazier folks, or perhaps folks interested in testing their skill, sometimes try to do it from a higher landing. According to the ordinances the pots are supposed to be kept covered, but this ordinance is too often honored in the breach. Children sometimes use the stairs to relieve themselves. This is occasionally done, I gather, as a game, the winner being decided by the greatest number of stairs soiled.

"Ho there," said an unpleasant voice, from the top of the landing. We looked up into a pool of floating light, from a lifted lantern.

"Tal," I said.

"He is not here," said the fellow.

"Who?" I asked.

"Anyone," said the fellow.

"There is no one here?" I asked.

"Precisely," he said.

"We should like to rent a room," I said.

"No rooms," said he. "We are filled."

"I can be up the stairs in an instant," said Marcus, "and open him like a bag of noodles."

"Whom are you looking for?" asked the fellow, who perhaps had excellent hearing.

"Renato the Great," I said.

"The villain, the fat urt, the rogue, the rascal?" asked the fellow.

"Yes," I said. "He."

"He is not here," he said.

I supposed the fellow was fond of him, and was concerned to protect him. On the other hand, perhaps he had not yet collected the week's lodging. That, in itself, might be a good trick.

"Do not be dismayed by our armbands," I said. "We do not come on the business of guardsmen."

"You are creditors then," he said, "or defrauded bumpkins intent upon the perpetration of dire vengeance."

"No," I said. "We are friends."

The pool of light above us seemed to shake with laughter.

I drew my blade and put it to the bowl of the lamp, on its small shelf in the hall. With a tiny movement I could tip it to the floor.

"Be careful there," said the fellow. His concern was not without reason. Such accidents, usually occurring in the rooms, often resulted in the destruction of an *insula*. Many folks who lived regularly in *insulae* had had the experience of hastily departing from their building in the middle of the night. There was also the danger that such fires could spread. Sometimes entire blocks, and even districts, are wiped out by such fires.

"Summon him," I said.

"It is not my building" said the fellow. "It belongs to Appanius!"

"Ah, yes!" I said.

"You know the name?" asked Marcus.

"Yes," I said. "Do you not remember? He is the owner of Milo, the handsome fellow, the actor who played the part of Lurius of Jad in the pageant, and is an agriculturalist, an impresario, and slaver. That explains, probably, his interest in this establishment, and his catering to a certain clientele." I looked up at the pool of light. "It is that Appanius, is it not?" I asked.

"Yes," said the fellow, "and a powerful man."

I lowered the blade. I had no wish to do anything which Appanius might find disagreeable, such as burn down one of his buildings. He was undoubtedly a splendid fellow, and, in any case, I might later wish to do business with him. I sheathed my sword.

"Appanius is not one to be lightly trifled with!" said the fellow, seemingly somewhat emboldened by the retreat of my blade.

Marcus' blade half left its sheath. "And what of heavily trifling with him?" he asked. "Or trifling with him moderately?" Marcus was still not well disposed toward most fellows from Ar, and did not seem prepared to make an exception in favor of the fellow on the landing. I pushed Marcus' blade back down in its sheath.

"This," I said, indicating a cord and bar to one side, "is undoubtedly the alarm bar, to be rung in the case of emergency or fire."

"Yes?" said the voice from the pool of light.

"I am pleased to see it," I said. "This will quite possibly save me burning down the building."

"Why do you wish to see Renato?" asked the fellow, nervously. I think he did not relish the thought of being on the landing if the occupants of the building should suddenly, in their hundreds, begin to stream forth in vigorous, or even panic-stricken, haste, down the stairs.

"That is our business," I said.

"You are not going to lead him off in chains, are you?" he asked. "He owes two weeks' rent."

I surmised that more than an occasional lodging fee had in such a manner escaped the agent of Appanius.

"No," I said.

"Hah!" he suddenly cried.

"What is wrong?" I asked.

"It is the same trick!" he said. "I see it now! The same trick!"

"What trick?" I asked.

"The rogue last year pretended to have himself arrested and led away, but it turned out to be by members of his own troupe, and thus they all escaped without paying the rent!"

"And you took him back in?" I asked.

"Who else would give such a rogue lodging but Appanius?" said the man. "But he made him pay double, and for the time before, too!"

"Interesting," I said. "But we wish to see him on business, now."

"We can force the doors, one after the other," said Marcus.

"There are at least a hundred rooms here," I said. "Perhaps more."

"Which is his room?" asked Marcus. "And we shall rout him out ourselves."

"I would have to consult the records," said the fellow. "He may not even be rooming here."

"But surely you have one or more of his slaves chained somewhere as a surety," I said.

The fellow made a tiny, angry noise above us.

I saw I had guessed right. The only slave of the ponderous fellow I had seen in the show had been the one he was now calling Litsia. I expected he had one or more elsewhere. For example, I had not seen a certain blonde about whom he often used in his dramatic farces, in various roles, such as that of the Golden Courtesan. She, and perhaps one or two others, I did not know, were in this very building, or elsewhere, chained or caged, as a surety for the lodging fees. If he wished to use one of them in some farce, or such, he would perhaps take that one, and leave another, say, Litsia, as he now called her, with the agent, or his men. Such women, being properties, may be used as sureties, to be taken over by the creditors of their former masters in the case of default. They are usually then sold, the proceeds from their sales, minus various fees, being used to satisfy, in so far as this is practical, the claims of the former master's creditors. There are many variations on this sort of thing. For example, it is not unknown for one fellow, desiring the slave of another, to advance his fellow money, perhaps for gambling, in the hope that he may not be able to pay it back, in which case the creditor, in accord with the contractual arrangements, may claim the slave. Also, of course, it is not unusual, in serious cases, for a debtor's properties to be seized and auctioned, that his debts may be satisfied. These properties include, of course, his livestock, if any, which category includes slaves. Daughters, too, in some cities, are subject to such seizure and sale. Also, a female debtor, in many cities, is subject to judicial enslavement, she then coming rightlessly and categorically, identically with any other slave, into the ownership of the creditor.

"Shall I tell him that two guardsmen are asking after him?" asked the fellow.

"No, just say, 'two friends'," I said.

"I am not his friend," said Marcus.

"One friend," I called.

"I see," said the fellow from above, carefully. "There are two fellows calling for him, who do not wish him to know they are guardsmen, one of whom is his friend, and one of whom is not, and both of whom are armed, and seem ready to unsheath their weapons at a moment's notice, if not earlier."

"I am sure he is here," I said. "So do not return and tell us he is not in."

"Shall I go up with him?" asked Marcus.

"No, no!" said the fellow above, quickly.

"You realize," said Marcus, "that the fellow may elude us, over the roofs, or climb out on a ledge, and fall to his death, or lower himself by means of a rope to the alley from the room?"

"Or disappear into thin air?" I asked.

"Possibly," grumbled Marcus, who had not yet, I fear, been persuaded to an attitude of skepticism in such matters.

"I have it," I said. Then I called up to the fellow on the landing. "Tell him," I said, "that the world's worst actor desires to speak with him."

"That seems a strange request," said the fellow with the lantern.

"Not so strange as you might think," I said.

"Very well," he said. He then turned about and began to climb the flights of stairs upward, toward the least desirable, hottest, most dangerous levels of the *insula*. We watched the flickering light of the lantern making its way irregularly up the walls on either side of the staircase, and then, eventually, saw it fade and disappear.

"He whom you seek is now doubtless making his exit," said Marcus.

An urt hurried down the stairs and darted along the side of the wall and through a crack in the wall.

Marcus swiftly drew his sword.

"No," I said, staying his hand. "That is not he."

"Are you sure?" asked Marcus.

"Pretty sure," I said.

"Perhaps we should wait out back," said Marcus, "to close off his retreat."

"It's dark out there," I said.

In a moment, however, we heard the stairs shaking and creaking, from flights above, and then, in a bit, apparently feeling his way by the walls at the sides of the stairs, down came the bulk of the large fellow, his paunch swaying, his robes flying behind him.

"He moves with great rapidity," said Marcus. "Perhaps he can see in the dark?"

"No," I said.

"Perhaps he is part sleen," he said.

"Some have claimed more than a part," I said.

Marcus whistled softly, to himself.

"He knows the stairs," I said, somewhat irritably. "So, too, would you, if you lived here."

Then the great bulk was on the floor of the hall, rushing toward me. Without a moment's hesitation it seized me in a great embrace.

Then we joyfully held one another at arm's length.

"How did you know it was me?" I asked.

"It could be no other!" he cried, delightedly.

"Who is this?" he asked, regarding Marcus.

"My friend, Marcus," I said, "of Ar's Station."

"The state of knaves, traitors, and cowards?" inquired the ponderous fellow.

I restrained Marcus.

"I am pleased to meet you!" said the ponderous fellow, extending his hand.

"Beware," I said to Marcus, "or he will have your wallet!"

"Here is yours," said the fellow, handing mine back to me.

"That was very neatly done," I said. I was genuinely impressed. "Is there anything left in it?"

"Almost everything," said the fellow.

Gingerly, standing back, Marcus extended his hand.

The ponderous fellow seized it and shook it vigorously. It was Marcus' sword hand. I trusted it would not be injured. We might have need of it.

"How did you know where to find me?" asked the ponderous fellow.

"Inquiries, and a couple of silver tarsks, at the theater," I said.

"It is good to know one has friends," he said.

"Do you do your wonders by magic or trickery?" asked Marcus.

"Most often by trickery," said the fellow, "but sometimes, I admit, when I am tired, or do not wish to take the time and trouble required for tricks, by magic."

"See!" said Marcus to me, triumphantly.

"Really, Marcus," I said.

"It is as I told you!" he insisted.

"If you would like a demonstration," said the large fellow, solicitously, "I could consider turning you into a draft tharlarion."

Marcus turned white.

"Only temporarily, or course," the fellow assured him.

Marcus took another step back.

"Do not fear," I said to Marcus. "There is not enough room in the hall for a draft tharlarion."

"You are as practical as ever!" said the large fellow, delightedly. Then he turned to Marcus. "When a wagon would be stuck in the mud, it was always he who would first discover it!

When there wasn't enough to eat, it would be he who would be the first to notice!"

I did have a good appetite, of course.

"I do not wish to be turned into a draft tharlarion," said Marcus.

"Not even temporarily?" I urged.

"No!" said Marcus.

"Have no fear," said the fellow. "I couldn't do that if I wished."

"But you said—" said Marcus.

"I said I could consider turning you into a draft tharlarion," he said, "and that is quite easy to do, considering such a matter. The difficulty arises in accomplishing it."

"Am I mocked?" asked Marcus.

"Actually his name is 'Marcus'," I said.

Marcus regarded me, startled.

"I see that your wit is as sharp as ever!" said the ponderous fellow.

"Thank you," I said. I thought the sally had been deft. I am not sure Marcus knew what to do in the presence of two such fellows as we.

"And what do you do?" the fellow asked Marcus. "Do you juggle, do you walk a tightrope? Our friend Tarl here was excellent at clinging to a wire with great tenacity. It was one of his best tricks."

It was not my fault if I were no Lecchio.

"I am of the warriors," said Marcus.

"How unfortunate," said the fellow, "our military roles are all filled. We already have our captain, our imperious general, and two spearmen."

These would be Petrucchio, Andronicus, Lecchio and Chino.

"I am not an actor," said Marcus.

"That has never been essential for success on the stage," he was assured.

It might be noted also, of course, that unusual talent did not guarantee success either. For example, I had not been notably successful on the stage.

"Consider the fabulous Milo," said the fellow to Marcus.

Marcus looked at me, with a malicious grin. He did not much approve of Milo. Or perhaps it would be more correct to say that he did not much approve of Phoebe's approving of him.

"I think Milo is an excellent actor," I said.

"You see?" asked the fellow of Marcus.

"Yes," said Marcus.

"Did you see him in the pageant about Lurius of Jad?" I asked.

"Yes," he said. "It was on the basis of that performance that my opinion was formed."

"I see," I said. How ugly, I thought, professional jealousy can be.

"Milo," he said, "has the flexibility, the range, the nuance of a block of wood!"

"Many folks find him impressive," I said.

"So is the fountain of Hesius," said the fellow, "but it can't act either."

"He is thought to be the most handsome man in Ar," I said. "Or among the most handsome," I added, reflectively.

"Your qualification is judicious," said the fellow.

"Certainly," said Marcus, apparently also giving the matter some thought. I said nothing more then, modestly. Nor, as I recall, did they.

"Have you lost any Home Stones lately?" the fellow asked Marcus.

Marcus' eyes blazed.

"Beware," I said. "Marcus is a touchy fellow, and he is not overly fond of those of Ar."

"He does not know what noble, good-hearted, jolly fellows we are," said the large fellow.

"Why have you changed your name?" I asked.

"There are various warrants out for me," he said. "By changing my name that gives the local guardsmen on Show Street an excuse for taking my bribes with a good conscience."

"The others, too, have changed their names?" I said.

"For now," he said.

"His Litsia was once "Telitsia," I said to Marcus.

"That is not much of a change," he said.

"But then she has not changed much," said the large fellow.

'Litsia', in any case, is a shortened form of 'Telitsia'. It would not be unusual to take a name such as 'Telitsia' which is most often a free woman's name and give it a shortened form, a more familiar form, perhaps one more fitting for a well-curved, delicious slave animal. The names of slaves, of course, may be given and taken away at will, as the names of other sorts of animals.

"It is my hope that I can be of service to you," said the fellow. "But unfortunately as we are not now on the move, there is little current scope available for the exercise of your special talents."

"What special talents?" asked Marcus.

"He can lift a wagon single-handedly on his back," said the fellow. "He can thrust in the pegs of a temporary stage with the heel of his hand!"

"He jests merrily," I informed Marcus. It was not that I could not do such things, depending on the weight of the wagon and the various ratios involved, those of the diameters of pegs and holes, and such, but I did not want Marcus to get the wrong impression. I did not wish him to think that my theatrical talents might be limited to such *genres* of endeavor.

"But nonetheless," he said, "we are eager that you should share our kettle, and for as long as you wish."

"Thank you," I said.

"The others, too, will be delighted to see you," he said. "For example, Andronicus complains frequently of the burdens of manual labor."

"I can imagine," I said. Andronicus was a sensitive fellow, with a delicate sense of what was fitting and unfitting for an actor of his quality. He had been one of the bearers of the palanquin. The others had been Petrucchio, Lecchio and Chino. Also, in spite of his considerable stature, he regarded himself as somewhat frail. Were I a member of the troupe I had no doubt but what he might have been persuaded to step aside, withdrawing from the role of bearer in my favor. I think I could have pulled it off. The ponderous fellow had once assured me that he had seldom seen anyone do that sort of thing as well.

"You will come up?" asked the fellow. "And the knave from Ar's Station, home of traitors and cowards, is welcome as well, of course."

"Back, Marcus!" I said. "No," I said. "Our renewed acquaintance must be kept secret from the others."

"But surely you wish to hide out with us?" said the ponderous fellow.

"No," I said.

"The authorities are seeking you?"

"Not exactly," I said.

"We could conceal you," he said. "We have all sorts of boxes and trunks which could serve the purpose quite well."

Marcus shuddered.

"No," I said.

"You are not fleeing from authorities?"

"No," I said.

"This is a social visit?" he asked.

"Not really," I said.

"Business?"

"Yes," I said.

"Secret business?"

"Yes," I said.

"Dire business?" he asked.

"Pretty dire," I admitted.

"Speak," he said.

"We have a job for you, and I suspect you are one of the fifty or so men in Ar who might accomplish it."

"Is this a dangerous job?" he asked.

"It is one involving great risk and small prospect of success," I said. "It is also one in which, if you fail, you will be apprehended and subjected to ingenious, lengthy and excruciating tortures, to be terminated doubtless only months later with the mercy of a terrible death."

"I see," he said.

"Are you afraid?" I asked.

"Of course not," he said. "Beyond what you describe there is little to fear."

"It is a dire business, truly," said Marcus, grimly.

I hoped that Marcus would not discourage him.

"Moderately dire, at any rate," the fellow granted him.

"I know that you always claim to be a great coward, and act as one at every opportunity," I said to him, "but long ago I discerned the foolhardy hero hidden beneath that clever pose."

"You are perceptive," said the fellow.

"I myself would never have guessed it," said Marcus, awed.

"You are interested, aren't you?" I asked. I now had him intrigued.

"You should consider a future in recruiting," said the fellow, "say, one of those fellows who recruits for the forbidden arena games, held secretly, those in which almost no one emerges alive. At the very least you should consider a future in sales."

"Would you care to hear what we have in mind?" I asked.

"If there are some fifty or so fellows in Ar," said the fellow, "who could do this, why didn't you ask one of them, or perhaps you have already asked them."

"No," I said. "And you are the only one of those fellows I know. Besides you are my friend."

He clasped my hand warmly.

"Where are you going?" I asked.

"Upstairs, to bed," he said. "Telitsia will be moaning by now."

"But you have not yet heard our proposition," I pointed out.

"Have you considered what my loss to the arts might mean?" he asked.

"I had not viewed the matter from that perspective," I admitted.

"Do you wish to see the arts plunged into decline on an entire world?"

"Well, no," I said.

"A decline from which they might never fully recover?"

"Of course not," I said.

"I wish you well," he said.

"Let him go," said Marcus. "He is right. The task we have in mind is no task for a mere mortal. I consented to have the subject broached only because I still suspected he was a true magician."

"What's that?" asked the paunchy fellow, swinging about.

"Nothing," said Marcus.

"What you have in mind you regard as too difficult for one such as I to accomplish?"

"Not just you, any ordinary man," said Marcus.

"I see," said the fellow.

"Forgive me," said Marcus. "I meant no offense."

"Ah, yes," I said, suddenly. "Marcus is right, of course. No ordinary person could hope to perform this task. It would require brilliance, dash, flair, subtlety, skill, even showmanship. It would require a master to pull it off. Nay, a master of masters."

"And what do you think I am?" asked the fellow.

"This task," I said, dismally, "would require flexibility, range and nuance." It seemed I had heard these words recently. They seemed useful at the moment. I seized upon them.

"But I am a master of flexibility," said the fellow, "I have enormous range, from one horizon of the theater to another, I have a grasp of nuance that would shame the infinite shades of the spectrum, in all their variations in brilliance, saturation and hue!"

"Truly?" asked Marcus.

"Of course!" said the fellow.

"We really need an army," he said.

"In my youth," said the fellow, "I was a one-man army!" In Gorean theater armies are usually represented by a fellow carrying a banner behind an officer. In the pageant we had seen earlier in the year, of course, hundreds of actors had been on the stage in the great theater.

"You could never manage it," I said.

"You are craftier than a battering ram," he said, "and your subtlety would put to shame that of most tharlarion of my acquaintance, but this young man is serious."

Marcus looked at him, puzzled.

"Do you not know who I am?" he asked.

"A wondrous magician?" asked Marcus, hopefully.

"The least of my accomplishments," said the fellow.

"If anyone could accomplish the task, I would suppose it must be one such as you," said Marcus.

"Do you wish to know what the task is?" I asked.

"Not now," he said. "Whatever it is, I shall undertake it speedily and accomplish it with dispatch."

Marcus regarded him with awe.

"What is it?" asked the fellow. "You wish the Central Cylinder moved? You wish the walls of Ar rebuilt overnight? You wish a thousand tarns tamed in one afternoon?"

"He is a magician!" said Marcus.

"You wish Ar to escape the yoke of Cos?" I asked the fellow.

"Certainly," he said.

"What we have in mind may help to bring that about," I said.

"Speak," he said.

"You know that Ar refused to support Ar's Station in the north and that her loyalty to the state of Ar cost her her walls and her Home Stone?"

"Yes," he said. "I know that, but I am not supposed to know that."

"Ar owes the fidelity and courage of Ar's Station much," I said.

"Granted," he said.

"Would you like to pay back a part of the debt which Ar owes to Ar's Station?" I asked.

"Certainly," he said.

"And would you like to take a trip to the north with your troupe, a trip which might eventually bring you to the town of Port Cos, on the northern bank of the Vosk?"

"They are staunch supporters of the theater there, are they not?" he asked.

"It is a rich town," I said.

"Staunch enough," he said.

"In which, if you accomplish this task, you will be hailed as heroes," I said.

"We are already heroes," he said. "It is only that we have not been hailed as such."

"If you undertake this task," I said, "you will be indeed a hero."

"Port Cos?" he said.

"Yes," I said.

"That is where the survivors of Ar's Station are, is it not?" he asked.

"Many of them," I said.

"What do you have in mind?" he asked.

"The Delta Brigade," I said, "is restoring courage and pride to Ar. The governance of the city, under the hegemony of Cos, wishes to discredit the Brigade by associating it in the popular mind with Ar's Station, which the folks of Ar have been taught to despise and hate."

"That has been clear to me for some time," said the fellow, "at least since noon yesterday."

"Do you think most folks in Ar believe, at least now, that Ar's Station is behind the Delta Brigade?" I asked.

"No," he said. "It is supposed almost universally that it is an organization of delta veterans."

"What do you think would happen," I asked, "if the Home Stone of Ar's Station would disappear, from beneath the very noses of the authorities?"

"I do not know," he said, "but I suspect it would be thought that the Delta Brigade, the veterans, rescued it, and this might give the lie to the official propaganda on the subject, and even vindicate Ar's Station in the eyes of the citizenry, that the Delta Brigade chose to act on her behalf. At the least, the disappearance of the stone would embarrass the governance of the city, and Cos, and cast doubt on their security and efficiency. Its loss could thus undermine their grasp on the city."

"I think so, too," I said.

"You wish me to obtain the Home Stone of Ar's Station for you?" he asked.

"For Ar," I said, "for Ar's Station, for the citizenry of Ar's Station, for Marcus."

"No," he said.

"Very well," I said. I stepped back. I had no wish to urge him. Nor had Marcus.

"You misled me," he said.

"I am sorry," I said.

"You told me that the task was difficult, that it was dangerous," he said, scornfully.

I was puzzled.

"Do you not know that the stone is now on public display," he asked, "for Ahn a day?"

"Yes," I said. "We know that."

"It is in the open!" he said.

"In a way," I said.

"It is not locked in a tower, encircled with a moat of sharks, behind ten doors of iron, ringed by deadly osts, circled by maddened sleen, surrounded by ravening larls."

"No," I said. "Not to my knowledge."

"I shall not do it!" he said.

"I do not blame you," I said.

"Do you hold me in such contempt?" he asked.

"Not at all," I said, puzzled.

"Do you ask me, me, to do such a thing?"

"We had hoped you might consider it," I said.

"Never!" he said.

"Very well," I said.

"What slandering scoundrels you are, both of you," he said, angrily.

"How so?" I asked.

"It is too easy!" he said, angrily.

"What?" I asked.

"It is too easy," he said. "It is unworthy of me! It is beneath my attention. It would be an insult to my skills! There is no challenge!"

"It is too easy?" I asked.

"Would you come to a master surgeon to have a boil lanced, a wart removed?" he asked.

"No," I admitted.

"To one of the Builders to have a door put on straight?"

"No," I said.

"To a scribe to read the public boards!"

"No!" said Marcus. I myself was silent. I sometimes had difficulty with the public boards, particularly when cursive script was used.

"Let me understand this clearly," I said. "You think the task would be too easy?"

"Certainly," he said. "It requires only a simple substitution."

"Do you think you could manage it?" asked Marcus, eagerly.

"Anyone could do it," he said, angrily. "I know of at least one, in Turia."

"But that is in the southern hemisphere," I pointed out.

"True," he said.

"Then you will do it!" I said.

"I will need to get a good look at the stone," he said. "But that is easily accomplished. I will go and revile it tomorrow."

Marcus stiffened.

"It is necessary," I said to Marcus. "He will not mean it."

"Then," he said, "once I have every detail of the stone carefully in mind I shall see to the construction of a duplicate."

"You can remember all the details?" I asked.

"Taken in in an glance," he assured me.

"Remarkable," I said.

"A mind such as mine," he said, "occurs only once or twice in a century."

Marcus had hardly been able to speak, so overcome he was.

"Do you, lad, know the stone fairly well?" he was asked by the paunchy fellow.

"Yes!" said Marcus.

"Good," said the paunchy fellow.

"Why did you ask that?" I asked.

"In case I forget the color of it, or something," he said.

"You do realize, do you not," I asked, "that the stone is under constant surveillance."

"It will not be under surveillance for the necessary quarter of an Ihn or so," he said.

"You will use misdirection?" I asked.

"Unless you have a better idea, or seventy armed men, or something."

"No," I said.

"There will be many guards about," said Marcus.

"I work best with an audience," said the ponderous fellow.

I did not doubt it. On the other hand he did make me a bit nervous. I trusted he would not try to make too much of a show of it. The important thing was to get the stone and get it out of the city, and, if possible, to Port Cos.

"Sir!" said Marcus.

"Lad?" asked the ponderous fellow.

"Even though you should fail in this enterprise and die a horrible death, I want you to know that you have the gratitude of Ar's Station!"

"Thank you," said the fellow. "The sentiment touches me."

"It is nothing," Marcus assured him.

"No, no!" said the fellow. "On the rack, and under the fiery irons and burning pincers, should such be my fate, I shall derive much comfort from it."

"I think you are the most courageous man I have ever known," said Marcus.

"Twice this evening," said the fellow, turning to me, "it seems my well-wrought sham of craven timidity, carefully constructed over the period of a lifetime, has been penetrated."

"Do you plan to seize the Home Stone by trickery or magic?" asked Marcus.

"I haven't decided," said the fellow. "Which would you prefer?"

"If it does not the more endanger you," said Marcus, grimly, "I would prefer trickery, human trickery."

"My sentiments, exactly," said the fellow. "What do you think?"

"Whatever you wish," I said.

"By using trickery," said Marcus, earnestly, "we are outwitting Ar, making fools of them, accomplishing our objective within the rules, winning the game honestly."

"True," said the fellow. "I have nothing but contempt for those magicians who stay safe in the towers of their castles, consulting their texts, uttering their spells and waving their magic wands about, spiriting away valuable objects. There is no risk there, no glory! That is not fair. Indeed, it is cheating."

"Yes," said Marcus. "It would be cheating!"

"You have convinced me," said the fellow. "I shall use trickery and not magic."

"Yes!" said Marcus.

"There is danger," I said to the ponderous fellow.

"Not really," he said.

"I am serious," I said.

"If I thought there were the least bit of danger involved in this, surely you do not think I would even consider it, do you?"

"I think you might," I said.

"It all depends on the fellow involved," he said. "If you were to attempt to accomplish this, with your particular subtlety and skills, there would indeed be danger, perhaps unparalleled peril. Indeed, I think I would have the rack prepared the night before. But for me, I assure you, it is nothing, no more than a sneeze."

"He is a magician," Marcus reminded me.

"But he is only planning on using trickery," I reminded Marcus, somewhat surlily.

"True," said Marcus, thoughtfully.

"Would you wait outside, Marcus?" I asked.

"Certainly," he said, exiting.

"A nice lad," said the fellow.

"There are serious risks involved," I said to the fellow.

"For you perhaps," he said. "Not for me."

"We have gold," I said, "obtained in the north."

"And you do not know better than to try futilely to force this wealth upon me, even against my will?" asked the fellow.

"I would like you to consider it," I said.

"That is the least I can do for a friend," he said.

"It will help to defray the expenses of the troupe in the north," I said.

"It is then a contribution to the arts?" asked the fellow.

"Certainly," I said.

"And you would be grievously offended if I did not accept it?"

"Certainly," I said.

"Under those conditions you leave me no choice."

"Splendid," I said.

"The amount, of course, I leave to your well-known generosity."

"Very well," I said.

"It should be commensurate, of course, as you are the patron, with your concept of the risks involved and not mine."

"So much gold," I said, "is not on Gor."

"Really?"

"Yes."

"Then I trust that my estimate of the risks involved is a good deal more accurate than yours."

"It is my fervent hope," I said.

"Do you think an entire gold piece, say, a stater, or a tarn disk, would be too much in a cause to perpetuate and enhance the arts on an entire world?"

"Not at all," I said.

"What about two gold pieces?"

"It can be managed," I assured him.

"In that case perhaps you can return the young fellow's wallet to him." He handed me Marcus' wallet. I felt quickly for my own. It was still in place.

"It is all there," he said, "what there was."

"Very well," I said. Marcus and I did not carry much money about with us.

"Be careful," I said to him.

"If I were not careful," he said, "there would be a great deal more than eleven warrants out on me, and I would have a great deal more creditors than the twenty-two who know where to find me."

I was silent.

"I must go upstairs now," he said, "and content Telitsia. Since she has become a slave she is quite different from the free woman you once knew."

"I am sure of it," I said.

In bondage, the once proud, arrogant Telitsia, of Asperiche, had learned slave arousal. I could imagine her upstairs now, probably chained by the neck to a ring, probably stripped, given the heat of the higher apartments, probably lying on the floor, where she had been put, near the ring, her small hands on her neck chain, or her fingers on the ring, now and then moaning, and turning about, or squirming, with a movement of chain, awaiting the return of her master.

"I wish you well," I said.

"I wish you well," he said.

He then turned about and, with considerably less speed than he had manifested in his descent, began to climb the stairs. In a moment or two, as he was not carrying a light, he had disappeared in the darkness. I listened, however, for some time, to his climbing. I then went outside and rejoined Marcus.

"Do you know who that was?" I asked.

"A magician," he said.

"Here is your wallet," I said.

"Ai!" said Marcus, slapping at his belt.

"Supposedly its contents are unrifled, or at least intact."

"It was wafted away by magic," said Marcus.

"Sometimes I believe him to be more light-fingered than is in his own best interest," I said.

"No," said Marcus. "I felt nothing. It was magic. He is a true magician!"

"Perhaps he is a bit vain of his tricks," I said.

I could well imagine many Goreans leaping upon him with a knife under such circumstances. or, at any rate, looking him up later with that in mind, having discovered their loss in the meantime.

"Perhaps we should encourage him to use magic in his attempt on the Home Stone," said Marcus. "I would not wish him to be torn to shreds on the rack."

"His mind is made up," I said. "He would not hear of it."

"Such courage!" cried Marcus.

"Do you know who he is?" I asked.

"Renato, the Great," said Marcus.

"That is not his real name," I said.

"What is his real name?" asked Marcus.

"In an instant you would know it, if I told it to you," I said. "You would be astonished that such a fellow has deigned to help us. He is known far and wide on Gor. He is famous. His fame is spread throughout a thousand cities and a hundred lands. He is known from the steaming jungles of Schendi to the ice packs of the north, from the pebbly shores of Thassa to the vast, dry barrens east of the Thentis range!"

"What is his name?" inquired Marcus, eagerly.

"Boots Tarsk-Bit!" I said.

'Who?" asked Marcus.

"Put your wallet away," I said.

"Very well," he said.

I also checked my own wallet, again. It was in place, and its contents were in order.

19 The Field Slave

"That is she," I whispered to Marcus.

We were astride rented tharlarion, high tharlarion, bipedalian tharlarion. Although our mounts were such, they are not to be confused with the high tharlarion commonly used by Gorean shock cavalry, swift, enormous beasts the charge of which can be so devastating to unformed infantry. If one may use terminology reminiscent of the sea, these were medium-class tharlarion, comparatively light beasts, at least compared to their brethren of the contact cavalries, such cavalries being opposed to the sorts commonly employed in missions such as foraging, scouting, skirmishing and screening troop movements. Rather our mounts were typical of the breeds from which are extracted racing tharlarion, of the sort used, for example, in the Vennan races. To be sure, it is only select varieties of such breeds, such as the Venetzia, Torarii and Thalonian, which are commonly used for the racers. As one might suppose, the blood lines of the racers are carefully kept and registered, as are, incidentally, those of many other sorts of expensive bred animals, such as tarsks, sleen and verr. This remark also holds for certain varieties of expensive bred slaves, the prize crops of the slave farms. Venna, a wealthy town north of Ar, is known for its diversions, in particular, its tharlarion races. Many of Ar's more affluent citizens kept houses in Venna, at least prior to the Cosian war. To date, Venna, though improving her walls and girding herself for defense, had not been touched in the Cosian war. This is perhaps because it is not only the rich of Ar who kept properties within her walls, but those of many other cities, as well, perhaps even of Kasra and Tentium, in Tyros, and of Telnus, Selnar, Temos and Jad, in Cos. We were some pasangs outside Ar. We wore wind scarves. Dust rose up for feet about us. The season was dry. Where our beasts trod the prints of their feet and claws remained evident in the dust. In places the earth cracked under their step.

"Are you sure?" he asked.

"Yes," I said.

"I saw her only once before," he said, "on a fellow's shoulder, in Ar, in our district, carried in slave fashion, her upper body wrapped closely in the toils of a net."

"Helpless," I said.

"Utterly," he said.

"She had been taken," I said, "only moments before."

"You are sure it is she?" he asked.

"Yes," I said.

"Her head was completely enclosed in a slave hood, buckled shut," he said.

"It is she," I said. "I saw her before, in the room. I recognize her."

"I am not sure I understand your plan," he said.

"Let us approach," I said.

We had left Ar early in the morning, and had circled the remains of her walls to the west and then took smaller roads into the hills to the northeast. We then, after noting the travelers on the road, particularly on the more isolated roads to the northeast, running through the villa districts, doubled back. In this fashion one tends almost automatically to cancel through the large numbers of coincidental travelers and detect those whose relationship with you is likely to be more purposeful, those who are following you. The likelihood of a given individual following you in both directions is small. Similarly, there is small likelihood of having someone or other constantly behind you on isolated roads. This helps to compensate for the possibility that the trackers might be acting in relays or shifts, one picking up where another turns aside.

We turned the tharlarion toward the fields where the girl was filling a vessel with water.

Her figure, extremely female, exquisitely curved, was rather like the figure of another girl we had encountered earlier in the morning, some pasangs to the northeast of the city, on one of the isolated roads winding through the hills, among which, nestled back, almost out of sight, were set a number of small, white-washed villas. Apparently she had come from some stream or rivulet, or public place, where she had been laundering, for she had had in her possession a basket filled with dampened clothes. Her, hair, too, which she had apparently recently washed, was wet. This sort of thing would normally be done at a cemented pool within the walls of the villa, to the back, but, I had gathered, given the dryness of the season, the villa resevoir might be being reserved for drinking water.

We had come upon her as she was about to turn into the path leading toward one of the small villas.

"A pretty one," commented Marcus.

"Hola," had called I, "slave!"

She immediately stopped and put down the basket, and hurried to the side of the road where we waited.

"Yes," I said. "She is indeed a pretty one."

She did not dally in kneeling. I noted with approval the position of her knees.

"Quite pretty," I said.

She looked up. Perhaps free men wished to inquire directions of her? Then she looked down. I saw that she would be quite lively in a man's hands. She had a common band collar, flat, close-fitting. She wore a brief tunic of white rep-cloth. She was barefoot.

"You are a girl of this house?" I asked, indicating the villa behind her.

"Yes, Master," she said.

"You have the look of a woman who is well and muchly mastered," I said.

She smiled suddenly, charmingly, gratefully, in embarrassment.

"It seems you have been laundering," I said.

"Yes, Master," she said.

"I see that the water source is not far away," I said.

"Yes, Master," she said.

"Your tunic is still damp," I said.

"Yes, Master," she said, shyly.

"And it seems you are a careless laundress," I said.

"Master?" she asked.

"The tunic is quite wet," I said.

She lifted her right hand a bit from her thigh, as though she might cover herself, but quickly returned it to position.

"The wet tunic sets you off well," I commented.

"Forgive me, Master," she said, frightened.

"Perhaps your master will notice it," I said, "as you return flushed from your labors, delighted, your hair washed, your body freshened."

She put down her head, quickly.

"But doubtless it is not the calculated act of a scheming slave girl, one cleverly aware of what she is doing," I said. "Doubtless it is a mere inadvertence, a merely accidental calling to your master's attention of your beauty, a totally unintentional, never-dreamed-of reminder to him of the promise of its delights."

She would not raise her head.

"What a clever little slut she is," said Marcus.

"But she did not plan on meeting two strange fellows on the road," I said. "Did you, slave?" I asked.

"No, Master!" she said.

"Do you fear our armbands?" I asked.

"Yes, Master," she said.

"Do not do so," I said.

"Thank you, Master," she whispered. Some apprehension on her part was not irrational. Those of Cos, and in the pay of Cos, could do much as they pleased in Ar and its environs, and particularly in the case of slaves. Who would have the courage, or foolishness, to gainsay them the use of such an object, to challenge the employments to which they might put such a mere fair article of property? Too, she was barefoot and slave clad. And in the garmenture of female slaves, even in spite of its customary scandalous brevity, nether shielding is almost never provided. In this way the girl is kept aware of her vulnerability and is immediately available to the attentions of the master. Also, out here, in the vicinity of the villa of her master, I doubted that she was in the iron belt. Also I did not detect, beneath her dampened tunic, any sign of the close-fitting apparatus, no sign of either its horizontal component, usually a bar or metal strap tightly encircling the waist, nor of its vertical component, usually hinged to the horizontal component in front and swung up, then, between the girl's legs, to the back, where the whole is usually fastened together, there, at the small of the back, with a padlock. She blushed, perhaps sensing the current purport of my scrutiny. She was lovely, and much at our mercy. Her apprehension was not irrational, as I have mentioned. It would not have been difficult to have her and then, with a few horts of binding fiber, leave her behind in the ditch, bound hand and foot, at the roadside. More alarmingly, we might have confiscated her, in the name of reparations, or such, bound her and put a rope on her neck and led her off, at my stirrup. In the last few months that sort of thing had happened to hundreds of slaves in Ar who had happened to catch the eye of one fellow or another. Too, if one tired of them, they could always be sold afterwards.

"Do you think I would object," I asked, "to a slave girl's desire to please her master, to call herself to his attention, to signify to him her desire, to request his touch, to beg him for her mastering?"

"I think not, Master," she said, shyly.

"Is it not the same as the wearing of the bondage knot in the hair, the offering of fruit, the serving of wine, the moaning, the prostrations, the obeisances, the gentle, supplicatory licking of the feet?"

"Yes, Master!" she said.

"What is your master's name?" I asked.

"Teibar," she said, "of Ar."

"And what are you called?" I asked.

"Tuka," she said, "if it pleases master."

"I have seen you before," I said, "months ago, outside the walls, at the camp of refugees."

She looked up at me.

"You dance well, slave girl," I said.

"Thank you, Master," she said.

"You dance better than many women I have seen in taverns," I said.

"Thank you, Master," she said.

"But perhaps you, too," I said, "once so danced." I could well imagine her in such a place, in a bit of silk, belled, with bangles, pleasing men.

"Yes, Master," she said. "Once I so danced."

"And do you now so dance?" I asked.

"When my master chooses to put me forth," she said.

"Doubtless upon occasion," I said, "you dance privately for your master?"

"It is my hope that I please him," she said.

"And if you did not please him?" I asked.

"He would whip me," she said.

"He is strong?" I asked.

"Yes, Master," she said.

"You love to dance?" I asked.

"Yes, Master," she said.

"But as a slave?" I asked.

"It is what I am, Master," she said, looking up at me.

"I see," I said.

"Surely all women desire to appear before men as a slave, and to so move, and so serve, and to dance for them, to please them."

"Do you suggest that all women are slaves?" I asked.

"It is what I am," she said. "I do not presume to speak for all women."

"You have an accent," I said.

"Forgive me, Master," she said.

"Where do you come from?" I asked.

"From far away, Master," she said.

"What is your native language?" I asked.

"I do not know if Master has heard of it," she said.

"What is it?" I asked.

"English," she said.

"I have heard of it," I said.

"Perhaps Master has owned girls such as I?" she asked.

"Yes," I said.

"From Earth?"

"Yes," I said.

"I have heard of it," said Marcus. "It is far away."

"Yes," I said.

"It is an excellent source of female slaves," he said.

"Yes," I said.

"Thank you, Masters," she said.

"What was your name on Earth?" I asked.

"Doreen," she said. "Doreen Williamson."

" 'Doreen'," I said.

"Yes, Master," she said.

"Is that a slave name?" I asked.

"It was the name of a slave," she smiled. "Though at that time I was not yet collared and branded."

"So you are from Earth?" I said. I had, of course, noted her vaccination mark at the camp outside Ar months before. By such tiny signs may an Earth female be recognized among other Gorean slaves.

"Yes, Master," she said.

'What are you now?" I asked.

"Only a Gorean slave girl," she said.

I regarded her. It was true.

"Master," she said, timidly, looking up at me from where she knelt by the roadside, to where I was high above her, in the saddle of the tharlarion.

"Yes," I said.

"Forgive a girl who does not wish to be punished," she said, "but I suspect that Master may not be native to this world either."

"He is from the place called "Earth", too," said Marcus. Marcus, of high caste, was familiar with various tenets of the second knowledge, such things as the roundness of his world, its movement in space, and the existence of other planets. On the other hand he remained skeptical of many of these tenets as he found them offensive to common sense. He was particularly suspicious of the claim that the human species had an extraterrestrial origin, namely, that it did not originate on his own world, Gor. It was not that he denied there was a place called "Earth" but he thought it must be somewhere on Gor, perhaps east of the Voltai Range or south of the Tahari. Marcus and I had agreed not to discuss the issue. I had no ready response, incidentally, to his suggestion that the human race might have originated on Gor and then some of these folks, perhaps transported by Priest-Kings, had been settled on Earth. Indeed, although I regarded this as quite unlikely, it seemed an empirical possibility. For example, anthropoidal fossils can be found on Gor, as well as on Earth, and so on. At any rate, Marcus found it much easier to believe that magic existed than that his world was round, that it moved, and that there might be other worlds rather like it here and there in the universe. In fact, in his philosophy, so to speak, the universe was still of somewhat manageable proportions. Sometimes I rather envied him.

"It is true," I said. "I am originally from Earth." Undoubtedly she had detected my accent, as I had hers. To be sure there are many accents on Gor which are not Earth accents. For example, not everyone on Gor speaks Gorean. There are many languages spoken on Gor. For example, most of the red hunters of the north do not speak Gorean, nor the red savages of the Barrens, nor the inhabitants of the jungles east of Schendi.

"Strange, then, Master," she said, "that we should meet in this reality, I, once a woman of Earth, as now no more than a kneeling slave before you, once a man of Earth."

"Do you find it unfitting?" I asked.

"No, Master," she said.

"It is as it should have been on Earth," I said.

"Yes, Master," she said.

"But such considerations need not concern us," I said. "They are in the past. They belong to a different world. You are now of Gor, and only of Gor."

"Yes, Master," she said. "But if I am not mistaken, it is not I alone who am now no longer of Earth, not I alone who am now of Gor, and wholly so."

"Oh?" I said.

"It seems that we are both now of Gor, and wholly so."

"Yes," I said. It was true.

"I as a slave," she said, "and you as a master."

"Yes," I said.

"I am not discontent," she said.

I was silent.

"Of men who are Goreans, and such as Goreans," she said, "women are the rightful slaves!"

"And is your master such?" I asked.

"Yes!" she said, fervently.

"Do you love your master?" I asked.

"Yes, Master!" she said.

"Are you happy?" I asked.

"Yes, Master!" she said. "I am happier than I ever knew a woman could be!"

"But you are a slave," I said.

"It is what I am!" she said.

"Perhaps that is the explanation for your happiness," I said.

"It is, Master!" she said.

"The collar looks well on your throat," I said.

"It belongs there, Master!" she said. "All my life I was craving and desiring total slavery, and now I have it!"

"That is why you are so happy?" I said.

"Yes, Master!" she said.

"And has your master something to do with this?" I asked.

"Doubtless, Master," she said. "He is the most wonderful of masters!'

"But what if you had a harsh master, one cruel or unfeeling."

"I would still be a slave," she said. "I would still love my condition. It is what I am."

"I see," I said.

Her knees squirmed a little.

"She is uneasy," said Marcus.

"Yes," I said.

"May I speak, Masters?" she asked.

"Yes," said Marcus.

"I fear my master will wonder what has become of me," she said.

"Do you fear you will be whipped?" asked Marcus.

"Yes, Master," she said.

"You are not yet dismissed," said Marcus.

"Yes, Master," she said.

"Your tunic is still quite damp," I said.

Her hands moved a little on her thighs, but she retained position.

I considered her slave curves, which would not in any event be well concealed by rep-cloth, and certainly were not so now that it had been splashed with water, even soaked by it.

" 'Tuka'," I said, "is a very common slave name."

"It is fitting for me, Master," she said, "who am a common slave."

"What is your brand?" I asked.

"That of most girls," she said, "the common Kajira mark. It is fitting, as I am a common girl."

"You regard yourself as a common slave?" I asked.

"Yes, Master," she said.

"Yet," I said, "I think you would bring a good price, stripped, and on the block."

"I would try to perform well," she said.

"Tuka!" we heard. We looked up to the villa. From where we were, over the white-washed wall, we could see the veranda of the main building, where it was nestled back, in the side of a hill. On the veranda there was a well-built fellow, with dark hair.

The girl looked up at us, frightened, agonized.

"Your master?" I asked.

"Yes, Master!" she said.

She squirmed. She looked about. In the beauty there was great agitation. Obviously she wished to rise up and run to her master, hurrying as she could. Slave girls do not dally when their masters call. That call takes precedence, of course, over a detention by strangers, but it is a rare girl who will simply leap up, not dismissed, and flee from the presence of free men.

"You may go," I said.

"Thank you, Master!" she cried, and leaped up. She was in such a hurry that she sped past the basket of laundry a pace or two, but then, suddenly recollecting it, hurried back, picked it up, and then, balancing it on her head with two hands, sped through the gate of the villa and up the path to the house. The fellow had, in the meantime, seeing her approach, withdrawn into the house. We saw her on the veranda, where she turned once, to look at us, and then hurried within.

"A superb slave," said Marcus.

"Yes," I said.

"I expect she will be cuffed a bit," he said, "either for dallying or for permitting herself to be seen so provocatively on on the road, with a dampened tunic."

"I expect you are right," I said.

"To be sure," said Marcus, "he will doubtless understand that she did not expect to meet folks about, surely not at this Ahn, and that the tunic was dampened for his benefit."

"He will presumably, if he pleases, take such matters into consideration." I said.

"By now she has probably been cuffed," he said.

"I would suppose so," I said.

"Or stripped and lashed," he said.

"Perhaps," I said.

"And now who knows to what lingering, pleasurable purposes she is being put?"

"I do not know," I said, "but it is my conjecture that she will serve well."

"I do not doubt it," said Marcus.

I looked about, turning in the saddle of the tharlarion. "I see no one on the road," I said. "Let us now retrace our steps. By noon I wish to be southwest of Ar, in the vicinity of the sul fields."

* * *

"That is she," I had whispered to Marcus.

"I am not sure I understand your plan," he had said.

"Let us approach," I had said.

The sun was now high overhead. It was much hotter here, in this area, and at this time of day, than it had been earlier in the villa districts, in the hills northeast of Ar, the Fulvians, foothills to the Voltai.

In the softness of the dust, then among the vines, moving across the field, our tharlarion in stately gait, we approached the girl, she at the large wooden tank, filling the vessels which would be slung over her yoke. She wore a brief, brown rag, perhaps from some other girl who had been given something better. Her hair had been cropped rather closely to her head, as is not uncommon with field slaves. She was barefoot and her feet and calves were white with dust. She lifted the large vessel from the tank with both hands, and then, her head down for a moment, rested it on the rim of the tank. She then, after a time, carefully, slowly, lowered it to the ground. It would not do to spill the water. She moved slowly, as though her body might be stiff and sore. I conjectured that her muscles ached. She was not accustomed, I supposed, to such labor.

As it was shortly before noon the shadows were small, and behind us, but she heard the movement of the feet of the tharlarion in the dirt behind her and spun about, frightened, immediately kneeling, putting her head to the dirt.

We halted the beasts some feet from her. She trembled. It would have done her no good, of course, to have run, even would it have been permitted that she do so. She could have been easily overtaken or ridden down, even trampled. It would not have been difficult to head her off or turn her back, or to have her between us in sport, like some object in a game, a terrified, confused quarry, buffeted, or struck to the ground, again and again, until perhaps she lay quietly in the dust, trembling, and the tharlarion would come and gently, firmly, place its great clawed foot on her back, holding her in place for our binding fiber. Also, had we been slavers, she might, in her hasty flight, as we overtook her, have been roped or netted. In the south, the Wagon Peoples sometimes use the bola in such captures, the cords and weights whipping about the girls legs and ankles, pinning them together, hurling her to the ground, where, in an instant, before she can free herself, the captor, leaping from the saddle, is upon her.

I let her remain in her current posture for a time. It is a good for a master to be patient. Let the girl well understand the meaning of such things.

"You may look up," I said.

She kept her head low, but turned it, looking up at us. Her hair was light brown, much lighter than that of the girl we had encountered to the north, in the Fulvian hills. That girl's hair had been very dark. I remembered it from the camp outside Ar long ago. This morning, as we had seen it, freshly washed, and still wet, it had seemed almost a glossy black. They were, as I have mentioned, similarly bodied. This girl, however, I would have supposed, was not a dancer. To be sure, she could undoubtedly be trained as such. As the female by nature has feminine dispositions, needs, instincts and aptitudes, such things being genetically coded within her, functions of her behavioral genetics, as opposed to her property genetics, controlling such matters as eye and hair color, there is a template, or readiness, for self-surrender, service, sensuousness and love within her. These are, of course, familiar aspects of the female slave. Accordingly the readiness for, and the aptitude for, slave dance, so intimately associated with beauty and sexuality, displaying the female in her marvelousness, excitingness and need, scarcely need be noted. These things, incidentally, fit into a harmonious physical and psychological dimorphism of the sexes, in which the male, unless reduced, denied or crippled, is dominant. This sexual dimorphism and the dominance/submission equations do not require institutionalized slavery. It is only that that institution is an expression within the context of a natural civilization of certain primal biotruths. In this sense civilization need not be the antithesis of nature but can represent its natural enhancement and flowering.

"Kneel straight," I said.

She knelt then with her back straight, and looked up at us.

I stared down at her, at her knees, not speaking.

She put her head down, quickly, and spread her knees more widely. They made two small furrows in the dust, and there was now a ridge of dust on the outside of each knee. Did she not know how to kneel before men?

She looked up, and then lowered her head again, spreading her knees even more widely.

She looked up again, frightened, anxiously, seeking my eyes. Then she shuddered, in relief. Her position was now acceptable.

Her skin was burned from the sun. It was red and rough, peeling. In places it was cracked from the heat and wind.

I glanced to the two vessels, to the side, now filled with water, and the associated yoke, thrice drilled, with slender leather straps wrapped about it, at the center and near the ends. The wooden vessels would be heavy in themselves for such a small, lovely creature, let alone when weighted with a filling of liquid. She, too, following my eyes, regarded these things. "Your labors seem arduous," I said.

"It is as my master pleases," she said, looking up at me once more.

"And your day is long?" I asked.

"As my master pleases," she said.

"You are a field slave," I said.

"Yes, Master,' she said.

"And that, too," I said, "is as your master pleases."

"Yes, Master," she said, "that, too, is as my master pleases."

"Your hair has been cropped, as is not unusual for a field slave," I said.

"That it might be sold, master," she said.

"But doubtless it will grow again," I said.

"Yes, Master," she said.

"And it may then be again shorn," I said.

Tears sprang to her eyes.

"Verr are shorn," I said, "and so, too, is the bounding hurt."

"Of course, Master," she said.

"Do you object?" I asked.

She sobbed.

"Your head could have been shaved," I said.

She looked up at me. I gathered she had not thought about that.

"Are you not grateful your head was not shaved?" I asked.

"—Yes, Master," she said.

"Say it," I said.

"I am grateful that my head was not shaved," she said.

Whereas a girl's hair might be cropped, just as her head might be shaved, as a punishment, such a punishment would be quite unusual. After all, the master commonly delights in the long lovely hair of a slave. Indeed, in most cities, long hair is almost universal with slaves. There are many things that can be done with such hair. Not only can it please the master by its beauty and feel, but it can serve to secure the slave, to gag her, and so on. The major reason for cropping the hair of field slaves, both male and female, and certain other forms of work slaves, is to protect them from parasites. For a similar reason the bodies of the women transported on slave ships are almost always shaved, completely. Even then it is common, shortly after debarkation, and this is required by the rules of many port authorities, to subject them to an immersion in slave dip.

"Whose fields are these?" I asked, looking about.

"The fields of my master, Appanius," she said.

"He is a rich man?" I asked.

"Yes, Master," she said.

"And he has many girls," I asked.

"Yes, Master," she said.

"He must have a great many girls," I said.

She looked up at me.

She had a common black, strap collar on her neck, no more, really, than a strap or plate of black iron. It was riveted shut, behind the back of her neck. I had noted this earlier, given the shortness of her hair, and her earlier position, facing away from us as she drew water. The legend would probably be a simple one, not even containing the girl's name, probably something like "I am the property of Appanius."

"That a woman such as you is in the fields," I said.

Tears coursed down her cheeks.

"Keep your knees spread," I warned her.

Swiftly she once more increased the angle between her knees.

She certainly did not seem to me a field slave. Rather she seemed to me the sort of woman one would have expected to find in a house, hurrying about barefoot on the tiles, one ankle perhaps belled, in a bit of silk, serving, a small, luscious woman, well curved, smooth-skinned, and soft, her body perfumed for the pleasure of men, the sort of woman one keeps in mind, the sort of woman who is difficult to forget, the sort whom one might wish to keep close by, perhaps keeping her at night at the foot of one's couch, on her chain.

"What is your name?" I asked.

"Lavinia," she said.

"That seems a rather fine name for a slave," I said, "particularly for a field slave."

"It was my name as a free woman," she said.

"Then it is a different name now," I said, "put on you as a slave name."

"Yes, Master," she said.

"Stand, Lavinia, slave," I said, "and turn slowly about, and then resume your present position."

She obeyed.

"You have good legs," I said.

She did not speak. Her legs were a bit short, but excellent, rather like those of the girl we had seen earlier. Such legs are excellent for slave dance.

"I suspect you were once a rich free woman," I said. That seemed to me likely. Surely only such would have been likely to have managed a tryst with the famous, handsome Milo. She did not know, of course, that I had witnessed her netting, and taking.

She looked up at me, puzzled. "Yes, Master," she said.

"But you are not rich now," I said.

"No, Master," she said, putting her head down. Now she would not own even the rag she wore, or her collar. Such things, as simple as they were, were, like herself, the property of her master.

"I suspect you were a spoiled, rich woman," I said, "much used to having your own way."

"Perhaps, Master," she said.

"And doubtless one muchly pampered," I said.

"Yes, Master," she said.

These conjectures seemed to me sensible, for it would be likely to be only such a woman, spoiled and pampered, who would seek to have her way with the famed Milo.

I regarded her short-cropped hair, the simple collar on her neck, her scanty rag, her reddened, roughened skin, blistered and burned, peeling and cracked, from exposure, from the sun, wind and heat. "You you do not seem spoiled and pampered now," I said.

"No, Master," she said.

"How came you to be a slave?" I asked.

She looked up, her eyes clouded. She bit her lip.

"Consider your reply carefully," I said.

"I was taken in the levies," she said.

"You have earned yourself discipline," I said.

"Please, no!" she cried. "Have pity on me! I am only a poor slave!"

"Do you think it is permissible for you to lie to a free man?" I asked.

"No, Master!" she said. She put down her head, her head in her hands, and sobbed.

"Your reticence is interesting," I said. "The matter is doubtless entered in your papers."

"Yes, Master," she sobbed.

"Speak, girl," I said.

"I was taken pursuant to the couching laws," she said.

"I see," I said. Any free woman who voluntarily couches with another's slave, or readies herself to do so, becomes the slave of the slave's master. By such an act, the couching with, or readying herself to couch with, a slave, as though she might be a girl of the slave's master, thrown to the slave, she shows herself as no more than a slave, and in this act, in law, becomes a slave. Who then should own her, this new slave? Why, of course, he to whom the law consigns her, the master of the slave with whom she has couched, or was preparing to couch.

"With what slave," asked I, "did you couch?"

"I was only preparing to couch!" she said.

"But that is sufficient,' I said.

"Yes, Master," she said.

It seemed then that the rich beauty had received very little of Milo, scarcely the least of his favors. Perhaps, however, for what it might have been worth, she might have managed to receive a woeful glance or two, or a kissing of her gloved fingers. It is hard to say. How proud she might have been that she, of all women, as far as she knew, had managed to attract the marvelous Milo! Then, when she had kept the tryst, entering into the assignation, and had stripped herself and knelt on the couch, eager, waiting, amorous, careless and adventurous, the net had fallen upon her. Shortly thereafter her neck was in the collar. She was, it seems, to have been denied the caresses of Milo. The slave's master, and then hers, as well, Appanius, had decided it. It would be the coils of the slave net which would tighten upon her body, not the arms of the handsome bondsman. Perhaps this seemed fitting to Appanius, that the new slave, prior to her public imbonding, should be so served. Perhaps he found it amusing. Or perhaps he was jealous of his slave, and wished to reserve his caresses for himself. Or it could have been all three. One did not know.

"What was the name of the slave?" I asked.

"Milo," she said.

"The well-known Milo," I asked, "the actor?"

"Yes," she said.

"Did you not think he would have his pick of slaves in the house of Appanius?" I asked.

"I did not know," she said.

"Beautiful slaves, silked for a man's pleasure, perfumed for his delight, eager, needful, helplessly responsive, trained to please in a thousand modalities?"

"I did not know," she said.

"Did you think to be able to compete with such women?"

"I did not know!" she wept.

"Do you invite further discipline?" I asked.

"I was free," she said. "I thought that I was somehow special, or better!"

I smiled. Marcus laughed, and struck the side of his saddle twice, so amused he was.

She looked up at us, angrily.

"But you are not free now," I said.

"No, Master," she said.

"Do you still consider yourself better than slaves?" I asked.

"No, Master," she said, "for I now, too, am only a slave."

"And only a field slave," I said.

"Yes, Master," she said.

Female work slaves, field slaves, stable slaves, and such, like kettle-and-mat girls, are usually considered the lowest of slaves. At any rate, they commonly bring the lowest prices in the markets.

"You are now quite different from what you were as a free woman," I said.

"Yes, Master," she said.

"But now that you are slave, even a field slave," I said, "you are better prepared to compete with other slaves for the attention of a man than would be a free woman."

She looked up at me, puzzled.

"You at least know what is your business with men," I said, "to please them, and as a slave."

"Yes, Master," she said.

"Your life could depend on it," I said.

"Yes, Master," she said.

"Do you doubt your attractiveness?" I asked.

"Yes, Master," she said.

"Do not do so," I said.

"Master?" she asked.

"You are beautiful," I said, "or could be beautiful."

She was silent.

"Consider yourself," I said.

She put her hands up to her cropped hair, and then touched the tiny, torn brown rag she wore, and then, again, put her head down, and placed her hands on her thighs.

"Have you seen yourself in a mirror lately?" I asked.

"I have looked upon my reflection in water," she said, "in the tank."

"You are interested in such things?" I said.

She was silent.

"Speak," I said.

"Yes, Master," she said.

"As are other slave girls," I said.

"Yes, Master," she said.

"And what do you see in the water?"

"A slave," she said.

"A field slave?" I asked.

"A pleasure slave," she said.

"Ah!" laughed Marcus.

"But yet you are in the fields," I said.

"Yes, Master," she said.

"Do you think it strange that you, who were a free woman, should look upon your reflection, and see in it a pleasure slave?"

"No, Master," she said.

"From your collaring," I said, "you have seen in your reflection this pleasure slave?"

"I have seen her there for years," she said, "not just since my collaring."

"A bold confession," I said.

"I am a slave girl," she said. "I must speak the truth."

"But once before, it seems, earlier, in the matter of how you came to be a slave, you did not speak the truth."

"No, Master."

"But it is your intention now to speak the truth?"

"Yes, Master!"

"Keep the angle between your knees," I said.

"Yes, Master!" she said. Once again then, she knelt suitably.

"Is the pleasure slave whom you see in your reflection beautiful?" I asked.

"It is my hope that she is," she said.

"She is," I said.

"Thank you," she said, "—Master."

"Do you think you are the only woman who has been brought into bondage by means of the attractions of Milo, the slave?" I asked.

"No, Master," she said. "Apparently there have been several others."

"Trapped dupes," said Marcus.

"Yes, Master," she said.

"Snared as easily as vulos," he said.

"Yes, Master," she said.

"As you were," he said.

"Yes, Master!" she said.

"And doubtless there will be many more," I said.

She looked up, tears in her eyes. "Yes, Master," she said. "Doubtless."

"Do you know of others?" I asked. "Say, in the fields?"

"They were commonly sold out of the city," she said. "But apparently that is more difficult now, with the Cosians in power. That is probably why I am here, in the vicinity of Ar. I know of none in the fields other than myself. There are two others, however, in the house."

"Then you have been in the house," I said.

"Yes, Master," she said. "Only in the last few days have I been in the fields."

This did not surprise me, as her mien had suggested to me earlier that she might be new to the onus of such labors. This was also suggested to me by the condition of her skin, which had not yet browned, darkening and toughening.

"How did you get on with the other slaves in the house?" I asked.

"The three of us who owed our collars to Milo hated one another," she said. "The other slaves held all of us, recent free women, in contempt."

"Interesting," I said.

"We, too, now were only slaves, and inexperienced slaves," she said.

"True," I said.

"But they need not have been so cruel!" she said.

"Perhaps you behaved around them as though you might still think of yourselves as free women," I said.

"We did that scarcely at all," she said, "only a little at first, I think, and then we did not do it again, for they whipped us. After that, for the most part, they ignored us."

"They did not teach you their secrets then," I said, "such things as how to please men?" There are hundreds of such things, of course, ranging from the dressing and care of the hair, the application of cosmetics, such as lipstick and eye shadow, commonly thought improper for free women, and the judicious selection of jewelry, silks and perfumes, to physical and psychological subtleties, both behaviors and techniques, which can drive a master almost out of his senses with pleasure, and all this by a female totally at his disposal, one whom he can command, as it pleases him, one who is legally and literally owned by him, and in every way.

"They would not do so," she said, "though we begged them!"

"Did you put yourself as a slave before them?" I asked. "Did you weep and beg, kneeling before them and licking their feet? Did you make it clear to them that your entreaties were those of one like themselves, only another slave? Did you offer to work for them? Did you do so? Did you serve them, and wait upon them, on a lengthy probationary basis, as though you might be their own slave, that they might assess your earnestness, your sincerity and zeal?"

"As a new slave, I too much feared them," she said.

"Perhaps it is just as well," I said. "You might have been whipped."

"I think so, Master," she said.

"Perhaps, after a few months, after they had become used to

you as only another slave amongst them, no more or less, things might have been different."

"Perhaps, Master," she said.

"You seem to me a highly intelligent woman," I said.

"Master?" she asked.

"Surely you were aware of the couching laws?"

"Yes, Master," she said.

"You expected to violate them with impunity?"

"I gather so, Master," she said.

"You did not expect to be betrayed, or discovered?"

"I do not think so, Master," she said.

"And yet," I said, "as a highly intelligent woman, you must have realized that some danger would be involved."

"Perhaps," she said. "The matter is unclear to me now."

"That in itself is interesting," I said.

"Master?" she asked.

"It seems you were very careless," I said.

"Perhaps, Master," she said.

"That seems to me very interesting," I said.

"Master?" she asked.

"What was your first emotion," I asked, "when the net descended upon you?"

"It does not matter," she said.

"Surely you realized it was a slave net?"

"A capture net of some sort," she said.

"What was that first emotion?" I asked.

"It does not matter!" she said. "It was a momentary reaction, a sudden, fleeting, wild thing!"

"What was it?" I asked.

She looked up at me, agonized, miserable. She was quite lovely.

"Keep your knees widely separated," I reminded her.

Again the whitish dust, a hort deep, was pushed to the sides, to bank against the outside of her knees.

"Consider your reply carefully," I said. "You have already incurred discipline."

"Elation!" she said.

"Of course," I said.

"Then I was terrified!" she said. "I realized what had happened! I was caught! I had been discovered! I was trapped! I was within the toils of a net! I burned with shame, with embarrassment. It seemed I was afire! I choked with misery! I was naked! Men were moving about! They could see me! What of my reputation? I struggled! I was afraid! I was angry! I was outraged! I was miserable! I had been betrayed! I was helpless! I fought the net! I fought the net! But I could not free myself!"

"And what later," I asked, "in the edifice of the magistrates?"

"I was in a cell," she said, "naked, lying on some straw, chained by the neck to a wall."

"And your emotions?" I asked.

She looked up at me.

"My thigh was sore," she said. "I had been branded."

"Of course," I said.

"There were two collars on my neck," she said, "a light, temporary slave collar, identifying me as a slave provisionally in the custody of magistrates, and, over it, a retaining collar, that by means of which I was fastened to the wall."

"Go on," I said.

"I felt the collars on my neck," she said. "The temporary collar was flat and close-fitting. It was the first collar I had ever worn. It was put on me after my branding. The retaining collar, too, was close fitting, scarcely less so, it seemed, than the collar it covered. It was heavy and thick. The chain to it was heavy, too, with thick links. It was about four feet long. it was fastened to a stout ring in the wall, about a foot above the floor."

"And your emotions?" I asked.

"I lay there," she said, "my fingers on the chain, near the retaining collar."

I looked at her.

"Serenity, contentment," she said. "Happiness. The fighting was over."

"When did you receive the collar of Appanius?" I asked.

"The next day," she said, "affixed on me by one of his agents. Later I was called for at the edifice of the magistrates by one of his slaves, driving a tharlarion wagon. He tied my hands behind my back and put a rope on my neck, by means of which he tied me to the back of the wagon. I was not to ride in the wagon. I was a female slave. I would follow it afoot, on my rope. It was thus, naked, that I was conducted to the house of my master. Twice in the streets I was struck by free women. My introduction to slavery had begun."

"Were you angry with the slave who bound you?" I asked.

"No," she said. "Rather I was afraid of him. He was a male. Too, I realized I could be given to him for his pleasure, if my master wished."

"I gather that," I said, "in spite of the doubtless large numbers of beautiful slaves in the house of Appanius, you were to be trained as a house slave."

"Yes, Master," she said.

"Do not doubt, then, your desirability and beauty," I said.

"I tried to do well," she said, "to learn self-effacement and deference, to serve ably, silently and unobtrusively. I think I did well. I hardly ever felt the stroke of the house master's switch."

"And were you silked?" I asked.

"As befits slaves," she said, "clad for the pleasure of masters."

"How came you to the fields?" I asked.

"One night I, and two others, were serving not in the main halls, as we commonly did, but at a late supper, a small, private supper, laid in the very quarters of my master, Appanius. It was well after the curfew, and the closing of the theaters. There were only two at this supper, the master, Appanius, and Milo, his slave, whom you have heard of, who had returned from a performance in the great theater."

"Appanius and Milo must be on intimate terms," I said.

"Yes," she said. "The master treats him almost as though he might be a free man. They discuss matters of business and the theater. Even in the great hall, at the common suppers, he has Milo above the salt and at his right hand."

"You must have served Milo at the common suppers then?" I asked.

"Yes," she said.

"And as only another deferential slave," I said.

"Of course," she said.

"You must hate him," I said.

"Why?" she asked.

"It was through his collusion," I said, "that you came into the collar."

"Then I should be grateful to him," she said, "for I have known for years that it is in the collar that I belong."

"I see," I said.

"Besides," she said, "he, too, is a slave. He must act on behalf of Appanius. He, too, even though he is the great Milo, must obey. Do you think he wishes to be thrown to sleen?"

"I would not think so," I said.

"I am far from bearing him ill will," she said.

"I gathered that," I said.

"Indeed," she said, "it was my hope that I might be thrown to him, that I might at last feel his touch!"

"I see," I said.

"He is beautiful!" she said.

"Not a bad looking fellow," I granted her.

"And there I was," she said, "kneeling half naked in slave silk, collared, in bangles, waiting to serve, so close to him I could reach out and touch him, almost alone with him."

"Continue," I said.

"And then they began to discuss a free woman, I do not even remember her name, objectively, casually, as though she might be an animal, a mere slave, like myself. I could hardly believe my ears. And then I realized that at one time I, too, had doubtless been so discussed."

"You were angry?" I asked.

"Not then," she said. "I think I was rather more scandalized that the woman should be discussed in that fashion. After all, she was not, as I, an animal, a slave."

"But perhaps she was an animal, a slave," I said, "only one not yet in her collar, as once you were not yet in your collar."

"That is undoubtedly true!" she laughed.

"But you became angry later?" I said.

"Yes!" she said.

"At whom?" I asked.

"At both of them!" she said.

"Because of the trickery they would practice," I asked, "because of the toils of the slave net?"

"No," she said. "It was rather that I did not want Milo to have anything to do with that other woman, whoever she was! There were already enough women so captured in the house! What if she were more beautiful than I? What if he liked her, when he saw her naked in the net?"

"You were jealous of a possible rival," I said.

"Perhaps," she said.

"You would have preferred to be the only female in Milo's net?"

"Yes!" she said.

"But there have apparently been a great many," I said.

"I was distraught," she said. "I was furious! My heart was beating wildly. Then I felt futile, helpless and miserable. I could do nothing! Such as I are are completely at the mercy of our masters! I was only a slave! And then there were tears in my eyes, and Milo was so beautiful! I wanted him to see me, to notice me. I did not wish to be just another slave in the background, unrecognized, so simply taken for granted, serving but almost unnoticed, present but scarcely seen. I reached out, with tears in my eyes, and put my fingers on his arm."

"Continue," I said.

"He seemed startled that I had done this, as though he might not believe it. I looked at him, tears in my eyes, kneeling there, appealing to him, that he might take notice of me, though I were only a slave."

"Yes?" I said.

"This was noted, of course, by my master, Appanius. Apparently I had not realized the grievousness of what I had done. He leaped to his feet. His eyes blazed. He was beside himself with anger. 'Guards! Guards!' he cried, clapping his hands. I knelt small there by the table, trembling, my head down. I knew I had done wrong, daring to touch Milo, I, he so favored by the master and I only a house slave, but I had been unable to help myself. I so wanted to be brought to his attention! But never yet had he requested me, nor had I been put naked to my knees before him, my hands bound behind me in slave bracelets, the key about my neck, for his pleasure. I knew I had done wrong, but I had not understood that it was so terrible. I had only wanted to call myself to his attention, and had hoped doubtless that he might sometimes be moved to take pity on a poor slave. 'Guards! Guards!' cried Appanius. I was terrified. I trembled, not understanding the immensity of his anger, the enormity of his response to my tiny, pathetic deed. Guards rushed into the room, blades free of scabbards, the doors bursting open. Perhaps they had feared an attempt was in progress on the master's life. In a moment they were about me. I feared I was to be cut to pieces. He struggled, it seemed, to control himself. 'Forgive me, Master!' I wept. I crawled to him, my head down. 'Forgive me, Master!' I wept. I kissed his feet, fervently. He pulled away, in anger. He moved to the side. He kicked me twice, in fury. I returned to him on my belly, and showered my hair upon his sandals, and then again kissed his feet, again and again. 'Forgive me, Master!' I wept, an errant slave, one who had done wrong, pleading for mercy and forgiveness. He pulled back, away from me again, and then stood there, some feet before me, looking down at me. I was still on my belly. I looked up at him, a slave regarding her master with terror, lying before him, his property, on the tiles of his house. 'Have her lashed,' he said. 'Then have her hair cropped, and send her to the fields!' "

"And it was thus you came to the fields," I said.

"Yes, Master," she said.

"And how did Milo respond to all this?" I asked.

"Imperturbably," she said. "I was, after all, only a female."

"Do you think that Milo finds you attractive?" I asked.

"Master?" she asked.

"That he would like to strip you, collar you and throw you to the furs at his feet, there to vent his lust upon you, his slave?"

"I do not know if his drives are that strong, Master," she said.

"Would you object?" I asked.

"No, Master," she said. "It has always been my hope that I

might prove attractive enough to provoke such desire. I am a slave girl. I live to be the obedient, grateful, vulnerable object of such lust and power. I have always dreamed of it. I wish to be choiceless, to be overpowered and made to serve!"

"Milo must have exhibited some interest in you, or seemed to exhibit some interest in you," I said, "if only during the period of your seduction, when you were being trapped."

"Yes," she said, "then."

"But after you were in the house as a slave, collared, scantily clad, utterly vulnerable?"

"No, Master," she said.

"He never asked for you to be brought to him?"

"No, Master."

"Why do you think that is?" I asked.

"I am insufficiently beautiful," she said.

"Did he call for other women?" I asked.

"I do not know, Master," she said.

"Did you not see names written on the call boards in the kitchen?"

"No," she said.

"Interesting," I said.

"One of the girls, another one of we three who had been trapped by Milo, claimed to have been with him, but it was proven that she had lied. She had been chained in the stable that night. The house master found out about it and she was whipped, before us all."

"As far as you know, then," I said, "none of the girls of the house were put with Milo."

"As far as I know, not," she said.

"But surely there would be no cause for secrecy about such a matter," I said.

"I would not think so," she said.

"Milo was important in the house," I said. "He is famous. He is of great value to Appanius."

"Certainly, Master," she said.

"It would make sense then," I said, "to suppose that a girl would be sent to him, at least once in a while."

"Perhaps, Master," she said.

"So much is done even for quarry slaves," I said.

"Yes, Master," she said.

"But as far as you know this was never done?"

"Not as far as I know," she said.

"And if it had been done," I said, "it is my speculation that you would have heard of it, such gossip flowing quickly through the corridors of such a house."

"I suppose so," she said.

"If Milo had requested a girl, do you think he would have received one?"

"I would suppose so," she said, puzzled.

"Perhaps he did not request one," I said.

"Master?" she asked.

"Possibly Milo does not find women attractive," I said.

"Master?" she asked.

"Nothing," I said.

"Yes, Master," she said.

"Are you a virgin?" I asked.

She laughed. "How long can a slave remain a virgin, Master?" she asked.

"Whom have you served?" I asked.

"Mostly men in the house, on the staff," she said, "those who wanted me for the night. We are free to them, you know. I was muchly cuffed at first. I was clumsy. I knew so little."

"You are more accomplished now?" I asked.

"One learns quickly under the whip," she said.

"And in the fields?"

"Mostly the whip masters," she said. "But twice I was tied to a stake, for the field slaves."

I noted that her knees had moved a little further apart, probably unconsciously, or without really thinking about it, after she had said this. In such ways can a slave, sometimes not even conscious of what she is doing, or fully conscious of it, beg. I glanced to Marcus, and he smiled. He, too, had noticed the tiny movement.

"May I speak, Masters?" she asked.

"No," I said.

She put down her head.

"Have you experienced slave arousal?" I asked.

"Master?" she asked, looking up.

"Have the slave fires been lit in your belly?" I asked. She was, after all, a relatively new slave, and had been a house slave, apparently primarily consigned to domestic duties, serving table and such, and was now a field slave, whose primary services would presumably lie in such labors as the carrying of water and the hoeing of suls. It was not as though she had been in the attentive and exacting ownership, for example, of a particular master, who would see to the summoning forth and cultivation of these intimate, exquisite, exigent latencies which once initiated seem to blossom and grow of their own lovely, imperious will, which cannot be suppressed or silenced, and which make a girl so much their prisoner, more so than collars and chains.

"Sometimes," she said, "I sense their beginnings in me."

"How do you feel about them?" I asked.

"I love them," she said, "but I am afraid of them."

I nodded. Well she might be.

"May I speak?" she asked.

"Very well," I said.

"Who are you?" she asked. "Are you men of my master, Appanius?"

Perhaps she thought we had come from her master, to question her. But surely, too, our armbands should have suggested to her that our origins, and intents, were not indigenous to the house of Appanius.

"No," I said.

"You are not slavers, are you?" she asked.

We did not speak.

"Please tell me!" she begged.

"It is not in that modality that we have come," I said.

"You are members of the caste of slavers!" she said.

"No," I said.

"But you are slavers!" she said.

"Do not concern yourself with the matter," I said.

"Yes Master," she said.

The distinction, of course, is between belonging to the caste of slavers and being a slaver. Whereas members of the caste of slavers are slavers, not all slavers are members of the caste of slavers. For example, I am not of the slavers, but in Port Kar I am known as Bosk, and he known as many things, among them pirate and slaver. Too, both Marcus and myself were of the warriors, the scarlet caste, and as such were not above taking slaves, Such is not only permitted in the codes, but encouraged by them. "The slave is a joy and a convenience to the warrior." Neither of us, of course, was a member of the caste of slavers. It, incidentally, is sometimes regarded as a subcaste of the merchants, and sometimes as an independent caste. It does have its own colors, blue and yellow, whereas those of the merchants are yellow and white, or gold and white.

"Have you come to collect taxes?" she asked. "Have you come from the levies?"

"No," I said. Her questions were doubtless motivated by our armbands. It was not unknown in recent months in Ar and her vicinity for properties of various sorts, including such as she was, to be taken for taxes, Too, of course, there might have been new requisitions from Cos, or even from the camp of the polemarkos, calling for new levies of women, both free and slave.

"You are not going to carry me off are you?" she asked.

"Curiosity is not becoming in a kajira," I said.

"Forgive me, Master," she said. She squirmed in agitation. It would not be difficult, of course, to carry her off. With our armbands we could have done so with impunity. In a matter of moments she could have been ours, gagged, hooded and bound. There are a great many ways in which a girl may be carried captive by a mounted warrior, and many saddles have been designed with the accommodation of such a prisoner in mind. Some of these arrangements are quite simple and others are complex. Perhaps the simplest is to have the girl mounted before you with her hands tied to a ring before her body. Some of the more complex involve saddle cages and nets. A reasonably common arrangement, and that with which our saddles were equipped, involves paired rings, one on each side of the saddle. With this arrangement the usual technique is as follows: The girl's hands are tied before her and then tied, in turn, to a ring on the left side of the saddle. When she is thusly fastened, her hands up, tied together and fastened to the left saddle ring, she is lifted up and put over the saddle, on either her back or belly, as pleases the captor, after which her ankles are fastened together on the other side, then, of course, also lashed to the ring there, the second of the pair of rings, that on the right side of the saddle. In this arrangement the girl is quite safe, protected against the danger of a fall. She is also, of course, completely helpless.

"Would you not like to be carried off?" I asked.

"No!" she said.

"But surely you are not so enamored of the labors of the field slave," I said.

"No," she said.

"And you have already begun to sense in yourself the beginnings of slave fires," I said.

She looked up at me, and then put her head down, quickly. She clenched her small fists.

"Speak," I said. "Have they not already begun to burn in your belly?"

She looked up, agonized, her small fists clenched.

"Remember," I said, "you have already incurred discipline."

"Yes, Master!" she sobbed.

"Good," I said.

She put down her head, sobbing. How helpless one must feel at times, I thought, as a female slave. But such admissions are good for the development of their character, and their discipline. Too, they are very helpful and beneficial for the slave.

They help them to understand who and what they are, and who is master.

"I would think you would be an excellent house slave," I said, "silked, pattering about, perhaps belled, serving, heated and excited by the nearness of your master."

She looked up.

"Perhaps you might even be chained to his slave ring at night, at the very foot of his couch."

"It is such things I want!" she said.

"It is easy to imagine you kneeling before him, begging for his touch."

"Yes, Master!" she said.

"And will he consent to content you?" I asked.

"It is my hope that he would take pity on one who is only his slave."

"Yes," I said, "I think you would be hot, devoted and dutiful."

"Yes, Master!" she said.

"I think you would make an excellent house slave," I said, "indeed, an excellent pleasure slave."

"Oh, yes, Master!" she said.

"And perhaps in time," I said, "even a love slave."

"It is thusly that I want to live!" she said.

"Then surely you wish to be carried off," I said.

"No," she said. "No!"

"Why not?" I asked.

She sobbed.

"Ah," I said. "It seems you do not wish to leave the vicinity of the house of Appanius."

"No, Master," she said. "I do not wish to leave the vicinity of the house of Appanius."

"Apparently you are very devoted to your master," I said.

"I do not even know him," she said, "except as I, and others, are utilized for such purposes as serving his table. Even when he passes us in a hall we kneel in obeisance, our heads to the floor."

"Still," I said, "it seems you must be very devoted to him."

She put down her head.

"But in any event," I said, "your wishes are unimportant. You are a female slave. It will be done with you as men, and masters, please."

"Yes, Master," she said.

"I wish certain details as to the techniques utilized by Appanius and Milo in the capture of free women, thence to be enslaved."

"Master?" she asked.

"Surely from the conversation which you overheard, and from your own experience, you have some ideas of what these must be."

"Surely master can have no interest in such things," she said.

"You have now twice incurred discipline," I informed her.

"Forgive me, Master!" she said.

"How will you speak?" I asked.

"Fully, and perfectly, to the best of my knowledge!"

"As befits what you are?"

"Yes, Master!" she said.

"Which is?" I asked.

"A slave girl, Master," she said, "only that!"

"Who initiates these relationships?" I asked.

"In one of two ways, I think, are they initiated," she said. "In the first, the free woman puts herself in Milo's way, she compliments him, she calls herself to his attention, perhaps she lowers her veil a little, perhaps her tones to him are soft, and special, making clear to him that there is an eager lover awaiting him beneath her veils and robes, perhaps she even lets him lift and kiss the coverlets of her palanquin, near her feet, such things. These advances, so calculatedly ambiguous, and yet so obvious and meaningful, are reported to Appanius. He then makes a judgment as to whether they are to be encouraged or not, and then, later, perhaps after she has lowered her veil for Milo, and let him gaze upon the revelation of her beauty, and he has seen her move in the palanquin, apparently inadvertently, but in such a way that he can conjecture something of the fairness of her limbs beneath her robes, and has perhaps even seen her ankles, a second judgment, this again from the reports of Milo, is made by Appanius. If this judgment is favorable and it is decided that the female, after having been perhaps subjected to a rigorous regimen of dieting, exercise, training and discipline, might not preposterously be put upon a slave block, the arrangements for her capture are completed. In the second way the matter is initiated by Appanius himself, he himself selecting a candidate for approach, scrutiny and cultivation."

"On what grounds initially?" I asked.

"Usually from rumors of a certain free woman's beauty," she said.

"I see," I said.

"Too," she said, "it is my understanding that information is sometimes furnished, for a fee, by some of the female proprietors of women's baths in Ar. Too, in some cases, Appanius is permitted to observe the women from a secret coign of vantage."

"In what way did you come to attention of Appanius?" I asked.

"In the first way, doubtless," she smiled, "as I did not frequent the public baths and I doubt very much that rumors of my beauty were abroad in the streets."

"They might have been," I said.

"Master is kind," she said.

"Continue," I said.

"Although master might regard me as having been a spoiled, pampered free woman, and although that was undoubtedly true," she said, "I was nonetheless too shy in the beginning even to approach one such as Milo. Certainly there must be free women richer and more beautiful than I in Ar. Accordingly, in the beginning, I only worshipped him from afar. I attended his performances. I dreamed of him. But I did not dare call myself to his attention."

"In the beginning," I said, "your responses to Milo were more humble and slavelike?"

"Yes, Master," she said. "I even dreamed of crawling to him, putting my head down and kissing his feet."

"Continue," I said.

"But soon, of course, the free woman in me became outraged at such things! They were too feminine! I was not a slave!"

"So what did you do?" I asked.

"I told myself that I was a free woman, and rich, and could do as I pleased, and that he, Milo, for all his beauty and fame, was only a slave! He should be grateful if I so much as permitted him to crawl to my feet!"

"And you became bolder?"

She laughed. "Well," she said, "perhaps not so much bolder. But I would station myself and my attendants where he might pass, if only to catch a glimpse of him between the curtains of my palanquin."

"In effect," I said, "your responses were still shy, and slavelike."

"Yes," she said, angrily.

"You felt you belonged at the feet of such a man?"

"Perhaps," she said.

"But you truly belonged at the feet of any man," I said.

"Yes, Master," she said.

"Continue," I said.

"Certainly he must soon note my palanquin," she said. "Surely it was often enough in his way, outside the great theater, on streets which he frequented, even in certain markets. At that time, perhaps he had reported to Appanius, and his agents had ascertained my identity, that of the owner of the palanquin. To be sure, such thoughts did not occur to me then. Rather I castigated myself for my timidity, and reminded myself, again and again, that it was I who was the free person, I who was in control, I who was in command, I who could have my way, as I pleased. Then I took to having the curtains of the palanquin opened, that I might be seen within, in my most beautiful robes and veils, as though I might wish fresher air and greater light, paused there perhaps in the midst of some business, waiting for some acquaintance. I even let him see me glance at him once and then turned my head away, quickly, too quickly, as I now realize. Perhaps I should have behaved more like a free woman, and had him ordered to the side of my palanquin, to kneel there and be questioned as a slave. Doubtless some women did, arrogating to themselves, as free women are free to do, the prerogatives of males. I wonder how they felt when the net descended on them. At least I was not a slave. I could be forward, I could call myself to his attention, demanding it, as I wished."

"Slaves," said I, "as you must now know, have many ways of calling themselves to the attention of a man, subtly, effectively, pleadingly, vulnerably, helplessly, deferentially, humbly."

She looked up at me.

"The palms of your hands are facing upward," I said.

"Oh!" she said, and quickly turned them downward, and clutched her thighs. The rag she wore, given her knee position, that of a pleasure slave, was high on her thighs. Her hands, her fingers on her thighs, digging into them, as though they would anchor themselves there, half covered it. Her grip was partly through the cloth and partly on her thighs. Midway in her grip came the garment's frayed hem, pressed down on her fair, sweet thighs. The contrast was attractive, like slave silk against flesh, or a narrow cord sustaining such silk at the shoulder, perhaps an inch from a disrobing loop, or the metal of slave bracelets locked on small, downy wrists, a rope on a waist, snug above a sweetly rounded belly, or a collar on the neck.

"Indeed," I said, "slaves, in their subtle, vulnerable, helpless ways, in their beggingness, in their humbleness, in their deferentiality, in the very nature and entirety of their condition, have many better ways of calling themselves to the attention of a man than a free woman."

"But I did not understand that at the time," she said.

"I would suppose not," I said.

"Free women," she laughed, "are not likely to whimper and lick ankles."

"They do so quickly enough after they have become slaves," I said, "and have experienced slave arousal, and realize their need and helplessness, and their dependence on the master."

"Yes, Master," she said. "And I sense the beginning of such things in myself."

"So what did you do?" I asked.

"Actually," she smiled. "I had to do very little. I have little doubt now that I had been discussed by Milo and Appanius. Milo approached my palanquin when I had the curtains back, begging for forgiveness for approaching me, proposing even that he be beaten by my bearers for his boldness, but that he could not help himself, that for days he had struggled with himself, but now, regardless of what sorry consequences might ensue, even though it might mean he be hurled to sleen, that he had at last, against his sternest will, been drawn irresistibly to my side, as though in chains by tharlarion. Then, tears in his eyes, he begged liberty only to salute my beauty, and then hurry away, in joy."

"You were fully veiled?" I asked.

"In my most beautiful robes and veils was I bedecked," she said.

"You wore your street veil," I said.

"I had had the curtains of the palanquin drawn in the journey through the streets," she said.

"You did not wear your street veil," I said.

"No," she said.

"Then," I said, "I suspect that you were veiled in such a way that the lineaments of your visage might, though perhaps with some difficulty, be discerned."

"Yes!" she said, tossing her head.

"What a slave you were!" laughed Marcus.

"And am!" she said.

"Yes, and are!" laughed he.

Now no longer need the lovely Lavinia concern herself with matters such as veiling. She was slave. Would you veil a she-tarsk, a she-sleen?

"And so he saluted your beauty?"

"Yes," she said, "with a beautiful gesture."

"And it did not occur to you that he probably had numbers of sinuous little sluts in the house of Appanius who would snake about his legs and feet, and lick and kiss, and beg to serve him in any way he might desire, to his heart's content?"

"I did not think of such things," she said.

"He then hurried away?"

"Yes," she said. "Obviously he was in consternation, and in terror at the affrontery he might have offered me, or so I thought."

"And what had you said?"

"Nothing," she said. "I was as tongue-tied as a new slave girl thrown for the first time before her master."

"I see," I said.

"Afterwards I was frantic that I must set him at his ease, that I must let him know that I was not offended. I must encourage him to return. I must see him again! I sent him a note, informing him that I would permit him to speak with me."

"And then?"

"He did not come for two days," she said, "and when he came he contritely confessed that he had lacked the courage, he so unworthy, to approach one such as I, so high born and free. Soon one thing led to another, he even claiming that he was my slave in right, and in his heart, and not that of Appanius, his legal master. I was overcome. What free woman has not coveted such adulatory attention, though in her heart she knows it is she who in nature belongs worshipfully at the male's feet? Oh, yes, I was a pretty little vulo, ripe for the snare. There is a special room in which we agreed to meet."

"I know the place," I said.

"Oh?" she asked.

"Yes," I said. "It is in the Metellan district."

"Yes," she said. "Well, it was there that the net fell. Now I am in a collar."

"Yes," I said.

I looked down at her, she kneeling so far below us, in the hot, whitish dust.

"Where I belong," she said.

"True," I said.

"May I be of further service to Masters?" she asked.

"I have obtained from you the information I wished," I said.

"Then a girl is pleased," she said.

I then slipped down from the saddle of the tharlarion.

"Master?" she asked. She had moved suddenly, almost involuntarily, as though she might have thought of leaping to her feet and fleeing, as I had dismounted, but she had had the good sense to think the better of it. Certainly she had not received permission to break position. She then knelt there, her back very straight, trembling.

"Lift your head," I said. "Look up."

She did so. Her lower lip trembled.

I regarded her short brush of hair, the brief, tattered rag, scarcely more than a ta-teera, which was her only garment, the simple collar, no more than a strap of black iron curved about her throat, its small, right-angled, pierced terminations flush to one another behind the back of her neck, held together by the rivet, her blistered, burned skin.

"Field slave," I said.

"Yes, Master," she said.

"You have lied to free men," I said.

She regarded me in terror.

"You told us that you had been brought in as a consequence of the levies, whereas it was in consequence of the couching laws."

"Forgive me, Master," she whispered.

"But I am not particularly angered," I said.

"Thank you, Master!" she said.

"You hastened to rectify your account."

"Yes, Master!" she said.

"And were on the whole exact, voluble and diligent in your subsequent responses."

"Yes, Master!" she said.

"Do you think you would have lied to me, if I owned you?" I asked.

She looked up at me. "No, Master!" she said.

"I do not think you would have either," I said.

She shuddered.

"But, of course, I do not own you."

"No, Master," she said.

"But as you know, an errant slave may be disciplined by any free man."

"Yes, Master," she said.

"For example, her master might not be present."

"Yes, Master," she whispered.

"Her slavery does not exist only in his presence," I said.

"No, Master."

"It is uncompromised, categorical and absolute, at any moment, wherever she is," I said.

"Yes, Master."

"And thus it is fitting, is it not, that she be subject to the discipline of any free man?"

"Of course, Master."

"And Marcus, my friend, and I are free men."

"Yes, Master."

"And you are thus subject to our discipline."

"Yes, Master."

"And you lied to us."

"Forgive me, Master!" she begged.

"If I were your master," I said, "I do not know what I would have done with you. It is an interesting question. Surely, at the least you would have been stripped and tied, and given a lashing."

She swallowed, hard.

"And I do not think you would soon forget it," I said.

"No, Master," she said.

"Do you think you would then lie to me again?"

"No, Master!" she said.

"You would attempt to improve your behavior, in all ways?"

"Yes, Master."

I regarded her.

"Master?" she asked.

"I am thinking that since we do not own you that perhaps it might be fitting if your discipline were decided by your master, the noble Appanius."

"Please, no, Master!" she said.

"It would be easy enough," I said, "to strip you and tie your hands behind your back, and then write upon your body some brief but suitable message."

She seemed to pale beneath her burns.

"The left breast, as you know," I said, "is the usual place for such messages." This is, one supposes, because most masters are right-handed.

"Please do not inform my master, Appanius!" she wept.

"You seem to fear him," I said.

"Yes!" she wept.

"It is good for a girl to fear her master," I said.

"You do not understand!" she said. "I have already it seems muchly displeased him. Already I have been shorn and put in the fields! If I gave him further cause for displeasure I do not know what he would do with me!"

"You might be whipped?" I said.

"He might have me thrown to the eels in his pool!" she said.

"Have no fear," I said, "you have been helpful and cooperative, and I have obtained much of value from our conversation, more doubtless than you understand. Similarly, as this is the first time we have met, at least formally, I am inclined, somewhat against my better judgment, to be initially lenient. It might be pointed out, for example, that you did not know the sort of men we were. Perhaps some men ignore lies in a slave, pretending not to notice them, or, mistakenly, graciously accept them as trivial, as merely a girl's peccadilloes. But we are not such men. We are not patient with such things. Even had you lied about something as small as a candy or pastry we would not have accepted it. We approve of, and expect, truth from a slave. In short, had you known the sort of men we are, it is my speculation that you would not have lied to us."

"No, Master," she said.

"But, as I have suggested, I am inclined to be lenient, in this first offense."

"Thank you, Master," she said.

"Also, of course," I said, "we are not your master, and it seems that serious or grievous disciplines should be the prerogative of the master. These prerogatives we do not desire to usurp."

"No, Master!" she said.

"Accordingly," I said, "your discipline is to be light."

"Thank you, Master!" she said.

I then lashed her head back and forth, first with the palm of my right hand, and then its back. Then, with the last backhand stroke, I struck her from her knees, to her side, and she was lying on her side, twisted, her palms down in the white dust. She looked back at me, disbelievingly, startled, tears in her eyes, over her right shoulder.

"Position," I said.

She crawled back to where she had knelt, and resumed her former position, her head bowed.

I walked about her and then crouched before her.

I put my hand under her chin and lifted it. Her face was red from the cuffing. There were tears on her cheeks. Her lip was swollen. There was some blood at the side of her face. I removed my hand, and let her once again lower her head.

"Oh!" she said.

"You have a good belly," I said.

"Ai," she said, softly.

"And an excellent figure," I said.

"Oh!" she exclaimed, softly, helplessly.

I removed my left hand from the small of her back, where I had held it, that she might not draw back more than I would permit. "And you have at least the glimmerings of slave vitality," I said.

She moaned.

"You are not going to lie to us again, are you?" I asked.

"No, Master!" she sobbed.

I then rose to my feet and stepped back a little.

She squirmed a little. "May I speak?" she begged.

"Yes," I said.

"That was light discipline?" she asked.

"Yes," I said, "naught but a mere cuffing."

Normally, or course, one cuffs with a single blow. She had,

however, lied. Even so, I had, of course, pulled the strokes. One does not wish to injure the slave, only punish her. Had I struck her heavily, with the force easily summonable by a strong man, I might have broken her neck.

"I am sorry, if I have displeased Masters," she said.

I did not speak.

"But Masters are wrong in one thing," she said.

"What is that?" I asked.

"I have in me more than the glimmerings of slave vitality," she said.

"It seems so to you now," I said, "but in some months, when you are truly helpless under the lash of your needs, and you understand the prison in which they have placed you, you will better understand my words."

"Even so!" she wept.

Her eyes pleaded with me.

"You may break position," I said.

She flung herself to her belly before me, and pressed her lips to my feet. "Please," she said. "Please!"

"You grovel as a slave," I said.

"I am no longer a free woman," she said. "I no longer have to pretend. I no longer have to lie."

I looked down at her, pondering her needs. Her lips were soft on my feet, timid, petitioning.

"I am now half naked and in a collar!" she sobbed. "I am at your mercy. Take pity on me!"

"You wish to placate masters?" I asked.

"If I have displeased them, yes!" she said.

"You would like to escape further punishment?" I said.

"Surely it is understandable that a girl such as myself, one so helpless, one in bondage, would seek to avert the wrath of men, that she would seek by her curves, her service and love to soften the hearts of masters."

Yes, I thought, that is understandable. Slave girls are, when all is said and done, in spite of their beauty, so vulnerable, so owned, so ultimately helpless.

"Please, Master," she said.

"You wheedle and beg well," I said.

She looked up at me.

"Doubtless you learned that in your first days as a slave, in the house of Appanius, perhaps desiring to be fed."

"I am begging!" she said.

I looked down at her.

"Surely master understands for what I am begging," she said.

"Oh?" I said.

"Command me to strip," she wept. "There is shade on the other side of the tank. The dust is cool there. You do not need a blanket or a wrap. Put me in the dust itself!"

I did not speak.

"If you wish," she said, "I shall serve you here, in the hot dust, in the glare of the sun."

"A begging slave," I commented to Marcus.

"Yes," he said.

"Please," she said.

"Kneel over here," I said. I indicated a position near the yoke and the buckets, near the tank. Quickly she rose up and went and knelt where I had indicated. I then lifted up the yoke, which, as I have mentioned, was thrice drilled, once in the center, and once near each end. At these points leather thongs were wound in and around the yoke.

"Master?" she asked.

I put the yoke across her shoulders.

"Master!" she said.

I loosened the thongs at the center of the yoke and then, by means of them, looped about her neck and tied, fastened the yoke on her. I then used the thongs on her right to fasten her right hand to the yoke there, and then, to her left, similarly served her left hand. I then stepped back to regard her, fastened in the yoke, her hands widely separated.

"As you may recall," I said, "you incurred discipline twice, once for lying, for which you were cuffed, a preposterously light discipline considering the offense, and secondly for daring to suggest that a master might not be interested in the answer to a question which he had asked."

"Forgive me," she said.

"It is your business to answer questions, with exactness, and with the fullness desired," I said, "not to comment on such matters as their propriety or appropriateness."

"Yes, Master," she said.

"Your needs are apparently on you," I said.

"Yes, Master!" she said, delightedly. "But I am helpless!" She moved her head about a little, turning it a little from side to side, her neck within the loops of the thongs; too, she moved her hands a little, futilely, they held back against the wood, by the thonged wrists.

"Surely you are aware that a woman may be used in a yoke," I said.

"Yes, Master!" she said.

Indeed, it is quite pleasant to use a woman in a yoke. Too, a girl is sometimes given to field slaves that way, cords attached sometimes to the ends of the yoke, that she may be pulled about, turned this way and that, and, in general, moved about and controlled as the slaves wish, until they weary of the sport and choose to have their way with her. I gathered, however, that this had not been done, at least as yet, with the lovely slave before us. She had, apparently, been tied to a stake for the men once or twice. The usual procedure, of course, is simply to put the girl in the common kennel after dark, where she is utilized, serving muchly, sometimes being handed about, from man to man.

"But that is not our intention," I said.

"Master?" she said.

I put one of the vessels of water on the yoke. She had to bend down, that its weight was on the ground. Then I put the other vessel, too, on the yoke.

She squirmed in the yoke, she sobbed.

"What is to be my second discipline?" she asked.

"Stand," I said.

With difficulty she stood. She could hardly stand upright. She wavered a little.

"Am I not to serve?" she asked.

"No," I said.

She looked at me in misery.

"That is the second discipline," I said.

She closed her eyes, and tears forced themselves between those clenched eyelids.

"I am not a free woman!" she said. "I am a slave. I need your touch!"

"It is the second discipline," I said.

"Please, please!" she wept.

"You are dismissed," I informed her.

"Please, Master!" she wept.

"Turn about, and be about your labors," said I, "field slave."

She moved then a little from the vicinity of the tank, a few steps. The weight was considerable for her. She staggered once or twice. She turned, to regard us, pathetically.

"Away, field slave!" I said, with a gesture.

"Yes, Master," she sobbed, and turned away. We watched her moving slowly away, staggering at times, across the fields.

"How could you do that to her?" asked Marcus.

"Cuff her?" I asked, puzzled.

"Of course not," he said. "That was nothing."

"She thought it something," I said.

"She was let off easily," he said.

"True," I said.

"Doubtless she will in time, in trembling gratitude, realize how easily she was let off."

"Even as easily as she was let off," I said, "I do not think she will soon again consider lying to a free man."

"Probably not," he said.

I took saddle.

"What would you have done?" I asked.

"I would have put her under the belt," he said.

"And had it been Phoebe?"

"Phoebe knows better," he said.

"But if it had been her?"

"A number of disciplines," he said, "over successive days."

"What did you mean then," I asked, " 'how could you do that to her?' "

"Sending her packing," he said, "rather than putting her to use."

"Should you speak that way," I asked, "of the former free woman, Lavinia of Ar?"

"Be serious," he said.

"Was it not merciful?" I asked.

"Certainly not," he said.

"As a discipline?" I asked.

"No," he said.

"Speak," I said.

"You dominated her, making her feel her womanhood, and its relationship to the male," he said, "and then, her belly ready, aching, vulnerably aflame, helplessly stirred, you sent her packing."

"What would you have done?" I asked.

"Nothing so heartless, so cruel," he said.

"You are speaking of the second discipline," I said.

"Of course," he said.

"What, then?" I asked.

"I would have whipped her," he said. "Then I would have flung her to the ground, thrust her about, let her feel the side of my foot, such things, and then, when I wished, I would have knelt her, her head to the ground, and used her."

"In such fashion?" I asked.

"Yes," he said.

"I see," I said.

"Slaves understand such things," he said.

"Of course," I said.

"And I do not think she would have been likely to commit the same error again."

"Probably not," I said.

"No," he said. "I do not think so."

"You grant, however," I said, "that my discipline is also likely to be effective?"

"I would think so," he said. "But I think mine might have been measured more perfectly to the slave, her needs and her act."

"You would have subjected her to use discipline?"

"Of course," he said.

"But we do not own her," I said.

"It does not matter," he said.

"True," I said.

Use discipline is within the prerogatives of a free person.

"You think my discipline was too severe?" I said.

"Yes," he said.

"I know a place," I said, "where such would commonly not be thought to be discipline at all but an escape from one."

"That is hard to believe," he said.

"A place in which it is culturally acceptable for the most basic needs of females to be denied, frustrated and ignored."

"Do not jest about matters of such gravity," he said.

"There are complex ideologies involved," I said, "the purport of which is that nature and biology are mistaken, and the ideologies, whatever they happen to be, for there are several of them, even if contrived and inconsistent, are correct."

"Such a mad place cannot exist," he said.

"Perhaps not," I said.

"Surely you grant that your discipline, denying her slave use, was severe."

"She is a slave," I said. "Anything could be done with her."

"By her master," he said. "Not just anyone."

"True," I said. One did not have the right, for example, to kill or maim the slave of another, any more than any other domestic animal which might belong to someone else. In this sense the slave is accorded some protection from free persons who do not own her in virtue of certain general considerations of property law. The power of the master over the slave, on the other hand, is absolute. He can do whatever he wishes with her. She belongs to him, completely.

"You do grant then," he said, "that your treatment of her was severe?"

"But intentionally so," I said, grimly, looking after the girl, now small in the distance.

"Unnecessarily severe?" he asked.

"No," I said. "Aptly severe."

"I do not understand," he said.

"It was measured perfectly to her, and her act, and my plans."

"Your plans?" he asked.

"Yes," I said. "That is the difference between your measurements and mine."

"I do not understand," he said.

"I wish her to understand what can be done to her," I said.

"You speak as though you intend to own her," he said.

"I do intend to own her," I said.

"Oh?" asked Marcus.

"Yes," I said. "She will figure in my plans."

"I see," he said, softly.

"She is a field slave," I said. "I would suppose that Appanius, who does not seem enamored of her, will let her go for a pittance, perhaps no more than a handful of copper tarsks."

"That is a curvaceous female to acquire for a few copper tarsks," he said.

"You noticed?" I said.

He laughed.

"There she is," I said, pointing.

"Yes," he said.

Her figure was now tiny, far away. She had stopped at the crest of a small hill, and was kneeling there, wearily, apparently to rest, her head down. The vessels of water were on the ground.

"I am touched by your concern, or reservations, pertaining to the severity of my discipline for her, denying her slave use," I said.

He shrugged.

"Perhaps it is motivated by your well-known kindness toward animals," I said.

"Perhaps," he said.

"But I wonder, too, if your concern might not have been self-regarding in some respect, motivated at least in part by a certain disappointment that you were, in accordance with my decision, denied an opportunity to search out, locate and exploit the vulnerable pleasures of the slave?"

"Perhaps" he laughed.

"She is struggling to rise," I said. The small figure was trying to get her legs under her, and rise in the yoke, lifting the vessels. One does this by crouching and lifting up, trying to do most of the work with the legs.

"The weight is really too much for her," he said. "She is not large enough and strong enough for such labors."

"But those are the labors to which she has nonetheless been

set by her master, Appanius, and the whip masters in the fields."

"She does not belong in the fields," he said, "she belongs in bangles and a scrap of silk, if that, in a house."

"Much must she have offended Appanius," I said.

"Apparently," he said.

"She is on her feet now," I said. She stood, unsteadily, the vessels swinging on the yoke ends.

"Yes," he said.

"Did you think she was pretty?" I asked.

"Very much so," he said, "even in her present wretched condition, shorn, roughened and burned."

"Look!" I said.

"I see," he said.

The girl, at the crest of the hill, had thrown her head back, to the sky. We could not hear her, of course, but she must have cried out, or sobbed, with misery and frustration. Her shoulders shook. Her small arms moved, at the yoke, pulling. But she could not, of course, free them, fastened as they were in place, by her wrists, widely separated, at opposite ends of the yoke, thonged back against the wood.

"Her needs are still much upon her," said Marcus.

"Apparently," I said.

Then she staggered down the other side of the small hill, and disappeared from sight. The sun was now well behind us.

"Surely she would make an exciting, squirming armful of slave," I said.

"You noticcd?" he asked.

"Yes," I said.

"Do you not think it was cruel not to put her to slave use?" asked Marcus.

"Not nearly so cruel," I said, "as it might be a few months from now, when she will have been longer a slave."

"True," he said. Slave needs tend to develop and deepen in the course of a girl's bondage. At Lavinia's present stage of bondage she could not begin to suspect what her needs would be like later, how helplessly she would become their prisoner, how hopelessly they would put her at a master's mercy. In the face of such needs, the stoutest collars, the heaviest chains, are but as gossamer. The depths of a slave's sexuality, and love, I think, have never been sounded.

"She was cruelly deprived, even so," he said.

"We will make it up to her," I said.

"Oh?" he asked.

"Well, perhaps we will," I said.

"Oh?" he asked.

"Assuming, of course, that the intensity of her zeal, and the perfection of her service, warrants it."

"You are serious then," he said, "about bringing her within the scope of your whip?"

"Quite," I said.

"How does she figure in your plans?" he asked.

"You will see," I said.

He wheeled his tharlarion about, and dust rose.

"Where are you off to?" I asked.

"I want Phoebe!" he said.

"It seems then," I said, "that it is not only the lovely Lavinia, former free woman of Ar, who has been frustrated."

"True," he laughed.

"But she is helplessly yoked, and must depend upon men, even to be released," I said, "while you are free to ride to your slave."

"And what of you?" he asked. "Are you so unmoved by the charms of your little field slave?"

"I?" I said. "I think I shall to a paga tavern."

I, too, then turned my tharlarion.

"And perhaps some former free woman of Ar in such a place will have five pierced metal tokens, purchasable for so little as a tarsk bit, threaded on her ankle cord tonight?"

"I shall race you to Ar!" I said.

Losing not a moment then, eager and laughing, we raced toward Ar.

20 The Slave Will Obey

"I love my collar!" she wept. "I love my collar!"

"You understand what you are to do?" I asked.

"Yes, yes, yes!" she wept. "Do not stop!"

I lifted my hand and her body leaped up, to resume contact with it.

But I pushed her down, my thumb on her belly, to the blanket, spread on the floor of our quarters in the *insula* of Torbon, in the Metellan district. She squirmed, writhing there in frustration. I held her in place with my thumb. She looked up, wildly.

"Please!" she wept.

She drew back her left ankle and there was the sound of the links of chain rattling and scraping on the floor, that chain run betwixt her ankle ring and the stout slave ring, anchored in the floor.

"Oh, yes!" she wept, softly, in gratitude. "Oh, yes, my master! Oh, yes, my master!"

"She is pretty," commented Marcus, from the side of the room.

"Yes," granted Phoebe, kneeling nearby, some sewing across her knees.

"Thank you, Mistress," said the slave. Phoebe, of course, was first girl.

"For a cheap slave," said Phoebe.

"Yes, Mistress," said the girl. "Oh! Oh!"

The slave looked up at me in wonder and joy. Slaves are lovely.

"How you own me!" she wept. "I did not know it could be like this! How you have made me feel! How you have trained me! How much you have taught me! How much better a slave I am now!"

"Some women," I said, "think that the joys of bondage are primarily those of submission and selfless service, the loving and the unstinted giving, the surrendering to the master, the being wholly his, but now you see that there are additional feelings as well."

"Yes, Master!" she cried. "Please do not stop!"

"Her hair is too short," said Phoebe.

"Free women know nothing of this!" wept the slave. "They cannot begin to understand the raptures of bondage!"

"I think they are not as ignorant as you think," I said. "And surely you can recall your own speculations, and suspicions, and sensings, and dreams, when you were free."

"Only glimmers of terror, and longing," she said.

"Speak," I said.

"Of course in my belly," she said, "I felt the appeal of bondage. I was intrigued by thoughts of it, and lured by them. Often did I linger lovingly upon such thoughts. Often was I fascinated to consider how it might be with me if I should become a slave, be owned and have no options but to obey."

"Then you did understand much of these things," I said, "even when you were a free woman."

"No," she said, "I understood nothing, nothing!"

"Oh," I said.

"Aiii!" she wept, rearing up. "Nothing! Nothing! Oh, my

master, thank you, thank you! Be kind! Be kind to your slave, she begs you!"

I was silent.

"How helpless I am!" she said.

The chain moved a little again, on the floor. I glanced to her ankle. The ankle ring looked well there. She reached up, to put her arms more about me. She was stripped, save for her collar and the ankle ring.

"I desire to be found acceptable, Master," she whispered.

"You are acceptable," I assured her.

"Her skin is blotchy," said Phoebe.

"Steady," I whispered to the slave.

"Master?" she asked.

I put her arms gently away from me. I moved my right hand. "Oh!" she said. I felt the pressure of her left thigh against my hand. I moved my hand again. "Oh," she said softly. The chain moved on the floor. I moistened my tongue. I lowered my lips to her lower belly.

"Oh, Master," she whispered.

"Steady," I said.

She moaned, given no choice but to submit to the pleasure I chose to inflict upon her.

"Steady," I cautioned her.

"You know I shall not be able to resist you," she said.

"You will be whipped, if you even try," I said.

"Yes, Master!" she said, in joy. I felt her small fingers, clutching, in my hair. "Oh, Master!" she suddenly wept. And then she began to twist and moan, and try to remain still, and thrust against me, and to hold my head where it was not letting it go and her fingers were tight in my hair and this hurt but I did not beat her but relished her so moaning and then bucking and trying to remain still and thrusting against me and how needful and helpless she was and so much in my power and so responsive and how such helpless movements and cries could be elicited by such tiny, persistent, patient, delicate attentions and she cried out begging me and I took her hands from my hair and looked down into her wild pleading eyes.

"What is it you wish?" I asked.

"I juice, my master! I gape, my master!" she said.

"Do you wish to serve?" I asked.

"Yes," she said. "Yes!"

"Do you beg to serve?" I asked.

"Yes, Master," she said. "I beg to serve." She lifted her belly, piteously.

I looked down upon her.

"Please, Master," she said.

I was silent.

"I am only a slave," she said. "You have done this to me! I am only a girl in a collar. I am helpless. I belong to you! I am yours to do with as you wish! I will do anything for you! I beg you to have pity on me!"

"I have tested your responses, slave," I said.

"Oh, Master!" she wept, in misery.

"I have found them satisfactory," I said.

"Thank you, Master," she said.

"Once triggered," I said, "they were involuntary, reflexive, beyond your control."

"Yes, Master," she wept.

"Such responses will much improve your value," I said.

"I am pleased, Master," she wept.

"And they appear still beyond your control," I said. I regarded her.

"They are, Master!" she said, tears in her eyes. Her body moved. She squirmed. Even to look upon her seemed to make her move. She was aroused, clearly, simply finding herself under the eyes of the master.

"But surely," she said, "you have not addressed these attentions to me merely to assess the nature and specificity of my slave responses?"

"No," I admitted.

"Let me serve! Let me serve!" she begged.

I regarded her.

"I beg to serve, Master!" she said.

I entered her.

"My Master!" she said.

I then informed her, in a modality of the mastery, of my ownership of her.

"I yield me yours, your slave!" she cried.

Then I held her quietly, her body trembling in my arms. "Ecstasy, ecstasy," she breathed.

"You see," I said, "there are feelings involved."

"It was unbelievable," she said.

"You are just learning to feel," I said.

She looked at me, startled.

"It is true," I said, "You are still a new slave."

"Then I think I must just die," she said.

"Slaves have survived such things, and more," I said.

She laughed softly, and pressed against me.

"There have been slaves for thousands of years," I said.

"And there is another now," she said.

"Yes," I said. There was no doubt about that.

"I have never been so happy in my life," she said.

"Your feelings do not matter," I said.

"Master?" she asked.

"They are those only of a slave."

"Yes, Master," she said.

She then lay quietly beside me, her head on my chest.

"But if free women could understand these things," she said, "they would all put themselves to the feet of men and beg their collars."

"But they cannot understand them," I said. "They are not slaves."

"I assure you that I had some understanding of this sort of thing when I was a free woman," she said.

"Anything like the understanding you have now?" I asked.

"No, Master," she said. "Nothing like my understanding now!"

"That is my point," I said.

"Yes, Master," she said.

"The experience is a totalistic one, which occurs in an entire context," I said. "It is thus that a woman does not fully understand what it is to be a slave until she becomes a slave. Once she is owned, of course, and subject to the whip, she will learn her condition. Kneeling before her master, she will soon apprehended something of its joys, duties, and terrors."

"It is true, Master," she said.

"Kneel," I said.

"Yes, Master," she said.

I lay on one elbow, regarding her.

"It is my hope that I have pleased my master," she said.

"You have pleased me," I said.

"Then the slave, too, is pleased," she whispered.

"She is very pretty," said Marcus.

"Her skin is still blotchy," said Phoebe.

"It is much better now," I said. We had purchased soothing, healing lotions.

"And her hair is much too short," said Phoebe.

"That is true," I said.

The slave kept her head down.

"But I suppose she is pretty enough," said Phoebe, "for a cheap girl."

"Thank you, Mistress," said the slave.

"What did you cost?" asked Phoebe.

"Oh, come now," said Marcus, irritatedly. Phoebe knew very well, of course, what I had paid for her. Indeed, she had not rested from the moment we had brought her in, braceleted and on a leash, until she had learned, and to her immense satisfaction, how little it had been.

"Five copper tarsks, Mistress," said the girl.

"I myself," said Phoebe, "sold for a hundred pieces of gold."

"That was under very special circumstances," I said.

"But that is what was paid!" she said.

"True," I said.

Much of the weightiness of this was lost on the new slave, of course, for she had very little notion of the prices of women. As she had come into the keeping of Appanius in virtue of the couching laws, she had had only one sale, that to me for a few copper tarsks. She would, of course, recognize that a hundred pieces of gold was an incredible amount of money. In a sense a women is worth as much or as little as someone is willing to pay for her. In typical markets, if it is helpful for purposes of comparison, an excellent woman, suitable, say, for the paga taverns, would sell for between one and three silver tarsks. In such a market I thought that Phoebe would probably go for something like two or two and a half silver tarsks, and that the other girl, if her hair was grown out and her skin healed, for something like two silver tarsks.

"Mistress is very pretty," said the slave.

Phoebe tossed her head, smoothing her hair about. She was pretty. I had always thought so.

"I did not know Cosian girls could be so pretty," said the slave.

Phoebe cried out with rage, and rushed to the wall to seize up a switch there. She rushed to the new slave, the switch raised. The new slave cried out in misery, putting her head down. But no blow fell. Marcus had intercepted Phoebe's descending wrist. Phoebe cried out in pain and dropped the switch. But she looked down at the new slave. "Cos defeated Ar!" she said. "That is clear!"

"No longer are you of Cos," said Marcus, sternly. "Nor is she any longer of Ar. You are both only slaves, only animals!"

Phoebe struggled, angrily, in his arms..

"Is it not true?" he asked.

She looked up at him, her eyes blazing. "Yes, Master!" she said.

She struggled a bit more, but was now pinioned tightly in his grasp. She could do little more now than squirm, futilely. She made a tiny, angry noise. As well might her lovely body have been wrapped in cables of iron. The sewing she had been attending to had been spilled to the side, when she had leaped up to seize the switch. Originally Phoebe had known little, if anything, of sewing, but when she had become slave she must learn such things. Indeed, we had even rented a girl to give her some lessons. The new slave, too, knew little of such labors. I would see to it that she received instruction of Phoebe. One expects a slave to know such things.

Phoebe ceased struggling and Marcus released her, stepped back a pace and regarded her.

She stood before him, angrily, defiantly, her small fists clenched.

"I suppose you could be thought of, as of Cos," he mused, "in the sense that you were once of Cos."

She trembled.

"So in that sense," said he, "take off your clothes, female of Cos, and get to your belly, with your legs widely spread."

"I am not of Cos!" she said, suddenly. "I am only a slave, Master!"

He regarded her, unwaveringly.

Swiftly she drew off her tunic, over her head, and put herself to her belly, and as he had stipulated.

He looked down upon her.

She sobbed, subdued.

The other slave was very quiet. It seemed she scarcely dared to breathe.

"Perhaps the wrong girl is first girl," mused Marcus.

Phoebe sobbed, her head to the side.

"May I speak, Master," whispered the new slave.

He looked at her. "Yes," he said.

She went to her belly before him and reached out her tiny hand, timidly, to touch his foot.

"Yes?" he said.

"Please have pity on her, Master," she said.

"You would speak for her?" asked Marcus.

"Yes, Master," she said.

Phoebe looked at her, in wonder.

"It is only that she loves you so much," she said.

"I do not understand," said Marcus.

Phoebe sobbed, looking away.

"She is telling you that Phoebe is jealous of her," I said.

Marcus crouched down beside Phoebe.

"Is that true?" he asked.

"Yes, Master," sobbed Phoebe, her eyes closed.

"But you are my love slave," he said to her.

She sobbed, with joy. He touched her and she trembled beneath his touch like a vulo.

He then rose to his feet, and removed a coiled slave whip from the wall. This he threw down beside Phoebe, the coils of the leather cracking on the floor, beside her head, to the right.

"You will serve," he said.

"Yes, Master!" she whispered.

He then put his hand to her hair, letting her feel the tightness of his grasp, and turning her head from one side to the other. Then he put his hand on the back of her neck, letting her feel this grip. He then took her right ankle in his hand and lifted it, bending her lower leg, his grip like an ankle ring, toward her body. Then he released it, and let it return to its former position. She lay there very quietly. Then she made a soft noise, as he had begun to caress her, audaciously and masterfully.

I went over and picked up the sewing which Phoebe had dropped to the floor, when she had leaped to her feet. It was a tunic resembling that of a state slave, done in the new fashion. The garmenture of the state slave, that of a girl owned by the city itself, some time ago, had been brief, sleeveless and gray, slashed to the waist. The collar worn by such slaves had been gray, matching the tunic, and it had been customary to lock about their left ankle a steel band, also gray, from which depended five small bells, also of gray metal. Fashions in such things tended to change, of course, even in normal times. For example, the hemlines might go up and down a bit, the garments might be accented or trimmed with color, or not, the number of bells on the ankle might be increased, say, to seven, or be returned to the original five, and so on. Currently, however, the garmenture of the state slaves, as one might have expected, given the defeat of Ar and the hegemony of Cos, had been considerably altered. No longer were the tunics slashed to the waist. Now the necklines were high, and about the throat. Similarly the hemlines had been considerably lowered, to just above the knee. These alterations had been introduced to assist in the subjugation of the men of Ar, by seeking to depress their sexual vitality. Similarly, of course, no longer were the left ankles of the slaves belled. The sound of slave bells on a woman's ankle tends to be sexually stimulating to a male. To be sure, of late, with the rise of the Delta Brigade, and the undercurrent of unrest in Ar, there seethed in the city, doubtless to the dismay of Cos, a surgency of male energies. As I have mentioned earlier, many masters, now, no longer sent their slaves unescorted about the city, until they had fastened them in the iron belt. The slave tunic of the state slave was still sleeveless, however. That is common with slave garments.

I looked down at the new slave, who was lying on the

blanket, on the floor. I gestured that she should stand. When she had done so, I handed her the tunic. "Hold this against you," I said.

She did so, with both hands, closely, one above her breasts and one below.

I regarded her.

"Master?" she asked.

"You could make a rock sizzle," I said.

She flushed. "Thank you, Master," she said.

I continued to regard her.

She would be fetching, indeed, in that tunic. The Cosians, I thought, had to some extent miscalculated. Did they really think that the excitingness of a slave could be reduced by such a triviality as the addition of a few horts of material to a tunic? Did they not realize it would still be the single garment she wore, the one piece of cloth she was permitted, and that it would have no nether closure? And even more significantly did they not understand that her true excitingness did not depend on such things as a collar and a particular sort of livery, as telling, and revealing and lovely, as these things were, but on her condition itself, that she was slave? That she was slave, the essence and perfection of the female, was what made her such an extraordinary, special, incomparable object of desire, and that would be so whether she were kneeling in a ta-teera, clad in an evening gown or concealed from head to toe in the dark haik of the Tahari, peeping out through a tiny screen of black lace. I then, in a moment, took back the garment, and dropped it to the side, where Phoebe had been working, near the small sewing basket there. I indicated that the slave might kneel and she did, her hands on her thighs, her knees in the appropriate position.

Phoebe was now gasping at one side of the room.

"Master?" said the new slave.

"Yes?" I said.

"Was I pleasing?"

"Yes," I said.

"Do you think another man might find me pleasing, as well?" she asked.

"It is possible," I said.

"I am not now as stupid, as ignorant, as I was, am I?" she asked.

"No," I said.

"I am a much better slave now, am I not?"

"Yes," I said.

"I am grateful for my training," she said.

"It is nothing," I said.

"It is my hope that I have profited from it," she said.

"You have," I said, "considerably."

"Then you think I might not, under certain circumstances, at least, be found displeasing by another man?"

"No," I said.

She put down her head, shyly.

"I would not get my hopes up," I said. "It is your business to obey me, and your primary objective, in the first phase of our operations, is merely to deliver the message."

"I understand, Master," she said.

"In the course of this delivery," I said, "you may behave much as you wish. That I leave to you."

"Yes, Master," she said, shyly.

There was a sudden noise at the side of the room and I looked there, quickly. Marcus, turning, rolling, Phoebe locked in his arms, had struck into the wall there.

"Approach me, on all fours," I said to the new slave. She did so, dragging the ankle chain behind her.

I indicated a flat leather box to one side. "Knee crawl," I said. "Fetch it here."

She went to the box on her knees and picked it up, and returned to a place before me. It had been a simple knee crawl. I was briefly reminded, however, of the Turian knee walk, sometimes used by slave dancers. I considered the slave. I did not doubt but what she might be taught to dance.

"Master?" she asked.

"Give it to me," I said.

But I did not take it.

She looked at me, puzzled.

"Forgive me, Master!" she said.

She then, kneeling before me, her knees widely spread, lifted and extended her arms, proffering me the box. Her head was down, between her lifted, extended arms.

"It seems you still have much to learn," I said.

"Forgive me, Master," she said.

I took the box.

She then knelt back, her hands on her thighs, her head still bowed.

"Your training will continue," I said.

"Thank you, Master," she said.

"But it seems that perhaps it should be sharpened with the whip," I said.

"As master wishes," she said, trembling.

The whip is an excellent mnemonic device. The girl who receives a lash, or lashes, for an error, seldom repeats it.

"To all fours," I said. "And stay here close, where I can reach you."

I then put out my hand and touched the collar on her neck. It was one of three collars I had for her. The other two, with their keys, were in the flat box. The collar on her neck bore the legend, "RETURN ME TO TARL AT THE *INSULA* OF TORBON." I then removed the first of the other two collars from the box and, reaching out, put it on her neck, next to the other collar, but ahead of it, closer to the chin. I snapped it shut. It fit well. It was now on her, locked. Its legend read, "RETURN ME TO THE WHIP MASTER OF THE CENTRAL CYLINDER." I then turned it and, inserting the key, opened it, and removed it from her neck. I then lifted the second collar from the box, putting the first, with the key, back in it. This second collar I then put on her neck, next to the original collar, and ahead of it, closer to the chin, as I had the one a moment before. Then I snapped it shut. It, too, fit well, and was now on her, locked. Its legend read, "RETURN ME TO APPANIUS OF AR." I then let her remain that way for a little while, on all fours, in the two collars.

Phoebe was moaning to one side. She turned her head from one side to the other, her eyes closed. She was delirious with pleasure, slave to her master.

I then took the key to the second of the two collars which had been in the box, that which I had put most recently on her, the Appanius collar, and removed it from her neck. I put it back in the box, under the first collar. I dropped the key in the box. I closed the box.

"Claim me!" wept Phoebe. "I beg it! I am your slave! Use me as the helpless vessel of your pleasure!"

"Do not move," I said to the new slave.

She remained as she was, on all fours.

"I yield me your slave!" wept Phoebe. "I yield me your slave!"

Then she was trembling, and gasping for breath, clinging to Marcus. He, too, gasped, and then suddenly he laughed, a mighty laugh, almost a roar, a laugh of triumph, like an exultant larl, joyful in his mastery of the beauty.

"Such may be done to slaves," I said to the new slave.

"Yes, Master," she said, on all fours.

"The other garment, I take it," I said to the new slave, "is finished."

"Yes, Master," she said. "Mistress finished it yesterday."

"Put it on for me," I said.

"Yes, Master," she said. She rose to her feet and went to the side of the room where she knelt by a chest and took from it a white garment, of the wool of the bounding hurt.

I looked away, as she stood up, to slip it over her head and arms, and smooth it down on her body. I did not wish to look until it was on her.

"Master," she announced.

"Excellent!" I said.

It came to a bit above the knees, and had a high, modest neckline. In some respects it was rather in the style set for the tunics of state slaves. That I thought might fit in well with my plans.

"Turn," I said.

"Yes," I mused. "Excellent." Perhaps even more importantly it was the sort of garment in which a slave might might dare to appear before a free woman. It was not the sort of garment that would be likely to excite the envy or anger of free women. It was not the sort of garment which sometimes provokes free women to rush at slaves in the street, crying out and lashing at them with switches. It was decorous, and yet clearly the garment of a mere slave.

"Mistress has sewed it," she said.

"You have done well, Phoebe," I said. "It is perfect."

"Thank you, Master," gasped Phoebe. She was lying next to Marcus. She was covered with a sheen of sweat. Her body was covered with red blotches, from the recent racing of her blood, the excited distention of thousands of capillaries. Her lovely nipples were not yet subsident.

"Your skin is blotchy," I said to Phoebe.

She laughed, ruefully. "Yes, Master," she said.

The new slave, her head down, smiled.

"Remove the garment," I said to her. "Replace it in the chest. Then resume your position here, beside me, on all fours."

"Yes, Master," she said.

I then again, in a bit, regarded her. No longer was she in the dignity of a garment. Her breasts, in her present position, that which I had dictated, were beautifully pendant.

"Can you write?" I asked her.

"Yes, Master," she said.

I reached to her.

"Oh," she said, softly. "Oh!" I had taken her nipples gently, first one and then the other, between my thumb and forefinger. They, too, it seemed, had not forgotten their state of but a few moments ago. Or, perhaps it was but the fact that the meaning of her present position was intrusive in her consciousness.

"Surely you are interested in the nature of the messages you will carry," I said.

"Yes, Master!" she said. I had touched her, lightly, at the side of the waist.

"One need not concern you," I said, "as you will be the mere instrument of its delivery. On the other hand, I think you will have a little doubt as to its general import."

"Yes, Master," she said.

"You will deliver it to the female I designate," I said, "and to her personally."

"Yes, Master," she said.

"To make it more likely you will be admitted into her presence, the message will be carried about your neck, in a message tube, and your hands will be back-braceleted."

"As Master wishes," she said.

"But even so," I said, "before being admitted to her presence, you may be double leashed, one on each side, that you cannot touch, or approach, the woman, except as permitted."

"I understand, Master," she said.

"Do you think she will be admitted to her presence?" asked Marcus.

"Given her story, and her collar," I said, "I think so."

"The note she carries is to be written in a man's hand," said Marcus.

"Of course," I smiled.

"Doubtless in your deft script," he said, lying on his back, looking at the low, peeling ceiling above him.

"I was hoping someone might be prevailed upon to provide a more convincing communication," I said.

"Oh!" said the new slave. She moved uneasily, tensely, but did not break position.

"The handwriting must suggest a correspondent who is educated, charming, witty, elegant and suave," I said.

"That sounds like a job for your own block script," he said. "It has many virtues. I have known peasants who could not do as well. Or, if you prefer, you could use your inimitable cursive script, with its unusual alternate lines. Its humorous suggestion of complete illiteracy adds to it a piquant charm all its own."

"My master has an excellent hand!" volunteered Phoebe.

"Were you asked to speak?" inquired Marcus.

"No, Master," she said. "Forgive me, Master." She then lay small and quiet beside him. She did not wish to be cuffed or whipped.

"It was my hope, Phoebe," said I, "that your master, exactly, might be prevailed upon to lend his expertise to this endeavor."

"Yes, Master," she whispered.

"I write a simple hand," said Marcus.

"Perhaps you could add a few flourishes, or something," I suggested.

"No," said Marcus.

"Do you want me to write it?" I asked.

"That would be disastrous," he said.

"Also," I said, "my handwriting might be recognized."

"I hadn't thought of that," said Marcus.

"You will do it then?" I said.

"I will write only my own hand," he said.

"That will be perfect," I said.

"What if she has seen the handwriting of the putative correspondent?" asked Marcus.

"That is highly unlikely," I said. It was unthinkable that the putative correspondent would initiate such a correspondence. In such a relationship the first note, if there were to be notes, given the risks involved, would surely issue from the free person.

I touched the slave near me, on all fours, on the side of the leg.

"You," I said to her, "will be under no doubt, however, as to the contents of the other message."

"Yes, Master," she said. She moved, uneasily. I moved a bit, and looked at the ankle ring on her left ankle. I then put my hand on the ring, and then pressed my thumb a little into her leg. I then turned the ring a little on her ankle, shifting it a bit. There was about a quarter of an inch of slippage between the metal and her ankle. I then lifted the chain, a little, one of its links hammered shut about the ring's staple, and let it drop to the floor. She shuddered at the tiny sound. I then jerked twice, softly, on the chain, that she might feel this small force exerted on the ring, and subsequently on her ankle, within it. Below the ring, behind it, her foot was small and soft. I regarded it, the heel, the sole, her toes. It was a small, shapely, lovely foot. And then, above it, close about the ankle, locked, was the ankle ring. I then touched her collar, and turned it a little, back and forth. She was very quiet while I did this. It, like the other collars, was an excellent fit. I then readjusted it, carefully. The lock was now again centered, at the back of the neck. I then touched her. "Oh, oh!" she said.

"Steady," I said.

She moaned.

"Because," I said, "you will write it."

"Yes, Master," she said.

"I will dictate the contents to you," I said, "or, if you wish, you may compose it, subject, of course, to my approval."

"As master wishes!" she said.

"Do not break position," I warned her.

Marcus and I had agreed that Phoebe would not write the letter. It was better that it was done by a woman who had been at one time a citizeness of Ar, her penmanship influenced by the private schools of the city. It is a well-known fact, on the world, Earth, that the cursive script of diverse nationalities, such as the English, French and Italian, tend to differ in certain general ways, quite aside from the individual characteristics of particular writers. Certain letters, for example, tend to be formed differently, and so on. Much the same thing, predictably, and perhaps even more so, given the isolation of so many of her cities, occurs on Gor. For example, Phoebe had a beautiful, feminine hand, but it was natural for her, and easiest for her, of course, to write in Cosian script. It was not that Cosian script, was illegible, say, to folks of Ko-ro-ba or Ar, but rather that it was recognizably different. Thus, rather than have Phoebe try to disguise her hand and write in the script of Ar, Marcus and I had decided that the note, or letter, would be written by the new slave, whose background, and education, were of Ar, the same as those of the putative writer of the note, or letter. In the formation of most cursive letters, incidentally, there are few, if any, differences among the various cities. The differences tend to have more to do with the "cast" of the hand, so to speak, its general appearance, a function of a number of things, such as size, spacing of letters, linkages among them, length of loops, nature of end strokes, and such. Also, certain letters, at least for commercial or legal, if not personal, purposes, tended to be standardized. An excellent example are those standing for various weights and measures. Another familiar example is the tiny, lovely, cursive 'kef' which is the same whether it is put on a girl in Cos, or Ar, or Ko-ro-ba, or Thentis or Turia.

"Oh, Master!" sobbed the slave.

"Master!" said Phoebe, suddenly, taken by Marcus and thrust down, forcibly, to the boards. He looked down into her eyes, fiercely. "Yes, Master," she said, lifting her arms to put them about his neck.

"When do you think your friend, the noble Tarsk-Bit, will be prepared to act?" asked Marcus, evenly.

"Please enter your slave, Master," said Phoebe.

"Do not be angry with him," I said. "He had to revile the

Home Stone to see it, to examine it." I had encouraged Marcus not to be present when this was done, but he had, of course, insisted upon it. In so far as it was practical it seemed he wished to be present at, and, in a sense, supervise, all phases of this delicate and, I thought at least, perilous operation. No detail was too unimportant for him to overlook. What could compare in importance for Marcus, for example, to the recovery of his Home Stone, its rescue from its captivity in Ar? To be sure, I think Boots had overdone the matter a bit. He, exuberant in his performance, probably did not realize that I was struggling a few yards behind him to keep Marcus from leaping upon him, blade in hand. Most of those about, of course, also taking no note of the reactions of Marcus, the fire in his eyes, and such, had been muchly amused. Boots had made a great show of his contempt for the Home Stone of the treacherous Ar's station. His insults had been numerous, well thought out, stinging, and delivered with flair. He had even been applauded. It was fortunate that Marcus had not reached him. In so simple a manner had Boots, unbeknownst to himself, escaped unscathed, for example, without having had his heart slashed out of his living body.

"When will he be prepared to act?" asked Marcus.

"He did not mean it, what he said," I said.

"He sounded convincing," said Marcus, grimly.

"Would you have preferred that he sounded unconvincing?" I asked.

"Master," begged Phoebe.

"Master!" said the new slave, suddenly. She must not, of course, break position.

"When will he be prepared to act?" asked Marcus.

"The facsimile must be prepared," I said. "That takes time."

"When will he be prepared to act?" asked Marcus.

"Soon, I am sure," I said.

"Perhaps he has already left the city," said Marcus.

"No," I said.

"Your slave begs," said Phoebe to Marcus.

"Your slave begs, too!" said the slave near me.

The new slave, beside me, was on all fours. She was in this position by my will. I had been keeping her in this position. It is a position which a woman understands. I had, furthermore, checked her ankle ring, and collar. Such things are very meaningful to a woman. Such attentions, seemingly small in themselves, subtly, explosively, erupt in the cognizances of her belly. By means of them is her bondage recalled to her. By means of them she understands herself the better, and to whom she belongs. Also, such things would commonly be checked as a simple matter of course, just as one might check the tether on a verr, or the chain on a sleen. Beyond this, of course, I had, from time to time, as I had spoken with her, and discussed matters with Marcus, touched her, sometimes almost idly, while concerned with other matters. But now her body was tense. "Oh!" she said. Her lovely flanks quivered. She could not resist my touch, even involuntarily, as her knees and the palms of her hands must remain in contact with the floor.

"He had better not," said Marcus.

"He will not," I said. "But if he chose to do so, surely one could not blame him. It is not his Home Stone. He is not a soldier. You are not his officer, or Ubar, or some such."

"True," said Marcus.

"Be grateful," I said, "if he is willing to be of assistance."

"I wish to owe him little," said Marcus. "I will see that he is well paid."

"Very well," I said.

"Do you think he can be prevailed upon to accept money?" asked Marcus.

"Doubtless, if we are strenuous enough in our insistence on the matter," I said.

"Good," he said, grimly.

"He is really not a bad fellow," I said.

Marcus made an angry noise.

"I think it would be better if you were not present when he makes the attempt on the Home Stone," I said.

"I will be there," said Marcus. "He may need help."

"It will not be much help," I said, "if you drop him on the spot."

"What do you mean?" he asked.

"If he does manage to obtain the Home Stone and you run him through, and it drops out of his cloak on the street, and it becomes immediately apparent to the guards about that there appear to be two Home Stones of Ar's Station in the vicinity, what then?"

"I shall seize it up and make away," he said.

"There may be a hundred guards about," I said.

"Doubtless you will be at hand," he said.

"But what if there are one hundred and one guards about?" I said.

"You jest," he said.

"What do you think your chances will be of getting the stone out of the city, let alone to Port Cos?"

"I do not know," he admitted.

"The alarm would be sounded within Ihn," I said.

"Doubtless," he granted.

"You would be fortunate if you managed to get the stone as far as the Teiban Market," I said. "If I did not know your skill with the sword I would have placed a bet you would not get it as far as Clive." This street actually entered the Avenue of the Central Cylinder, from the west.

"I have nerves of steel," said Marcus. "I can control my emotions with perfection."

"As five days ago?" I asked.

"He needn't have been as ribald as he was," said Marcus.

"There are at least two reasons for what he did," I said. "First, the length of his tirade gave him time to study the Home Stone, in all its details. Secondly, it established a character. If he comes back during the same watch, as he presumably will, the guards will remember him, and expect a show."

"Then they will be more attentive," said Marcus.

"But to him, not to the Home Stone," I said.

"You said 'at least two reasons,' " said Marcus. "That suggests there might be at least one other."

"Perhaps," I said, evasively.

"What?" he asked, not pleasantly.

"He was enjoying himself," I said.

"He should have been impaled!" said Marcus.

"Master," begged Phoebe.

"I should have run him through!" exclaimed Marcus.

"Master!" whimpered Phoebe.

The new slave whimpered, too, urgently, helplessly, plaintively, to call her needs, and herself, to my attention.

"I think it would be better if you were not present when the attempt is made on the Home Stone," I said.

"You are in one of your rational moods," said Marcus, disgustedly.

"Almost everyone has them occasionally," I said. "Also, I thought you were supposed to be the rational one."

"I shall think about it," he said.

"The important thing here," I said, "is not your sense of honor, which seems a bit touchy, but the rescue of the Home Stone."

"This is more of your Kaissa," he said.

"If you will," I said.

"Master," begged Phoebe.

He looked down at her, fiercely.

"A slave begs," she said, "that her master consent to enter her."

"Oh!" she cried, as Marcus, fiercely, took her in his arms. "It is I who am impaled," she laughed. "It is I who am run through!"

"But as befits female slaves!" he said.

"Yes, Master!" she laughed. Then she closed her eyes. "Oh, yes!" she said. She gasped. She sighed, softly. "Deign to use me, unworthy slave though I am," she whispered, "as the cover for your spear, as your sheath and scabbard."

"And it is done, is it not?" he asked.

"Yes, Master!" she said.

"And in the manner befitting female slaves?" he asked.

"Yes, Master!" she said.

He kissed her, his head down, fiercely about her throat.

Her head was back. Her eyes were closed. "I have received my master," she said.

"I, too, would receive my master," whispered the new slave.

"I will write the letter for you," mumbled Marcus, his words lost somewhere in Phoebe's neck.

"I will require further assistance, as well," I said.

"It is yours," he said.

"I do not think it will interfere in any way with the recovery of the Home Stone," I said.

"Yes," mumbled Marcus. "Yes, yes."

I regarded the new slave. She turned her head toward me. Her eyes were filled with tears. She whimpered. I seized her, turned her and threw her to her back, with a sound of the chain, beside me, on the blanket, spread over the boards. I touched her, lightly, and she lifted her body, piteously. She looked up at me. She whimpered. I gently touched her breasts. Again she whimpered. They were very beautiful, and their condition, like that of her whole body, signified her readiness, and need. Tears of supplication welled in her eyes.

I touched her lightly about the waist, and she moved almost as though she might have been burned. Even the chain had jerked.

"You are a hot slave," I said.

"Yes, Master," she said.

I touched her.

"Oh!" she said.

"And you juice exceedingly well," I said.

"Thank you, Master," she said.

I looked down at her. How amazing, how astonishing, and wonderful are female slaves. How, too, this woman's life had changed! What a dramatic *volte-face*, from a free woman to a slave! How different she was from a free woman, this slave, hot, needful, beautiful, owned, obedient, begging. Too, she had not been that long in bondage.

I looked down upon her.

"Are you a slave?" I asked.

"Yes," she whispered. "Subjugate me."

I then took her in my arms.

"Now I, too, am impaled," she whispered. "Now, I, too, have been run through. Now, I, too, have received my master. Now, I, too, am cover to his spear. Now I, too, serve him as sheath and scabbard!"

"But such things in manners befitting the female slave," I said.

"Yes, Master," she whispered, ecstatically.

"You may move as you wish," I said.

"Yes, Master!" she said.

"Hold!" I said.

"Master?" she asked.

"Hold, a little," I said.

"Yes, Master," she moaned.

"You squirm well," I said.

"Thank you, Master," she said.

"It seems you are already on the brink," I said.

"I was there even before you put me to my back," she said.

"Even from such small things as keeping you in a certain position, checking your ankle ring and collar, touching you a little now and then, here and there?"

"It is not just such things," she said. "Even more, it is my entire condition!"

"Interesting," I said.

"I have become hot, submissive, sexual and obedient," she said.

"I see," I said.

"I am a slave, and needful," she said.

"I see," I said.

"You have done this to me!" she said.

"I?" I asked.

"You, and others," she said. "Men, masters."

"These things are within you," I said. "They are born in you. Surely you have sensed them in yourself, or hints of them, even when you were a free woman."

"Then I have always been a slave," she said.

"Yes," I said. "It was only that you were waiting for a master, or masters."

She was silent.

"Too," I said, "even though these things are within you, they did not have their beginning with you. They are very ancient things. They go back at least to the cave and the stone knife."

"Master?" she asked.

"Never mind," I said.

"As master wishes," she said.

How far we were from the cave and the stone knife, I thought, and yet, again, in a way, how close! Could one not see in the blade of steel, so much keener and more dangerous, the knife of stone? Could one not recollect in the spacious courts of the palace the dim recesses of limestone caves? And who moves barefoot and graceful upon the tiles of the palace? Is it the hunter's mate, clad in her skins, kept, and cuffed and obedient, cowering lovingly at her master's feet, his in the sense of rain and stones? No, it is the curvaceous, perfumed, silked, collared slave, owned in law, hurrying to do her master's bidding.

"You may now again move," I said.

"Oh, yes, Master!" she said, gratefully.

But in a short while I counseled her once again to desist, which she did, reluctantly.

"Surely you did not learn to move and moan like that as a free woman," I said.

"No, Master," she said.

"Speak," I said.

"I am excited, and cannot help myself," she said. "It is muchly reflexive, involuntary."

"I see," I said.

"I beg my master's pardon," she said. "The sensations, the feelings, are incredible! Then my movements become such that I cannot even control them. It is not like it is I who move, but rather than it is I who am moved. It is like hands jerking me about. I am wild inside and helpless and my body cries out silently and moves as it wishes! Sometimes it is almost as though I were being beaten, or struck!"

"They are simple slave reflexes," I said. "I effect nothing critical."

"Thank you, Master," she said.

"Have you ever seen slave dance?" I asked.

"No, Master," she said. "But I have heard of it."

"You have no idea, then," I said, "of its incredible sensuousness and beauty, and of how a woman appears in it, how exciting, desirable and owned, and of how men, seeing it, can cry out with need?"

"Only what I have heard," she said.

"As you were in the house of Appanius, who is a rich man," I said, "it is surprising that you never observed such dancers."

She was silent.

"Surely he could have afforded to bring them in, or even to own his own."

"I would think so, Master," she said.

"Not even at the banquets?" I asked.

"No," she said.

"Or at the small suppers, later to be chained to rings near the guests?"

"No," she said.

"I see," I said.

This information fitted in with certain surmises I had formed earlier. If my surmises were correct, it would fit in well with my plans.

"Why does Master ask?" she asked.

"Curiosity is not becoming in a kajira," I said.

"Forgive me, Master," she said.

"My question was suggested to me," I said, "by the helplessness of your slave responses."

"I do not understand," she said.

"There are various movements in slave dance," I said, "of the hips, the belly, and such, indeed, of the entire body, which are clearly akin to, and reminiscent of, the movements of love and need."

"Yes, Master?" she said.

"To be sure, in the dance," I said, "these movements tend to be under much stricter control. The dance is, after all, an art form. Nonetheless it is clear that the sexuality of the dancer is not uncommonly aroused. After all, it is hard for a woman to be beautiful and sensuous without feeling beautiful and sensuous, and it is hard for her to feel beautiful and sensuous without having her sexuality ignited. Indeed, few are the dancers who have not upon occasion, even in the dance itself, succumbed to orgasmic helplessness. This can occur to them while they are on their feet, but more often it will occur during floor movements or when they are on their knees."

"Yes, Master," whispered the girl.

"And your movements," I said, "suggested to me that you might make a dancer."

"I see," she said.

"You also have an excellent body for a dancer," I said.

"Yes, Master," she whispered.

"Would you like to trained for the dance?" I asked.

"I do not know, Master," she said, frightened.

"Or would you dare to be so beautiful?"

"I am a slave," she whispered. "It will be done with me as masters wish."

"But would you like it?" I asked.

"Perhaps, Master," she whispered, fearfully.

"It is something to keep in mind," I said.

"Yes, Master," she whispered.

Phoebe was moaning to one side, locked in the arms of Marcus.

I moved a little.

The girl in my arms gasped. "Oh," she whispered. She looked at me, beggingly. "Please," she whispered.

"Yes?" I asked.

"Please continue my subjugation," she said.

"Are you certain you wish it?" I asked.

"Yes!" she said.

"Why?" I asked.

"I am a slave," she said. "It is appropriate that I be subjugated!"

"I see," I said.

"I understand my sex, and its meaning," she said.

"In bondage," I said, "you have discovered these things?"

"Yes, Master," she said.

"I see," I said.

"And I have been given little choice, Master," she smiled.

"True," I said.

"Please!" she suddenly wept.

"Incidentally," I said, "when you kneel before the free woman, in your carefully prepared modest garb, fit for a lowly slave, as you must soon do, to convey to her the message which will be inserted in the message tube about your neck, be certain to kneel with your knees closely together."

"Certainly, Master," she said. "She is a female, not a male."

"But even more importantly," I said, "insofar as you can, before her, and before any other free women who might be in attendance upon her, conceal your sexuality. Do not let them suspect it. Let them think that you are as inert and meaningless as they are."

"That is common by slave girls before free women, Master," she said. "It does not take us long to learn that, once we are in the collar."

"I see," I said.

"But I do not think they are always fooled," she said.

"Perhaps not," I said.

"Even as long ago as in the house of Appanius," she said, "I was twice switched by free women who had come to see him on business."

"Do the best you can," I said.

"Yes, Master," she said.

"Seem to be merely a modest, deferential girl, demurely clad, awed perhaps, discharging your errand."

"Have no fear," she said, "but what I shall be awed in such a presence."

"She is only another woman," I said, "and if she were stripped and in a collar, she would be no different from you."

"Master!" protested the slave.

"Indeed, you might be first girl over her," I said.

"Please, Master!" she protested.

"It is true," I said.

"Yes, Master," she said.

"Another thing," I said. "I do not think it would be in your best interest for you to convey to her in any way, inadvertently or otherwise, even in feminine vanity, the hint, to be sure, the false hint, that there might be anything between you and the putative author of the note you bear."

"Yes, Master," she said.

"You are to be only a humble messenger."

"Yes, Master," she said.

"I would not wish for you to be cut to pieces, or boiled in oil," I said.

"No, Master," she said.

"What is wrong?" I asked.

It seemed to me that tears had sprung afresh in the eyes of the slave.

"No more need I fear, Master," she said, "that I might be of interest to he who is to be the supposed author of the note in question. Now I am only a lowly slave. At best I could expect only to be spurned by his foot from his path."

"I see," I said.

"But I would be grateful to him," she said, "for even so small a touch."

"I see," I said.

"I would kiss the unstrapped, discarded sandal that had kicked me."

"You may move," said I, "Lavinia," for that was the name I had kept on her.

She then, released from the enforced, tense quiescence I had imposed upon her, clutched me gratefully, sobbing with relief and joy. In a few moments she wept, "I yield me, Master!" and I then held her like iron and cried out with joy and she sobbed

"I am helpless and taken!" and Phoebe, too, in the arms of Marcus, cried out, herself as well taken, and he, too, uttered a wild cry and a then sudden, low, satisfying growl, and the sounds of Phoebe and Marcus and of Lavinia and myself mingled in the tiny room and it had been done to the slaves once more.

"I am yours," said Phoebe to Marcus.

"I am subjugated, and am your slave, Master," said Lavinia to me.

"Tomorrow," I said, "our project begins."

"Yes, Master," she said.

"You will obey," I informed her.

"Yes, Master," she said. "Your slave will obey."

21 I Receive The Report Of A Slave

"I am terrified, Master!" said Lavinia.

I thrust her into our small room, in the *insula* of Torbon, on Demetrios Street, in the Metellan district, and closed the door behind us.

"How went it?" I asked.

"I am frightened!" she said.

"Why?" I asked.

"How dare I be seen before him," she asked, "as what I am now, a slave?"

"You will be in the modest livery of a state slave," I said, "not even belled."

"I am frightened," she said.

"Pull off the cloak," I said.

She put to one side the cloak which she had clutched about her, concealing her garment of white wool and the collar on her neck. To be sure, her exposed calves and bared feet had left no doubt in the streets as to her status.

"I would not even dare to lift my eyes to his, to look into his eyes," she moaned.

"You must do so, if he commands it," I said.

"Yes, Master," she said, in a misery.

"But it may not be necessary," I said.

"Yes, Master!" she said.

"Change your clothing," I said, "quickly."

She drew off the modest garment of white wool, and, then,

just for an instant, perhaps hardly even aware of it, she stood before me, naked, and looked at me.

"Vain slave!" I laughed.

She blushed, and quickly put down the garment of white wool, and fetched the gray garment of the state slave.

I smiled.

Well had she displayed in that brief moment her master's property.

In an instant she had drawn the tunic of the state slave over her head and was smoothing it down about her hips.

I regarded her.

She stood before me.

"Excellent," I said.

She smiled.

I then fetched the collar, designed to resemble a state collar, from the flat leather box. I went behind her and locked it on her neck, above the Appanius collar. She now wore two collars. I then removed the Appanius collar from her neck. In this way there was no moment in which she was not in at least one collar.

"Do you know what time it is?" I asked.

"No," she said. "I hardly know what I am doing, or where I am."

"Kneel," I said.

Chronometers exist on Gor, but they are rare and valuable. Marcus and I did not have any, of intent, at the time, among our belongings. They would not have seemed to fit in well with our guise as auxiliary guardsmen. In many cities, of course, including Ar, time tends to be kept publicly. Official clocks are adjusted, of course, according to the announcements of scribes, in virtue of various astronomical measurements, having to do with the movements of the sun and stars. The calendar, and adjustments in it, are also the results of their researches, promulgated by civil authorities. The average Gorean has a variety of simple devices at his disposal for making the passage of time. Typical among them are marked, or calibrated, candles, sun dials, sand glasses, clepsydras and oil clocks.

She was breathing deeply.

I sat down, cross-legged, opposite her.

"Master, too, seems apprehensive," she said. "Forgive me, Master."

"Catch your breath," I said.

"Thank you, Master," she said.

She had not neglected to have her knees in proper position. She was, after all, before a free man.

We must soon to the theater of Pentilicus Tallux, the great theater, which was more than two pasangs away.

"I am frightened," she said.

"How went it?" I asked.

At this point the eleventh bar rang.

"It is only the eleventh bar," she said, gratefully.

"Yes," I said.

She closed her eyes in relief.

"You are frightened, aren't you?" I said.

"Yes," she whispered.

She was entitled to be frightened, I supposed. She was, after all, only a slave.

"Why are you frightened?" I asked.

"Because of he before whom I must shortly appear, and as only a slave!"

"Ah, yes," I said. I myself would have thought her terror might more plausibly have been motivated by what had occurred earlier this morning.

"Tell me of what occurred in the Central Cylinder," I said.

"It was much as you had anticipated," she said. "I approached the Central Cylinder. I knelt before the guards, my head down. The capped message tube even touched the stones. I looked up. I made known my errand, that I bore a private message emanating from the house of Appanius for the Ubara. They read my collar. It seemed then surely that I was a girl of Appanius. The guards were skeptical that I would be admitted. However, to their surprise, I was to be permitted to enter the presence of the Ubara."

"That the message might emanate from a particular person in the house of Appanius, and presumably not Appanius himself, who would not be likely to have any direct business with the Ubara," I said, "was what gained your admittance. The Ubara would suspect, and perhaps even hope, from whom the message might come. Too, of course, that the message was considered "private" would tend not only to confirm her suspicions, but to excite and intrigue her."

"Yes, Master," said the girl.

She had, of course, reported to the guards at the Central Cylinder back-braceleted, with the message tube about her neck. In this way, she could not have uncapped the tube and read the message. She would presumably be in ignorance as to its contents. Indeed, in a sense she was ignorant of its contents as Marcus and I, with Phoebe's expert assistance, as it turned out, had composed it yesterday evening, while she had been scouting the public boards for us, for any news that might be of interest. It is best for slaves to approach the public boards in the evening or very early morning, when it is less crowded in their vicinity. In that way they are less likely to be beaten. She did know, of course, its general purport, and its role in our plans. The letter itself, of course, had been written by Marcus. I had removed the bracelets from her and the thong, the tube attached, from about her neck, of course, when we had had our rendezvous, after her departure from the Central Cylinder. I had given her the cloak then and we had made our separate ways back to the *insula* of Torbon.

"Go on," I said.

"My bracelets were checked," she said. "It was found that I was perfectly secured."

"Yes," I said. Having her back-braceleted, of course, was also a convenience to the guards. That would save them putting her in their own bracelets, before conducting her into the presence of the Ubara.

"Then I was double leashed," she said.

"A single metal collar," I said, "with chain leashes on each side?"

"Yes," she said.

There are several double leashing arrangements, sometimes with two collars, and sometimes with a single collar, with leash rings on opposite sides. The collars are usually of leather, metal or rope. The leashes, too, are of similar materials. Some collars, stocklike, are of wood. The point of double leashing is security and control. A prisoner is not likely to be able to pull away from two leashes. At least one is likely to restrain him. Similarly, by two leashes he can easily be immobilized, kept in place, held, say, between two leash masters, unable to reach either of them, or a third person. In the case of females double leashing is primarily aesthetic. Certainly a girl would not be likely, more than once, at any rate, to attempt to attack a leash holder, say, to bite or kick. That is something she would never do again. On the other hand, in Lavinia's case, clearly the guards would not wish to risk her approaching the Ubara too closely, even back-braceleted.

"I was then conducted by five guards within the double gate of the Central Cylinder," she said. "The leader went first. Two were with me, one on each side, each holding a leash. Two followed, with spears. Inside the double gate, I was hooded, and then I was led through what seemed to be a maze of passageways, and levels, and turnings. Sometimes I was even spun about. I had no idea where I was in the Central Cylinder. Then I was told to kneel and my leashes seemed to be fastened down, on either side of me. 'Bring me the message from my dear friend, Appanius,' said a woman's voice."

"What was the voice like?" I asked.

"It seemed friendly, even kindly, and charming," she said, "but, somehow, underneath, cold, or cruel."

"Continue," I said.

"I felt the tube being taken in hand, and uncapped, and heard the message being removed from it. The leader of the guard, I presume, did this, and then delivered it to the woman. For a time I heard nothing. Then she spoke again. 'It is nothing,' she said, 'this little note from my dear friend, Appanius, news of a coming play. But leave us now, alone. And before you go, unhood the slave. I would see her.'

"I was unhooded.

"I was kneeling in what appeared to be a private audience chamber. It must have been well within the cylinder. It was lit by lamps. The hangings were scarlet and magnificent. There was a dais a few feet before me, and on this dais, resplendent in robes of concealment, beautifully veiled, on a curule chair, there sat a regal figure. I was speechless.

" 'We await without,' said the leader of the guard. He then, with his men, withdrew.

"The hood which had been removed from me lay to one side. The message tube, with its cap, attached by its tiny thong, was still about my neck.

"I looked timidly to the woman on the curule chair. It seemed she did not notice me. She read the letter in her hands over and over, seemingly avidly.

"The chain leashes attached to the leash rings on the metal collar I wore were fastened to rings on each side of me. I was held in place. I could not rise to my feet.

"The woman on the curule chair looked down upon me. I put my head down to the floor. The message tube then, on its throng, was on the floor as well.

" 'Is that how you kneel before a free woman?' she asked.

" 'Forgive me, Mistress!' I wept. 'The guards were about!'

" 'They are not about now," she said, 'and even if they were, it is I who am Mistress here, not they.'

" 'Forgive me, Mistress!' I begged.

" 'You will kneel before me demurely," she said.

" 'Yes, Mistress,' I said. You can now well imagine how modestly and humbly, and demurely, I then knelt before her."

"I warned you about that sort of thing," I reminded her.

"Am I to be beaten?" she asked.

"No," I said. "Such knee positions become almost instinctive in a female slave, and I would not wish to complicate your training by punishing you for having failed to alter them in a particular case. I do not want your dispositions to respond to become too complex, or inconsistent."

"Thank you, Master," she said.

"Too," I said, "the guards were men, and had been present."

"Yes, Master!" she said.

"But for your own sake, when you are before free women," I said, "I would advise you to be alert to such matters."

"Yes, Master!" she said.

"Continue," I said.

"The woman looked down at me. I scarcely dared look at her. Muchly did I keep my head down. I even trembled. You can well imagine how small, and meaningless, I felt there."

"Certainly," I said, "in such a place, in the presence of such a personage, the Ubara of Ar herself."

"Oh, yes, Master," she said, "certainly that. But it was not just that."

"Oh?" I said.

"I think it was even more that she was a free woman, and that I was before her, only a slave."

"I see," I said.

" 'This note does not come from Appanius,' she said to me.

" 'No, Mistress,' I said.

" 'Do you know from whom it comes?' she asked.

" 'From the beautiful Milo,' I said.

" 'Do you know its contents?' she asked.

" 'No Mistress,' I said.

" 'Can you read?' she asked.

" 'Yes, Mistress,' I said.

" 'But you have not read it?'

" 'No, Mistress,' I said.

" 'Have you some concept of its contents,' she asked, 'any inkling as to its purport?'

" 'I fear so, Mistress,' I said.

" 'Do you know who I am, girl?' she asked.

" 'The majestic and beautiful Talena,' I said, 'Ubara of Glorious Ar.'

" 'He could be slain for even thinking of writing such a letter,' she said.

"I was silent.

" 'He has even signed it,' she said.

"I was silent.

" 'What a fool,' she said. 'What a poor, mad, infatuated fool.'

"I was silent.

" 'How could he do anything so compromising, so foolish, so utterly mad?' she asked.

" 'Perhaps he has been driven out of his wits by some brief glimpse of the beauty of Mistress,' I whispered."

"Excellent, Lavinia," I commended her.

" 'Speak,' she commanded me.

" 'He has given performances in the Central Cylinder,' I continued, 'readings, and such. Perhaps in one of these times, due to no fault of Mistress he was charmed by her voice, as by the songs of the veminium bird, or again, by her grace and manner, the consequences of a thousand generations of elegance and breeding, or again, once more through no possible fault of Mistress, perhaps in a moment of inadvertent disarray he was so unfortunate as to glimpse a portion of her briefly unveiled features, or note a width of slender wrist betwixt cuff and glove, or even, beneath the hem of her robes, fearful to contemplate, the turn of an ankle?'

" 'Perhaps,' she said. "And I had no doubt, Master, that the royal hussy had seen to it that such signals, such signs, such intriguing glimpses, such supposed inadvertencies, and such, had abounded!"

"In this," I said, "perhaps she was not so different from you."

"Master!" cried Lavinia, scandalized.

"At least," I said, "she never knelt at his side, in bangles and slave silk, and reached out to touch him."

"Had she been in my place, and only a slave," she said, "she might have done so!"

"Perhaps," I said.

"I think so, Master!" said Lavinia.

"And perhaps have found herself in the fields?"

"Perhaps, Master," smiled Lavinia.

The thought of the regal Talena shorn and in the fields was indeed an amusing one.

"Master?" asked the slave.

"Continue," I said.

" 'Do you know that he dedicated the first performance of his "Lurius of Jad" to me?' she asked.

" 'Yes, Mistress,' I responded.

" 'It is said to have been his finest performance,' she said, the she-sleen!"

"Come now, Lavinia," I said.

" 'Yes, Mistress,' I said.

" 'And he has dedicated many other performances to me, as well,' she said.

" 'Yes, Mistress," I responded.

" 'Hailed as inspired performances,' she said.

" 'Yes, Mistress,' I said. Surely, Master, she must understand the political aspects of such things!"

"Continue," I said.

" 'But then I have inspired many artists,' she said."

"Continue," I said. I smiled to myself. I wondered if the Ubara could be taught slave dance. If so, she might learn what it was like, truly, for a woman to inspire men. To be sure, the beauty of almost any slave is seldom ineffectual in such matters.

" 'I should destroy this letter,' said the Ubara to me. 'I should burn it in the flame of one of these tiny lamps.'

" 'Yes, Mistress,' I said.

" 'It could mean his death if it were so much as glimpsed by one of the Council, or by Seremides, or Myron, or his master, or perhaps any free man,' she said.

" 'Yes, Mistress,' I said. But, Master, she did not destroy the letter! She folded it carefully, and concealed it within her robes!"

"I understand," I said. I suspected that that letter was too precious to the Ubara for her to destroy it. Perhaps she would treasure it. I wondered what she would do if she learned that it had been written by Marcus. For a brief instant, a rather unworthy one, I was pleased that my own handscript was so poor, particularly with respect to alternate lines. To be sure, it also, theoretically, gave her great power over the innocent Milo. If such a letter fell into the wrong hands it was not unlikely he would find himself keeping an appointment with sleen at dinner time. Marcus might not have objected to this, but I would not personally have approved of it. I bore Milo no ill will, though he was a rather handsome fellow.

" 'Milo presumes outrageously above his station!' she said to me.

" 'Yes, Mistress,' I said. But I think she was pleased."

"He is, after all," I reminded the slave, "one of the most handsome men in Ar."

"*The* most handsome man in Ar!" said Lavinia.

"What?" I asked.

"Surely one of the most handsome men in Ar!" she said.

"Well, perhaps," I said.

" 'What a mad fool he is!' she exclaimed.

" 'Perhaps he finds Mistress irresistible,' I suggested. 'Perhaps he cannot help himself.'

" 'Yes,' she said. 'It can only be that.' "

I myself was wondering if the Ubara could be taught to writhe in chains, or to move on the floor in such a way, so prettily, that the master would not lash her for clumsiness.

"Is Master listening?" asked Lavinia.

"Yes," I said.

"She then rose up from her chair, and came down to where I knelt, back-braceleted and fastened to the rings.

" 'Of what house are you?' she asked.

" 'Of the house of Appanius, Mistress,' I said. But surely that would have been suggested by my collar! Surely she had been apprised of this sort of thing by the guards, even when I was still on the street outside!"

"Continue," I said.

" 'Kneel straight, and lift your chin,' she said. 'Put your head further back!' she said. She then bent down, and put her hands on the collar, and checked it. 'RETURN ME TO APPANIUS OF AR' she read. 'A suitable legend for a collar,' she smiled, straightening up, 'fitting for an animal.'

" 'Yes, Mistress,' I said.

" 'You are an animal, you know,' she said.

" 'Yes, Mistress,' I said.

" 'Incredible,' she marveled, 'the difference between one such as I and one such as you.'

" 'Yes, Mistress,' I said.

" 'What are you called?' she asked.

" 'Lavinia', I said.

" 'That is a pretty name,' she said.

" 'Thank you, Mistress,' I said.

" 'And you are a pretty girl, Lavinia,' she said.

" 'Thank you, Mistress,' I said.

" 'Very pretty,' she said.

" 'Thank you, Mistress,' I said.

" 'Do not dare to bring your head forward!' she said.

" 'No, Mistress!' I said.

"Then she took my collar in her hands and held it, and looked down, angrily, into my eyes. 'Meaningless, collared chit!' she exclaimed.

" 'Yes, Mistress!' I gasped, frightened. But, Master, if she were in a collar, do you think she would be so much more than I?"

"No," I said.

"It would be as fixed upon her as upon me! She would be as helpless in it as I! She would be no more able to remove it from her neck than I!"

"No," I said. "Such collars are not made to be removed by girls."

" 'What are you to Milo?' she asked, suddenly.

" 'Nothing, Mistress!' I cried. 'Nothing, Mistress!'

" 'How is it' she asked, 'that you have brought this message? Keep your head in position!'

" 'I have been assigned by my master, Appanius, to Milo, to be a personal serving slave to him, to clean his quarters, run his errands, and such.'

" 'And does he sleep you at his slave ring?' she asked.

" 'No, Mistress," I gasped, 'he sleeps me on my mat, in the corner of his room, and I am not permitted to leave it until morning!'

" 'Absurd!' she said.

" 'No, Mistress!' I said.

" 'And has he never touched you, in the way of the man?' she asked.

" 'No, Mistress!' I said.

" 'Do you expect me to believe that?' she asked.

" 'Yes, Mistress!' I begged.

"She glared down at me.

" 'I am to Milo only a meaningless serving slave,' I said.

" 'But you would be more!' she said.

" 'Please do not make me speak!' I wept.

"She looked down upon me, and laughed. Oh, Master, how that laugh cut me! How deeply was I wounded by that sound!

" 'Do not presume above your station, silly little slave girl,' she said.

" 'Forgive me, Mistress," I said. Why was she so cruel to me, only a slave?"

"Continue," I said.

" 'Your hair is too short," she said to me.

" 'Yes, Mistress,' I said. 'I served in the fields.'

" 'You are pretty to have been put in the fields,' she said.

" 'I was punished,' I said. 'I served the paga of one of my master's retainers at an incorrect temperature.'

" 'Stupid slave,' she said.

" 'Yes, Mistress,' I said.

" 'And after your time in the fields you were returned to the house, and assigned to the quarters of Milo?'

" 'Yes, Mistress.'

" 'Keep your head in position,' she said.

" 'Yes Mistress,' I said.

" 'And Milo has never touched you?' she said.

" 'No, Mistress,' I said.

" 'Interesting,' she said.

" 'I fear he has thoughts, and eyes, for only one woman,' I said.

" 'Oh?' she said.

" 'Yes, Mistress,' I said. 'And I fear it is she, and she alone, to whom his heart belongs.'

" 'And who might this woman be?' she asked.

" 'Perhaps Mistress can guess,' I said.

" 'He is a fool to write such a note,' she suddenly said, touching her robes, within which she had concealed the note.

"I did not respond, Master, but surely Milo is no fool!"

"I do not know if he is a fool or not," I said, "but he did not, at any rate, write the note."

"True," she said.

"Continue," I said.

" 'Are we the only ones who know of this note,' she asked, 'Milo, I and yourself?'

" 'I think so, Mistress,' I said.

" 'Then,' she said, 'perhaps I should have your tongue cut out, and then have you skinned alive."

"She would not do that," I said, "as she would need you as a go-between."

"I trust Master is correct in his assumption," said Lavinia.

"I would think so," I said.

"That would seem to borne out by her subsequent remark, that she herself would not be so foolish as to have written such a note."

I nodded. "After a time, she said, 'You may bring your head forward.'

" 'Thank you, Mistress,' I said.

" 'Do you think we should have our mad, rash boy, Milo, burned alive?' she asked.

" 'I would hope,' I said, 'that Mistress would to some extent, in view of her fabled beauty and the damage that even the thought of it it may wreak in the hearts of poor men, be rather moved to pity, be rather moved to look leniently on this bold transgression.'

"She smiled.

" 'Is morning to be blamed that it should glow in the light of the sun, or the tides that they are drawn by the moons, or oil that it cannot help but burn at the touch of fire?'

" 'Perhaps not,' she said, the vain, haughty thing!"

"Continue," I said.

" 'Whereas you must understand that I am not personally in the least interested in matters such as these,' said she, 'there may be a woman of my acquaintance to whom such attentions may not be entirely unwelcome.'

" 'Mistress?' I asked. She thought I would believe this!

" 'I shall have to consult with her' she said.

" 'Yes, Mistress,' I said.

" 'Ludmilla, of Ar,' " she said."

"Ah!" I said.

"This is meaningful to Master?" asked the slave.

"I think so," I said. "I am not sure. It is something I have long suspected."

"Master?" asked the slave.

"In any event," I said, "that is apparently the name she will use for her intrigue."

"That I had gathered, Master," said the slave.

"I do not think, at any rate," I said, "that it is a mere accident that that name occurred to her, as on the spur of the moment."

"Perhaps not, Master," said the girl, puzzled.

To be sure, there are many Ludmillas in Ar, as there are many Publias, Claudias, and so on. Indeed, there are doubtless several Talenas.

" 'But it is you, Mistress,' I protested, 'not some other, for whom the beautiful Milo pines, as a sickened verr.'

"She laughed. She thought me stupid, doubtless."

"Continue," I said.

" 'You will speak to him of Ludmilla,' she said. 'He will understand.'

" 'How shall I know this Ludmilla, or he know her?' I asked.

" 'You will report to me,' she said. 'All matters will be arranged through me.'

" 'Yes, Mistress,' I said.

" 'And the first thing you will tell him is that Ludmilla scolds him for his foolishness in sending such a note, and warns him to quake in terror of having incurred her displeasure for having done so,' and then she added, thoughtfully, 'and yet that she is inclined, as is her nature, to be merciful, indeed, that she is not altogether unmoved by his plight.'

" 'But should Mistress not confer with the noble Ludmilla before conveying these sentiments on her behalf?' I asked."

"Beware, Lavinia," I smiled. "You are treading on dangerous ground."

"But she is such a haughty slut, Master!" said Lavinia.

"You speak of her as though she might be a slave," I said.

"I think she is a slave," said Lavinia, "but in the robes of a Ubara!"

"Perhaps," I said.

" 'I can speak for her,' she said.

" 'Yes, Mistress,' I said.

" 'This will save time,' she said. 'I have decided it.'

" 'Yes, Mistress,' I said."

"Apparently the Ubara is eager," I said.

"Yes, Master," said the slave.

" 'Tell him, too,' said she, 'that his plaint may not have been altogether ill received.'

" 'Yes, Mistress,' I said.

" 'Put your head to the floor, slave girl,' she said.

"I obeyed, and sensed the lowering of her veil, the soft sound of rustling silk.

" 'You may look up,' she said.

"I looked up, Master," said the slave. "I gasped. I could not even speak. I was awed. She was more beautiful than I had imagined! She was more beautiful than I could have dreamed! She was utterly beautiful!"

"Much was doubtless a function of the context," I said, "she in the robes and veils, so colorful and resplendent, and silken, and being Ubara, and you on your knees before her, merely a slave. The comparison is not really fair to you."

"She is very beautiful!" said Lavinia.

"She has been said to be the most beautiful woman on Gor," I said, "but there are thousands upon thousands of incredibly beautiful women on Gor, perhaps millions, most of whom are in collars where they belong."

"But surely she is one of the most beautiful women on Gor!" said Lavinia.

"I would not even be sure of that," I said.

"Master?" said Lavinia.

"She is pretty," I said, "and is, or was, the daughter of a Ubar. Such things tend to increase one's reputation in such matters."

"She is surely one of the most beautiful women on Gor!" said Lavinia.

"I am inclined to doubt it," I said. "Still she is pretty. I recall that I once found her of interest."

"Master knows the Ubara?" she asked, in awe.

"Once, long ago," I said.

"Does the Ubara recall Master?" she asked.

"If she were to see me," I said, "I think it possible she would recall me."

"She is very beautiful," said Lavinia, softly.

"That I think is true," I said. There could be no gainsaying that. On the other hand, it is one thing to be very beautiful, and another to be one of the most beautiful women on a planet. I would have surely granted that Talena was very beautiful, but I would really doubt that she might have counted in among the most beautiful women on Gor. This is not to deny that she would bring a high price in a market, nor that her alcove space on holidays might have been signed up early in the evening.

"She is so beautiful!" said Lavinia.

"Suppose," I said, "that she were not free, that she were not Ubara. Suppose, rather, that she were one slave among others, lovely slaves all, chained to a wall. Or suppose that she was paraded in a line, with other slaves, excellent slaves all, on all fours, in neck coffle, the chains going back under the slaves' bodies and between their legs, rising to the collar of the next in line, and so on, before a conqueror's chair. Would she then seem so outstanding? Or might not other girls, here and there, more appeal to one man or another?"

"I see what Master is saying," said Lavinia.

"If she were a captured Ubara," I said, "and auctioned before Ubars, doubtless her price would be high, perhaps thousands of tarn disks, but if she were unknown, and only one slave on a chain with others, and it were she alone, the girl alone, only herself, so to speak, who was to ascend the block, hurried by the gesture of the auctioneer's whip, what would she bring?"

"I do not know, Master," said Lavinia.

"Perhaps two or three silver tarsks," I said.

"Surely Master jests," she said.

"Remember," I said, "it is only she being sold, not her reputation, not her political importance, not her symbolic value as an acquisition, not her value as a trophy, not her possible historical interest as a collector's item, and such, but only she, only the girl, only another slave."

"I see, Master," she said.

"And, I would conjecture," I said, "for two or three silver tarsks."

"Possibly," mused Lavinia.

"Indeed," I said, "it is possible that you would bring a higher price."

"I?" exclaimed Lavinia.

"Yes," I said. "And do not forget to keep your knees properly positioned."

"Yes, Master!" she said, delighted, hastily readjusting the position of her knees.

"Do you really think I compare in beauty?" she asked.

"Yes," I said. Indeed, I thought it might be interesting to see both in slave silk, hurrying about, barefoot, perhaps belled, fearing the whip, striving to serve well, hoping to found pleasing by masters.

"Thank you, Master!" she said.

"Continue," I said.

"As you will recall," she said, "I had just been permitted to glimpse the beauty of the Ubara."

"Yes," I said.

"Why did she show herself to me?" asked Lavinia.

"I suppose," I said, "because she was jealous of you, and wished, in a sense, to awe you with her own beauty."

"I thought so," said Lavinia. "What a vain creature!"

"She is a female," I said.

"Yes, Master!" said Lavinia.

"Like yourself," I said.

"Yes, Master!" laughed Lavinia. "Well, I assure you, Master, she was successful in her intent for I could not even speak for a moment. This pleased the Ubara certainly. She saw that I was much impressed with her beauty."

"That your awe was genuine," I said, "was much in your interest."

"Do you truly think my beauty compares with hers?" asked Lavinia.

"Certainly," I said, "assuming, say, that you were both on the slave block, that you were both chained to a ring, that you were both serving, and so on."

"Then it truly compares with hers," she said, "as female to female, as beauty to beauty?"

"Yes," I said.

" 'Surely the Lady Ludmilla,' I said to the Ubara, when I could gather my wits and speak, 'could not begin to compare in beauty with Mistress!' "

"Again you were on dangerous ground," I observed.

"Perhaps, Master," smiled the slave.

" 'She is every bit as beautiful as I,' she said.

"That makes sense," I said.

"Well, then, Master, she smiled, muchly pleased, and readjusted her veil, and told me that I would be admitted to her presence immediately any time of the day or night."

"Excellent!" I said.

"But I was to approach, and be exited from, an inconspicuous side gate, no more than a postern."

I nodded.

"She then clapped her hands, recalling the guards. She spoke to them briefly, primarily, I gather, pertaining to her policies with respect to my access to her presence. In a few moments I was again in the passageways outside the audience chamber, hooded, and double leashed. I was freed of the hood and leashes outside the gate, this time the main gate, by means of which I had entered."

"Of course," I said, "as you had entered through that gate this time."

"Yes, Master," she said.

"You are now the go-between in an intrigue, my dear," I informed her.

Just then the twelfth bar rang.

She looked up, frightened.

"It is late now," I said. "We must be on our way."

I rose to my feet and indicated that she should do so, as well. She had already donned the livery intended to resemble the state livery of Ar, and I had earlier put on her neck the collar designed to resemble a state collar. Indeed, I had even a few days ago, stopped a state slave, to check her collar. "RETURN ME TO THE WHIP MASTER OF THE CENTRAL CYLINDER" read the legend on the collar. I picked up the small cloak she had worn, and put it about her shoulders. I smiled to myself. It was much like a fellow helping a young lady on with her cloak, or coat. Yet what a difference there was here. I could do what I wanted with her. I owned her. We then, I first, she following behind at an interval, left our small room, in the *insula* of Torbon on Demetrios street, in the Metellan district. I was pleased, for my own purposes, at any rate, that state slaves in Ar were no longer belled, a consequence of the misguided and unsuccessful policies of Cos to devirilize, and thus make more manageable, the men of Ar. Thus that the slave, Lavinia, beneath the cloak, was in state livery, you see, would not be suggested to any in the streets outside.

22 My Plans Proceed

"The door opens, Master!" said Lavinia.

"I shall draw back," I said.

We were behind the great theater, near one of its rear entrances. Lavinia well knew the portal. There were various folks about, mostly coming and going, workmen, bearers of burdens, and such. One fellow was drawing a two-wheeled cart, loaded with basketry. There were loungers in the vicinity, as well, interestingly, among them, some free women, in habiliments suggesting diversities of caste, and one level or another of affluence. Two palanquins, too, set down, the carrying slaves about, were behind the theater, their curtains partly parted.

"It is he!" said Lavinia.

She backed against the wall, her hand, clutching the note, at her breast.

I walked back, casually moving away. I would stay in the vicinity, not really far away, but not so close that I might hear what transpired. I doubted that converse would flow unimpeded if one were within clear earshot.

A few yards away I turned, to observe. Lavinia was where I had left her. She seemed rooted to the spot. Her heart, for whatever reason, I suspected, must be rapidly palpitating. I could see the suggestion of agitation, if not of terror, in the heaving of her bosom. She clutched the note. I trusted that it would not be crushed and soiled in that sweet sweaty little palm of hers.

The fellow, with two others, had emerged from the rear portal.

Lavinia did not move.

I was curious to observe this small encounter, but I had come mainly to protect her, if it seemed necessary. I was not certain as to how her approach, and overture, might be received. She was, after all, even though in the seeming livery and collar of a state slave, still only a slave. Too, she might be remembered from the days of her freedom, when her person had been sacrosanct and inviolate, and her will selfish and imperious, and this might earn her some abuse, perhaps to assuage lingering resentments, accrued from formerly endured affronteries, or perhaps merely, for the agent's amusement, to remind her of her present vulnerability and station, of her change in condition, that it was not now she who was to be pleased but rather that now it was she who must please. Too, she might be recalled, as well, from her days as a house slave in the house of Appanius. There, of course, particularly as a new slave, she would have been at the mercy of the men of the house, and, I supposed, of even the higher slaves. They might have formed the habit then of treating her poorly, or venting spite and frustration upon her. Accordingly, I would stay in the vicinity. I had no objection to the fellow kicking her, or cuffing her about a bit, of course. Indeed, such things are good for a slave. But I did not wish any serious injury to be inflicted upon her. That might lower her price, for example.

But Lavinia had not moved from the spot!

Her immobility exasperated me, but, on the other hand, perhaps it was just as well. Four or five of the several free women who were about hurried forward to throng about the fellow. Others hung back. The palanquins did not move. Various veils, I thought, were not as carefully adjusted as they might have been. The hem of more than one robe was lifted up a little as the women hurried forward. Surely this was interesting, as the alley was dry. I detected, at any rate, neither mud nor puddles in their path. Doubtless they wished in their haste to avoid stirred dust, hoping to keep it from their robes. There were some lads about also. Perhaps they had come to witness what revelations might be betrayed by a subtly disarranged veil, or to see if one might not, if sufficiently alert, and if one were so fortunate, catch a glimpse, perhaps no more than a flash, of an ankle. To be sure, they might, as they wished, feast their eyes on slaves.

I growled to myself in frustration. On the other hand, it would not have done for Lavinia to rush up to the fellow, competing for his attention with free women. That would have been extremely unwise, and even dangerous. She was in a collar.

The fellow was very patient with the free women who clustered about him, as I suppose it behooved him to be. They were very close about him, and some even touched him. Their eyes shone as they looked up at him. Several could scarcely speak. He was a tall fellow, and towered above them. I considered them in their robes. They might make a group of lovely little slaves, I thought.

I looked over to Lavinia. She was standing so close to the wall that she might almost have been attached to it by a fixed neck ring.

After a time the two men with the fellow, apparently with soft words, and certainly with gentle gestures, began to suggest that the fellow be permitted to continue on his way. The women did not seem much pleased with this. Some uttered little noises of dismay, of protest. Surely they must have a few moments more to cluster about him, to touch him, to utter their compliments. Was it so soon that they were no longer permitted to bask adoringly in the warmth of that bright smile? Then they drew back, standing behind, looking after him, longingly, as he continued on his way.

I looked to Lavinia. Still she did not move!

More than one of the women left behind was now repinning her veil, almost as though in embarrassment. How had it slipped so?

Then some of the more timid women who had not dared to approach the fellow hurried to him, one after another, to be alone with him, if only for a moment. He would smile upon them, and kissed the gloved hand of one.

He was preceding on, heading in my direction. Lavinia was now well behind him. I looked at her. Did she think she was chained to the wall there? I made a tiny, almost imperceptible gesture. She moved a bit from the wall, as though to follow behind the fellow and the others. At the same time one of the bearers of one of the palanquins approached the fellow's party and knelt, and indicated the palanquin. Lavinia quickly moved back. I was now growing impatient, but, surely, I would not want her to compete in these matters with the occupant of the palanquin, who was doubtless a wealthy free women. The palanquin, at any rate, did not appear to be a rented one or its bearers rented slaves. It would be all I would need for Lavinia to be beaten by the bearers and the note lost somewhere in the dust of the alley.

I scuffed about for a time in the dust of the alley. The woman in the palanquin must indeed be wealthy, or well-fixed, or something. The two men with the fellow even withdrew so that he might converse with the palanquin's occupant. I saw, too, after a time, him bow his head and place to his lips the fingers of a small, gloved hand extended between the curtains of the palanquin.

This probably did not please the occupant of the other palanquin. She, incidentally, for I assumed it to be a she, from the décor and style, and closed nature, of the palanquin, had not only bearers with her, but one or two free men as well. I wondered if the bearers of these palanquins, on behalf of their mistresses, occasionally interfered with one another in the streets. I supposed it not impossible. On the other hand, things seemed relatively civilized this afternoon.

When the fellow then took to his way again this second palanquin, in a fashion I thought rather reminiscent of the investigatory movements of the nine-gilled Gorean marsh shark, slowly, silently, and smoothly turned in his direction.

I made an impatient gesture to Lavinia.

How helplessly distraught was the beauty!

The fellow with his attendants passed me. Briefly did our eyes meet. Hastily did they look away. In a few moments the second palanquin, too, had passed, nosing after the fellow and his small party. Lavinia, then, timidly, left the vicinity of the wall, and began to follow in the wake of the palanquin and its putative prey. As she passed me I took her by the arm and pulled her to the side. "What is wrong with you?" I said. "I await my opportunity, Master!" she said, looking not at me, but rather after the party down the street. I released her arm. To be sure, there was no real point in being angry with her. She, a mere slave, had had as yet no suitable opportunity to make her approach. I think rather my being somewhat out of temper was the result of my fear that she might bungle the matter, as simple as it was, because of some inexplicable emotional upheavals or unrests, or, perhaps, it was merely that I was anxious for the business to be successfully and expeditiously completed.

Lavinia, released, hurried away, to follow in the wake of the palanquin and its putative prey.

I looked suddenly at a fellow nearby, which opportunity he seized to remark interesting arrangements of tiles on various nearby roofs. When he had completed these architectural inquiries he found my eyes still on him.

"Yes?" I said.

"That was a state slave," he said.

"A branded slut is a branded slut, even if she is owned by the state."

"True," he said, agreeably.

"So what is your point?" I inquired.

"It is just that it may be improper to accost them while they are on their errands."

"Do you think that at night when they are chained at their slave rings the state caresses them?" I asked.

"No," he said.

The lot of a state slave can be one of great deprivation. Indeed, I fear it often is. Certainly it is commonly regarded as an extremely unenviable slavery by most slaves. To be sure, they are occasionally made available to male slaves, guards and such. Some state slaves, of course, usually girls of unusual beauty, are used at state banquets, to serve and entertain. But even there the state not unoften utilizes trained feast slaves, rented from various establishments or, upon certain occasions, even the girls from a Ubar's own pleasure gardens.

"Thank you for your observation," I said.

"It is nothing," he said.

We looked after Lavinia, hurrying down the street.

"She is a pretty one," he said.

"Yes," I said.

I then turned about and went down the same street.

I was not really displeased. The fellow had taken Lavinia unquestioningly for a state slave. That was reassuring, and was in its way a compliment to Phoebe's skill as a seamstress, which skill she had primarily acquired following her collaring. Too, he had reminded me that some folks, in particular, guardsmen, often disapproved of interfering with such a girl in the pursuit of her duties. This policy, incidentally, makes it difficult for such slaves to obtain simple, basic female gratifications, such as being caressed in the chains of a master. It was difficult for them, for example, to enter into, arrange or conduct affairs, even of the brief dark-doorway variety. On the other hand, the policy might prove useful, from my own point of view. In virtue of it, I thought I might be able to defend Lavinia, if necessary, without calling too much attention to myself, in particular, without identifying myself as her likely master. Who knows? I might be merely a civic-minded citizen, or perhaps a fellow spoiling for a fight, or one who might find it in his interest, on a certain occasion, to seem to be such.

In a few Ehn, on Aulus, in the vicinity of Tarn Court, I saw one of the free men accompanying the palanquin hurry forward to stay the fellow with his two companions. Lavinia was about thirty to forty yards beyond the palanquin. I was about ten yards or so behind her. Stayed, the small group awaited the arrival of the palanquin, which now approached them in a stately fashion, the bearers impressive in their lack of haste, befitting the undoubted dignity of the palanquin's occupant. In a moment or two the palanquin had been set down on its legs, on the shady side of Aulus, near a wall covered with theater posters, many of them faded, tattered, overlapping and half torn away.* Many Gorean advertisements, incidentally, though not in this area, are written on the walls themselves, sections of the wall occasionally being whitewashed to make room for new entries. Some shopkeepers, householders, landlords and such rent space on the streetsides of their buildings for this purpose. Needless to say, many advertisements, notifications and such, are not, so to speak, authorized. Some of these notifications, and such, perhaps inscribed by the proprietors of certain taverns or their agents, sing the praises of various slaves. I wondered if the fellows passing these notifications, and such, recounting, say, the charms of a certain Tania or Sylvia, of such-and-such a paga tavern, ever considered the possibility that these might be former free women of Ar, perhaps women thitherto unapproachable, once haughty, vain women, women courted in vain by many, perhaps even by themselves, who had now become slaves, women who must now, in their collars, answerable to the whip, to the best of their ability, serve

*Twice in the manuscript, later, Cabot refers to a "Flute Street." From the context it seems clear that this is "Aulus." I have accordingly edited the manu-

masters. Perhaps they could even arrange for the purchase of one of them, not to free her, of course, for it is said that only a fool frees a slave girl, but to take her home and keep her for themselves. Graffiti, too, in Gorean public places, as the markets and baths, is not uncommon. Whereas this graffiti is mostly of a predictable sort, as one might expect, names, proclamations of love, denunciations of enemies, obscenities, and such, some of it is, in my opinion, at least, of quite high quality. For example, poets not unoften use the walls to publish their work, so to speak. Indeed, it is said, though I do not know with what truth, that Pentilicus Tallux, for whom the great theater is named, first inscribed his poetry on walls. Needless to say, readers then often feel free to write their own comments on the poems, or even to edit them. More than one critic, I fear, has been found bloodied at the base of such a wall. Indeed, there is a story abroad that Pentilicus Tallux himself, whose work is noted for its restraint and delicacy, figured in more than one fracas of that sort. One story has it that he slew seven men in formal duels alone.

The palanquin now having been set down, its bearers, its accompanying free men, and the two men who had accompanied the fellow from the theater, withdrew. This left the fellow in a position to conduct some form of tête-à-tête with the palanquin's occupant, of the privacy of which she would presumably

script in the interests of consistency, changing "Flute Street" to "Aulus." My interpretation is supported by information supplied by a colleague in the Classics Department, to the effect that there is a Greek expression for a flute which might be transliterated as *aulos*. I think we may assume then, apart from contextual considerations, that "Aulus" and "Flute Street" are the same street. My conjecture is that *aulos* was absorbed into Gorean as 'Aulus'. An additional consideration is that "Aulus" is one of the streets bordering the great theater, that of Pentilicus Tallux. Flute music is apparently extremely important in Gorean theater. Indeed, we learn from Cabot's miscellaneous notes that the name of the flute player usually occurs on theatrical advertisements immediately after that of the major performer or performers. It seems the flute player is often on stage and accompanies performers about, pointing up speeches, supplying background music and such. This is accepted as Gorean theatrical convention, it seems, much as background music is accepted in Twentieth Century films, even in such unlikely locations as city streets, airplanes, life rafts and deserts. Various "modes" are supposed, as well, to elicit and express various emotions, some being appropriate for love scenes, others for battle scenes, etc. Lastly it might be mentioned that 'Aulus' can also occur as a Gorean masculine name. This sort of thing is familiar, of course, in all languages, as Smith, Cooper, Chandler, Carpenter, Carter, and such, stand for occupations, and names like Hampshire, Lake, Holm, Rivers, and such, stand for places, and names like Stone, Hammer, Rock, and such, stand for things.

—J.N.

wish to be assured. I wondered if this fellow commonly ran such a gantlet on his way back from the theater to the house of his master, Appanius of Ar. When the palanquin stopped, Lavinia did, too, naturally, and, of course, some yards behind her, so, too, did I. While the fellow was engaged in discourse with the palanquin's occupant one of the free men, the fellow who had gone on ahead to call upon the fellow and his companions to wait, took notice of Lavinia and began to approach her. She must have seen him coming, for she reacted in fear, and turned about. She cast a wild glance toward me, but I pretended not to notice. She began to come back, back down Aulus, in my direction, but he called out, "Hold, female slave!" I was afraid for a moment that she might panic and bolt in which case he would presumably have her in custody in a moment and she would have been beaten. If he did not catch her I would have to beat her tonight, for having disobeyed a command of that sort, from a free person. Such are not to be disobeyed. But, to my satisfaction, accosted, although she had apparently been momentarily gripped with fear, she had the good sense to turn about and kneel. Also, as he was a man, she had her knees in proper position. One of the advantages of that position, aside from its general suitability and its effect on the female, is that it commonly has placatory value. The fellow had, I assumed, noted her lingering about, too, in the vicinity of the theater, and had probably noted that she was following them, or, more likely, he whom they were following. Perhaps, while he was waiting, in order to while away the time, it was his intent to draw her aside, into a doorway, and thrust her back against the door or wall, for a bit of brief sport. I did not think I would object to this, if no danger came to the note. Too this might fit in with her guise as a state slave, for such are often not averse to such attentions, and have something of a reputation of provoking them. As I have earlier indicated the state is generally heedless of the sexual needs of its state slaves. At any rate, it seldom seems inclined to make any adequate provision for the satisfaction of these very real, and very profound, needs. To be sure, what does it matter, as the women are only slaves? On the other hand, it might be noted that state slaves being sold into the private sector often bring good prices. They seem eager to become private slaves, with a given master, whom they may then try to serve with such perfection and devotion that they may hope to exert some influence, however small, on the quality of their lives, for example, with respect to the nature of the contentents they may receive, those which their master may deign to bestow upon them. On the other hand, his mien seemed hostile, so I moved somewhat closer. He stood now before Lavinia, angrily, who, wide-eyed, kneeling, quaked before him. She spread her knees even more. I saw now that it was apparently his intention to protect his employer's interests, as he saw them, that he wished to warn her away. That would not do. He drew back his hand to cuff the slave. As his hand came forward I intercepted it, and held it, by the wrist, in midair. "Ai!" he cried out, in surprise, in anger, in pain. When he ceased to struggle I released his hand. He pulled his wrist away, angrily, rubbing it.

"What is the meaning of your interference?" he snarled.

"What is the meaning of yours?" I inquired, eagerly.

He backed away a step. "Mine?" he asked.

"Interfering with a state slave," I said.

"She is following us!" he said.

"Why?" I asked.

"Well," said he, "not us, but another."

"Who?" I asked.

"He," he said, indicating the direction of the palanquin.

"What business is it of yours?" I asked.

"My employer would not approve of her pursuit," he said.

"And is your employer a competitive slave girl?" I asked.

"No!" he said. "She is the Lady——"

"Yes?" I said.

"It does not matter," he said, irritatedly.

"Perhaps her master has not yet given her a name?" I said.

"You can see she carries a note!" said the fellow, gesturing to Lavinia.

"Give me the note," I said to Lavinia.

"It is private!" she said.

I put out my hand, and she put the note in my hand.

"It is nothing," I said, glancing at the note, and handing it back to Lavinia.

"Let me see!" he said.

"You dispute my word?" I said, eagerly.

"No!" he said.

"Draw!" I said. My hand went to my tunic.

"I am unarmed!" he said. "It is the law! We of Ar may not carry weapons."

"Let us then adjudicate our differences with our bare hands," I said.

"You are drunk!" he said, stepping back.

"If true, that will give you an advantage," I said.

"It is unseemly for free men to squabble before a female slave," he said.

"I shall send her away then," I said.

"No, no," he said, anxiously. "She is doing no harm."

"You would keep her here, away from her duties?" I asked, eagerly.

"No," he said. "No!"

"Glory to Talena, Ubara of Ar," I said.

"Yes, glory to Talena, certainly!" he said.

"Glory to Seremides, first minister to the Ubara, high captain, commander of the Taurentians, to Myron, polemarkos of Temos, to Lurius of Jad, Ubar of Cos!" I said.

"Yes, yes," he said, "glory to them, glory to them all!"

"Glory to a fat tharlarion!" I said.

"If you wish," he said, "yes, of course!"

"You are very agreeable," I said.

"I try to be congenial," he said.

"I think that I shall make the acquaintance of your lady," I said.

"Do not!" he said.

"To complain of your interference with the duties of a state slave," I said.

"She is in converse!" he said.

"No matter!" I said.

"Do not interrupt her!" he said.

"Perhaps you wish to stop me?" I said.

"No!" he said. He then turned and hurried away, toward the palanquin.

"It is my recommendation," I said to Lavinia, "that you route yourself about and rendezvous with our quarry on Tarn Court, underneath the bowers. As I understand it that is his accustomed path. Also, in this way it will seem as though I sent you away, hurrying you back to your proper business."

"Yes, Master," she said.

"Tuck the note in your tunic," I said. "Deliver it when the opportune moment arises."

"Yes, Master," she said. She kissed the note, and then thrust it into her tunic.

"It is a well-written note," I said.

"Thank you, Master," she said. She herself, as it had turned out, had written the note, it compliant, of course, with my directives and objectives. Marcus and I had struggled with the note for a time and then, for all practical purposes, had given it up. Lavinia had then composed it. It was sensitive, lyrical, tender, poignant and touching, the desperate, pleading letter of a highly intelligent, profoundly feminine, extremely vulnerable, extremely needful woman hopelessly in love, one eager to abandon herself and to surrender all to the lover. Both Marcus and myself were astonished that Lavinia did such an excellent job with it. It was almost as though she were writing the letter in her own behalf, and not as part of a plot. Only Phoebe had not seemed surprised, but had merely smiled. She did make a couple of suggestions about the formation of certain letters, but, as it turned out, such things were common in the cursive script of Ar, a point in which Marcus concurred with Lavinia. The script of Ar's Station is, apparently, for most practical purposes at any rate, the same as that of Ar. There are some differences in speech, that is, in accent, but even they tend to be negligible. For example, whereas Marcus' speech would have attracted immediate attention in Tyros or Cos, or even in the western Vosk basin, it attracted little, if any, attention in Ar.

"You understand why I did not permit the fellow to cuff you, do you not?" I asked.

"To protect me, Master," she said.

"Not really," I said. "There are other sorts of points more involved. First, there is a consideration of fittingness. For example, whereas others, particularly on certain occasions, and in certain circumstances, may, and should discipline you, this did not seem to me to be such an occasion, or such a set of circumstances. For most practical purposes, you see, you are primarily mine to cuff, or beat, as I might please, and not others."

"Yes, Master," she said, swallowing hard.

"Secondly," I said, "I do not want you to present yourself before our quarry with, say, a scarlet cheek, or a swollen, bloodied lip, such things. Such might provoke distractive speculation."

"I understand, Master," she said.

I glanced down Aulus, to the palanquin, still in its place. "You speed about," I said to Lavinia. "Our quarry will be along shortly. His conversation with the lady in the palanquin, although she is perhaps unaware of it, is about to conclude."

"What if I cannot do it, Master," suddenly wept Lavinia.

"I do not understand," I said.

"What if I should die of fear, not even daring to approach him?"

"I am prepared to take that risk," I told her.

"Master!" she said. "I am serious."

"I doubt that you can manage to die of fear in this business," I said, "but if you should manage it, I shall just have to find another girl."

"I see," she said.

"So, rest easy," I said. "As you see, there is nothing to worry about."

"I am much set at my ease," she said.

I crouched down before her.

"What are you?" I asked.

"A slave," she said.

"What else?" I asked.

"Only that," she said. "A slave, and only that."

"That is what you must remember," I said to her, softly. "When he approaches remember that, and its truth, in your mind, your heart and belly, that you are a slave, and only that."

"I see, Master," she smiled, through tears.

"I do not think you will fail," I said, "and if you do, do not fear, you will be severely beaten."

"I do not think I will now fail, Master," she smiled.

"Good," I said, standing up.

"You are kind," she said.

"It seems you do wish to be beaten," I said.

"No, Master!" she said.

Then I waved my arm, back down Aulus street. "Do not dally here, slave girl," I said, loudly. "Be off. Be about your duties!"

"Yes, Master," she said, springing up, and hurrying back down Aulus.

I had decided that it would be better for her to carry the note in her tunic, in order that it not attract attention. The free man, for example, had noticed it. It had been all right for her to carry it in her hand, I had thought, when we had hoped that she would be able to deliver it almost immediately, say, behind the theater, but it seemed now she would have to wait a little, say, until our quarry reached Tarn Court, which, if I had anything to do with it, would not be long.

I turned and looked to the palanquin. In a moment I was beside it.

"One side," I said to the handsome interlocutor standing beside the palanquin.

"Oh!" said the woman within it, drawing back.

"I feared this," said the free fellow I had talked to earlier, up the street.

The handsome interlocutor, our quarry, of course, did not interfere, but stood back. Had I insisted on it, he must kneel. He was slave.

"What is the meaning of this!" exclaimed the woman, hastily raising her veil, holding it about her face.

"This fellow," I said, indicating the free fellow with whom I had held brief converse but a moment or so ago, "interfered with the progress of a state slave."

"Be off!" said the woman.

"I thought you would like to know that," I said.

"Pummel him!" she said to the free fellow.

"That might not be wise," he said. He glanced to the other free fellow with the palanquin. Their exchange of glances suggested that his fellow fully corroborated his speculation.

"Will no one protect a free woman?" she inquired.

The handsome interlocutor, at this point, seemed for a moment undecided. He might even have been considering the wisdom, all things considered, of hastening forward. I said to him, rudely, I fear, considering his indubitable fame and talent, controversial though the latter might be, "Kneel!"

Immediately he did so.

"Oh!" said the woman in dismay, seeing the handsome fellow put to his knees.

The two fellows with the handsome fellow, both free men, started forward a little at this point, but I threw them a welcoming, menacing glance, and they, looking to one another, decided to remain in the background. After all, on what grounds should they object to a legitimate command issued by a free person to one who, after all, was but a slave?

"Attack him!" said the woman to the free men with her.

"He is armed!" said the fellow I had met earlier.

Actually I was not armed today, as I was not in uniform, not wearing, that is, the armband of the auxiliary guardsman, and I did not want to be stopped by guardsmen, line or auxiliary, as being in possible violation of the injunction against unauthorized weapons in the city, that injunction which placed a populace at the mercy of anyone armed. When I had reached to my tunic earlier, of course, I had merely meant to convey the suggestion to the fellow that I had a concealed weapon there. This suggestion he, a bright fellow, had been quick to accept. To be sure, had I been really armed, I would not have cared to be he, calling the bluff.

"Be off!" cried the woman. "Or I shall set my bearers on you!"

"You would set your slaves on a free man in the streets?" I asked.

Her eyes flashed.

"Who are you?" I asked.

"That is none of your business!" she cried.

"It will surely be of interest to guardsmen," I said.

"Go away!" she said.

"They will wish to ascertain what person ordered slaves to attack a free man, an innocent fellow merely engaged in reporting a misdemeanor."

"Begone!" she cried.

"Besides," I said, "if I disembowel a couple of these fellows, how will you get home? I do not think that you would care to walk through the streets, perhaps soiling your slippers." The slippers were well worked, colorful and intricate with exquisite embroideries. Slave girls, on the other hand, commonly walk the streets barefoot, sometimes with something on an ankle, usually the left, a few loops of cord, an anklet, bangles, a tiny chain, such things.

"Also," I said, "what were you doing here, accosting a male slave?"

"Oh!" she cried, in anger.

"Do you not think guardsmen will be interested in that?" I asked.

"Beast!" she said.

"But then perhaps you are a slave girl," I said.

"Beast!" she said.

"Are you branded?" I asked.

"No!" she said.

"Why not?" I asked.

"Sleen! Sleen!" she said.

"Then I gather you are not branded," I said.

"No," she said. "I am not branded!"

"I see," I said. "Then you are an unbranded slave girl."

"Sleen!" she wept.

"There are doubtless many of those," I said.

"Sleen! Sleen!" she cried.

I reached to her veil, and tore it away, face-stripping her. She seized the veil in my hands but, as I held it, she could do nothing with it. Indeed, she could not, as she held the veil, even draw her hood more closely about her features. She looked at me in disbelief, in astonishment, in fury. Her features, though distorted by rage, were of interest. They were well formed, and exquisite. "You are very pretty, slave girl," I said.

She released the veil, cried out with misery, turned about in the palanquin, and threw herself down in it, covering her face with her hands, hiding it from me. Her head was now toward the foot of the palanquin, and her knees were drawn up. This well displayed her curves to me, even beneath the robes of concealment. "You apparently have an excellent figure," I said to her. "It would be interesting to see how it might look in a bit of slave silk."

"Take me home! Take me home!" she wept.

One of the free men with her, the one with whom I had earlier held converse, signaled to the bearers, and they lifted the palanquin. Soon it was on its way. He drew shut its curtains as it moved down the street. But I did not doubt but what he, too, before he drew shut the curtains, had formed some conjectures of his own on the lineaments within, and how they might appear if properly clad, in slave silk.

I glanced to the fellow kneeling there on the stones. "You may rise," I informed him.

He stood up.

"Kneel," I said to him, sharply, angrily.

Immediately, startled, he went again to his knees.

The two fellows with him started forward, but I warned them back with a look.

"Do you not know who that is?" asked one of them.

"A slave," I said. Then I turned to the slave. "Let us now try this again," I said. "You may rise."

"Yes, Master," he said. "Thank you, Master."

He then rose properly to his feet, humbly, permitted.

More than one person about gasped.

I think, as well, that this was not a familiar experience for the fellow.

The slave, of course, need not verbally respond to all such permissions, and such, but it is expected that his behavior will be in accord with the decorems of obedience.

"You may continue on your way," I said to the three of them, releasing them from the custody of my will.

"Come along," said one of the two fellows to the slave. The three of them then, together, lost little time in making their way down Aulus street. I noted that the fellow had not responded deferentially to the summons to come along, but then I did not think that that was my business. If the two fellows were disposed to treat the slave as though he might not be a slave, I did not think that that need be considered my concern. The interaction had not taken place with me, for example. Also, of course, I had upon occasion, though quite infrequently, to be sure, on this world, remarked an instance in which a slave had seemed to me at least minimally deficient in deferentiality to a master. In such instances, of course, one does not desire to usurp the prerogatives of the master, even if he is a weakling. One may always hope that he will eventually understand what must be done, and reach for the whip. Needless to say, all Gorean slave girls find themselves sooner or later, perhaps after a renaissance of manhood in the master, or a new sale, or some change of hands, kept under perfect discipline. It is the Gorean way. Only one can be master. The fellow did turn once, and look back at me, as though puzzled, and then, with the others, he continued on his way. I suspect he had not been reminded that he was a slave for a very long time. Perhaps Appanius had let that slip his mind. In my opinion, that would have been a mistake. At any rate I had seen no reason for doing so, particularly in the light of my plans. I did not think it would take them long to reach Tarn Court. Also, as I had cut short the fellow's conversation with the free woman in the palanquin, I had surely saved them a little time. I neither expected, nor wished, thanks for this, however. Briefly I recollected the free woman in the palanquin. Surely I had given her something to think about. Perhaps she was now curious as to what she might look like on a sales block, or what the nature of the bids might be.

As Lavinia was cognizant of the usual itinerary of the fellow from the theater to the house of Appanius and she had gone about to Tarn Court, on the way, and was presumably stationed there, to the east, under the bowers, I took a similar route, rapidly striding. In this fashion I would appear to be moving in the direction opposite the fellow and his two companions. I could then renew my contact with them from a distance, discreetly observing the encounter between that party and a girl seemingly in the garments of the state slave. In a few Ehn I was on Tarn Court, following the fellow and his companions. Once off Aulus, and perhaps being confident that they were not followed, they had slowed their pace. Tarn Court is a wide street, or, at least, wide for a city street on Gor. Several blocks east of Aulus, before noon, it is the location of a vegetable and fruit market. In the areas of the market, stretching almost from the north to the south side of the street, the street is shaded by a large number of vine-covered trellises, creating bowers, which provide protection for the produce and, later in the day, shade for pedestrians. Many Gorean streets, incidentally, are almost always in shade because of their narrowness and the encompassing buildings. A result of this is that one is not always clear as to the position of the sun and, accordingly, it is easy to lose one's orientation, even as to the time of day. The fact that not all Gorean streets have generally accepted or marked names can add to the confusion. To one who knows the area this presents little difficulty but to a stranger, or one unfamiliar with the area, it can be extremely confusing. Interestingly enough many Gorean municipalities intentionally resist the attempt to impose some form of rational order on this seeming chaos. This is not simply because of the Gorean's typical reverence for tradition but because it is thought to have some military advantage, as well. For example, portions of invading forces have upon several occasions, in one city or another, literally become lost in the city, with the result that they have been unable to rally, rendezvous, group and attain objectives. Cases have been reported where an enemy force has literally withdrawn from a city and some of its components have remained in the city, wandering about for a day or two, out of communication with the main forces. Needless to say, the military situation of such isolated contingents is an often unenviable one. More than one such group has been set upon and destroyed. To be sure, invaders usually supply themselves with fellows who are familiar with the city. It is illegal in many cities, incidentally, to take maps of the city out of the city. More than one fellow, too, has put himself in the quarries or on the bench of a galley for having been caught with such a map in his possession.

I was about fifty yards behind the group of three fellows, who were sauntering east on Tarn Court. For a long time I did not detect the presence of Lavinia. Then, some seventy yards or so ahead, and to the right, near a wall, before the eastern termination of the trellised area where the morning market is held, from a patchwork of lights and shadows, I picked her out. She, after entering from the south, from a side street, had apparently hurried on ahead. In this fashion she could make certain that she would not miss the group when it passed. She would also have time to prepare herself, and regain her composure. She had positioned herself on her knees, at a wall, near a slave ring. This was fully appropriate. Too, it added to the effect which her appearance must have on all males who saw her, her beauty, her collar and a slave ring. The ring was about level with her neck. To such rings, of course, a master may fasten or chain a girl while he busies himself elsewhere. I was pleased that she had had the intelligence not to act as though she had been put at the ring "bound by the master's will" because her leaving the ring might then have elicited astonishment or comment. There are many ways of putting a girl at the ring "bound by the master's will." One typical way is to stand her at the ring and have her place her right hand behind her back through the ring and grasp her left wrist. Another typical way is to kneel her at the ring and have her put her right hand through the ring, grasping her left wrist. One of the simplest and perhaps the most typical way of "binding by the master's will" is simply to have the girl grasp her left wrist with her right hand behind her back. Needless to say whatever amusement, pleasure or convenience this may afford a master it can be exquisitely frustrating to a slave to strive desperately and in terror to maintain this position while, say, being subjected to various attentions typical of the mastery. Most masters, in such a situation, would simply bind the girl, tying or braceleting her hands behind her back. In this fashion she knows her struggles will be unavailing, that she is helpless and cannot escape. She may then without fear or hesitation open herself completely to the joy of her subjugation, to the rapture of her conquest, to the bliss of her surrender.

When the party of three, the handsome fellow, and his two companions, were within a few yards of her, she rose lightly, gracefully, to her feet. They noted this movement, of course, and doubtless had observed her earlier. Certainly it is difficult for a kneeling slave, and one of such beauty, as they could now detect, even given the mixtures of light and shadow beneath the trellises, to be ignored. Their eyes met, and then she lowered her head, humbly. This contact, however, brief as it was, gave them to halt. In it she had conveyed to them that she had been waiting for them, and would approach. The two fellows with the handsome slave looked to one another. This girl who had been waiting was a state slave. Could she bear a message from someone in the Central Cylinder, say, from one of the many free women in the entourage of even the Ubara? Too, they may have remembered her from the theater, and from Aulus. Certainly the slave had bided her time discreetly. Could something sensitive be afoot? There were few about. The street was muchly deserted. The market was closed. The day was hot, even under the trellises. I lounged against a wall, several yards away, near a doorway. I did not think it would be easy to pick me out, even if one were interested in doing so, given the variegated patterns of light and shade, and the dangling vines. Too, between us, here and there, were some of the posts supporting the overhead trelliswork. The fellow said something to them. The two men immediately drew back. That interested me. It seemed that no official note was to be taken of this encounter, or, at least, that its content was to be accorded the delicacy of privity, at least in theory.

I watched the girl approach the slave.

She approached with rapid, small steps, her head down, her hands to the side, slightly extended, palms back. When near him she lifted her head slightly, hardly daring to meet his eyes, and then she knelt before him, as before a master, doing obeisance onto him, her head down to the stones before his golden sandals, the palms of her hands, too, on the stones. This was not inappropriate, of course, even though both were slaves, as she was female and he male, and the obeisance thus, manifested in this instance in the persons of slaves, might be regarded simply as that of that of femaleness to maleness. The perfect obeisance, of course, the natural obeisance, that most in accord with nature, and most perfectly manifesting it, is that of the female slave to the free male. What surprised me about Lavinia's obeisance was that it seemed so perfectly to exemplify that of the female slave, literally that of the slave to her master, though it was performed before a male who was not only not her master, but himself a slave. That I found of interest. Did she think he owned her? Too, she did not have to perform such an obeisance in this context. It was not, for example, required by custom or prescribed by ordinance. Too, as he did not own her nor expect to encounter her he would not have had an opportunity to specify certain details of her relationship with him, for example, his preferences with respect to her manner of presenting herself before him, the nature of the rituals of deference or submission to be expected of her, and such. He was, after all, only a slave, too. Indeed, sometimes female slaves are quite cruel to male slaves, taunting or mocking them, and such. Let the female slave hope, in such a case, that she does not find herself braceleted and put to him in his cell, a whip tied about her neck. In such a case he is as master to her.

Lavinia looked up at him, tears in her eyes. He then, I think, from his reaction, clearly recognized her, well recollecting her from the capture room in the Metellan district, as one who was once a free female, whom he, as a seduction slave, had entrapped for his master, Appanius. He seemed stunned. I did not know if this were merely his surprise at seeing her here, again, from so long ago, so unexpectedly, she now in her collar, or if the startled response to her might be more the result of recognizing the incredible transformation which had taken place in her, that the mere free woman he had entrapped had now become, in her bondage, so astoundingly fascinating and beautiful. Perhaps it was both. Lavinia then, seemingly overcome, trembling, put herself to her belly before him, her lips and hair over his sandals, and beggingly, timidly, as though she feared she might be struck or kicked, began to kiss and lick his feet. I myself, I am sure, was little less startled than the fellow to whom these attentions were addressed. I had expected Lavinia to kneel before him and give him the message, little more. Indeed, I was not certain that she would have been permitted to do even this. I had thought it possible that she might be kicked back or cuffed away from him, if not by him, then by the fellows with him. She was, after all, a slave. If this sort of thing occurred, I would not be likely to interfere, of course, for that might reveal, or suggest, my connection with her, a relationship which I was eager, at this point, to conceal. I did not anticipate, of course, that she would be subjected to much more abuse than is natural to, or fitting for, a female slave. I was prepared, of course, to interfere if it seemed likely she might be in danger of disfigurement or serious injury. After all, she was not without value in a market, and one would not wish anything to happen to her which might lower her price.

She slowly moved to her knees again, her head down, licking and kissing, and then, her knees under her, she began to raise her ministrations to his shins and calves. She looked up at him, again. It seemed he could not move, so stunned, so startled, he was. Tears were in her eyes. Then she put her hands on his legs, and began to kiss him about the knees, and then above the knees. She now, kneeling before him, close to him, had her arms lovingly about his legs, her head down, shaking as though with sobs. She then looked up at him again. It seemed there was no other place that she would rather be. She then, again, lowered her head, and was kissing and licking delicately at the sides of his legs. To serve him and give him pleasure seemed as though it might be her desire, her happiness, her meaning and destiny in life. Did she think she was his slave? Again she looked up, this time pleadingly. I saw the two fellows in the background exchange alarmed glances. Was the handsome fellow in some sort of danger? Were there risks involved which might be clear to them, if not to others? She then put her head to the side, brushing up the purple tunic with the side of her head, kissing and licking at his thigh beneath the tunic. At this point one of the fellows rushed forward with an angry cry and seized her by the hair. "Lewd slave!" he cried. He hurled her, she crying out with pain, to her side on the stones of the street. He then rushed to her and she curled up, making herself small, and kicked her, twice, to which blows she reacted. She was then on her right thigh, and the palms of her hands, half sitting, half lying, on the street. She looked at them. The handsome fellow had not moved. He stayed where he was, as though rooted to the spot. "Away, lewd slave!" snarled one of the men with the fellow. "Begone!" said the other.

At this point Lavinia swiftly knelt, her knees in proper position, that of the female slave who is used also for the pleasure of men, reached to her tunic, and from within it, from where she had concealed it, from where it rested, at her bosom, withdrew the note which she then held, her arm extended, to the handsome fellow. One of the other two strode forward to seize the note but Lavinia drew it back, clutched in her tiny fist, held it to her body, and shook her head vigorously, negatively. This note, it seemed, was to be delivered to the slave alone. The fellow reached for it again and she put down her head to the stones, rather as in common obeisance or in kneeling to the whip, holding the note beneath her. "No, Master!" she said. "Forgive me, Master!"

"Slut!" he cried, and kicked her, again.

"Hold," said his fellow. "You are under orders?" he asked the slave.

"Yes, Master!" said the girl. "The note may be given to one, and one alone!"

"Very well," said the second fellow.

Lavinia then, gratefully, rose to her feet, and went to kneel before the slave. How well she knelt before him! How well she looked at his feet, though he were only a slave. She then lifted the note to him, her head down between her extended arms, holding the note in both hands, proffering it to him, much as in the manner in which a slave offers wine, and herself, to a master. The fellow gasped, and seemed shaken by this, the sight of the beauty so before him. I almost feared he might fall, so beautiful she was. Never I suspect had he had a woman so before him. In that instance I think he may have first begun to sense the glories, the exultancies, the fittingnesses, the perfections and powers of the mastery. I watched Lavinia surrender the note to him. It was almost as though it were her own note, offered pleadingly to him on her own behalf, and not putatively the note of another, in whose transit and delivery she was merely humble courier. To be sure, she had written the note herself. I was much puzzled by her behavior. I was also much impressed by it. I had never hitherto realized she was that beautiful.

"You have delivered your note, slut!" said one of the men, angrily. "Now, be off with you!"

"Yes, Master!" she said.

He drew back his hand, angrily, as though contemplating giving her a cuff.

"Yes, Master!" she said, and scrambled to her feet, not at all gracefully, in her haste, and raced past me, going west on Tarn Court. Clearly she would not have relished further attentions from the fellow. Already she was a bruised, thrice-kicked slave. I do not think that he intended striking her that time, incidentally, but was only threatening to do so. The threat, however, had been sufficient to speed her on her way, and had she not leaped up and departed with suitable dispatch I did not doubt but what her lovely face in an instant, flashing and burning scarlet, might have suffered the sting, and perhaps more than once, of that ready, harsh masculine hand.

"She is pretty," said one of the fellows, he who had questioned her, looking after her.

"But she is only a female," said the other, he who had threatened her.

"And a slave," said he who had questioned her.

"Yet they are the prettiest, and best," said he who had threatened her.

"Yes," said he who had questioned her. "There is no comparison."

The handsome slave stood in the street, under the trellises, in the light and shade, looking after the slave, wonderingly. In his hand, neglected, was the note. It seemed he could not take his eyes off the retreating figure of Lavinia. Could it be that he found her of interest, and in the most profoundly sexual way in which a man may find a woman of interest, of slave interest? I had not counted on that. I trusted that this would not disrupt my plans.

"Read the note," ordered one of the fellows.

Absently, almost as though not aware of his surroundings, except for the now tiny figure of the slave, hurrying away, he opened the note. He could, apparently, read. I had counted on that. He was a high slave. Too, it would have been difficult for him, I supposed, as he was a well-known actor, to have learned parts without being able to read. To be sure, some actors do, having the parts read to them, and they memorizing them from the hearing of the lines. This is particularly the case with women, as most parts of women on the Gorean stage, other than those in high theater, which tend to be acted by boys or men, are acted by female slaves, many of whom cannot read. Also, of course, as is well known, singers, scalds in the north, and such, transmit even epics orally. Because there are many Goreans who cannot read, many stores, shops, and such, will utilize various signs and devices to identify their place of business. For example, a large, wooden image of a paga goblet may hang outside a tavern, a representation of a hammer and anvil outside a metal-worker's shop, one of a needle and thread outside a cloth-worker's shop, and so on. I have known extremely intelligent men on Gor, incidentally, who could not read. Illiteracy, or, more kindly, an inability to read and write, is not taken on Gor as a mark of stupidity. These things tend rather, in many cases, to be associated with the caste structure and cultural traditions. Some warriors, as I have indicated earlier, seem to feel it is somewhat undignified for them to know how to read, or, at least, how to read well, perhaps because that sort of thing is more in the line of, say, the scribes. One hires a warrior for one thing, one hires a scribe for another. One does not expect a scribe to know the sword. Why, then, should one expect the warrior to know the pen? An excellent example of this sort of thing is the caste of musicians which has, as a whole, resisted many attempts to develop and standardize a musical notation. Songs and melodies tend to be handed down within the caste, from one generation to another. If something is worth playing, it is worth remembering, they say. On the other hand, I suspect that they fear too broad a dissemination of the caste knowledge. Physicians, interestingly, perhaps for a similar reason, tend to keep records in archaic Gorean, which is incomprehensible to most Goreans. Many craftsmen, incidentally, keep such things as formulas for certain kinds of glass and alloys, and manufacturing processes, generally, in cipher. Merchant law has been unsuccessful, as yet, in introducing such things as patents and copyrights on Gor. Such things do exist in municipal law on Gor but the jurisdictions involved are, of course, local.

"What does it say?" asked the fellow.

The slave clutched it to him. "It is private," he said, "and, I fear, personal."

"Let me see," said one of the fellows.

"Better that only I and Appanius see this," he said. He seemed white-faced, shaken.

"Very well," said the fellow who had spoken, stepping back. He had judged from the slave's response, it seemed, that the matter was not one for just anyone to press.

"Is it important?" asked the other fellow.

"I am afraid," said the slave.

"Let us return to the house," said the first fellow.

They then again took their way east on Tarn Court and, in a bit, once beyond the trelliswork, went to the right side of the street, which now, given the lateness of the afternoon sun, was the shady side. Normally Goreans keep to the left sides of streets and roads, as is proper, given that most men are right-handed. In this fashion the sword arm is on the side of the stranger. A similar, interesting historical detail, though not particularly pertinent to Gor, as most Gorean garments lack buttons, is that, on Earth, men's shirts, jackets, coats, and such, have the buttons on the right side, so that the opening of the garment is held down, and to the right. This is because the sheath of the knife or sword is, by right-handed men, commonly worn on the left, faciliating the across-the-body draw to the right. In this arrangement of the garment's fastenings, thusly, the hand, or sleeve, or guard of the weapon, will not be caught or impeded in its passage to the ready position. A similar provision does occur, incidentally, in various Gorean garments, having to do with pins, brooches and such. Also the male tunic of the wraparound variety has its overlap to the right, presumably for a similar reason. Warriors, in situations of danger, commonly carry the scabbard over the left shoulder. The scabbard is held with the left hand and the draw takes place with the right. The scabbard and strap is then discarded, to be recovered, if practical, later. Obviously the scabbard attached to a belt is not only an encumbrance but it is something which someone else might seize, cling to, and perhaps use to his advantage.

I watched them withdraw. I was not even certain that the slave would show the note to Appanius. On the other hand, since he had been witnessed in receiving it, which I had not known would happen, it seemed highly likely he would do so. My plans, as I had laid them, of course, did not require that the note be seen by Appanius. Appanius did, of course, figure significantly in my plans. The note did not, as far as Appanius was concerned. It could do its work with or without his knowledge.

I now went west on Tarn Court.

In a few Ehn I had come to the rendezvous point, on Varick, west of Aulus, which I had arranged with Lavinia. I waited there, near some doorways. She would not be loitering in the vicinity, of course, as that would attract attention. She would, rather, pass this point at certain intervals, in one direction or another. She may have passed it once or twice already. I would then, in the concealment of one of the doorways, put her in the small cloak she had worn before, now folded in my wallet, and we would then make our way home.

I observed her approaching.

How beautiful she had been, how fetching she was now.

"Master," she said.

"In here," I said, gesturing to the doorway.

She stepped within the sheltered area and I took her by the upper arms and turned her about, and thrust her back, sharply, against the wall, to the right.

"Master?" she said.

I looked down into her eyes. I held her by the upper arms, facing me, slave close. It is not unpleasant to hold a woman thusly. There were the tracks of tears, some only half dried, on her cheeks. She had thus wept even after leaving Tarn Court, probably while hurrying along.

"You are fortunate that you were not cuffed," I said.

"Yes, Master," she said.

"You are not unattractive," I said.

"Thank you, Master," she said.

I stepped back a little, not releasing my hold, and looked down at her.

"Even in such garments," I said.

"Thank you, Master," she said.

The recent garments prescribed for state slaves, of course, as such things went, were quite modest. They had their supposed role to play, doubtless, in the attempt on the part of Cos to depress the sexual vitality of the males of Ar, to devirilize them and make them easier to manage. That program, of course, as I have indicated, was unsuccessful. That the female is a slave is far more important than her garmenture, pleasant as that may be, dressing her in one manner or another for your pleasure, for example. That the female is a slave can double or treble, or more, the sexual interest and vitality of the male. It also has a considerable effect, an astounding effect, on the sexuality of the enslaved female, as well. The reasons for this have to do with the order of nature.

"Is Master angry with me?" she said.

"Stand back against the wall," I said. "Put the palms of your hands back, against the wall. Hold them there. Do not move."

"Yes, Master," she said.

I touched her.

"Ohh," she said, trying not to move.

"You are still hot," I said.

"Forgive me, Master," she said.

"No forgiveness is necessary," I said. "Being hot is commendable in a female slave. Indeed, she may be whipped if she is not."

"Yes, Master," she said, swallowing hard.

"And recently," I said, "if I am not mistaken, you were steaming, and oiled."

"Do not be angry, Master," she begged.

How exciting she had been on Tarn Court! How beautiful she had been on Tarn Court! I had been tempted to rush forth and seize her, putting her to my pleasure, I owning her. I had not, of course, done so. That would surely have interfered with my plans.

"Do not be angry with me, Master!" she begged.

"To whom do you belong?" I asked.

"To you, Master!" she said.

"And to whom else?" I asked.

"To no one else!" she said.

I regarded her.

"The slave hopes that her master is not displeased with her," she said.

I then took her once more by the upper arms and drew her, again, close to me. I held her in this fashion for a few Ihn, and then she made a tiny noise, and turned her head to the side, to her right.

"You feel my closeness?" I asked.

"Yes, my master," she whispered.

"And you grow excited," I said.

She looked up at me. "Yes, Master," she said.

"And you cannot help yourself?" I said.

"No, Master," she said, looking away.

"And I could be any man?" I asked.

"Yes, Master," she said.

"But I am your master," I said.

"Yes, my master," she said.

"You are a female slave," I said.

"Forgive me, Master," she said.

"I effect nothing critical," I said. "Your sexuality has been taken away from you, and out of your control."

"Yes, Master," she whispered, frightened.

"Do not be troubled," I said. "It is appropriate that a female slave be sexually alive, vital and responsive."

"Yes, Master," she said.

"Even required," I said.

"Yes, Master," she said.

"You would not wish to be whipped for insufficient heat, would you?"

"No, Master!" she said.

"Think no more about it then," I said. "Surrender, rather, as you now must, and wish to do, to your deepest needs and desires, to your most profound and helpless passions, to those truths hitherto concealed in the most secret recesses of your belly."

"Take me somewhere, Master!" she begged. "Take me somewhere!"

"You are somewhere," I informed her.

She looked wildly at me, and I then, by the upper arms, lifted her up, against the wall.

She looked down at me. "Master!" she begged.

I kept her to the wall with my body, and, in an Ihn or two, got my hands to her waist, lifting her up. She put her arms about my neck, sobbing. "Oh, yes, Master!" she breathed. "I yield me, as a slave, your slave!"

For an Ehn or two I held her.

"Aiiii," I breathed, gasping.

"I am yours," she whispered, "your slave!"

"Yes," I said. "Yes, you are."

Shortly thereafter I became aware of a presence behind me. I I turned. There was a guardsman there, a regular, not an auxiliary. I had never seen him before. He did not seem angry. I lifted Lavinia upward. "Ai!" I said, softly. I then put her to her feet in the doorway. She kissed at my arm, and kept her arms about me. Surely she was aware of the observer, as well. "Do you not know enough to kneel in the presence of a free man?" I asked her. Quickly she removed her arms from my body, smoothed down her tunic, and knelt, properly, in the doorway.

"Does the whip master know where you are?" asked the guardsman of Lavinia.

"No, Master," she said.

"You are pretty," he said.

"Thank you, Master," she said.

"These state sluts are all the same," said the guardsman.

"Oh?" I said.

"I liked it better when they were belled," he said.

"That was nice," I said.

"It made it easier to keep track of them, in alleys, in doorways, and such."

"Doubtless," I granted.

He looked at Lavinia, who lowered her head.

"I suspect it is lonely for them, in their chains, at night," he said.

"I suspect so," I said.

"She has duties," he said. "Do not stay here long."

"We shall be gone in a moment," I said.

He then turned about and went south on Varick.

Lavinia was trembling.

I had her rise and put the short cloak about her. Then, on a thought, as it pleased me, I had her adjust the hem of the garment she wore so that it was slave short. I then, too, adjusted the cloak so that it barely covered the raised hem of the garment. She would hold the cloak high, bunched, about her neck, to cover the collar. In this fashion it was concealed that she wore a garment resembling that of a state slave and her legs, quite contrary to the intent of the statelength garment, were extensively and delightfully bared.

"I delivered the message," said Lavinia to me.

"I know," I said.

"You saw?" she asked.

"Yes," I said.

She looked down.

"Do not be afraid," I said.

"I could not help myself," she whispered.

"I effect nothing critical," I said.

She looked at me.

"You are a female slave," I said.

"Yes, Master," she said, wonderingly. "That is it. I am a female slave. I have now become a female slave."

"Do you object?" I asked.

"No, Master," she said. "I love it!"

"You did your work well, excellently," I said. "I am very pleased."

"Thank you, Master!" she said.

I then looked out from the doorway. The guardsman was nowhere in sight. Indeed, the street was deserted.

"We will now return to the *insula*," I said.

"Shall I heel my master?" she asked.

"No," I said. "Precede me."

"Yes, Master," she smiled.

23 A Message Is To Be Delivered.

"The dung of tharlarion be smeared upon the Home Stone of Ar's Station!" cried the portly fellow. "Let it be spattered with the spew of urts!" He seized up the Home Stone from the plank on which it sat, the plank resting on two inverted wastes vats, of the sort used in *insulae*, in the park of the Center Cylinder, within which lies the Central Cylinder. "Not even jards of stone would pick the bones of this loathesome rock!" cried the fellow. There was laughter at this by the guards about, and several other folks, too, outside the roped-off enclosure, within which was the Home Stone on its mock pedestal. Indeed, several fellows, expecting some sort of show, had hurried to stand outside the rope, to watch. The guards, too, it seemed, remembered this fellow, and egged him on with their cries. There was a line, as well, behind the fellow, awaiting its turn to enter the roped-off circle, and, one by one, express their contempt for the "Traitress of the North" as Ar's Station was now referred to on the boards.

"Surely I should kill him!" hissed Marcus to me.

"You are under no obligation to do so," I assured him, irritatedly.

"Honor deems it necessary," said Marcus, grimly, his hand going to the hilt of his sword.

"Nonsense!" I said.

"Yes!" he hissed.

"Not at all!" I insisted.

I was now alarmed. When Goreans get the idea that honor is involved they suddenly become quite difficult to deal with. Moreover, Marcus, an agile fellow, could make it over the rope and get to the vicinity of the Home Stone in something like one or two jumps.

"Certainly!" he said.

"Shhh!" said a fellow, turning about. "I wish to hear this!"

I hooked my right hand in the back of Marcus' knife belt. This made it difficult for him to move forward, let along get the elevation necessary for leaping over the rope.

"That was a nice blow," said a fellow nearby, turning to me, "the concept of a stone jard and likening the Home Stone to unfit mineral carrion."

"Yes," I agreed. "Deft." The jard is a small scavenging bird. It commonly moves in flocks.

"Even brilliant," said the fellow.

"I agree," I said. Boots Tarsk-Bit was also, quite unwitting of the fact, playing with his life.

"That is you holding the back of my knife belt, I trust," said Marcus, not looking about.

"Yes," I said, "it is I."

He did not remove his eyes from Boots and the Home Stone. His gaze was intense, fixed and fierce.

"Would you mind unhanding it?" he asked.

"Not at all," I said, "but not just now."

"Not even the slime slugs of Anango would take shelter beneath this rock!" cried Boots Tarsk-Bit, waving the stone about in his two hands.

"Well done!" cried a fellow, congratulating Boots on this sally.

I felt Marcus tugging at the belt.

"I told you not to come," I said to Marcus. "Then I told you to stay back."

"But then I would not have been cognizant of these insults!" said Marcus.

"That is true," I admitted.

"Seremides," cried Boots, "tried to throw this miserable rock into a wastes vat. Do you know what happened? The wastes vat threw it back!"

There was laughter.

Marcus made a strange noise. Hitherto I had heard such sounds emanating only from larls and sleen.

I tightened my grip on his knife belt.

"Note these wastes vats," cried Boots, indicating the two inverted vats on which the plank rested, on which the Home Stone was kept. "They are taking no chances!"

There was more laughter, even applause, at this.

"That is enough," said Marcus, grimly.

I restrained him from lunging forward.

Boots turned his head to one side and sneezed.

"At least he missed the Home Stone," said Marcus.

"Do not be too sure," I said.

"There is a line," said the officer of the guard, his eyes filled with tears, so amused had he been. "I do think another should now have his turn."

There were some cries of protest, even of dismay, about the outside of the roped-off circle.

"No, no!" called Boots to the crowd, cheerfully, pacifying it. "It is true. The general is quite right! Let others have their chance, as well. Let me not monopolize time better distributed amongst the needs of my fellow citizens of free and glorious Ar! Let not this loathesome particle of disgusting gravel, fitting Home Stone for knaves and traitors, receive the impression that it might be I alone to whom the perfidy of its city is evident!"

He then moved about, bowing graciously, to one side or another, acknowledging applause and comments, smiling, waving, touching people here and there, and then took his way from the roped-off circle.

I removed my hand from Marcus' knife belt.

Marcus stood there. Now he seemed not angry, but shattered.

"Come away," I said.

"He failed," said Marcus to me.

"Come away," I said. I literally drew Marcus away from the rope. We then walked away, across the park and thence across the Avenue of the Central Cylinder.

Another fellow was now within the circle. He was spitting, and crying out insults.

"We must go back, and try with blades," said Marcus, suddenly.

"No," I said. "We have been through that. That is not practical."

"Then he must try again, tomorrow!" said Marcus. "He must make a new attempt!"

"No," I said.

"No?" asked Marcus.

"No," I said.

"We must have the stone!" said Marcus. "I shall not leave Ar without it!"

"Concern yourself with the matter no longer," I said.

"I should have let him use magic," moaned Marcus.

"What?" I asked.

"In recommending that this be done by mere trickery," said Marcus, "we have lost the stone!"

"Oh?" I said.

"He could have done it by magic," said Marcus, angrily. "And it was I who discouraged him from doing so!"

"Do not be too hard on yourself," I said.

"Surely you remember his recounting of his powers? Surely you remember him asking if I wished the Central Cylinder moved, if I wished the walls of Ar rebuilt overnight, if I wished a thousand tarns tamed in one afternoon!"

"Yes," I said. "I think I recall that."

"Yes," he said, miserably.

"Perhaps you should have asked for the Central Cylinder to be moved, instead," I said.

"Purloining the Home Stone would be child's play," he said, "compared to moving the Central Cylinder."

"Probably," I admitted.

"I would think it very likely," he said.

"You are probably right," I said. "But I am not an expert on such matters."

"It is all my fault," he said.

"Recall clearly now," I said. "He only asked you if you wished the Central Cylinder moved, and such things. Certainly it would have been easy enough for you to have wished for that, and such things."

"What?" he asked.

"He did not say he would move it or could move it."

"What?" asked Marcus.

"It is obviously one thing for him to find out if you wished to have the Central Cylinder moved, and quite another for him to move it."

"I do not understand," he said.
"It is not important," I said.
"It is all my fault that we do not have the stone," he said.
"How do you know we do not have it?" I asked.
"Do not jest," he said, angrily.
"I am serious," I said.
"I saw," he said. "I watched. I did not take my eyes from him. I watched with care. I watched with attention. I watched closely. I watched like a tarn. Nothing escaped me. Nothing, not even the tiniest of movements!"
"You did watch carefully," I said. I certainly had to give him that. He would have been watching more carefully than anyone there, unless perhaps myself. The others about, of course, would not have been watching as we were. They would not have known anything might be afoot. They would not have been suspecting anything, or looking for anything.
"Yes," he said.
"But perhaps you did not watch as carefully as you thought," I said.
"No," said Marcus. "I watched very carefully."
"But perhaps you were carefully watching in the wrong place at the wrong time," I said.
"I do not understand," he said.
"It is not important," I said.
"I must have the stone," said Marcus. "I shall not leave Ar without it!"
"I do not think you will have to," I said.
"I do not understand," he said.
"Perhaps we have the stone," I said.
"No," said Marcus. "Even from here I can see it, on its plank."
"You see some stone," I said.
"It is the Home Stone of Ar's Station," he said.
"Are you sure?" I asked.
"It has to be," he said. "I did not take my eyes off it the whole time.
"Perhaps you only think you did not take your eyes off it the whole time," I said.
"This is not a time for joking," he said.
"Sorry," I said.
"I am prepared to rush forth and seize the stone," he said. "Are you with me?"
"No," I said.
"Then I shall go alone," he said.
"I would not do so, if I were you," I said.

"Why not?" he asked.

"I really do not think it is necessary," I said.

"Why not?" he asked.

"I think we have it already," I said.

"What?" said Marcus.

"Just that," I said.

"Tal, gentlemen!" beamed Boots Tarsk-Bit, waddling up to us.

"I wanted to kill you," said Marcus to him.

"Any particular reason?" inquired Boots.

"For insulting the Home Stone of Ar's Station," said Marcus, grimly.

"I trust that your homicidal urges have now subsided," said Boots.

"Considerably," said Marcus. "Now I am depressed."

"You seem in good spirits," I said to Boots.

"What did you think of my performance?" he asked.

"I thought it marvelous, brilliant, unparalleled, incomparable!" I said.

"Only that?" he asked, hurt.

"Better than that, if possible," I assured him.

"Incomparably incomparable?" asked Boots.

"At least," I said.

"Yet I expect to exceed it," he said.

"You will try again, then?" asked Marcus, eagerly.

"Hold," I said. "How can you exceed the incomparably incomparable?"

"Easily," said Boots. "All that is required is that in each of one's performances one exceeds all one's previous performances, as well as those of everyone else. Thus I set new standards as I go along."

"And thus," I said, "in that fashion, it is possible for the incomparably incomparable to be outdone by the even more incomparably incomparable."

"That is it," said Boots.

"You will then try again?" asked Marcus, eagerly.

"Try what again?" asked Boots.

"To obtain the Home Stone of Ar's Station," said Marcus.

"What for?" asked Boots.

" 'What for?'?" asked Marcus.

"He already has it," I said.

Boots opened his cloak, briefly.

"It is the Home Stone?" whispered Marcus, reverently.

"I certainly hope so," said Boots.

"Do you not remember what he said in his *insula*," I asked

Marcus, "that it was nothing, that it would be no more than a *sneeze*?"

"Yes," said Marcus. That is a Gorean expression, incidentally, that something would be no more than a sneeze.

"A *sneeze*," I said. "A *sneeze*! Do you not grasp it, the the audacity of it, the humor of it?"

"No," said Marcus.

"That is when the wily rogue did it," I chuckled, "when he sneezed. We were watching him, not his hands, and that is when the substitution was made!"

"Quite wrong," said Boots.

"Oh?" I said.

"Yes," he said. "The substitution was made quite early in the performance, when I looked up at the clouds, speculating that they would be unlikely to bother raining on such an unworthy stone. You remember, in the jokes about why they had to take it indoors and make it a Home Stone, there being nothing else to do with it, because it was causing a drought in the countryside?"

"That is not true, of course," said Marcus.

"No, of course not," said Boots. "It is really a quite nice stone."

"And it could be rained upon like any other stone," said Marcus.

"Of course," agreed Boots.

"It comes from a very well-watered area, in the Vosk Basin," said Marcus.

"I am sure of it," said Boots.

"I remember," I said. "The substitution was made so early?" I asked.

"Yes," he said.

"Not when you sneezed?" I said.

"No," he said. "It is often my practice to make the substitution early, before the audience is really ready to watch for it. They are not yet that alert. Then one acts as though the substitution, if it is a magic show, is to take place later. One may even hint at times and ways of doing it, and have the audience crying out, thinking they have caught you, but then they are mystified when you show them that things are not as they thought. Also, if the substitution is made late, people may remember more clearly what you did later than earlier, and perhaps even recall, remembering things they did not pay attention to at the time, or deduce what must have occurred. Thus, you wish to give them a great deal to think about after the actual substitution. One does not just do the substitution and rush off. That might suggest the time at which, for example, and perhaps even the manner in which, the substitution had taken place. To be sure, this was not really a performance of that sort because no one, except you two, I suppose, was expecting anything of the sort. Indeed, it was, all things considered, little more than a brief, startling revelation of comedic brilliance, with a casual substitution thrown in. You will never know the temptation I felt to show both Home Stones afterwards, so that the audience might come to a fuller appreciation of the entire matter."

"It is good that you resisted that temptation," said Marcus.

"I think so," said Boots.

"You might have been roasted alive within the Ahn," said Marcus.

"In my thinking on the matter I did not neglect to take such considerations into my calculations," said Boots. "I permitted them to exert their influence, to add their weight, so to speak, to the scales."

"Know that we, for what it is worth, and all those of Ar's Station," said Marcus, "appreciate your brilliance!"

"Thank you," said Boots.

"We salute you!" he said

"Thank you," said Boots.

"You did not do it when you sneezed?" I asked.

"No," he said.

"Why then did you sneeze?" I asked.

"My nose itched," he said.

"Then," said Marcus, pleased, "if the substitution was made early you were not, most of the time, reviling the actual Home Stone of Ar's Station."

"True," said Boots.

"And I almost killed you for nothing," marveled Marcus.

Boots shuddered.

"You nose itched?" I asked.

"Yes," said Boots.

"I think," I said, "that you should prepare to leave the city as soon as possible."

"No," said Boots.

"Tonight," said Marcus.

"No," said Boots.

"Marcus is going to assist me tomorrow," I said. "But he will catch up with you, with a slave, Phoebe." I looked at Boots. "No?" I asked.

"No," said Boots. "Tomorrow night is better. If the substitution is discovered today, on the same day I was within the circle, and I left the city today, this might seem too improbable to be a mere coincidence. It seems likely that it might be conjectured I was in flight."

"He is right, of course," I said.

"Yes," said Marcus, in anguish.

Both Marcus and I, of course, now that the Home Stone was in our keeping, were anxious for it to be on its way north.

"Perhaps it is just as well," I said. "Then, if all goes well, Marcus and Phoebe can leave with you tomorrow."

" 'If all goes well'?" asked Boots.

"You need not assist me, of course," I said to Marcus.

"I will assist you," he said.

"My thanks," I said.

"What of you?" asked Boots.

"Do not concern yourself with me," I said.

"You are remaining in Ar?" asked Boots.

"For the time," I said.

"If the fraudulent Home Stone is a plausible duplicate," said Marcus, "it should not matter too much. The substitution might never be discovered."

"Ah," said Boots, beaming. "But the substitution will be discovered, and probably quite soon, doubtless within a few days at the most."

"What?" Marcus.

"You do not wish the duplicate to be a plausible duplicate," said Boots. "If it were, Seremides, and the Ubara, and their minions, could pretend it is still the Home Stone of Ar's Station. Indeed, they might challenge the authenticity of the stone which reaches Port Cos, should we make it that far."

Marcus regarded him, astonished.

"It must be clear to everyone," said Boots, "that the true Home Stone of Ar's Station has been snatched from under their very noses."

"Such things would surely weaken the grip of Cos in the city," I said. "Such things would surely give heart to Ar. Indeed, such things have toppled regimes."

"I have made certain that there are many small discrepancies between the original and the copy," said Boots, "but mostly they are such as would be noticed only by one quite familiar with the Home Stone of Ar's Station."

"And few of Ar's Station are in Ar," said Marcus, "and of those of Ar's Station who might be in Ar, presumably few would would approach their Home Stone under these circumstances, when expected to revile it."

"And if they did notice these differences," said Boots, "one might plausibly suppose they would not hasten to bring them to the attention of the guardsmen."

"I would think not," smiled Marcus.

"But then," I said, "if these differences are subtle, might not authenticity be claimed for the fraudulent stone?"

"I can guarantee that it will not be," said Boots.

"How can you guarantee that?" I asked.

"If you have noticed," said Boots, "and I certainly have, for I made it a point to note such things, and over a period of several days, almost no one *touches* the Home Stone. I was very unusual in picking it up and handling it. It is flat, and it lies flat on its board."

"Yes?" I said.

"So I took the liberty," he said, "in the fraudulent stone, of cutting a message into its under surface, and, indeed, of even coloring the lettering."

"What is the message?" I asked.

"It is simple," said Boots. "It says 'I am not the Home Stone of Ar's Station.' "

"That seems clear enough," I said.

"And I took the further liberty," said Boots, "of adding an additional remark."

"What was that?" I asked.

" 'Down with Cos,' " he said.

"Flee now," said Marcus, in dismay.

"But think," said Boots. "If you were in the guard, and you discovered that the stone was fraudulent, surely you would fear either that the stone had been stolen in your watch, or would be thought to have been stolen in your watch."

"Yes!" I said.

"Accordingly," said Boots. "It seems to me more likely that the guards would manage to overlook the matter, and turn over the stone to the next watch, as though nothing were amiss, thus letting the next watch, or the next, and so on, worry about the matter. Certainly it would be embarrassing, if not absolutely dangerous, to have the substitution discovered during, or at the end, of one's tour of duty."

"You are a clever fellow, Boots," I said.

"Also, the guards are mostly fellows of Ar," said Boots. "Thus I do not think they would take the same offence or manifest the same zeal in these matters as might be expected of Cosians."

"They might even relish the matter," I said.

"Possibly," said Boots. "On the other hand, I do not think

they, either, would be eager for the substitution to be discovered on their watch."

"No," I said. "I would not think so."

"Accordingly," said Boots. "I think we need not fear that the substitution will be too promptly discovered."

"Or, at any rate," I said, "too promptly reported."

"Precisely," smiled Boots.

"You will arrange your rendezvous tomorrow evening with Marcus?" I asked.

"Of course," said Boots.

I pressed a heavy purse into the hands of Boots Tarsk-Bit.

"The weight of this suggests a great many copper tarsks," said Boots, surprised.

"Count it later," I said. "Conceal it now."

"My robe does contain a few interior pockets," he said. The purse disappeared inside the robe.

"I shall not enter into the details of this," I said, "but in the north, last summer, in virtue of an unusual combination of circumstances, Marcus came into the possession of a large fortune, one hundred pieces of gold."

"One hundred?" asked Boots, startled.

"Yes," I said, rather pleased that I had, for once, managed to startle the great Boots Tarsk-Bit, or Renato, the Great, as he now called himself.

"But he gave me the hundred pieces of gold," I said, "for a slave."

Boots regarded Marcus, aghast.

"She is worth ten thousand, and more," said Marcus, defensively.

"It is not that he is really insane," I said. "There are special circumstances involved."

"Too," said Marcus, angrily, "I did not know at the time that she was a Cosian!"

"That does make a great deal of difference," said Boots.

"Else a copper tarsk or two might have been too much," said Marcus.

"Doubtless," said Boots.

"You see," I said, "there are special considerations here. You note the discrepancy between, say, ten thousand pieces of gold, or more, and one or two copper tarsks."

"She is not for sale, anyway, for any price," said Marcus.

"Though I am not of the scribes," said Boots, "I did note the discrepancy."

"And that is how I obtained one hundred pieces of gold in the north," I said.

"And you wish us to convey this paragon of beauty to the north?" asked Boots.

"You do not object, do you?" I asked.

"Certainly not," said Boots. "After all, that will give us something to do in leisure moments, fighting off armies from all directions, fending away clouds of mercenaries, battling bands of brigands, attempting to turn back innumerable waves of eager, lustful ruffians, and such."

"I do not understand," I said.

"I do," said Marcus, pleased.

"I agreed to transport a Home Stone to Port Cos," said Boots, "not to risk traveling with one of the most fabulously desirable and beautiful women on Gor in my train."

"She is certainly that," agreed Marcus. "You could always keep her in a box, or sack."

"I am certainly eager to see this slave," said Boots.

"Despite the convictions and the enthusiasms of Marcus in this matter," I said, "well warranted though they doubtless are, I should make clear to you that they might not be shared, at least to his extent, at first sight, by all casual observers."

"I suppose that is possible," said Marcus, reflectively, in a mood of uncommon charity.

"This is not to deny that the girl is an exquisite slave," I said, "and Marcus is training her very well."

"What would she sell for?" asked Boots, bluntly.

"In a common market," I asked, "with nothing special known about her?"

"Yes," he said.

"I would guess for something like two or two and a half silver tarsks," I said.

"She is quite lovely then," he said.

"Yes, but there are thousands upon thousands like her on Gor," I said, "and it is not like armies of tarnsmen would be launched to acquire her."

"I see," said Boots, relieved.

"What do you think Telitsia would sell for?" I asked.

"Probably about the same," he said.

"But you would not sell her?"

"No," smiled Boots. "She is not for sale.

"Then it is the same," I said.

"Not really," said Boots. "Telitsia makes an excellent Brigella, and she is excellent about one's feet and thighs. She is devoted, and loving, and it is hardly ever necessary to whip her now."

"It is seldom necessary to whip Phoebe either now," said Marcus.

"Yes, yes," I said. "I am sure they are both excellent slaves."

"I trust," said Boots, "that the purse I have received, which was unusually heavy, contains the equivalent of at least a gold piece."

"Surely you trust me," I said.

"I trust you," said Boots. "It is only that I am wary of your mathematics."

"Have no fear," I said. To be sure, there was more to what Boots was saying than might be evident at first sight. It was not that I had difficulty in adding and subtracting, of course, but rather that I was not always as knowledgeable as I might be about the relative values of various coins, of numerous cities, which, of course, depended on such things as compositions and weights, and exchange rates, which might fluctuate considerably. For example, if a city debases its coinage, openly or secretly, perhaps as an economy measure, to increase the amount of money in circulation, or there is a rumor to that effect, this will be reflected in the exchange rates. Many Gorean bankers, not only the fellows sitting on a rug in their booth on a street, their sleen about, but also those in the palaces and fortresses on the "Streets of Coins," work with scales. Too, sometimes coins are literally chopped into pieces. This is regularly done with copper tarsks, to produce, usually, the eight tarsk bits equivalent in most cities to the copper tarsk. Every year at the Sardar Fair there is a motion before the bankers, literally, the coin merchants, to introduce a standardization of coinage among the major cities. To date, however, this has not been accomplished. I did not feel it was really fair of Boots to call attention to my possible lack of expertise in these matters. I was not, after all, of the merchants, nor, among them, of the coin merchants.

"The purse contains no copper tarsks," I said.

"What?" said Boots.

"Of the hundred gold pieces we acquired in the north, we had only some ninety left," I said. "I am sorry. You must understand, however, we have had expenses, a long journey, that prices in Ar are high, particularly for decent food and rented lodging, that we have needed money for bribes, for example, to obtain information, and such, that we have given some away, and so on. I have put half of those, forty-five pieces of gold, in the purse. They are yours."

"I do not understand," said Boots.

"I have kept the other forty-five," I said, "because I may need them, tomorrow. I do not know."

"That is too much money," said Boots.

"Do not be concerned for us," I said. "We have other

moneys, as well, from donations received, so to speak, from a fellow or so here and there, usually met in remote areas in dark places, and from fees taken in service."

"We agreed on two pieces of gold," said Boots, "at most."

"So we now break our agreement," I said.

"You would do that?" he asked.

"We might," I said.

"Scoundrels," he said.

"Simply suppose that we are mad," said Marcus. "Just take them, and with them, our undying gratitude, and that of Ar's Station."

"I cannot take so much," said Boots.

"You are Boots Tarsk-Bit?" I asked.

"I think so," he said. "At least that is what I have suspected for years."

"Then take the money," I said.

"Give me a moment," he said. "Let me collect myself. Let me recall myself to myself. I did not expect this. Give me time. My greed has been taken unawares. It staggers. It reels. Such generosity would give pause to even the most robust avarice."

"We obtained the money with little effort," I said. "It is not as though a village of peasants had hoed suls for it, for a century, or anything."

"I am relieved to hear it," said Boots. "I had been much concerned with that."

"Indeed," I said, "it is, in a sense, purloined treachery money, from traitors in Ar."

"It is my duty to accept it?" asked Boots.

"Certainly your right," I said.

"Perhaps I might be persuaded to accept it," he said, "for the arts."

"Be persuaded then," I said, "for the arts."

"Done!" said he.

"Excellent," I said.

"The arts and I thank you," he said.

"You are welcome," I said, "all of you."

We clasped hands.

"I can double this overnight at the gaming tables," he said.

"But do not do so until after delivering the Home Stone to Port Cos," I said.

He looked at me, stricken.

"Yes," I said, sternly.

"Very well," he said.

We then again clasped hands. In a moment Boots had hurried off.

"The Home Stone must reach Port Cos," said Marcus.

"You can help to assure it," I said. "You will travel with them, as I once did, as a roustabout, leaving tomorrow evening."

"I am pleased," said Marcus, "that we managed to persuade him to accept the money."

"It was difficult," I said. "But we won out."

"Largely," said Marcus, "it was due to your persuasive powers."

"Come now," I said. "You were quite persuasive yourself."

"Do you think so?" he asked.

"Certainly," I said.

"I was afraid for a time he would refuse to accept the fortune we urged upon him."

"Yes," I agreed. "It was nip and tuck for a time."

"But that business about the arts," said Marcus. "That is what did it."

"Yes," I said. "That is his weak spot."

"What now?" he asked.

"I must arrange for a message to be delivered to Appanius," I said, "tomorrow morning."

24 Staffs and Chains

"You understand what to do?" I asked her.

"Yes, Master," said Lavinia, kneeling beside me. She trembled, slightly.

I looked down at her. She was now in a short cloak, held about her neck, and, under it, in a tiny, loose, beltless rep-cloth tunic, fastened only at the left shoulder. The cloak, held as it was, concealed her collar. She was now in the collar that read "RETURN ME TO TARL AT THE *INSULA* OF TORBON." She was thus now well identified as my slave. The tunic's fastening at her left shoulder was a disrobing loop. That was important. I wished her to be able to disrobe on an instant's notice.

"The timing of these events is extremely important," I said.

"Yes, Master," she whispered.

"If you do not do well," I said, "I will have you fed to sleen."

She looked at me, white-faced.

"I will," I said.

"I will do my best, Master," she said.

I had made certain, in my rehearsals, that she could remove both cloak and tunic expeditiously.

Marcus, sitting to one side, sharpening his sword, lifted his head.

"That is the fifth Ahn," he said.

I nodded. We could hear the bars, even at a distance of over a pasang.

We were in a room in the Metellan district. I had sealed the shutters, and blocked them, on the inside, so that no one might, from the outside, through the cracks, observe what occurred in the room. In the center of the room there was a large couch, a round couch, some seven or eight feet in diameter. It was well cushioned, and covered with furs, and was soft and inviting. At one point, in its side, there was a slave ring. We had set a small table near the couch, bearing a decanter of wine, with glasses, and a small, tasteful array of sweets. The room was lit with a small tharlarion-oil lamp. I had already tested the apparatus in the adjoining room. It was activated by a simple wooden lever, and the weights would do the rest. I had also brought along some other articles, which I thought might prove useful.

"You informed the slave," I said to Lavinia, "that the plans had been advanced, and that he was now to be here at half past the fifth Ahn?"

"Yes, Master," she said.

"He thinks that is the new time of the assignation?"

"Yes, Master," she said.

"And he has not had time to convey this information to his master, as far as you know."

"I should not think so, Master," she said.

"He will then presumably regard it as his work to keep the free woman, whoever she turns out to be, here until Appanius and the magistrates arrive."

"I would think so, Master," she said.

"Which arrival, as he understands it, will be in the neighborhood of a half past the sixth Ahn?"

"Yes, Master," she said.

"Good," I said. The original time of the assignation, conveyed to the slave, which he, in turn, would have conveyed to his master, was the seventh Ahn. Accordingly the master, and presumably two magistrates, who would act as official witnesses and be officers versed in certain matters, would wish to arrive early, presumably about half past the sixth Ahn, or, at any rate, at a decent interval before the seventh Ahn. The free woman might very well, of course, not appear precisely at the seventh Ahn. She might prefer to let her putative lover wait, perhaps torturing himself with anxieties and doubts as to her intent to appear at all. This is very different from a slave, of course. The slave must be instantly ready to serve the master, and at so little as a whistle, a gesture or a snapping of the fingers.

"But," I said, "I have sent a message to Appanius myself, an anonymous message, on which I think he will act. He should, then, if all goes according to my plans, not arrive at half past the sixth Ahn, as the slave expects, but shortly after the slave himself arrives, which should be shortly."

"I think," said Marcus, "we should consider withdrawing."

"True," I said.

Marcus put away his sharpening stone.

He wiped the blade on the hem of his tunic.

"Do you expect to use that?" I asked.

He sheathed the blade. "I do not know," he said.

"The slave is likely to enter through the main door?" I asked Lavinia.

"I do not know," she said.

"He was here when you arrived?"

"Yes," she smiled. "I made him wait."

"But you entered through that door?" I asked.

"Yes," she said. "That is the door by means of which I was entered into this room. Appanius, and the magistrates, and others, apparently had entered through the back, or some side entrance."

"There is such an entrance," I said. "It lets out into an alley, a little further down the street. One then comes back to the street between buildings."

"That is, I believe," she said, "the way I left the premises. To be sure, once out in the street I was almost instantly disoriented."

I nodded.

"I did not even know where I was," she said, "until I was unhooded, and found myself chained by the neck in a magistrate's cell."

"Good luck," I said to the girl.

Marcus preceded me. We would leave through the back. "Remember the sleen," I said.

"Yes, Master!" she said.

How marvelous she looked, slave, the collar on her neck!

In a moment or two Marcus and I were on the street, outside the room.

"There!" said Marcus.

"The hooded fellow, in the robe?" I said.

"That is our friend, I am sure!" said Marcus.

"It is his size, at any rate," I said. The golden sandals, too, suggested it was he for whom we were first waiting.

"He is going between the buildings," said Marcus. "He will use the side entrance."

"I trust that Lavinia will not be too disappointed," I said.

"Why should that be?" asked Marcus.

"Nothing," I said.

"He will think he has at least an Ahn alone with her," said Marcus.

"Even if he is not in the least interested in her," I said, "Lavinia knows what to do."

"Why should he not be interested in her?" asked Marcus. "She is a well-curved slave."

"It is just an apprehension," I said.

"You certainly went into it in great enough detail," said Marcus.

"It is important to be thorough," I said.

"I never saw a woman get undressed so fast," he said.

"It may have to be done between the sound of a footstep and the bursting open of a door," I said.

"I myself prefer a more graceful, sensuous disrobing on the part of a female slave," he said.

"I would generally agree," I said, "if there is time." It is a delight, of course, to have a slave disrobe before one, gracefully, sensuously, displaying herself, revealing her master's property to him. Women are excellent at this sort of thing. They seem to have an instinct, or a natural sense, for it. And I think that they are not always averse to noting the effects of their unveiling upon the master, to note how they, in this revelation of their beauty and loveliness, can drive him wild with desire. In such things I think a slave has great power. Yet, in the end, it is still she who is owned. In slave pens, incidentally, girls are trained to disrobe, and, indeed, robe gracefully. Slave girls are not permitted to shortchange their beauty. They must fulfill its promise. There is something to be said in favor of the swift disrobing in certain contexts, of course, aside from its more unusual employments, as in plans such as mine. For example, a master, whip in hand, may order a slave, usually a new slave, to disrobe instantly, and then robe, and then disrobe, and so on. This may be done fifteen or twenty times in a row. This is useful in teaching her that she is now a slave. It also, of course, gets her used to disrobing before her master. Another use is when the slave desires to surprise her master with her beauty, perhaps before begging use. She might then utilize a particular moment to disrobe, perhaps one in which he has merely turned away. When he turns back, she is naked. She then kneels before him.

"Ah!" said Marcus. "What a shame!"

"What is a shame?" I asked.

"The poor fellow will have almost no time with her," he said.

"Yes," I said. "Here, if I am not mistaken, comes Appanius, and he has men with him."

"You will approach him?" asked Marcus.

"Certainly," I said.

"Hold!" I said, angrily, stepping forth. "Are you Appanius, he of well-known house of Appanius?"

"Who are you?" said he, angrily.

"By my armband you see I have authority to stop you," I said, not pleasantly. Both Marcus and I, of course, as we usually did, wore our armbands, signifying our status as auxiliary guardsmen. A major advantage of this, of course, is that it entitled us to go abroad openly armed.

Appanius lifted his staff, angrily.

I took no note of the raised staff. I could, of course, at that point, have killed him. My codes permitted it.

"Tread softly, Appanius," warned one of his retainers. There were four such with him. They, too, carried staffs. Other than this, however, in accord with the weapons laws, they were not armed. Two also carried chains.

"You have been questioned," I reminded Appanius.

He lowered his staff, angrily. "Yes," he said, "I am Appanius, of that house, best known for his agricultural enterprises."

"Do you own a disobedient, wayward slave?" I asked.

"I do not understand," he said.

"I have a little slut named Lavinia," I said.

"Lavinia!" he cried, in fury.

"Recently purchased," I said.

"The lewd little baggage!" he said.

"A fellow, whom I gather from others is your slave," I said, "has apparently seduced her."

"Impossible!" he said.

"You know this Lavinia?" I asked.

"I am sure it is the one!" he said. "I should have sold her out of the city as a pot girl months ago!"

"They have apparently been seeing one another," I said. That was true enough, of course, as Lavinia, in the garment resembling that of a state slave, and in what seemed to be a state collar, had been in contact several times with the slave, carrying verbal messages, and arranging the details of the putative assignation of this morning. Too, of course, she had been similarly in contact with the Ubara, only in that role, of course, in a collar purporting to be that of the house of Appanius.

"I cannot believe that!" said Appanius, angrily.

"Why are you here?" I asked.

"You!" he cried. "It was you who sent me the message of this morning?"

"Yes," I said. "I have followed him. They meet somewhere around here. I am not sure where."

"If this is true," cried Appanius, "I know where!"

"Your slave should be disciplined," I said.

"It is your slave who should be disciplined!" he said. "Mine is innocent!"

"Mine is only a female slave," I said.

"Only a female slave! Only a female slave!" he exclaimed. "That is exactly it! She is a female slave! They are all the same. They all have hot little bellies and can't help themselves. They are always licking and kissing and begging! And that Lavinia is one of the worst! She is a seductrix, I tell you. They are all seductrices!"

"I have heard that it is your slave who is a seduction slave!" I said.

"Who has said that?" he cried.

"I have heard it said secretly in the city," I said.

"It is false!" he said. "False!"

"Nonetheless," I said, "it is your slave who is at fault."

"No," he said. "I know your Lavinia. It is she, the lewd little baggage, who is at fault!"

"She is only a female," I said.

"But a female slave!" he said. "Whip them and chain them, I say! Keep them in the kitchens and laundries, in the fields, put to labors as is fit for the little beasts! Keep them from honest men! Let honest men be protected!"

"At any rate," I said, "it seems they have been seeing one another."

"It cannot be!" he said.

"Your slave, it seems, has been carrying on a shameless affair with her."

"That cannot be," he said.

"I have seen him," I said. "He is a big, handsome fellow. Why could it not be?"

"He would not betray me!" he said.

"I do not understand," I said.

"I trust your little slut is on slave wine," he said.

"Of course," I said. "I have not chosen, at least as yet, to have her mated."

"You should keep her shackled," he said.

"To protect her from your slave?" I asked.

"Do you know who my slave is?" he asked.

"He is known in Ar?" I asked.

"Somewhat," said Appanius.

"I am not from Ar," I said.

"I gathered that," he said. "Were you from Ar you would know that a slave of my slave's quality could not be interested in the least in a meaningless little pot girl."

"You are sure of it?" I asked.

"Certainly," he said.

"Yet you have come here, with men," I said.

"That his innocence may be proved," he said.

"Is that why your men carry staffs and chains?" I asked.

"You are an insolent, surly fellow!" he cried.

"Beware, Appanius," said one of his retainers. "He is of the police."

"We could make a clear determination on this matter," I said, "if we could only locate them."

"You do not know where your slave is," he said, scornfully.

"How should I know where she is?" I asked.

"If you kept her at home in close chains, so she could hardly wriggle, and fastened to a ring, you would know," he said.

"And so, too," said I, "you would know the location of yours, if you had kept him in his cell!"

"It was your mistake," he said, "to let a slut like Lavinia off her chain!"

"What of you," I asked, "letting your fellow wander about Ar like a vulo cock?"

"My slave is innocent, honest and trustworthy!" he said.

"And that is why you have brought men, and staffs and chains?" I asked.

"Sleen!" cried Appanius.

"Caution, Appanius," said one of his retainers. He was not unaware, as apparently was his employer, of Marcus, behind them, his hand on his sword. Marcus, I conjectured, could probably cut through the neck vertebrae of two of them before they could break. Also he could probably apprehend at least one of them, assuming they started off in different directions, as would be in their best interest. I, on the other hand, might hope to catch up to the other one, after dropping Appanius where he stood. If I had had to wager on the matter I did not think any of them would escape. The staff, except in the hands of an expert, is not a weapon to put against the blade.

"At any rate," I said, "I trailed Lavinia to this area, and I saw your slave about, too, and then, somehow, it seemed they disappeared."

"You did not actually see them together?" he asked.

"No," I said.

"Then they are not together!" he said.

"I am sure they are together," I said.

"No!" he said.

"It seems both just disappeared," I said.

"Do you not think they might not be, separately, of course, in nearby buildings?" asked Appanius.

"How could that be?" I asked. "Slaves do not just walk into buildings without some business there. Too, folks do not just welcome strange slaves into their houses, greeting them and inviting them to share their kettles. And I would assume they had no money to bribe free persons for a room, for their clandestine rendezvous. Certainly Lavinia had no money."

"Have you counted your coins lately?" asked Appanius.

"Have you counted yours?" I asked.

"My slave has spending money," he said.

"Then they could be anywhere," I said, angrily.

"No," he said. "He is too well known."

"Where then?" I asked.

"There is only one place!" he said.

His retainers exchanged glances, and nodded.

"Where is that?" I asked. To be sure, we were within ten yards of it, though of its front entrance, not its side or back entrance.

"That is," said Appanius, "there is only one place where my slave might be. I do not know where your slave is. She, the baggage, the chit, the tart, the wench, the use girl, might be slutting about anywhere, clutching at someone in a doorway, writhing on a discarded mat, squirming in an alley behind garbage containers, moaning in a dark corridor, who knows?"

"I wager," said I, "that if we locate your slave we will also locate mine."

"I know where mine would be," said Appanius, defensively. "He has gone to a place where he may study his lines in privacy."

"His lines?" I asked.

"He is an actor," said Appanius.

"Well," I said, "if he is currently studying lines, I have little doubt that they are those of my Lavinia."

"Sleen!" said Appanius. The fellows with him shifted, restlessly. Two of them glanced back uneasily at Marcus, much as they might have at a larl behind them.

"I think they are together," I said.

"No!" said Appanius, "That could not be!"

I shrugged.

"Follow me!" he said. He started for the street entrance of the room.

I trusted that Lavinia would have time to throw off her cloak and get at the disrobing loop on her tunic before the door could be opened. She could then fling her arms about the slave, protesting her love, and such. I hoped she could manage to do this believably.

At the street entrance of the room, however, Appanius stopped. It seemed he was considering something. "Open it," I said, "if this is the place." I certainly did not want them sneaking about to the rear or side entrance and coming on the two slaves without warning. That would not give Lavinia time to disrobe. If they were found yards apart, fully clothed, engaged in exchanging comments on the state of the theater in Ar under Cos, or something, I might as well forget my plans. I strode to the door, and raised my fist, to pound on it, and then, an Ihn or two later, I would kick it in.

"No," whispered Appanius, seizing my hand. We then, I rather disgruntled, stepped back a little, a few feet from the door.

"Yes, Appanius," said one of his retainers. "It would be better to go around the back. In this fashion one may observe through the observation portals the front room."

"Observation portals?" I said.

"Thus," continued the retainer, softly, suavely, "one need not disturb him while he is reading his lines, as he undoubtedly is, and, more importantly, he will never know of our coming and going. Thus, he will never suspect that you might have been jealous, or ever suspected him of any unwonted treachery."

" 'Jealous'?" I asked. " 'Treachery'?"

"My thoughts, exactly," said Appanius. The retainer, I saw, was not only a retainer, but an able courtier. Those fellows have a talent for telling important people what they wish to hear. To be sure, such fellows have occasionally been responsible for the downfall of Ubars, and themselves, because of their desire to protect the throne from unwelcome truths. Serenity has reigned in more than one royal residence while a country's borders crumbled. I myself, however, was about ready to strike the fellow. I was plunged into despair.

"Come with me," said Appanius. "Move quietly."

"Of course," I said, through gritted teeth.

I glanced at Marcus.

He smiled.

This made me angry. Did he not realize that my plans might now, in a moment, be destroyed?

I turned back, to pound on the door, but he took me firmly by the arm and we followed Appanius and his retainers back down the street, until we turned left, and made our way through an opening between two buildings.

25 Bracelets and Shackles

"So," shrieked Appanius, "this is how you betray me!"

Lavinia had screamed when the net had descended, and the slave with her had cried out in dismay.

An instant or so before I had seen the face of Appanius grow livid with rage at the observation portal and he had seized at the wooden lever and thrown it, dropping the net with its weights over the couch. Almost at the same time, weeping with misery and rage, he had rushed into the front room, his staff raised, followed by his four retainers, all seemingly sharing their employer's wrath and indignation, as befitted such fellows. I myself had not had an opportunity, nor had Marcus, of utilizing the observation portals, of which there were two, the first of which had been commanded by Appanius, and the second by his chief retainer. I had not, accordingly, been able to see what was going on in the front room.

Almost instantly however I, Marcus behind me, had rushed to the front room.

There, clinging together, terrified, helpless, entrapped in the toils of the net, threatened by the staffs of Appanius and his retainers, were the slave and Lavinia.

"Treacherous, treacherous slave!" wept Appanius.

I saw the two slaves within the heavy toils of the net, the reticulated pattern of cords close about them. He kept his arms about her. Both were naked.

"Treacherous slave!" screamed Appanius.

Marcus looked at me, and grinned. He was not surprised at this. I, on the other hand, was. It had been my anticipation that Lavinia would have to do all this by herself, get her clothing off and cling to him, presumably by the door, he fully clothed, and hope to convince Appanius that their presence together was by mutual arrangement, and indicative of mutual interest and desire. On the other hand, I found her in the center of the room, on the couch itself, in his arms. Saving for being on a couch instead of on furs on the floor she might have been any alcove slut in a paga tavern. The short cloak and tunic had been discarded to the side. There was no sign that either had been hastily removed. The cloak had apparently been slipped off, and dropped behind her, to reveal her shoulders and tunic. The position of her tunic suggested she had dropped it, doubtless by means of the disrobing loop, about her ankles, and then stepped from it. I suspected she had then entered his arms, and that he had then, a little later, lifted her up and carried her to the couch.

"You have betrayed me!" wept Appanius.

Marcus looked at me, puzzled. I shrugged. If I had been wrong about one thing, it seemed to me only fair if Marcus might be wrong about another.

"Traitorous slave!" wept Appanius.

Lavinia's body was a mass of contradictory colorations. Apparently but moments before it had been red with excitement, love and yielding, and had then, in the sudden surprise and shame of her discovery, flushed scarlet, blushing literally from head to toe, and then, almost instantly later, in the tumult, had begun in terror to drain of color, she suddenly realizing that she was now a discovered slave, a vulnerable, caught girl, apprehended in a situation of great compromise by a man such as Appanius, her former master. Once before, as I understood it, for so little as timidly touching a certain slave she had been sent to the fields. Now she had been discovered naked in his arms.

"How could you have done this to me?" wailed Appanius.

Lavinia's nipples were still erected. They were very lovely.

"How could you do this to me?" begged Appanius.

The male slave did not respond to these questions.

I thought that Lavinia was exquisite, naked, collared, in the net. I had once told her she could make a rock sizzle. Surely that was true.

"How! How!" demanded Appanius.

Lavinia was very exciting in the net. I felt like pulling her out and using her myself.

"Surely it is not hard to understand," said Marcus. "She is very pretty."

I did not think that this was a judicious remark on his part, but then who am I to judge?

"Master, no, Master!" cried the male slave.

Appanius then, with a cry of rage, seizing his staff with both hands, struck down with it, smiting the male slave on the shoulder. He then, again and again, struck him, about the back and shoulders.

The female slave began to sob and it seemed she would try, within the net, to put her body between that of the male slave and the lashing staff, but he turned her, forcibly, away from the staff, holding himself over her, sheltering her. I found this of interest. Seven or eight times the slave received heavy blows from the staff. In a moment there were long, dark welts on his body. These were the only marks on his body. I gathered he might have been a pampered slave. Appanius then seemed to realize that he was sheltering the girl and, angered by this, he rushed about, to strike, too, at her, but, again, the fellow turned, in the net, sheltering her. "No!" he said. As Appanius, crying out again with rage, again attempted to circle about, so that he could strike the girl, the fellow became tangled in the net and could no longer protect her. "It is my fault!" he cried. "I am to blame!" he cried. "Do not strike her!" he begged. Appanius, then, in fury, jabbed at Lavinia, and she cried out, hurt. "No!" wept the fellow. "Do not hurt her!" Appanius drew back the staff again to thrust at Lavinia, but then I managed to get my hands on it, and held it back, away from the slaves. Appanius could not wrest it from my hands. He sobbed with frustration. His retainers neither used their staffs to punish the two slaves nor came to the assistance of their employer. I think this might have been because of their sensing the mood of Marcus, that he was more than ready to spill blood. Indeed, although they would not know this, it was even his plan to leave the city this evening. "You see," I said to Appanius, "I was right."

"She seduced him!" screamed Appanius.

"Nonsense," I said, though to be sure a candid observer might have admitted that there might be some sense to Appanius' asseveration.

"Appanius!" said the male slave.

"Do not dare speak my name to me," he wept, "slave!"

"Forgive me, Master!" said the slave.

I released the staff of Appanius, as the slave had dared to address the master by the master's name. To be sure, he might have become accustomed to doing so in the past but that was no excuse for permitting such boldness in the future. It was time the slave learned his condition, and was taken in hand.

Five times then the master struck the slave, and tears pressed from between the eyelids of the punished slave.

"Please, Master," wept Lavinia, "do not let him so strike him!"

"Did you not hear?" I asked. "He used the master's name to him. He is to be beaten as an errant slave."

"Master!" she wept.

"Be silent, slave girl," I said.

"Yes, Master," she wept.

Twice more the staff fell on the male slave, who now shuddered in the net.

Appanius, too, interestingly, was weeping. He then raised his staff against Lavinia.

I held the staff. "No," I said. "Her discipline is mine."

"I should have sent her out of the city on the first night I owned her," he said, "after having cut off her ears and nose."

Lavinia shuddered in the arms of the male slave.

"She is not yours," I said. "She is mine."

"Seductrix!" he said to her.

She made herself as small as she could, in the net.

"If you had listened carefully," I said, "you would have heard your slave admit his guilt in this matter. Clearly he turned the head of my little Lavinia."

"Look at her!" cried Appanius. "See the sleek, curvaceous little thing, naked, in her collar! Do you truly think she is guiltless in this matter?"

"Perhaps she is a little to blame, or, at any rate, her wanton, owned slave curves."

"Look there," said Appanius. "See the wine, the sweets, on the table, there, beside the couch! Do you doubt that this has been arranged?"

"That is an interesting point," I said.

"Slut!" said Appanius.

"Yes, Master!" she said.

"These things," he said, "or the moneys with which they were purchased, did they come from the resources of your master?"

"Yes, Master," whispered Lavinia.

"See!" said Appanius.

"Yes," I said.

"Forgive me, Master!" said Lavinia to me.

"Do you doubt her guilt now?" asked Appanius.

"No," I said.

"It is I who am wholly guilty," said the male slave.

"He spoke without permission," I said. "Also, in the light of your point, he has lied."

Appanius then, as Lavinia wept, struck the male slave twice

more with his staff for speaking without permission, and twice again, for lying.

He moaned in the net, beaten.

"Get him out of the net," said Appanius, angrily, "and chain him."

In a moment the male slave lay on his stomach on the furs, chained, hand and foot. A heavy collar, too, was locked on his neck. To this was attached a chain leash. He was then drawn from the couch and put on his knees, at the feet of his master. Lavinia, still under the net, knelt to one side on the couch. I went to her and extricated her from the net, dropping it to the side. She then, frightened, wide-eyed, knelt near me.

"Master?" she asked, looking up.

"Be silent," I said.

"My Milo, my Milo!" wept Appanius, looking down at the much-beaten slave. "The most beautiful slave in Ar! My beloved slave! My beloved Milo!"

"He has betrayed you," said one of the retainers.

"How could you do it?" asked Appanius. "Have I not been good to you? Have I not been kind? Have you wanted for anything? Have I not given you everything!"

The slave kept his head down. I think he was sick, and I did not much blame him. He had taken a fearful beating. His back and shoulders were covered with welts. I did not think that anything had been broken. I wondered if he had ever been beaten before. Perhaps not. I myself had doubtless been responsible for a few of those blows, but then they had been appropriately administered. His behavior, after all, had contained errors.

"He is an ungrateful slave," said another of the retainers.

"Send him to the fields," said one of the retainers.

"Sell him," said another.

"Make him an example to others," said the first retainer.

"We can find you a better, Appanius," said another.

"One even more beautiful," said one.

"And one with appropriate dispositions," said another.

"And he, too, if you wish, can be trained as an actor and performer," said another.

Marcus looked at me, puzzled. He did not really follow this conversation. I did not react to his look.

"What shall I do with him?" asked Appanius.

"Let all your slaves learn that they are your slaves," said one of the retainers.

"Speak clearly," said Appanius.

"Rid yourself of him," whispered the fellow.

"Yes," said another.

Appanius looked down at the chained slave.

I now had some understanding of the jealousy of the retainers for the slave. The slave had doubtless enjoyed too much power in the house, too much favor with the master. They were eager to bring him down.

"How?" asked Appanius.

"He has been unfaithful to you," said a retainer.

"He has made a fool of you, *with a woman*," said another.

This remark seemed to have its effect with Appanius.

"If this gets out, you will be a laughing stock in Ar," said another.

I doubted this. It is natural enough for a male slave to have an eye for female slaves, and it is not unusual for a female slave to occasionally, say, find herself taken advantage of by such a fellow. To be sure, it is much more dangerous for a male slave to accost a female slave than for a free man to do so. Unauthorized uses of female slaves are almost always by free men. They have little, or nothing, to fear, for the girls are only slaves. The masters, if they are concerned about such things, may put the girls in the iron belt, particularly if they are sending them on late errands, or into disreputable neighborhoods.

Appanius seemed to be becoming angry.

I looked at the slave. His hands were manacled closely behind his back. The chains on his ankles would hardly permit him to walk. The chain leash dangled to the floor, where it lay in a rough coil.

"So, Milo," said Appanius, "you would make of me a laughing stock?"

"No, Master," said the slave.

"One can well imagine him laughing about how he betrayed you *with a woman*," said one of the retainers.

"It will be the whip, and close chains for you, Milo!" said Appanius.

"No," said one of the retainers. "Let him serve as an example to all such slaves as he!"

"Yes!" said another retainer.

"Let it be the eels!" said another.

"Yes!" said the fourth.

"No!" screamed Lavinia. "No!" She leaped to her feet and ran to Milo, to kneel beside him, holding him, weeping. She turned then to Appanius. "No, no, please!" she wept. "No! Please!"

I took her by the hair and threw her back, away from Milo, to the floor, where she scrambled to her knees and, tears in her eyes, frantic, regarded us.

Many estates, particularly country estates, have pools in which fish are kept. Some of these pools contain voracious eels, of various sorts, river eels, black eels, the spotted eel, and such, which are Gorean delicacies. Needless to say a bound slave, cast into such a pool, will be eaten alive.

I looked closely at Appanius. He was white-faced.. As I had suspected, he was not enthusiastic about this proposal.

"It must be the eels," said the first retainer.

"Nothing less will expunge the blot upon your honor," said another.

"What blot?" said Appanius, suddenly, lightly.

The retainers regarded him, speechless.

"What is it to my honor," asked Appanius, "if I have been betrayed by an ungrateful, worthless slave? It is scarcely worth noting."

"Appanius!" said the first retainer.

"Do you wish to buy a slave?" asked Appanius of me, as though lightly. But I saw that he was desperate in this matter. Indeed, I was touched. His problem was a difficult one. He wanted to save both his honor and the life of the slave. As outraged as he might be, as angry, as terribly hurt as he was, even as sensitive of his honor as I supposed he might be, he was trying to save the slave. I was startled by this. Indeed, it seemed he might care for him, truly. That development I had not anticipated. I had thought that things would have worked out much more simply. I had expected him to be outraged with Milo and be ready, in effect, to kill him, at which point I was prepared to intervene, with a princely offer. If he were rational, and the offer was attractive enough, as it could be, as I had a fortune in gold with me, I could obtain the slave. That is the way I had anticipated things would proceed. If Appanius would not sell Milo, then I could simply keep Appanius, and the others, with the exception of Milo, bound and gagged somewhere, say, in the pantry in the back, and use Milo, still the slave of Appanius, to achieve my objective in a slightly different fashion, one then merely involving two steps rather than one. If he would not sell Milo, certainly he would be willing to sell another, one who might, for a time at least, be too dangerous to acknowledge, too dangerous to free, too dangerous to keep.

"Perhaps," I said.

"I have one for sale," said Appanius.

"No, Appanius!" said the first retainer.

"He is cheap," said Appanius, bitterly.

"How much?" I asked.

"He is the cheapest of the cheap," said Appanius, bitterly.

"Do not sell him, Appanius!" said the first retainer.

"He is the most valuable slave in all Ar!" said another.

"To me," said Appanius, "he is worth less than the lowest pot girl."

"How much do you want?" I asked, warily. I had some forty-five pieces of gold with me.

"He is worthless," said Appanius. "He should be cast away."

"Throw him to the eels, Appanius," whispered the first retainer.

"No," said Appanius, "rather let him know my estimate of his worth."

"How much do you want?" I asked.

"A tarsk bit," said Appanius.

The retainers cried out with horror. The slave looked up, startled, trembling. Lavinia gasped.

"A tarsk bit," repeated Appanius.

The slave wept in shame, and jerked at the manacles in frustration. But he could not free himself. Well were his hands confined behind him.

"I think I can afford that," I said.

"That is the most valuable slave in Ar!" said one of the retainers.

"No," said Appanius. "It is the most worthless slave in Ar."

I removed a tarsk bit from my wallet and gave it to Appanius.

"He is yours," said Appanius.

The tarsk bit is the smallest-denomination coin in common circulation in most Gorean cities.

"You do not mind filling out certain pertinent papers, do you?" I asked. I had brought some sets of such papers with me.

"Common slave papers?" he asked.

"Yes," I said.

"It is not necessary," said one of the retainers.

"Not at all," said Appanius. "You do not have an appropriate collar at hand, I gather."

"No," I said.

"If I am not mistaken," said Marcus, "ink and a pen are in the back."

"Interesting," I said. To be sure, they had been here when we had scouted the compartments. Doubtless they had been used before, in the course of Appanius' acquiring new slaves. Slave papers, too, were in the back, although I had brought my own. Hoods, gags, ropes, and such, were in the back, too.

"Give me the papers," said Appanius.

I handed him a set.

"I will fill these out in the back, and you, Lucian, will witness them."

"Yes, Appanius," said one of the retainers, dismally.

"You will wish to bind him," said Appanius.

"No," I said. "If he attempts to escape, his throat will be cut."

"Remove his slave bracelet, and his chains," said Appanius to another retainer.

"Yes, Appanius," said the fellow.

"I foolishly neglected to have him branded," said Appanius.

"I have noted it," I said.

"As he is a cheap and common slave," said Appanius, "I would have him put under the iron before nightfall."

"I shall consider the suggestion," I said.

Appanius went to the back, to complete the papers.

The slave looked up at me while the retainer removed his chains, and the identificatory slave bracelet, of silver, which he had worn on his left wrist. The retainer also gathered up his clothing, the golden sandals, the purple tunic, the robe, with the hood. Such things I had not purchased. I had, however, anticipated such things, and had brought, among several other things, some suitable garments with me, from the *insula* of Torbon.

"To whom do you belong?" I asked.

"To you, Master," he said.

"Remain on your knees, slave," I said.

"Yes, Master," he said.

Lavinia looked wildly at me, and then at the slave. And he looked at her, and at me. They both knew that they were now of the same household. They both knew that they now belonged to the same master.

In a few moments Appanius and I had concluded our business. The papers had been signed, and witnessed.

Appanius, returned to the front room, looked down at the male slave. "Do you wish to beg the forgiveness of your former master for what you have done?" he asked.

"No, Master," said the slave. "Not for what I have done.".

"I see," said Appanius.

"But I beg your forgiveness, if I have hurt you," he said. "That was not my intention."

"As I have not been hurt," said Appanius, "no forgiveness is necessary."

"Yes, Master," said the slave.

"I see that you are at last learning deference," said Appanius.

"Yes, Master," said the slave. "Thank you, Master."

Appanius then turned toward Lavinia. "You are a pretty slut," he said.

She threw herself to her belly before him, in terror. She looked well there, on the tiles, naked, the collar on her neck.

Appanius, then, with a swirl of his robes, exited. He was followed by two of his retainers. The other two lingered, momentarily. Among them was the first retainer. "We have spoken among ourselves, the four of us," he said. "We will give you a silver tarsk for Milo."

"You are very generous," I said. "That is a considerable profit for me."

"You accept?" he asked.

"No," I said.

"Why not?" he asked.

"There are free women in Ar," I said, "who would pay a thousand pieces of gold for him."

The two retainers exchanged glances. It seemed I knew more of this fellow than they had understood.

"Could you have afforded that much, Lavinia?" I asked.

"No, Master," she said. "I could not have afforded that much."

"Position," I snapped.

Instantly Lavinia rose from her belly to her knees, placing herself in a position common among Gorean pleasure slaves, kneeling back on heels, back straight, head up, palms down on thighs, knees spread.

The male slave gasped, seeing how beautiful she was, and how she obeyed. Perhaps then he sensed something of the pleasures of the mastery, what it can be to own a woman.

"Do you dare look at a female slave?" I asked him.

"Forgive me, Master!" he said, lowering his head. Much had it doubtless cost him to avert his eyes from the beauty.

"What of ten thousand pieces of gold?" asked the first retainer.

"You have so much?" I asked.

"I think we can raise it, forming a company to do so," he said.

"I do not think you could raise it in Ar today," I said. "Perhaps a year ago, or two years ago."

"We have in mind contacting men in several cities," he said, "even in Tyros and Cos."

"So much money would pay the mercenaries of Cos for a year," I said.

"Perhaps," he said. "I do not know."

"Not even Talena, in a golden collar, would bring so much," I said.

"But she is a female," he said.

Actually I thought Talena might bring that much, not as a common slave, of course, but perhaps in some situation of great dignity, as, say, a stripped, chained Ubara, being bid on in a private sale, perhaps by the agents of Chenbar, the Sea Sleen, Ubar of Tyros, and Lurius of Jad, Ubar of Cos. It was my intention, of course, to see to it that she would become such that it would be unfitting for her to be accorded this dignity.

"That is your price then?" asked the other retainer.

"He is not for sale," I said.

"I see," said the first retainer.

"You will not get more," said the other.

"I do not expect to," I said.

"Appanius would not sell him either," said the first retainer to the other.

"But he did," I reminded him, "for a tarsk bit."

The two retainers then, angrily, left. They left in the same fashion as had Appanius, and the other two, by the front entrance.

"What time do you think it is?" I asked Marcus.

"It is surely past the sixth Ahn," he said. The fifth Ahn marks the midpoint of the morning, betwixt the Gorean midnight and noon, as the fifteenth Ahn marks the midpoint of the evening, between noon and midnight. There are twenty Ahn in the Gorean day, as time is figured in the high cities. These Ahn, in the high cities, are of equal length. In certain cities, interestingly, the length of the Ahn depends on the time of year. In these cities, there are ten Ahn in the day, and ten Ahn in the night, and, as the days are longer in the summer and shorter in the winter, so, too, are the Ahn. Correspondingly, of course, the Ahn are shorter in the summer night, and longer in the winter night. The day as a whole, of course, including both day Ahn and night Ahn, comes out to the same overall length as it would in one of the high cities.

I looked down at the male slave.

"You do not look well," I said.

"I am sick, Master," he said.

He had taken a splendid drubbing, to be sure.

"Do you think that what has occurred here this morning is unaccountable?" I asked.

"Master?" he asked.

"That this is all a matter of chance, and unexpected?" I asked.

"I do not understand, Master," he said.

"It is not," I informed him. "You have been acquired as the result of a plan."

He looked at me, startled.

"You have been seduced," I said, "that you would be brought into circumstances of great compromise, circumstances the outcome of which would be to bring you to your present condition, as my slave,"

"Aii," he wept.

"The female slave, of course," I said, "was acting under my orders."

He looked at Lavinia.

"Have you received permission to look at her?" I asked.

Quickly he averted his eyes.

"You may look at her," I informed him,.

He turned to Lavinia, stricken.

"May I speak?" he begged.

"Yes," I said.

"Do you not care for me?" he asked the slave.

"She has not received permission to speak," I informed him.

Lavinia looked at me, pleadingly, her lower lip trembling. I would permit her to speak later.

"She is pretty, isn't she?" I asked.

"Yes, Master," he said, in misery.

"She is a seduction slave," I said.

Lavinia sobbed, and shook her head. A tear coursed down her cheek.

"Are you not, Lavinia?" I asked.

"Yes, Master," she sobbed.

"You should not object to this," I informed the male slave. "You yourself, often enough, if I am not mistaken, have acted in the role of the seduction slave. Surely it is only fair that the tables have now been turned, and that it is you, so to speak, who now finds himself in the net."

He could not take his eyes from Lavinia.

"She acted under your orders?" he said.

"Of course," I said.

He moaned.

"And is there not a rich joke here," I asked, "for, as I understand it, it was you who, as a seduction slave, were responsible for first bringing her pretty little neck into the collar. Is it not only fitting then that it be she, now a slave, whom I used for your acquisition?"

"Yes, Master," he said.

"Doubtless she finds her triumph rich and amusing," I said.

"Please, Master, may I speak?" begged Lavinia.

"No," I said.

She sobbed.

"You did your work well, pretty little seduction slave," I said to her.

"Please, Master!" she begged.

"No," I said.

"I had hoped you cared for me," he said.

She threw back her head in anguish.

"I had hoped you cared for me," he said. "I had never forgotten you!"

She looked wildly at him.

"You seemed so tender, so real, so helpless!" he said.

"Surely, as one who has had, as I understand it, experience on the stage," I said, "you can understand such things."

"She was responsive!" he said.

"She had better have been," I said. "Indeed, slave girls are trained to helpless responsiveness. They can juice, for example, in a matter of Ihn."

"She responded!" he said.

"She is a slave," I said. "She has strong and recurrent needs. Indeed, she is the prisoner, and victim, of such needs. Why should she not have utilized you to temporarily satisfy them?"

"Please, Master," wept Lavinia.

"No," I said.

"Well did you trick me," he said to the girl.

She regarded him with anguish.

"I do not blame you," he said. "You must do as your master commands."

I smiled to myself. I myself, despite my remarks to the male slave, had little doubt of the genuineness of Lavinia's words, her protestations, and such. The authenticity of a slave's words and responses, of course, are attested to by numerous bodily cues, many of which they are unaware of, and cannot control. A master who is alert to these can then determine, particularly over a period of time, whether or not the slaves's words, feelings and responses are genuine or not. The alternatives accorded to the Gorean slave girl are, in effect, to become an authentic slave, or die. Interestingly this understanding, particularly on the part of a woman who has been the victim of an antibiological conditioning program, as some Earth females, can be received as a liberating and joyful revelation, permitting them then in good conscience to yield at last, as they have long wished, to their femininity. Most women, of course, including most Earth females brought to Gor, as slaves, for that is the usual reason for which one is brought to Gor, do not need anything of this sort. Most are so joyful to find themselves on a natural world where their beauty, their dispositions and feelings are meaningful, that they can hardly wait to fulfill their depth nature, to be at last the women they are in their hearts, and bellies, and have always desired to be.

"She is not hard to take," I said.

"No, Master," he said.

"And if you had to be seduced," I said, "surely you must not object to my using her for the purpose."

"No, Master," he said.

"Indeed," I said, "perhaps you commend my perception, and generosity."

"Yes, Master," he said.

"Now," I said, "you both belong to me."

They looked wildly at one another.

"And I expect, seduction slave," I said to the girl, "that he will be good for your discipline. If you are not pleasing, perhaps I will throw you to him."

"Yes, Master!" she said. "Chain me, and throw me to him. Let me be his to do with as he pleases!' '

The male slave gasped, staggered with the thought of such power over the beauty.

"But then, on the other hand," I said, "I do not know if I would permit dalliance among my slaves."

He could not but drink in the beauty of Lavinia.

"Look away from her," I commanded.

With a moan he averted his eyes.

"To be sure, I might upon occasion," I said, "let you look upon one another, each chained to an opposite wall, or perhaps I might even allow you each enough chain to approach, but not touch, one another. Too, of course, I might have you chained helplessly and then have her dance naked, in her own chains, before you, thence to be dismissed to her kennel."

He put down his head, in misery.

"No," I said to Lavinia, reading her anguished expression. She put her palms down, again, on her thighs. Tears were upon her cheeks and breasts.

"You noted when you saw her this morning, of course," I said, "that she was not in seeming state garb."

"Of course, Master," he said.

"Nor in a collar, to be sure, one she could not remove, seemingly one of the state."

"Yes, Master," he said.

"Did this excite your curiosity?" I asked.

"No, Master," he said. "As this was the morning of the putative assignation, I supposed it might be a disguise prescribed by her Mistress, that the curious, if they saw her in this neighborhood, would not be likely to link her with the Central Cylinder."

"That was an intelligent conjecture on your part," I said.

"And doubtless one on which Master counted," he said.

"Yes," I said.

"It did excite me," he said, "to see her not in the drab state garb, but in the tunic she wore, with the disrobing loop."

"Did she drop the tunic well?" I asked.

"Yes, Master," he said. "She is a superb seduction slave."

Lavinia sobbed.

The male slave looked up at me. "I am an actor," he said. "Master does not appear to be of the theater."

"No," I said, "I am not of the theater."

"I do not understand why master has brought these things about," he said, "why he has brought me into his possession. Of what possible use can I be to master?"

"Perhaps I could sell you to the quarries, or into the fields," I said. "Perhaps I could take you to the Vosk, or the coast, and sell you to a captain. You might look well, chained to the bench of a galley."

"I do not think it was for such purposes that master purchased me," he said.

"You think you are valuable?" I asked.

"Surely master thinks so," he said. "I heard master himself conjecture that there were free women in Ar who would pay a thousand pieces of gold for me."

"And there are perhaps men," I said, "who would pay fifteen hundred."

"Yes, Master," he said, putting his head down, and clenching his fists. Then he looked up. "But master did not sell me, nor offer me for sale," he said.

"No," I said.

"But surely I have been purchased on speculation," he said, "for resale?"

"Do not concern yourself with the matter," I said.

"Does master intend to keep me long in his possession?" he asked.

"Do not concern yourself with the matter," I said.

He looked at me.

"Curiosity is not becoming in a kajirus," I said.

"Yes, Master," he said. This was a play, of course, on the common Gorean saying that curiosity is not becoming in a female slave, or kajira. One of the traces of Earth influence on Gorean, incidentally, in this case, an influence from Latin, occurs in the singular and plural endings of certain expressions.

For example, 'kajirus' is a common expression in Gorean for a male slave as is 'kajira' for a female slave. The plural for slaves considered together, both male and female, or for more than one male slave is 'kajiri'. The plural for female slaves is 'kajirae'.

"Straighten your collar," I said to Lavinia.

Instantly, embarrassed, self-consciously, she lifted her hands to her collar. Then she looked at me, for a moment puzzled. To be sure, it was almost perfect. Then, shyly, with seeming demureness, but with a slave girl's sense of self-display, she, her chin level, her back straight, her shoulders back, centered the lock, with both hands, delicately, carefully, at the back of the neck. This lifted her breasts, beautifully. "Are you looking at her?" I asked the male slave.

"Forgive me, Master!" he said.

"To be sure," I said, "it is hard not to look at her."

"Yes, Master," he said, putting his head down.

Lavinia, too, lowered her head, smiling.

"As I mentioned earlier," I said, "you do not look well. This is doubtless because of having been well beaten. Indeed, from the marks, I suspect the staff of Appanius to have been cored with lead. I recommend you get up now and go to the alley. You may wish to heave there, once or twice. Then, return. In the back you will find water and a towel. Clean yourself. Then come back here and kneel again, as you are."

"Yes, Master," he said, rising to his feet.

For a moment Marcus blocked his exit, but then Marcus, with a look at me, stepped aside.

"I should go with him," said Marcus to me.

"No," I said.

"Do you think he will come back?" he asked.

"Certainly," I said. "I do not think he wishes to run naked about Ar. He is well known, and would doubtless immediately be in ropes." Nudity is often used on Gor as a uniform, so to speak, of prisoners and slaves. Too," I said, "I doubt that he wants his throat cut."

"Probably not," granted Marcus.

"May I speak, Master?" asked Lavinia.

"Yes," I said. Let her tongue now be freed. It was acceptable to me.

"Would you do that?" she asked.

"Yes," I said.

She shrank back, white-faced.

"He might try to make it to the house of Appanius," said Marcus.

"He would be bound, and neck-roped, within two blocks," I said.

"Suppose he makes it to the house of Appanius," he said.

"Yes?" I said.

"If I am not mistaken Appanius would welcome him back."

"I think so," I said.

"He may wish to buy him back anyway."

"Perhaps," I said.

"For perhaps five thousand gold pieces, or more."

"Perhaps," I said.

"He might hide him," said Marcus.

"He would not be an easy slave to hide," I said. "And we have papers on him. Sooner or later I think we could get his throat to our blade."

"Oh, Master!" wept Lavinia.

"What is wrong with you?" I asked.

"Let me stand surety for him!" she said.

"I do not understand," I said.

"If he runs, kill me, not him!" she said.

"No," I said.

She put down her head, weeping.

"He is not going to run," I said.

She looked up, red-eyed.

"Surely you are aware," I said, "that even were it not for the impracticality of escape, he would return."

"Master?" she asked.

"He has a motivation," I said, "which in itself would be sufficient to bring him back."

"What, Master?" she asked.

"Can you not guess?" I asked.

"No, Master!" she cried in protest.

"Yes," I assured her.

She put her hand to her breast. "But I am only a collared slave!" she said.

"And they are the most beautiful and exciting of all women," I said. "Wars have been fought for them."

She gasped. "He is so beautiful!" she wept.

"He is a reasonably handsome fellow, I grant you," I said.

"He is the most beautiful man in all Ar!" she said.

"Surely you do not think him as handsome as I?" I asked.

She looked at me, startled.

"Well?" I asked.

"Master jests," she said.

"Oh?" I said, not altogether pleased.

"Apparently Master wishes to beat his slave," she said, uncertainly.

"Why?" I asked.

"If I tell the truth," she said, "it seems I shall displease my master and be beaten, and if I should not tell the truth, it seems I must lie to my master, and then, a lying slave girl, be beaten, or worse!"

"You think he is more handsome than I?" I asked.

"Yes, Master," she said. "Forgive me, Master!"

"But not more handsome than I?" inquired Marcus.

"Yes, Master," she said. "Forgive me, Master."

"What does a slave girl know?" I said.

"True," agreed Marcus.

"Surely many women of Ar would agree!" she said.

"You are a meaningless and lowly slave," I said. "Be silent."

"Yes, Master," she said.

"Besides," I said, "what do they know?"

"They are women," she said. "Surely they are entitled to form an opinion on the matter."

"Perhaps," I said, begrudgingly.

"Surely you believe that men are entitled to form an opinion on the beauty of women," she said.

"Of course," I said. "And it is important that we do so. In many cases, we must buy and sell them."

"But then" she said, "if men may form opinions on the beauty of women, so, too, surely, women may form opinions as to the handsomeness, or beauty, of men."

"Very well," I said. "Your point is granted."

"Thank you, Master," she said.

"But your opinion, even if it might be shared by some others, is still only the opinion of a lowly and meaningless slave."

"Yes, Master," she said.

"And it is thus of no significance," I said.

"Yes, Master," she said. "Master," she said.

"Yes," I said.

"Do not think poorly of Milo," she begged.

"I do not think poorly of him," I told her.

"Did you not see his "Lurius of Jad"?" asked Marcus.

"I thought it was rather good," I said.

"It was terrible," he said.

"You are just not an enthusiast for Lurius of Jad," I said. "Besides, you are angry that Phoebe liked it."

"Your friend, Boots, would not have liked it," he said.

"Probably because his Telitsia would have liked it," I said.

"Do not be jealous of Milo, if he is more handsome than you," said Lavinia.

"Very well," I said, "—if he is."

"Excellent," she said. "If he is more handsome than you,

then you will not be jealous of him, and if he is not more handsome than you, then, as there would be no need, you will not be jealous of him."

"Of course," I granted her. The logic here seemed impeccable. Why, then, was I not better satisfied? Whereas intelligence in a slave is commonly prized on Gor, it is not always without its drawbacks.

"Am I to be whipped?" she asked, suddenly.

"No," I said.

"Thank you, Master," she said.

"At least not at the moment," I said.

"Thank you, Master," she said.

"It is nothing," I said.

"Do not fret, Masters," she said. "Even if you are not Milos, you are both strong, handsome, attractive men. Too, there is something different and special in you, something distinguishing you from many other men. It is the mastery. Women sense in men such as you, or can come suddenly to sense in men such as you, sometimes to their terror, their masters, and this makes you unbelievably exciting and attractive to them. This puts you beyond compare with other men. Women then wish to kneel before you and serve you, to please you and love you. And that has nothing to do with the regularity or smoothness of one's features, which may characterize even weaklings."

"All men are masters," I said.

"I do not know," she said. "But that is what the woman desires, her master."

"Why were you on the couch when I entered the room?" I asked.

"He put me there," she said.

"Very well, I said. One might have expected her to have been put on the floor, on furs, at the foot of the couch, as she was a slave.

"The slave is returning," said Marcus.

"Of course," I said.

Lavinia gasped with relief. I recalled that she had been ready to die for him. Too, I recalled he had, to the best of his ability, attempted to shelter her from the blows of the irate Appanius. These things I found of interest. To be sure, I did not think I would encourage dalliance among my slaves. It might be interesting, of course, to keep them within sight of one another but in anguished separation.

In a few moments Milo had washed in the back and returned to kneel in the front room.

"Put your head down and extend your left wrist," I said to him.

He did so, and I locked a silver slave bracelet, resembling the one he had previously worn, on his left wrist. On this bracelet, in fine, tiny lettering, were the words "I belong to Tarl of Port Kar."

I then threw him a common tunic, one of the things I had brought with me. "Put it on," I told him.

"Yes, Master," he said.

"What time do you think it to be?" I asked Marcus.

"It must be near the seventh Ahn," he said.

"The magistrates should arrive any moment," I said.

"Presumably they will come to the back," he said.

"I would think so," I said. Surely they would have been here often enough in the past. Too, it did not seem likely they would wish to be seen entering by the street door. They would be, as far as they knew, keeping their appointment with Appanius and his men. When they arrived, of course, they would discover that a change of plans had occurred, and that it would not be Appanius for whom they would render their services, but another.

"Are you looking at the female slave again?" I asked the male slave.

"Forgive me, Master," he said.

"Keep your head down," I said.

"Yes, Master," he said.

"I will explain to you in a moment what I wish you to do," I said.

"Yes, Master," he said.

"In the meantime," I said to Marcus, "let us readjust this net."

"Did you bring the bracelets, with linked shackles?" asked Marcus.

"Of course," I said.

26 A Free Woman; A Female Slave

"You may assist me with my wrap," she informed the handsome slave. "Your hand trembles," she smiled.

In the back room I tracked these matters by means of one of the observation portals. One of the two magistrates, he who was senior, Tolnar, of the second Octavii, an important *gens* but one independent of the well-known Octavii, sometimes spoken of simply as the Octavii, or sometimes as the first Octavii, deputy commissioner in the records office, much of which had been destroyed in a recent fire, was at the other portal. His colleague, Venlisius, a bright young man who was now, by adoption, a scion of the Toratti, was with him. Venlisius was in the same office. He was records officer, or archon of records, for the Metellan district, in which we were located. Both magistrates wore their robes, and fillets, of office. They also carried their wands of office, which, I suspect, from the look of them, and despite the weapons laws of Cos, contained concealed blades. I was pleased to hope that these fellows were such as to put the laws of Ar before the ordinances of Cos. I had requested that they dismiss their attendant guardsmen, which they had done. I did not anticipate that they would be needed. Whatever force, if any, might be required could be supplied by Marcus and myself. Similarly it seemed that Marcus and I could handle any other matters of the sort in which they might customarily have been utilized. Too, certain matters might prove sensitive, and I saw fit to limit the number and nature of witnesses.

"Must I remove my own wrap?" she inquired.

"No, no, Mistress!" said the male slave.

" 'Mistress'?" she said. "It seems you have learned deference."

"Yes, Mistress," he said. He knelt quickly, trembling, his head down.

"It is not like you," she said.

"Forgive me, Mistress," he said.

"But I find it charming," she said. "And you look well, my dear Milo, on your knees."

"Thank you, Mistress," he said.

"But I do not understand this new deference," she said.

"What but deference," said he, "could be in order, before one such as you?"

"I think we shall get along very well," she said.

He was silent, kneeling before her, bent at the waist. He kept his head down. He trembled. I did not really blame him.

"It is as though, suddenly, it had been recalled to you, that you are a slave," she said.

"Yes, Mistress," he said.

I was pleased that his back had not been opened by the staff of Appanius. It would not have done, at all, if stripes of blood had appeared on the back of his tunic, soaked through.

"Interesting," she said.

"Before you," he said, "what man could not be a slave?"

"Flatterer!" she chided.

I smiled to myself. He had a nimble, flattering tongue. He was able in his work. Doubtless he had been of great value to Appanius, in many ways. Then I smiled grimly to myself. How susceptible was the chit to his blandishments. How little she understood of herself. Before what man, I wondered, could *she* not be a slave? Indeed, before what man, I wondered, should she not be a slave? Indeed, before any man, she, and other women, should be slaves.

"My wrap!" she said, irritably.

He leaped to his feet, and delicately, courteously, removed her outer cloak, with its hood. She had been well covered in it, from head to toe. He put this on a peg to one side.

"Your guards are without?" he asked.

"I have come alone," she said. "Surely you do not think me a fool?"

"No," he said.

She brushed back the light inner hood and unhooked the collar of her robe.

"You will never believe the difficulty I had in escaping from the Central Cylinder!" she said. "It is almost as though I were a prisoner there. Seremides is so careful! His spies are everywhere. Who knows who they are, or which of them is watching you at any given time? Whom can I trust? It is hard to leave without an escort of a company of guardsmen. What do they fear, I wonder. The people love me."

"You are too glorious and marvelous to risk," said Milo.

"Alas," she said, "sometimes I myself grow weary of the preciousness and dignity of my person. It seems it has always been thus. Long ago when I was a girl it was the same, and then, in my time of troubles, after the misunderstanding with my dear father, Marlenus, I was sequestered, and then, later, now that the war has been concluded to the mutual benefit of Ar and Cos, with victory for us both, thanks to the mercies of Cos, and the noble Lurius of Jad, and we have become allies with our former enemies, now our dearest of friends, the Cosians, it seems the same again."

"Mistress is Ubara,' said he. "Simply order them to desist from their attentions."

"Of course," she smiled.

The handsome slave regarded her, puzzled.

"But I eluded the guards," she said. "It was not really too difficult. They are men, and stupid."

"How did Mistress outwit them?" asked the slave.

"As you will note," she said, "I wore a common street cloak

and hood, secured for the occasion. A departure was arranged for a putative maid, supposedly one of my retinue, on personal business, and it was as such a one that I was passed through the guards."

"Mistress is to be praised for her discretion and cleverness," he said.

"Who will remove the veil of a free woman?" she laughed.

"Who, indeed?" inquired the slave, awed.

"And few," she laughed, "are even aware of the features of the Ubara!"

"True, wondrous Mistress," he said.

She laughed.

"How grateful and humbled I am," said he, "that I, only a slave, at three suppers, was permitted to look upon them."

"You dared to look upon me?" she asked.

"Forgive me, Mistress," he cried. "I had thought that perhaps it was for that reason that Mistress had lowered her veil."

"It was warm, those evenings," she said.

"Of course, Mistress!" he said.

"But, to be sure," she said, "I did fear that looking upon me, you might fall under my spell."

She then, gracefully, reached to the pins at the left side of the veil and unpinned it. A moment later she had lowered it, gracefully.

"Aii!" said he, softly. "What man could not fall under the spell of such beauty?"

"Think you so?" she laughed, delighted.

"Yes!" he said. "Surely Mistress is the most beautiful woman on all Gor!"

I glanced down at Lavinia. She was kneeling on the floor, to my left. I thought her lip trembled, and a tear formed in her eye.

"I feel like a slave girl," said the free woman, "running about, sneaking here and there, to keep a rendezvous."

Milo gasped. I conjecture he had just considered how exciting the female might be, if she were truly a slave, slave clad, slave collared, and such.

The Ubara looked at herself, in the mirror at the far end of the room.

"Sometimes I envy the meaningless property tarts," she said, "running about much as they please, here and there, in all their freedom, in their short skirts and collars. Sometimes I think that they have more freedom than I, that I, a free woman, indeed, one who is Ubara of Ar, am more slave than slave."

"Do not even think so!" said Milo.

"It is true," she said, dismally.

The male slave was silent.

The Ubara continued to regard herself in the mirror. I wondered how she saw herself, really, in that reflection. Did she see herself in the mirror as she now seemed, moody, and attired as befitted a woman of high caste, or did she see herself there otherwise, perhaps in a ta-teera or tunic, as men might choose to keep her.

"If I were a slave," she said, "and I were here, what do you think would be done with me?"

"Mistress is not a slave!" cried Milo, aghast.

"But, if I were?" she asked.

"And you were caught?" he asked.

"Of course," she said.

"Mistress would be severely punished," he said.

"Even though I am so beautiful?" she asked, skeptically.

"Especially so!" said he.

"Oh?" she said.

"Yes, Mistress," he assured her.

"Interesting," she said.

"But Mistress is not a slave!" he said.

"Lashed?" she asked.

"The least that might be done to Mistress," he said, "would surely be that she would be stripped, and tied, and lashed. Too, she might be bound, and subjected to the bastinado."

The free woman shuddered.

"And I do not think that Mistress would err in such a fashion again," he said.

"Perhaps not," she said.

I glanced over at Tolnar, at the other observation portal. He looked over to me, and I returned my attention to the portal.

The Ubara, moving very little, was still regarding herself in the mirror.

She seemed moody.

"Mistress?" asked the male slave.

"You do find me attractive, do you not?" she asked.

"Of course, Mistress!" he said.

"And do you not think other men might do so likewise?" she asked.

"Certainly, Mistress!" he said.

"Some think me the most beautiful woman in all Ar," she said.

"You are surely," said he, "the most beautiful woman on all Gor!"

Near me Lavinia put down her head. A tear fell to the floor.

"And I am Ubara!" said the free woman.

"Yes, Mistress," said the slave.

"A Ubara, too," she said, "is a woman, and I have a woman's needs."

"Yes, Mistress," said the slave.

The Ubara then, bit by bit, piece by piece, looking at herself from time to time in the mirror, the slave standing back, removed her outer garments. When she had stepped forth from her slippers, she stood before the mirror, barefoot, in a one-piece, white, silken, wraparound sliplike garment. It came slightly above her knees. She then unpinned the dark wealth of her hair, and shook her head, and then, with both hands, lifted it, and then swept it back, behind her shoulders. She regarded herself in the mirror. It was all I could do not to rush forth into the other room and seize her. About her neck, on a leather thong, there was a small, capped leather cylinder. I was confident I knew what it contained. Milo, on the other hand, would not. Milo had not had with him, I had determined, the note which had putatively come to him from the Ubara, that which had been written by Lavinia. I supposed he had destroyed it, as it might prove dangerously compromising. Neither the Ubara nor Milo, of course, knew of the notes which they themselves had supposedly written. All communications between them other than these had been effected by Lavinia, to the Ubara in the guise of a slave of the house of Appanius, to Milo in the guise of a state slave, with the exception of their rendezvous this morning. With Lavinia as go-between, under my instructions, matters had proceeded expeditiously, culminating apace, save for some delays on the part of the Ubara, presumably to increase the anxieties of, and torment, the poor slave, in the arrangements for this assignation.

"I wonder if I am truly the most beautiful woman on all Gor," said the Ubara, looking into the mirror.

"Certainly," said Milo.

Near me Lavinia had her head down, and in her hands.

"How could one doubt it?" asked Milo.

Near me Lavinia wept, silently. Tears had trickled down her wrists, and to the floor. I noted that her knees were in proper position, spread, given the sort of slave she was.

"And you, Milo," said the Ubara, "are a handsome brute."

"I am pleased if Mistress should find me not displeasing," he said.

"And surely," she said, "you are the most handsome man in all Ar."

"Mistress," he said, softly, coming close to her.

"Serve me wine!" she snapped.
"Mistress?" he asked.
"Is that not wine, and assorted dainties," she asked, "on the table by the couch, that which I see behind me, in the mirror?"
"Yes, Mistress," he said.
"And certainly female slaves humbly and beautifully serve their masters in such a way," she said.
"Yes, Mistress," he said.
"Must a command be repeated?" she inquired.
"I am a male slave," he said. "I am not a female slave."
"Surely you are aware that male silk slaves are trained in such things as the serving of wine to their mistresses," she said.
"I am not a silk slave," he said.
"I see that a command must be repeated," she said.
"No, Mistress!" he said. He hurried to the small table and put a tiny bit of wine into one of the small glasses. He then returned, and knelt before her. He then, holding the tiny glass in both hands, his head down between his extended arms, proffered her the beverage. But she did not receive it as yet at his hands. "Look up," she said. He did so. She fingered the small, capped cylinder at her neck. "Surely you know what is contained in this capsule," she said.
He did not respond.
She uncapped it, and moved the tiny rolled paper a hort from the capsule, that he might see it. Then she thrust it back in, triumphantly, and recapped the cylinder.
"You are a better actor than I gave you credit for," she said.
He had remained impassive.
"You will obey me in all things, and not merely because you are a slave," she said, "but because of this." She tapped the tiny cylinder twice. "I now hold all power over you, my dear Milo, even though I do not own you. It is given to me by this note. Should it come to the attention of Seremides, or Myron, or the high council, or an archon of slaves, or perhaps even a guardsman, you may well conjecture what might be your fate."
He looked up at her.
"How foolish you were, to write such a note," she laughed. "But then you are a man, and men are stupid."
He put down his head, and, again, lifted the wine to her.
He would not recognize the note, of course, but he would immediately realize it must have had some role in my business, in which he was now so deeply involved. Too, almost simultaneously, he would doubtless suspect that the note which he himself had originally received might very well not have come from the Ubara herself. Surely it would now seem to him

unlikely that she, so obviously aware of the danger of such notes, would have sent one herself. Surely it would have been at the least politically compromising, if it fell into the wrong hands. He did not glance toward the back room. I myself, incidentally, did not think it impossible that the Ubara herself, in certain circumstances, might be so indiscrete as to write such notes. She was, after all, a woman with feelings, desires and needs. She was quite capable, I was sure, in their cause, of throwing caution to the winds. On the other hand, in this case there had been no need for her to do so.

She let him hold the wine for a time, and then, reaching out, she took the glass.

He kept his head down, and put his hands, palms down, on his thighs.

She lifted the glass to her lips. She took no more, it seemed, than the tiniest of sips.

"Replace the glass," she said. "Then return and kneel as you are now."

She was standing before the couch.

She watched him, in the mirror, replace the glass on the tiny table.

In a moment then he had returned to kneel before her.

"You are the idol of thousands of women in Ar," she said, "but it is my beauty which has conquered you."

He was silent.

Lavinia looked up at me, red-eyed.

"It is my beauty to which you have succumbed," she said.

He was silent.

"It is I before whom you kneel," said the Ubara.

He did not respond.

"You look well there," she said, "on your knees, before me."

He was silent.

"That is where men belong," she said, "on their knees, before women."

He kept his head down, and did not respond.

"You may look up," she said.

She turned about then and went to the couch. She stood there for a moment, beside it, regarding him.

Then, with a graceful movement, she removed the white, silken, sliplike garment, letting it fall about her ankles.

"Ai!" said the male slave, softly.

She then, swiftly, with a smooth, silken movement, ascended the couch and lay curled upon it, near its foot, watching him.

"Mistress!" he said.

"Do not dare to rise to your feet without permission, slave," she said.

"Yes, Mistress," he said.

She laughed, softly.

He looked away.

"Do you have the needs of a male?" she asked.

"Yes!" he said.

"Sometimes female slaves," she said, "after their slave fires have been ignited, after the poor things have begun to learn their collar, after they have become sexually helpless, are deprived of sexual experience," she said. "Did you know that?"

"I have heard so," he said. "Perhaps as a cruelty, to teach them the master's power or that they are slaves, or as a punishment, or to ready them for a successful performance on the block, such things."

"Are such things done with male slaves?" she asked.

"Perhaps," he said.

She laughed.

He did not look at her.

"Look at me," she commanded.

"At least upon occasion," he said.

She laughed again, merrily.

This was true, incidentally. Tauntings, it might be mentioned, are usually involved in such denials. On the other hand, male slaves have much the better of it, in my opinion, in these matters. Sexual gratification is seldom denied to them for long periods. They, like male sleen, tend to become not only restless and aggressive, but dangerous. Accordingly, it is common to see that they are permitted to periodically access a female, almost invariably a slave. No such provision, on the other hand, is prescribed for the female slave. She, as her needfulness increases within her, as she becomes more lonely and miserable, more desperate, is left much on her own, to wheedle and beg, and such. To be sure, most female slaves enjoy an enormous amount of sexual experience. This is largely because they are beautiful and exciting, and slaves.

"You may rise, handsome slave," said she, amused.

"Yes, Mistress," he said.

"But stay where you are," she added.

"Yes, Mistress," he said.

She lay on her side, watching him. "You are indeed a handsome brute," she said.

"Thank you, Mistress," he said.

She then lay on her back, toward the foot of the couch, and stretched, luxuriantly, indolently, before him, savoring the feeling of the fur, the delight of her own movement. She looked upward, lazily. She did not detect the net, of course, as she was not looking for it, and it was recessed in the structure of the ceiling, the ceiling having been designed for its concealment.

She had the palms of her hands facing upward, at her sides. Her left knee was lifted.

I thought she would look well in a collar.

She moaned, softly.

She turned her head to the side, toward him. "Sometimes I feel," she said, "as I think a slave must feel."

The net, concealed, was above her.

He made as though to step toward her.

"Do not approach!" she warned him.

He stood still.

She laughed, and rose, facing him, to her hands and knees, on the couch. She then backed away from him, toward the center of the couch. In this way, unwittingly, she positioned herself under the center of the net. To be sure, it had been designed to cover the entire couch.

"You may approach," she said. "No nearer!" she said.

He then stood near the foot of the couch.

"It seems, Mistress, has come to this room to torture a poor slave," he said.

She then slipped to her left side, propping herself up with her left elbow, and, her knees drawn up, regarded him.

"Poor Milo," she said, sympathetically.

He was silent.

"There are slave rings on the couch," she said. "Perhaps I shall chain you to one of them."

"As Mistress pleases," he said.

"What woman of Ar would not desire you as her conquest," she mused.

He was silent.

"And you are mine," she said. "Conquered by my beauty."

He was silent.

"You have told me," she said, "that you have the needs of a male."

"Yes, Mistress," he said.

"Is it true?" she asked.

"Yes, Mistress," he said.

"I am Ubara," she said.

"Yes, Mistress," he said.

"But I am also a female," she said, "and I have a female's needs."

"Mistress?" he asked.

"Yes, Milo," she said. "It is true."

He looked down.

"Happily, of course, they are not those of a female slave," she said. "That, fortunately, has never been done to me."

"Yes, Mistress," he said.

In her last words her voice had almost broken. In them was betrayed a seething half-suspected emotional sea. In the Ubara, it seemed, might be latent depths on the shores of which she stood frightened, and in awe. In her, it seemed, might be revelations, discoveries, and enforcements that in her state of inert freedom could scarcely be conjectured. And well might she have feared such things. How helpless she might be, if she found herself in their chains. The slave girl is the helpless prisoner of her sexuality.

"Surely you understand the purport of my words," she said, angrily.

"Surely I dare not explicitly conjecture," he said.

"Why do you think I have come here?" she asked.

"To torture a poor slave, it seems," he said.

"That I could do in the Central Cylinder," she said.

"What more could there be?" he asked.

"Can you not guess?" she said.

"Mistress is free, and Ubara," he said.

"Look upon me," she commanded. "What do you see?" she asked.

"The Ubara of Ar," he said.

"And a female?"

"Yes, Mistress," he said.

"You are a man," she said. "When you arranged this meeting, surely you must have had hopes."

He put down his head.

"And you, shameful, arrogant slave, have presumed far above your station. I should have you boiled in oil!"

He kept his head down.

"But I am prepared to be merciful," she said.

"Mistress?" he asked, looking up.

"I am prepared to extend to you the extraordinary and inestimable privilege," she said, "of entering upon the same couch with me."

He looked at her.

"Yes," she said.

"I am unworthy!" he said.

"Are the sluts, thrown by the hair to their masters' couches any the more worthy?" she asked.

"No, Mistress," he said.

"Do not concern yourself then with such matters," she said.

"But so much honor!" he said.

"Do not consider it," she said.

"But I am only a slave," he said.

"That is known to me," she said.

"I have a master!" he said.

"Of course," she said.

"And mistress does this of her own free will?" he said.

"Yes," she said.

He was silent.

She gestured to the furs beside her. "I invite you to share my couch," she said.

He hesitated.

"I am lying here before you," she said, " 'slave naked', as you vulgar men might say. Do you dally, handsome Milo?"

"Mistress invites me to share her couch?" he asked.

"Yes," she said.

"Mistress is then preparing to couch with me?"

"I am not only preparing to couch with you," she said. "I am prepared to couch with you." She then knelt on the couch, and back on her heels.

I glanced to Tolar, the magistrate. He nodded.

"You may approach me," she said. She extended her arms, opened to him, as she knelt. "Come, handsome slave," said she. "Come, couch with me!"

I threw the lever, releasing the net.

It fell over her beautifully.

She screamed in surprise and fear, as its toils dropped about her. She tried to spring to her feet on the couch, clawing at it, but fell. Milo, doubtless practiced in the matter, expertly brought it together and whipped it about her and, in an instant, on her belly on the couch, she was helpless in its folds. Almost instantly, too, Marcus entered the front room, followed by Tolnar and Venlisius. I had remained for a moment or two at the observation portal. Then I, too, followed by Lavinia, entered the room. Although she may have been aware of my movement, that of another man entering the room, she did not, in her consternation, and in her attention to Marcus and the magistrates, before her, really look upon me, or recognize me. I was then in back of her, with the bracelets and linked shackles. Milo, his work done, stood now to one side.

"What is the meaning of this!" she cried, on her belly, turning her head to the right, lifting it from the furs, squirming in the toils of the net.

I, behind her, gathered the net more closely about her,

jerking her legs more closely together, wrapping the net more closely about them. A naked woman, on furs, netted, helpless, is quite lovely.

"Sleen! Sleen!" she wept. She lifted her head, as she could, from the furs, looking at the magistrates who, in their robes, with their fillets, with their wands of office, regarded her. "Sleen!" she screamed at them. They did not strike her. She did not seem to realize that she had now become a slave. "Release me!" she demanded. "Release me!"

"What was your name?" inquired Tolar. "We shall wish it for the records."

"I am Talena!" she cried. "I am Talena, Ubara of Ar! Down on your knees before me! I am Talena, Talena! Ubara of Ar! I am your Ubara!"

"You may, of course, attempt to conceal your former identity," said Tolnar. "At this point it is immaterial."

"I am Talena!" she cried.

"Perhaps you might think to delude a poor slave," said Tolnar, "but we are free men."

"Fools!" she wept.

"What was your name?" he asked.

"My name is Talena!" she said. "I am Ubara of Ar!"

"You would have us believe that Talena of Ar is a sensuous tart in need of sexual relief, a mere chit who would condescend to keep a rendezvous so shameful as this?"

"I am Talena!" she cried, squirming in the net. "Release me! I shall scream!"

"That would be interesting, if you are Talena," said Tolnar. "You would then choose to publicize, it seems, your whereabouts. You would choose to be discovered naked and netted, before magistrates, in a room in the Metellan district, having been prepared to couch with a slave?"

She threw her head down, angrily, on the furs. "I am Talena," she said. "Release me!"

"What is more pertinent to our purposes," said Tolar, "is your legal status, or, in this case, it seems, your former legal status."

"Release me, fools!" she said.

"What was your legal status before you entered this room?" asked Tolnar.

"I was, and am, a free woman!" she said.

"Of Ar?" he asked.

"Yes!" she cried, angrily.

"That is the crux of the matter," said Tolnar. He glanced to Venlisius, who nodded.

"Do you doubt that I am Talena?" she demanded of Tolnar.

"Surely you must permit me to be skeptical," he smiled.

"I am she!" she cried. Then she looked wildly at Milo. "You know me!" she wept. "You can attest to my identity! You have seen me in the Central Cylinder! So, too, has that slut of a slave!"

"Stand," said Tolnar to Lavinia, who immediately complied.

"Please, Milo," begged the netted beauty, helplessly, pathetically, agonizingly, "do not lie! Tell the truth!"

He looked at her.

"Please, Milo!" she begged. "Tell them who I am!" How much she felt then dependent upon him, how much in his power! How different this was from her former mastery of him! How terrified she was that he might, for one reason or another, lie to the magistrates, putting her then before them as no more than a common, captured, compromised female.

"Who was she?" asked Tolnar of Milo.

"Talena, Ubara of Ar," said Milo.

"Ah!" she wept in relief.

Tolnar and Venlisius exchanged glances. They did not much relish this development.

"Release me, you sleen!" wept Talena, struggling futilely in the net.

"And you?" asked Tolnar of Lavinia, who was looking on the netted captive, indeed, a prisoner of the same cords which, months before, had held her with such similar perfection.

"Master?" asked Lavinia.

"Who was she?" said Tolnar.

"That, too, is my understanding," said Lavinia. "Talena, of Ar."

"Release me!" demanded the captive.

"What difference does it make," asked Marcus, "if, indeed, she is Talena of Ar?"

"Fool!" laughed the netted captive.

"From the legal point of view," said Tolnar, "it makes no difference, of course."

"Release me!" she said. "Do you think I am a common person? Do you think you can treat one of my importance in this fashion! I shall have Seremides have you boiled in oil!"

"I am of the second Octavii," said Tolnar. "My colleague is of the Toratti."

"Then you may be scourged and beheaded, or impaled!" she wept.

"You would have us neglect our duty?" inquired Tolnar. He was Gorean, of course.

"In this case," she snapped, "you are well advised to do so."

"That is quite possibly true," said Tolnar.

"The principle here, I gather," said Marcus, "is that the Ubara is above the law."

"The law in question is a serious one," said Tolnar. "It was promulgated by Marlenus, Ubar of Ubars."

"Surely," said Venlisius to the netted woman, "you do not put yourself on a level with the great Marlenus."

"It does not matter who is greater," she said. "I am Ubara!"

"The Ubara is above the law?" asked Marcus, who had an interest in such things.

"In a sense, yes," said Tolnar, "the sense in which she can change the law by decree."

"But she is subject to the law unless she chooses to change it?" asked Marcus.

"Precisely," said Tolnar. "And that is the point here."

"Whatever law it is," cried the netted woman, "I change it! I herewith change it!"

"How can you change it?" asked Tolnar.

"I am Ubara!" she said.

"You were Ubara," he said.

She cried out in misery, in frustration, in the net.

"Interesting," said Marcus.

"Release me!" demanded the woman.

"Do you think we are fond of she who was once Talena," asked Tolnar, "of she who betrayed Ar, and collaborated with her enemies?"

"Release me, if you value your lives!" she cried. "Seremides will wish me free! So, too, will Myron! So, too, will Lurius of Jad!"

"But we have taken an oath to uphold the laws of Ar," said Tolnar.

"Free me!" she said.

"You would have us compromise our honor?" asked Tolnar.

"I order you to do so," she said.

Tolnar smiled.

"Why do you smile?" she asked.

"How can a slave order a free person to do anything?" he asked.

"A slave!" she cried. "How dare you!"

"You are taken into bondage," said Tolnar, "under the couching laws of Marlenus of Ar. Any free woman who couches with, or prepares to couch with, a male slave, becomes herself a slave, and the property of the male slave's master."

"I, *property*!" she cried.

"Yes," said Tolnar.

"Absurd!" she said.

"Not at all," he said. "It is, I assure you, all quite legal."

"Proceed then with your farce!" she cried. "I know Appanius well, and his position in this city is much dependent upon my support! Have I not freed him of numerous burdens? Have I not adjusted his taxes? Have I not spared his house, and those of other favorites, the exactions of the levies?"

"You acknowledge, then," asked Tolnar, "that you are a slave?"

"Yes," she said, angrily, "I am a slave! Now, summon Appanius, immediately, that I may be promptly freed! Then you will see to what fates I shall consign you!"

"But what if Appanius wishes you as a slave?" asked Marcus.

She laughed. "I see you do not know our dear Appanius," she said. "The most he would want from a woman would be to have her do his cleaning and scrub his floors!"

"But what if that is precisely what he has in mind for you?" asked Tolnar.

She turned white.

"Doubtless she would look well, performing lowly labors in chains," said Marcus.

"Perhaps, unknown to you," said Tolnar, "Appanius is a patriot."

"Never!" she said. "Bring him here!"

"What if he would keep you in his house as a slave?" asked Marcus.

"Perhaps you think you could make your former identity known," said Tolnar. "That might be amusing."

" 'Amusing'?" she asked.

"Who would believe that once you had been Talena, the Ubara of Ar?" asked Tolnar.

"More likely," said Venlisius, "you would be whipped, as a mad slave."

"While," said Tolnar, "another woman, suitably coached, and veiled, would take your place in the Central Cylinder. From the point of view of the public, things would be much the same."

"Bring Appanius here!" she cried. "I know him. I can speak with him. I can make him see, I assure you, what is to his advantage! This is all some preposterous mistake. Free me! This is all some terrible misunderstanding! Bring Appanius here! I demand it!"

"But what has Appanius to do with this?" asked Tolnar.

"I do not understand," said the woman.

Tolnar regarded her.

"He has everything to do with it," she said. "He is Milo's master!"

"No," said Tolnar.

The prisoner turned her head about, not easily, in the net. "Appanius is your master!" she said to Milo.

"No," he said.

"Yes!" she cried. "He is your master. He is also the master of that short-haired slut!"

"No!" said Lavinia.

"You did not call me 'Mistress'," said the prisoner.

"Why should I?" asked Lavinia.

"It is true that you belong to the master of Milo," said Tolnar, "but it is false that the master of Milo is Appanius."

"To whom, then, do I belong?" she asked, aghast.

"Let the papers be prepared, and the measurements, and prints, taken," said Tolnar.

"Yes, Tolnar," said Venlisius.

"Papers! Measurements! Prints!" she protested.

"I think you can understand," said Tolnar, "that in a case such as this, such documentations, guarantees and precautions are not out of order."

"No! No!" she cried.

Tolnar and Venlisius put their wands of office to the side and went to the back room, to obtain the necessary papers and materials.

"You!" cried the prisoner, looking at Marcus. "It is then you to whom I belong!"

He merely regarded her.

"Who are you?" she cried.

"It does not matter," he said.

"I will buy my freedom!" she said. "I will give you a thousand pieces of gold! Two thousand! Ten thousand! Name your price!"

"But you have nothing," he said. "No more than a kaiila, or sleen."

"Contact Seremides!" she said. "Contact Myron, polemarkos of Temos! They will arrange my ransom."

"Ransom or price?" asked Marcus.

"Price!" she said, angrily.

"But you are not, as of this moment, for sale," he said.

"Sleen!" she wept. She struggled but I, behind her, kept her well in the net.

At this point Tolnar and Venlisius reentered the room and, in a few moments, were in the process of filling out the papers.

These included an extremely complete description of the woman, exact even to details such as the structure of her ear lobes. Tolnar then, with a graduated tape, reaching in and about the net, and moving the woman, as necessary, took a large number of measurements, these being recorded by Venlisius. Additional measurements were taken with other instruments, such as a calipers. With these were recorded such data as the width and length of fingers and toes, the width of her heels, the lovely tiny distance between her nostrils, and so on. The result of this examination, of course, was to produce a network of data which, to a statistical certainty, far beyond the requirements of law, would be unique to a given female. Then, one hand at a time, pulled a bit from the net, then reinserted in it, her fingerprints were taken. Following this, her toeprints were taken. Then, the woman shaken, tears on the furs, was again fully within the net, on her belly. Her fingers and toes were dark with ink, from the taking of the prints. I had taken care, behind her, holding her, and such, to see that she had not seen me.

"You will never get me out of the city!" she said, suddenly, to Marcus.

"Do you really think it would be difficult," he asked her, "gagged, hooded, perhaps in a slave sack?"

"Already the alarm may be out for me!" she said to him.

"I have not heard the alarm bars," he said.

"Do not be naive," she said. "Even now, a secret alarm, a silent alarm, may be out. Even now guardsmen may be turning Ar upside down, looking for me."

"If you have planned your putative dalliance as well as you would have led us to believe," he said, "I doubt that you have even been missed. Indeed, perhaps you will not be missed until morning!"

She moaned.

"Thus, we would have plenty of time to get you out of the city, as merely another slave. If we have a tarn waiting, you could be a hundred pasangs from here by nightfall, in any direction, and by morning, with a new tarn, five hundred pasangs from there, in any direction, and in another day, who knows?"

She lifted her head with difficulty in the net, to look at him. His face was stern. She put down her head, frightened, lying on her left cheek.

"But perhaps," said he, "we have no intention of taking you from the city."

"What?" she said, frightened, lifting her head again, with difficulty regarding him. Her eyes went to the dagger at his belt. His fingers were upon it. "No!" she said. "Surely you are not assassins!"

He merely looked at her, his hand on the hilt of the dagger.

"Surely you do not intend to kill me!" she cried.

He regarded her, not speaking.

"Do not kill me!" she wept. It was not irrational on her part, of course, to fear an assassination plot. Even if she believed herself generally popular within the city, perhaps even much loved within it, she would realize that these sentiments might not be universal. For example, the increasing resistance to Cosian rule in the city, the growing insurgency, the actions of the Delta Brigade, would surely have given her cause for apprehension, if not genuine alarm. "Surely," she said, "I have not become a slave, simply to be slain?"

He did not speak.

"Do not kill me!" she begged. It must have been painful for her to hold her head up, as she was, on her belly, in the furs, in the net, to look at Marcus.

He did not speak.

"Please do not kill me," she wept, "—*Master*!"

"I am not your master," he said.

She looked at him, wildly. "Who, then," she said, "is my master?"

"I am," I said.

I seized her by the upper arms, from behind, and half lifting her, pulled her up, and back, to her knees, tangled in the net. She turned wildly in the net, to see me over her right shoulder, and our eyes met, and she recognized me, and she gasped, and half cried out, and then I had to hold her on her knees, as she had fainted. I lowered her to the furs. I then threw the bracelets with the linked shackles on the furs to her left. I then removed her, carefully, from the net. Then, in a moment, she was in the bracelets, back-braceleted, with her ankles, shackled, pulled up, and back, attached by a short chain to the linkage of the bracelets.

"I shall sign the papers," I said to Tolnar.

"And I shall stamp, and certify, them," he said.

27 We Take Our Leave

"Extend your left wrist," I said to Milo.

He did so, and I unlocked the silver slave bracelet there, and handed it to him, with the key.

The new slave, the dark-haired, olive-skinned beauty who

had but recently been the Ubara of Ar, was still unconscious. I had removed her from the couch and put her on the floor, on the heavy, flat stones, on her side, some feet to the left of the couch, as one faced it, from the foot, her wrists behind her, braceleted, chained to her ankles, her neck fastened by a short chain to a recessed slave ring. Near her, but not yet fixed upon her, were the makings of a gag.

"I do not understand," said Milo.

"It is silver," I said. "Perhaps you can sell it."

"I do not understand," he said.

"And these papers," I said, "are pertinent to you. They are all in order. I had Tolnar and Venlisius prepare them, before they left."

"Papers, Master?" he asked.

"You can read?" I asked.

"Yes, Master," he said.

"Do not call me 'Master'," I said.

"Master?" he asked.

"The papers are papers of manumission," I said. "I am no longer your master. You no longer have a master."

"Manumission?" he asked.

"You are free," I told him.

Lavinia, kneeling nearby, gasped, and looked up, wildly, at Milo.

"I have never been free," he said.

"You are now," I said. "You will have to make the best of it."

"Surely master jests," he said.

"No," I said.

"Does master not want me?" he asked.

"I do not even have a theater," I said. "What do I need with an actor?"

"You could sell me," he said.

"You are not a female," I said.

He looked down, wildly, at Lavinia.

"Now that," I said, "is a female. That is something fit for sale."

"But your loss is considerable," he said.

"One tarsk bit, to be exact," I said.

He smiled.

"For so little," I said, "one could purchase little more than the services of a new slave for an evening in a paga tavern, one still striving desperately to learn how to be pleasing."

"Women are marvelous!" he exclaimed.

"They are not without interest," I granted him.

Lavinia put down her head, as it had been she upon whom his eyes had been fixed when he had uttered his recent expression of enthusiasm. To be sure, when one sees one woman as beautiful, it is easy to see the beauty in thousands of others.

"I have always been a slave," he said, "even when I was a boy."

"I understand," I said.

"I was a pretty youth," he said.

"I understand," I said.

"And I have always been denied women, warned about them, scolded when I expressed interest in them, sometimes beaten when I looked upon them."

"I know a world where such things, in a sense, are often done," I said, "a world in which, for political purposes, and to further the interests and ambitions of certain factions, there are wholesale attempts to suppress, thwart, stunt and deny manhood. This results, of course, also in the cessation or diminishment of womanhood, but that does not concern the factions as it is only their own interests which are of importance to them."

"How could such things come about?"

"Simply," I said. "On an artificial world, conditioned to approve of negativistic ideologies, with determination and organization, and techniques of psychological manipulation, taking advantage of antibiological antecedents, they may be easily accomplished."

"Even deviancy, and madness, threatening the future of the world itself?" he asked.

"Certainly," I said.

He shuddered.

"Some people are afraid to open their eyes," I said.

"Why?" he asked.

"They have been told it is wrong to do so."

"That is insanity," he said.

"No," I said. "It is cleverness on the part of those who fear only that others will see."

He shuddered again.

"But perhaps one day they will open their eyes," I said.

He was silent.

"But put such places from your mind," I said. "Now you are free. No longer now need you deny your feelings. No longer now need you conceal, or deny, your manhood."

"I am truly free?" he said.

"Yes," I said. I handed him the papers, and he looked at them, and then put them in his tunic.

"I do not know how to act, how to be," he said.

"Your instincts will tell you, your blood," I said. "Their

reality transcends your indoctrinations, presented under the colors of reason, as though reason, itself, had content."

"I am a man," he said.

"It is true," I said.

"You would touch my hand?" he asked.

"I grasp it," I said, "in friendship, and, too, in friendship, I place my other hand on your shoulder. Do so as well with me, if you wish."

We held one another's hand, our hands then clasped. My left hand was on his right shoulder, and his on mine. "You are a man," I said. "Do not fear to be one."

"I am grateful," he said, "—sir."

"It is nothing," said I, "sir."

"I think it would be well for him to leave soon," said Marcus. "For all we know Appanius may have repented of his indiscretion and be returning with men."

Lavinia looked up, agonized, at Milo.

"I liked your 'Lurius of Jad'," I told him.

"Thank you," said Milo.

"I didn't," said Marcus.

"Marcus is prejudiced," I said.

"But he is also right," he said.

"Oh?" I said.

"They were, on the whole, inferior performances," he said.

"Oh," I said.

"You see?" said Marcus.

"I liked it," I said.

"I am not really an actor," said Milo.

"Oh?" I said.

"No," he said. "An actor should be able to act. What I do is to play myself, under different names. That is all."

"That is acting, of a sort," I said.

"I suppose you are right," he said.

"Of course, I am right," I said.

"You are a wonderful actor, Master!" exclaimed Lavinia to Milo. Then she put down her head, quickly, fearing that she might be struck.

"You called me 'Master'," he said to her.

She lifted her head, timidly.

"It is appropriate," I said. "She is a slave. You are a free man." She had, of course, spoken without permission, but it seemed almost as though she had been unable to help herself. Considering the circumstances I decided to overlook the matter. To be sure, it would not do for her to make a habit of such errancies.

"Forgive me, Master!" she whispered to me.

"You may speak," I said.

"It is only," she said, "that I think the great and beautiful Milo is a wondrous actor. It is not that he acts a thousand roles and we cannot identify him from one role to the next. It is rather that he is himself, in a thousand roles, and it is himself, his wondrous self, that we love!"

"There," I said to Marcus. "See?"

" 'Love'?" said Milo, looking at the kneeling slave.

"Of course my opinion is only that of a slave," she said, looking down.

"That is true," I admitted.

" 'Love'?" asked Milo, again, looking at the slave.

"Yes, Master," she said, not raising her head.

"Get your head up, slave," I said to her.

Lavinia raised her head.

"Put your head back, as far as you can," I said.

She did so. This raised the line of her breasts, and prominently displayed the collar.

"She is pretty, isn't she?" I asked.

"She is a beautiful slave!" said Milo.

Tears of vulnerability, and emotion, filled Lavinia's eyes.

"Milo had best be on his way," said Marcus.

"Yes," I said.

Lavinia sobbed, but she could not, of course, break position.

"But moments ago," said Milo to me, "you owned us both!"

"True," I said.

"You should leave," said Marcus to Milo.

Again Lavinia sobbed, a sob which shook her entire body, but again she could not break position.

"I think,, said Milo to me, "that I would fain remain your slave!"

"Why?" I asked.

"That I might upon occasion, when permitted," said Milo, "have the opportunity to look upon this woman."

"Do you find her of interest?" I asked.

"Of course!" he said, startled.

"Then she is yours," I said.

"Mine!" he cried.

"Of course," I said. "She is only a slave, a property, a trifle, a bauble. I give her to you. Here is the key to her collar," I pressed the key into his hand. "You may break position," I said to the slave.

She flung herself to her belly before me, covering my feet with kisses. "Thank you! Thank you, Master!" she wept.

"Your new master is there," I said, indicating Milo.

Quickly then she lay before him, kissing his feet. "I love you Master!" she wept. "I love you!"

He reached down, awkwardly, to lift her up, but it seemed she fought him, struggling, and could not be raised higher than to her knees, and then, he desisting in amazement, she had her head down again, to his feet, in obeisance, and was kissing them. She was laughing, and crying. "I love you, Master!" she wept. "I love you! I will be hot, devoted and dutiful! I am yours! I will live to please you! I will live to love and serve you I love you, my master!" She kissed him again, and again, about the feet, the ankles, the sides of the calves. Then she looked up at him, timidly, love bright in her eyes. "I will try to be a good slave to you, Master!" she said.

"Surely I must free you!" he cried.

"No!" she suddenly cried, in terror.

"No?" he said.

"No!" she said. "Please, no, my Master!"

"I do not understand," he stammered.

"I have waited too long for my slavery! It is what I have desired and craved all my life! Do not take it from me!"

"I do not understand," he said, haltingly.

"I am not a man!" she said. "I am a woman! I want to love and serve, wholly, helplessly, unquestioningly, irreservedly, unstintingly! I want to ask nothing and to give all! I want to be possessed by you, to be yours literally, to be owned by you!"

He was speechless.

"My slavery is precious to me," she said. "Please, Master, do not take it from me!"

"What should I do?" he asked me, wildly.

Lavinia, too, kneeling before him, her arms now about his legs, looked at me, wildly, pleadingly, tears in her eyes.

"What do you want to do?" I asked him.

"Truly?" he asked.

"Yes," I said.

"She is beautiful!" he said.

"Of course," I said.

"I want her," he said.

"Subject to what limits?" I asked.

"To no limits," he said.

"Then it seems you want her wholly," I said.

"Yes," he said, "*wholly*."

"There is only one way to have a woman wholly," I said "and that is for her to be your slave, for you to own her."

"Please, please Master!" wept Lavinia, looking up at Milo. "Please, Master!"

"Do with her what you wish," I said. "But she is a slave. It is the only thing which will truly fulfill her. It is the only thing which will make her truly happy."

"I do not know what to do!" he said.

"What do you want to do?" I asked.

"I want to own her!" he cried, angrily. "I want to own every inch of her, every particle of her, every bit of her, totally, every hair on her head, every mark on her body, all of her, all of her! I want to own her, completely!"

"Yes, Master! Yes, Master!" said Lavinia.

"It is what you want, and it is what she wants, too," I said.

"You understand," said he to Lavinia, "that if I make this decision, it is made."

"Yes, Master!" she said.

"Once it is made, it is made," he said.

"Yes, Master!" she said.

"And that is acceptable to you?" he asked.

"She is a slave," I said. "It makes no difference whether it is acceptable to her or not. You are the master."

He looked down at Lavinia.

"He is right, of course, Master," she said. "My wishes are nothing, as they are only the wishes of a slave. My will is nothing, as it is only the will of a slave. I am at your mercy, totally. I am in your power, completely."

"Aii!" he said, understanding this.

"Master?" she asked.

"You are my slave," he announced, accepting her.

"I love you, Master!" she wept, putting her head against his thigh.

"I own you," he said, softly, wonderingly.

"Yes, Master," she said.

"Truly," he said.

"Yes, my master!" she said.

"It is one thing to own a woman," I said, "and it is another to have her within the bonds of an excellent mastery."

"Undoubtedly," he said.

"I do not think you have had much experience at this sort of thing," I said.

"No," he admitted. "I haven't."

"Perhaps you, slave girl," I said to Lavinia, "can teach him something about the handling of slaves."

"Of course, Master," she smiled.

"You must make certain that you get everything you want

from her," I said, "and then, if you wish, more, even a thousand times more."

"Aii!" he said.

"All is your due," I said. "She is a slave."

"How can I believe such happiness?" he asked.

"Do not yield to the temptation of being weak with her," I cautioned him. "She loves you, but she must also fear you. She must know that you are not to be trifled with. She must know herself to be always within your discipline."

"I understand," he said.

"And as she is female," I said, "she may occasionally, curious, foolishly, particularly at first, wish to test the strength of your will, to discover, if you like, the boundaries of her condition."

"Master!" protested Lavinia.

"It is then up to you to teach her what they are, promptly, decisively, unmistakably."

"I understand," he said.

"She wants to know, so to speak, the length of her chain, the location of the walls of her cell. Too, she wants to be reassured of your strength. She wants to know that you are her master, truly, in the fullness of reality. Having learned this, she need not be so foolish in the future. She will have discovered that stone is hard and that fire burns. Thenceforth she will be in her place, pleased and content."

"The whip, tell him of the whip, Master!" said Lavinia.

"It is a symbol of authority, and an instrument of discipline," I said. "The slave is subject to it. Some masters think it is useful to occasionally use it on a slave, if only to remind her that she is a slave."

"How could anything so beautiful be touched with the leather?" he asked.

"That we learn to obey, and who is master!" laughed Lavinia.

"Buy a whip," I advised him.

"Yes, Master," said Lavinia.

"You wish me to have a whip?" asked Milo of the slave.

"Yes, Master!" she said.

"But, why?" he asked.

"So I well know that I must obey, and be pleasing!" she said.

"I see," he said.

"And that you will have a convenient implement at hand for enforcing my discipline," she said.

"A whip, of course, is not absolutely necessary," I said. "There are many other means of enforcing discipline."

"True," said Lavinia.

"But there is much to be said for the whip," I said. "It is perhaps the simplest, most practical device for such purposes. It is also traditional. Also, of course, it has symbolic value."

Lavinia, on her knees, looked up at Milo, her master. "Yes, Master!" she said.

"You truly think I should get a whip?" asked Milo. I was pleased that he had addressed this question to me, and not to Lavinia. He was beginning, I noted, to get a sense of the mastery. The decision in such matters lay among free men, not with slaves. Lavinia looked up at me, smiling. She, too, to her delight, recognized that she had been left out of the matter. Milo was learning, quickly, how to relate to her, namely, as her master. She was a slave. Such decisions would be made by others. She would not participate in them, but, as was appropriate for a slave, simply abide by their consequences.

"Certainly," I said.

He pondered the matter.

"And," I said, glancing down at Lavinia, "if she is not pleasing, use it on her, liberally, and well."

He swallowed, hard.

She put down her head, shyly.

"She is a slave," I said, "not a free companion, who may not be touched, to whom nothing may be done, even if she turns your life into a torture, even if she drives you mad, even if she intends to destroy you, hort by hort."

"She is so beautiful," he said. "It is hard to think of touching her with the whip."

"Sometimes," I said, "it is the most beautiful who are most in need of a whipping."

"May I speak?" asked Lavinia.

"Yes," said Milo.

"Too, Master," said Lavinia, "I love you, so I want you, sometime, or sometimes, to whip me."

He regarded her, puzzled.

"I want to know I am your slave," she said.

"I do not understand," he said.

"Teach me that you are my master."

"I do not understand," he said.

"It has to do with being subject to the master," I said, "with being truly his."

"Interesting," said Milo.

"For a female," I said, "I would recommend the wide-bladed, five-stranded whip."

Lavinia looked up, startled. She had not anticipated, it seemed, that whip. Doubtless she already regretted her recent tolerances and enthusiasms. If it were to be to that particular implement that she was to be subject, matters, it seemed, were to be viewed suddenly in a quite different perspective. On Gor, slave girls live in terror of that whip. It is designed for the female slave, to correct her behavior with great effectiveness while not leaving lasting traces, which might reduce her value.

"Is anything wrong?" I asked Lavinia.

"I will try to be pleasing to my master," she said.

"I am sure of it," I said.

"It seems she knows that whip," he said.

"She has at least heard of it," I said. "With it on your wall, I have little doubt she will prove to be a most excellent slave, particularly if she has once felt it. It is an excellent tool. You can buy one for as little as one or two copper tarsks."

"If I should come into some money," said Milo, "I shall certainly consider it."

"You are going to come into some money," I said.

"I do not understand," he said.

"You are well advised to leave Ar," I said.

"Undoubtedly," he said.

"For this," I said, "you should have money.".

"But alas," smiled Milo, "I have no money."

"Here," I said, "are ten pieces of gold." I counted them out, into Milo's hand. He looked at me, disbelievingly. I had already given fifteen pieces to Tolnar and Venlisius each. They had upheld the laws of Ar and preserved their honor. They would also file the papers, and several certified copies of them, in various places, and, by courier, with certain other parties, official and unofficial, in various cities. It would be next to impossible, for, say, Seremides, to recover them all. I retained my copies, of course. Both Tolnar and Venlisius, with my concurrence, thought it wise to remove both themselves and their families from Ar. Fifteen gold pieces each was a fortune. It would enable them to relocate with ease and reestablish themselves much as they might wish, wherever they might wish. At the time Boots Tarsk-Bit had obtained the Home Stone of Ar's Station I had had something like ninety gold pieces left from the one hundred gold pieces I had obtained in the north. I had given Boots half of these, forty-five gold pieces, and had retained the other forty-five. I had then given fifteen each to Tolnar and Venlisius. I had now given ten to Milo, and had retained five. Five pieces of gold, in its way, incidentally, is also a fortune on Gor. One could live, for example, in many cities, though not in contemporary Ar, with its press on housing and shortages of food, for years on such resources.*"

"Permit me," said Milo, "to return one of these gold pieces to you."

"Why?" I asked.

"You paid a tarsk bit for me," he smiled. "Thus I would not wish you to lose money on the arrangement."

"He learns honor, and generosity, quickly," I said to Lavinia.

"He is my master," she said.

I showed the coin to Marcus. "You see," I said to him, "I have made a considerable profit."

"You should be of the merchants," he assured me.

The new slave, she in the bracelets and shackles, lying on her side, chained by the neck, to the ring, near the couch, made a tiny sound.

I put the gold piece back in my wallet.

"You should leave," said Marcus to Milo.

"But a moment," I said.

I looked down at the new slave, whom I had decided to call 'Talena', which slave name was also entered on her papers, in the first endorsement, as her first slave name pertinent to these papers, and by means of which she could always be referred to in courts of law as, say, the slave who on such and such a date was known by the name 'Talena.' This did not preclude her name being changed, of course, now or later, by myself, or others. Slaves, as other animals, may be named, or renamed, as the masters please. Indeed, if the master wishes, they need not be named at all. She made another small sound, like a tiny moan of protest. She stirred, a little. I saw her hands twist a little, behind her, her wrists locked in the bracelets.

*Although it is not my policy to include Cabot's marginal notes, jottings, etc., which are often informal, and apparently written at different times, in the text of his accounts, I think it would not be amiss to hypothesize certain approximate equivalencies here. To be sure, much seems to depend on the city and the particular weights involved. For example, a "double tarn" is twice the weight of a "tarn." It seems there are usually eight tarsk bits in a copper tarsk, and that these are the result of cutting a circular coin in half, and then the halves in half, and then each of these halves in half. An analogy would be the practice of cutting the round, flat Gorean loaves of sa-tarna bread into eight pieces. There are apparently something like one hundred copper tarsks in a silver tarsk in many cities. Similarly, something like ten silver tarsks would apparently be equivalent, depending on weights, etc., to one gold piece, say, a single "tarn." Accordingly, on this approach, the equivalencies, very approximately, and probably only for certain cities, would be eight tarsk bits to a copper tarsk; one hundred copper tarsks to a silver tarsk; and ten silver tarsks to a gold piece, a single tarn. On this approach there would be, literally, 8,000 tarsk bits in a single gold piece. —J.N.

I went to the table at the side of the couch and lifted up the decanter of wine. I then stood near the slave and poured the wine out, upon her. She jerked under the thin, chill stream, awakening, discovering herself chained.

"Who dares!" she cried.

I handed the decanter to Marcus, who put it to the side.

"You!" she cried, lying on her side, turning her head, looking up at me. "Is it truly you?"

"On your knees, slave girl," I said, lifting her to her knees.

"It is you!" she cried, wildly, now kneeling.

"Your name is 'Talena'," I said. "That is the name I have put on you."

"Sleen!" she said. She could not rise to her feet, as she was back-braceleted, with her ankles shackled closely to her wrists.

"Lavinia," I said. "Come here, and kneel beside the new slave."

Lavinia obeyed, but with obvious uneasiness.

"She-sleen!" cried the new slave.

Lavinia kept her eyes straight ahead.

"Sleen!" cried the slave, Talena, to Milo.

"I was a seduction slave," he said to her. "I obeyed my master."

"Sleen! Sleen!" she cried.

"Beware," I said to Talena, "you are addressing a free man."

"You are free?" she said to Milo.

"Yes," he said. "I am free."

"Impossible!" she cried.

"No," he said. "Now it is I who am free, and you who are the slave."

" 'Slave'!" she cried. "How dare you, you sleen!"

"Now we have the two slaves kneeling side by side," I said, "both well exposed to view, both suitably slave naked."

Talena tore at the bracelets.

"You may chafe your wrists," I warned her.

"Sleen!" she wept.

"One is mine, and one is yours," I said.

"Yes," said Milo.

"I now offer you an even trade," I said. "If you wish, you may have this female, whom I have decided to call "Talena," and I shall have your Lavinia.

Talena looked suddenly, disbelievingly, at me, and then, as suddenly, wildly at Milo. "Accept me!" she cried. "Accept me! I will make it worth your while! I will give you thousands of gold pieces. I will reward you with villas! I will give you a hundred beautiful women as slaves. If you wish I will give you boys! I will give you high posts in Ar!"

"No," said Milo.

"Surely you do not prefer a naked slave to me!" she cried.

"But you, too, are a naked slave," he said.

"But you think me the most beautiful woman on all Gor!" she said.

"No," he said.

"But you said such things!" she said.

"Did you believe me?" he asked.

She regarded him, in helpless rage.

"I was a seduction slave," he said.

"Who is more beautiful than I?" she demanded.

"Lavinia," said he.

"Master!" breathed Lavinia, radiant.

"That slave!" cried Talena.

"That other slave," he said.

"Preposterous!" cried Talena.

"It is she who is the most beautiful woman on all Gor," he said.

"Master jests," laughed Lavinia.

"To be sure," he granted her, "I have not seen all the women on Gor."

Lavinia laughed, delightedly.

"But of those I have seen," he said, "it is she who is the most beautiful!"

"Really, Master," said Lavinia, shyly, chidingly.

"It is true!" he said.

"But at least I will do?" she asked.

"Yes," said he, softly, "you will do, beautiful slave."

"I love you, Master!" she said.

"Am I not beautiful?" demanded Talena.

"You are not unattractive," said Milo.

" 'Not unattractive'!" she said.

"No," he said.

"I am beautiful!" she said.

"You would probably bring your master a satisfactory selling price," he said.

"Thousands of gold pieces!" she said.

"For your femaleness alone, in chains?" I asked, skeptically.

"Of course!" she said.

"Are you trained?" I asked.

"Of course not!" she said.

"Probably you would go for something in the neighborhood of two or three silver tarsks," I said. That seemed about right, given the condition of the current markets.

"Absurd!" she said.

"Remember," I said, "they are only buying a female, and what you are good for."

"Sleen!" she said.

"Milo had best be on his way," said Marcus.

"Yes," I agreed.

"You would truly prefer this chit of a slave to me?" asked Talena of Milo, unbelievingly.

"Yes," said Milo.

"To the other chit of a slave," I said.

"Yes," said Milo.

"Sleen!" said Talena.

"Another has been chosen over you," I said.

She looked at me, in rage.

"Do not be distressed," said Lavinia to her. "We are only slaves, and men may look upon us, and pick us, and sort amongst us, as they please. In another time, in another place, their choices might be different."

"She-sleen!" hissed Talena.

"We must go," said Milo.

"I am unclothed, Master," said Lavinia.

"Dress," I said. "Take the garments you wore here, and those, too, of the former Ubara of Ar."

Talena looked at me in anger.

"Consider them paid for with moneys from the gold piece returned to me," I said.

"Excellent," said Milo.

Lavinia scurried to gather up garments.

"Do not neglect the tunic with the disrobing loop!" Milo called to her.

"Yes, Master!" she laughed, snatching it up.

"It would probably be good for her to disguise herself as a free woman," I said.

"Yes," agreed Milo. He pointed to the garments near his feet, which had been removed earlier by the former Ubara. Lavinia, from the side of the couch, hurried to them, and fell to her knees, to sort through them. This put her, again, of course, on her knees, at Milo's feet. She looked up at him, happily, in her place. Then she bent again to her work.

"There is a purse here!" she said.

"It is mine!" cried Talena.

"It is heavy," said Lavinia.

"Give it to your master," I said.

He regarded me.

"Keep it," I said.

"It is mine!" said Talena.

"Slaves own nothing," I said. "It is they who are owned."

Milo dropped the purse inside his tunic. Some numerous

coins, of smaller denomination than gold pieces, I thought, might be useful to him.

"And do not forget this," I said, lifting up the small, capped leather capsule on its thong which the former Ubara had worn about her neck, which contained the compromising note, which had given her such power over him when he was a slave.

"My thanks!" said he.

Talena struggled a little, helplessly, futilely.

The capsule disappeared in his tunic.

"And what of the note you received?" I asked. "I trust that it was destroyed."

"It was too beautiful to destroy," he said. "I tied a thread about it and inserted it between two stones at the theater. I can retrieve it by the thread."

"Do so," I said.

"I will not leave it in Ar," he said.

"Lavinia composed the note, and wrote it out," I said.

"I had gathered during the events of the morning," he said, "that it had not been written by Talena of Ar."

"By that slave over there?" I asked.

"When she was Talena of Ar," he said.

Talena looked away, angrily.

"I am pleased to learn," said Milo to Lavinia, "that you did the note."

"I am pleased, if master is pleased," she said, shyly.

"It is beautiful," he said.

"I meant every word of it," she said, looking up at him.

"It was exquisite," he said.

"In it," she said, "I poured out my heart to you. I bared my thoughts, my dreams, my hopes, my feelings, my emotions, my heart, to you. I made myself naked before you. I put myself at your feet, at your mercy."

"It was like the letter of a slave girl to her master," he said.

"That is what it was," she said, softly.

"Dress, slave," he said.

"Yes, Master," she said.

In a bit Lavinia was bedecked in the robes which had been worn by Talena.

"That is my clothing!" said Talena. "Tell that slave to take off my clothing!"

"I think she will attract little attention in the streets," I said. "Indeed, I do not think that the great Milo in the company of a free woman in the streets will come as any great surprise to passers-by. To be sure, the woman would presumably take great pains to make certain that she was discretely veiled."

"I shall, Master!" said Lavinia.

"She-sleen!" said Talena.

"And if any know the tricks of Appanius," I said, "they will presumably smile to themselves, thinking that this mysterious free woman may find herself, perhaps even in a short while, clad somewhat more revealingly, indeed, perhaps in little more than a slave collar."

Lavinia laughed. Already, of course, within the robes, she was in a slave collar.

"And if anyone saw the new slave enter here earlier, when she was a free woman, they will presumably believe it to be her exiting, as well."

Talena sobbed with fury.

Lavinia stood before us. She was clothed now, save for her veiling, and the adjustment of the hood.

"How do you like your free woman, Master?" she asked Milo.

"You are not my free woman," he said. "You are my slave."

"But I am in the robes of a free woman," she said.

"I shall enjoy removing them from you later," he said.

"I shall look forward to it," she said.

"You must leave," said Marcus to Milo.

He nodded.

Lavinia then knelt before me. It seemed paradoxical to see a woman in the robes of concealment kneeling. "Thank you for giving me to Milo, Master," she said to me. She then, softly, in gratitude, kissed my feet. She then kissed those of Milo, her master. "I love you, Master," she said to him.

"Veil yourself," he said.

Then, kneeling at our feet, she veiled herself, and then adjusted the hood.

"I wish you well," I said to Milo.

"I wish you well," said Marcus to him.

"My thanks for everything," said Milo.

"It is nothing," I assured him.

We looked down at Lavinia. She, over the veil, from within the hood, looked up at us.

"Do not forget to buy a whip," I said.

"I will not," he said.

"If I do not please you," she said to Milo, "punish me so terribly that I know I must please you."

"I will," said Milo.

She lowered her head, in submission.

"You are both wished well," said Milo to us. We then, in turn, Milo and I, and Milo and Marcus, clasped hands.

"Do not leave me here with these men, alone!" called Talena.

But Milo, followed by his slave, had gone.

We then turned to face Talena.

She shrank down a little, in her chains.

"You will never get away with this," she whispered.

"I have already gotten away with it," I said.

"I do not understand," she said.

"You belong to me," I said. "You are now my slave."

She looked at me with fury.

"Hail Talena," I said, "Ubara of Ar."

"Yes!" she said.

"No," I said.

" 'No'?" she said.

"No," I said. "Do you not know you are mocked, slave?"

"It is a technicality!" she said.

"Not at all," I said. "You are my slave, in full legality."

She looked at me, in fury.

"Your slavery is complete," I said, "by all the laws of Ar, and Gor. Your papers, and certified copies thereof, will be filed and stored in a hundred places."

"You will never get me out of the city!" she said.

"That can be arranged in time," I said, "when I come for you."

" 'When you come for me'?" she said.

"Yes," I said. "Tomorrow I will have your whereabouts conveyed to Seremides by courier."

"I do not understand!" she said.

"He will not know that you have been enslaved," I said. "He will think only that you were foolish enough to leave the Central Cylinder without guards and perhaps fell in with brigands and were robbed. Surely you can invent some plausible story."

"He will rescue me!" she said.

"You will then resume your role as Ubara of Ar," I said. "Things will seem much the same, but they will be, of course, quite different. You are now, you see, my slave."

"You are mad!" she said.

"And you will not know when I will come for you."

She looked at me, frightened.

"And I will come for you," I said. "I promise you that."

"No!" she said.

"Yes," I said, "I will come to claim my slave."

"I will be in the Central Cylinder!" she said. "I will be surrounded by guards!"

"You will know that one day I will come for you," I said.

"Why will you not keep me now?" she asked.

"My work in Ar is not yet finished," I said.

"Your work in Ar?"

"Cos must be cast out of Ar," I said.

"Seremides will hunt you down! I will see to it!" she said.

"The downfall of Seremides," I said, "has already been arranged."

Marcus looked at me, puzzled.

I nodded to him. "Myron will accomplish it," I said.

"I do not understand," he said.

'You will see," I said.

"Kaissa?" he asked.

"Of a sort," I said.

"Guardsmen will turn Ar upside down for you!" she said.

"There is one place I do not think it is likely that they will look," I said.

"What place?" she said.

"Curiosity is not becoming in a kajira," I said.

She jerked at the bracelets, angrily.

That place, of course, would be within their own ranks.

"Cos can never be cast out of Ar!" she said. "Cos is too strong! Cos is invincible!" she said.

"Ar was thought to be invincible," I said, "once."

"Ar will wear continue to wear the yoke of Cos!" she said.

"Do not be too sure of that," I said, "and, too, as you are a slave, it is you who may find herself in a yoke."

"I am not a slave!" she said.

"Amusing," I said.

"Recall the papers!" she said. "I shall buy my freedom."

"You have nothing," I said.

"Seremides can arrange for their recall," she said.

"You would let him know that you are a slave?" I asked.

She blanched. Then she said, "Yes, if necessary!"

"But it does not matter," I said.

"I do not understand," she said.

"You are not for sale," I said.

She looked at me, angrily.

"At least not now," I said.

"Sleen!" she wept.

"She is going to be here until sometime tomorrow," I said to Marcus. "Accordingly I will now feed and water her."

" 'Feed and water me'!" she said, angrily.

"Yes," I said. "By tomorrow, at noon, I am sure you will be grateful to me for having done so.' '

"You are kind," she said, acidly.

"On the whole," I said, "if a slave is pleasing, and is striving to serve with perfection, I believe in treating her with kindness."

"I hate you!" she cried.

I went to the table and picked up the tray of dainties. "The wine is gone," I said to Marcus. I had poured it out on her, to rouse her. "Would you fill the decanter with water, from the back?"

"Yes," he said.

I, then, in a moment, crouched beside Talena.

"Do not touch me!" she said.

"You are not interested in offering me your favors, to buy your freedom?" I asked.

She looked at me, suddenly, sharply.

I regarded her.

"Perhaps," she said, coyly.

I put the tray of dainties on the floor to my left. The makings of the gag I had prepared for her were a bit behind her, to her left.

She inched forward, toward me, on her knees. She put her head forward, toward me, her lips pursed, her eyes closed.

I did not touch my lips to hers.

She opened her eyes.

"I had once thought," I said, "that Marlenus had acted precipitately in disowning you, but I see now that he, though your father, understood you far better than I. He recognized that his daughter was a slave."

She drew back in her bonds, in fury.

"You look well as a slave," I said. "It is what you are."

"I hate you!" she said.

"And as for your favors," I said, "do not concern yourselves with them. They are mine to command, as I please."

She shook with rage.

"She belongs in a collar," said Marcus.

"You have been watching?" I said.

"Yes," he said. He had the wine decanter with him, now filled with water.

"And eventually I will have her in one," I said. "And then it will be clear to all the world, and not just to us, that she is a slave."

"You are both sleen!" she wept.

"Open your mouth," I said. "Eat."

She looked at me.

"Yes," I said, "you will be fed as what you are, a slave."

I then put one of the tidbits into her mouth, and, in a moment, angrily, she had finished it. It is not unusual for a slave's first food from a new master to be received in a hand feeding. It may also be done, from time to time, of course, with all, or a portion, of a given snack, or meal. This sort of thing expresses symbolically, and teaches her also, on a very deep level, that she is dependent upon him for her food, that it is from his hand, so to speak, that she receives it.

"Although this doubtless does not compare with the provender of the Central Cylinder," I said, "which is reputed the best this side of the palace at Telnus, it is such that you should not come to expect it as a slave."

She finished another tidbit.

"We do not have any slave gruel on hand," I said.

She shuddered.

"That is enough," I said. "We must be concerned with your figure. You are a little overweight, I think. In a paga tavern or brothel, you would have to be trimmed down a little."

"Do not speak so of me," she said.

"Surely you would wish to look well, curled on the furs, at a man's feet, in a lamplit alcove."

"I," she said, "in an alcove?"

"Certainly," I said.

"Never!" she said.

"I wonder how you would perform," I said.

"I would not "perform," " she said.

"Oh, yes, you would," I assured her.

She looked at me.

"There are whips, and chains, there," I said.

She turned white.

"Yes," I said.

"And for whom would I be expected to perform?" she asked.

"For any man," I said.

"I see," she said.

"And to the best of your abilities," I said.

"I see," she said.

"Perhaps, someday, Tolnar, or Venlisius, might be interested in trying you out, to see if you were satisfactory."

She looked at me.

"If you were not," I said, "they would doubtless have you severely punished, or slain."

"I do not understand them," she said. "To uphold the law they have jeopardized their careers, they have entered into exile!"

"There are such men," I said.

"I do not understand them," she said.

"That," I said, "is because you do not understand honor."

"Honor," she said, "is for fools."

"I am not surprised that one should hold that view, who is a traitress."

She tossed her head, in impatience.

"You betrayed your Home Stone," I said.

"It is only a piece of rock," she said.

"I am sorry that I do not have time now for your training," I said.

" 'My training'?" she asked.

"Your slave training," I said.

She stared at me, disbelievingly.

"But it can wait," I said.

"You amuse me," she said, "you who come from a world of weaklings! You are too weak to train a slave."

"Do you remember our last meeting?" I asked.

"Of course," she said.

"It took place in the house of Samos, first slaver of Port Kar," I said.

"Yes," she said.

"You were not then on your knees," I said.

"No," she said, squirming a little.

"But you were in a slave collar."

"Perhaps," she said.

"At that time I did not realize how right it was on you," I said.

She looked away, angrily.

"As it is on any woman," I said.

She pulled a bit at the bracelets, angrily.

"I could not then rise from my chair," I said. "I had been cut in the north by the blade of a sword, treated with a poison from the laboratory of Sullius Maximus, once one of the five Ubars of Port Kar."

She did not speak.

"Perhaps you remember how you ridiculed me, how you mocked and scorned me."

"I am now naked, and on my knees before you," she said. "Perhaps that will satisfy you."

"That is only the beginning of my satisfaction," I said.

"Do not pretend to be strong," she said. "I know you are weak, and from a world of weaklings. You come from a world where women may destroy you in a thousand ways, and you are forbidden to so much as touch them."

I looked at her.

"I hold you in contempt," she said, "as I did then."

"Did you think I would walk again?" I asked.

"No," she said.

"Perhaps that explains the license you felt, to abuse me," I speculated.

"No," she said. "That you were confined to a chair was amusing, but I knew that you would free me, that I could do whatever I pleased to you, whatever I wished, with impunity. I despise you."

"I do not think it would be so amusing to you," I said, "if it were you in whom the poison had worked, paralyzing you, making it impossible for you to rise from the chair."

She didn't answer.

"Doubtless such toxins still exist," I mused, "and might be procured. Perhaps one could be entered into your fair body, with so small a wound as a pin prick."

"No!" she cried, in alarm.

"But anything may be done to a slave," I said.

"Please, no!" she said.

"But then," I said, "I think I would rather have your lovely legs free, that you might hurry to and fro, serving me, or be able to dance before me, for my pleasure."

" 'Dance'!" she wept. " 'For your pleasure'!"

"Of course," I said.

She regarded me, aghast.

"Such practices are surely not unusual among slaves," I said, "such things as dancing before their masters."

"I suppose not," she said.

"For they are owned," I said.

"Yes," she said.

I was silent.

"What are you thinking of?" she demanded.

"I was thinking," I said, "that a special chair might be constructed, a holding chair, a prison chair, so to speak, into which you might be inserted, it then locked shut about you for, say, a few months. More simply, you might be simply chained in a chair for some months. This would give you, I would think, something of the sense of one afflicted with such difficulties. Then again, of course, you might consider how amusing you might find it."

"Do not even speak so!" she said.

"I would speculate," I said, "that after only a few Ahn in such a predicament you would be eager to be freed, that you would soon beg piteously to be permitted to dance, to run and fetch, to serve, such things."

"You can walk now," she murmured.

Much the same effect, of course, can be achieved in many ways, for example, by close chains, by the slave box, by cramped kennels, tiny cages, and such. These devices are excellent for improving the behavior of slaves.

She put her head down. I saw that she was frightened, that she was no longer certain of me.

"I received the antidote in Torvaldsland," I said, "brought to me from far-off Tyros, and, interestingly, as a matter of honor."

She lifted her head.

"Do you understand honor?" she asked.

"No," I said.

"How, then, can you speak of it?" she asked.

"Once or twice I glimpsed it," I said.

"And what is it like?" she asked.

"It is like a sun, in the morning," I said, "rising over dark mountains."

"Fool!" she cried.

I was silent.

"Weakling!" she said.

I was silent.

"You are a weakling!" she said.

"Perhaps not so much now as I once was," I said.

"Free me!" she said.

"Why?" I asked.

"Before," she said, "you freed me!"

"I am wiser now," I said.

"Cos can never be driven from Ar!" she said.

"The might of Cos on the continent," I said, "as opposed to her naval power, is largely dependent on mercenaries."

"So?" she asked.

"Mercenaries, on the whole," I said, "saving some companies with unusual allegiance to particular leaders, such as those of Pietro Vacchi and Dietrich of Tarnburg, are seldom trustworthy, and are almost never more trustworthy than their pay."

"It matters not," she said. "Their pay is assured."

"Is it?" I asked.

"Ten companies could hold Ar," she said.

"Perhaps," I said. "I am not sure of it."

"Is it truly your intention to call my whereabouts to the attention of Seremides?" she asked.

"Yes," I said.

"He will rescue me," she said.

"No," I said. "In a sense he, or Myron, or others, will merely be keeping you for me, rather like your being boarded at some commercial slave kennels."

"What a beast you are," she said.

"Indeed," I said, "they will be saving me your upkeep."

"I shall be restored to the honors of the Ubara!" she said.

"No," I said. "You are now a slave. A slave cannot be Ubara. You can do no more now than pretend to be the Ubara. In a sense you will be an impostor. And let us hope that no one detects your deception, for, as you know, the penalties for a slave masquerading as a free woman are quite severe."

She looked at me, in fury.

"To be sure," I said, "few, at least at present, are likely to suspect your bondage. Most, seeing you participate in state ceremonies, holding court, opening games, and such, will think you are truly the Ubara. Only a few will know that you are my slave girl. Among these few, of course, will be yourself, and myself." .

"It interests me," she said, "that you will not try to smuggle me now out of the city."

"You are only a slave girl," I said. "You are not that important."

"I see," she said.

"It would be rather pointless to take you now, and I do not find it convenient to do so."

'I see," she said.

"Other projects, you must understand, are of much higher priority."

"Naturally," she said.

"You can wait to be collected."

"Of course!" she said.

"Besides," I said, "it amuses me to think of you in the Central Cylinder."

"Oh?" she asked, angrily.

"Waiting for me to come for you," I said.

"Absurd!" she said.

"Particularly as you grow ever more apprehensive, and more frantic, sensing Ar slipping away from you, and your power collapsing about your ears."

"You are mad!" she said.

"But now I must water you," I said. I lifted up the decanter of water. "There is a good deal of water here," I said, "but I want you to drink it, as you will not have another drink until sometime tomorrow. Put your head back."

I set the opening of the bottle to her mouth, but scarcely had she dampened her lips than she drew back her head.

"What is wrong?" I asked.

"This water has been drawn for days," she said. "Surely it is not fresh!"

"Drink it," I said. "All of it."

She looked at me.

"Your head can be held back by the hair," I said, "and your nostrils can be pinched shut."

"That will not be necessary," she said.

I then gave her of the water.

"Please," she protested.

But I did not see fit to permit her to dally in the downing of it.

I then set the decanter to the side, empty.

"That is a nicely rounded slave belly," said Marcus.

I patted it twice. It sounded not unlike a filled wineskin. Too it bulged out, and reacted not dissimilarly.

She drew back.

"If you were to be sold in a Tahari market," I told her, "you might find yourself forced to drink a large amount of water, like this, shortly before your sale."

She crept back, on her knees, apprehensively, putting a little more distance between us.

"Do not fear," I said. "I have no intention at present of testing you for vitality."

I then picked up the makings of the gag which were to her left, the wadding and the binding.

She eyed them, apprehensively.

"This is not the first time you have been a slave," I said. "Once, I know, you were owned by Rask of Treve."

She looked up at me.

"Did you serve him well?" I asked.

"He put me often in slave silk, and jewelry, to show me off," she said, "as it amused him, he, of Treve, to have the daughter of Marlenus of Ar for a slave, but he did not make much use of me. Indeed, I served him, by his will, almost entirely in domestic labors, keeping his tent, and such. This he seemed to feel was appropriate, such demeaning, servile labors, for the daughter of Marlenus of Ar. But, too, I do not think he much cared for me. Then, when he got his hands on a meaningless little blond chit, a true slave in every hort of her body, named El-in-or, he gave me away, to a panther girl named Verna, to be taken to the northern forests. I served panther girls, too, as a domestic slave, and was later sold, at the coast, where I came into the collar of Samos, of Port Kar."

"It is difficult to believe that Rask of Treve did not put you to slave use," I said.

"He did, of course," she said.

"And how were you?" I asked.

"He told guests that I was superb," she said.

"And were you?" I asked.

"I had better have been," she said.

"True," I said. I had twice met Rask of Treve, both times in Port Kar. He was the sort of fellow whom women strove to serve unquestioningly to the best of their abilities.

"Surely you learned much of the arts of the slave in his tent," I said.

"No," she said. "I was more of a prize, or a political prisoner. I was more like a free woman in slave silk than a slave, in his camp."

"Then, in effect," I said, "aside from having worn the collar and such, you have never experienced what one might call a full slavery?"

"Like a common slave slut?" she asked.

"Yes," I said.

"No!" she said, angrily.

"That would seem to have been an oversight on the part of Rask of Treve," I said.

"Perhaps," she said, angrily.

"Perhaps other masters can remedy that oversight," I said.

"I am the Ubara of Ar!" she said.

"No," I said. "You are a slave girl." I then gagged her.

I then stood up, and looked down at her. "Tomorrow," I said, "guardsmen will come to free you of your bonds, and return you to the Central Cylinder. You must not forget, of course, even in the Central Cylinder, that you are my slave girl. Too, you must remember that I will come for you. When will it be? You will not know. Will you fear to enter a room alone, or a corridor unescorted, for fear someone may be there, waiting? Will you fear dark places, or shadows? Will you fear high bridges, and roofs, and promenades, because you fear the loop of a tarnsman tightening on your body, dragging you into the sky, his capture? Will you fear even your own chambers, perhaps even to open the portals of your own wardrobe, for fear someone might be waiting? Will you fear to remove your clothing, for fear someone, somehow, somewhere, might see? Will you fear to enter the bath, for fear you might be surprised there? Will you fear to sleep, I wonder, knowing that someone might come to you in the night, that you might waken suddenly to the gag, and helplessness?"

I looked down at her. There were tears in her eyes, over the gag. She looked well in bonds. She was a pretty slave.

"Let us go," I said to Marcus.

We then left the room.

28 The Room

I lay on a blanket, in the small room, in the *insula* of Torbon, on Demetrios Street, in the Metellan district.

Outside, the city was generally quiet.

I looked up at the darkness of the ceiling.

It must have been in the neighborhood of the twentieth Ahn. By now Milo and Lavinia must have left the city. Too, Boots Tarsk-Bit, with his troupe, would be on his way north, perhaps on the Viktel Aria. Somewhere, hidden among their belongings, would be an obscure item, a seeming oddity, a stone. To look at it one might not know it from many other stones. And yet it was different from all other stones; it was special. I wondered about the Home Stones of Gor. Many seem small and quite plain. Yet for these stones, and on account of these stones, these seemingly inauspicious, simple objects, cities have been built, and burned, armies have clashed, strong men have wept, empires have risen and fallen. The simplicity of many of these stones has puzzled me. I have wondered sometimes how it is that they have become invested with such import. They may, of course, somewhat simply, be thought of as symbolizing various things, and perhaps different things to different people. They can stand, for example, for a city, and, indeed, are sometimes identified with the city. They, have some affinity, too, surely, with territoriality and community. Even a remote hut, far from the paved avenues of a town or city, may have a Home Stone, and therein, in the place of his Home Stone, is the meanest beggar or the poorest peasant a Ubar. The Home Stone says this place is mine, this is my home. I am here. But I think, often, that it is a mistake to try to translate the Home Stone into meanings. It is not a word, or a sentence. It does not really translate. It is, more like a tree, or the world. It exists, which goes beyond, which surpasses, meaning. In this primitive sense the Home Stone is simply that, and irreducibly, the Home Stone. It is too important, too precious, to mean. And in not meaning, it becomes, of course, the most meaningful of all. It becomes, in a sense, the foundation of meaning, and, for Goreans, it is anterior to meaning, and precedes meaning. Do not ask a Gorean what the Home Stone means because he will not understand your question. It will puzzle him. It is the Home Stone. Sometimes I think that many Home Stones are so simple because they are too important, too precious, to be insulted with decoration or embellishment. And then, too, sometimes I think that they are kept, on the whole, so simple, because this is a way of saying that everything is important, and precious, and beautiful, the small stones by the river, the leaves of trees, the tracks of small animals, a blade of grass, a drop of water, a grain of sand, the world. The word 'Gor', in Gorean, incidentally, means 'Home Stone'. Their name for our common sun, Sol, is 'Tor-tu-Gor' which means 'Light upon the Home Stone'.

A wagon trundled by. I heard the snort of a tharlarion. There were not so many wagons now. There was less need. Ar was by now muchly looted, stripped of her gold and silver, her precious items, even of many of her women, and slaves. The wagon, at any rate, would be some sort of official carrier, or licensed, or authorized, as such. It was after curfew.

I thought of a slave. Tonight would not be a comfortable night for her, or, I supposed, the better part of tomorrow. I had already arranged that a sealed message, conveyed by courier, would reach the Central Cylinder tomorrow, after the tenth Ahn. I wondered if she had been yet missed. Quite possibly. If not now, surely by morning, when her women would arrive for her robing, her bathing, the breaking of her fast, her morning audiences. How frantic would then be the Central Cylinder. Well could I imagine Seremides storming about, striking subordinates, denouncing his staff, threatening his officers, and all Ar, overturning furniture, tearing down hangings, picking up the pen, putting it down again, spilling ink, shouting orders, rescinding them, issuing them again, demanding that word not be sent to the camp of Myron, not yet, not yet. How eagerly they would seize on any clue. How swiftly, how desperately, would the simple message be received, specifying her location. They would rush there and find she whom they took to be their Ubara chained in place, as though she might now be no more than someone's mere slave girl. How they would rejoice upon her recovery, and would hasten to cover her, and send for one of the metal workers, to relieve her of her effective, shameful bonds. They would then convey her back to the Central Cylinder, secretly, that none in Ar might know what had occurred. She would then, within an Ahn or two, be restored to the role of the Ubara, and perhaps even be seated again upon the throne. I wondered if she would be uneasy, or perhaps even terrified, realizing the folly in which she was now enmeshed, daring to ascend the dais, not to lie on its steps as a half naked slave, collared, at a Ubar's feet, an item of display, but to sit upon the throne itself. Surely she must be aware of the presumption of this act, of the insolence, and fearful peril, of it. One could scarcely dare conjecture the punishments which might be attendant upon it, she only a slave. Well must she be concerned to keep her bondage secret. Yet she must know that some in Ar would know that secret, that some would even have access to the papers involved in its proof.

I heard someone outside, down in the street, doubtless a guardsman, cry, "Halt! Halt!" There was then the sound of running feet. Guardsmen in the Metellan district, as now in Ar, generally, went in pairs. Some fellow, I gathered, had been spotted, violating the curfew.

No, the slave would not spend a comfortable night, lying on the flat flooring stones, naked, her wrists chained closely to her ankles, kept in place by a neck chain, fastened to a floor ring. It would be something of a change for her, from the comforts, and cushions, of the Ubara's couch. But I thought this might be good for her. Long ago, when she had been the slave of Rask of Treve, she had been, I gathered, treated as something rather special, kept less as a slave than as a free woman kept, for his amusement, in the shame of slave garb. There, I gathered, she had been kept more as a prize, or trophy, than a slave. She there, though certainly technically in bondage, had, it seems, been pampered. That did not displease me. Let this night, however, teach her what can be the lot of a more common girl, such as she was.

I looked up at the ceiling.

I did not think she would forget this first night in my keeping.

I smiled to myself.

Let her sit again upon the throne of Ar. Beneath the robes of the Ubara, in all their beauty, complexity and ornateness, she would be no more than my naked slave.

I heard a sound outside, on the stairs.

I thought that perhaps she might, in time, tend to forget that she was now a slave and come again, on the whole, to think of herself as the Ubara of Ar. On the other hand, surely, from time to time, perhaps in an uneasy or frightening moment, she would recollect that she was my slave. Sometimes at night, I did not doubt, she would start at some small noise, and lie there in the darkness, wondering if she were alone. Or perhaps I had come for my slave, with gag and bonds, to claim her.

I considered Ar, and its condition. I thought of the delta of the Vosk, and the disaster which had occurred there, and of the veterans returned from the delta. How angry I was, even though I was not of Ar, that they had, for all their loyalty and sacrifice, for all their service, courage and devotion, received little but scorn and neglect from their compatriots, a scorn and neglect engineered by factions hoping to profit from the perversities of such politics, using them to further their own ends, among these ends being to put Ar and those of Ar into a condition of even greater weakness and confusion, to undermine their will and sap their pride, to put Ar and those of Ar even more at the mercy of their enemies. And interestingly, it seemed that many of Ar, particularly the young, the less experienced, the more gullible, the more innocent, and, too, perhaps, the most fearful of hardship, responsibility and danger, and their attendant risks, those unaccustomed to such things, those who had always received and never given, those who had never sacrificed anything, were among those most ready to lap up the sops of Cos, clinging to excuses for their cowardice, indeed, commending their lack of courage as a new virtue, a new, and improved, convenient courage. Yet how unfair was this to the perceptive young, piercing the propaganda, scorning the public boards, recognizing without being told what was being done to them and their city, smarting with shame, burning with indignation, recollective of Ar's glory, the young in whom flowed the blood of their fathers, and the hope of the city's future. Perhaps there was not, after all, young and old, but rather those who were ready to work and serve, and those who were not, those who preferred to profit from the work and service of others, risking nothing, contributing nothing. But even so, how odd, I thought, that those who did not wade in the delta, facing the arrows of rencers, the spears of Cos, the teeth of tharlarion, should profess their superiority over those who did, indeed, by their work and service sheltering and protecting those who, obedient to the subtleties of Cos, heaped ridicule and abuse upon them. Why did such men return to such an Ar, one so unworthy of them? Because it was there that was their Home Stone. But the veterans now, within Ar, were a force. Indeed, Cos must now try anew to demean them, to undermine their influence, to once more turn people against them. Perhaps it could be done. Perhaps it was only necessary to cloak the ends of Cos in moral rhetorics. That had worked in the past. Perhaps it would work in the future. Those who control the public boards, it is said, control the city. But I was not sure of this. Goreans are not stupid. It is difficult to fool them more than once. They tend to remember. To be sure, Cos could certainly count on those who regarded their best interests as being served by Cosian rule, and many of these were highly placed in the city, even in the Central Cylinder. Too, the conditionings of Cos, verbal, visual and otherwise, surely would not be entirely ineffective. Such programs produce their puppets, legions of creatures convinced of values they have never reflected on, or examined in detail. There would always be the dupes, of one sort or another, and the opportunists, and the cowards, with their rationalizations. But, too, I speculated, there would be those of Ar to whom the Home Stone was a Home Stone, and not a mere rock, not a piece of meaningless earth. And so I thought of Ar under the yoke of Cos, and of hope, and pride, and of the Delta Brigade. I thought, too, of the mercenary might that held Ar oppressed. I thought of Seremides, whom I had known as long ago as the time of Cernus. I had spoken boldly to the slave in the room, but who knew what the future held. I wondered, too, of Marlenus of Ar, doubtless slain in the Voltai range, in his punitive raid against Treve. Doubtless his bones lay now in some remote canyon in the Voltai, picked by jards. Else what force, what might of man or nature, could have kept him from the walls of Ar?

There was now a small sound, outside the room. I had heard the creak of boards on the landing.

I lay very quietly.

The weight was now outside the door.

I rolled to the side and reached for the knife beside the blankets. I located it. I removed the knife from the sheath, putting it beside the sheath. I wrapped the blanket about my left forearm. I picked up the knife. I rose quietly to my feet. I did not think I would care to be the first person through the door. There was no light beneath the door, so whoever was outside was not carrying a lamp. I did not stand directly behind the door. The metal bolt of a crossbow, fired at close range, some inches from the other side of the door, that light a door, a sort not uncommon in the poorly built *insulae* of the Metellan district, could splinter through and bury itself in the opposite wall.

I heard the handle of the door, a lever handle, fixed crosswise in the door, move.

It moved only a little, of course, as the bolt was thrown, the lock peg in place. Two crossbars, too, had been set across the door, in their brackets, one about the height of a man's chest, the other about the height of his thighs. The door was thus both locked and barred. It would have to be burst in, breaking loose the brackets from the wall on my side. Normally this sort of thing is done with two or three men, one or two trying to burst in the door, in one attack upon it, and the other following, immediately, armed, to strike. Yet I was sure there was only one man on the other side of the door.

I then heard a tapping, softly, on the other side of the door.

I did not respond.

I waited.

Then, after a pause, there came four taps together. This was repeated, at intervals.

I was startled.

I discarded the blanket. I put the knife in my belt. I pulled loose the lock peg. I lifted the two bars from the door. I stepped back. The door opened.

"It is safe to come in, I trust," said a voice.

"Yes," I said. I myself might have been similarly reluctant to enter a dark room in an *insula*, late at night.

"I was careless," he said. "I was seen by guardsmen."

"Come inside," I said.

"I managed to elude them," he said. "I took to the roofs. They are searching to the west."

"What are you doing here?" I asked.

"I was not sure you would still be here," he said.

"I did not think it would be wise to suddenly change my residence," I said.

"I trust you can afford the rent on your single salary," said the voice.

I fumbled with a lamp, lighting it.

There had been, after the first knocking, alerting the occupant of the room, taps in groups of four. The fourth letter in the Gorean alphabet is the delka.

"Why have you come back?" I asked.

"I never went," he said.

"Where is Phoebe?" I asked.

"Back-braceleted, hooded, and chained by the neck to the back of one of the wagons of your friend, Tarsk-Bit," he said. "I so secured her with my own hands."

"She thinks you are with them, too, then?" I said.

"She will discover differently in the morning," he said.

"She will wish to come after you," I said.

"She is a female," he said. "Chains will keep her where I wish."

"She will be distraught," I said.

"The lash can silence her," he said.

"You are crying," I said. The lamp was now lit.

"It is the smoke from the lamp," he said.

"Of course," I said.

"She will be kept under exact discipline and in perfect custody," he said. "I have given orders to that effect. Moreover, if she is troublesome in any way, she is to be sold enroute for a pittance, the only condition being that her new master is neither of Ar, nor has dealings with that city. Her only hope then to see me again, if she should wish to do so, is to accompany Boots Tarsk-Bit and his party in perfect docility to Port Cos."

"I am sorry for her," I said.

"Do not be," he said. "She is only a slave."

"What will you do for a slave?" I asked.

He was a Gorean male.

"Doubtless there are other sluts in Ar," he said.

"Doubtless," I said.

"Is there anything to eat?" he asked.

"Some bread," I said, indicating a wrapper to one side.

He attacked the bread.

"It seems the lamp is still smoking," I said.

"I hadn't noticed," he said.

"You came to Ar to recover the Home Stone of Ar's Station," I said. "You have done so. Your work here is finished. You should go back to Port Cos."

"I do not think my presence with the troupe of Tarsk-Bit would make much difference," he said.

"Nonetheless," I said, "your work here is finished."

"You have acquired the female for whom you came to Ar," he said. "She is now your slave. Indeed, you could go fetch her now, from where she lies, chained and helpless. You could get her out of the city. You could carry her off. But you did not choose to do so. Rather you are letting her go."

"I look upon it differently," I said. "I look more upon it as giving her, for a time, the run of her tether."

"You finished your work in Ar," he said. "Why have you not left, taking your slave with you, if you wished?"

"She is not important," I said. "She is a mere slave girl."

"But you came to Ar for her," he said. "And you let her maneuver herself perfectly, and helplessly, into your hands. It was a coup. She is yours."

"I think that I shall stay in Ar, for a time," I said.

"Why?" he asked. "You are not of Ar."

"Why have you come back?" I asked. "Are you so fond of Ar?"

"I hate Ar," he said.

"Why, then, have you returned?" I asked.

"Because you are still here," he said.

"I, too, am hungry," I said.

He tore off a piece of bread. "Here," he said.

"I am grateful, Marcus, my friend," I said.

"It is nothing," he said.

We then, in the light of the small lamp, ate together.

Presenting JOHN NORMAN in DAW editions . . .

☐ **HUNTERS OF GOR**	UE2205—$3.95
☐ **MARAUDERS OF GOR**	UE2025—$3.50
☐ **TRIBESMEN OF GOR**	UE2026—$3.50
☐ **SLAVE GIRL OF GOR**	UE2027—$3.95
☐ **BEASTS OF GOR**	UE2028—$3.95
☐ **EXPLORERS OF GOR**	UE1905—$3.50
☐ **FIGHTING SLAVE OF GOR**	UE1882—$3.50
☐ **ROGUE OF GOR**	UE1892—$3.50
☐ **GUARDSMAN OF GOR**	UE1890—$3.50
☐ **SAVAGES OF GOR**	UE2191—$3.95
☐ **BLOOD BROTHERS OF GOR**	UE2157—$3.95
☐ **KAJIRA OF GOR**	UE1807—$3.50
☐ **PLAYERS OF GOR**	UE2116—$3.95
☐ **MERCENARIES OF GOR**	UE2018—$3.95
☐ **DANCER OF GOR**	UE2100—$3.95
☐ **RENEGADES OF GOR**	UE2112—$3.95
☐ **VAGABONDS OF GOR**	UE2188—$3.95
☐ **MAGICIANS OF GOR**	UE2279—$4.95

Other Norman Titles

☐ **TIME SLAVE**	UE1761—$2.50
☐ **IMAGINATIVE SEX**	UE1912—$2.95
☐ **GHOST DANCE**	UE2038—$3.95

NEW AMERICAN LIBRARY
P.O. Box 999, Bergenfield, New Jersey 07621

Please send me the DAW BOOKS I have checked above. I am enclosing $________ (check or money order—no currency or C.O.D.'s). Please include the list price plus $1.00 per order to cover handling costs. Prices and numbers are subject to change without notice.

Name ____

Address ______________________________________

City ________________ State ________ Zip ________

Please allow 4-6 weeks for delivery.

SHARON GREEN

takes you to high adventure on alien worlds

The Terrilian novels

☐ THE WARRIOR WITHIN (UE2146—$3.50)
☐ THE WARRIOR ENCHAINED (UE2118—$3.95)
☐ THE WARRIOR REARMED (UE2147—$3.50)
☐ THE WARRIOR CHALLENGED (UE2144—$3.50)
☐ THE WARRIOR VICTORIOUS (UE2264—$3.95)

Jalav: Amazon Warrior

☐ THE CRYSTALS OF MIDA (UE2149—$3.50)
☐ AN OATH TO MIDA (UE1829—$2.95)
☐ CHOSEN OF MIDA (UE1927—$2.95)
☐ THE WILL OF THE GODS (UE2039—$3.50)
☐ TO BATTLE THE GODS (UE2128—$3.50)

Diana Santee: Spaceways Agent

☐ MIND GUEST (UE1973—$3.50)
☐ GATEWAY TO XANADU (UE2089—$3.95)

Other Novels

☐ THE FAR SIDE OF FOREVER (UE2212—$3.50)
☐ LADY BLADE, LORD FIGHTER (UE2251—$3.50)
☐ MISTS OF THE AGES (UE2296—$3.95)
☐ THE REBEL PRINCE (UE2199—$3.50)

NEW AMERICAN LIBRARY
P.O. Box 999, Bergenfield, New Jersey 07621

Please send me the DAW BOOKS I have checked above. I am enclosing $________
(check or money order—no currency or C.O.D.'s). Please include the list price plus $1.00 per order to cover handling costs. Prices and numbers are subject to change without notice.

Name ____________________________

Address ____________________________

City ______________ State ________ Zip ________

Please allow 4-6 weeks for delivery.

DAW

NEW DIMENSIONS IN MILITARY SF

Timothy Zahn
THE BLACKCOLLAR NOVELS

The war drug—that was what Backlash was, the secret formula, so rumor said, which turned ordinary soldiers into the legendary Blackcollars, the super warriors who, decades after Earth's conquest by the alien Ryqril, remained humanity's one hope to regain its freedom.

☐ THE BLACKCOLLAR (Book 1) (UE2168—$3.50)
☐ THE BACKLASH MISSION (Book 2) (UE2150—$3.50)

Charles Ingrid
THE SAND WARS

He was a soldier fighting against both mankind's alien foe and the evil at the heart of the human Dominion Empire, trapped in an alien-altered suit of armor which, if worn too long, could transform him into a sand warrior—a no-longer human berserker.

☐ SOLAR KILL (Book 1) (UE2209—$3.50)
☐ LASERTOWN BLUES (Book 2) (UE2260—$3.50)

John Steakley
☐ **ARMOR**

Impervious body armor had been devised for the commando forces who were to be dropped onto the poisonous surface of A-9, the home world of mankind's most implacable enemy. But what of the man inside the armor? This tale of cosmic combat will stand against the best of Gordon Dickson or Poul Anderson.
(UE1979—$3.95)

NEW AMERICAN LIBRARY
P.O. Box 999, Bergenfield, New Jersey 07621

Please send me the DAW BOOKS I have checked above. I am enclosing $________ (check or money order—no currency or C.O.D.'s). Please include the list price plus $1.00 per order to cover handling costs. Prices and numbers are subject to change without notice.

Name ________________________________

Address ________________________________

City ________________ State ________ Zip ________

Please allow 4-6 weeks for delivery.

DAW

A Writer of Epic Fantasy in the Grand Tradition

Peter Morwood

THE BOOK OF YEARS

☐ **THE HORSE LORD: Book 1** (UE2178—$3.50)

Centuries ago, the Horse Lords had ridden into Alba to defea an evil sorcerer and banish magic from the land. Now ar ambitious lord has meddled with dark forces, and the ancien evil is unleashed again. Rescued by an aging wizard, young Aldric seeks revenge on the sorcerous foe who has slain his clan and stolen his birthright.

☐ **THE DEMON LORD: Book 2** (UE2204—$3.50)

Aldric must undertake a secret mission that will lead him to the troubled border provinces. There he finds unexpected allies: a mysterious, not-quite-trustworthy Demon Queller, and the beautiful young heir to a demon-possessed citadel. Together, they journey to the fortress of Seghar to challenge the demon spiri that holds it in its wrathful grasp.

☐ **THE DRAGON LORD: Book 3** (UE2252—$3.50)

As a warrior's honor leads Aldric into the heart of the Drusalar Empire on the king's orders, unbeknownst to him, the king has betrayed him into enemy hands. Slowly the trap closes about him, while powerful allies are riding to his aid: the wizard Gemmel anc the mighty warrior Dewan. But can even they help Aldric agains dark and deadly sorcery and a monstrous dragon?

NEW AMERICAN LIBRARY
P.O. Box 999, Bergenfield, New Jersey 07621

Please send me the books I have checked above. I am enclosing $________
(please add $1.00 to this order to cover postage and handling). Send check o money order—no cash or C.O.D.'s. Prices and numbers are subject to chang without notice.

Name______________________________

Address______________________________

City ____________ State ____________ Zip Code ________

Allow 4-6 weeks for delivery.